DIRTY WILD TRILOGY

DIRTY
WILD
TRILOGY

paige press

DIRTY WILD TRILOGY

Laurelin Paige

NEW YORK TIMES BESTSELLING AUTHOR
LAURELIN PAIGE

Copyright © 2021 by Laurelin Paige

All rights reserved.

No part of this book may be reproduced in any form or by any electronic or mechanical means, including information storage and retrieval systems, without written permission from the author, except for the use of brief quotations in a book review.

Cover: Laurelin Paige

Editing: Erica Edits

Proof: Michele Ficht and Kimberly Ruiz

Ebook ISBN: 978-1-957647-29-6

ALSO BY LAURELIN PAIGE
WONDERING WHAT TO READ NEXT? I CAN HELP!

Visit www.laurelinpaige.com for content warnings and a more detailed reading order.

Brutal Billionaires

Brutal Billionaire - a standalone (Holt Sebastian)

Dirty Filthy Billionaire - a novella (Steele Sebastian)

Brutal Secret - a standalone (Reid Sebastian)

Brutal Arrangement - a standalone (Alex Sebastian)

Brutal Bargain - a standalone (Axle Morgan)

Brutal Bastard - a standalone (Hunter Sebastian)

The Dirty Universe
Dirty Duet (Donovan Kincaid)

Dirty Filthy Rich Men | Dirty Filthy Rich Love

Kincaid

Dirty Games Duet (Weston King)

Dirty Sexy Player | Dirty Sexy Games

Dirty Sweet Duet (Dylan Locke)

Sweet Liar | Sweet Fate

(Nate Sinclair) Dirty Filthy Fix (a spinoff novella)

Dirty Wild Trilogy (Cade Warren)

Wild Rebel | Wild War | Wild Heart

Men in Charge
Man in Charge

Man for Me (a spinoff novella)

The Fixed Universe
Fixed Series (Hudson & Alayna)

Fixed on You | Found in You | Forever with You | Hudson | Fixed Forever

Found Duet (Gwen & JC) Free Me | Find Me

(Chandler & Genevieve) Chandler (a spinoff novel)

(Norma & Boyd) Falling Under You (a spinoff novella)

(Nate & Trish) Dirty Filthy Fix (a spinoff novella)

Slay Series (Celia & Edward)

Rivalry | Ruin | Revenge | Rising

(Gwen & JC) The Open Door (a spinoff novella)

(Camilla & Hendrix) Slash (a spinoff novella)

First and Last
First Touch | Last Kiss

Hollywood Standalones
One More Time

Close

Sex Symbol

Star Struck

Dating Season

Spring Fling | Summer Rebound | Fall Hard

Winter Bloom | Spring Fever | Summer Lovin

Also written with Kayti McGee under the name Laurelin McGee

Miss Match | Love Struck | MisTaken | Holiday for Hire

Written with Sierra Simone

Porn Star | Hot Cop

This book may contain subjects that are sensitive
to some readers.
Please visit www.laurelinpaige.com/dirty-wild for content warnings.
May include spoilers.

WILD REBEL

ONE

I paced the length of Donovan's office, then checked my watch for the third time in as many minutes. She wasn't late yet, but there was a boulder of doubt in my stomach that had me sure she wouldn't come at all. It was a natural assumption after last time. How long had I waited that night? At what point had I known for sure that she was going to ghost?

I'd been more optimistic then. I'd waited hours. Now I relied on experience. If she were planning to show at all, the Jolie I'd known would have been early.

But I hadn't known her for a long, long time.

And the name was Julianna, not Jolie. No one called her Jolie but me, and I refused to call her that now. She didn't deserve it. In the week since I'd gotten her email, I'd practiced it over and over. *Julianna, Julianna, Julianna.* She wasn't Jolie anymore. Jolie disappeared the night I waited for her in a run-down pickup in the parking lot of a CTown Supermarket. Jolie was gone.

Again, I checked my watch. Not even thirty seconds had passed. Time was moving at a snail's pace. I cracked my neck from side to side before loosening my tie. I'd already taken off the jacket, and I was still sweating. It was a Saturday in December, for fuck's sake, and I was the only one in the Reach office. Did the guys keep the heater on over the weekends? No wonder the New York overhead was so high.

I crossed to the thermostat and was surprised to find it was actually set at an arctic temperature that only an asshole penny-pincher would have thought was acceptable, which made sense because Donovan and I were alike in that area. When we'd worked the office together in Tokyo, we'd had the trimmest budget of all the Reach locations. It had risen a bit when he'd moved to the States since I no longer had the time to keep a close eye on it. I hadn't really examined the New York numbers in a while, but I had a feeling they'd probably improved with his presence.

Regardless of company spending and the perspiration beading on my forehead, the current setting was not all that friendly. I'd be a bad host to leave it there. I considered doing just that before begrudgingly switching the heater on full blast. Hopefully, it would do something before Jolie showed up.

Not Jolie.

Julianna.

Fuck, this was a giant mistake. This whole thing. I shouldn't have opened the email. I shouldn't have responded. I shouldn't have told her I was going to be in New York for a wedding that I'd had no prior plans to attend. I most definitely shouldn't have dropped everything, boarded a plane, and flown halfway across the world to impatiently pace Donovan's office, waiting for her to show. Especially knowing she had a record for *not* showing.

If I'd been intent on justice, I would have ghosted *her* this time.

But it wasn't justice I needed most from Julianna Stark. It was closure. And that's why I was there—for me, not for her. And so help me God, if she'd stood me up again...

I forced myself to sit on the edge of the desk. It wasn't exactly a relaxed position, but it was better than wearing a hole in the carpet. Still antsy, I pulled out my phone and reread her email, even though I could recite it by heart without looking.

. . . .

CADE,

I know I have no right to reach out to you like this, but there's no one else I can turn to...

MY GAZE SKIPPED down to her signature. She'd used the name I refused to call her. The one meant to tug at my emotions. Fuck her for that. Fuck her for all of it.

My agitation renewed, I stuffed my phone back in my pocket and took a deep breath. I refused to be riled up when she got here. With my palms settled on my thighs, I traced the tattoos on the back of my hands with my eyes. It was a trick I'd taught myself a decade or so ago, back when the pressure of some of my bigger jobs got the best of me, and I needed something to help me focus. I hadn't had to use it since going into business with Donovan and the guys. Advertising was definitely a high-stress career, but it was legit, and that made it a walk in the park compared to what I'd done before.

The trick still worked. By the fifth sweep of my eyes along the inked skin, I was breathing more regularly, and even though the heat had kicked in, I was feeling cool enough to reach for my jacket.

Just as I fastened the button of the navy blue Armani, I heard the ding of the elevator arriving. Then the sound of two sets of footsteps clicking on marble flooring echoed through the hallway.

She was here.

Fuck. She was here, and I was going to keep it together, whatever it took.

I ran my hand over my beard, straightened my tie, then with a final curse under my breath, I clicked the button that turned the glass wall from opaque to transparent and moved to stand in front of it.

There wasn't a direct path to the elevators from Donovan's office, so I had to wait until the pair turned down the corridor, and then it was Fran that I saw first, the security guard that I'd tipped a hundred in exchange for personally walking my guest to the back office. Was it necessary? Probably not. I told myself I was being hospitable. Truth was, I didn't want to be alone when we first saw each other.

And when Jolie—I'd given up on calling her Julianna in my head—followed Fran around the corner, I knew I'd made the right choice because, even with her head bent and her eyes fixed on the floor, Jolie was a lodestone, and I was fighting really hard not to be iron. If it had been just the two of us, I wasn't sure I would have been able to resist her pull.

I wasn't sure I'd be able to resist her pull even with Fran between us.

Thank God for the glass wall.

Showing up now doesn't make up for not showing up back then.

In case that wasn't enough of a reminder, I forced myself to remember what had happened when I'd gone after her. My ribs hurt with the vividness of that memory. My shoulder throbbed where the bone had once been broken. My chest ached with the pain of a fractured heart.

And just like that, her pull on me diminished.

"I think she has it from here, Fran," I called out. The glass was between us, but the office door was open, so I could be heard. "Thank you."

At the sound of my voice, both women came to a halt. Fran had already been looking at me, but my gaze settled past her, watching as Jolie's head lifted, her eyes swiftly meeting mine, and much as I told myself not to look for anything from the past in her face, I immediately saw the girl she'd been back then. Her cheekbones were sharper, sure. Her curves were more filled out, her naturally dark hair had been dyed blonde and cut to her shoulders, and I hadn't remembered her eyes being so light, and yet, I would have recognized her anywhere.

So much for convincing myself she was someone new.

"Sure, sure," Fran said with a tone that said she was positive she hadn't earned the generous tip I'd given. She lingered a couple of seconds, as though trying to decide if she should give the money back or make peace with the unbalance. "Tell you what—you let me know when you're on your way out, and I'll come back up for a thorough sweep and set the alarm for you."

"Will do." I could turn the alarm on and off with the push of a button on my phone, but if it made her feel good enough to leave, then fine. I'd wanted her there as a buffer, but the foolishness of that notion was clearly evident. Now as then, when Jolie was in the room, the only person I saw was her.

Her gaze seemed just as intent to stay locked on mine.

Seconds passed like hours. Vaguely, I was aware of Fran turning around, of the clop, clop, clop of her footsteps as she made her way back to the elevator. The ding of its arrival had sounded and gone silent before either Jolie or I said a word.

"Hi." She was the one who spoke first because I was a fucking chickenshit, though even through the glass, I could hear a rasp in her voice that said this likely wasn't easy for her either.

I cleared my throat as if I could clear the scratch in hers for her. "I'm sure you'll be more comfortable sitting down." I gestured for her to join me. It was smugly satisfying that she had to be the one to walk to me.

Her plump lips curved down, and she nodded, as though realizing the tone of this meeting had been set and with that nod she'd accepted it. "Yes. Sitting down for this is probably best."

The disappointment in her tone was jarring—apparently I hated it as much now as I had then—and for the briefest of moments, I wished I'd said something else, something more inviting, something sentimental.

But then I told myself to fuck that regret. This wasn't a nostalgic reunion. This was an ending, and the sooner we got to her asking for her favor, the sooner that conclusion would come.

I knew that, yet as she walked toward me with the same brisk energy she'd had when we were younger, I found myself wishing she would slow down so I could stretch this moment to its limits. It had to last forever. It had to make up for so much lost time.

Fuck, I was in trouble.

Disgusted with myself, I moved away from the glass and had made it to the bar by the time she came in. "Have a seat," I said, busying myself with empty glasses. "Can I get you something to drink?"

"Water would be fine."

I opened the mini fridge, happy to have an excuse to keep my back to her. "Sparkling or still?"

"Either."

I grabbed a bottle of sparkling for her and abandoned my impulse to pour a whiskey for myself. I needed to keep a clear head.

But then I had to get close enough to her to hand her the water, and suddenly I regretted not having the alcohol.

She'd taken her coat off and draped it on the back of the chair with her purse, but she was still standing, despite my invitation to sit, which somehow made it worse when I crossed to her. I would have preferred looming above her. I would have preferred to not have to look her in the eye. And though I purposely made sure we didn't have physical contact, I could feel the spark between us all the same, as though she was lightning and the bottle between our fingers was a rod, and every part of my body lit up like the Christmas tree in the building lobby.

I let go immediately and took a step back.

"Thanks." She didn't open the bottle. I stared where her fingers wrapped around the cylinder shape, noting the lack of a ring where one should be if she were married. That was satisfying, at least.

Except a bare finger didn't necessarily mean anything, and I didn't care about her marital status, and I definitely didn't want her thinking I did, so I pushed my eyes up to hers where I found her attention was completely on me. She took in every change in my appearance—the beard, the tats, the muscular build I'd worked for in my twenties, the hard expression that was permanently etched on my face. "You look good," she said finally.

I didn't look good. I was jet-lagged and haggard, but when she said it, I believed her because that was just what I'd always done, and old habits die hard. "You look the same."

She made a noise that could almost be called a laugh. "I don't, but thank you."

I shrugged, not sure how else to respond. She did look the same, in all the ways that mattered, and that was a real fucking problem for me. It kept me looking at her when I should have been looking anywhere else. It kept me standing within arm's reach when I should have been stepping away.

"I'm underdressed," she said, looking down at her jeans and sweater. It was definitely more casual than anything she'd ever worn as a teenager, but we'd spent most of those days in a school uniform, and her father dictated what she wore the rest of the time, so it was impossible to know what her true style would have been.

It fit her, I realized. Fit who I'd imagined her to have grown up to be, someone who didn't try to impress anyone. Someone who dressed for practicality and comfort. Someone who didn't care about anyone else's opinion.

Except maybe she cared about mine because she seemed to be seeking reassurance. While I didn't care about making her feel better, the comment begged a response. "You're dressed appropriately for the weather."

"I didn't expect to see you all decked out in a suit."

"I have a wedding after this," I reminded her. A wedding I wasn't going to make it to since it started in twenty minutes. But I hadn't really ever planned on going anyway.

"Oh, yeah. That's right." Instead of taking that as a cue to hurry this along and sit down, she scanned the room and strolled toward one of the bookcases. Immediately, she found the one picture on Donovan's shelf that included me. She smiled as she leaned in to study it, and fuck if that smile didn't do something profound to my insides. Like her lips were razor blades cutting through the darkest parts of me, letting in sunshine that had no business brightening the gloom.

I willed myself to shut it out.

And still I found myself standing behind her, looking at the image over her shoulder, trying to imagine what it was she saw that she thought deserved that grin. It was of the five of us guys—Donovan, Weston, Nate, and Dylan—all of us dressed in our best suits and puffing cigars.

"I never pictured you as a cigar smoker," she said.

Probably because I'd been a cigarette smoker when she'd known me. I'd quit more than a decade ago, but strangely I found myself jonesing for a cigarette now. Funny how people from the past brought you back to the person you were when you knew them.

I wondered if she'd quit as well or if she had a pack buried in that oversized purse of hers. It was tempting to ask just to have her dig it out and hand it over, just to feel my lips on something that she'd touched.

"We were celebrating," I said, trying to rein in my wandering mind.

"Celebrating what?"

"The opening of this office."

"Was this the first location you opened? You said you were in Tokyo."

I found the words spilling out before I could stop them. "We planned to have three locations from the beginning. New York opened first, then Tokyo three months later, and London a few months after that."

"A global phenomenon." She sounded proud, and I liked that.

I hated it at the same time. She had no right to be proud of me. She had no right to care how I'd turned out. She had no right to smell the way she did—familiar and new all at once, a scent that made my head cloud and my pulse race and my chest feel like it was breaking in two.

She turned her head toward me, and we were so close I could make out the spattering of freckles on her cheeks, the ones she'd always hated. The ones that formed a constellation in my sleep. "I always knew you'd end up someone important," she whispered.

I *had* been someone important. I'd been hers.

And that hadn't been enough for her.

Abruptly, I moved back. "How about you tell me what it is you need from me, *Julianna*?" I said her name pointedly, proud that I hadn't tripped over it when it crossed my lips.

She turned to face me, her tongue sweeping across her lower lip. "Actually, it's Jolie now. I didn't change it legally, but I may as well have. It's what I go by."

As difficult as it was to think of her by any other name, this new bit of info pissed me off. Unreasonably so. I'd been the only one to call her that once upon a time, and while I didn't expect to still get to indulge in that honor, I sure as hell wasn't happy about discovering that the honor now belonged to everyone.

I definitely wasn't calling her that now. "Whatever you want to go by, I have that wedding to get to, so if we could hurry this along..."

"Right. Sorry." She still had that ability to close off in an instant. Like someone pulling down the blinds. One minute you could see deep inside her, the next she was shut up tight.

For the best, I reminded myself.

But damn if I didn't need a cigarette.

She walked past me and sat primly on the edge of the chair, the way her father had always professed that proper young ladies should sit, her hands laid casually in her lap. I followed after her, circling behind the desk, but instead of sitting, I stood, my arms folded over my chest, a posture her father would most certainly have found disrespectful.

It was a belligerent stance on my part, one that Langdon Stark probably deserved more than she did, but in a lot of ways, Jolie and her father were inseparable in my mind. The complicated feelings I had for one of them more often than not extended toward the other.

Except that I'd never loved Headmaster Stark. That emotion had belonged to Jolie alone. Still did, I supposed, since there hadn't been anyone I'd said the word to since her.

Which was why I needed closure.

I nodded toward her, a silent prompt to get on with it.

"You probably want to be sitting for this," she suggested.

"I'm fine like I am."

"All right." She let out a sigh. "I, um. I need to ask you for your help."

She hesitated, so I prodded her on. "Something only I can help with, you said. I have to be honest—I'm curious. It's hard for me to believe I'm the only one you can turn to when I haven't seen or heard from you in close to two decades. Surely there are other men you've strung along since me. What could this favor possibly be?"

The barb did the trick. She stopped hedging and spit it out. "I need you to help me kill my father."

TWO

She was right—I should have been sitting down.

I sat now with a chuckle as I ran my hand over my beard. I was hearing things. "I'm going to need you to say that again. For a second there, I thought you said you wanted me to help you kill your father."

Her expression stayed even. "That's what I said."

I held her gaze, impossibly trying to read somebody that I used to know. She looked sincere.

But, hell, I'd thought she meant the things she said to me back then, too.

I pressed back in the chair as much as it would give. Donovan apparently preferred sitting straight and tall. I was more of a lean kind of a guy, but when *the* woman from my past was sitting in front of me asking the outrageous, the lack of mobility was a nuisance that barely registered. "What is this? Some kind of practical joke?"

"It's not a joke."

"You want to kill your father."

She shifted uncomfortably in her chair. "You don't have to keep saying it."

That almost had me laughing again. "You can't even hear it, and you think that's what you want. Nice try." Condescending, yes. I could be an ass, really without even trying.

Teenage Jolie wouldn't have stood for being patronized. Adult Jolie was a whole different organism. "It's not a decision I came to lightly."

"Well, that's heartening. A good murder plot really should involve at least one night of restless sleep."

She gave a sarcastic smile, then immediately dropped it. "Go ahead, get all the wisecracks out. I'll wait."

"It's not a wisecrack. This is not something to joke about."

"But you aren't taking me seriously."

I studied her for several seconds, sure I was still missing the punchline, but she remained somber, not a trace of humor anywhere in her countenance.

She was dead serious, no pun intended.

And I was thrown harder than I'd been thrown in years. "Fuck, Julianna. What do you expect me to say?" I was pretty sure that I couldn't even Google an appropriate response.

"It's Jolie," she corrected. "And you're right. It's brazen of me to be here at all, let alone to ask for you to help me with something so diabolical. But I hoped—I *hope*—that you will realize I wouldn't be here if I thought I had any other options."

"I'm a last resort, then." She'd basically laid that out in her email. And still, it stung. Stupidly. Like what answer would I have preferred? That she'd reached out because she needed me, and no one else could meet that need?

Obviously, I should have done a better job at managing my expectations.

She must have heard the bitterness in my tone. "I didn't mean..."

"No, I got it." Last thing I needed was a pitying platitude. Too fucking little, too fucking late. "I would never assume it was anything else."

Her mouth tightened, and as curious as I was to find out what comment she was biting back, I was more interested in controlling the conversation. Her silence gave me the reins, and with them, I took a hard turn. "Why?"

"Why...which part?" She crossed one jean-covered leg over the other, and I wondered if she knew how sultry she looked with the simple action or if she was completely unaware.

More likely it was the former. She'd known how to weaponize her femininity when she was just a kid. All these years later, I imagined she'd probably honed the skill.

I needed to remember that. That she'd never been innocent.

"How about we start with why you think you want your father dead?" I pointedly used the D word. I wasn't fucking changing my language to make her feel better. If she really was considering murder—which she couldn't be. Not really. The girl I knew wouldn't have been capable, and people didn't change that much—but if she was bold enough to be here talking about it out loud with a man who was, for all intents and purposes, a stranger, then she needed to be able to deal with the fucking terms.

Maybe she realized that, because though she cringed, she didn't remark on my choice of words. "You really have to ask?"

"Yeah. I really do."

"You, of all people, know what a monster he is."

"I know what a monster he *was*. Seventeen years ago."

"And you think he's changed?"

No, I didn't think he'd changed. Just like I didn't think she'd changed. But the fact of the matter was..."It's not my problem anymore."

She tsked. "That's not you. You're not that dismissive."

I wasn't sure what pissed me off more—her presumption that she knew shit about anything or her attempt to use it over me. "Don't pretend you fucking know anything about me. Do it again, and this conversation is finished." I managed to keep my voice low and steady, but there was no question that I'd drawn a line.

I half expected her to fall over herself with apologies or to take a step back. At least, try another tactic.

But she was Jolie fucking Stark, and backing down had never been her style. "It was an observation based on your actions. You tried to press charges against him a couple of years after..." She cleared her throat. "After you left."

It surprised me that she knew, but I refused to let on. "If you know that then you know that there was no case to be had. Might have been a different story if there had been someone to corroborate."

"They wouldn't have believed me any more than they believed you."

"I'm not sure how you could know that for sure without—"

She went on as if I hadn't spoken. "Which is why he has to be dealt with in other ways."

I could have argued the point further, but she was right. Not about murder, but about the limits of the law. The main reason my case was thrown out was because the accusations looked like an attempt at retribution against a man who hadn't wanted me anywhere near his daughter. Any charges Jolie brought up would have faced the same scrutiny.

And besides, she'd tried to report him once. Before I'd appeared on the scene. From what she'd told me, it was a mistake she had vowed not to make twice.

Once upon a time, that might have been reason enough for me to consider offing her old man. But all we'd had to do was make it to graduation to be free of him. We'd done that. We'd survived.

Then when she'd had the chance to walk away, she'd chosen to stay.

"So, next why—why now? You're an adult. You aren't living under his roof anymore. Not subject to his discipline. Surely you aren't just now concerned about what he might be doing to other students—"

"He didn't," she interrupted. "What he did to me—he wasn't like that with his students."

"Oh, right. It was just me." Lucky old me.

It wasn't completely true that it was just me and her who suffered. He might not have left physical marks on anyone else, but

Headmaster Stark knew how to fuck with people in other ways. He was a true sadist—not particular about what methods he used to bring about agony, and I had no doubt that there were dozens, if not hundreds, of students who had suffered under his tutelage since our class.

Unfortunately, the mind fucking was even harder to prosecute than the physical abuse.

"I'll repeat the question—why now?"

For the first time since she'd dropped her bombshell, she looked away. "It doesn't matter."

"It sure as hell does. You want me to have this conversation with you, you at least have to have a motive."

Her head turned back toward me. "Isn't it better if I don't? No reason to suspect me."

"Yeah, that's not how it works. There obviously is a motive or you wouldn't be here, and I don't want to hear about it first from a cop who comes knocking at my door asking questions, so you might as well tell me now what they'd try to say." Not that I was seriously entertaining any of this.

"I guess they'd say I'd finally traced the source of all the shit in my life. Everything that has ever mattered to me, everything good that I've ever lost, it's been because of him."

God, she was good. With all the innuendo and subtext, wanting me to think she was talking about us. That she was talking about losing me. That right there was class A emotional manipulation.

Like father, like daughter, right?

"Have you lost something *recently*? Because if not, I'm going to ask once again—why now?"

She blinked once before answering. "It's complicated."

The fuck with *complicated*. It was a word I'd heard all my life—from my mother, from Jolie, from the lawyer who had tried to represent my case. I was tired of complicated being an excuse to end a conversation. I'd been tired of it so long that I had purposely set my life up to be simple. No ties. No obligations. Even my contract with the guys had a clear escape clause. Whatever I did, whomever I did it with, there was always a clear path out.

I didn't do *complicated* anymore, and if I was in my right mind, that would have been the moment to show her the door.

If I was in my right mind, I wouldn't have even answered her email. Out of the blue, after all these years? It might as well have said "complicated" in the subject line.

Against better judgment, I was here.

Which led me to the most important why. "Why me?" I sat forward, suddenly afraid of the answer, and asked something better. "In fact, why anyone at all? You want the man gone, why not just do it yourself?"

"I can't figure out how. A registered gun is too easy to trace back to me, and I don't know the first thing about how to get one on the black market. I considered poisoning, but I don't have access to poison him, not on my own. Beyond that, I'm not creative enough to come up with a plan."

In other words, she wasn't a killer. Which I already knew.

"And when you realized you needed help, you thought, 'Who do I know who is capable of murder?' And then you thought, 'Oh, I bet Cade Warren would be up for that. He always did have that rebellious streak.' Should I be flattered?"

Really, I was surprised. Because I might have been trouble, but I hadn't been a guy who could kill back then. I'd come pretty close a couple of times, when the low-life job I'd had before Donovan "rescued" me had found me in some pretty shady circumstances, but that had been after Jolie. There wasn't any way she knew about that.

"I didn't reach out to you because I thought you'd be..." She let out a frustrated sigh. "That's not why."

"Then why? Why me, Julianna?"

She flinched at the name. "I thought two heads were better than one, and like I said before, you had reason enough to hate him."

"Reason to hate him? Yes. Reason to *kill* him?" I left that question unanswered because it shouldn't need voicing. Sure, I'd imagined it enough times over my life. I'd imagined it in detail. I could write a book about all the ways I'd killed Langdon Stark in my head, but that didn't mean I'd ever actually do it.

"And if I did want the man dead," I went on, realizing there was another more pertinent part of this question, "why would I have waited nearly twenty years to do it? You couldn't have thought I was just sitting around waiting for someone to give me permission. If I'd wanted that motherfucker dead, he'd be dead. I wouldn't need you to tell me to do it."

"I know," she said solemnly. "I know I'm asking you to do this for no other reason than because I need someone to help me. I know I have no right. I know, Cade. I know."

"You know, and yet you're still asking."

"I am."

There was one more why—why did she think for one minute that I'd agree? But I didn't have to ask. The answer was right there, evident in her hopeful eyes and her pleading tone and her unsaid words. She thought I'd agree because she assumed that now, as then, I would do anything for her.

"You know what, Julianna? Nope."

"Nope?"

"Nope." After breaking her promise? After standing me up? After pushing me away, ignoring my attempts to reach out? After disappearing? After seventeen years? "Nope. And fuck you for even asking."

She drew back slightly. "I deserve that."

Yeah, she did. She deserved a whole hell of a lot more, as far as I was concerned.

"While we're at it"—I stood up, wanting the full advantage of my height—"fuck you for disappearing like you did. And fuck you for showing up out of the blue thinking that I owed you something—"

"I don't think that," she interjected.

"Then fuck you for thinking there was any chance in hell that I would do your dirty work for you—"

"Not *for* me. I'd do it with you."

"And fuck you for trying to sell that lie. To me. Of all people. You can't even squash a beetle under your shoe, and you expect me to think you could have any part of ending someone's life? It's bullshit. All of this is bullshit. I'm not going to be your fall guy—" She opened her mouth, and I put up a finger to silence her. "And I'm sure as fuck not going to be your knight in shining armor. I tried to play that part once, and I got burned. You don't know anything about the man that made me, so I'll lay it out—I'm not anyone's hero. But if I were going to start being one today, it sure as shit wouldn't be for Julianna Stark."

I hadn't planned to tell her off. As many times as I'd played it out in my daydreams, I hadn't wanted her to see me that affected. It was the weaker hand. Anger/hurt/resentment—showing any of those emotions proved she still had a hold on me, and while I knew she did, the last thing I'd wanted was for her to know that.

Despite that, it felt damn satisfying. Might have felt better if she'd broken down into tears, or, the jackpot, if she'd gotten down on her knees and begged, but her despondent silence was a hell of a gratifying end to our relationship. I was taking it as a win. A big fat fucking score.

Without saying anything, she reached out to Donovan's desk and grabbed a piece of paper off his notepad and a stray pen. "It's Jolie," she said as she jotted something down.

"Not ever calling you that."

She ignored the barb. "Here's my cell phone number." She set the paper and pen on the desk and stood before gathering her coat and her purse. "I'll be in town for a few days, if you change your mind."

"Not going to change—" But I was talking to her back now, so I didn't bother finishing the statement since she was obviously done listening.

Which made all that smug satisfaction fizzle away like a punctured tire. This was supposed to be *my* closure, and yet goddamned Julianna Stark had managed to once again have the last word.

THREE

Past

I hissed as I pulled my T-shirt over my head, then craned my neck, trying to see the marks on my back. They burned like a motherfucker, like my entire torso had been lit on fire, and though I couldn't see anything, I was sure I was probably bleeding.

Though my shirt was relatively clean. It was black, which made it hard to tell for sure, and the whole thing felt damp, but I'd been sweating. If I'd been wearing my uniform dress shirt like I was supposed to, I would be able to see better.

If I'd been wearing the dress shirt, I wouldn't have been in this position at all.

I reached an arm back to feel and cringed at the brush of my fingers across newly torn skin. When I brought my hand back, there was blood. Not too much, but enough. I twisted my neck again to look. Dammit, I needed a mirror.

I froze at the sound of the door as it squeaked open, my head angled over my shoulder. My breath sat trapped in my lungs until she slipped in, shutting the door behind her. Jolie. Kind eyes. Soft lips. My angel. My savior.

And the last person who should be here right now.

"You shouldn't be here." My voice was cautiously low, and despite my words, it was evident I was relieved to see her.

"Where else would I be, you moron? Turn around. Let me see."

I hesitated, not wanting her to see me like this—weak and wounded. She'd seen me like that so many times, I shouldn't have felt ashamed. And I didn't. Not really. Just.

I wanted to be different for her.

And as many times as I swore that I would be, her father still got the better of me.

"Come on, Cade," she said soothingly. "Let me."

Slowly, I turned, keeping my head craned so I could use her expression as a mirror. She barely flinched, but I saw it before her mask of compassion swallowed it up, and all I saw was love.

"It's not really that bad," she said.

"You're a bad liar." Actually, she was a good liar. I would have believed her if I couldn't feel the evidence to the contrary.

"I'm not lying. Most of them aren't even bleeding."

"Seriously? It feels like my whole back was torn open."

"I know." She tugged my T-shirt from my hands and patted it gently on a spot that must have been oozing.

I bit my cheek so I wouldn't cry like a big baby.

"They're really thin. Like cat scratches. I bet they don't even scar."

Probably why Headmaster Stark was so fond of the skinny-tailed whip. That and because it hurt the most.

I let my breath out slowly before attempting to speak. "That's not fair. I deserve a souvenir."

She forced a laugh and pulled a small tube from the pocket of her skirt. "You'll remember it. Trust me." She was still in her uniform, but her tie was loose, and even though class hours were over and we were no longer required to be in dress, I instinctively wanted her to fix it, just in case there was a chance she'd face the same punishment I'd faced.

Concern over her outfit got pushed away as she delicately rubbed the ointment along one of the stripes on my back.

"Holy fuck." So much for taking it like a man.

She winced. "I'm sorry. I don't want them to get infected."

It was hard to concentrate on words, the pain too blinding to think about much else. "Right. That's, um. Thanks. Good. Good thinking. Oh my fucking hell almighty Christ!"

"Shh." She was trying to be comforting but also reminding me to watch my volume.

It also reminded me of the risk she was taking just by being here. Tears pricked at the corners of my eyes, and I wasn't sure if they were from the pain or because she was helping me. There hadn't been much kindness in my world before her.

It was still hard to believe she was real. Hard to believe she was mine.

Of course, she was forbidden, so it wasn't like anyone knew she was mine. But she was all the same.

I blinked away the moisture in my eyes. I hadn't cried when I'd been beaten, I wasn't going to start now.

She finished applying the antibiotic and pressed her lips on one of the wounds, so gently that it barely stung. Then she snuck her arms around me, her hands moving low toward the crotch of my khaki uniform pants.

"Jolie," I warned. It would have been a perfect distraction from the agony of my wounds—her in my lap, my cock buried inside her, my kisses swallowing the sound of her moans.

But the risk...

"It would be worth it," she murmured, reading my mind.

I was hard when her hand cupped my bulge, but I put my palm over hers to stop her before we got carried away. Then I pulled her around to my front and settled my hands on her hips, holding her at arm's length. "We can't," I whispered sternly.

She glanced toward the door, seeming to assess the threat. Then she sighed. "I wish..."

"I know."

She looked up at me with yearning, the flecks of brown in her eyes more present at the moment than the green or the blue. She had kaleidoscope eyes, the colors always changing, and what I wouldn't give to spend hours lost inside her gaze, studying every shift of pigment. I wanted that even more than the hastily stolen moments we'd shared. Wanted to just be with her, seeing into her the way she always saw into me.

My resistance was weakening. I pressed my forehead against hers. "How can we live like this?"

"Like caged birds?" She brought her hands up to my cheeks, tilting my face so she could look at me directly. "It's not too hard if we just keep thinking that eventually we'll fly free. And we will, Cade. We won't be trapped like this forever."

I brushed my knuckles across her cheek. She had such delicate features, but in reality, she was so much stronger than me. So much braver. Sometimes I swore she had courage enough for both of us.

I bent in to graze my lips against hers, but halted at a voice calling from outside the room. "Julianna?"

Her body tensed in recognition of her name. It was still far away though. She had time.

"Go," I said, ushering her toward the door. "Before he catches you here."

She took two steps away, then hurried back to press a fast kiss on my mouth and a half empty pack of cigarettes into my hand. "One day. We'll fly."

Then she was gone, out of the room before I could say anything else. I rushed after her and pressed my ear against the door, listening.

"In my office now, Julianna."

I couldn't tell if he was close enough to know where she'd just come from, or if he suspected. Her, "Yes, sir," gave nothing away.

My fingers curled into a fist at my side, ready to punch a hole in the wall, but I stopped myself, my wounds too fresh of a reminder about the consequences of rebellion.

I forced myself to take deep breaths instead, and held tight to the promise of *one day*.

FOUR

Present

I sat at Donovan's desk for a long time after Jolie left, my mind in a strange fog. There was so much new that I couldn't process, and I found myself back in the past.

We'd been so young. Made so many promises. I'd believed with every fiber of my being that she'd meant them at the time. So why hadn't she flown away with me?

It was a question I had never been able to answer, which was why I tended to avoid looking back at all costs.

Currently, the past felt surer than the present. I may have been wrong in the long run, but in that moment, when she'd risked everything to be at my side, I'd known what was between us. Known what we were. Known what I'd felt for her. Known I could trust her.

Now, I didn't know anything. I was blank. My body numb. The only feeling I could identify was the decade-long forgotten urge for a smoke.

"I saw your lady friend leave a while ago and wondered if I'd missed you," a voice said.

The unexpected company snapped me out of my daze, and I looked up to find Fran standing in the doorway.

I must have been truly out of it. I hadn't even heard the elevator ding, let alone the clomp of her thick heels.

"Not so sure she's a lady. She's definitely not my friend." I stood and crossed to the closet, hidden in the bookshelves, and grabbed my coat. Now that I was in motion, I needed to stay in motion. "You good to lock up?"

"That's why I'm here."

"Thanks." I patted my coat pockets, as if I'd find a pack of cigarettes tucked away in one of them, an old reflex that had me cursing under my breath as soon as I realized it had kicked in. Then, ignoring the piece of paper with her phone number scrawled on it, I headed to the door, snagging one of Donovan's cigars on my way out. I wasn't much for the fancy shit he liked to puff on, but maybe it would satisfy the craving.

Once on the street, I realized I should have grabbed a lighter as well.

With another curse, I tucked the cigar in the breast pocket of my suit jacket and hailed a cab to the Park Hyatt. I'd missed the wedding ceremony at this point, but the reception would be going on for hours. Plus, I was staying at that hotel.

I considered bailing on the festivities altogether. Weston and I were both partners in the firm, but we weren't that buddy-buddy, and it was a fake wedding at that, some marriage-of-convenience scheme Donovan had concocted to help expand Reach in Europe. Honestly, business and money were probably the smartest reasons I could think of to get married, and in many ways I was more supportive of this union than most because of that. But since the parties involved considered it all for show, it wasn't like anyone would care if I ditched.

When I walked into the hotel lobby, though, I realized that if I didn't go to the reception, I'd end up at the bar. And ending up at the bar would be a sign that I wasn't okay, and I needed very much to be okay.

Another benefit of the reception? The booze was free.

Despite suggesting to Julianna that I'd dressed in my suit for the wedding, I'd actually rented a tux—or rather, Donovan had rented me a tuxedo. I'd found it waiting in my room when I'd checked in the day before. I was of half a mind to ignore the monkey suit and just go in what I was wearing. But I had my coat to deal with, and I didn't want to check it, so I headed up to my room to ditch it and ended up changing into the tux as well.

While I was up there, I lit the rich-ass cigar, ignoring the no-smoking sign blatantly posted in my suite with each puff. Serious cigar smokers don't inhale, but I sure as hell did, praying it would get me buzzed. The numbness was wearing off, and if I was going to feel, I wanted to be in control of what kind of feeling I had.

The cigar wasn't quite the fix I wanted, but I was a different kind of jittery when I found myself downstairs in the Onyx Ballroom—thank God for no line at the bar. The place was decked to the nines in luxury. Everything from the jazz band to the gift bags for the guests was Grade A wedding material, and even if the marriage hadn't been Grade A fake, I would have been nauseated at the sight.

A couple swigs into my beer and the urge to puke faded away, as did the urge to smoke. The itchiness of the tux remained, but that had nothing to do with the event itself. Tuxes were always too constraining. I'd learned that the hard way when an art auction in Thailand had gone south. I'd left that situation with a busted kneecap and a bruised kidney that I was certain I could have prevented if my attire hadn't restricted movement. I'd hated the fancy-ass get-ups ever since.

At least Donovan had known well enough not to get me a cummerbund.

I did a quick scan of the room, looking for a familiar face, not expecting to find too many—the pompous wedding was mostly meant to appease the bride's family, so most of the guests were on her side. Plus, I hadn't been in New York in years, and I wasn't the type who had many connections to begin with. But it didn't take too long before I spotted Donovan with a hot brunette cozied up to him.

I paused a minute to take that in before approaching them. I'd known Donovan now going on seven years. In that time, I'd seen him with plenty of women—the man wasn't a whore, but he kept himself entertained. Never had any of those women been more than arm candy and (presumably) a good lay. He'd certainly never looked at anyone the way he was looking at this chick.

Of course, no chick had been *this* chick. He'd been carrying a torch for this one for the last decade. I didn't know a lot about her beyond a few drunken exchanges over the years, but I recognized in him what he probably recognized in me. There's a specific type of wariness in those who have loved and lost. Like speaks to like. We understood each other well.

But now the girl he'd pined for was in his arms, carrying the torch along with him.

And I was...

I wasn't going there, was where I was.

It took another swig of beer to loosen the tightness in my chest and another after that before I approached the couple. "Then the rumors are true," I said, startling them out of their embrace. "Donovan Kincaid has found himself a girlfriend."

Said girlfriend backed away from him as fast as a teenager caught making out by dad.

Maybe not *that* quickly. If anyone would know that panic, it was me.

"I'm the one who told you that rumor, you asshole," Donovan said, clapping his hand on my back.

He'd dropped it like a bomb, actually, when I'd called Tuesday to tell him I was coming to town. *"Great. You can meet our new director of marketing strategy. Oh, and by the way, she's my girlfriend."*

Unable to get more from him, I'd asked Weston about it when I'd called with my late wedding RSVP. He'd filled me in with as much as he knew, which wasn't a hell of a lot that was meaningful. He had more to say about his own tryst with the woman than Donovan's relationship with her. Too much to say about her, really. I hadn't needed the intimate details. But that was to be expected—Weston liked to gloat about his conquests, and Donovan was tight-lipped.

Truth was, I hadn't needed to hear anything from either of them to put together that this girlfriend was *the* girlfriend. The fact that Donovan had abandoned me in Tokyo and moved back to the States as soon as this woman from the past was hired told me everything I needed to know.

"Sabrina, this is Cade Warren," Donovan said, making the official introduction. "Cade, I told you about Sabrina."

It was possible he was hinting for me to play that up, make the girlfriend feel all warm and fuzzy because her boyfriend had been talking about her. If he was, well, he had to know me better than that. "No. *You* told me about our new director of marketing strategy. Weston told me about Sabrina."

I shook her hand, taking in her features as I did. Big brown doe eyes, rail thin frame. The kind of beautiful that turned heads. No wonder the boys had both been into her. "Pleasure to meet you. Everything I've heard has been quite...complimentary."

I was a little more friendly with her than necessary, forcing myself to be present for reasons beyond seeing if it would rile Donovan up.

Apparently it did. "Cade's story that he's here for the wedding is only a cover," he said pointedly. "He's really in the States to meet up with a woman from the past."

I narrowed my eyes. "Hey—"

"Payback's a bitch." He wrapped his arm around Sabrina's waist and pulled her closer like he owned her, which knowing him, he probably thought he did.

"That was supposed to be a secret." I made sure my tone reminded him that I was still someone to be afraid of. In case he'd forgotten that I hadn't been innocent when he'd met me. He knew the kinds of things I could do to people. The kinds of things I'd done.

Not murder, though. I'd never gone that far.

Could I go that far? Would I, if...?

"Sabrina and I have no secrets," Donovan said, and as soft as it made him sound, I had the gut feeling that *he* would kill if he had to. For her.

But I wasn't Donovan. And Jolie wasn't in my arms. And I sure as fuck wasn't killing anyone for her.

And even if, once upon a time, I was the type of guy who would have killed for her, this share-all-my-secrets-pussy-whipped bullshit was not ever going to be my scene.

I rolled my eyes. "Well, isn't that precious?"

"Don't worry. Your secret is safe with me." At least Sabrina seemed to understand I was a man not to reckon with.

Though, I wasn't sure it was that important to keep the meeting with Julianna on the down low. At first, I hadn't wanted people to know because who would understand besides Donovan? Now that I knew what she'd wanted from me, it was a different story. If I were going to help her, any communication with her could incriminate me.

I wasn't going to help her, obviously. But if she went through with it herself and someone later had questions for me...Yeah, that was a whole can of worms I didn't want to get involved with. Best to keep it hush.

I needed to clue Donovan in on that so he wouldn't mouth off to anyone else, and I planned to do that as soon as I had the chance. With how tightly he gripped his "girlfriend," and the office staff now gathered around us, it wasn't going to be anytime soon.

Good thing I had my beer.

FIVE

Another twenty minutes of chitchat and mingling with staff, and I was beyond ready to get the fuck out of that ballroom. Free booze or no, the lovey-dovey vibe had me twitchy as shit. Although I'd met most of the employees at one time or another, I hadn't worked with any of them enough to be able to hold a meaningful conversation, and I was...distracted.

Distracted by light eyes and womanly curves and dyed blonde hair that somehow looked more natural than the brown I'd been used to imagining. Distracted by a request that I could never take seriously and the secretive reasons behind the request and the goddamned proof that the woman I'd once loved still existed in this world.

So much for fucking closure.

I needed to be drunk. And for as drunk as I planned to be, I was going to need to eat something more substantial than the fancy hors d'oeuvres the caterers were serving. Time to think about getting out of there.

The universe rarely worked in my favor, but just then the speaker system announced Mr. and Mrs. Weston and Elizabeth King, and finally—since I'd been informed by Donovan that I had to wait until they'd arrived to take off—I was closer to escape. Hallelujah.

"They do a lineup or something, don't they?" I finished my beer with one long swallow. Maybe I could rush through it, give my congrats, and let them know the gift was in the mail (then remember to call my assistant and make sure she'd sent something in my name).

I'd meant the question for Donovan, but it was Roxie, Weston's secretary, who answered. "I think they plan to mingle."

For the first time since I'd arrived, I sized up the crowd. Jesus, the place was packed. There were already several small bunches gathered near the bride and groom, people waiting for their turn to coo over the couple. The rest of the afternoon would be like this, Weston and his new wife the center of attention while they cut the cake and did the dance and threw the garter. Were they doing all that traditional bullshit?

Another unbidden memory popped in my head. Jolie in my arms, her cheek pressed to my chest. *"We can't have a wedding,"* I'd told her, and I remembered feeling disappointed by that. *"We'll have to elope. There won't be a big ceremony. No reception. None of it."*

"I don't care about that. All I care about is being with you."

I shook the memory from my thoughts, but the essence of it lingered like a bad scent after the garbage had been taken out. "Fuck this. It will take forever for them to get through all these people. I'm taking off."

I tossed my bottle into a nearby trash can, then crossed to my business partner, interrupting another session of canoodling with a tap on his shoulder. "Can I borrow you for a moment, Donovan?" I forced myself to acknowledge his woman, even though all I wanted to do was get some place that didn't feel so claustrophobic. Some place I could breathe. "It was nice meeting you, Sabrina. I'll probably see you around the office before I head back to Tokyo."

She said, "Ditto," but I was already walking away, Donovan in tow.

"I want to hear this," he said when he caught up to me, "but make it quick."

Not even two seconds away from his girl, and he was already on edge. "You're so fucking pussy whipped."

"You want to know something, Cade?" When I turned my head toward him, he flipped me the bird.

Neither of us spoke again until we were outside the ballroom in the lounge. It wasn't as empty as I would have preferred, but it would do for the conversation I needed to have now. The rest could wait. "You didn't tell anyone else why I was in town, right?"

"You mean that you were in town for Weston's wedding? I told the whole goddamn office because, as you seem to have correctly assumed, I talk about you nonstop."

I gave him an impatient glare. I wasn't in the mood for his sarcasm.

He returned the glare with his who-do-you-think-I-am look. "I didn't tell anyone, you moron."

"Except Sabrina."

He didn't roll his eyes, but his expression had the same effect. "Except Sabrina, and you were right there in the room when it happened."

"Good, good." I'd thought the confirmation would calm me, but my shoulders felt just as tightly drawn as before. "You're sure she won't tell anyone?"

"She won't."

"You'll make sure?"

"I'll make sure. What the hell happened when you saw her?"

He would have wanted to know no matter what, but after my paranoid interrogation, he had to be even more piqued. For as much as the asshole had done for me, he did deserve an explanation.

I glanced around the space. "Not here."

Donovan gestured to a room nearby, the door slightly open. "The bride used it to get ready. Bet it's empty now."

If I got started, I wasn't going to stop. I'd need copious amounts of liquor for that, and I doubted the dressing room had a suitable minibar. Besides, Donovan had already spelled out his desired time frame for this interaction.

"I'll fill you in later. When we're somewhere else."

He narrowed his eyes, reluctant to let it drop. "She showed, though?"

I nodded and did another scan of the lounge. Experience and necessity had turned me into a vigilant man, but I recognized I was probably being overly cautious. Talking about her always felt unsafe, not just today. She'd been my secret too long for me to feel any other way about her.

But now she didn't need to be my anything. I'd seen her, and I could stop looking for her and move on. "You can take that PI of yours off the job."

"You don't want him to do any more digging? He was waiting for her after your meeting. I'm sure he's got more—"

"No. Call him off." I wasn't even sure why I'd had the guy look in the first place. Years of coming up with nothing had only driven my curiosity to keep searching.

"Did you get a phone number, at least? My guy could probably get you a whole background from that, as long as it's not a burner phone."

I thought briefly about the note she'd written, still sitting on Donovan's desk. I should have torn it up and thrown it away. I should have destroyed it.

Because right now that simple sheet of paper called to me like a siren song, begging me to return so it could destroy *me*.

"I don't care anymore." I told myself I meant it.

"You're sweating and twitchy and smell like one of my Fuentes—you're welcome, by the way. You'd never reach voluntarily for a cigar unless you were worked up. That doesn't seem like a man who doesn't care."

Reading between the lines was Donovan's superpower. Normally, it was something I admired. Today, his perception made me want to snap. "I don't care about her," I reiterated with finality.

"Whatever you say."

Hearing myself, I wouldn't buy it either. "Just cancel the PI, okay? And don't tell anyone about me seeing her. Not Weston, not Nate—no one. I mean it."

"Okay." He studied me for several seconds. "Something big happened, didn't it?"

Even without her insane—not to mention illegal—request, "big" was an understatement. I hadn't had time to process it yet, hadn't let myself begin. The numbness had completely worn off, though, and in its place was a tar pit of emotion. As soon as I started walking through it, I knew I was going to be stuck.

Stuck was where I'd been for years. Was I really just right back where I started?

"I'll tell you about it tomorrow," I assured him. "All of it."

"Stop by my place in the afternoon."

"Fine." Without a goodbye, I spun away from him. I'd spent as much energy on him as I could. The rest I needed to keep myself from falling apart.

"Cade," he called after me.

It took more strength to turn and listen than to keep going, but I forced myself to stop all the same. "What?"

"Don't do anything stupid."

It was hard not to laugh at the late warning. She'd reached out, and I'd come running. What could be more stupid than that?

SIX

"Re-al li-fe," the girl said slowly, her head tilted to read the letters spelled out across the back of my fingers. "Real life."

"Yep. Real life."

"It's a bitch sometimes," she said with a wink.

My chuckle disappeared behind a swig of bourbon. What did she know about it? She was only twenty-two according to the bartender's pronouncement. He'd read it out loud when she'd handed her ID over the first time, and he'd been the one to wink when he'd passed it back. He made no bones about his intent to seduce her, hinting more than once that his shift was over in an hour. He probably wasn't much older than she was.

I, on the other hand, had thirteen years on her, which meant she was at least three years too young, and that was definitely one of the reasons she was coming back to my room with *me*. She had bad decision written all over her, and that couldn't have been a better match for my mood.

Tough luck, my bartender friend. I'd leave him a big tip to make up for stealing his conquest.

"Do your tattoos go all the way up?" the girl asked now, fondling my arm.

"What do you think?" My bicep flexed instinctively under her hand, and she practically purred.

I'd probably get her to meow when we were both naked. If she wasn't too drunk.

If *I* wasn't too drunk.

And fuck. I was headed for too drunk if I wasn't there already.

"Hmm. I have a guess. Maybe I'll get to find out if I'm right." She ran her hand down my sleeve before dropping it to pick up her cosmo. I still wore the tux jacket, but I'd managed to lose the stupid bowtie—and by lose, I meant cutie pie next to me had it wrapped around her neck like a choker. It gave her a sexy playgirl look that had my cock interested, even if the rest of me was somewhat numb to her charm, but that was the way with most of my encounters with women. It was the head in my pants that did the scoping out and drove the pickups. Generally, he liked the ones that didn't talk so much. The ones that didn't giggle. This chick was out of the norm because she did both, but he perked up whenever she tossed her hair over her shoulder, which was quite often.

Seemed we liked blondes now. That was new.

"I wonder if blondes really do have more fun."

The memory stormed in without warning—Jolie standing in front of a mirror, holding her hair up with one hand. A fingerprint-shaped bruise on her neck that made me want to ask questions that I didn't need to ask.

"Don't even think it. I like it dark," I'd said. But I'd been focused on that bruise, not her hair, and even though I knew it wasn't worth getting her upset, I had a sick impulse to hear about every pain that monster inflicted on her. If she had to suffer it, I needed to suffer it too.

"Like I'd ever get away with it. Just let me dream for a minute."

I'd reached my hand out to press gently against the marked skin, erasing her smile from her face. She dropped her hair and put her hand on my wrist. *"Let it go, Cade."*

"I need to know."

"You already know."

I'd bit my cheek until it bled, the familiar coppery taste reminding me that I hated telling her about my bruises too.

With a sigh, I'd let my hand fall. *"You should dye it as soon as we leave."* I didn't believe blondes really had more fun, but I'd figured she deserved every chance at happiness she could get.

And now Jolie was away from her father, and her hair was lighter like she'd wanted, and I hadn't seen any bruises, but if she was anything like me, she still wore them under her skin. My insides were even more marked up than my outsides.

That wasn't something I planned on sharing with a girl I'd just met in a bar.

Forcing my attention back to her—the current blonde at my side—I turned in, and the jostle of someone stepping up to the bar behind me gave an excuse to step an inch closer, staking claim. "Do you have any?"

"Have any what?" She blinked up at me, her eyes glossy, and it occurred to me she was on her way to too drunk too, which was fine. It would make it a fairer coupling.

"Tats."

"Oh! Tattoos! Yes."

I wasn't really precious about my own ink. Only a couple held any meaning. The rest were acquired to help create an image—*respect* written on my forearm, *beast* down my bicep, the cross-shaped dagger on my hand. Looking tough had been an essential part of my former job. It was a wonder Donovan had seen past it, but I was lucky he had. My current career was more satisfying, not to mention safer. Oh, and one hundred percent legal.

Though no longer necessary for work, I'd learned that talking about tats was a handy topic for hookups. "Where they at?" After a second, I added, "The tats," in case she'd already forgotten again.

"I have a butterfly across the top of my foot. It hurt so bad I'm scared of getting another."

"Because it's near the bone." The bartender set another cosmo in front of her. "On the house." Either he'd missed my stake and was clueless or he was cocky enough to not care.

"Next time get one where there's lots of flesh." My innuendo was as much for her as for the bartender, to let him know he wasn't the only one seducing.

"It hurts less on the fleshy parts?" Another toss of her hair. Another twitch of my dick.

"Presumably."

"You'll have to show me a good spot, then, Cade."

She got points for remembering my name. I didn't remember hers, and wouldn't if she repeated it, so I didn't bother asking. It had been years since I remembered any name besides Jolie. Not likely I'd start now.

"The tat on the outside of my arm wasn't bothersome." The bartender busied himself with wiping down the counter, an obvious excuse to keep talking to Blondie. "Inside hurt a bit more."

Blondie considered. "I don't think I'd get a tattoo on my arm."

"Mine wasn't too bad," a voice came from behind me. A woman inserting herself into a flirty conversation meant one of two things to my drunken brain—either she was hitting on the bartender, or she was hitting on me.

I supposed it was possible she was hitting on Blondie. I was already thinking threesome as I turned to include her in the conversation, my mouth opened to spout off some provocative quip.

It shut without a word uttered when I realized the other woman was Jolie.

Not Jolie. Julianna.

Too late, I realized her voice had been familiar. If I'd been sober, I would have placed it sooner, and what would that have gained me? Because whether I recognized it sooner or not, she'd still be here, and I'd still be speechless, and drunk as I was, I wasn't drunk enough to not have feelings about that.

What those feelings were was harder to identify.

"Where is it?" Blondie asked across me, her world continuing to spin while mine had stopped.

"My right hip," Julianna answered.

"And you said it didn't hurt?"

"Not any more than a bee sting."

"Bee stings hurt." The girl pouted.

I took another swig of my bourbon. Then another. Hoping each swallow would settle the thump of my heart. Each swallow failing.

She'd tracked me down. Of course she had. I hadn't said whose wedding I was here for, but it wouldn't have been too hard to figure out since Weston's was publicized heavily. A simple Google search for Reach would have probably brought it up. That had to be how she found me.

I couldn't decide how I felt about the fact that she'd been looking.

"And what are you having, pretty thing?"

I should have been glad that the bartender now had his sights fixed on Jo—on Julianna, but for some reason it just made me want to punch a hole through the counter. Or through his face.

"Martini. In and out with the vermouth." She handed over her ID when he asked for it with a roll of her eyes. "You probably want me to take that as a compliment, but all I see it as is a hassle."

His expression went cold. "Just following the law, ma'am."

"Well, follow it with a little less smarm, will you?"

Yeah, that hookup wasn't happening. Fuck me for almost smiling.

Another swallow. Of all the gin joints, in all the world...

"Did yours hurt?" The slight pressure of Blondie's hand back on my forearm drew my attention back to her.

That's it. Focus on her. But her question didn't make sense in my stupor. *Did it hurt?* Yes, goddammit, it hurt. After all these years, after all the booze, it still fucking hurt, and it wasn't fucking fair.

"Your tattoos," she clarified. She placed her palm over the back of my hand and laced her fingers through mine. "Lots of bone here. Did it hurt?"

My dick didn't even register her touch, but I flirted back, interested now in the hookup to prove something rather than to get off. "I'm a man. Which means I was crying like a baby."

She laughed. "No, you weren't."

"No, I wasn't." Each time I'd sat under the needle, I'd welcomed the pain, curious to see if this time I'd feel something new.

But the only thing I ever felt was the same old constant ache. It never varied. Never dulled. I'd carried it so long now, it was as much a part of me as any ink on my skin. I barely noticed it these days.

With *her* back in my life, sitting close enough that her arm brushed against mine, that ache burned as though it were new.

I turned my hand over so that Blondie and I were now palm to palm and imagined the dagger drawn on the back plunging through the heart of the woman on my other side. If only it had the power—if only *I* had the power to inflict pain on her.

I didn't believe for a minute that I did, but it felt damn good to pretend.

Blondie moved close enough that her breasts pressed against my bicep. "What other tattoos do you have?"

"That's the kind of question better answered with my clothes off."

"But the tux makes them look so hot."

"They're just as hot without. Trust me." I hadn't reached the level of drunk that I'd been aiming for, but it was about time to take this to my suite. The only thing keeping me was wanting a reaction from the woman next to me. She might not be at all bothered by me slutting it up in front of her, but she had to be irritated that I'd barely spared her a glance. She'd come looking for me. She at least wanted my attention.

The bartender returned with the martini. "Charge it to your room?"

I held my breath waiting for Julianna's answer, praying she hadn't gone so far as to book herself in the Park Hyatt. When she threw down a twenty, I was surprised to not feel more relief.

"What's yours?" Blondie asked the bartender. "You said it was on your arm?"

I guess we were still talking about tats.

"Tribal design. It goes all across here." He gestured with his hand, indicating he had a half sleeve.

Tribal design. If I weren't so intoxicated, I'd kick his ass just for being predictable.

But since I was intoxicated, and because I was obsessed and had been for years, I suddenly couldn't think about anything other than the flesh above Julianna's hip.

"What's yours?" I asked, the question out before I could stop myself.

If she was surprised I'd spoken to her, she didn't show it. "That's the kind of question better answered with my clothes off."

Direct hit.

Fuck her for landing it.

Fuck her for making me steal a glance at her, and fuck my head for the split second of thinking about her naked.

Remembering her naked.

I finished off my bourbon, then pushed the glass toward the bartender. "Another."

So much for taking off soon.

SEVEN

At the realization that there would be at least one more drink before the action started, Blondie leaned in to whisper in my ear. "I'll be back. I need to head to the ladies'."

I smiled like she'd said something dirty. Then, before she'd walked too far away, I pulled her back and kissed her. PDA wasn't generally my M.O. Frankly, neither was kissing. I preferred to have as little of it as possible when I fucked.

But this kiss was about making a point—the point that I was fine and desirable and not affected.

I didn't know if I was making that point for Jolie or for me.

Blondie was breathless by the time I let her go, at any rate. My breathing had been erratic before our lips locked and had nothing to do with her. I didn't even watch her walk away, when normally, if the woman from my past hadn't shown up, I would have followed after for a quickie in the restroom.

It was a couple tense seconds later that I realized that my much needed distraction had just walked away.

I chugged down half the glass of bourbon the minute the bartender set it down.

Maybe she'd leave.

Maybe she wouldn't say anything.

Maybe she...

"She's right," she said. "The tats are potently sexy combined with the tux."

I told myself not to engage.

I didn't listen. "I suppose that's why I chose to wear it."

"To show off your tats?"

"Yep." Short. Clipped. The message clear: this conversation was done. She and I were done.

"That's a lot of fuss to show off a bit of color. And you can't really see anything besides the ink on your hands—I'm assuming you have more underneath. You'd think you'd wear something that you could roll up. Show off the art on your arms or your chest. More likely, I'd say you probably wore the tux for some other reason. A wedding perhaps?"

I felt tense all over, pissed off that she thought we could sit here and chat like there was nothing between us. Like we were strangers who'd just met at the bar.

I dared another glance, allowing myself to check her out like she was just that—a stranger that I'd never seen before. She wore a black, spaghetti-strap dress with a slit up the thigh, the material sheer enough that I could see a hint of areola.

Shit, she was hot.

Not just woman-I've-been-fantasizing-about-for-eons hot, but grab-every-dick-in-the-rooms-attention hot. If she'd been a stranger who'd popped up at the bar—and if she hadn't been interested in a threesome—I would have dumped Blondie for her.

I probably would have dumped the idea of a threesome no matter what. Stranger in black made it impossible to see anyone but her once I was looking.

What could have happened between us if this was when and how we'd met? No doubt I would have asked her to my room. Would she have come?

Maybe because I was drunk or because I was fucked in the head or because there were parts of me that had longed to be in her presence for too long to walk away without more words exchanged, whatever the reason, I found myself turning toward her. Found myself putting on the charm. Found myself dipping a toe into the stranger fantasy. "I'd never let an event dictate my dress code."

"You dress for the ladies," she said smoothly, as though we'd both been playing the fantasy all along.

In a way, we had been. We were more strangers than anything else after all these years. It really didn't take much pretending. "Definitely for the ladies. This look is a chick magnet."

"Does it really work?"

"Seems to be working just fine." I waited for her to protest, to say that she wasn't drawn to me. Dared her with my stare to say it.

She didn't blink, but her eyes drifted toward the exit where Blondie had disappeared a few minutes before. "I think that one's drunk enough to not care what you're wearing."

"Is that a judgment?" I wanted it to be jealousy.

She hesitated before grinning. "It's an observation."

"You hand out observations to all the men you happen upon at bars?"

"If they're hot." Blondie had already referred to me as such tonight, yet it felt like it was the first time I'd ever heard it. "If it will start a conversation."

"Judgy observations are an obnoxious way to get noticed. I'd recommend another tactic."

"I don't know. Seems to be working just fine." She smiled smugly this time, and I couldn't help returning it. Her eyes had lit up, and it was even easier to look at her than it had been, and it had been very easy before.

The banter was easy as well. Too easy. We could anticipate each other's rhythm. There was no learning curve, just a fall into familiar patterns. If she were fishing in this pond, I'd already be in her bucket.

I wasn't sure if she *was* fishing. There was every chance she wanted to forget our past as much as I did, that she also sought closure. Leave it to her to go for the hot, sweaty ending. There might be benefits to fucking her out of my system. I could do that. All night long, if that's what it took.

It was more likely she was only trying to seduce me into helping her deal with her daddy issue.

I took a sip of my drink, rerouting my thoughts. Reminding myself she was a stranger. "So you have the conversation started. Are you as good at keeping it going?"

"I tend to find that starting is all I really need. After that, who needs talk?"

She did this too well—the stranger game. The seduction. I wondered how often she did this sort of thing and hated myself for wanting to know all the names and details of every man she'd ever hit on, ever sucked off, ever let inside her, just so I could track them down and bash each and every one of their heads into the ground.

I would not kill for her. Not even in a jealous rage. Not even just in my head.

"Pro at pickups, are you?" My tone was cool.

"Never said that."

"You don't have to."

"Really? Now who's making judgments?"

"Just observing, baby. Just observing." I was such a liar. I was all judgment and jealousy, and even if I could successfully compartmentalize and separate the woman in front of me from the one from the past —from the one even this morning—that only worked for my head. These emotions were too primitive for reason.

Still, I couldn't tear myself away. "What about you? Why do you look so..." *Sexy, spectacular, devastating.* "Fancy?"

She looked down at her outfit as if she'd forgotten what she put on. "Not sure a basic black dress counts as fancy."

"Huh. Just a basic black dress." Now who was lying? That dress was anything but basic. That dress was a well-chosen weapon.

But she kept up the ruse. "Heels and red lipstick. It's a magic trick."

My eyes had a mind of their own, wandering down to where her steepled nipples pressed the fabric away from her body. God, in the right light, that dress was obscene. Made me want to do obscene things. "You use the magic trick for yourself or for someone else?"

"I was hoping to run into someone."

"Then I'm getting in the way." But I took a step closer.

"You aren't getting in the way at all."

For a handful of seconds I really considered it. Considered forgetting that I was the someone she'd been hoping to run into. Considered really letting myself be someone different. Considered slipping my arm around her waist and escorting her to my room for a night with no names and no strings and no baggage.

But she'd expect there to be strings in the morning.

And the baggage was sewn into me.

And I knew her name better than I knew my own.

I shot back the rest of my drink and slammed the empty glass on the bar so hard that eyes turned in our direction. I ignored them as I lay into her. "Why don't you go by Julianna anymore?"

There was a lot to be angry about when it came to her. Her name was only the first one to make it to the tip of my tongue, probably because it was the latest of the hurts she'd doled out over our lifetime, salt on a wound that would never ever heal.

Her face fell, but she quickly recovered, and now she was the woman she'd been in the office. Softer. Provocative, but only because she couldn't not be rather when seconds before it had been on purpose. "Julianna isn't who I wanted to be."

"But that's who you chose to be."

"I didn't choose anything," she snapped, as if I didn't know anything about her.

"Didn't you?" My voice was a blade. "You had the chance to be Jolie. You didn't take it."

"I know."

"You don't get to pretend everything is water under the bridge."

She looked guiltier with this. "I know."

Her acknowledgments weren't satisfying. Not when I wanted to fight. "You don't get to pop up suddenly and try to tell me that's who you are now."

"But it is," she said, her blue-green eyes flashing. "It's who I've always been. Since you gave me that name."

Now it was her with the blade, its tip held at my gut as she tried to tell me that Jolie had existed all these years without me. Trying to tell me that there was a very real part of her that was still mine.

I wouldn't hear it. Couldn't. "That girl is gone. Honestly? I'm not sure she ever really existed."

Without giving her a chance to say anything else, I pushed away from the bar and crossed the lounge to meet Blondie returning from the restroom. "Let's get out of here, baby," I said.

"Mm. Yes."

I grabbed her ass, glancing over my shoulder to be sure blue-green eyes were watching as I steered her toward the elevator. I could still spend tonight fucking Jolie out of my system.

I'd just do it fucking some other girl.

EIGHT

I woke up with regrets.

My neck ached from my awkward sleeping position. For some crazy reason, I'd decided to pass out on the couch. The hangover wasn't too bad, at least. I knew well enough how to handle my liquor and had made sure I was plenty hydrated before I crashed.

Nevertheless, my mouth tasted like shame, and my body ached with remorse.

I shouldn't have gone to the bar. I should have drunk myself into a stupor in the safety of my room. I shouldn't have been somewhere that I could be found.

I shouldn't have come to New York in the first place.

Movement from the suite's bedroom reminded me why I'd ended up out here.

"You're awake," Blondie said, walking out with the sheet wrapped around her body, mascara streaked and her eyes bleary.

I'd forgotten about her.

I'd forgotten about her when I was with her, to be honest. She was naked underneath that sheet, and I was fully aware I'd been the one who'd gotten her that way, but she hadn't been who I'd been thinking about when I did. The woman I'd pictured underneath me had slightly smaller tits and specks of green in her blue eyes and a gaze that saw right into me.

Yeah, I was a real piece of trash.

I scrubbed my hand over my face. "Yeah. I'm awake."

"Sorry again about putting you out of a bed. You could have slept with me." She was bashful with her flirting, not like she was trying to be coy, but like she was nervous about the morning-after routine.

I wasn't used to it myself. Generally, I was the asshole who made them go when the performance was through. Blondie was only here because she'd left her purse with her ID, phone, and room key at the bar, and by the time we'd gotten around to noticing, the place was closed up for the night. Since the front desk wouldn't give her another room key without identification, I'd let her stay.

Guess I wasn't a *complete* asshole.

"I don't sleep well with others," I told her, which was what I'd said last night as well as the truth. "It's a me thing, not you."

She scanned the room, as though it was easier to look anywhere but directly at me. "Well. The restaurant should be open now. I'll get dressed and get out of your hair."

She was hoping the purse had been tucked away in the restaurant safe rather than stolen, counting on it even since she refused use of my laptop when I offered so she could put a stop on her credit card.

I didn't have quite such an optimistic outlook on humanity. "If you wait until I get some things together, I'll go down with you in case it's not there."

I wasn't sure what I'd offer to her if it wasn't. I wasn't going to leave her completely stranded, but I was also long past ready for her to be out of my hair.

She shut the door to get changed, even though I'd seen everything, and I was grateful. If she'd left it open, it would have been an invitation, and I didn't want to deal with hurt feelings when I turned it down. I wasn't a fuck-every-chance-you-get kind of guy like Weston was. I had to be in the mood for sex, and for the most part, that mood only struck when I was lonely and liquored up.

Or, apparently, when I was trying to distract myself from someone else.

Shaking off thoughts of *her*, I pulled on the jeans and sweater I'd brought out from the bedroom the night before. Then I went to the closet by the front door to grab my duffel bag with gym clothes. There was a fitness center in the hotel, but I needed more than a treadmill and rowing machine. Fortunately, I'd located a boxing club a couple blocks away when I'd made my reservation, and I'd come prepared, suspecting I'd need to burn some energy off on this trip.

By the time Blondie came back out, I had my shoes and coat on, ready to go. She'd scrubbed her face and pulled her hair back into a bun held with the complimentary hotel pen and didn't look like a woman who had partied too hard. Even so, the dress from last night was too much bling for daywear, making her walk of shame obvious.

I considered loaning her my coat, but I needed my coat, and I didn't owe her anything, so I didn't feel too bad about not making the offer. With a nod, I gestured to the door and followed her out. Thankfully, she didn't attempt to make small talk, and we managed to get in the elevator and travel to the lobby floor in silence.

There was a group of people waiting for the elevator when the doors opened. I put a gentlemanly hand at Blondie's back to steer her around them, and so that's how we were when Jolie saw us.

Actually, I saw her first, which was why I didn't drop my hand immediately.

She was impossible to miss, her voice raised as she argued with the front desk clerk. "No, it's not fine. I need the room until Friday."

I couldn't hear the clerk's response. I wasn't sure she heard it either because that was the moment she looked up and saw me, my arm around the woman from the night before, and for a full second I gloated. How many times had I wished for exactly that scenario? To bump into Jolie with a younger, prettier woman on my arm. To show her I was doing better than fine and she could eat her heart out.

It only lasted that second, though, before it fizzled into misery. Blondie wasn't prettier by a long shot, and even if she were, she didn't mean anything to me, and I wasn't doing fine, and it was highly unlikely Jolie would ever eat her heart out over me. That was me that did that. That was still doing it.

I dropped my hand, and Jolie turned her focus back to the clerk. Her voice softer now, but still discernible. "Could you try it again? I know you already did, but just once more?"

It wasn't my business. Whatever she was fussing about, I wasn't part of it. I needed to keep walking.

"Hey, uh." I stumbled since I didn't have a name to end the statement with. "How about you go on ahead? I'm going to be..." I nodded at the desk. At Jolie.

"Oh, the woman from last night!" She surveyed the situation, quickly catching on. "You gonna rescue her? Look at you being everyone's knight in shining armor."

I cringed. I was not a hero. I was definitely not Jolie's hero.

What I was, apparently, was a masochist, because I kept finding myself drawn to the woman who had become synonymous with pain. "Let me know if you don't find your purse," I said dismissively.

Jolie had angled her body after spotting me so she didn't notice me come up until I was already there. "What seems to be the trouble?" I did that douchebag man thing where I addressed the clerk instead of her. To be fair, it wasn't because she was a woman—it was because she was her.

"It's nothing, Cade. A problem with my card." Jolie dismissed me without even looking at me.

She wanted me gone, and for some fucked-up reason, that was exactly the reason why I stayed.

NINE

"I've tried three times," the clerk said patiently, handing the credit card back to Jolie. "It's still showing..." He lowered his voice, trying to be discreet. "Declined."

Her cheeks flushed, but her expression stayed cool. She took the card back and pulled another from the wallet open on the counter in front of her. "Please, can you run this one instead?"

"Yes, Ms.—"

She cut him off sharply. "It's Jolie. Please."

"I'll try it right now, Jolie."

"Thank you." I could feel her vibrating with anxiety as the clerk ran the card through the reader.

I stepped closer, needing to soak up her energy. Not because I thought I could take it from her or because I liked negative emotions, but because it was palpable and hers, and I'd spent so many years yearning to be close enough to her to know what she was feeling that I couldn't help being drawn into it now.

Her eyes flicked to me, then back to the clerk. "Go away, Cade."

I didn't move. The clerk, on the other hand, looked up, assessing the situation, probably trying to decide if he should interfere with whatever was going on between the guests standing in front of him.

After a beat, he smiled brightly. "Give me a moment. It might be the machine. Let me try another."

Without waiting for a response, he took Jolie's credit card and disappeared into the back room under the pretenses of trying to run it again. I strongly suspected he was giving us time to resolve our altercation on our own so he wouldn't have to deal with me. People often found me intimidating like that.

As soon as he was gone, I turned to Jolie. "Are you strapped—"

She wouldn't let me even finish the sentence. "This isn't your problem. You don't need to get involved."

It was a little nervy for her to push my help away a day after she'd come begging for it. "Little late for that, don't you think?"

"No, I don't think. You made it blatantly clear that you had no interest."

It didn't matter that she was speaking fact. Being dismissed pissed me off all the same. Unreasonably. I huffed, trying to come up with some pointed comeback when I caught the eye of Blondie returning from the bar. She held her purse up for me to see and gave me a wave.

At least that was resolved. I'd have my suite back to myself.

When I waved back, Jolie followed my eyeline to see Blondie scurrying to the elevator.

"Is she your girlfriend?" Her voice was even tighter than before.

I considered for a moment, trying to decide if I wanted to answer what Jolie had asked or give her the answer I was sure she wanted. "Not really," I said, not feeling generous enough to tell her I didn't do girlfriends.

She rolled her eyes. "Oh, one of those." I didn't get a chance to drill her on her meaning before she asked, "What's her name?"

"Cassie," I said, thinking quickly.

"Weird that her purse has Addie stitched across it."

I squinted toward my one-night stand waiting for the elevator. "You couldn't see that from here."

"I saw it last night."

Cassie/Addie. Close enough. More importantly... "If you already knew her name, why did you ask?"

"I wanted to see if you knew it." The triumphant look on her face was so familiar, reminding me how she always loved to be right, and how she loved to revel in her victory, and how I loved to kiss that look right off of her lips.

Her lips were just as plump and tempting as they'd been back then.

Fuck her and her lips and her trap to one-up me. "Seems weird that you noticed her purse."

She turned away from me, facing straight ahead, her triumph tempered with a mask of disinterest that she couldn't quite pull off. "Why? Girls notice each other's things."

"In my experience, they only notice when they're being catty." I was pulling shit from my ass, but I liked how it sounded. "Why would you be spiteful to a girl you just met? Are you jealous?"

Her head turned toward me so fast, her hair swung. "Jealous?! You've got to be kidding me."

I hadn't believed it when I said it. I was just trying to poke her a bit because I resented her and enjoyed seeing her provoked.

But the way she reacted—her face red, her eyes blazing—I almost wondered if there was something to it.

No way I wasn't leaning into that. "I think it's a reasonable enough question. Can't figure why else you'd care. And your reaction now confirms it."

"There was no reaction. I was curious. Politely curious. And now I'm—"

The clerk returned, and her expression quickly shifted to something friendlier. "Did it work?"

Her tone said she knew it hadn't gone through before the guy answered. "I was able to get your current room charge to go through, but it won't accept the prepayment for the rest of your stay."

Two credit cards with no credit available.

"You don't have money?" It came out like an accusation. I hadn't meant that exactly. I was more just...surprised. I had a real nice bank account now, but when I'd known her, she'd been the one with money. Her father, anyway. A decent amount, too. The kind of amount that made him look noble for continuing to headmaster the school that had been in his family for generations instead of hiring someone else to do it. The kind of money that would not be used up before he died.

So why the hell was Old Man Stark not taking care of the daughter he'd always been so protective of?

Things were beginning to click. "Is that why...? Because you need his—"

"I don't want to discuss this here," she snapped. "Please."

Fair enough.

"We're going to get the bill covered," I said to the clerk, ignoring Jolie's attempt to disagree. "We just need a moment to discuss the finances. Be right back. I'm leaving this for insurance." I didn't know if he actually needed insurance, but I dropped my duffel bag on the counter all the same.

"All right. Sure." The clerk appeared relieved to see us go as I grabbed Jolie's elbow and pulled her with me down the hall, trying the handles of closed doors, searching for one that would open to someplace private where I could drill her more thoroughly.

She fought me verbally the entire way. "Where are you taking me? Let me go. This isn't any of your business, Cade. Stay out of this."

Despite her protests, she didn't once try to yank her arm away. She was wearing another weather-appropriate sweater, material much thicker than the thin dress Blondie/Cassie/Addie had been wearing, but my hand felt the heat of her skin. Heat so intense my palm burned, and I wondered if I'd ever be able to let it go or if I'd be fused to her forever.

Eventually, one of the doors I tried was unlocked. I opened it, glancing at the sign that said Business Center before stepping in and pulling her with me, then turning us so that my back was blocking the door.

"What is your problem?" Now she jerked her arm and stumbled, apparently surprised when I let her go right away.

I guess that answered that question.

I shoved my still burning hand into my pocket. "I don't have a problem. You, it seems, do."

"It's not a problem that needs you."

"It's not? I thought I came to New York specifically so you could ask me to help with your problem."

"I don't need help with money."

"Is this why you want him gone? Because he cut you off?" That son of a bitch, if he did. I was beginning to want him dead after all.

"It's not that simple." Her mouth quivered, and I recognized it as a gesture she made when she was on the edge of breaking down.

God, if she cried...

I might kill *her* if she pulled that on me. I couldn't deal with tears from anyone, least of all her. Especially when I couldn't know if they were real or a manipulative tactic.

I leaned my back against the door, getting comfortable. "Tell me the complicated version then."

She folded her arms across her chest and shot me a death glare. After a long, silent minute, she spoke. "You can't keep this room blocked off forever."

I surveyed our surroundings. For a nice hotel, it was a pathetic business center. Just a desk with two computers and a printer on it. Most likely, the type of clientele that stayed here had the hotel concierge handle any of their needs for them.

In other words, we weren't going to be bothered anytime soon. "Let's just see if I can't. I'm waiting."

"You'll be waiting a long time then because I don't owe you any explanation."

I could have begged to disagree.

But she was right about one thing—I couldn't keep her in this room forever. Because every second that passed with her two feet away—her cherry-blossom scent tickling my nose, her lips trembling and tempting, her eyes big and penetrating—was a torturous second. Her features and gestures were too achingly familiar. The longer I stood in here with her, the closer I was to giving in.

Giving in to what, I didn't know. Giving in to everything.

I needed another tactic before I lost my grip. "You told the clerk you need the room until Friday. Is that when you're leaving New York?"

She sighed. "My flight home is Friday night."

I didn't let myself wonder where *home* was. "You can't change your flight?"

"Not without an outrageous change fee." Now that I wasn't asking about the particulars of how she got in her situation, she seemed more forthcoming.

"And you don't know anyone else in town?"

Her arms dropped to her sides, and she shook her head slowly, reluctantly, as though it cost her something to let me know that.

Probably because that meant she'd come just for me. She'd booked a whole week here, just for me.

She seemed to read my mind. "I didn't know how much time it would take to get you on my side."

"Seems you didn't count on me shutting you down on day one."

She shrugged, and I had a feeling the shrug meant she hadn't really accepted yet that I had shut her down. She sure as hell wasn't going to be closer to accepting it if I stepped in and helped her out.

Don't do it. Do not do it.

Just like that, I was back there again, to the past. *"He has money in his safe at the cabin. Gobs of it. I'll give you the combo. Take all of it, Cade. Every penny."*

It hadn't been hers to offer, but if she'd had money of her own, she would have drained her piggy bank for me. Whether or not she'd ever planned to leave with me, I knew she wouldn't have let me go empty-handed.

Without that stolen cash from her father, I would have had to do a lot uglier things than I had to survive.

With a groan, I wiped my palm over my beard. The money might have saved me, but I didn't owe her shit. Still, I couldn't leave a woman stranded in New York City. Not even her. "I'll pay your hotel bill. Let me get to a cash machine, and I can give you some extra for anything else you need."

And I could take the next flight out to Tokyo and not think about her ever again.

Her eyes flashed with the spitfire temper I remembered from her. "No way. I'm not a charity case."

I laughed. "You'll ask me to commit murder, but you can't take my money?"

"I was hoping you'd be invested in that for yourself." Her arms were folded across her chest again, in just the right way so it propped up her breasts, and fuck, I did not need to be thinking about her tits right now.

I focused my eyes on hers, refusing to let them drift lower. "Well, I'm not, and if the whole reason you want your father dead is because you need money, then you should just cut out the murder part and take mine." I'd give her more than what I'd offered. I'd write her a blank check.

I seriously hated myself for it, but it was true.

"I don't need your money." She stuck out her chin. Insistent. "I do fine."

"'Fine,' but you're getting kicked out of your hotel room—"

"Fine doesn't mean I can spare the money for an impromptu trip to NYC and a fancy hotel room. Regular people don't have gobs of cash lying around."

The comment about regular people hit me in the gut. Because I'd always been the regular one, and she'd never been anything close to "regular."

But I understood what she was saying. She wasn't desperate. She could take care of herself. She just couldn't take care of *this*, and to make matters worse, the reason she'd splurged on *this* was because she'd put all of her hope in me saying I'd help her out, and I refused.

"Then let me pay for the room," I said, softer. I didn't have any reason to feel guilty, and I didn't, but I could help her out. It wasn't a rescue. It was being a good human.

"You're not paying for my room."

"Let me—"

"I said you're not paying for my room."

"Then you can stay in my room." It was out of my mouth before I had time to think it through. I imagined I looked as shocked as she did about it.

She had the decency to realize it was something I never should have said. "I can't stay with you, Cade."

She was right. She couldn't. Worst idea on the planet. "It's a suite. There's plenty of space."

"I...can't..."

"I'm either paying for your room or you're staying in mine. Choose, Jol—." I caught myself. "Choose."

"You're not paying for my room." Stubborn, defiant. Like she'd always been.

Well, she'd made her choice.

And I was as stubborn and defiant as she was.

I whirled around, opened the door, and trekked down the hallway back toward the front desk.

"Cade? What are you doing now? Whatever it is, no." She followed after me, skipping now and then to keep up.

Ignoring her, I pulled my wallet out of my back pocket, went up to the desk clerk, and laid my ID and a hundred in front of him. "Add her to my room. She'll need her own key. Then have a bellhop help her move her stuff over."

It was outrageous and showy to give a hundred dollar tip, but I had a point to prove. I had money. Helping her out like this was nothing. She could have just let me pay for her room.

She stood next to me, silent, vibrating again, this time with rage, but also relief. I could feel it, and if I didn't know her better—and it could be argued that I didn't know her at all—I might have thought I'd been conned.

"Thank you," she said when it was all settled, and the clerk had called a bellhop and given her a key. I could tell it was hard for her to say it, but it didn't make me any less pissed.

I picked up my duffel bag. "You're sleeping on the couch."

"Of course."

"I'm sure you can find your way to the room on your own." I turned toward the front doors, needing the boxing club more now than ever.

Before I'd taken a step, she put a hand out on my bicep to stop me. "I want to be honest with you. It's like you said—I'm still here because I'm hoping you'll change your mind. I want you to know I'm going to take advantage of this situation."

I should have been scared. Instead, I took it as a challenge. "Go ahead and try."

I could take advantage of the situation too, I told myself as I stormed out into the cold December day. I could learn her secrets. I could leave no reason to still be curious. I could get my closure.

Or I could end up right where I'd always been—on my knees in love with a woman who would never love me back.

TEN

"Oh, it's you." Sabrina appeared just as surprised to see me when she opened Donovan's door as I was to see her. "I thought you were our lunch."

She stepped back so I could walk in past her. "Domesticating together already?" I'd known Donovan long enough to know he'd never had women in his apartment. He didn't even let them in for a romp before kicking them out. He didn't let them in period.

Based on Sabrina's outfit, which consisted of men's boxer shorts and an oversized T-shirt, it was obvious she'd stayed the night. And she was still here in the afternoon.

When the man said "girlfriend," he went all the way.

Sabrina apparently wasn't yet comfortable with their relationship status. "Uh...I mean, um. We had some work to go over..." She couldn't look at me, her cheeks bright pink.

I chuckled. "It's okay. Don't worry about it. No explanation needed. Is he here?"

"In his office." She nodded toward the stairs, but I was already headed in that direction. I knew the layout of the place, having stayed there several times over the course of our relationship. I was probably more familiar with the place than she was.

I bounded up the stairs two at a time, then knocked once on the closed door. I didn't wait for a reply before I opened it.

Donovan glanced up from his computer without moving his head. "I thought it was too fast for the food to be here. You're here sooner than I expected as well."

I looked at my watch. I'd spent a couple of hours at the boxing club, then hit the sauna before heading over to his building. Still, it was early in the day, only a little past one. "You said afternoon. It's after noon."

"Not complaining." He closed out of whatever he was working on and swung his chair to face me. "I just figured you'd be battling a mighty hangover today."

"Fuck you. I've even been to the gym already." I'd rented a locker at the club so I didn't have the duffel to prove it.

"Good for you. Have a cigar." He picked up the ornate box from the corner of his desk and handed it toward me.

I shook my head. "You look cozy. Playing house with her, are you?"

He set the cigar box down and pulled one out for himself before giving me a look that said I'm-not-discussing-my-girlfriend-with-you.

"And yet you want me to discuss Jolie with you."

He bit off the end of his cigar, then pointed it at me. "The difference is you don't want to hear my shit with Sabrina. I do want to hear your shit with Jolie. So you gonna lay it on me or what?"

I couldn't protest because it was true. I didn't want to hear about his happy love life. I was too bitter and jealous. Fuck him for being lucky enough to have everything work out. Must be fucking nice.

My expression must have told him exactly what I was thinking.

"Oh, come on," he said, standing up. He walked around the desk to me and stuck the cigar in my face. "Sit down. Smoke with me. You want to tell me, and I want to hear. Don't make me have to work to get it out of you."

I held my scowl for another few seconds before taking the offering and putting it in my mouth. Donovan was there instantly with a light. I puffed, getting the cherry nice and red while he returned to his chair and lit one for himself. "I hate these, you know."

"But you enjoy burning up my cash. These are Gurkhas. Seven-fifty a stick. Hate it less now?"

He knew me so well. I really did get a kick out of wasting his money. I cracked a small smile as I sat down in his leather armchair. "Marginally."

"That's what I thought."

The room filled with the scent of cognac and tobacco as we puffed silently. I knew where to start, and as he'd guessed, I was anxious to tell him, but now that I was here sitting down with him, it felt a little less urgent. Like maybe I'd made it all up in my mind. Not her visit, because that had definitely happened, but the atrocity of her request. Was I making it a bigger deal than it was? I'd told her no, I meant no, was there really anything to say about it?

I supposed that was what I was here to figure out.

"She wants my help with something," I said eventually, glad that Donovan hadn't pushed me to say it before I was ready.

"Figured as much. She disappeared for all these years. Couldn't imagine she'd pop up again unless she was desperate. Are you going to help her?"

"You're not even going to ask what it is?" I was sure he would have wanted to know that first thing. Here he was jumping past the most important part.

"The favor is less interesting than your response."

"But how can you decide if my response is justified if you don't know what the favor is?"

He tapped his finger on his cigar, then leaned forward. "You really are going to make me work for this." There was the Donovan I knew.

I inhaled deeply on my cigar, taking in more tobacco than I needed, but damn the buzz felt good. "She wants me to kill her father."

He didn't bat an eye. "Does he deserve it?"

"Uh. Does anyone?"

"Yes. There are most definitely people who deserve it, and you know that as well as I do. You've worked with a fair number of them."

Sure, I'd worked with some despicable men in my life, but I hadn't ever sat around contemplating a death wish list. "I've never thought it was my responsibility to make it happen."

"It's not. Unless you decide it is. Have you decided it is this time?"

"I can't believe you're calmly sitting there, casually asking me if I'm going to murder my ex-girlfriend's prick of a father."

"If that was the entire extent of the relationship you had with Stark, I'd maybe be more worked up about it." He considered his words. "Nah. Probably not."

I wasn't sure what I'd been expecting. Calm, collected, cool-as-a-cucumber Donovan Kincaid didn't get in a fuss about much of anything. Why had I thought this would be any different? "She should have asked you to help her out."

"She still could. Want me to find someone?"

I couldn't decide if he was messing with me or if he was sincere. Or if he actually knew someone who did that kind of job.

Whatever the answer, my response was the same. "You helping her is the same as me helping her, and I'm not fucking helping her."

"Because the favor itself turns you off or you don't want to help her at all?"

"Both." It wasn't true. I wanted it to be, but I'd offered her money and a place to stay within twenty-four hours of our initial meeting. "The first one. Frankly, you should be turned off by it too."

He ignored my attack on his morals. "Then if she'd asked something else, something less..."

"Illegal," I filled in for him.

He gave me a knowing glare. He knew legality had never been a problem for me. "Something less *life ending*, you would have helped her out."

I didn't know how to answer that. Honestly, I was appalled she had the gall to ask for anything from me at all, and if her favor had been anything else—if she'd asked for me to give her a recommendation or sign a get well card, anything at all—I would have probably turned her down. Because she deserved to be the disappointed one this time. Because how dare she?

The only reason I'd helped her out today was because it hadn't been as satisfying to turn her down yesterday as I'd wanted it to be.

"I don't know, Donovan. I don't know what I would have said if her request had been something reasonable. I think I would have turned her down no matter what."

"But you'd still be thinking about it today."

I didn't have to respond. I was here, wasn't I?

ELEVEN

"So I'll ask again—does he deserve it?"

It was a moot point as far as I was concerned, since there was no way I was helping, but as long as Donovan wanted to go down this road, well. It could be interesting to see where it led. "Stark was...not nice."

"So I've gathered from what you've said in the past."

"Abusive for sure. Physically. The kind of abusive that Child Protective Services would want to put behind bars."

"But you could never prove it."

"No."

"And he wasn't like that with other students?" He was familiar with the charges I'd tried to bring against my former headmaster, though I'd never gone into detail. It seemed he'd done some research of his own, or had at least figured out enough of the parts I'd left out to know what to ask.

"Nope. I was special." The wrong kind of special.

"Yeah, well, you know why that is."

I was quiet for a second, remembering all the reasons that man had hated me from day one. "Yeah. I suppose I do."

"Not your fault. You dealt with the cards you were handed." He rolled his cigar between his lips. "But you're saying he wasn't really a danger to anyone after you were gone?"

My instinct was no. Though I couldn't have said what he'd done after I'd left.

There was also a chance I'd been a buffer for his brutal nature. And with me gone, he could very well have gotten his sadistic kicks elsewhere, including on Jolie.

My mind started to wander to someone else who might have been his victim, someone other than Jolie, but I shut that line of thinking down right away, unwilling to follow it. It was bad enough thinking he might have used his daughter for his punching bag with me gone. I didn't have room to worry about anyone else.

But Langdon Stark's danger didn't just lie in his hands. "On paper, no. He was a model headmaster who ran a model school. He produced the best students who got into the best colleges. The parents who sent their kids there didn't care about methods. They wanted results."

"So they didn't care if the guy in charge smacked them around a bit?"

"No, not that. I really don't think he laid a hand on anyone else. At least, I couldn't find anyone who would admit it when I was looking for corroboration when I filed charges. But he was..." I paused, trying to think how to describe it. The man was a gaslighter and a master manipulator. Looking back, it was just as hard to identify what was so horrible about him as when I'd been in the middle of it.

"This one time, for instance," I said, deciding it was better to give him an example. "I was still new to the place, but a couple of the guys were feeling me out. Seeing if I was worthy of their time or friendship. This kid, Birch—I don't remember his first name. He was a total asswipe. So of course he was popular. He liked to write these horrid stories about the people he didn't like. He thought they were funny, and of course anyone he shared them with would laugh like they were because he was a guy with that kind of power, but they were really just mean. Stories about how slutty the girl in math class was or how the kid with the glasses had a limp dick.

"So this day, he wrote a particularly nasty thing about the fat kid. Presley." I'd never forget him—wide eyes hidden behind round glasses that only made his face look heavier. Smart, but shy. Decent. Nice. "I mean, this story went on and on about Presley's size, how he'd never get laid, and if he even tried he'd end up rolling over on the girl and killing her with his weight."

"Sounds like we need to take a hit out on this Birch guy," Donovan said. As though taking a hit out on someone was everyday for him.

"Eh. Birch was a prick, but he was harmless for the most part. Most of his victims never knew they were being made fun of. Except this time, the story had been passed to me, and I was reading it behind my history book, pretending to laugh as I did so he'd think I was cool. Or maybe I really did think it was funny. It's hard to have that perspective in the aftermath. Anyway, Stark was subbing for the professor that day, and he caught me."

"Uh-oh."

It had been ridiculously stupid for me to have been acting up in front of him. I should have been on my best behavior the minute he'd walked in the room. Even new, I'd figured that much out in my encounters with him.

But I'd been seventeen and a rebel, and I'd wanted to fit in, and that need outweighed any sense of survival. "And instead of just sending me to detention or dealing with me privately later on, he turned the whole thing into a spectacle. Brought me up to the front of the class. Made me read the whole thing out loud."

"Okay...and?" Donovan seemed to need help seeing the point.

"And it was awful. Not for me, necessarily—though yes for me, too, because like hell was I saying who really wrote it, and so of course most everyone thought it was me. But the worst part was that Presley was in the class, and he had to hear it. I could understand the nature of the punishment, truly I could. But as soon as Stark heard what sort of story it was, he should have stopped me and dealt with me later. That's what a decent educator would have done.

"Not Stark. He prodded me on. He made me read every cruel

word, made Presley listen as I made fun of his size in every wicked way possible. Made me keep going, even after Presley had started to openly cry. I tried to keep my eyes on the paper so I wouldn't see his face, but I couldn't miss the sound of his sobbing. And when I glanced at Stark, praying he'd let me stop, he had the most gleeful look in his eyes. Orgasmic. Like he was in heaven."

"Sounds like a true sadist." Donovan tapped the growing ash off the end of his cigar into an ashtray.

"Mm," I murmured in agreement. Then I dropped my own cigar in the tray, feeling too sick from the memory to smoke anymore. "I could recount a dozen stories like that. He didn't lay a hand on his students, but he was psychologically abusive."

"Psychological abuse is quite often worse than physical."

"But harder to identify." I waited a beat, then added, "Harder to justify murdering over."

Donovan raised a shoulder as though not quite sure he agreed. "I imagine his treatment of his students isn't the reason Jolie wants him gone."

It was my turn to shrug. "She wouldn't say why."

"She wouldn't?" Finally, Donovan seemed surprised.

"Wouldn't tell me why now or why me."

"Hard to ask someone for such a heavy favor without having a reason. She offer to pay you?"

"No, no. No." I paused, not sure I wanted to say more. But it was Donovan, and I always told him everything. "I think she's broke, actually. Might be why she came to me. Because she thought I might do it for her without compensation. I was probably one of a whole list of ex-boyfriends she approached to do the deed."

He shook his head. "I doubt that. Still seems hard to expect you to be motivated without more information."

"Right."

"Has to be something pretty important though. Something specific. To bring her out of hiding."

I leaned back in the chair, considering. This was what I liked about my partnership with Donovan—he thought differently than I did. He looked at the whole picture while I was focused on the minutia. He followed trails of thinking that I would never see and ended up with an understanding of situations that was often out of my scope of comprehension.

Regardless...

"It doesn't matter what her reason is. I'm not helping her, and I'm not covering for her if someone comes asking me questions later on."

"Then that's it. Your decision's made." He didn't sound like he was trying to dispute me. More like he was trying to confirm.

"Yep."

"Great. You're done with this and her; you can move on."

"Yeah. Exactly how I was looking at it." Well. Except. "Actually, not quite done with *her* yet..."

He raised a quizzical eyebrow, and with his black turtleneck and slacks, he looked more like a behind-the-scenes mastermind than usual.

For some reason, that made it harder to want to admit my fuckup. But he'd find out one way or another. Donovan had a way like that. "Like I said, it seems she's got a money problem. Couldn't afford to keep her hotel through until she leaves. Refused to take money from me for it. So I told her she could stay with me." I said the last part fast. Like ripping off a Band-Aid.

Now both of his eyebrows rose. "Seems you weren't opposed to helping her after all."

"It's barely helping her," I protested. "I wanted her off my conscience. That's all." It had nothing to do with the way my chest felt tight when I was near her or the way her gaze pierced into my soul.

"Off your conscience, into your bed. Sounds right."

I gave him a stern stare. "I'm not going to fuck her."

"Want to bet on that?"

Last time I'd made a bet with Donovan, I'd ended up with *Gangster* tattooed across my back. I vowed never to make that mistake again.

But it was impossible not to want to show him up. He always acted so superior. Like he knew everything and everyone better than they knew themselves. And maybe if I had a bet with him, I wouldn't be tempted to even consider letting something sexual happen with Jolie.

Not that I was considering sex as it was. I definitely wasn't.

"Sure thing. I win, and you get the tattoo of my choice this time." I already had it planned out—a heart with flowers and the word *Mom*.

"When I win, that will be two tattoos you don't want on your skin. You ready for that?"

"Not going to lose, and I'm definitely ready to see you in ink."

"You're on." He was too far away to shake on it, but a nod sealed the deal. He grinned like I was a fool. "This day just took an eventful turn. Glad to have you back in town. How long are you here?"

I hadn't booked a return flight yet. Every instinct said I should get on a plane sooner rather than later. If I got something out tonight, I could stop by the hotel, gather my things, and not have to see Jolie ever again. I'd picked up the phone to make a reservation at least three times since I'd first had the thought. Twice I'd started a text to have my assistant do it.

Then I'd think about what was waiting for me at home—enough work to keep me busy. Designer sheets that only ever smelled like me. A list of revolving hookups who didn't mind meeting in hotel rooms.

Arguably the perfect life.

I had no logical reason to stay, and a million good reasons to run, but I was stuck again in that tar pit that surrounded Jolie. Desperately wanting to get out but unable to make myself move.

"I guess I'm leaving Saturday," I said. She'd be gone then. I'd be able to leave.

"Jolie must be flying out Friday." His grin widened. "Got any blank skin on your torso? I want to pick the best spot for your new art."

"Fuck you."

"You mean fuck her."

I refused to reply. We sat quietly again, and I mulled over everything we'd talked about, trying to decide if I'd gained any perspective from our conversation. Usually talking with Donovan helped shift my view, but everything looked exactly the way it had when I'd walked in.

I was just as adamant that I wasn't going to kill Stark as when I'd arrived. I was just as pissed that she'd asked me. I was just as determined to hate her forever.

Fucking her hadn't crossed my mind before Donovan put the idea in my head, but I was just as resolute about that as well.

"Do you have to kill him literally?" Donovan asked, interrupting my what-a-waste-of-time thought spiral.

He was always trying to figure out the way that most of the people involved came out a winner, usually with him the biggest winner of them all. It was abnormally altruistic for him to care when he wasn't eligible for a prize.

His question was intriguing, though. "What do you mean?"

Before he could answer, the buzzer rang. "Food must be here," he said but let Sabrina answer it. He put his cigar out. "You can stay. We ordered extra yakisoba in case you came by."

It was tempting. It had been the better part of the year since I'd had a meal with my friend, and nothing sounded more relaxing than kicking back with a beer and shooting the shit with him over Japanese.

But he was with Sabrina now. And I had Jolie to deal with. Or rather, Jolie to avoid. With our bet made, it was unlikely Donovan would be supportive in that endeavor.

"Next time," I said, standing up. "You have house to play. Should we wager how long before there's a ring on her finger?" I held out my hand to shake goodbye if he didn't take me up on the bet.

"Not a chance," he said, taking my hand. "Unlike you, I know when the odds are against me."

He didn't fucking know anything. Not a single goddamned thing.

But I was definitely going to stay away from my suite for the rest of the day, just to be sure.

TWELVE

I spent the rest of the afternoon back at Reach, using Weston's office so I didn't have to be reminded of the last time I was in Donovan's. After that, I joined Nate at the gentleman's club the guys liked to frequent, which wasn't the worst of distractions, despite the fact that he had a new lady he couldn't shut up about.

At least his lady wasn't the lady I was trying to not think about, and so I endured the torture until well after midnight when I finally gave up the battle and headed back to my hotel.

Headed back to *her*.

Outside my room, I took a beat to prepare myself, then opened the door to the best case scenario—a dark living area, suggesting my guest was already asleep. Just as I'd hoped.

I avoided looking at the direction of the sofa as I headed toward my room. A lamp had been left on, and the low murmur of voices told me I'd left the TV on as well. I didn't have a chance to realize I hadn't turned on the television before I'd made it to the doorway and saw who apparently did: Jolie. Asleep. On my bed. Wearing nothing but a T-shirt and panties.

Emotions crashed through me like lightning, striking and disappearing so fast, I barely had time to acknowledge them. Once upon a time, this was supposed to have been our life. Her, sleeping in my bed like it was no big deal. Me, eager not to disturb her as I gazed down at her soft features.

But we hadn't gotten the happily ever after.

And this was not our life.

"What the fuck, Julianna? I said sleep on the couch." My voice boomed loud enough to wake her with a start.

She blinked, confused for a moment. Then she saw me and stretched. "Hey! You're here." There was a note of relief in her tone. As though she were glad I'd shown up. As though she'd been afraid I wouldn't.

It was fucked up how the instinct to run to her was still so easily triggered in my body.

I was as mad at that response as I was her. "Yeah. Because it's my room. If you wanted to treat it like your own, you could have stayed in yours, like I originally offered."

"No. This is good. This is great. I mean the couch is great." She jumped off the bed and gathered herself before explaining. "The TV out there isn't working. I have a hard time sleeping when I'm alone unless it's on, so I figured I'd just hang out here until you got here. I didn't mean to fall asleep. I'm sorry."

It was after one in the morning. Of course she was falling asleep.

There was no accusation in her tone, though, which almost pissed me off even more.

But also, I didn't trust her.

"The TV doesn't work?" I flicked on the light switch, noting that the couch hadn't even been made into a bed yet, then stomped over to the living area television set, ready to call bullshit. While I wasn't sure that she was particularly manipulative, she *had* said that she'd try to take advantage of this situation, and seduction had always been her weapon of choice. The broken TV seemed like an awfully convenient setup.

But when I tried the power button, sure enough, it didn't turn on. I found the cord behind the set and followed it to the wall.

"It's plugged in," she said from behind me.

Yeah, but had she tried it in another outlet? I unplugged it and scanned the wall for another place to try it.

"I checked the outlet too. My phone cord works in it, so it's not that."

"You should have—"

She cut me off, reading my thoughts. "I called the front desk. They came up and fiddled with it and said they'd have a new one delivered tomorrow. They offered to give us a different room, but I didn't want to make that decision for you."

So not a scam then.

I looked around for something else to be mad at and found it easily. That T-shirt she was wearing? It was mine. "It's hard to not think you're up to something when you're lounging around on *my* bed, wearing *my* clothes."

"You're so very perceptive. I was very much up to something. Want to know what it was?" She'd sauntered toward me while she spoke, and now she was an inch away, leaning in like she was about to share her greatest secret.

I could barely breathe. "What?"

"Sleeping." She flashed a huge smile, popping the tension like it was a balloon and she was a pin. "I'm pretty transparent, Cade. I've already laid out what I'm up to, and save for a couple of personal secrets, I'm not really hiding anything."

She was definitely not hiding a lot dressed like that. Her legs were long and toned and curved in just the right places. It was hard to ignore how beautiful she was. How beautiful she'd always been.

I wasn't distracted enough by her looks, though, to miss the implication of her words. She was basically inviting me to ask her anything. Anything at all. I could have all the answers I'd been seeking. I could ask about all the unknown details of her life that had kept me awake for countless nights over the years. The bits of Jolie trivia that had driven me crazy with burning curiosity.

Or maybe that was her game. Lull me into a false sense of trust. Then attack.

I refused to let my guard down. "Okay, then, so you won't mind telling me why you're wearing my shirt."

She took a step back and leaned against the arm of the couch. Comfortably, not seductively. "It's not as exciting as the reason you're alluding to. I usually sleep in just..." She gestured to her panties. Cotton and plain, like the kind she'd worn as a teen. "All the clothes I brought with me are weather appropriate. Sweaters. Jeans. Nothing comfortable enough to sleep in."

"So you went through my stuff?"

That smile again. "I don't remember you being so suspicious and melodramatic."

"I don't remember you having a total lack of respect for privacy."

Her smile faded then because we were talking about my things, but we were talking about her secrets too. If she wanted me to respect her boundaries, she had to respect mine. "I opened one drawer and took the first shirt I found. That's it. I can give it back—" She grabbed the hem and lifted it high enough that I saw the bottom curve of her breasts.

My pants felt tighter.

"Stop." I looked away in case she didn't. "Keep it. Keep it for the week." I almost offered to let her take it with her when she left, but the plain black T had suddenly become one of my favorites.

"Thanks." Her smile was back, more contained than before, but genuine. "And for the room. I really do appreciate it."

I was still pissed. Anger was my security blanket, and if I let it go...

Well, I didn't want to think what I'd be left with then. So I didn't accept her apology or her gratitude. I just stood there feeling gruff and raw and turned inside out and let her make of it what she would.

"I'll, um, just..." She stood and nodded toward the couch behind her.

It was my cue to leave. To go hole up in my bedroom, with the dresser pushed against the door if necessary.

But that luxury room, with its king-size bed and thousand-thread-count sheets, suddenly seemed lonely. And just like she'd needed the TV on for companionship, I wanted to linger in her presence. "Here, I'll help you set it up."

I crossed to the opposite end of the couch and reached for a cushion. She hesitated only a beat before joining me, tossing cushions to the floor, then hefting the metal frame out of the enclosure. The mattress inside was bare, but I found a bag of bedding in the coat closet that included a bed sheet. I unfolded it and handed her an end.

Then together we spread it across the mattress, tucking the ends around the corners so it would stay. I'd never made up a bed with someone before. This was the spot where she'd sleep. Where she'd spend hours at her most vulnerable. It was intimate in a way I hadn't expected. More intimate than sex even. I'd fucked a lot of women. Jolie hadn't even been my first. But for this, she was the only one.

I peeked over at her as we tucked the top sheet in. Her gaze brushed over mine in periphery, then caught it full on. My breath felt lodged in my chest, and I cleared my throat, as though that would help.

It didn't. But the noise strengthened her attention, and now I felt obliged to do something with it. "You're here a week," I said, not sure where I was going with the remark.

"Yeah."

"Because you thought that would be enough time...?"

"Enough time to convince you to help me?" She pulled a pillow to her so she could put on a pillowcase. "I hoped it was enough time."

I tried to consider her position and what she knew of me. What she knew of the boy I'd once been. That kid, would he have helped her? How long would it have taken for him to be convinced?

Not even a full minute.

"I could already have been on my way out of the city by now. How could you be sure I would even be here for a full week?"

"It's a long flight. The odds seemed to be in favor that you wouldn't just turn around and go back."

"But we had no arrangements to see each other again. As far as you knew, you had that one meeting. That's all I'd given you."

She smiled guiltily. "Why do you think I made sure I was staying in your hotel?"

A hotel with a near thousand-dollar-a-night price tag. She probably would have had enough to charge the whole week if she'd booked something on Priceline.

It had been an expensive gamble on her part. "That's a lot of guesswork. A lot of things had to fall into place to be sure you saw me again."

"Hard to knock my plan when I'm staying in your room."

I caught myself before I laughed out loud. Admittedly, she was cute —had always been cute. A little full of herself. A lot full of determination. I'd already spent enough time with her to see that hadn't changed. As much as I refused to acknowledge it, there was a lot of that girl I'd known still in this woman, and that realization made me nostalgic.

Made me start thinking things I shouldn't.

I was grateful when Donovan's words from earlier butted into my thoughts. *Do you have to kill him literally?*

"Why do you need him to be dead? Are you that set on revenge?" I was an idiot. Practically asking her to change my mind.

"Not just revenge."

"Then what? Money?"

She shook her head as she unfolded the comforter. "I need him out of my life. Can you take the end?"

I took the other side of the blanket and spread it over the bed, but I ignored her attempt to change the conversation. "Do you still live near him? Do you need help moving away?"

Headmaster Stark was a prominent figure in his community. She was a full-grown woman, but if they lived in the same town, there was no way she could really escape him. Was that all it was? She had enough money to live, but maybe not enough money to reestablish herself away from him?

"No, I've lived in Boston for about ten years."

Boston.

One word, but it was a puzzle piece I'd been searching for for so long that I couldn't help but hold on to it once she'd given it. *Boston.* All this time, she'd been in Boston.

Boston wasn't that far from Connecticut, though. "Is he bothering you? Showing up on your doorstep?"

"It's not quite that simple—"

"You keep saying that. I have resources that can handle complicated."

The blanket in place, she stood up straight. "I need him out of my life *for good.*"

There was desperation in her voice that I recognized because it was exactly the desperation I'd felt back then, when I didn't see any escape from her father's abuse. She'd suffered at his hand too, but I'd never seen the despair in her that I saw now.

What hold did he still have over her?

Trying to convince myself I didn't care was futile. At the very least, I was curious. "What did he—"

She cut me off. "I'm not going to say any more than that, Cade. Please don't ask."

Transparent, my ass.

Fuck her.

"Looks like you're good here. I'll leave you to it."

I brushed off her good night and walked around the bed to head to my room without a word. I did look back, though. Not to check out her ass, but since she was reaching across the bed to straighten the edge of the comforter, that's exactly what I saw.

And then I froze, my eyes pinned on the art inked at her hip, visible as the shirt rose with her stretch.

Before I knew what I was doing, I was at her side, tugging down the side of her panties far enough to see the whole thing.

"Hey!" She was startled but not incensed. In fact, once she realized what I was looking at, she lifted the shirt so I could see the full-color design better—a bird cage, the bars torn open in one spot, one bird outside the cage in flight, another still sitting inside.

I knelt down at her side, my breath caught in my chest, my heart pounding in my ears. Wordlessly, I swept my finger across her skin. Goosebumps broke out underneath my touch. Strange, since my finger felt like it was burning as it moved over the broken cage. Over the bird in the sky. Over the bird behind the bars. I lingered here the longest, tracing the creature's wings.

Why hasn't she flown away?

I would have traded places with her. If one of us had had to stay, I would have done that. If that had been an option. If that had been the price for her freedom.

Her belly rose with an intake of air, and I realized she'd been holding her breath. Realized I was touching her. Realized I was on the brink of falling apart.

I stood up quickly, careful not to meet her eyes. "Hey, how about you go ahead and take the bedroom? So you can keep the TV on," I added, so she wouldn't think the offer was for any reason other than practicality.

She tugged her shirt—my shirt—down, and folded her arms across her chest, as if by covering up, I could unsee what I'd seen. "I'm not doing that."

"You said you can't sleep."

"I should be better knowing you're in the next room. If not, I'll put YouTube on my phone."

She wouldn't look at me either. God, she was so frustrating. "Just take the room, Jo—" I caught myself. "Julianna."

Now her eyes hit mine, and I could practically hear her thoughts. *"It's Jolie now."* But she managed to refrain from saying it.

And I managed to refrain from saying the other thing pressing on my tongue, that I could take the room with her. That I could make her feel less alone. That I could still help her fly.

"Just for tonight," I insisted. Needing her in that other room as soon as fucking possible. "Okay?"

If she had fought with me right then, I didn't know what I would have done, but I had a feeling it would have been something impossible to come back from.

Fortunately, she didn't fight. I sat on the couch bed and busied myself with taking off my shoes, not looking up again until after I'd heard the click of the door shut behind her.

THIRTEEN

I slept fitfully, and not because the bed was uncomfortable, though it really was too small for my height. It was her keeping me up. She was quiet as a mouse, the only sound coming from the bedroom the low drone of the television. But I *felt* her. And every time I started to drift off, I jerked awake, as though my brain had determined I couldn't waste a single second of being in her presence with sleep.

I must have slept eventually because sometime around seven in the morning I woke up. There was no foggy daze where I temporarily forgot she was in the next room. As soon as my eyes opened, my ears were straining, listening for any of her sounds, imagining I could hear the soft rhythm of her breathing.

Cursing at myself, I rolled out of bed and tugged on last night's clothes so I wouldn't have to deal with her. Thankfully, the bathroom wasn't an en suite, and I was able to slip in, relieve myself, and freshen up without disturbing her.

I was out the door before she made a single peep.

The boxing club was busier at this time of the day. Being Monday didn't help; the place filled with Midtowners getting a workout in before heading to the office. Somehow, I managed to get a bag to myself, and I set out to keep my thoughts from overtaking me with pure aggression.

But even after an hour of beating the shit out of my imaginary opponent, I had enough energy to scare myself. Twice, I was invited into the ring for a real fight. Twice, I declined, afraid I'd kill someone.

Kill the *wrong* someone.

Fuck, I couldn't escape it, couldn't escape *her* or her damn favor. Couldn't punch away the thoughts and the memories and the desires. The desire to save her. The desire to fix her. The desire to have her as mine again.

I was sore and exhausted by the time I finally gave up and changed out of my gym clothes. After the long workout, the cold outside felt good, and I loitered outside the club, letting the nine-to-fivers hurry past while I soaked in the chill.

Not too much later, someone else paused as he stepped out of the club, long enough to pull a smoke out of his pocket and get it lit.

"Can I bum one?" I hadn't even made the conscious decision to ask before the words were out.

The guy looked me over, probably deciding if I meant to mug him or if I really just wanted a cigarette. Then he pulled the pack out and handed me one followed by his lighter.

"Thanks, man." I inhaled just enough to light the end before handing the lighter back. When he was on his way and I was alone again, I took a long drag and inhaled deeply.

Instantly, I was back there. Back to the night she'd kissed my stripes. She'd slipped out later to meet me at our spot. As she crouched down next to me, I handed her the cigarette I'd been smoking, then lit another for myself.

She hadn't had to say anything for me to know he'd punished her too. For what, it didn't matter. For helping me. For being caught with me. For something else entirely.

"Was it...terrible?" *I cringed because of course it was terrible. It was always terrible.*

She stared out into the distance and didn't answer, which wasn't unusual. She didn't like to talk about the punishments. Fortunately, she didn't get them very often. Not as often as I did anyway. Headmaster Stark must have really been on a tear today.

I reached a hand out to settle on her arm. "Do I need to be putting antibiotic on your back?"

She took a drag off her cigarette, then blew it out before answering. "He doesn't like to leave marks on me."

I wanted to hold her, but she didn't like to be held when she was in this mood. She seemed to think it was a suffering she had to handle on her own, and no matter how many times I tried to tell her differently, tried to tell her we were in this together and she didn't have to take it on alone, I'd yet to convince her.

It tore me up inside that I couldn't bear it for her. It was agony worse than any punishment her father could give.

"We're going to fly away, Jol," I said, wanting to give her the hope she'd given me earlier. It sounded stupid when I said it to myself, but out loud to her, it was a promise.

She looked at me then, looked at my hand resting at my side next to hers. Then she linked her pinkie in mine, and I wondered if she knew that she'd saved me, just by being there, just by being who she was, and I prayed with all my soul that I could do the same for her.

Praying had obviously gotten me nowhere.

Or was it only now that those prayers were being answered?

I tossed my unfinished cigarette in the snow. My muscles were stiff from the cold, but I pushed them forward, trucking back to the hotel at top speed, urgency buzzing in my blood.

I pushed through the breakfast crowd in the lobby and hit the elevator button over and over, willing it to get there faster. Then once inside, I hit the floor button with as much vigor. Finally, I was bursting into the suite, then throwing open the bedroom door.

She was awake, but from the glazed way she looked at me, just barely.

"We won't kill him," I declared. "We'll destroy him."

Her brows furrowed as she tried to get context. Then she frowned. "But—"

"He'll be out of your life. For good." Whether we had to set him up or dig up a real scandal, we would bring Langdon Stark down.

I waited for her to argue. I could feel her on the brink of it, but if she was really as desperate as she said she was, then she'd take what she could get, and this was what I could give.

She must have realized that because all she said was, "Okay."

Then before she got all weepy or grateful, I set the record straight. "And I'm doing this for me. Not for you. Got it?"

"Okay."

"Okay," I repeated.

"Okay," she said again, the corners of her mouth lifting in a wary smile.

Okay. We were doing this. Okay.

Our eyes locked, and I could practically hear her echoing thoughts. *Finally, we're doing this. Okay.*

"Good. Get dressed. We leave in ten." I tore my eyes away, but not before noticing she'd lost the shirt sometime during the night and now only had the sheet wrapped around her.

No time for thinking about that. We had work to do. We had someplace to be.

And if we were going to do this, we were going to need Donovan.

FOURTEEN

Donovan's office wall was opaque, and his door was shut when we arrived. Which meant he was either with a client or he was in a mood.

I hoped it was the former.

"He alone in there, Simone?" I asked his secretary, the same one he'd had in Tokyo, so I knew her well.

"He is, but—"

There wasn't any but between partners. Still, it was probably best to go in by myself first in case he was rubbing one out under his desk. "Hang here a second," I told Jolie, then entered Donovan's office without knocking, ignoring Simone's protests.

He was at his desk—both hands visible and working, thank God—and only gave me a fleeting glance before turning back to his computer. "I don't have time for it."

I guffawed. "You don't even know what *it* is."

"Doesn't matter what it is, unless you're here to help me, and if you are I'm grateful for the offer, but seeing how you're dressed..." He gave a disapproving frown at my hoodie and jeans. "That doesn't appear to be the case, so go away."

His dismissive tone would have sent most of his subordinates scurrying away.

But I wasn't a subordinate. "You forget I've worked with you long enough to know you can handle a day's load in an hour and spend the rest of the day busying yourself with your other interests. Whatever side project you're obsessed with today, I have one that will top it."

It was the right bait, and he hesitated before shaking his head. "I have *actual* work to do. Weston's out on his honeymoon—"

Oh, whoa. Wait. "He's going on a real honeymoon for a fake wedding?"

"Would you quiet down?" He gestured toward the door, which I'd left slightly ajar. "And yes. It needs to look legit."

I kicked the door the rest of the way closed. "He's heard of internet, right? Surely he can still handle putting together marketing packages from a beach."

"Sabrina and I can handle it. But that means I need to be actually handling *it* and not *you*."

I bit my cheek so I wouldn't go off on his inference that I needed to be handled. "I'll pitch in with Weston's shit. Throw me at whatever. I'm yours to command."

Again, he looked tempted. I very rarely offered assistance. He had to be itching to take advantage of that.

But after a few seconds, he shook his head. "It'll be easier to just do it all myself."

I swallowed a growl and the urge to kick him in his arrogant nutsack, and forced myself to be on my best behavior. To be fair, I was showing up unannounced, expecting him to drop everything to dig up a scandal on a man who had tormented me almost two decades ago.

On the other hand, this was exactly Donovan's jam.

"Look, D, I wouldn't be here if I had another option. We need your help. The kind of help only you can give."

Finally, his hands moved off the keyboard. He swiveled in his chair, giving me his full attention. "You decided to do it?"

Got him.

I tried not to be too smug. "We're not going to kill him literally. We're going to kill him in the figurative sense."

"What a brilliant idea. Wonder where you got it?" Donovan didn't bother hiding his smugness at all. His eyes narrowed, his jaw working, and I knew he was already seven steps ahead of me, various ideas of vengeance playing out in his mind. "You're doing all the advertising performance reports."

Shit. Advertising reports were the fucking worst. "Fine."

"There's a significant stack."

He was gloating, but I refused to appear fazed. "Cool. Whatever." I opened the door, stuck my head out, and found Jolie sitting on the waiting area sofa. I gestured for her to join us and turned to Simone. "Make sure we aren't disturbed."

Simone was a professional who somehow managed to work with the likes of Donovan. Partner title or not, she wasn't about to take orders from me, and her single-raised eyebrow made sure I knew it.

Fortunately, her real boss intervened. "No disruptions unless it's Sabrina," he called out.

The guy was definitely whipped.

He defended himself without me saying anything. "She's been thrown into her boss's job. I'm not leaving her to that alone. It would be bad for the company."

"Right. It's about the company." I dropped it, though, as Jolie stepped in the room, passing by me. I hadn't given her a chance to shower, but she must have freshened up her perfume because that cherry-blossom scent drifted to my nose, mixed with the familiar scent of her, and while I'd never been a delicate kind of guy, my knees actually felt like they might buckle.

I pulled the door shut behind her, glad I had the knob to hold on to for support.

"Wasn't that wall see-through the other day?" she asked, first noticing the clouded glass before the domineering dickwad behind the desk.

I could have kissed her for that blow to Donovan's ego.

Not literally, of course.

Though now I was thinking about her lips when I had no business thinking about them.

"It transforms at the push of a button," Donovan explained as he came around his desk and walked over to us. "I prefer the opaque when I'm working. Less of a distraction." He threw a glare in my direction that I didn't have a chance to decipher before he stuck his hand out toward Jolie. "And since it doesn't look like this asshole is going to do it, I'm Donovan Kincaid."

Oh, right. Introductions. He already knew so much about her, it felt like they'd already met.

With a warm smile, she put her hand in his. "Jolie—" She stopped abruptly, as though she were about to say her last name and decided against it for some reason. "Jolie."

"Julianna Lucille Stark," I corrected. Because she might be trying to run away from who she'd been, but who she'd been was entirely the reason she was here right now.

Her smile went from warm to tight. "I go by Jolie now."

"Ah. So that's why we couldn't find you." He'd already considered the possibility, of course, and had suggested it numerous times. *Maybe she changed her name.*

"But wouldn't there be a record?" It hadn't occurred to me that she might have done it unofficially.

She turned her gaze toward me for the first time since meeting Donovan. "You looked for me?"

Her tone was genuinely surprised, which in turn, surprised me. I'd always assumed the reason I couldn't find her was because she hadn't wanted me to find her. But that presumed she'd expected me to look.

There was probably more to it to wonder about, but I was more concerned with what Donovan's slip gave away about *me*. Like the impression that I cared.

I did, obviously.

Or I had. I wasn't sure anymore which it was, but I was sure I didn't want her help figuring it out.

I shrugged, trying to blow it off. "Didn't look that hard. I don't talk to my mother anymore. Thought you could give me a bit of news from the home front." Plausible. Likely, even.

She held my gaze, though, looking at me in a new way, as if she saw more to me than she saw before. More than I wanted her to see.

Fucking Donovan.

I shot him daggers, which he returned with a smirk.

"Anyway, it's nice to meet you, Jolie. Let me take your coat." He helped her with it while I took off my own. "Ready to get started? I imagine we have a lot to get through."

He handed her coat to me to hang up, like I was the unnecessary component of this meeting, and ushered her to take a seat before returning to the other side of his desk.

Like I said before, fucking Donovan.

"I don't know what you've been told..." she said, twisting in her chair so she could see me at the closet.

See? I was still important here. "Assume Donovan knows everything. If I haven't already told him, he's figured it out on his own. He has a knack for..." I trailed off, weighing the desire to tell the truth with how much trouble it might get me in with him to say it.

"Knowing things?" he offered when I took too long.

"I was going to say getting involved in other people's shit without their invitation. But that works."

It earned me a glare. "It's that knack that's helping you right now, so I'd be careful with your attitude."

I shut the closet door harder than need be. I'd helped him out a time or two or seven. Perhaps I needed to remind him.

"Thank you for this," Jolie said sincerely. "If he hasn't said it yet."

"He hasn't. But I'm pretty sure I owe him one so there's no need." No reminder necessary, it seemed.

"Only owe me one?" I perched on the arm of the sofa.

He stared at me for a beat. "If we get into the game of who owes whom, Cade, we're going to waste a lot of valuable time, but if you want to play, by all means."

There was more to the admonishment than appeared on the

surface, and I deserved the callout. Here I was, picking at him after I'd practically begged him to help. It wasn't him who I resented. It wasn't even Jolie.

It was myself.

I hated myself for getting involved when I'd been set on closure. The thing was, and I hadn't yet been able to admit it, I was beginning to realize I couldn't have closure without first getting involved.

So I needed to just fucking commit and stop being a dick about it. "We're cool. Let's get on with this."

"Great." He opened a drawer and pulled out a notepad wrapped in a pretentious executive style cover and dropped it on the desk. "What can you tell me, Jolie?"

She looked at me again, and I could read her question without her having to say it.

"You can trust him," I said, fully aware that her need to hear that meant she trusted *me*.

Ironic, wasn't it? That she had all the faith in me now that I'd wished she'd had back then. I didn't know how to feel about that, so I tried my best to pretend I didn't feel anything.

Thankfully, her attention was now on Donovan, so she couldn't see how badly I failed. "What is it you need?"

Donovan grabbed a gold-coated ballpoint pen from his front jacket pocket and removed the cap. "Information. Leads. I need to see where the opportunities are to find dirt on your father."

"What if what you find isn't enough to destroy him?"

"We'll make sure it does," Donovan assured.

Determined to play nice, I backed him up. "D has a knack for that as well."

"Seems you're a talented man." She practically purred, which was her way with people in general, but it made my hands bunch into fists all the same. "And you run a marketing firm? Why do I have a feeling you missed your calling?"

He pointed a finger to correct her. "I run an *international* marketing firm. But don't worry—I have plenty of other hobbies."

"I like this guy," she said with a wink.

"Don't." So much for playing nice.

"Can't help it."

"He's taken."

"That's not what she likes about me, Cade. Don't get your panties in a bunch." Wisely, he didn't give me a chance to bite back. "So opportunities for dirt—as you've likely realized by now, accusations of abuse aren't strong enough to do the kind of destruction we're looking for. Too much he said/she said involved, and there are statutes of limitations. We need something with meat—money laundering, theft, bribery, gambling, or a sex scandal could have potential. He hasn't happened to murder anyone, has he?"

"Um." She glanced at me as if to ask *Is he for real?* I nodded. "Not that I'm aware of."

"Too bad. That would be a nail in his coffin for sure." He jotted something down on his notepad. "Still might be something we could explore. Does he have any enemies?"

Okay, maybe I was looking for reasons to crap on his ideas now, but this had to be said. "We're not going to kill someone just to frame him. The whole reason we're here is to *not* kill someone."

"I wasn't suggesting that we kill anyone. Just, you know, some people end up dead all on their own."

I gave him a glare that I hoped he understood as *knock it off.*

Jolie didn't seem bothered by the exchange or by our attempts to out-piss each other. Or she was too busy considering options for destruction to really pay attention. "Isn't a sex scandal another he said/she said kind of thing?"

"You're correct there. But if there's any chance he's fucking minors... That would be a tough one to sell if it's not true, though, and you'll need a bunch of victims or hardcore evidence to pull it off." Her brow wrinkled, and he added, "Like bastard children. Semen on a blue dress from the Gap isn't going to get him more than a slap on the wrist."

Her lips twitched with a smile that couldn't quite force itself to form. "I guess that takes sex scandal off the list. Sad, isn't it? That fucking with people's money holds more weight than fucking with people's kids?"

Donovan grew gravely serious, which was saying something since the man was pretty serious in general. "It's not just sad, Jolie, it's disgusting. Which is why I have no qualms about creating a scandal from scratch, if need be."

"That's comforting." Another trusting glance toward me. "I think."

"It's this or murder," I said, laying down the facts. I didn't need to add that if she chose the latter, I was out.

She nodded. "I'm good with this."

"So tell me about him." Donovan propped his pen up, ready to write. "Who does he spend time with? Who are his friends? Who does he not seem to like? What are his hobbies? What does he do with his days off?"

Jolie chuckled. "Oh, is that all you want to know?"

"Sweetheart, that's only the beginning," he replied. "Better buckle in. It's going to be a long morning."

FIFTEEN

Two hours passed. Two hours of Donovan drilling for the particulars of Langdon Stark's life. Two hours where every one of Jolie's answers took me to a time in the past.

My short time at Stark's school had been completely unforgettable. I still remembered how the classrooms smelled. The sound of footsteps crossing the forbidden great hall remained distinct in my mind. Every encounter with Jolie—every stolen kiss, every shared dream—was etched permanently in my brain.

Or so I'd thought.

Now, as she sketched out the life of my once headmaster, events and details I'd neglected came rushing back. How had I forgotten Stark's weekly interstate private school committee meetings? Or that he'd liked to play Chopin's Death March during dinner? And that he imposed a "fine" for students who walked across the front lawn? (Students who weren't me, anyway. I got the beating plus the fine.)

There were new things I learned too. Family members of Jolie's that I hadn't been aware of. Friendships I'd heard nothing about. Side projects that hadn't come about until after I'd left.

"How about his money?" Donovan asked as we entered our third hour. "Does all of it come from running the school?"

"About fucking time we got to something significant." For the most part, I'd stayed silent, letting Donovan decide what he needed to ask, but I was starting to get restless, and the walk down memory lane was taking a toll.

My partner glared, but neither he nor Jolie addressed me. "We have family money," she said. "The school was founded by my great-great-grandparents as a philanthropic endeavor. It wasn't intended to be the foundation of the family income, but every generation after them had at least one child that made it a primary focus. Since my father was an only child, it all rested on him."

More information I hadn't been aware of, which stemmed a new thought. "It will be yours one day."

This time she shifted to look at me. "It will."

I didn't know why it had never occurred to me. Is that where her loyalty had lain? With the school rather than her father? "Will you run it?"

"I was supposed to take over when he retired. But I won't step foot there as long as he's still around."

There was no way he would make any transition of power easy. He was not a man who stood idly in the wings, and I was surprised retirement had ever been discussed at all.

But if he stepped down, and she refused, who would run it then? Jolie was proud of the Stark contributions to education. I couldn't imagine her giving away the family legacy without a fight. Was that the reason behind her wanting her father gone?

The possibility had me softening toward her. Reluctantly.

"So your father has outside investments?" Donovan's tone made it clear he didn't appreciate the deviation from his line of questioning.

Jolie thought for a moment. "He must have. He never talked money with me, so I'm only guessing. He was very private about it."

"If he did have other investments, and if that was where his money truly came from, wouldn't it be odd that he still stayed so involved with the school? He could have handed it off to a board to run." Donovan tapped his pen against his notepad as he made each point.

"You mean, maybe we hadn't really been as wealthy as he made it seem? Maybe he relied on the income from the school?"

"I don't know. You tell me."

The man was good. He could have been a detective. Or an interrogator for the CIA. Or the mob.

"I never saw any indication that he was worried about money. There were never phone calls from collectors. There was never a concern about how often we ate steak. He spoiled me on occasion, and we always had nice things and went on nice vacations. Some years it did seem we might have had an influx of cash. We have a cabin in the woods that he bought out of the blue when I was ten, and he bought a beach house in Key West and a yacht when I was nineteen."

His eyes glinted as though he'd hit a jackpot. "Sounds like he definitely has access to other money. Running a private school doesn't buy you third homes and yachts, no matter how prestigious the place is."

"I really don't think this is going to lead you anywhere. I'm pretty sure we just had enough passed down to pay for all the extras." She paused, a flicker of doubt crossing her features. "I'd always assumed that, anyway."

"Possible. But then I'm back to questioning why he stayed personally involved at the school. Why not pay for someone else to do it and enjoy living life as a philanthropist? Does he enjoy being an educator?"

"I don't think he ever enjoyed anything besides being cruel," she said, and though she didn't look at me, it felt like a shared moment of honesty. No one knew her father's cruelty better than the two of us.

Donovan had spared me very little acknowledgement over the morning, but he looked at me now before replying. "Yes, Cade told me he was a sadist."

She fidgeted with the collar of her sweater. We'd never used that word outright. Donovan had been the first to say it to me, and of course that's what Langdon Stark was. It was odd having a term for it. It felt minimizing. Like he simply suffered from a personality disorder and wasn't really a malicious, inhumane monster.

No, he was still that. He would always be that. The word didn't take away his cruelty.

If Jolie found the term hard to reckon with, she didn't show it. "Kids find school torturous. Maybe that was enough for him to want to be hands on."

"Maybe so." Donovan wrote something down. Then, after a beat, wrote several more things down.

"Sorry I don't know more about his money."

"It's fine. I'll get my guy to look into it." He was still taking notes, preoccupied with his thoughts instead of us.

"Ferris won't have a problem with any of this?" I asked when he'd been silent for a while. The PI had been on our payroll for years, but he'd been searching (unsuccessfully) for Jolie, not hacking into financial accounts. It might not be in his area of expertise.

Donovan didn't look up from his notepad. "We can't use Ferris. He's doing surveillance on someone else right now."

"On whom?" I'd only told him to drop the guy two days ago. What other job did he get him on since then? Something for the firm?

"Me, if you must know."

"He's doing surveillance on you? *For* us?"

"For Sabrina, actually." There was plenty to follow up with after that comment, but Donovan waved his hand like he was flicking away a bug. "Never mind that. I have someone else. Someone more suited to this type of work. He'll be able to track all his accounts and when money was put in and taken out. We'll have a better idea what we're looking at once he gets an initial report back to me." Finally, he returned his focus to the woman beside me. "You do realize this might take some time?"

She sat up straighter, and I could feel panic emitting off her. "How much time? I'm only in town until Friday."

"It's a long shot to say that we'll have what we need by then. Is this urgent?"

"I want it done as soon as possible."

My partner glanced toward me, and I took the cue. "I think he's asking if you're safe."

I felt my chest tense as I waited for the answer. I'd wanted to know about this since she'd first told me she wanted Stark dead, but she hadn't been forthcoming with her motives, and asking outright had felt somehow too personal.

Or maybe I was afraid of what she'd say.

"Oh. Yeah. I'm safe." Seeming to sense it wasn't enough assurance, she added, "My father doesn't know where I live. He hasn't been part of my life in ten years."

My muscles relaxed, and once again air flowed in and out of my lungs. She hadn't been ready to leave when I'd left, but seventeen years had passed. Of course she'd gotten away eventually.

But then my relief took on a new shape as I realized the implication of her statement. "Years? Is any of this information you've given today still accurate?"

"We don't need recent information to find something in the past." Donovan not only didn't seem to think it was a problem, he also didn't seem surprised.

I was already feeling pissy because of all the memories that had been drudged up and wasn't in any mood to realize Donovan had put things together that I'd missed. Adding to my annoyance was recognition that my knowledge of Jolie was hollow. There was so much I didn't know about her. So much of her life that I'd missed. So much of her life that she'd kept me out of.

I turned my wrath where it belonged—on her. "What are we even doing here, Julianna? If you haven't talked to him in years, then why do you suddenly—?"

She cut me off but addressed Donovan. "Do you have to know my reasons to make this happen?"

"I do not," the traitor said. "I just need to know what the time frame has to be. I'll push to have things happen as fast as possible, but no promises. And if safety becomes a concern, we'll want to rethink our plan."

"Sure. Thank you."

I shook my head, my fingernails digging into my palms, wondering if I should think about hitting the boxing club again later.

Donovan turned unexpectedly to me. "Need to walk it off, Cade? You could take a trip to the vending machine if you need to blow off some of that hot energy. Weston still has that dartboard in his office, if you'd prefer."

I would prefer punching him in the jaw.

"I'm good." I gave him a forced smile. I wasn't about to let him look like he was the tough one, and fantasizing about kicking his ass was already calming me down.

"Glad to hear. We're nearly done anyway. Any other details you can tell me? Anything odd? Anything at all out of the ordinary ever happen at school or at home?"

"Um..." Jolie sighed, the first sign that this conversation was exhausting her as well. "Someone gave him a car once."

"*Gave* him a car?" His reaction suggested he thought this was something he might have been told earlier.

"Yeah. A Land Rover."

"A parent? A bribe for school entrance?"

"I don't know who gave it to him. I don't think it was a parent, but maybe. I don't know." She seemed flustered. Embarrassed maybe for not bringing it up before or for not having better answers.

"Definitely worth looking into." He made a note.

"Yeah, his wife wasn't too happy about it." She looked at me. I could feel her eyes even though I refused to look in her direction.

"I'll bet." He circled whatever he'd written before. "What else?"

"He owns a gun. He owns several guns for hunting, but he always kept those at the cabin, and this one wasn't for hunting. It's a revolver."

"Legally registered?"

"I think so."

My entire body tensed at the thought of that man with a gun in his hand.

"When did he purchase it?"

"Uh, when..." She didn't want to say it, which told me everything.

"He got it when I left, right? He get it for me? In case I came back?"

She nodded, her mouth tight. "He keeps it in the nightstand by his bed. Or he did. I don't know if he still does."

"Loaded?" I asked, surprised at how calmly I was discussing a man wanting me dead.

"No, but the bullets are in the same drawer."

"Good to know," Donovan said, like we were talking about double A batteries instead of bullets. Like I hadn't just realized how close I'd come to probably losing my life. The number of times I'd considered going back, the number of times I'd actually started out in that direction...

I'd thought I was a coward for staying away. Turned out I'd also been smart.

But I'd left her in that house with that man and a gun.

I didn't want to think about that and was grateful Donovan took another road of thinking. "What did your mother die from, Jolie?"

"Not a gunshot. Brain aneurysm when I was four."

"You're sure that's what she died from and not just a story he told you?"

Her frown said that it had never occurred to her to question it. Hadn't occurred to me either.

"I'll have my guy follow that up too." He made a note. "Anything else?"

She shook her head, wrapping her arms around herself like a hug, and I wondered what she was feeling. She hadn't hated her father like I had. She hadn't liked him either, but her feelings toward him had been more complicated. While she'd never told me about the times she'd been punished, I was sure it had been abusive. But she hadn't gotten punished often. He'd also doted on her. Heaped her with praise. Treated her like a princess. They'd been close in a way I'd never been with my mother, despite the fact that I'd also grown up in a single-parent home.

I'd resented her for that. For having something I'd wanted and for not being able to hate the man the way I had.

What had I expected from her? To run off and leave him forever? What a fucking child I'd been.

What a fucking child I was.

Thinking of running away abruptly brought another thing I'd forgotten to mind. "There was that kid that went missing the year I was there. Bernard Arnold?"

"He was just a runaway," Jolie explained. "Not that unusual. Teens do that sometimes."

Donovan wasn't so dismissive. "He ran where? Back home?"

"No. Just away."

"They ever find him?"

"I'm not sure."

Once again, Donovan and I exchanged glances. It wasn't something I'd thought was suspicious before. Like Jolie had said, teens run away. I'd considered running away more than once.

He said what I was thinking. "Any chance he ran away because of your father? Is it possible he doled out punishment to him as well?"

"I guess." She didn't seem to buy it. "But for real—kids run away. It wasn't unusual. Two seniors took off when I was a freshman too."

Donovan opened his mouth, but already presuming he was going to ask for more information, she beat him to speaking. "Two girls. It's possible they had an altercation with my father, but the rumor was they were in love. It's more likely they ran off to be together."

This time I was the one boring my eyes into her, and she was the one who refused to look at me. "Huh. Who would have thought escaping was an option?"

She flinched but still wouldn't look at me. "And cruel as Daddy was with his mind games, I never once heard anyone mention anything about physical punishments. Other than Cade, I mean. And obviously he had reason and opportunity with Cade that he didn't have with others."

"You might not have been the girl kids shared that kind of rumor with," Donovan said bluntly. "Being his daughter and all."

I had a feeling she doubted that. She'd prided herself on being informed when it came to the student body. I'd always suspected it was one of the reasons she'd had the reputation with the boys that she'd had when I arrived on the scene. That rep had always bothered me, but I'd understood her motives. She'd wanted to be someone they could trust. She'd wanted to keep tabs on what her father might be doing to them. She'd wanted the attention to make her feel like someone cared.

But Donovan had a point.

"I never heard anything either," I volunteered.

"You might not have been considered a safe person either, all due respect."

Okay, that was another good point.

"Do you remember the girls' names? I'll check them out as well."

She rattled them off. Donovan jotted them down.

He was still looking at his notepad when he asked his next question. "You said he hasn't been part of your life in ten years. I'm assuming that's when you moved away?"

"Correct. I know my information isn't necessarily accurate anymore."

That wasn't where Donovan was going with his line of questioning. "He didn't *try* to keep in touch or you didn't *let* him?"

"I didn't tell him where I went. I found someone to give me a fake ID and was able to enroll in college under that name. Paid my own way with student loans."

I folded my arms over my chest, pretending this wasn't interesting to me in the slightest.

"And you've been using that identity since? You didn't legally change it?"

She shook her head. "I didn't want to be traceable."

"So now you live your life under the name Jolie?"

"Yeah."

"Jolie...what?"

I recognized what he was doing. He'd pushed me to have Ferris look into her now that we knew where to look, and I'd resisted. Donovan could never resist knowing all, though.

But Jolie had never been a dummy. "Why are you focused on me all of a sudden? I haven't been in his life in a decade. I'm not going to be able to give you anything that I haven't already given you."

He produced his most innocent look, which wasn't very innocent at all, but managed to win over a surprising amount of people. "I'm only trying to see if there are opportunities surrounding your estrangement that you might not have thought about. It seems safe to assume that something occurred that made you decide to cut him off."

"He was a strict man who brought out a belt anytime the dishes weren't stacked correctly in the dishwasher. Does there have to be another reason?"

"There does not." Donovan knew when he'd met a wall.

I wasn't surprised by it. That was how she'd always been, whenever I tried to actually talk about what we were going through back then—cold and closed off. I'd had to put the pieces together about her father myself. I imagined she'd learned early that her father demanded perfection. She'd learned to always stack the dishes correctly before I ever met her. Without her giving him excuses to be punished, he had to look elsewhere.

To be fair, I'd gotten cold when she'd tried to get me to open up about it too. We lived it together. We didn't need to talk about it.

As perceptive as Donovan was about hitting barriers, he was also fond of trying to bulldoze through them. "But you were an adult. You weren't living with him anymore. Presumably he wasn't still punishing you for how you did the dishes."

If the answer to this related to her reasons for wanting her father gone, I expected she wouldn't respond.

But after a tense beat passed, she did, though reluctantly. "No. He wasn't."

"Then was there something that motivated your leaving?"

Her head shook, barely perceptible. "Delayed reaction, I guess."

Another beat. "And if he *had* still been abusive, it wouldn't matter because, like you said earlier, he said/she said won't get us anywhere."

"I did say that."

"And you said you didn't need to know my reasons."

"I said that too." For a second, I thought he'd leave it alone. "But we might be able to use your leaving. Could blame it on something else. Say you discovered something he'd done. Were afraid for your life."

"Would that be helpful?" There was a raw note in her timbre that suggested saying she'd been afraid wouldn't have been a lie, and that bothered me more than I wanted to admit.

"I don't know yet." His intercom buzzed. "I need more information before I can tell you that." He put his phone on speaker. "This better be urgent, Simone."

"Sabrina says there's a client who's demanding to see Weston. She explained he wasn't available, and now he wants to see you."

Donovan rolled his eyes. "Tell her I'll be right there." He pressed the button to end the call. "How does Weston always draw out the crazies, even when he's not here?" He stood up and buttoned his jacket. "I should have enough to get us started. Sorry to run out like this. I'll be in touch."

He scurried out of the room, letting the door shut behind him.

We'd been dismissed, which was good because I'd officially reached a point where I couldn't hear anymore. It was hard enough grappling with the past shit that I'd been a part of. I didn't know where to begin processing the new revelations.

Had she been afraid?

I'd always believed he hadn't treated her as cruelly as he'd treated me. She'd learned how to live within the lines, or he was easier on her because she was a girl, or no one had ever made him as pissed as I had.

Truth was, I'd let myself believe that my leaving had to have calmed him down.

Wishful thinking, perhaps.

Self-centered, definitely.

My leaving also may have had the opposite effect. I'd taken away his favorite punching bag. Had she become my replacement?

The possibility nagged at me as I brought her coat to her and held it out for her to put on. Her brow rose in surprise. Then she stood and let me help her put it on, one arm, then the next.

The scent of blossoms infiltrated my senses, but I didn't step away. Even after her coat was on. Instead, I turned her around, and pulled the fur edges together to button her up.

"Did he get worse, Jolie? After I'd gone?" I'd whispered it, afraid that if I spoke too loudly, I would scare her truth away. That she'd turn cold on me too. I didn't even care that she'd heard me call her by that name. I was too anxious about the answer.

Her gaze locked onto mine, and she brought her hand up to cover my own. "You know he was never as hard on me as he was on you." Her voice was equally soft.

"That doesn't tell me anything."

"What do you want me to say? That he became a sweet, loving man the minute you left? He was still him. Quick with his tongue. Quicker with his hand."

Years of separation disappeared, and all the distance between us now was a few inches. Whatever shit had kept us apart felt insignificant in the moment. We had shared something that so few people were unfortunate enough to share. Lucky enough to share, too. Once we had been everything that mattered to each other. It had been the two of us against the world. Against him. That had bonded us in a way that couldn't be ignored, no matter what else had happened between us, and with that recognition, a sudden overwhelming wave of guilt washed over me as well.

"You should have come with me." I tugged her closer, holding her coat as though keeping her here now could have kept her with me then. "Even if you hadn't wanted to be with me. I would have gotten you out of there. I would have gotten you free."

Her breath stuttered as she drew in. "It wasn't your job to be my savior."

"But I wanted to be."

I had wanted to save her and fix her and give her safety and a life that was better, and as angry as I had tried to be with her for not letting me do those things, I also knew I hadn't fought hard enough. I'd failed her.

I didn't want to fail her again.

She reached her fingers up to brush across my cheek, her stroke burning into my skin with a welcome fire. "Cade...?"

I didn't know what she was asking, but I knew what she needed. After all this time, I could read her body language like we'd invented it together.

I needed it too. Needed to feel her lips on mine. Needed to see if kissing her now held the magic and escape that kissing her then had.

I started to lean in.

And the door burst open. "Apparently, I need my wallet. This jackoff is expecting me to take him to lunch."

I jumped back from Jolie like she was forbidden. Old habits die hard. Donovan didn't make any indication that he knew what he'd interrupted, but he wasn't the kind of guy who missed anything. It was unusually generous for him not to gloat about it, considering our bet, so I tried to be generous in return. "Do you need me to step in?"

"I don't think it's an occasion for a heavy hand." He pulled his coat out of the closet and patted the pocket to be sure his wallet was there. "Sabrina is coming as well. It won't be all terrible. Especially if I can convince her to let me finger her under the table."

Knowing Donovan, Sabrina wouldn't really have a say.

"Sorry for the crass language," he said, remembering Jolie was there. "I'm in love."

As if that was an excuse.

He turned back to me. "Besides, you have a stack of performance reports to work on. Don't worry. I'll bring you something back."

I'd forgotten about the promise to help him.

It was a blessing, actually. Because then I could send Jolie away and lose myself in paperwork and ignore the feeling that I was once again about to lose myself in her.

SIXTEEN

Hours later, I closed the folder on the last performance report and pushed it aside. Donovan hadn't been lying when he'd said there'd been a stack of them. All of us preferred to keep what work we could digitized, but a stubborn portion of our clients still wanted a hardcopy printed and signed off on each quarter. These were the reports we tended to leave until the last minute possible. Weston had pushed them off, then left the contiguous United States.

When I'd still had quite a few to go through by the time Donovan was ready to leave the office, I'd piled the rest in a recycling shopping bag I'd found in the office kitchenette and taken them back to the hotel. A bigger man would have taken the project up to his room. Instead, I'd commandeered a table in the restaurant and both hoped and dreaded that Jolie would eventually come down for dinner.

It was close to ten, and she hadn't made an appearance. Did that mean she'd gone somewhere else to eat or ordered room service?

Fuck. Why did I even care?

I scrubbed a hand over my face then picked up my phone to text Donovan.

> Reports done. Should I bring them to you or the office?

He didn't need them until the morning, but I could drop them off tonight. It would give me another excuse to avoid my hotel room, and since my skin started to buzz every time I thought about going up—every time I thought about *her*—it seemed like a good idea to try to make sure she was asleep before I returned.

Not that I was worried anything would happen with her.

I'd been seconds from kissing her earlier—and kissing her was one thousand percent not something I needed to be doing—but that had been a fluke of circumstances. We'd been talking about the past, and I'd been caught there. The idea of kissing her had seemed natural in the moment. It wasn't something I was still thinking about. It wasn't something I planned to think about ever again.

Still. Distance did seem prudent. In case *she* had other ideas.

I started to gather the reports to put in the bag when Donovan replied.

> I sent someone to pick them up from your room.

I couldn't get my fingers to type fast enough.

> Too much trouble. I'll drop them off.

> It's already done.

Barely any time had gone by since I'd sent my first text. Surely there was time to reverse his orders.

But that would mean explaining to Donovan why I needed an excuse to avoid my hotel room, and considering the bet we had going, there was no way he was going to support me. Probably why he'd sent someone in the first place. Because he wanted me alone with Jolie.

Alone with no distractions. Alone with nothing to think about but each other.

I swallowed a groan and signaled the waitress over to close out my tab. If Donovan was sending one of his lackeys to my room, I'd better be up there to meet them.

Ten minutes later, I was standing outside my door, feeling déjà vu. Hadn't I done this whole get-myself-together-before-seeing-her routine last night? It was stupid and unnecessary. Without hesitating, I swiped my key card and pushed into the room.

Like the night before, I was met with the low murmur of a television set, but this time the TV was on in the living area. Apparently, the hotel staff had it switched out during the day, which meant there was no reason to give Jolie my room tonight, and the couch bed was already pulled out, so it seemed she was planning to sleep there. There was a half-eaten burger and salad on a tray on the desk, too, so I knew she'd been in for most of the night and that she'd gotten something to eat.

Only, she wasn't there now. A peek into my bedroom told me she wasn't there either.

Irrational panic ticked up the rate of my pulse. I dropped the bag and my coat on the floor by the couch and headed toward the only other room in the suite, the bathroom. I was halfway there when I realized the water was running.

She's here. She's fine. Just taking a shower.

As my heart calmed, I walked to the wall and banged my head against it. What the fuck was wrong with me? She'd said it herself—it wasn't my job to save her. And there was nothing to save her from here anyway. It had to be old instincts kicking in. That never-ending trepidation that had underscored every other emotion back in those days. *Be careful. Watch your back. Don't get too comfortable.*

It had been years before I'd felt any sort of peace. Nowadays, fear was foreign. Then as soon as Jolie was back in my life, I was right where I'd been at eighteen.

No. I refused. I was a different man now. She wasn't going to change that.

And I definitely wasn't going to think about the fact that she was currently down the hall naked.

The sound of knocking prevented me from exploring that last thought further.

I shouldn't have been surprised to see Simone standing there when I opened the suite door. "Daddy has you working overtime too?"

Simone was the type who could be dangerous—a provocative beauty with black frizzy hair and dark features who would do anything for Donovan Kincaid. She worshipped him, and not even necessarily in a sexual way. She just seemed to be into the kink of submission, with or without the sex, and since we'd made it a rule not to bang our subordinates, her relationship with her boss had gone without.

But he could get that woman to do anything without any fuss, including going to Midtown at ten o'clock at night to pick up a bunch of non-urgent performance reports.

Simone made a sultry harrumph sound and pushed past me into the suite. "I might have volunteered for the job." She peeked over her shoulder to see my reaction, batting her lashes, and now I understood her motives for volunteering went beyond pleasing her boss. "You barely looked at me today at the office, Cade Warren."

At the time it was made, the rule of not banging our subordinates had included not banging each other's subordinates, which was why Simone and I hadn't ever fooled around. She'd made it clear she'd been interested. Of course I'd been interested—I wasn't an idiot. But I'd been respectful of my partner and our agreement and had kept my hands off.

Now that Donovan was with Sabrina—who was Weston's subordinate—it seemed which subordinates were hands off had been redefined. And with Simone and I no longer working in the same office, all the obstacles that had prevented us from getting it on before had been removed.

Her body language said that she was fully aware our situation had changed.

Well, shit. That altered my plans for the rest of the night.

Except, actually, it didn't.

The flick of her tongue over her lips thing she was doing would have had me jumping last week. This week, the only lips on my mind belonged to the woman currently naked in my shower, and my cock had been sporting a semi before I'd even known who was at the door. It was possible that fucking Simone could help redirect my thoughts—an erection worked the same no matter where the inspiration came from—but banging Blondie the other night hadn't helped get my mind off Jolie. It was unlikely Simone would be any different.

I crossed to the bag, picked it up, and held it out for her to take. "I appreciate what you're offering, but it's not a good time."

Her mouth turned down into a pout. I'd expected that. I hadn't expected her to reach out, ignore the bag, and lift the edge of my hoodie to get her hands underneath.

"Excuses, excuses. We should put all those aside for the night. It's the holidays. Give yourself a present." Now she was tugging at my belt. "Give me one too while you're at it."

"Oh, hey, no thanks." I tried to take a step back and bumped against the side of the sofa. "Really. This isn't hap—"

She cut me off with a kiss. At the same time she shoved a hand down my pants in search of my still semi-aroused manhood.

And of course that was exactly the second that Jolie would walk down the hall, her hair dripping wet, wearing nothing but a big, fluffy, complimentary hotel robe. "Oh. I didn't realize you had company."

Simone broke the kiss and stepped back, the additional person in the room apparently more motivating than my protests. "Whoops. I didn't mean to intrude." In true Simone fashion, she didn't sound all that sorry.

"I'm the one intruding, it seems." Jolie smiled, but her tone was bitter, and much as this whole situation sucked, I did like imagining the bitterness had something to do with jealousy. "I'd planned to sleep out here tonight, so if you'd like to move this to the bedroom... Or I can just grab my things and go in there myself. You won't even know I'm here."

"How modern-relationship," Simone quipped.

Before she started getting any ideas of how modern my supposed relationship with Jolie was, I shoved the bag of reports in Simone's hand. "Simone was just going." Glad she hadn't gotten around to taking her coat off yet, I turned her around and ushered her toward the door.

"I don't have to be going. I can be quiet." Her whisper was loud enough for Jolie to hear, which made her argument less believable. "Or I can be loud, if that's what you prefer."

She winked, and suddenly I wasn't sure if she really had been coming on to me or if this had all been some sort of ploy set up by Donovan to stir trouble. I didn't put it past him, though I did question what his reasoning would be. Sending his drop-dead gorgeous secretary to seduce me in front of Jolie hardly seemed the best strategy for getting me to take my former lover to bed.

Whatever Simone/Donovan's objective had been, I could use it to my advantage. Let Jolie think she was in the way. Remind her I had every intention of keeping her at a distance. Motivate her to stay away.

If it also made her jealous, even better.

"Sorry, sweetheart," I said as I opened the door. "I'm trying to be a good roommate. Next time I'm in town, okay?"

"Don't change your plans because of me," Jolie called from behind me. "I have earbuds."

There went the jealous-ex-girlfriend vibe I'd been digging.

Simone trailed a single finger down my chest. "We could have a good time..."

"Go." I practically pushed her into the hall. "Thank you for coming by. It's always nice to see you, Simone. Good night."

I didn't let her respond, pulling the door shut and letting out a deep breath when the lock clicked in place.

"You both seemed cozy."

I turned to find Jolie bent over her suitcase, searching for something in the contents. She wasn't even looking at me, as though the preceding incident had not only not bothered her, it also hadn't deserved her interest.

The sharp edge in her tone said otherwise.

Jealous-ex-girlfriend vibe was back in full force.

"We've worked together. That's all." I played it cool, toeing off my shoes, making myself comfortable.

"You invited her to your hotel room. It seems there was definitely more to it than that."

Of course she hadn't realized that we hadn't come back to the suite together. I'd parted with Jolie hours ago, staying at the office to work. It probably looked like I'd spent the rest of the day and evening with Simone.

I had no reason to correct that assumption. "I suppose I wasn't thinking. Forgot I wasn't rooming alone. I don't usually have to worry about that."

She stood up. The T-shirt she'd stolen from me was clutched in one hand, a pair of flimsy see-through panties in the other.

Fuck. Now I was thinking about those panties. And the fact she wasn't wearing any underneath that big fluffy robe. My cock jerked to attention.

Good thing it wasn't my cock making decisions around here. His reaction was definitely my signal to call it a night.

Or maybe take a shower myself. Temperature set to cold.

I was already headed toward the bathroom when Jolie stopped me. "You know, Cade..." She sounded tentative. "I understand you are used to living a certain kind of lifestyle."

Certain kind of lifestyle? Was she calling me a manwhore? I was intrigued enough to turn around and face her.

"And I realize that having me here is probably getting in the way of that lifestyle." She paused.

"Go on."

Hesitantly, she approached me, her cheeks rosy, her lips wet. "If you really need to...you know. I don't have to be an inconvenience. I'm here. You're here. There's no reason I couldn't help out with...your needs."

I blinked incredulously, not sure she was talking about what I thought she was talking about but unable to figure out what else she could possibly mean. "I'm fine. Thanks."

She eyed the bulge in my jeans. "You sure about that?"

Okay then. She was definitely talking about what I thought she was talking about.

I choked back a laugh. "Uh, no. Definitely not."

She took another step toward me. Now we were close enough that I could feel her exhale. "Why not? I'm a woman, you're a man. No-strings hookups seem to be your M.O. Me being here is preventing you from going after that. Might as well be useful."

Any other beautiful woman saying those words to me, and I'd be stripping already.

Those words coming from Jolie made me wince. She was not my usual M.O. She was not disposable. Or forgettable. She was not string-free.

How could she even consider putting *me* in that box?

Still, I was trapped in place. Glued to the spot. She placed her hand on my chest, and even through the hoodie, my skin scorched.

"Stop it," I warned, my restraint thinning.

"Hell, it could be fun. Everyone wants a night with an ex-lover, don't they?"

"No fucking way." I wasn't even thinking about the bet with Donovan. It was a matter of self-preservation.

"Because we're not strangers? After all these years, we kind of are. That's your type, right? Someone you don't know? Or is it because you can't separate now from the past?"

All my blood was running south, but I managed to come up with a decent argument. "How about because you think that sex equals love? Is that reason good enough?"

"Ouch." She blanched and moved away. Only one step, but her heat went with her, and she suddenly felt a mile away. "That was a lot of years ago, you know. I'm sure your innocence has faded too. You probably don't still think love can save the day, for example."

It stung more than it should have, which was fair since I'd set out to hurt her first. It angered me that she could still understand me so well, and I'd lashed out. I didn't really believe she was still that naive. I certainly wasn't.

But that was who she'd been when I'd met her—a girl seeking affection in whatever way she could get it. She'd been the school's official boy toy when I'd transferred in, and while I was pretty sure she hadn't slept with most of her conquests, she'd been on her knees enough to make it a sore spot to my ego. Particularly when I'd never been one of the boys who'd been lucky enough to receive one of Julianna Stark's famous blow jobs.

I hadn't really wanted that from her then. I'd wanted to be special to her. I'd wanted to treat *her* special. I'd wanted to give her more than praise spouted out in a moment of fleeting euphoria.

For all the good it did. Here we were, strangers, like she'd said. I wasn't special to her.

She didn't have to be special to me.

And hadn't I earned a turn with her on her knees?

She must have read my thoughts because she stepped forward, and now she was close again. "Look. It doesn't have to be a big deal." She fingered the button of my jeans, but unlike when Simone had her hands in the vicinity, this time my cock reacted.

"I'm not asking you to do this." I put my hand on her wrist, meaning to push her away, but instead just stilling her.

"You're not asking. I'm offering. With all you're doing for me, I owe you this. I think you need it. Let me give it to you."

Everything she said pissed me off.

Worse, it turned me on. Made me unimaginably hard. Made my thinking originate from my little head instead of my big. She wanted me to treat her like those boys had? She wanted to minimize everything that had been between us with something transactional? She wanted to feel cheap? She wanted to be used?

Fine. I could do that.

I could use the hell out of her and feel fucking good about doing it too.

SEVENTEEN

"Kneel down." The order flew from my mouth, harsh and impossible to disobey.

Jolie's pupils got wide and dark. The surprise, I understood. I hadn't been like that with her before. Back then, I'd been sweet and adoring and nice. Forceful tones had been part of our every day. There'd been no place for them in our lovemaking.

But this wasn't about love. This wasn't about nice. This was about justice. And closure. And basic, primal need, and the lust present in her dilated eyes said that maybe somehow this was meeting a need for her too.

"I'm not saying it again, Jolie. Get on your knees."

She fell to the ground instantly, her mouth open and waiting before I had to ask. I didn't want to think about all the boys who'd seen her like this back at school. I didn't want to think about any men who'd seen her like this after I'd left, but I forced myself to be aware of them all the same. *You're not special. You are one of a crowd.*

The acknowledgment made me even harder. Made me more desperate than ever to have my piece. My belt was still undone from Simone, so all I had to do was pop the button and unzip my fly, but I paused before I pushed my jeans down. "One more thing I need to make clear."

She nodded eagerly, and I wondered if she'd still be nodding when I said what I had to say. "This is for me, not for you. Got it?"

Her lips curled into a smile. "I didn't expect it would be any other way."

A sharp stab of pain shot through my chest until I shoved it aside and made myself stone. This was what we were now. This was all we could be.

With that settled, I pushed my jeans and underwear down together, just far enough for my cock to spring free and in her face.

Her breath drew in audibly. I hadn't reached my full potential by the age of eighteen. I'd had a significant growth spurt after I'd last been with her, and my cock had gone from a very normal width and length to a size that most called impressive.

I could sense the compliment on her tongue, and though I normally liked hearing it, I didn't want it from her. I was feeling mean and contemptuous. I didn't want her praise. I didn't want her awe. I wanted to shove my impressive cock so far down her throat that she couldn't breathe.

So before she could get out a single syllable, I was pushing my crown between her lips and into her lush mouth.

Fuck. Her mouth. Damp and hot. Heaven.

I'd planned to get in, fuck hard, and get right back out, but her tongue curled around my length as I pressed in, sending a storm of sensation down my spine. I closed my eyes and paused my stroke, trying to get my bearings before I exploded.

In my hesitation, she took over, wrapping her small hand around the base of my cock. Then she moved her mouth over me, sucking me in as far as she could before releasing me to the tip. Again. Again. Long, hard sucks that had me shivering.

After three trips up and down my cock, she swirled her tongue around my head, then started the whole pattern over again, bringing me closer to the edge on each round. Bringing me closer to erupting.

Bringing me dangerously close to losing my mind.

I closed my eyes hoping it would help. If I didn't see her, I could pretend I didn't know her. That she was a woman I'd just met in the bar. That I could get lost in the selfishness of pleasure and forget everything else between us.

But there wasn't any real forgetting.

Even if she had been another woman on her knees, it would still be her face in front of me, plastered on the back of my eyelids. Because it was always Jolie I thought of, even when I didn't acknowledge it to myself. She was always the undercurrent of every sexual encounter.

And even if she wasn't always the undercurrent of my sexual encounters, I wouldn't be able to pretend now. She felt familiar, despite never having taken me like this. The way she touched me, the sounds she made as she sucked me off, the smell of her own arousal wafting up to my nose—they were uniquely her, and there was no way not to feel a tug of emotion with each draw of her lips against my sensitive skin.

My world suddenly felt like it was spinning, and I urgently looked for something to steady me. My hands fell on her head, tangled in her hair, pulled at it from the roots. I opened my eyes, and they immediately crashed into hers. Green-rimmed pools of beauty held my gaze, probing me with intensity as she worked her jaw over my cock.

I hated her.

In that moment, I realized just how much I did. How much I had for years. I hated her for hurting me, and for letting herself be hurt, and for hiding, and for having the guts to face me again after all this time. I hated her for throwing away what we'd been and for not allowing us to find out what more we could be.

I hated her for not loving me enough.

I hated her because I'd loved her too much.

A blast of fury spread through my torso. I braced her face with my hands, holding her still so I could control the speed and depth of my next thrust. She didn't fight me. Her jaw went slack. Her eyes looked at me with something akin to trust.

"Did you learn this from them?" I drove in until my tip touched the back of her throat, barely letting her breathe when I pulled out before thrusting back in. "Birch and Wesley and Troy? Did they teach you how to take a cock like this?"

Her eyes watered, but the hitch in her breath made me wonder if the shaming aroused her.

I didn't want her to enjoy this, but the possibility that she did somehow made me even harder. I looked for more signs of pleasure. Besides her dilated eyes, her skin was flushed and splotchy. Her chest rose and fell with rapid breaths.

"Open your robe," I demanded.

She did without question, exposing plump breasts, and it was my turn to suck in a breath. I hadn't been the only one who'd had a growth spurt after high school. Before, she'd perfectly fit my palm. I didn't move my hands to be sure, but it looked like she'd spill over if I groped her now.

More provoking than the sight of her beautiful tits was the steepled nipples they sported. Two solid beehives, begging to be touched and sucked and pulled. Proving that her body was reacting to this blatant exploitation. Inviting me to use her in other ways. Inviting me to use her all night long.

I could do that. Easily. Could pull her up to her feet, kiss her until her knees buckled. Carry her to the other room and make her come a thousand different ways until morning.

But if I did, it would mean something.

Not because I couldn't separate the present from the past, but because in the present, I still loved her as much as I hated her. Nothing I did would ever change that. It was a commitment I'd made at the age of eighteen, and maybe Headmaster Stark had turned me into a masochist because I'd stuck miserably by that commitment for seventeen years.

There would never be closure. Not with Jolie.

Frustration threatened to distract me from orgasm, but one more glance at her face—tears streaming down her cheeks, her jaw struggling to take me all in—and I was almost there. Electric shocks ran down my cock and up my spine, radiated from my limbs. My torso spasmed like I'd been tickled. Two more pumps, and I was going to come.

And as much as I wanted her to suck me dry, that felt too good for her. Too intimate. She didn't deserve any more parts of me than she already owned.

Abruptly, I pulled out, wrapped my hand around my cock, and aimed at her breasts. As soon as she understood what I wanted, she stuck her chest out like it was an offering. Inviting me to defile her.

Three and a half strokes later, I was spurting white ropes across her tits, decorating her flushed skin with my cum as my body stuttered out my release. I grunted out a long curse word, adding way more vowels than normal. I forced my eyes to stay open, forced myself to memorize her like this—debased and dishonored and degraded.

"Feel better?" She sounded proud of herself, but not smug. Her smile seemed genuine. She stood up and pulled her robe back over her shoulders, leaving it open in front, probably so the garment wouldn't get dirty, but also giving me the advantage of seeing my artwork.

I thought about it a second. Actually, I *did* feel better. In the way that only a good orgasm could make me feel. Staring at the evidence of my release, my cock was already getting thick again.

And that made me not feel better anymore.

Because the fact was there was no end to this wanting. All these years, I'd told myself that if I just saw her again, if I just spoke to her, if I just knew how things had turned out then I could move on.

But I'd always known that was a lie. I would always want her. I would never be satisfied with just pieces. I would always want as much of her as she had of me.

And the real hitch of it all was that, even if she did say she wanted me too, I'd never be able to trust it.

It was a Catch-22. My own personal hell loop. One I was meant to suffer through alone.

I tucked myself away and pulled up my pants, not bothering to zip. "You need a wash rag to clean up?" I nodded toward the semen on her chest, but I didn't really look at her. I was already gone. My mind already safely shut behind the door to the bedroom with a couple of bottles from the minibar, ready to push her out of my mind and my heart with alcohol like I had so often over the years.

"I'll take another shower, if that's cool with you." Her tone was flat. Whether that was because I was listening to her from a distance or because she was disappointed that I was pulling away, I didn't know. I didn't care. It didn't matter.

What mattered was leaving the room.

"Good. That's a great idea. It's been a long day. I'm going to hit the sack now." I didn't listen for her response. I grabbed the liquor from the fridge and headed to my room, refusing to feel bad for making her sleep on the couch bed, or for leaving her a mess in my cum, or for not returning the favor.

There was only one thought of her I allowed myself as I disappeared behind a closed door and pushed her from my thoughts entirely: *See, Jolie. You're not the only one who can walk away.*

EIGHTEEN

I was used to waking up with morning wood and lingering dreams of Jolie.

I wasn't used to waking up that way with her in the next room.

It took a moment for the thought to register, but as soon as it did, I sat up straight and cursed.

Then I remembered what had happened the night before, and I cursed again.

What the fuck had I been thinking?

That's the thing—I *hadn't* been thinking. Now that I was thinking, I had a half-mile list of reasons why what had happened last night shouldn't have happened, starting and ending with *she was Jolie*. I couldn't even entertain it not mattering. Couldn't think for even a second, *is it really such a bad thing?* because every fiber of my being knew just how bad it was.

And also the reasons that it was so bad were not reasons I wanted to dwell on.

I needed closure for a reason—and in the daylight, I was no longer willing to believe that goal was impossible. Getting sucked off and jizzing all over her chest like I was marking my territory, though, was not very closure-esque.

I scrubbed a hand down my face. What was today? Tuesday? Three fucking days until she was out of here.

Three fucking days of trying to convince myself I didn't want to do a whole bunch of other bad things with her.

I grabbed my cell off the nightstand, scanned my email and messages, then not seeing what I was hoping for, called Donovan. "Any leads yet?"

"It's been one day, Cade." He sounded like that father who was tired from yelling every time his kids asked *are we there yet?*

To be fair, he sounded like that a lot when I called. "It should be a compliment that I think you can work so fast."

"Funny how your version of a compliment seems an awful lot like harassment." His voice got muffled like he'd turned his phone into his shoulder, but I could still make out what he said. "Is that still scheduled for ten thirty? Better make it ten forty-five."

I should have been sympathetic about his workload when I was sitting on my ass, shut behind a door, afraid of the woman on the other side.

But really all it made me feel was annoyed. "Is there something I can do to make things move along faster?" I'd even do more ad performance reports if it meant he'd get something concrete sooner.

I decided not to offer that specifically.

The muffled sound went away. "There is nothing you can do. There are things in motion. All we can do now is sit and wait for information to come in."

Pretty much what I'd expected, but not at all what I'd wanted to hear.

"What you're telling me is that twenty-four hours have passed, and you've got nothing?" Being irritated at Donovan was a lot more satisfying than being irritated by the situation.

"No, that is not at all what I'm saying. Hold on, no, Simone. I changed my mind. Move the Pritzogram meeting to after lunch, and then put the call with Dyson on at ten forty-five." This time he hadn't even bothered to mute me.

Obviously, he was busy.

Obviously, I didn't care. "So tell me what you found. I'll follow up."

I heard a door shut—his office door? Then he sighed. "There is nothing for you to follow up with, Cade. I gave the info to my guy as soon as I got back from lunch yesterday. Then I stayed up last night looking into a few things myself. Discovered a couple of other things for my guy to research—some out of the norm purchases, a pattern of runaways, etc., etc.—and as soon as he finds a single bit of useful information, he will get back to me, and I will get back to you. You get how that works? *I* call *you*. There wasn't a part of that scenario where you call me."

When Donovan got patronizing, it was time to hang up. Or punch him, but there was the whole we weren't near each other thing, and violence wasn't a real motivator where D was concerned.

But he'd said something I couldn't let slide. "A pattern of runaways? What's that supposed to mean?"

"Right now, it means exactly what Jolie said yesterday—teens run away. Ninety-nine percent of teens who do return home, even when abuse is involved, which is often. So even if Stark had pulled his shit with other kids, they would fit into the statistical data. Problem is, of all the runaways that have been reported at Stark Academy, I can only find one that's shown up again, and that's you."

Shit.

But data could be skewed. "Technically, I disappeared for a long fucking time too."

"I'm sure none of the other runaways shared your unique circumstances." He cleared his throat, and now he sounded like he was in motion, walking to his desk maybe. "Point is, it's unusual, and it's being looked into, and I will get you something eventually. Now's the part where you leave me alone and let that happen."

"Fine, fine. Fine." What other reaction could I have?

But that left me with nothing to do and a woman I needed to avoid in the next room. "I'll come by the office then to work. Put me on something to help with Weston being gone."

"Don't come in. Anything I have for you to do, I'd have to explain first, and that will take more time than just doing it. If you're here, you'll be in the way."

I resented that comment, but I'd have said the same thing if he tried to show up at the Tokyo office and help out, and he'd only been gone from there for six months.

Through the door, I heard the sofa bed creak. Then creak again. Jolie was awake, and panic returned. "What the hell am I supposed to do with her in the meantime?"

I could practically hear his smirk. "Holed up in a hotel room together? I'm sure you'll think of something."

I hung up with more cursing. *Fucking prick*. Was that why he didn't want me in the office? Was he withholding shit just to try to make his odds better on that stupid bet?

The only reason I didn't truly believe that was the case was because Donovan was too cocky to think his wagers needed interference. And to back up his point, he'd almost won last night.

Or, wait—*had* he won? Did BJs count as fucking?

Since we hadn't defined terms, I decided only fucking counted as fucking, which meant I hadn't lost, and I was resolved *not* to lose.

But I was also realistic—the two of us holed up in a hotel room together really wasn't working in my favor.

I leaned my head against the headboard, half listening as Jolie moved around the suite. The water turned on at the minibar. Making coffee, probably. The volume on the TV was turned up. The *Friends* theme song played.

The other half of my brain tried to remember back to when I was ten, and we'd moved to Poughkeepsie with Stan, my mother's boyfriend of the moment. Stan had been one of the more decent father figures in my life, which meant he didn't just ignore me or keep me locked in a bedroom all the time. It also meant he sometimes took me to the movies or let me go on day trips with the neighbor kids.

One such winter trip stuck in my head.

I picked up my phone and scrolled through a few things. Checked out my options.

Then I pulled on yesterday's jeans and a Henley from one of the dresser drawers and forced myself out of the bedroom.

As soon as I saw her, curled up in her panties and my T-shirt with a mug of black coffee in front of the television, I realized I should have taken a moment to prepare myself for being in her presence. Were we going to act like last night didn't happen? How was I planning to deal with the fact that every time I looked at her mouth, my dick got hard?

Fortunately, she decided the first answer for us. "Hey," she said, barely glancing at me before returning her gaze to her show. "There's still a pod of coffee if you want me to make some for you. Housekeeping only left two that aren't decaf, and I'm already drinking this one."

Normal then. We'd act normal.

"I got it. Thanks." Except this wasn't normal because there was no way I'd be making hotel coffee, and here I was, adding water to the machine. I peered warily at her like she was an unpredictable dog, one that I had to keep tabs on in case she suddenly decided to bite.

That wasn't fair.

So far, I'd been the one who'd done all the biting. She'd been perfectly nice. Nicer than necessary.

And now I was thinking about her on her knees again.

I forced my head in another direction. "So, uh, talked to Donovan. He's working on a few leads, but it's going to be a few days."

She didn't blink. "I figured."

"You planning on doing anything today?"

"Considering that I have two hundred fifty left in my account—that will probably pay for my meals this week with just enough left for the car ride to the airport—no. No plans." Abruptly, she turned her attention to me, as though she just realized I might be trying to get rid of her. "Do you need me to get out of your hair? I can find something to keep me occupied outside the room."

She started to stand up, but I waved her to stay put. "No, no. I wasn't getting at that." I concentrated on the task of coffee making, wondering why it was so hard to extend a simple invitation.

She seemed to sense I had more to say. "Do you need to go into the office? I'll be fine here alone if that's what you're worried about."

Come on, you pussy. Just fucking say it.

I turned to her. "Actually, I was thinking... Donovan doesn't need anything more from us, and sitting around here all day's just gonna make me stir-crazy. I don't know about you, but, um. We should just forget all the shit going on. For the day. Get out of here. Do something fun."

She looked at me in that way of hers, the way I'd never forgotten, where she made me feel like I was the only person that mattered on the planet. "Did you have something in mind?"

She wasn't flirting, really. Wasn't trying to be suggestive at all, and probably most definitely wasn't thinking about being spread out on that sofa bed so I could eat her like a breakfast buffet, so I made myself ignore the fantasy that had just popped in my head and focused on the idea I'd had when I brought the whole thing up. "Yeah. I think I do."

"Awesome. I'm game." Without even knowing what I had in mind, she was on board. Like she trusted me.

I had to not let myself think about that too long. "Cool. Dress warm."

I abandoned the tasteless coffee—we could pick up to-go in the hotel lobby on our way out—and went back in the bedroom so I could shoot Donovan a text.

> I'm going to need to borrow your car.

NINETEEN

An hour later, we were in Donovan's Jag, headed out of the city, and surprisingly, considering the fact that I hadn't been behind a wheel in years, I was managing the New York City traffic without any problems.

Donovan's threat to cut off my dick if I returned his car harmed in any way might have had something to do with my attentiveness.

Fortunately, concentrating on the task at hand made a good excuse for silence, but thirty minutes into the trip, we turned on I-87, and from there it was smooth sailing.

After that, the quiet between us might not have been awkward, but it did give me time to think, and the things my mind kept wanting to think about were complicated and heavy. Our past. Stark's future. Jolie's eyes. Jolie's lips.

Several times I found myself thinking about the night before, and not just the dirty parts, but the haunting parts. *You probably don't still think love can save the day,* she'd said. *You can't separate now from the past,* she'd said. *Because we're not strangers? After all these years, we kind of are.*

The last one was the one that tormented me most. Probably because it was the accusation that I felt I had the most control over. We were strangers, but we didn't have to be. We were strangers, but I could do something to change that.

Getting to know her might have seemed a counterintuitive way to go about getting closure, but in reality, not knowing her anymore was one of the things that stung the most about the status of our relationship. I used to know all of her. I'd wanted to know all of her for a lifetime. I'd planned on loving all of her forever.

Trying to hold her over the years had been like holding sand. Every day, some part of her slipped away, which had made me even more desperate to hold on to the parts of her that I still had.

So maybe if I didn't feel like I was clutching onto scraps, I could finally relax, open my fingers, and let her go.

Or maybe I'd just have more to clutch onto. Fuck if I knew. But it was as good of a plan as any.

I tapped the button on the steering wheel that adjusted the radio volume, and the You + Me Spotify list she'd turned on faded to background noise. She looked at me expectantly, assuming I must have something I wanted to say.

I really should have figured out what that was exactly before I'd turned down the sound. "You, um. You said we're strangers. It's weird. Thinking of you as a stranger."

Fantastic preface, asswipe. I was a bumbling teenager again, with absolutely no chill.

The corners of her mouth lowered, and she turned her head to look out the window. "That's my fault. I know that wasn't fair to you."

"That wasn't what." I glanced at the back of her head and resisted the urge to touch her to try to get her to look back. "I wasn't trying to place blame. I was saying that, um." Why was it so hard to have an honest conversation with her? "I'm saying I don't like it."

"Oh." She turned her face back to study me, again in that way that made me feel like I was everything. "I don't like it either," she said, and it felt like she was making a confession. As though she wasn't sure she had the right to feel that way.

I wasn't sure she had the right either.

But I was glad she didn't like it.

With both of us on the same page, conversation should have flowed easily from there. Yet a whole song had started and finished before either of us spoke again.

"I'm a teacher," she said.

"You are?" I'd been handed gold. That little bit of information, tiny and miniscule in the wording, filled an entire quadrant of the Jolie puzzle. From this, I could envision the structure of her days. Could see the makeup of her years. I could begin to imagine the pattern of her life that had for so long seemed like a deep black, shapeless sea.

"Yeah." She gave me her best smile, and I knew now that she also liked the job. "Middle school literary arts. But I've taught high school too. And filled in for the assistant principal for a semester while he was having back surgery. My bachelor's is in secondary education English, but my master's is in educational leadership and policy."

"So you could one day take over the academy?"

She nodded without really committing. "I mean, it was always in the back of my mind. Also, it just seemed like the most natural thing for me to do. Kind of in my blood."

"Yeah." When we'd been kids, we'd been so hell-bent on leaving everything behind that I'd never considered she'd follow the career path of her ancestors.

It made sense. From a practical, adult perspective, of course it did, and I was happy for her for finding her place like that.

But was it really her place? Or was it just a trap?

She had to know what I was thinking. "It was half the reason I hesitated too, Cade. I didn't want to have anything to do with the family legacy. I didn't want..." She shook her head, changing her course. "I didn't even go to college until I was twenty-five."

"Not really typical of a Stark alum." The academy promotional material bragged endlessly about the high percentage of graduates who pursued higher education.

"Not at all typical. I was proud of that. It felt rebellious, throwing away my potential and such." She picked up her phone from her lap and paused the playlist altogether. "Then I realized that throwing away my potential hurt me more than it hurt Daddy, and I was already working at the school so what was the point of avoiding it?"

"You *worked* at the academy?"

"I did. For a handful of years. Administrative stuff, mostly. Substitute teacher. Daddy didn't think a degree was necessary when the school was in the family. I didn't need any credentials. I was already hired. Which is bullshit, by the way, because you most certainly need credentials to run a school. But. Well. You know Daddy."

I did. But I didn't know what method he'd used to bully her into doing his bidding. Was it emotional and psychological manipulation? That seemed to be his favorite tactic with Jolie. Or had he resorted to physical abuse? She would have been an adult, but I doubted that would have stopped him from striking her if he'd thought it would be effective.

It was tricky wanting to know the present while having to dance around the past. It wasn't that her father or our time together was necessarily off limits, but I knew that if we went there, there was no coming back, and I wasn't sure that was a trip I wanted to take.

So I didn't ask the questions I wanted to ask and resigned myself to being content with what she chose to share on her own.

"When I finally decided to get a degree, I wasn't planning to ever go back to Stark Academy. But I kept returning to the education courses in the catalog. Like I said—it's in my blood. So I thought I'd try it until something else stole my interest, and no one else ever did."

My heart missed a beat.

I glanced at her and saw her cheeks pinken. "*Nothing* else ever did, I mean."

But now I wanted to know about her slip. Had she said that for a reason? Had there really been no one over the years? That couldn't be possible.

It would have been easy enough to ask. Natural, too. That was exactly the kind of thing a person asked about when catching up.

But I couldn't get myself to form the words, and then she was talking again. "I took a vacation week to come here. I don't have to be back until Monday, but I booked my flight for Friday because I thought I might need a couple of days after being here to..." *Recover.* She didn't have to fill in the blank. "There's only one more week before winter break, and I have more vacation. I could call in if we need more time. My lesson plans are already done."

No one else.

I could feel her eyes on me, waiting for an answer. "I think we need to wait until Donovan comes back to us before we think about that."

"Right. Sure." A beat passed, and I wondered if she knew what I was thinking. *No one else. No one else.* "What about you?"

There'd been no one else for me. Not anyone that I'd loved. Fucked, yes. Fucking wasn't the same.

But she couldn't be asking about that. What had she said before? "I'm one of the owners of my company. I get all the vacation I want."

She chuckled. "I meant..." She paused, as though trying to decide what exactly it was she meant. Then twisted in her seat to better face me. "How did you get involved with Donovan Kincaid?"

"He recruited me from, uh..." This wasn't necessarily safer ground. It would be if I stuck to my lie, the one I told most often when other people asked this question, but this was Jolie.

And I meant it about not wanting us to be strangers.

I went with the truth. "From dealing art. Forged art."

"Oh." My answer had startled her, but when she processed it, she had no judgment in her expression. "How do you get into a business like that? I'm sure there's not an application."

"You meet someone who knows a guy who knows another guy. I started out legit. Got a degree in international finance management. I was good at math in..." I didn't need to tell her my best subjects from school. "Well, you know. There's a lot of boring ways to use math, but I thought international would be an opportunity to get out of the country. But you can't really get anywhere without a master's, and when I graduated with my bachelor's, I had more student loan debt than I could afford, so when a guy I knew said he had a line on how to make some cash, I took the job."

"What did you do exactly? You didn't forge the art."

I laughed. We both knew I didn't have an artistic bone in my body.

But I also wasn't really interested in going into the specifics of what I'd done in the early days. The people I'd beat up. The ways I'd threatened men who got in our way. "Mostly, I was just there to look scary."

"I never thought of you as looking scary back in high school."

"Well, that's why I was intent on bulking up. I wanted to look scary." I'd been a scrawny teen who'd gotten his height before his width. I might have had a chance with Headmaster Stark if I'd looked like I did now.

She nodded, and I knew she understood.

"And you don't usually get to looking scary without actually *being* scary. I learned to fight. I can throw a pretty big guy around if necessary. I can also get someone to stay in line with just a look."

"No, you can't. Show me."

I tried for a full thirty seconds before giving up. "I can't do it." Even if I could stop smiling, I couldn't give "the look" on demand. Too bad because there were a shit ton of people I wished could have seen it from me. I'd imagined giving it plenty of times to the boys back at school. To her father. To her, sometimes. When I was feeling really bitter.

I wasn't feeling that bitter at the moment.

She squinted her eyes and studied me all the same. "Okay, I see it. You're...intimidating."

"Damn right I am. I'm also good at orchestrating people, it seems, so I moved up from heavy to management, and that's where I met Donovan."

"He was working management in illegal art? Or was he buying it?"

This was a detail I'd never been able to quite hammer out. "Not quite sure what his role was. Nate hooked us up. He's one of the other Reach owners. He was dealing art at the time, and when I got bumped up to the more civilized level of the business, our paths would cross now and again. Sometimes we'd go out drinking, get in trouble, or whatever, and this one night he brought along Donovan. Rich motherfucker, fresh out of Harvard with his MBA and fascinated with business strategy and structure, no matter what the field. Nate and I spent all night telling him about our jobs. Which was really bad judgment. We were lucky he wasn't an undercover because we told him everything."

"Why would you do that?"

I shrugged. "A lot of drugs and alcohol. And also Donovan has a way, if you haven't noticed."

"Oh, I've noticed."

Her tone made my chest tight with jealousy, and I both wanted to drill her about all the things she'd "noticed" about my asshole friend and also drive straight to the office and show Donovan "the look" and also maybe kick him in the nuts.

After a calming breath, I could live with doing neither. "It was a good thing we told him, in the end, because we impressed him. He told us both that he wanted to put something together eventually, some sort of business, and said he'd be back in a few years with an offer. Promised he'd have something to get me out of the States. Nate blew him off—he was too happy making money the way he was, though if you ask him about it now, he doesn't even remember the conversation. I thought it sounded like a nice way to eventually retire, and if he could get me someplace foreign, all the better. I still had a bunch of loans—I was making good money, but you don't want to pay off anything all in one bunch like that if the income isn't going to be reported on your taxes—but I was able to get them deferred and applied for more so I could get a master's in entrepreneurship. I wanted to be ready when he came back."

"You quit the other stuff just on this guy's maybe-someday offer?"

"Oh, no. I kept the day job. Or night job. Most of that work was in the dark. Plenty of time to go to school on the side." I could feel her eyes pinned on my profile, could feel her interest in my story. "I was just graduating when D came back a couple of years later with a basic idea to launch a worldwide international ad firm. Recruited me and Nate. Introduced us to his buddy Weston and his almost stepfather-in-law, Dylan—don't ask. It's complicated. The five of us sat down, made a plan together, and here we are. And yes, now I've quit the night work."

"That's crazy admirable." She sounded more impressed than I could have hoped for and also exactly as impressed as I'd always dreamed she'd be.

It *was* pretty impressive when I let myself remember where I'd come from. After I'd run away from Stark, I'd been dirt poor, living on the streets. I hadn't even had my diploma. I'd had to take the GED before college, and now I was co-owner of one of the biggest marketing firms in the world. I burned money just for fun. I wanted for nothing.

Well, that wasn't true.

"I'm not going to pretend I don't like having my ego stroked, but which part specifically was admirable?" I was a total glutton. No denying it. But also, I really wanted to know what she thought. Needed to know.

"All of it," she said. "*All* of it. Changing your look. Working your way up. Becoming somebody. Finding your people. But the part I really admire is the part where someone told you to trust in his vision, and you just...did."

That surprised me, and I was sure that it said something about her that I hadn't realized before. Something big. Another puzzle piece in my hand, but this one I couldn't quite place.

Besides, she was wrong. "Some people would say it was naive."

"But it wasn't naive. Donovan came back with a real plan."

"Some people would call that fool's luck."

She shook her head, adamant. "It wasn't luck. And you're not a fool. You just know how to let yourself believe."

She was still wrong, but I didn't argue. The truth was much more basic, and not impressive in the least. It hadn't mattered whether I believed in Donovan or not.

I just hadn't had anything left to lose.

TWENTY

"Skiing?" Jolie asked as I turned where the highway sign pointed toward Hunter Mountain. "You're taking me skiing? No way. I'm not skiing."

I chuckled as I resumed speed. "Calm your tits. I'm not taking you skiing. I didn't forget you don't know how."

She scowled at me again. "It's been a lot of years. I could have learned."

"But you didn't." It wasn't even a guess. I knew it like I knew anything.

Still, she held out for a beat before admitting I was right. "No, I didn't." Her forehead remained wrinkled in distrust. "You sure as fuck better not be trying to get me to take lessons. And I'm not snowboarding, either."

I tried to imagine that scenario, but it was too absurd to picture. Jolie was one of the strongest women I'd ever met, fearless too, in many ways, but she hated daredevil shit. Heights, fast speeds, anything reckless had always been a hard no. It had taken a lot of convincing just to get her to sneak out to her roof back in the day. I knew what her limits were.

That said, it was possible I was pushing those limits with my plans today. I reassured her all the same. "I'm not signing you up for lessons, and I'm not taking you snowboarding. Chill." As if I wasn't already pressing my luck, I added, "Trust me."

I immediately regretted the words, even as they passed my lips. I definitely deserved her trust, but I didn't like asking for it. I didn't want her to think she could count on me, which was irrational considering how I'd been doing nothing but showing her she could count on me since she walked back into my life.

But it was out there now. The words said, and as though she understood what it cost for me to say them, she answered earnestly. "I do."

She didn't ask again what we were doing at the resort, and we were silent as I found a rather fortunate parking spot near the lodge. Car off, keys in my coat pocket, I gave her my full attention for the first time since we'd started driving. Her expression was wary, but her eyes were bright. She meant it, I realized. That she trusted me. So easily after all this time, when she hadn't trusted me back then.

I didn't know what to make of that or of the way that revelation punched at my gut.

So I didn't try to analyze it. "Let's go."

She followed me without question as we walked up to the lodge and headed for guest services. "Two standard size tubes," I said, pulling out my wallet.

"We're going tubing?" Jolie sounded both intrigued and anxious.

"We'll stick to the kiddie hill. Even three-year-olds can handle it."

"I imagine they're sitting on a parent's lap when they do. They probably also have very little choice in the matter."

I took my card back from the customer rep, pocketed my wallet, then accepted the two passes before turning again to Jolie. "And neither do you it seems." She opened her mouth—to protest, most likely—but I didn't let her. "Here's the receipt so you can pick up our tubes at the counter outside. I'll meet you there in a few."

I left her still gaping and headed to the retail shop before she could argue.

Half of me expected her to follow, but when I chanced a glance over my shoulder a half a minute later, I saw her trudging toward the back doors of the lodge. It felt stupidly good that she would just do what I said without a fight.

Maybe having her trust wasn't so bad after all.

Quickly, I picked out what we needed, not being particular about what I grabbed, and paid for the items, declining a bag. Less than ten minutes later, I found Jolie outside with a blue and a red tube, each awkwardly tucked under an arm.

"Here," I said, throwing a scarf around her neck, then another around mine. I tucked the rest of the clothing into the crook of my arm while I pulled a beanie with the Hunter Mountain logo over her head. It was too intimate, and as my fingers let go of the edge of her hat, I found they were too close to brushing down her cheeks, red from the cold.

"Thank you." Her breath came out in a puff, but it was the color of her tone that was the warmest.

It was that heat that drew me into making another dangerous choice. "You can put those down." I waited while she set the tubes down, each balancing on end between us so they wouldn't be in anyone's way. The barrier between us was good and necessary, but I still resented it as I took one of her hands and put a glove on it like I was a goddamned lady in waiting.

Too close.

Too intimate.

Too fucking dangerous.

Her skin burned against mine as I tugged the waterproof fabric over her fingers. The small gasp she made at the contact told me she felt it too. I zipped the glove on, and without saying anything, she offered her other hand so I could clothe it as well.

Dumb. I was so incredibly dumb.

Especially because this time, I took my time, running the tip of my thumb over the backs of her bare knuckles before presenting the glove. I paused on one digit in particular. "This finger is bare," I said before I could think about it. The thought was a fly I'd tried to keep bottled up, ignoring how it had buzzed inside me, wanting to be free.

With my guard down and the distraction of silky skin, it escaped, and now it buzzed between us.

"It's always been bare."

She didn't belong to anyone. She'd never belonged to anyone.

A weight on my chest lifted, but the fly still buzzed, nagging to know more. "No one's ever tried to put a ring on it?"

"Once." A pause. "Wait. No. Twice."

Twice. Not one but two separate men had thought he was good enough to ask her to be his forever.

"What happened?" I hoped she said that they were both dead. That way I didn't have to go looking for them.

"I had no interest in the one."

Buzz. Buzz. Buzz. "The other?"

She frowned. She'd been solemn, but this was the first time the conversation seemed difficult for her. Her hand turned over so her palm was against mine. "I hurt him very much."

My breath stuck in my lungs. *Me.* She meant me. There was no way she didn't mean me, and acknowledging the past and the pain in that way let loose something in me that was far bigger than a fly. Something more the size of a beast with fangs and predator eyes. A beast that would tear us both apart if I let him.

I stepped back, snatching my palm from hers, and handed her the other glove to put on for herself. Putting on my own gloves and hat, though, I kept thinking about *then*, about the fucked-up proposal I'd made with a pipe cleaner I'd found in my mother's hobby box.

"One day it will be a real ring," I'd promised.

"It doesn't matter. You know I love you."

She'd been crying, and I'd thought for a long time that her tears had been for the situation. For fear of the unknown and where we would go and how it would possibly work out, but every now and then I wondered if they might have been a different kind of tears—the kind shed out of sentimentality and emotion too brimming to keep in.

The way things turned out, that notion seemed unrealistic, but I'd lived long enough to know the complexity of emotions. She could have been crying both kinds of tears all at once. She could have been crying out of happiness and still thrown that happiness away.

But if she hadn't? God, I would have loved her for a lifetime.

It was better not to think about that. Easier too, for both of us I was pretty sure, and when I swatted the fly away and let the topic drop, she didn't try to pick it back up.

The next couple of hours were lost to the stupid thrill of going up and down. The kiddie run was even more tame than I'd imagined, filled with lots of parents and children too young to remember to break for the bathroom without a reminder, yet it was fun all the same. Not much more of a ride than we would have gotten if we'd just gone to Central Park, but I was glad I'd dragged her farther away. The drive had eaten up time and psychologically the distance, made the day feel more like an escape.

She wouldn't talk to me about it, and I'd stopped pressing, but I would have been naive to think that Jolie wasn't carrying a burden at all times, despite the warmth in her eyes and the ease of her smiles. I'd lived a similar past, and I sure as fuck carried shit from those days, so it was a no-brainer that she'd feel the same.

Plus, there was the whole *help-me-kill-my-father* thing. People didn't come to those kinds of decisions without something weighing on them. Point being, she didn't have to say anything for me to know she needed a chance to set down her load and take a vacation from the strain.

Two straight hours of her infectious giggling, and I was confident the day's activity had done the trick.

"One more run?" I asked after we'd taken a break to warm up with hot cocoa in the lodge. We'd been frozen to the bone, despite all the layers, and jonesing to sit by a fire, but after twenty minutes in front of the roaring fireplace, I was thawed enough to go back into the cold.

I watched her as she considered. She'd taken off her gloves, and her scarf was open, revealing the hollow of her neck.

I'd never realized how sexy a throat could be, and I wasn't even thinking about when my cock had been buried inside it.

"Yeah. I could do one more."

I tore my eyes from her neck and took the empty Styrofoam cup from her hand to toss in the recycling along with mine. "One more good run, then we can pick up another round of cocoa for the drive home."

"Sounds perfect."

Outside, we stopped by the counter to get two new tubes, then headed to line up for the conveyor belt that would take us to the top of the hill.

"This was such a great idea," she said as we got in line, and my chest puffed out involuntarily from the praise. "How did you even know about this place?"

"Carla had a boyfriend we lived with for a while in Poughkeepsie. I came here once with some friends from school." I leaned around her to see how many people were in front of us. The crowds had gotten longer as the day had gone on and more skiers abandoned the slopes for tubing. I spied a shorter line next to us, one that led to a longer run. "Here, come this way."

She followed without question. "That's right. I forget that Carla had a life before she remarried."

"I do too." My mother had always been Carla between the two of us. Her days of being Mom had long passed by the time her choices had brought me into Jolie's world. I couldn't hate her for that, no matter what else it had brought me, because knowing Jolie had been the single most gratifying thing in my life. But I'd never forgiven Carla for the rest of it, and these days I rarely thought about her at all.

"I know you haven't talked to her. She's never tried to reach out?"

I glanced behind me at her as I stepped onto the magic carpet, partly to make sure she was still following, but also because of what she'd said. Since she'd been gone for so many years, I'd assumed she didn't have any news from home. "No, she hasn't, thank God. How do you know I haven't talked to her?"

"I went home recently."

She said it all casual, like it was no big deal when instead it was a big fucking clue. "You said you were hiding from your—"

"I was hiding. And then I wasn't."

I adjusted my tube and turned around so I was riding the belt facing backward. I had so many questions but was very aware that she would have told me already if this was stuff she wanted me to know.

But she was talking now. So did that mean she was ready to answer?

"He found you." Guessing felt more sure than questioning, but it still felt tentative. Like I was walking out onto a frozen pond, trying to decide how long the ice would hold.

She gazed in the distance to where the sun was starting to get low in the sky. "No."

"Something he did drew you out."

She avoided the question-not-question. "I didn't lie when I said I didn't know anything current about him. I wasn't home long enough to learn anything useful."

Asking what happened with Langdon was useless. I blew out a breath that steamed in the air like the exhale from a cigarette. "But you were home long enough to figure out I haven't talked to Carla?"

She gave a cute shrug, her lips puckering as she did. "I might have asked about you while I was there."

"What else do you know about me?"

"Hmm." Her cheeks went rosy. Probably from the cold and not the conversation. "I know you've never had a ring on your finger either."

"They know that much about my life?" I'd thought I'd gone as dark from the people back home as they'd gone for me.

"No, actually, that..." Now she definitely blushed. "I Googled. Public record says Cade Warren has always been single."

We were still moving, but I swore the earth stood still. I'd known she had to look me up in order to email me to meet with her. That didn't require looking at public records. She'd looked that up because she'd wanted to know.

Why had she wanted to know?

Why did it mean so much that she did?

My feet hit snow as the belt came to an end. Since I hadn't been watching, I hadn't been expecting it, and Jolie crashed into me. I put my arms out to steady her. To steady us. She shivered as my free hand found her waist, and after I stepped us to the side and out of the way, I left them there. She took a step in, bringing us even closer, despite the tubes we carried, and for a second I thought we were having a moment.

Then she realized we weren't at the top of the kiddie run.

"Hold on a minute." She walked out of my grasp, scanning the hill in front of us and the belt we'd just come up, obviously realizing she'd been tricked. "No way. Not a chance. I'm not going down that."

"You've been fine all day. Why suddenly get cold feet?"

"Because this run is twice as long!"

"Three times as long, I think." I wasn't helping myself. "Which means you have three times the fun."

"I don't think it works like that."

"It works exactly like that. Longer run just means extending the thrill."

"I was happy with the length of thrill before." She gave a tight smile to someone behind me. "Go ahead! We're not going down."

"Yes, actually, we are, but please go before us. We need a second."

The teens behind us grinned as they stepped around us, a blunt contrast to the glare Jolie gave me. "I'm not going down that hill, Cade. You can do whatever you want, but I'm not going down."

"I have news for you, sweetheart. There's not another way down."

She spun around to see if I was telling the truth, which I might not have been. It was possible there was a pathway that could be walked, but it wasn't obvious if there was.

Realizing that she'd have to ask, she stepped toward the attendant at the top of the run. "Excuse me?"

The kid—he couldn't have been more than twenty-five—answered with what he presumed Jolie wanted to know. "Sitting in the tube is all that's allowed. No belly rides. You can get in place here, and I'll get you started down the hill."

While he'd given his rote delivery, I'd taken the opportunity to pull a hundred out of my wallet and slapped it in his palm before Jolie could correct him with her real question. "Take care of this, will you?" I handed him my tube and took Jolie's from her.

She relaxed, assuming I was helping her find another way down the mountain, but instead of handing the man her tube as well, I plopped it on the ground and sat down, pulling Jolie in my lap. "Don't struggle if you want this to stay safe, and hold on tight."

"What are you—?"

I pushed off, sending the tube down the mountain, and her question turned into a high-pitched squeal.

"No lap riders over forty-four inches tall!" The attendant called after us, too late.

Seriously, what did he think the hundred had been for? Like I'd pay that much for him just to return my tube for me.

Whatever he thought, he'd lost his chance to stop us. We were tearing down the run at full speed, the wind whipping, Jolie screaming and laughing and screaming again. She clung onto the handles, and I clung onto her and tried to ignore her ass in my lap, and the way it rubbed against my cock whenever the tube took a little bit of a jump. I hadn't quite expected how bumpy the ride would be. Turned out the difference between the kiddie runs and the regular runs really was more than just length.

But God, it was fucking thrilling.

Because it was always thrilling to soar at a wicked speed through space, but we could have been sitting still, and I would have been just as thrilled because she was in my arms, and she was happy, and once upon a time that right there had been The Dream.

I wished the ride could have gone on forever.

At the bottom, after we scurried to our feet and rushed our tube out of the way as was protocol, I expected her to attack. A snowball in the face, maybe. At least a good tongue-lashing, even though she'd obviously had a good time and had most likely felt the evidence of my good time as I'd grown thick and hard beneath her.

Instead, when she'd caught her breath, her eyes were still gleaming and her smile still pasted to her face. My hands were still around her, too. Or around her again, and the way she kept looking at my lips, I wondered if maybe she was thinking about kissing me.

That might have been a real punishment.

Just thinking about it stole my own smile from my face. She sombered when I did, and then it felt even more likely that we might kiss.

I didn't think I could survive that.

It had been one thing to have her mouth wrapped around my cock. Her lips on mine was a whole other level of connection. One that would surely kill me.

And despite the danger, I couldn't fucking step away. "See?" I said, desperate for something safe to fill the silence. "Not so scary when it's both of us together."

She grew even more serious. "I forgot that. That I'm stronger with you."

"I didn't." Fuck. This wasn't safe at all.

"No, you always knew. I wish I'd thought that would have been enough."

Her regrets meant nothing.

Maybe that wasn't true. "I've been mad at you for a really long time because you didn't believe in us, Jol."

"And now?" It was a whisper, as though the question might break something if voiced too loudly. "Are you still mad?"

Fuck, yes, I was mad. Mad was all I ever was. It had been the only emotion I'd truly known for so long now that I didn't remember what it felt like not to be mad.

Except, all of a sudden, that wasn't true either. "I want to be," I said, and I was bare and naked now before her.

"But you're not?"

Everything about her was hopeful. Her expression, the way she held her body, the soft lilt in her voice. It was the perfect chance to say something hurtful to her, to get back for how hurt she'd once made me when I'd been full of hope and looking at her with the same trusting eyes.

Revenge had been a nice fantasy over the years. I'd conjured up many scenarios where I'd given paybacks. Both to her father and her. The times I'd dreamed about destroying her had been the most satisfying.

Right now, I couldn't imagine why I'd ever want to hurt her. Hurting her only meant hurting me, and hadn't I been hurt enough?

So where did that leave me emotionally? "I don't think I'm ready for what I feel."

She nodded. "I don't think I'm ready either."

Then, because she'd said she wasn't ready—because caring for her and protecting her was what I always did, what I'd always done—I stepped away, without kissing her, without even a last lingering glance at her mouth.

But if she thought I'd stepped away because I was protecting myself? Well. I kind of hoped that's exactly what she thought.

TWENTY-ONE

Past

I flattened myself against the roof and bent over the overhang, checking to make sure the window was slightly open before I knocked. That was our code—if the window was shut, it was a bad time. That way I didn't pop up when her father might see me. We'd become masters at secrecy. It was funny what skills necessity could instill.

Almost as soon as I rapped, as though she'd been waiting for me, her curtains parted, and Jolie lifted her window all the way. Carefully, I turned around and lowered my foot to the open ledge, then worked my way through the opening onto her bed, where she immediately threw her arms around me.

"I swear I can't breathe every time you do that."

I knew she was looking behind me, at the drop from the second floor to the ground. The height was even worse here than around the front of the house because the basement opened up to garden level on this side. No sane person would attempt to get to Jolie this way, which was probably why Headmaster Stark had put her in this room.

Headmaster Stark hadn't been counting on me.

"I could climb it in my sleep," I insisted. But I tore myself away from her and shut the windowpane because keeping it open felt like tempting fate.

I started to pull her back to my arms when she reminded me. "The dresser."

Stark was the kind of guy who locked his daughter in her room at night. Literally. The threat of her having no way out in a fire was apparently less frightening than the threat of her sneaking out. The high window took care of one possible route of escape—or so he thought. A lock on the outside of her door took care of the other route.

If he wanted to walk into her room, the only warning we'd get would be the click of the lock turning, and while both of us agreed it was highly unlikely he'd come to check on her in the middle of the night, Jolie insisted on taking precautions all the same.

And so her dresser was pushed in front of the door. It wasn't heavy enough to keep anyone out for long, but it could buy me time to go back through the window.

"One day, he's going to come up here because he hears us sliding the dresser against the door." I tugged it into place all the same while she pushed with her shoulder on the other side.

"It makes me feel better." It was what she always said, and I understood that too, but it was the same reason that made her feel better that made me hate the safeguard—I was the one who was protected. Not her.

But that was the price of her love. She looked out for me, and when it came to avoiding the wrath of her father, she was the expert. And as I moved with her back to the bed, I promised myself, as I always did, that one day I would be the one who did all the protecting.

Back in her arms, my lips found hers, teasing them open with soft kisses before claiming her with my tongue. I was at turns aggressive and gentle, a technique I'd only recently realized drove her wild—the chase, the retreat, the chase again. That was exactly how Jolie wanted to be pursued. She wanted to be wanted but couldn't handle being wanted all at the same time, and the push/pull seemed to allow her space to process both feelings separately.

Driving her wild, though, meant I'd just set the agenda for our tryst. I'd wanted to talk to her first. Truth was, I missed her. We'd been avoiding each other publicly the past couple of weeks, sure her father was onto us, a fear that could very well have been imagined. Regardless, we'd been playing it safe, and while I loved the physical with her—love wasn't even the right term; I craved it, needed it, depended on it for my survival—our connection went beyond that. I yearned to know every part of her, to be the keeper of her every secret, both the important ones and the trivial. My heart beat more steadily in her presence. Keeping my distance had been agony, and I wanted to catch up. There was the thing I wanted to ask her too, the pipe cleaner from my mother's craft kit burning like a hot coal in my pocket.

But I also wanted this—her panting and eager, her mouth everywhere, her hands tugging at my sweatshirt.

I broke away long enough to get the thing over my head. By the time I'd tossed it to the ground, she was already climbing onto me, straddling my lap, grinding her hips against the aching rod in my jeans.

With a grunt of satisfaction, I unthinkingly leaned back and jerked at the unexpected surge of pain as my body met the decorative framework around the window.

Jolie, of course, noticed. "Is it still really bad? Does it need more ointment? I'm pretty sure I could get an antibiotic if I faked a sore throat."

"Carla had something from her last toothache that she never finished. I stole those." Carefully, I repositioned myself so I was leaning against the flat of the wall instead of the uneven molding. "It's healing pretty well, I think."

It had been worse this time than usual. He'd brought out a cane instead of his skinny-tailed whip, and the single stripe he'd left had torn open and bled. It had been more than a week since I'd slept on my back, and only the last few days that I'd been able to go long stretches without thinking about it at all.

I downplayed the pain for her, though. Partly because it had been her father who'd made it, and I didn't want her to feel any guilt about that.

But also because I was ashamed of it. Ashamed that I'd been stupid enough to get myself in trouble. Ashamed of what had happened in that room after the cane had broken my skin.

I still hadn't told her all of it. She carried enough on her own. I didn't need her to feel this pain with me too.

"Turn around. Let me see it."

I shook my head and tried to pull her back toward me. The heat of the moment was ruined now, but if I let her examine me, she'd turn into my nurse, and I didn't need that kind of attention right now.

She resisted for a moment, then sighed and stretched out, her legs tangling with mine, her head resting on my chest. "How long do we have to hold on?"

"It's only two months. Less, actually. Seven weeks." I pressed my lips against her forehead and stroked her hair. "We just have to get through seven weeks, and then we're gone."

"Tell me again how we're going to do it."

This was becoming as routine as the window being left open and the dresser pulled in front of the door, me reciting how we'd eventually get away like it was her favorite bedtime story. "We'll walk the stage. We'll get our diplomas. Then after the ceremony, we'll leave. We won't even go to the after party. We'll just be gone."

"And we won't take his car."

"No. We won't take my mother's either."

"So they can't come after us saying we stole anything." This was one of the most important details to her, the part she went over and over. She rarely expressed fear where her father was concerned—because she'd learned to keep it buried, I suspected. Her hyperfocus on making sure there was no legal way her father could come after us revealed the terror she usually kept hidden.

"We won't take anything of theirs," I promised. "And you'll be eighteen then. He can't call you a runaway." Her birthday was only three days before graduation. I'd already had mine. Both of us would be adults in the eyes of the law.

"And you're sure Janice won't press charges about her truck?"

"Yes." I wasn't as sure as I pretended I was, but I felt good enough to count on it. Janice was the school's gardener. These days, she did more delegating than actual work, but she still occupied the cottage attached to the greenhouse on the edge of the school property. The truck we planned to take had belonged to her late husband and had sat unused in her garage since his death the previous year.

I'd heard all about it when I'd been sentenced to weed pulling for one of my punishments. Official punishment, anyway. The one that had been declared to my fellow schoolmates as a warning to not get caught with a joint. My real punishment had been doled out in the privacy of Stark's office, the door closed, my mouth biting down into my shirt so that I wouldn't be heard down the hall. Any sound at all would equal double the thrashing, so I tried extra hard to be quiet. I hadn't learned as well as Jolie had, but I'd learned some.

The greenhouse part of the punishment had ended up being more of a reward. Mostly I moved heavy bags of soil and dug holes, but it was calm and meditative, the hours filled with a gentle rhythm of work as Janice chatted about her husband and her refusal to learn to drive a stick and the truck that still worked but she hadn't gotten around to selling. More than once she said that I could buy it from her, and when I told her that I didn't have the money, she'd always say, "We'll figure something out." She'd even shown me where the keys were kept.

We could take the truck, I'd decided. We could write a note explaining. She wouldn't report us. I hoped.

"We'll send her money when we can," Jolie said, repeating the promise I'd made in the past.

"We will. We'll be fine."

"And where will we go?"

This was where the story changed from telling to telling. Sometimes I'd say we'd go to New York. Other times, Canada. On days when one of us was feeling especially pessimistic, I'd take us farther—to Europe. To Egypt. To Japan.

Truth was, where we went didn't matter. As long as I was with her.

I tipped her chin up toward mine so I could look her in the eyes when I said it. But then her mouth caught my attention as she swept her tongue over her bottom lip, and the hand she'd been lazily dancing over my abdomen suddenly felt like not enough touch.

I pressed my mouth to hers, pulling her leg astride me so that my cock could press against the warm spot between her legs. "I need to be inside of you," I whispered between drugging kisses. "That's the only place I want to go."

Sex was Jolie's love language even more than it was mine, and that was all I had to say before she was stripping off her girly nightie and scrambling out of her cotton panties. I toed off my shoes and stripped off my jeans. Digging for the condom in my pocket before I tossed them aside, my fingers brushed against the pipe cleaner, and I considered briefly if now was the time for my proposal.

But then she was naked, the moonlight streaming through the window like a spotlight on her beauty, and my cock turned so hard that it became the priority. I tore open the wrapper with my teeth, slid on the latex, and pushed her down to the bed.

She spread her legs to make room for me, and I climbed between and hovered over her, my weight balanced on my palm placed on the bed next to her head.

"Are you ready for me?" My free hand was checking even as I asked, slipping between her folds to find her wet and slick. She hadn't been the first girl I'd ever fucked—I hadn't been her first either—but she'd been the first girl I'd fucked long enough to actually feel like I knew what I was doing.

I had a pretty good feeling I was the first person who'd made it good for her, and that was worth more than being the only person who'd ever been inside her. I prided myself on making sure I always made it good for her, hoping that would keep me special, and so after finding her wet, I dragged my fingers up to swirl against her swollen bud.

"Are *you* ready for *me*?" she teased, her back arching as I hit an especially sensitive spot.

I was always ready for her.

And I never was.

It was a paradox. How those things could exist together and be true was beyond the capability of my teenage mind, but the reality of it sent a shiver of apprehension down my spine even as I rushed to get myself inside of her.

We were still clumsy at this part—one of us usually needing to use a hand to get my head notched up to the right place—and this time I was still in the process of lining up when she lifted her hips and pulled me inside her.

I shuddered at the sudden damp heat as I buried myself to my balls.

No, I was never ready for her.

But I was ready to be hers. For always. Ready for her to be mine. With each thrust, I felt more and more like we already belonged to each other, like each push into her was me giving her another piece of myself, and each pull out was me taking another piece of her.

And so what if I was only eighteen and sentimental? Some things deserved to be romanticized. Some moments deserved to be treasured. Some bonds deserved to be glorified and worshipped like the unbreakable covenant of a God to his people. That was the kind of connection we had. Fucking her was holy. The only communion I'd ever believed in. Sex, a sacred act that made us one.

"I love you." She brought her hands to my face and kissed me between breaths. "I love you so much."

Then I was coming, before I could say it back, before I could spend the time needed to make her come too, before I could register the rattle of the knob and the door knocking against the dresser.

"What the hell is this, Julianna?" Stark's voice hissed through the open crack.

We jumped apart. Scrambled like the breaking in a game of pool. I got my jeans on without removing the condom. My shoes, I grabbed without bothering to put on.

Meanwhile, Jolie opened the window and started looking for my shirt. "Where is it? *Where is it?*" Her whisper felt like a yell.

The dresser was moving. Slowly, but surely. Stark was putting his back into his push, cursing and demanding that Julianna *open the door right this instance*.

We didn't have any time.

"If you find it, stuff it under the bed." I was already sitting on the windowsill. I had to pull myself out, then crouch, placing my feet flat on the sill so I could reach up and hoist myself the way I came. Normally, I took my time climbing out. If I did it too fast and didn't have a firm grip on the overhang above me, I would fall to the ground below.

I glanced down.

I'd survive it. It would probably hurt, but I'd definitely survive.

I wasn't sure that would be the case if I stayed.

Jolie knelt on the bed, her face etched with terror, her eyes wide. "Be careful." She glanced to the door and back at me. "Be careful, but go!"

I hesitated, just long enough to give her a reassuring nod. I was going to be okay. She was going to be okay. She'd already had the foresight to make up a story about why she'd moved the dresser—*she'd heard a noise. She was scared.* Her father wouldn't know there was a boy creeping on the roof above them as she explained.

The hesitation was where I'd gone wrong—that damned desire to make sure she was okay, even when the best way to make her okay was to be gone. It was instinctive and my weakness.

In that half second of time, Stark got the door open and saw me hanging out the window without a shirt on, saw his daughter naked and trying to help get me out.

I'd thought I'd seen the man in all states of anger, thought I'd seen the worst of his wrath, but the look on his face expressed a whole new level of rage. "You're dead, Cade Warren."

Even without the venom in his tone, I knew he meant what he said.

He'd shown himself to be quite reliable when it came to follow-through on his threats.

With no time and no choice, I had no chance of climbing up.

I didn't let myself think.

I grabbed onto the bottom of the window, swung my legs out, and dropped to the ground.

TWENTY-TWO

Present

We spent the next two days avoiding each other.

I didn't know what was going on in her head, but I knew what was going on in mine, and what was going on was complicated. For the first time in years, I verged on optimism, and that felt dangerous and fragile. I'd gotten used to the idea that I'd always be alone. The possibility that I might have someone—that I could have *her*—thrilled me, but I didn't know how to let that notion sit in my head. My muscles literally tensed against it. As if they remembered the physical pain that came with feeling things for Julianna Stark.

My heart was a whole other sort of tense. I'd developed a constant ache in the center of my chest. It hurt to breathe, and both Tuesday and Wednesday nights, when I lay in the dark straining my ears to hear any sound from her in the next room, my lungs struggled to work altogether. Each intake stuttered as I fought to bring air in. Each exhale went so long I felt completely empty before I was able to attempt another draw.

I tried not to wonder if Jolie was going through something similar.

At the same time, I didn't believe she had the right to anguish. She'd been the one to desert me. What did she have to fear about reconnecting? What did she stand to lose that she hadn't willingly given up?

Whatever she was grappling with, it made her skittish and quiet. She left the hotel room for long stretches of time without saying a word about where she was going or when she'd be back. Not like I told her where I was going when I disappeared to go to the gym or the office or the hotel bar. I told myself I didn't care, but twice I found myself following her at a discreet distance. Once she ended up at the Midtown Library. The other time she slipped into a church. Both times I'd lingered outside in the cold, smoking from a pack of Camels that I'd finally broken down and purchased. Both times I psyched myself up, saying as soon as I got to the butt, I'd go in after her. I'd confront her with every tangled-up emotion. I'd force her to hear everything I had to say.

Both times, my will dissolved when the cigarette had turned to ash. I stomped out the cherry and left her for my own distractions.

By Thursday afternoon, the hotel suite had become a living hell.

I'd spent most of the day locked in my bedroom and tried to catch up on what was going on in the Tokyo office. Besides the fact that I couldn't concentrate, everyone on the other side of the world was asleep or trying to be, and after the third time I woke my assistant up to ask her a question that I should have been able to figure out on my own, I decided to give up on the attempt.

I shut my laptop and looked at the clock. A quarter past four. The hours were ticking down until Jolie left. With Donovan on board to help with her father, there wasn't any need for me to stay involved. She'd get on that plane, and we could go back to being strangers.

Was it too early to start drinking?

Close enough. The numb side effect of alcohol lured me to venture out of my room to the minibar. When I came out, she was on her bed, wearing nothing but my goddamn T-shirt and her panties, painting her toenails bright red. She glanced at me quickly before going back to her task.

Fuck, even that had memories attached. All the times she'd pull out a brightly colored bottle and decorate her toes, only to wipe them clean with acetone when she was finished since her father didn't approve.

One day, I'll always have painted toes.

I popped off the lid on a beer bottle and chugged a quarter of it down right there. I would have drunk more if my cell phone hadn't started ringing.

"What have you got?" I said when I saw it was Donovan.

Jolie returned her attention to me, either because she was nosy or because she suspected the call might be in regard to her. I turned my body so I wasn't looking at her, but I could feel her eyes boring into me all the same.

"I'd rather discuss it in the office." Donovan's tone refused any argument, which was a sure-fire way to make me combative.

"I can discuss things perfectly fine on the phone."

"I'm sure you can, asshole, but this isn't the kind of information that should be shared over unsecured lines. And the information isn't complete yet. I need you to run an errand first."

I muttered a curse under my breath. "Fine. I'll be there in a bit."

"I'm coming with," Jolie said as soon as I'd hung up.

I ran my hand over my beard and took another pull on the bottle, trying to decide if I should fight her on it. If it was about her quest, then she should probably be allowed to be there. But I'd spent the last two days trying not to be with her.

Being with her was also exactly what I wanted most.

As I shifted toward her, her eyes caught mine, and the decision was made. "We're leaving in twenty."

"Awesome." It was the first time I'd seen her smile since Hunter Mountain, and I suddenly couldn't remember how I ever existed without it. "Good thing that was the second coat."

I drank my beer and watched as she capped the polish, then walked carefully down the hallway. A few seconds later, I heard the hair dryer go on. Drying her wet nails, I suspected.

It almost had *me* smiling.

The impulse disappeared when my phone dinged with a text from Donovan.

> Come looking mean.

The skin at the back of my neck prickled. *Look mean* was code for *I need you to do something shady with some even shadier people*. I'd handled a few of these kinds of interactions for Donovan before. The man might have a dangerous brain, but I doubted he could throw a punch to save his life. He certainly didn't look like a threat.

My size was threatening on its own. Add the tats and my perma-scowl, and I could look very intimidating. It helped that I was rough around the edges, no matter how well I was dressed. In fact, while I'd spent my earlier days of thug life in black jeans and black T-shirts, I'd since found I was more menacing in a suit. Good thing I still had a clean one hanging in the closet.

But now I had a problem. Whatever Donovan needed me to do, I wasn't going to want Jolie with me.

I started down the hallway to tell her and stopped halfway there. Telling her she couldn't come would mean taking away that smile. A few days ago, I would have done it willingly. On purpose. Because I wanted her to feel as bad as I did every day.

When exactly had I stopped wanting that?

She could at least come hear what Donovan had dug up so far. No harm in that.

"MISSING TEENS?" Jolie looked to me, even though it had been Donovan who had delivered the information.

I hadn't told her about the pattern of runaways that he'd mentioned on Tuesday, not only because that would have required a conversation when I'd been avoiding her, but because it hadn't seemed like anything real yet.

Apparently, now it was.

"Thirteen in all. Fourteen if you count Cade, which I'm not. It wouldn't be notable if any of them had shown up again. As it is, there are thirteen teenagers who were last seen at Stark Academy and never again." He spoke in a hushed tone. It had been after five when we'd arrived, but Donovan had set the glass to the opaque setting and shut the door as soon as we had. The conversation was obviously one he didn't want overheard.

Understandably so. Since there was a real good chance we were talking about thirteen kids who were very likely dead.

"And you think my father has something to do with that?" Again she looked to me, as if I could somehow translate whatever it was that she was having trouble understanding.

Donovan gave a slight shake of his head. "Not necessarily. But if he isn't responsible, it's an opportunity to blame him."

This time I was the one who looked at her. I watched the color slowly drain from her face as she processed what he was proposing. It was one thing to destroy her father for the things he'd actually done. It was another to frame him for murder.

Personally, I didn't have a problem with it.

Jolie seemed to need to sit with it a minute.

"We don't have to decide what we do until we have more info," Donovan said in an attempt to soothe her. "We might get lucky and discover your father's responsible for all of it."

So much for putting her at ease.

"I'm sure your dad didn't...*hurt* them." I wasn't really sure of that, but I couldn't bring myself to say the words *murder* or *kill* or any other synonyms.

I actually wasn't sure he hadn't taken their lives. While I didn't think he was a secret serial killer, he had predispositions. He was a sadist. He liked to inflict pain. He got off on the sight of blood.

"On purpose, anyway," I amended. I could totally see a punishment gone too far kind of scenario.

But thirteen times?

Her skeptical glare said it was pointless to try to sell her a lie. She knew who her father was as well as I did. "You're sure they totally disappeared? Maybe they just changed their names. Didn't want to be found again. I know, thirteen kids is a lot, but it's not impossible."

"It's not," Donovan agreed. "I had my guy try to trace them down. Honestly, I expected it to take a while. This isn't the kind of investigation work that happens overnight, and if he were searching any of these kids individually, he probably wouldn't have found anything yet. But looking for them as a bunch, he stumbled upon something useful."

"That sounds ominous." I was beginning to regret having brought Jolie. As much as she wanted her father gone, I wasn't sure she wanted to know he'd been as much of a monster as Donovan was suggesting.

"My guy's contact says he has definitive proof of what happened to those kids. That's all I know. That's all he'll say until he's paid." He reached under the desk, brought out a black briefcase, and set it in front of him. He entered a code, and the case popped open, revealing stacks of money. "The contact has the code as well. He and I are the only ones able to open the case. He'll take the money, replace it with the proof we're looking for, then he'll lock the case again. Bring it back to me, and we'll go over it together."

Jolie's eyes were wide at the sight of the cash. "You're paying that much for this information?"

The money wasn't what had me bugged. I could pay him back without blinking. "We're the ones who want it. Why's he need to lock it?"

"Because I'm not just paying for info for you. He's handing over something for me as well. Which is why I have no problem paying the money."

In other words, it wasn't any of my business.

He'd been looking directly at Jolie. Now he stared at me. "The info is free of charge. As long as you do the collecting."

"Got it." My pulse had already ticked up with adrenaline the way it did before I stepped into a ring to spar. I enjoyed being behind a desk, managing people. Making legit money. But there was a part of me that felt more suited to being a heavy. A year spent as Stark's punching bag had given me a desire to possess the power of being on the other side, and while I didn't feel the need to pursue that full-time, I did love the thrill now and then.

Donovan shut the briefcase and reentered the code before handing it over to me. "Good. The meeting's set for six."

I checked my watch. "Cutting it close, aren't we?"

"Meetup is six blocks away. You can walk it in ten."

Jolie stood up before I did. "We should go now. Get there early."

Before I got the chance to correct her, Donovan did it for me. "Not you, kid. This is a job just for Cade."

The kid remark likely ruffled her as much as being told no. Especially since Jolie was a couple of years older than Donovan. Grateful as I was that I didn't have to be the one to ban her from the trip, I kind of wanted to punch him in the dick for patronizing her.

But Jolie could stick up for herself. "I'm not a kid, thank you very much, and I'm the one who is destroying my father, not Cade. He's *helping* me. Which means I go with him, and that's that."

Donovan glared at me, a look that could only mean *would you set the woman straight?*

I was of half a mind to let him work it out himself, but I knew how nasty he could get when he wanted to win, and I didn't have any intention of letting Jolie come. "He's right. This is just me."

"That's ridiculous. I don't want you doing me—" She cut herself off. "Hold on. Are you implying that this is dangerous?"

I'd thought that had been obvious. "That's exactly what I'm implying."

At the same time, Donovan said, "Not at all. Just very unnecessary."

His response was admittedly better. Gave her less to worry about.

"Right. What he said. It's cold out. I'll be in and out. Stay here, stay warm, and we'll open it up when I get back. I won't have anything before you do."

She wasn't fooled. "If it's dangerous, even more reason for me to go.

This is *my* thing, Cade. I know you said for you, not for me, but fuck that. I came to you. I'm not asking you to go into a dangerous situation on my behalf."

Donovan stood up to meet her at that level. "Look. I know you're trying to watch out for him, but he can take care of himself. Trust me."

Sure seemed like it too, with him defending me.

I stood to gain some power. "You didn't ask me. I'm choosing."

"I'm not *letting* you." Her eyes were pleading, her jaw set, and as much as I wasn't going to tolerate some woman telling me what I could and couldn't do, I did feel a tightness in my chest over her concern.

"You're not going, Jolie. Get that through your head now, or I won't share the information I get."

"You're destroying him without me now?"

"Sure. Why not? Like I said—like you reminded me—I'm not doing this for you." My eye twitched from the lie.

Which was weird because when had it stopped being the truth?

Fortunately, she couldn't read me that well anymore, and after a beat, her expression went hard. "Fuck you both very much." She grabbed her coat off the back of the chair. "I'm not waiting here for you while you traipse around the underworld, probably getting yourself killed. And I'm not spending another minute with *him*." She glared at Donovan. I would have been much happier about her being upset with him if she wasn't also upset with me. "I'll be waiting in the lobby." She stormed out the door, letting it slam behind her.

I'd started after her, without thinking, when he stopped me. "Let her go. She's upset, but she's safe. This is definitely not a meeting you want her attending."

It took a couple of deep breaths before I turned back toward him. "This guy's that scary?"

"Not sure. It's my first dealing with him. My contact vouches for him, but he also emphasized caution. The amount of money being exchanged and what I'm getting in return is enough reason to be wary." He moved to the bookcase while he spoke, where his safe was hidden behind a fake shelf. He opened it up and removed a loaded semi-automatic handgun. "Here's this, just in case."

I put my coat on before taking it, sticking it into the inside pocket that I'd had made specifically for hiding a gun. It had been a while since I'd carried one. The weight against my chest felt both exhilarating and foreboding. The thrill of danger was a nice perk of running Donovan's dirty errands. The actuality of it was the downside.

I was suddenly curious about what I'd be transporting. "What is it I'm bringing back to you?"

He waved his hand dismissively. "Nothing that interesting. It's the info you're getting about the kids that's valuable. Didn't want to worry your girl, but it took some heavy negotiating to even get the conversation started. Someone really doesn't want this information out."

He was feeding me some bullshit somewhere. Either he really didn't want me knowing what he was involved with or what he'd discovered about the missing teens was a whole lot bigger than Stark.

I knew him well enough to know he wouldn't tell me any more easily, and with twenty minutes left to six, I didn't have time to push. "Where am I meeting up with this guy?"

He gave me the info, along with a shot of whiskey. Liquor was always a good idea before these errands. Not too much to cloud the head, but enough to steady the nerves.

"Call me after. I can meet you at the hotel, if that's easier. I know you'll want Jolie with you when we open the case up. You know she's going to try to get you to let her come with you, right?"

I'd already considered that. "I'll put her in the cab myself." I straightened my collar, rechecked the gun, buttoned my coat, picked up the briefcase. "Oh, and Donovan? She's not my girl."

He threw out some rebuttal, but I'd already left.

And truthfully, I was having trouble finding the will to deny it.

TWENTY-THREE

"I'm going with you," Jolie said as soon as I found her in the lobby downstairs.

Sometimes I fucking hated it when Donovan was right.

Without saying anything, I ushered her out the main doors, pretending it didn't feel natural to touch the small of her back.

Outside, I dropped my hand and walked to the edge of the sidewalk so I could signal a cab.

She trotted after, pleading her case the whole time. "I'll be quiet. I won't interfere. I can stay outside if you really want me to. I won't be in the way. I just need to go with you."

Miracle of miracles, a taxi pulled over toward us immediately. I didn't speak until it was at the curb, and I had the door opened for her. "Where you need to go is back to the hotel."

She didn't move, her hands clenched into fists at her sides. "You can't keep me from going with you. I want to go. Why can't I go?"

"Why do you want to come?" I sounded tired and frustrated because I was. I needed to be getting my head in the right place, and she was distracting me, pulling my focus, throwing me off my game.

"He's my blood relative, not yours. I should take the responsibility of his sins."

"You took responsibility. You asked me for my help. So let me do the thing I'm good at, and wait for me at the hotel so we can go over what I come back with together."

"And if it's dangerous, you shouldn't go alone. You should have backup. You could get hurt. "

Like she could protect me.

But what I said was worse. "Since when do you care what happens to me?"

She retracted as though I'd slapped her, her eyes glistening. "Is that what you think? You think I don't care?"

The cab driver honked his horn, but I ignored him. "Have you given me any reason to think otherwise?"

She blinked several times, and her jaw got tight, her mouth a straight line. "I guess that's how you'd see it."

Damn straight. Because I wasn't an idiot. Because I'd been there.

"Hey, lady. You getting in or not?" The driver had his head cranked over his shoulder, waiting for Jolie's answer.

"She's getting in." This time when I pushed at her, she got in and hugged her arms over her chest, refusing to look at me.

Well, that was fine. She could be mad. Like Donovan said, she'd also be safe.

"She's staying at the Park Hyatt." I reached over her to hand the driver some bills. "This should cover the cost."

I hesitated for a moment before closing the door, wanting to say something, not sure what that something was.

After a beat, I figured it was best to let things lie. I shut the door and hit the roof of the cab, letting the driver know he could take off.

I was tempted to watch after her, but I knew that would be a mistake. Turning away from the street, I set down the briefcase, pulled a Camel from my pocket, and lit it. The rhythmic act of smoking was a great way to get focused. I needed to be on my toes. Needed to be completely in the moment.

Needed to stop thinking about what she'd meant when she said, *I guess that's how you'd see it.*

Why would I see it any other way? Had I missed something? Was she saying she *did* care?

It was a detail I could run away with, if I let myself.

I couldn't let myself.

Shaking my head of all Jolie thoughts, I took a long drag of my smoke, picked up the case, and set off toward my destination.

THE MEETING POINT was at the edge of Midtown, right where it met up with Hell's Kitchen. Admittedly, the area had a bit of grit, but the luxury apartment building across the street made it an unsuspecting location for dirty deals.

Truth was, the more upscale meetup spots were the ones that put me most on guard. Upscale meant money, and people with money were, in my experience, the most dangerous.

I slipped into the alleyway between a grocery store and a restaurant that served Cuban cuisine and counted doors until I came to the fifth one. My watch said it was a minute to six. Right on time.

I knocked.

A burly man in a black suit opened the door. He didn't make eye contact, scanning both directions in the alley behind me instead. "Entrance to the restaurant is round front. We don't take deliveries after five."

I responded with what I'd been instructed to say. "I'm here for Bishop."

With a nod of his head, Burly Man pushed the door open, his jacket lifting so I could see the glock he was packing. "Upstairs. You'll know the room."

I resisted the urge to pat my gun. It was a typical interaction for this sort of thing, and my spidey senses didn't detect anything out of the ordinary, but there was a reason I'd moved out of dirty work. Even typical interactions had the likelihood of going bad.

Cautiously, I stepped past him, scanning the room as he'd scanned the street. It was a typical back-of-restaurant loading area. I could hear the scrape of pots and pans from the kitchen just ahead, and beyond that, as a swinging door flew open, the buzz of New Yorkers hoping to finish their meal in time to catch a show.

The staircase ran to my left—a standard narrow corridor that practically gave a person claustrophobia to climb through. Of course the light was out, and the stairs were steep, and the briefcase bumped against the wall with each step, but I was at the top soon enough. There I found a dark hallway, the only light coming from a room at the end.

Aren't you supposed to not go toward the light?

I chuckled at the thought as I walked the hall, careful to make noise so I wouldn't surprise anyone. I stopped at the threshold, thrown a little off guard by the sight of five overtly armed men stationed around the room. A bigwig sat behind a desk at the far side. A skinny lackey type perched on the edge as though they'd been consulting on some matter.

All eyes were on me.

Now this was a little atypical. Usually these deals were conducted with even teams.

I reassured myself that Donovan knew what he was doing—fuck, he better know what he was doing—and addressed the bigwig. "You Bishop?"

It was the man I'd thought was the lackey who answered. "I'm Bishop. You Beasley's guy?"

"That I am." Beasley was the name Donovan used when he did shady deals.

Bishop, which was likely a pseudonym as well, gestured toward the briefcase in my hand. "That for me?"

"You have something for me in exchange?"

He worked his mouth like he had snuff tucked in his lip and ignored the question. "Put her here."

I paused. I preferred not to hand over money without seeing the goods first, but I wasn't sure I was in a position to have demands. I swept my gaze around the room, noting that though none of the heavies had a weapon drawn, they were each at the ready. It was a lot of protection for a simple exchange. What the fuck had Stark gotten mixed up with?

Or was it the information Donovan was seeking that was so valuable?

Either way, I needed to be cautious. "Seems I'm at a clear disadvantage here. I'm expected to hand this over with no promise I'll get what I'm after in return?"

"You want a promise? Okay, I promise." It was half-hearted at best.

"Yeah, we both know there's nothing keeping you to your word."

Bishop stood and turned to face me. "For what Beasley wants, this is how it works."

His patience was wearing, which was not ideal. And it was clear I had no power in the situation and no resources to play hardball.

Fine. Whatever. It was Donovan who'd be out cash if I returned empty-handed, something he surely knew when he made the deal. Goal was just to make sure *I* returned.

Whoa. That was new. Since when did I care about a potential risk to my life? My flippancy about death had been one of the reasons I'd been suited to this kind of job in the past.

I refused to let myself acknowledge when and why that had changed.

Keeping my senses on alert, I crossed to the desk, set the case down, and took a step back. Bishop bent to enter the combination. The lid flipped open, and he nodded to the guy who wasn't the bigwig saying, "Be sure it's all there."

I hadn't counted it in Donovan's office. It had been a lot, and I probably could have done some fast math if I'd wanted to, but I hadn't. Now that not-bigwig was thumbing through it, it was obvious just how much my friend was willing to hand over.

And it was a lot.

The minutes passed like hours as all the cash was counted and inspected with a digital light to be sure they were real and hadn't been marked. Finally, the goon announced it was all there and accounted for. "Plus $10K," he added.

I'd forgotten I was supposed to mention that. "That's a tip for the rush."

Bishop studied my face, as though he thought the extra money might have been a trick. "No tip necessary. But we'll keep it for a down payment for future interactions." He nodded to his guy to take the cash to a large safe on the floor behind him.

I fidgeted as I watched the money get packed inside, then breathed a sigh of relief when the guy returned to Bishop with a hard drive. "Real sensitive info on here," he said, holding it up. "Hope Beasley knows what he's getting into."

Jesus, so did I.

"It's password protected." Bishop dropped the drive in the case. "He knows what it is. Any problems getting into it, he knows how to reach me."

The hard drive could be blank. It could all be a scam. But thirty more seconds, and I'd have what I came for. I'd be back on the street within two minutes.

Except, just as Bishop started to close the lid, a noise came from the hallway behind me. Footsteps and a shuffling sound like one of the people walking wasn't coming willingly.

I wasn't facing the door and didn't turn because it was never wise to take eyes off the man in charge. But I knew.

Maybe it was the scent of cherry blossoms.

Or the muffled high-pitched scream.

Or maybe just that I fucking knew Jolie, knew that she never took kindly to a no, knew that she was stubborn as the day was long.

Whatever it was that made me certain, I didn't have to look to know that when all the men in the room pulled their guns out in alarm, they were aiming them at her.

TWENTY-FOUR

"Found her sniffing around the back door," Burly Man from downstairs said.

"I was looking for my cat?"

I cringed at the sound of her voice—confirmation that it was her and the ridiculous lie, one she couldn't even make convincing with the question at the end.

I turned just enough so that I could see her without putting my back to Bishop, slowly so as not to arouse a reaction from any of the gun-wielding men. Seeing her was both a relief and an ache. She was in one piece, didn't seem scuffed up in any way.

But she had a gun to her head, and it took everything in me not to rip Burly Man's arms off his body for being the one to hold it there.

I focused on her face, trying to blot out the Glock pointed at her temple. She looked scared, which did something to my insides, but not scared enough, which did something to my brain. *Fuck, Jolie. Why didn't you just do what I asked, for your own damn good?*

As if she could hear my thoughts, she mouthed a *sorry*.

"She's with me," I said, knowing I'd probably just screwed Donovan's deal out of existence.

"With you?" Bishop had already removed the hard drive from the case. Now it sat open and empty, the object of our pursuit in the hands of the man who'd counted the money. "There were strict instructions that you come alone."

Jolie opened her mouth to say something, but I shot her a silencing look. "You know women. They never listen."

I addressed her now with false admonition that would be very real later, when we got out of this. If we got out of this. "You were supposed to wait at the hotel, baby. I told you I'd be back later." I added the endearment for the men—an indication that she wasn't a threat to whatever business these guys were doing—but also it was for her. To give her some reassurance in whatever way I knew how.

"I got impatient." Her voice was tinier now, her eyes wider as she scanned the room and really took in the situation. She practically shrank in front of me. "I think I probably made a mistake."

You think?

Bishop narrowed his eyes. "She's...what? Your wife?"

I knew this kind of questioning technique. I'd used it many times in the past. He'd already checked out our bare left hands. He was trying to catch us in a lie.

"Girlfriend," I said.

At the same time Jolie said, "Fiancée."

She wasn't helping. I was going to kill her later for trying.

"Girlfriend," I corrected. "Stop getting ahead of yourself, baby. These men don't want to hear us get into another argument about it."

Except for the guy holding her, the others relaxed a bit, identifying with the nagging-lover trope, either for real or for show, as happens with men around their peers.

"If she's a problem, we could take her off your hands." It was the first time Bishop had smiled since I'd walked in the room, and now that he did, I saw I'd been mistaken in thinking he wasn't carrying. That smile was his own weapon, as threatening as any hardware.

Whatever he intended by the offer, it was clear that death would be the nicest of options.

I could hear my blood rushing in my ears. "I'll pass. I hate to say it in front of her, but I'm kind of attached."

He swept his eyes down her body, pausing too long at her curves. "Understandable." He stuck one hand into the pockets of his crisp suit pants and scratched at his bare chin with the other. "But you see, now we got a problem. You know what we do when someone doesn't follow the rules?"

He was going to tell me anyway, so I didn't answer. Thankfully, Jolie kept her mouth shut as well.

Again that evil smile. "Why don't you tell him, Ross?"

I looked to the goon who'd counted the money, thinking he must be who Bishop was addressing, but it turned out Ross was the burly man holding Jolie captive. "Sure, Bish. We shoot them."

Jolie let out an involuntary squeak. I saw the quiver in her lip just before she covered her mouth with her hand.

Finally, she was as scared as she ought to be.

It had been a long time, but now I was too. "All right, hold on. Let's not overreact here. She did something dumb. Real dumb. It wasn't intentional. Just let us go. You got our money. Let us walk out the door, empty-handed if you prefer. No harm, no foul, and you're up a lot of cash."

"I'm up the cash anyway." He was fully aware he held every card. But he did seem intrigued by something. "You're willing to walk out of here without Beasley's drive? That much money sent out with no prize in return, seems you'd be dead anyway."

Of course Bishop assumed that Donovan was my boss. He definitely didn't realize that I had twice the amount we'd handed over in my personal checking account.

All of which made me more of a threat than if I were simply an errand boy. In my eagerness to talk him down, I'd drawn suspicion. If we weren't worried about our lives, then who were we?

"No, no, no." Jolie's panic erupted before I'd thought through my next move. "We can't leave without the information, Cade. We have to—"

I winced as she used my real name. "Shut up, baby. I've got this handled." I didn't have this handled at all. I addressed Bishop. "Obviously, I'd rather we left with the drive. But if that's off the table, I'll take my chances with Beasley. At least that's not a sure step in the grave. But, really, do we need to be talking graves at all? For such a minor infraction, it doesn't seem like a reason to get blood on your hands."

On the outside, I was cool. As cool as I'd been the times I'd been the one throwing the threats. Nine times out of ten, that's exactly what they were—threats. Nothing more. Except for the extreme psychopaths and sadists—and there were far less in the underground than people imagined—no one actually wanted to exert force, no matter the form.

But I was the furthest thing from cool. Because that one time out of ten was enough to cry bad odds when Jolie was involved. Even as a kid shaking under the hand of Headmaster Stark, I'd never been this scared. Never felt this helpless. Never felt this on the verge of unleashing whatever beast lived locked up inside me.

They could do whatever they wanted to me. They could break me into a million impossible-to-identify pieces. But if they hurt one hair on Jolie's head...

I wasn't sure there was a word for the kind of fear-rage that inspired.

"He makes a point." The weaponized grin had been put away, but Bishop was still terrifying knowing it was in his pocket. "Lot of hassle, and probably not necessary. Especially since we've already been paid."

He considered a minute, then nodded to the money counter. "Put the drive back in the case." The goon did as he was told, then Bishop once again shut the lid. This time he entered the code locking the contents in place.

"You're letting us take it?" Rule number one in negotiating was not to sound unsure, and I'd fucking failed big time. It seemed too unlikely that we'd leave with the case. It still seemed unlikely that we'd leave at all.

"I am." Bishop took the case by the handle and stretched his arm forth, inviting me to take it.

I stretched my hand out, carefully, sure it was a trick.

It was.

As soon as my fingers were close to touching it, he pulled it back, out of reach. "But first, if we're going to let you two go, we have to be sure you aren't cops. I'm sure you understand. Ross, strip the lady. Check for a wire."

Without being told, like well-rehearsed choreography, one of the other men stepped in, pointing his gun so that Ross could pocket his and pull at Jolie's coat.

Renewed rage mingled with adrenaline-fueled panic surged through my veins. "Don't you fucking dare touch her!"

I rushed forward, only to be seized by two men, one at each arm.

And since Ross didn't take orders from me, he threw her removed coat to the floor and reached for the hem of her sweater.

"Please, don't." Jolie trembled, her arms folded across her chest as though that could ward him off. "Please. At least let me do it myself. I can show you I'm not wearing a wire."

That wasn't much better, but at least she wouldn't have their wretched hands on her.

"No can do," Ross said, immediately squashing that idea. "Who knows? You might have something hiding beneath all your clothes."

The way he said it made it very clear that Ross knew exactly what was under her clothes, and that was exactly what he planned to get his hands on.

"Don't fucking touch her!" I fought against the men holding me, almost breaking free before my arm was wrenched painfully behind my back.

Bishop chuckled, clearly amused. "You really are attached to her, aren't you? Maybe you should give her that ring she's after."

I flailed again, already planning Bishop's death. I'd slit his throat as soon as I finished ending Ross with a bullet between the eyes.

"You know what? I get it. I got a lady I like too. Cut it, Ross. Entertaining as this is, we should probably be respectful to Beasley's man if we want to do business with him again."

Ross hadn't gotten far with the sweater, thank God, and he stepped away immediately without arguing.

I didn't have time to examine whether or not I could trust this change of heart before he showed me that I couldn't.

"We do need to be sure she's not wearing a wire, though." Bishop almost sounded apologetic about it. "So I'm willing to let you conduct the search yourself."

"She's not wearing a goddamned wire," I said.

He ignored me. "Ross, bring the lady here so *Cade* can show us his woman's clean."

I didn't even blanch at the acknowledgment that he'd caught my name. I was too concerned with her, with what I was being asked to do to her.

Not asked. Told. There was no option for me to say no.

It was a game. That much was obvious. If it had been unacceptable for Jolie to undress herself, it should have been unacceptable for me to do it in her place. The whole thing was just some asshole power trip.

And it didn't matter. In this scenario, she and I held none of the power.

It was almost like being back in high school.

"I'm sorry," I said quietly, when Ross brought Jolie in front of me. "I'm going to have to."

"I know." Her throat sounded clogged with tears. "It's okay. It's my fault."

It *was* her fault, but I felt responsible too. For no good reason, except that I would have to do this to her. My insides were an aluminum can under the stamp of a foot. I was sure I looked misshapen on the outside, like everyone in the room could tell that I'd been sufficiently crushed. It was impossible that it wasn't obvious. I was pretty sure that was the entire point.

After a series of warnings, my arms were released. I cupped her cheek with my hand, a comforting gesture that likely held little weight considering our predicament.

"Nothing funny," Ross warned, pulling his gun back out. Now

there were two pointed at us, and the men who'd held me only feet away, ready to grab me again if necessary.

Taking a deep breath, I took the edge of her sweater in my hands and gently pulled it over her head. She reached her arms out to help me, and I wanted to kiss her for that—for being cooperative. For trusting me. For realizing there was no other choice.

Those weren't the only reasons I wanted to kiss her.

I could admit that here, under these circumstances, when that desire that had seemed so overwhelmingly frightening hours before suddenly felt like the least terrifying emotion I'd had all day. I threw her sweater to the floor and moved to the button on her jeans, promising myself that, if we made it through this, I would deal with this feeling head-on. I would even look forward to it.

I had the denim pushed down her thighs before I remembered her boots. I knelt down on the ground before her, wondering if later, when I could laugh about this, I'd find the humor in the fact that I'd been right when I'd worried she'd have me on my knees soon enough.

This hadn't been quite what I'd envisioned when the thought had crossed my mind, and then again, wasn't it exactly what I should have expected? Because this was where I'd always been drawn to. Because she'd always been my master and I a groveling servant at her feet who would lay down my life for hers if required.

I prayed it was only her clothes that would be asked for. I knew I'd give everything I owned if it wasn't.

After her boots, I removed her socks. Then her jeans came off, and she was standing in the chilly room wearing nothing but her bra and the damn cotton panties that had teased me all week.

I stood up, rubbing my hands along her goosebump-riddled arms.

"See. No wire." I didn't take my gaze off hers, conscious that she was half naked and that I was the only one still looking at her eyes.

"Need to see inside her bra," Bishop insisted. I knew he would, but I had to try.

"Need to see that pussy too," Ross said, his pants already tenting.

I bit the insides of my cheeks until I tasted blood.

"It's okay," she said again, trying to comfort me. But her eyes were spilling, and I knew that as strong as she was trying to be, she was the one who needed the comfort.

"Pretend it's just you and me." I spoke softly, but not too quietly, knowing it wasn't wise to appear like we were plotting something. I reached behind her and undid the clasp of her bra. "Just you and me, back at the hotel."

She nodded, her focus pinned right on me so I could count each and every tear that trickled down her cheek.

"We're alone," I continued as I pulled the straps down her arms, "and this moment is ours. We've waited so long for this. *I've* waited so long. And now we've reached the place where it's impossible to wait any longer."

Her bra was off, her breasts fully exposed to a room full of leering men.

They were there, but they weren't. We were in our own bubble, she and I, and as naked as she was, I was on the verge of baring more.

That seemed about right. That seemed exactly right.

"It feels like I'm underwater with you," I said as I tugged her panties past her hips, my fingers trembling as they brushed against her skin. "And there's a very good chance that I'm gonna drown. But sink or swim, baby. I'm holding on to you this time for dear life."

And now she was completely stripped.

And the way her face crumpled, the way her eyes remained only on mine—I was pretty sure she knew I was stripped too.

"Look at that. No wire," Ross said, amusement in his tone, a blunt reminder that her vulnerability was much more real than mine.

Instinctively, I moved to cover her as well as I could.

"Maybe we need to examine her a little more closely," someone else said.

Fortunately for him, before I could knock the man's eyes out, consequences be damned, Bishop had tired of the game. He went back to the desk, his back turned to me as he perched again on the edge. "Let her get dressed. Take your case, Cade, and get the fuck out of here. You've already wasted more of my night than I'd planned."

He was done with me, done with us, demonstrating with his quick readiness to move on that this whole charade had been nothing but a show of power. He hadn't even bothered to check me.

But I wasn't going to challenge him.

While Jolie pulled on her underwear, I retrieved her coat. She put her jeans on, then let me put her boots on her feet, not bothering with socks, while she pulled the sweater over her head. When she just had her coat to deal with, I crossed to grab the case.

"Beasley knows where to find me if he needs anything else." Bishop didn't look up as he delivered his parting words. "But also make sure he knows that any trouble that comes down from poking into this is his and his alone."

I didn't bother with a response. Grabbing the briefcase, I took Jolie's hand in the other and pulled her with me out of the room, down the stairs, and into the night, racing as though we could outrun any trouble that followed.

Wondering if she was as aware as I was that everything had changed.

TWENTY-FIVE

We didn't stop moving until we were getting into a cab.

I'd been shaken, and even now, sure that we'd left with our lives, I felt precariously held together. As much as I wanted to discover what was on the hard drive—if there was anything at all—I couldn't deal with Donovan until I'd had some time to unwind.

Knowing he'd be anxious, I sent him a quick text.

> Got the case. I'll meet up with you in the morning.

His reply came instantly.

> I can meet you at the hotel in thirty.

> Not tonight, D.

He'd know better not to push me, but I turned off my phone all the same.

"I didn't think it through," Jolie said when I'd pocketed my cell. "The taxi stopped at a light, and I saw you on the sidewalk, and I just...I just got out and followed you."

"We don't need to do this right now."

She went on as if I hadn't said anything. "I knew you didn't need my help. But I couldn't stand the thought of leaving you alone. Not again."

I closed my eyes, a blanket of exhaustion covering me. I didn't have strength in me to deal with these words. I didn't feel equipped to keep the flicker of hope from turning into a full-fledged flame. "I don't want to talk about it."

She didn't say anything after that, simply stared out the window, her expression unreadable, and it wasn't until we were halfway to our destination that it occurred to me that I'd been an asshole. *Too much* of an asshole. And if I'd learned anything from today, it was that I didn't actually want to be that with her.

"Hey, Jol? Are you okay?" My fingers were still threaded in hers, which I only just noticed, and now that I had, it was impossible not to be completely aware of it.

She turned her face from the window and blinked a few times, as though she were struggling to put me in focus. "Yeah. I think I am." She glanced down at our clasped hands, and when her eyes returned to the glass, I almost thought I caught a smile on her lips.

We stayed silent for the rest of the ride, our hands linked, until we got to the hotel, and I had to free myself to manage my wallet. Outside of the cab, I reached for her again, automatically. Like I'd done it a hundred times before.

She gave me her hand, but while I continued walking toward the hotel doors, she stopped, pulling me back toward her.

"Cade." Her expression was earnest, and I sensed an urgency in her, as though she feared that whatever she had to say couldn't be said once we passed from the cold night to the warmth of the lobby.

Or maybe she feared this truce we'd come to wouldn't last past the threshold of the doors.

To be honest, I feared that too.

But not as much as I feared what she was about to say. "Don't," I warned.

She held me tighter, grabbing my wrist with her other hand, and though I could easily pull free, I felt caught. Like a water pipe tangled in tree roots. A hard thing, hollow on the inside, unable to escape from this living intrusion.

Stay hard, I willed myself. *Stay hollow.*

"I didn't want—"

"Don't!" It was harsher this time. A threat.

"I didn't want you to leave me," she said, bulldozing through the words before I could cut her off again.

I stared at her, trying very hard to be that hard, hollow thing, knowing that she wasn't talking about tonight. Knowing these words could change everything if I let them. *Everything.*

And fuck if that didn't make me want to hit something.

Because no. She couldn't do this. It wasn't fair. She couldn't disappear for seventeen years and then show up all vulnerable and soft and unchanged and then try to change the narrative that she herself had written. A narrative that had made me what I was now. Cold and rigid and empty.

She had no right.

I yanked my hand away from her, knowing a physical escape wouldn't do any good. It didn't even matter that she followed as I stormed through the hotel doors, or that she would be in the suite with me upstairs. I could put a thousand miles between us, and I still wouldn't have outrun this.

Didn't mean I wasn't going to try.

I walked through the lobby with long strides that her shorter legs couldn't match. When she caught up with me waiting for the elevator, I ignored her, as though she were some random woman with no ties to me other than the fact that she was in my vicinity.

She gave me my space, quietly occupying the opposite side of the car, allowing me to ignore her existence, though it was possible she was reciprocating. And if she was, fine. I didn't care. I watched the numbers for each floor light as we went up, up, up, and focused on forcing every bit of consciousness into that one action so that there weren't any brain cells left for caring. Or analyzing or recalibrating. Or wondering what would happen if I stopped running. Stopped trying to escape. Stopped searching for closure.

I didn't wait for her to exit first when we reached our floor, ignoring the male rules of etiquette and stomping to our suite so far ahead of her that the door had almost closed behind me when she caught it and pushed in.

And when she did, as soon as I heard the movement of air as the door swept open, I dropped the case and turned, crossing toward her, so that by the time it did click closed, I had already taken her in my arms.

"You're going to wreck me all over again," I said before crashing my lips against hers, which wasn't really true because she'd already wrecked me all over again, and now I was pretty sure she was doing the opposite—putting me together. Finding jagged pieces of me that had seemed to have no place for so long, and matching them with uneven pieces of her. Fitting us perfectly together with her presence. And her patience. And her lips.

God, her lips.

Kissing her was both familiar and new. A dance I'd forgotten. I anticipated the tilt of her head, the flick of her tongue. The soft sigh in the back of her throat as I became more aggressive.

If she'd been surprised by my attack, she only showed eagerness and urgency that matched my own. She tasted like want and mint. Like that candy that I loved years ago that they didn't make anymore. She tasted like refuge and peace, and kissing her was like going home.

Which was surreal considering that I'd never thought I'd go home again.

I wasn't sure who started pushing at clothing first, but both our coats fell to the floor quickly. Her hands slipped under my sweater, her palms hot against my bare chest as she kissed along my neck.

I returned the favor, savoring the salty taste of her skin and marveling at her rapid pulse underneath my tongue. It beat in tandem with the bass drum at the center of my torso, and part of me wanted to bite into her flesh and rip at her artery as if that would end this connection that existed between us. That twisted, perverted bond that should never have been born.

But that was only a very small part of me. The bigger part wanted to endure the fate of our bond, would enjoy it even if it destroyed me.

With one arm wrapped tightly around her waist, I slid the other down over her ass and squeezed the plump curve. She was rounder here than she'd been when we were young, and I loved it. I wanted to learn this change. Wanted to memorize the new landscape of her body. I squeezed again, harder. Then, angry at the barrier of her jeans, I swatted her with my palm.

Impatiently, I undid her pants, only bothering to push them down to her knees. I needed her ass, needed her flesh in my hands, needed it so urgently that I didn't even try to take off her panties. I just pushed through the leg holes until I had a cheek in each hand and gripped tightly, peering over her shoulder at the erotic sight.

Damn, she felt good. Supple and pliable and, Jesus, I could become obsessed with this ass. I could make a full-time job of fondling and massaging and licking and fucking this gorgeous round ass.

This time when I spanked her, I was angry at myself. For wanting her so much. For letting her exceed my expectations. For being so goddamned fascinated with my reddened palm print on her ass. I slapped her again, sharply. And again.

She squealed at each strike, a sound that called directly to my already stiff cock, making him stand up as though Jolie was his drill sergeant, calling him to attention. He was ready to take her. He wanted nothing more than to bury into her pussy, reclaim her. Get lost there. Lose control.

But there was a risk to feeling so wild. Especially with her.

In an attempt to find my balance, I pushed her against the wall, startling her lips from my skin. I placed my hands at either side of her neck, fingers spread, and lifted her chin with my thumbs, then looked directly into her hooded eyes.

The thing was, me and Jolie—we were more complicated than a quick fuck or even a long fuck. I'd been a hypocrite calling her out for being someone who turned sex into something more. Anything that happened between us *had* to be more than just physical, not only because that was what I wanted, but because there wasn't any other way with her. With us. We'd always been more than what we should have been. It had been our curse.

It had been our fortune too.

I needed to know if she understood what this would be before it got too far to redefine. My mouth hovered inches above hers, our lips parted, and tried to stare into her. Was there any of what we used to be still inside her? Or was all of this one-sided? Was I carrying this fucked up torch on my own?

I wanted answers to questions I couldn't bring myself to ask, hoping I wouldn't have to. Hoping she'd just know, and I'd know in return.

But while I was searching her eyes, she brought her hand to the steel pole in my jeans and rubbed up and down the length with a pressure that made me insane, and after that, I couldn't concentrate on worrying about what this was or what this wasn't. My thoughts descended into a primal state, and all hopes of staying tame disappeared.

In a flash, her sweater was gone. Unlike when I'd removed it earlier, this time I gave all my focus to what was underneath, desperately kissing along the skin above her bra while my hands reached behind to undo the clasp. When the garment fell off her shoulders, I caught her breasts with my palms and plumped them a little harder than I should, unable to restrain myself.

She leaned into my touch and moaned, her fingers wrapping into my sweater and clinging for stability, and all I could think was *it's about fucking time*. It was her turn to be off-balance. Her turn to be reeling.

And bonus that she seemed to like the rough because I didn't think there was much chance I could be any other way. There was too much pent up inside of me. Too many years of longing. Too much resentment. Too much hate that might have been love or love that might have been hate, and I needed her to feel all of it, whether she understood it or not.

I pinched at a nipple, twisting it until she gasped, then tortured it with soft strokes of my tongue, then moved to her other breast and took that peak by my teeth, clamping down until she jerked back with a cry.

Even as she pulled away, she begged for more.

I'd imagined her pleading a million times, usually with my cock in my fist and my eyes shut tight. I hadn't been able to rely on memory for this. We'd been inexperienced lovers when we'd first been together, our sex talk sweet and awkward, matching the actual sex. I'd been long gone by the time my desires had turned dirtier, and when I'd placed her in my fantasies, she'd adjusted to fit my wants.

But my imaginings had never been half as tantalizing as the real thing—her eyes tearing, her lips swollen and quivering, her cheeks flushed as she cried, "Please, Cade. Please. Please, fuck me. Please, please, please."

As though we'd orchestrated it, while she pulled down her panties to join her jeans at her knees, I took the three steps to the minibar and grabbed what we needed, grateful for the modern-day hotel custom of stocking condoms.

Back in front of her, I ripped open the foil square while she unfastened my pants. She brought out my cock, her hands small and dainty compared to the red, veined stick she held. I handed her the condom and half watched her roll it on, half took in her half-naked state.

Earlier, in a room full of men who only wanted to objectify her, I'd wanted to be the one man to respect her. I'd been careful to only look at her eyes. Now I soaked up every inch of her like she was a Playboy centerfold, letting every lewd impulse have free rein of my mind. Her full, fuckable tits would feel spectacular in my hands. I could feast on her trim pussy. I could lick up the moisture glistening on her lips or gather it on my fingers to lube up her ass. I could use her and fuck her and destroy her in so many ways that she deserved. In so many ways that she didn't.

But then my gaze returned to her face, to the eyes that windowed into the soul of a woman that I would never stop crawling toward. She had a noose around my neck, leading me like a dog, and faithful pet that I was, I would always come back seeking her love, whether she was done with me or not.

Did she know? Did she have any idea at all?

She rose up on her tiptoes to brush her lips to mine. If she kissed me now, there would be no hiding. No more pretense. No way to hold back.

Not ready for that level of vulnerability, I refused her kiss and spun her around so she faced the wall. So she didn't face me. Reaching between her legs, I made sure she was as wet and ready as she'd looked, then when she pushed her ass back and begged again, this time for my cock, I notched my crown at the mouth of her pussy and drove in.

Being inside her, after all this time, was indescribable. Neither of us were the same. Our bodies had changed. Our behavior had changed.

And still there was an easiness to our fit. A rhythm that didn't have to be learned. Filthy as it was—her cheek pressed against the wall as I pounded into her, the slapping of our thighs, the gasping cries tumbling from her lips, the butterfly pulses of her pussy around my cock—it was far from the innocent lovemaking of our youth. I'd never fucked her like this. We'd never *fucked* at all.

And still, she was Jolie. She was *my* Jolie, and every part of my body acknowledged the difference between her and every other woman I'd been with. None compared to her. None were anything like this.

I tried to forget that and lose myself in *just another pussy*, an impossible task when she craned her head around in an attempt to recapture my lips. She managed a brief kiss that had my legs feeling like they might give out. That had my chest feeling like it might explode.

Capturing her hands, I turned her again to face the wall. I kept her like that, my fingers threaded through hers, holding her in place so I could fuck her with abandon while she alternated between pleading not to stop and begging for more.

Then her litany changed. "Touch me, Cade. Please, I need you to touch me." It wasn't only the words that were different in these pleas, but the texture of their sound. They were thin and stretched, like it had taken a lot to ask. Like she'd wanted to be selfless. Like she'd thought there was a reward in keeping her needs to herself, but finally, she couldn't stand it anymore and gave in to her craving.

There was a version of me that wanted to deny her pleasure. Not in a kinky, fun way, but in a way that made her feel insignificant and used.

But I was as selfish as she was, and I wanted to hear her come, wanted to feel her pussy squeeze me tight, wanted to make sure she remembered this fuck and that she got wet whenever she did.

So I moved one hand to pinch her tit and the other to rub between her legs.

It didn't take much after that. A minute or two of watching her cues, learning what got her going, then teasing her with that pressure while I drove into her over and over and over, until the painting began to thump against the wall, until I was sure the neighboring suite would call management to complain. Then, on a "Yes, Cade, fuck yes," her entire body stuttered, and her pussy clamped down on my cock.

The pressure and the flood of wet heat sent me tumbling after her, surprising me with the sudden intensity. I came long and hard, as though I'd stored it up for her. As though it had been years instead of days since I'd last released. As though there was no part of me that I wouldn't give my all of, and my cock knew that score, even if my head didn't.

Seemed about right.

Breathless, I pulled out of her. Stepped back until I was leaning against the counter by the bar. My pants hung at my hips, my cock sticking out, as hard and thick as before I'd entered her. I removed the condom, tying it off and throwing it in the trash nearby, and then I dared to look at Jolie.

She'd turned around, but her pants were still around her knees, her breasts still exposed, her face and chest flushed. Her face glistening with sweat.

She was fucking beautiful.

I wanted her all over again.

"Should we talk about this?" she asked, and I could tell from her inflection that she was leaving it up to me—what came next, what was said, what wasn't.

And I thought of all the things I'd wanted to tell her over the years, the things I needed her to know. The feelings that I was sure could only be sorted with her help.

And I thought about the way I hadn't been able to breathe when she'd shown up at that meeting, how it physically hurt to think what might happen to her. And I thought about the case. The secrets it held inside. The task I'd promised to help her do.

I thought about what day it was. Thought about the flight she'd board tomorrow, how she'd get on a plane. How soon I would be getting on a plane too, but my flight path would take me to the other side of the world.

I glanced at the bar next to me, saw there were three more condoms in the pack. "I'd rather do that again." I nodded toward her, so she'd have no doubt what "that" meant.

"Just once?"

I held up the condoms. "Or more."

"This time in a bed?"

I nodded. "This time without any clothes."

"Yeah, I can get behind that."

So I took her hand, led her to my bed, and pretended that the memories from a night of fucking could possibly fill the cavity she'd leave tomorrow when she flew away.

TWENTY-SIX

I squatted next to the bed and studied her sleeping features. Her face was soft, her lips curled into an almost smile. The small lines that indicated her age when she was awake were missing, and she looked more like the girl I'd fallen in love with than ever.

Spending an entire night with her in my bed had been surreal. I usually didn't let my conquests stay that long, and if they did, it was usually accidental—I'd been too drunk to push them out or the woman had already fallen asleep. I couldn't remember when I'd woken up to a woman that I'd invited to stay, if ever.

I hadn't just invited Jolie to stay—I hadn't let her out of my arms.

And there was the fact that she wasn't just any woman. She was *the* woman. Even with the proof of her in front of me, her naked chest rising and falling with the rhythmic breaths of sleep, it felt very much like a dream. The best dream.

I didn't want to wake up.

She stirred, a sigh passed her lips, and while I very much wanted to leave her to whatever was happening in her head, there was a clock ticking.

I swept a strand of her blonde hair off her face, noting her natural light brown coming in at the roots. "Hey, Jol."

Her eyelids fluttered, but she didn't open them.

I brushed my knuckles across her cheek, using the excuse of waking her gently as a chance to touch her. This did the trick.

"Hi," she yawned. The room was mostly dark, a lone beam of sun streaming through a crack in the blackout curtains the only indication that morning had occurred. She frowned all the same when she realized I wasn't in the bed with her. "You're dressed."

"Early riser. Bad habit."

She chuckled, and my cock twitched.

I told him to calm the fuck down. He'd gotten to run the better part of the night. In the daylight, there were other priorities. Much as I'd rather ignore them, they didn't go away. "What time is your flight?"

Her frown returned, and she pulled the sheet up to cover her breasts, as though she just now realized that what we were to each other this morning was likely not what we were to each other last night.

"Um. Five fifteen." I hoped her sullen tone meant she was as unhappy about the countdown as I was.

But we had time. Not a lot, but some. "You should leave here no later than two. We need to get the case opened before that. Sooner the better." Whatever the contents showed, we'd have to make a plan of where we went from here.

Where we went regarding her father, anyway.

I wasn't holding any hopes that there would be a conversation about the future of anything else. "Donovan should be in the office in half an hour. Do you want to go with me, or do you want to keep sleeping?"

"I want to come."

I stayed crouched at her side. Glad as I was that she'd be with me, I felt guilty for the faint circles under her eyes. "You didn't get much sleep. I'm sorry I kept you up."

"I'm not." Her cheeks pinkened, bold as she was.

I figured I'd only gotten about three hours of sleep myself, and I wasn't sorry either. Not one bit. If she hadn't looked so thoroughly exhausted the last time I'd made her come, I would have kept her up longer.

"You're not sorry either, are you?" It was more of a statement than a question, but I sensed her need to be sure.

I answered by leaning forward and pressing my mouth to hers.

What was meant to be a light, affirming kiss quickly turned into my hand sliding under the sheet in search of the warmth between her legs, and it was only the moan that escaped against my lips that brought me to my senses.

I pulled my hand away and broke off abruptly. "We'll lose the whole day if we get started."

Her mischievous smile said that wouldn't be the worst thing in the world.

"Uh-uh." I pushed up to my feet, hoping to eliminate temptation with distance. Also, to give my cock a little breathing room.

She widened her grin, her gaze planted squarely on the evidence of my arousal. "Not that I'm complaining, but I'd say you've got the stamina of a teenager if I knew for a fact that you weren't like this as a teen."

I tensed automatically, the way I always seemed to when we started talking about before. Despite what had happened between us last night, our past was still a minefield that had to be navigated carefully. It was easier to leave it alone altogether.

But something had changed between us. Because this time I didn't back away. "Given the chance back then, I would have fucked us both raw. I didn't have the opportunity."

"No, we didn't." Her blush was back, which didn't help the state of my cock. "I need a shower. Want to join me?"

We probably had time for whatever her offer would likely turn into. Considering we were out of condoms, a shower made sense. Pulling out would be easy cleanup.

God, I was tempted.

But losing time wasn't the only thing at risk. The transition to today's relationship status would only be harder if we tried to prolong last night's status. And I was already struggling with trying to figure out what was between us—what was new, what was old, what didn't matter, what did. I still carried very real wounds where she was concerned, and while the sex had been an incredible and much-needed distraction from the pain, it didn't mean those injuries were healed.

Maybe some of them were.

Maybe most of them were.

They certainly didn't feel as present today. Figured, didn't it? That just as I'd abandoned my need for closure, my wounds might finally be closed. Maybe that was exactly how closure worked.

I needed to work that out, and getting filthy in the shower was only going to cloud that analysis.

"You're thinking about it too hard," she said, climbing out of the bed with no concern for her nudity. "I'm going to jump in, and if you join me, you join me. If not, I'm not going to take it personally."

As always, she was less fucked up about us than I was. For once, I didn't resent her for it.

Progress.

But I forced myself to let her shower alone all the same.

BY THE TIME we arrived at Reach an hour later, we'd fully transitioned to our new status, whatever that was. I was able to look at her without wanting to bend her over every available piece of furniture, though maybe that was because I really wasn't looking at her very much. It was easier this way, with distance between us.

The hard part was not being bitter about it, but I was trying my best not to be an asshole.

Jolie, as always, seemed to be letting me have my space, which I appreciated. Though I wouldn't have minded if she'd stood a little closer in the elevator or reached for my hand when we walked down the hall to Donovan's office, especially when we got to Simone's desk. Stupid as it was, I would have preferred to face her under the guise of being off-limits, for no other reason than that I liked the idea of being off-limits because I belonged to Jolie.

I obviously still had work to do on the whole letting go thing.

"He hasn't arrived yet, but he'll be in shortly," Simone said, completely professional. As though she hadn't had her hands down my pants days before.

That was odd since it was a quarter to nine. Donovan was generally in before eight, and I'd messaged him that we'd be here.

Simone came around her desk and headed to his office, a key in hand. "He said you could wait in here. Can I get you anything? Coffee? Latte? Muffins?"

"We're good." I shooed her off as soon as she had the door unlocked. When it was closed behind us, I set the briefcase on Donovan's desk and apologized to Jolie. "I suppose I should have let you answer before sending Simone away."

"I'm happier with her gone. Thanks."

I'd seen her jealous before, years ago. When I'd made a spectacle of myself with another girl in an attempt to try to distract myself from the very forbidden Julianna Stark. She'd had the same upward tilt of her chin, the same triumphant gleam in her eye when I'd ended that mockery of a relationship as she did now.

Fuck if it didn't make me want to kiss the hell out of her.

I settled for taking her coat and then getting her a bottle of sparkling water from the mini fridge. Only when I sat down in the chair next to her and a few silent minutes had passed did I notice the cloud of things we needed to say hanging in the air between us.

Coward that I was, I ignored it.

But Jolie had always been braver. "Since we might not get the chance later...something should probably be said."

Her awkward approach encouraged me to grow some balls. If she could be hesitant and still take on the minefield, then so could I.

"Look, um." I leaned forward, bracing my elbows on my thighs, steepling my tattooed hands together. "I've been unreasonable. Holding you responsible for the past. We were kids. Holding a grudge for something that occurred when we were teens..." I cleared my throat. "I apologize for being immature."

I hadn't been facing her while I talked—because, chickenshit—but now I turned my head to her. The corners of her mouth weren't exactly turned down, but her forehead was wrinkled, as though she found what I'd said troubling, or at the very least, puzzling. "Is that what that was? Immaturity?"

"On my part, yes. What else would it be?"

"I was hoping it was..." With a shake of her head, she let out an embarrassed sort of laugh. "I guess I was hoping it meant you still had some sort of feelings for me. Ridiculous after all these years. After what I did. I'm the immature one it seems."

Just like that, everything stopped. My heart. The clock. The air in my lungs.

If she'd been hoping I had some sort of feelings for her, did that mean that she had some sort of feelings for me?

I was half a second away from pouring out every emotion I still very much felt for her when Donovan rushed through the door.

"You have the case?" He saw it on his desk before I had a chance to answer. "I'm a bit late coming in. Sabrina and I are leaving early today for Washington, and I needed to get some things taken care of on the way in so that our weekend would be possible."

"Going home?" I asked, knowing that Washington, Connecticut was where he grew up and seemed the more likely location for a getaway than Washington state, especially in the middle of December.

Though taking the girlfriend to meet the parents meant the guy was in deeper than I'd realized.

"Don't say it," he said, correctly guessing that I'd been about to mock him. He threw his coat on the back of his chair and reached for the case, but before he opened it he studied us, his eyes darting from me to Jolie to me again. "You're in no position to talk."

I felt my face heating although, seriously, there was no way he could know shit. Not just from glancing at us.

Moving on, he opened the briefcase and retrieved the hard drive.

After a quick inspection—which, what? Did he think it might be a bomb?—he plugged it into his computer and sat down at his desk.

"These guys you had me hook up with..." I said, remembering I hadn't talked to him at all about the insanity of the meeting. "Don't be surprised if that hard drive is blank."

"It's not going to be blank." He was more sure than he should be, in my opinion.

While he booted his computer, Jolie turned to me. "Did you tell him—?"

"That's a more in-depth conversation than I want to have at the moment." Mostly I was protecting her. I was sure he'd lay into Jolie if he knew she'd been there.

But later, I'd be sure to tell them these dudes were scary.

Of course Donovan missed nothing. He stopped typing. "What happened?"

I waved him off. "Not now. Let's just see if it was worth it."

He frowned, his expression skeptical. Then his curiosity about the contents of the drive seemed to overtake his curiosity about the meeting, and he turned his attention to the screen.

My own curiosity got me out of my chair and circling his desk to peer behind him. He located the hard drive on the search panel, clicked it, then paused before entering the password. "Do you mind?"

I did mind. Very much. After what we'd been through to get the stupid thing.

But that was Donovan, with his secrets and his need for control. I wandered back to the other side of the desk where Jolie was now standing too.

"Maybe it's porn," she said, not bothering to lower her voice. "Kinky-ass porn."

"Like with horses, you think?"

"Furries. Guaranteed."

Donovan shot us a look, but I could tell he wasn't entirely unamused. "The drive's not empty," he said. "And the folder with the info I'd asked for is on it."

He clicked his mouse, and I came around again to look over his shoulder, propping my arm on the desk as I leaned in. A second later, I felt Jolie pressing against my back, and I lifted my arm so she could come in front of me. When I lowered my arm again, my hand landed on her back.

Purposely.

As always, touching her was distracting, but what was on the screen was compelling enough to grab my attention. A list of Word docs showed up in the directory, each with strange names.

F-17-V-09
F-17-V-11
M-16-U-11
F-15-V-07
F-16-U-04

The list went on and on. Twenty-five of them? Thirty, maybe.

The codes meant nothing to me, yet I had a bad feeling all the same.

"Click on one," Jolie said.

Instead, Donovan changed the view. A preview opened up, and now there was an image of a teenage girl I'd never seen and a bunch of stats—height, weight, hair color, birthdate, dollar amounts.

He scrolled down to the next doc which had similar info. And the next, this time a teenage boy.

"The M and F are their gender. And the first number is their age." Jolie was figuring out the code of the document titles.

Donovan scrolled down again.

"I recognize her." Her eyes scanned the info. "She disappeared soon after I graduated. That last number is the year she went missing."

Donovan scrolled to the next. And the next. And the next. All held similar images, similar stats, similar dollar amounts.

"There's Bernard Arnold," I said when we got to the boy who'd gone missing the year I'd been there. When Jolie identified more of the pictures as students that had disappeared from Stark Academy, it was clear. "These are missing person reports."

All that identifying info, the kind that had once been seen on the back of milk cartons, it couldn't be anything else. And the dollar amounts had to be rewards offered for the teens' return.

Very high dollar amounts. Impressively high.

"Didn't you already recognize the pattern of runaways from researching public information? Why pay all that money for missing person reports?" Jolie's question was fair, though I suspected we weren't looking at just any reports. These were standardized. Organized. Like someone had broken into the FBI.

Donovan scrolled down again. "That's not what we're looking at."

Jolie looked back at me, her brow raised. I shrugged. When Donovan scrolled down again without saying more, I went ahead and asked. "Then what are we looking at?"

"Receipts."

The hair stood up on the back of my neck. "What do you mean receipts?"

"I mean exactly that," he said impatiently. "These are receipts. Bills of sale. Every one of them. These missing teens? They've been sold."

TWENTY-SEVEN

"Sold? Are you talking sex slavery?" Jolie sounded dubious, as though she thought Donovan was trying to sell us a conspiracy theory, and she was not buying.

If he was offended by being doubted, he didn't say. "Primarily, yes. Drug mules too. Whatever suits their owner's fancy."

She blinked. "You can't *own* a person."

"Unfortunately, some people believe you can," Donovan said.

"And you think my father is one of those people?"

Donovan and I exchanged a glance. Stark certainly had the opportunity. Even if he wasn't already my enemy number one, he would be the first person I'd look at given the evidence.

Our lack of response said everything, and guessing from her reaction, it wasn't what Jolie wanted to hear. "How do you know that's what this is? Who told you that? This could be what Cade said it was. This could be someone making a scandal out of nothing."

The way we planned to make a scandal out of nothing?

I didn't say it, though, because Jolie was obviously having a hard time processing the depth of the crimes we were talking about.

Donovan excelled at remaining objective. "It's possible. I haven't worked with Bishop before, but I trust those who recommended him."

"Is this Bishop guy part of this?" I asked. "People don't have these records without being involved."

"He has a membership to a pleasure island in the Caribbean where these kinds of deals are done on the regular. My understanding is that Bishop made a deal of his own to get these records—apparently there is a member of the ring that he's been blackmailing with this."

It dawned on me that the scope of our plans had changed. "This doesn't just involve Stark anymore."

"No. It doesn't."

"You're serious about this." Jolie looked from me to Donovan, understanding sinking in. "You're really saying these teens didn't run away. That they were abducted. That they were sold."

Again, silence was as good of an answer as anything else.

She blinked a few more times, her eyes darting as she absorbed the situation. Then she sank down in a chair and brought her hand up to her mouth. "Oh my God. The V stands for virgin."

The tingly sensation at the top of my spine said she was right. "The U then?"

Donovan rubbed his chin. "Undetermined?"

Jolie's color had left her face. "I'm going to throw up."

In a flash, Donovan grabbed the trash can from under his desk and handed it to me. I started to pass it over, but she shook her head. "Not really. I don't think."

I moved behind her and rubbed my hand over the muscles at her neck.

She tilted her head toward me. "Do you really think he could do this?"

Did I think Headmaster Stark was so vile that he'd traffic teens out of his school? Given my feelings toward the man, it deserved a moment to consider. It would be easy to say yes because I hated him. Because I wanted to believe the worst of him. Because I wanted to bring him down.

But just because he beat kids on the regular didn't mean he'd try to sell them into slavery.

Then again, Stark's crimes against me had gone further than simply losing his temper. I had no doubt that his morals, if he had any at all, were flexible enough to lower himself to this level.

"You do, don't you?" she guessed when I hesitated.

I didn't want to bullshit her. But I cared about being sensitive. "I think someone did this. And if your father is in any way involved, he needs to be stopped. He needs to pay for it."

"And if you did want to destroy him, this stuff is pretty damning," Donovan piped in.

"If he's not responsible though..." I could sense she was working out her own morals as she spoke. "Can I really pin *this* on him? Of course, five days ago I was ready to kill him myself. Why does that seem easier to reconcile?"

"Because that was just between you and him. Now there are other victims who can't fight him themselves. It's a lot of responsibility."

My hand dropped as she swiveled in her chair to face me. "Yes. That's exactly it."

Donovan let a beat pass, giving us time to absorb. "Obviously, this isn't information we can just ignore. Something has to be done with it. At this point, you're welcome to walk away. I can submit this to someone who will make sure a full investigation is opened up. We have to get someone rescuing these kids."

"They aren't kids anymore." My stomach churned thinking of how long these people had been missing. How many years of torture they'd endured. What that would do to a person. Were they even savable anymore?

"The point is that it needs to be stopped." I could tell from Donovan's tone that there was something he hadn't yet said. Something we hadn't yet thought of.

I tried to see what he was seeing. "So we can walk away, you take this to authorities, the whole ring comes down including Stark, and we don't have to have our hands in it at all?"

"Not exactly." He backpedaled. "I mean, I hope that's what happens. But this network has been running for a long time now. It's plainly very organized. Very well sheltered. It's possible authorities already know about it—I'd be more surprised if they didn't. Knowing about it doesn't mean it's easy to take down. These receipts don't implicate anyone. There's another folder in here with pictures of the same kids at 'time of purchase,' which should help prove this isn't just a collection of missing person stats. But even if this somehow leads to arrests, Stark has likely done quite a lot to distance himself from this ring. There's nothing assuring that he will go down with the ship."

"Are you saying this could all be for nothing? This horrible thing that's been happening under our noses for decades keeps happening, my father keeps living his perfect life, and I have to figure out how to live my life knowing the man who made me is a fucked-up, repulsive piece of shit?"

"That's not what he's saying," I assured her, not actually sure of that fact.

"I'm saying that's a possibility." Donovan was clearly less interested in comforting Jolie than I was. "Another possibility is that it gets taken down, but your father remains unscathed. Another possibility is that we make sure he doesn't."

Finally, I was catching up to my partner. "All right. Then we make sure this evidence is tied to Stark. How do we do that?"

He cleared his throat, and I could tell that the pause wasn't to give him time to think of the answer but meant to slow his brain down so he could bring us up to speed. "Financial records would be helpful. His large bank deposits don't line up with these receipts, either in amount or timing, but over a decade, the totals come close enough to be suspicious, particularly when we're adding in expenses he might have paid in cash such as purchase of a boat or a vacation home. He's been careful on purpose. He's been smart.

"If he was found with copies of these folders—the bills of sale along with the photos sent back from those who made the purchase—that would be quite incriminating. As I said, he might already have this. Do you know where he'd keep information like this?"

"His safe at the cabin." She looked toward me. "Did you see anything when you got into it?"

Christ, that was seventeen years ago.

She had the same thought. "It might have been actual papers. Or a floppy disc."

"I don't remember what else was in there," I said honestly. "All I was interested in was the cash."

It would have to be planted there then. To be sure.

"So you know the combo?" Donovan asked, picking up on the fact I'd opened the cabin safe before.

"It's not the same safe," Jolie said before I could reply. "He replaced it after the money was gone. The new safe has the same combo—because that's how original he is—but now it requires a key to get in as well. At least, that was what he had a decade ago. It's probably still the same. He's particular and doesn't like things to change."

Donovan seemed to be taking notes in his head. "Let's assume then that the combination is the same. Do you know where the key is kept?"

"There are two keys. He keeps one on his key ring. The other is locked in a drawer in his home office." She rubbed her eyes, the lack of sleep likely catching up with her.

"The cabin's in Sherman, right?" Donovan had done his research. "And the home office in Wallingford. What's that—an hour away?"

"An hour and a half." I remembered the drive well.

"It's going to be a task for a PI to get into the house where your father lives and then get into the cabin safe. Not impossible, but there are easier ways to do this." He was leading us to suggest it ourselves, so that he wouldn't have to.

And I didn't want Jolie to be the one either. "I should do it."

"It will be just as hard for you to break in as a PI," she said.

The cabin wouldn't be hard. It was the house that would be tricky, and we both knew it. "I won't break in."

Her head snapped toward me. "You're planning on just going up and knocking? You don't even know if they'll let you in."

"They'll let me in." Like I'd been doing all morning, I pretended I was more sure of that than I was.

She turned away, her finger running back and forth over her lip while she deliberated with herself. "It should be me."

"I don't want it to be you."

She shifted again to face me. "This whole thing started with me. This is my responsibility."

"Bringing Donovan in was my idea. You had no idea it would lead to this."

"Neither did you."

I opened my mouth to offer another protest, but she beat me to speaking. "They'll let *me* in."

They would. I knew it in my gut. Whatever falling out she'd had with her father, he'd always allow her to return. There'd be a price, but he'd let her pay it.

She knew that as well as I did.

And I knew that she'd made up her mind. That she'd decided this. That there would be no chance of talking her out of it.

"I'll go with you," I said, and it was settled. I was as decided as she was.

She didn't argue. "I need to cancel my flight and get a sub. Let me make a couple of calls." She plucked her cell phone out of her purse and walked out of the office.

By the time the door shut behind her, Donovan was handing me a flash drive. "I put the relevant files on here. It has an amnesiac installed on it so there will be no log of where the data came from."

I didn't know if I was more impressed that he'd managed the transfer so quickly or that he just happened to have an untraceable USB drive hanging around his office.

I took it from him without comment. He didn't need a bigger head than he already had.

"You're not driving with me to Connecticut," he said, reminding me he was also heading to the state for the weekend.

"Didn't ask." Washington and Wallingford weren't even on the same route. "We'll take the train. We can rent a car when we get there."

He nodded his approval. "You can borrow one of mine if you'd like. I'm taking the Tesla."

"Thanks for the offer, but I think we'd be better off if we were a little less conspicuous." And if our next stop was the cabin, I doubted his luxury vehicles could handle the mountain snow.

"I'm sure you're right." He looked thoughtful. "Is this going to be dangerous?"

We were adults now. Before today, I'd have said that Stark couldn't hold the same physical power over us that he once had.

Now that I knew how deep he was involved with the crime world, I felt less certain. "I'll take your gun."

Of course even with a gun, there was a mental risk to returning home. For both of us.

Donovan stood and picked up the coat he'd thrown over his chair when he arrived and took it to the closet to hang up. While he was there, he retrieved ours.

"I don't need to tell you to be careful," he said, handing them to me. A not-so-subtle cue that it was time to leave. "But I will tell you, while you're gone, I have something you should think about."

I took the coats and picked up Jolie's purse from the floor. "What's that?"

"Where you're going to put that new tattoo."

I didn't change gears as fast as he did, so it took me a second to understand what he was implicating. "How could you possibly know that—?" I cut myself off too late. I'd already confessed. "You know what? Fuck you." But also, I appreciated his attempt to lighten the mood. The morning had been heavy, to say the least.

"Yeah, yeah, yeah." He slapped me on the back as he ushered me out his door. "It's going to be a terribly embarrassing tattoo, Cade. Even so, you're going to think it was worth it."

As much as I hated it when Donovan was right, I had a feeling he wasn't wrong.

TWENTY-EIGHT

It wasn't until we were waiting in line at Avis in Grand Central that I had a chance to really think about what we were doing, what we were about to do. We were two hours away from where everything between us had started, and even with the drive ahead of us, I worried we didn't have enough time to form a plan. Or that we'd forgotten something. I wondered if we should stop and think.

But I also knew that given the chance to deliberate, I might not be able to force myself to go through with it. Acting quickly helped give me momentum. Jolie gave me the motivation. As much as I wished she hadn't decided to walk into hell with me, I recognized that I needed her at my side.

"You were able to change your flight?" I asked when I needed to get out of my head.

"Yeah. I had to pay a fee to cancel it. They gave me a credit that I can use later for my trip back home."

"Did you have enough to pay that? I can—"

"Stop." She nudged me with her shoulder as she said it, stepping closer to do so and staying closer afterward. "You've given me way too much this week, which I appreciate, but no. I'm good. I got paid today. Which means I'm paying for the rental car."

I started to protest because that was ridiculous, but she didn't let me. "Please? It will make me feel like I'm contributing."

It took a beat for me to wrestle through the urge to put my foot down, and another beat to consider what it meant that I needed to care for her so badly. And one more to decide it would be in my best interest to refuse that desire. "Just the car rental. Everything else is on me."

Then it was our turn to step up to the rental desk. The agent rattled off a memorized spiel about our options, not trying very hard to upsell us when we decided on the standard SUV rather than the premium. After fully grilling him, I felt confident the tires would make it up to the cabin, even if it snowed, and then it was time for Jolie to hand over her credit card and license.

Without hesitation, she opened her purse and pulled out her wallet. It was only after she'd opened it up that she paused. "Uh, Cade. I saw a vending machine in the hall outside. Would you mind grabbing me a water?"

"Here's one, complimentary." The agent pulled a warm bottle out from under his desk.

Her smile was uneasy. "It's okay. I'd prefer cold, if you don't mind."

"I'll take the warm one," I said, picking it up off the counter. "And I'll get you one that's cold. Watch my bag."

The agent stopped me. "Your license, sir! If you want to be listed as a driver, I'll need to see a valid license."

"He can probably enter in your info while you're getting my water," Jolie said as I pulled out my wallet and dropped my ID on the counter.

"I can," the man confirmed.

I glanced suspiciously at the agent, fighting off an unreasonable flash of jealousy. If the guy hadn't been as old as her father, I might have thought she was trying to get rid of me. "Must really be thirsty."

"Parched."

I left her and found the vending machine quickly, returning to the ticket counter just as the agent was handing over the paperwork. Jolie seemed tense, which was reasonable, considering where we were headed.

"Here's your cards," the agent said, pushing them over the counter. "And your keys. Enjoy your trip, Mr. and Mrs. Warren."

I chuckled as I reached for my ID, chiding myself for how natural the pairing sounded, and expected Jolie to refute it. When she didn't, busying herself with putting her ID and credit card away instead, I chided myself for thinking that might mean something.

But then in her haste, she dropped her license to the ground, and even though she rushed to grab it, I beat her to it.

I glanced at it as I handed it over, because of course I did, and when she snatched it out of my hand, it was too late. I'd already seen it. Her name. The first was Jolie, as she'd insisted it was, not Julianna. And her last name didn't say Stark. It said Warren.

She didn't look at me, slipping her ID in her wallet and her wallet in her purse. Organizing the paperwork the agent had given her and stuffing it in her bag as well, along with the cold water I'd brought her.

"Jolie *Warren*?" I hadn't ever put those two names together.

No, maybe I had. Years ago. When we were plotting our escape, but I hadn't said it enough to get used to the way it felt in my mouth. The way it rolled over my tongue.

The color seeped out of her face. She refused to look at me. "We're holding up the line."

Grabbing the handle of her suitcase, she towed it behind her as she headed out the door that led to the parking lot.

I jammed my license in my pocket and followed after. It was obvious she didn't want to discuss what I'd seen, but there was no way I was letting it go. "Why does your ID say my last name?"

She stopped outside to scan down the rows of cars. "G-3, G-3," she said, searching for where our vehicle was parked.

"Jolie?"

"I told you I changed my name so my father couldn't find me." She still wouldn't look at me. "Do you see row G?"

Fuck row G. "Why did you pick Warren? Out of all the names you could have picked. Why Warren?"

She let out a puff of air, her shoulders sagging in resignation before she turned to face me. "Because it was who I wanted to be, okay? I told you already."

I held her gaze, trying to find something in her eyes that could explain that to me. Could explain how she could refuse to leave with me and then seven years later choose my name as the one she wanted to live by. How she could then disappear. How she wouldn't seek me out until ten more years had passed.

She'd wrecked me when she'd told me she didn't want me. Why was she living like I'd been the one who wrecked her?

"You won't understand," she said, breaking our stare.

"I want to."

"I know you do. I just." She rubbed her hands over her face. Took a deep breath. Put herself back together. "Can we deal with this first? With my dad?"

It wasn't fair. It was never fair, how she got to set the terms. How I was always paying interest. How the balance never changed.

I couldn't keep doing it.

I wouldn't.

But fuck. Her bringing down her father required all our focus. And it wasn't just about us anymore.

"After your dad is dealt with, we talk." It wasn't a request.

It would give me time, too. To figure out what should happen next with us. Maybe by then I'd be able to admit what I wanted. "I mean it, Jolie. I need answers."

"We'll talk," she agreed, her tone heavy, as though the commitment would be hard to keep.

Her weariness made it easier to believe that she meant to follow through, at least. It didn't make waiting any less frustrating.

Snatching the keys out of her hand, I nodded to the right. "Row G. I'm driving."

When we found the SUV, I got her into the passenger seat before putting our bags in the back. We only had one each, so it didn't take long, but I took the opportunity to open up my suitcase and get Donovan's gun out of the hard-cased container he'd given me for transport. After loading the cartridge, I shoved it in my coat pocket.

"Everything okay back there?"

"Yep. Just digging out my sunglasses." I grabbed those from the side pocket of my bag and shut the hatch.

A few minutes later we were on the road. Once out of the city, it was a straightforward route, which made the drive easy, and though I wanted to push her about her name and her secrets, I forced myself to spend the time firming up our plan. We decided to say we'd both been in New York—me for a wedding, her for a weekend away—sticking to the truth for the most part. *"Seeing each other again took us down memory lane, and we decided on a whim to drive up to the academy."* We expected they'd entertain us in the living room. The conversation would be awkward and painful, especially painful for us. At some point, I'd excuse myself to use the restroom and slip into his office to get the key.

Jolie said she should be the one to do the snooping because she knew what the key looked like and where it was kept.

I argued that I was the one who knew how to pick a lock. Plus, it had been ten years, and everything might be different. He might have moved it.

Besides, if I was caught, I was the one who could defend myself. I didn't mention I had a gun on me.

She agreed reluctantly, then suggested we should both have our phones on so we could text each other if need be.

And if nothing went as planned, we'd improvise.

I preferred being more prepared; I didn't know if it even mattered. Honestly, I was still not entirely convinced we'd even be let in.

Once we crossed the city limits of Wallingford, we grew quiet. There was too much to take in outside of us. The roads that had changed. The parts of town that had expanded. The stores that were gone. The new stores in their place. It was an odd thing to return to haunted ground. The shape of the city had altered enough to almost convince myself the ghosts were gone. That they had never existed in the first place.

But then we were turning on the winding drive that led to Stark Academy, and each bend of the road was so achingly familiar, I could navigate the SUV with my eyes shut.

And closing my eyes was tempting. Because each sight held a memory, and each memory led down a spiral of emotions. Emotions too tangled to unravel.

I couldn't imagine how much worse it had to be for Jolie. Stark had only been my home for a year. It had been hers for most of her life.

Whatever she was feeling, she managed to put a mask on. Her face was unreadable as we passed the turnoff toward the main entrance in favor of the less-driven road that curled behind the boarding school, past the cook's residence and the gardener's and the lodgings for visitors and prospective students, ending at the three-story house at the back of the property.

I parked the car, careful not to block the garage—a habit that was beaten into me—but when I pulled the key from the ignition, neither of us moved to get out.

"I should go in first." She looked suddenly nervous. More nervous, since she'd been low-key fidgety the entire trip. "You know, in case...in case..."

"In case...what?"

She took a deep breath, then shrugged, "I just wonder what they'll bring up."

I almost laughed. Whatever they used to hold against us, it couldn't compare to their sins. Even with what I didn't know about Jolie and the years before she'd left Wallingford, I couldn't imagine she had anything to be ashamed of.

Stark would try, though. And it would be hard to listen to, so I didn't say anything.

"What do you think she'll say to you?"

I'd tried not to think about *her*. Now that I allowed the thought, I didn't know what to expect. "She might not say anything at all."

"It was always too big of a house for just me and my dad. When he got married again, it almost felt snug enough to be a home."

I nodded.

"What if they aren't home?"

"Then we'll wait."

"What if they don't let us in?"

"Then we'll come back when it's dark." I wondered for the billionth time if we should skip the face-to-face and just sneak in later, but then there was an alarm to navigate, and Jolie's father had always been a light sleeper.

She turned to look at me. "Is it surreal to be back here? Like out of a dream?"

"Like out of a nightmare, more like."

"Yeah. That's it. Except, with you here, it's not him I'm scared of. I'm scared of not getting what we need."

It was hard to admit, even to myself, that I was scared too. But I was more scared of the woman sitting next to me, of losing her all over again. That was always the nightmare. A recurring one over the years that I realized in that moment could very well come true.

Not giving myself time to overthink it, I took her hand and squeezed. "We'll get it. If we don't, we'll try again until he goes down."

"Okay."

"Okay."

I let go of her hand, stowed my sunglasses, and at the same time, we both pushed open our doors. Side by side, we walked up the stone steps to the front door.

Jolie hesitated, her hand stretched out above the handle. "Do we ring the bell or just walk in?"

It seemed odd as fuck to ring. "Maybe knock?"

Turned out she didn't have to. The door opened on its own, and there stood a woman I hadn't seen in seventeen years.

She looked Jolie over for half a second. Looked longer at me. "About time you came in. I thought you might sit in the car all evening. Just the two of you?" She wiped her hands on her apron, a newer one than she'd had when I was a kid, but a similar style, and peered behind us as if expecting there were more ghosts from her past waiting to haunt her.

Instinctively, I peered too, my eyes following her gaze to the empty car. She got her answer faster from looking before I could summon up one with words. "Dinner's almost ready. There should be enough."

Jolie glanced at me, her expression showing even less confidence than she'd shown in the car.

I offered a tight smile and hoped it was encouraging. Truth was, my stomach had turned into a knotted rope, and every breath I tried to take in went shallow.

"Hi, Carla," Jolie said, and I had to give her credit for not calling her mom. Her father had required that she did when he'd remarried, an expectation that she'd fulfilled even though she'd hated it.

But instead of completely snubbing her with the dropped title, Jolie leaned in and gave her a half hug that was surprisingly returned before she walked inside past her.

I couldn't bring myself to be that affectionate. It already felt like I was on the verge of losing my grip, a grip I'd never been sure I had in the first place.

But I did address her as I walked past, using the name I'd called her once upon a time. Before Wallingford. Before Langdon Stark. "Hi, Mom."

Then I followed Jolie into the house where it all began, where I'd spent the best and worst year of my life being beaten by my stepdad and falling in love with his daughter.

WILD WAR

ONE
JOLIE

Past

I dropped my highlighter at the slam of a car door, perking my ears for more tell-tale sounds of my father's arrival. I'd barely been able to concentrate on my Advanced Biology textbook, and the dread of being unprepared began to turn solid like a rock in the pit of my stomach. Daddy would quiz me on the reading, and with him, the only acceptable option was to have the right answers.

There was no exception for special occasions like today. He hadn't even acted like there was anything out of the ordinary about his trip to Bradley International. As if he went to pick up a new member of the household every day.

My window faced the backyard, so I couldn't see the car, and even if I could, the smart thing would be to stay at my desk and focus on my homework until I had it memorized instead of peeking out. Years of living alone with a cruel man had taught me well to make wise choices; had taught me the consequences of choosing otherwise.

It had also inspired a rebellious streak that dared walk an often dangerous line.

I eased my chair out from my desk, quietly so the legs wouldn't screech across the wood floor, and tiptoed to my bedroom door. He hadn't locked it before he'd left for the airport. Before Carla, he would have. It was one of the first things that had changed when my stepmother had moved in four months ago, a sign that he might be different with someone else in the house.

That hope had been short-lived. Things had gotten easier, at least. His attention wasn't always on me. He noticed less the rare times that I fell out of line.

What would he be like now that our household of three was going to be four?

As I eased the door open, I told myself that was the main reason behind my intrigue—it was about self-preservation. Nothing more.

But the truth was, I was deeply curious about Carla's surprise son. I'd only found out about him after she'd officially taken the title of wife. I wasn't clear when my father had learned about him—before or after they'd gotten married—but it had definitely been he who'd insisted on bringing him to live with us now, two weeks into the new school year. So he could win points with his new bride, I imagined. Or so he could show off how transformative his methods of education could be. Or so he could have himself a whipping boy.

It certainly wasn't out of the kindness of his heart. He didn't seem to have one.

Outside my room, I crossed to the balcony and stooped down to peer between the rails. Even on my knees, I could only see the bottom of Carla's body as she stood at the front door, her back pressed to it to hold it open.

"Why didn't you park in the garage?" she called out. She had to know by now that my father rarely parked in the garage unless it was winter, but that didn't stop her from the occasional nag.

Not for the first time, I wondered how long my father would let that go on before he put a stop to it. For now it seemed they were still in the honeymoon period.

If he answered her, I couldn't hear it, and I was more interested in the boy who followed my father in, heaving a large duffel bag along with him.

"Hey," Carla said, stopping him before he'd walked in far enough for me to see more than from his waist down. She let the door go so she could cross to him. "Aren't you going to say hello to me?"

He dropped his duffel, and it landed on the floor with a plop. "Hello, Carla." His tone was bitter, his voice deeper than most of the guys at school with a subtle rasp. Warm, though. A much different timbre than my father's whose tone was clipped and hollow.

"That's not how you talk to your mother."

I tensed. My father rarely issued warnings.

The boy couldn't know that, though, and he smarted off again. "I didn't realize I still had a mother."

I could tell from Carla's shaky sigh that he'd hit her where he meant to, but before she had a chance to say anything, I heard a distinct thud that I recognized as the sound a hand made when struck against the back of someone's head.

"I won't say it again, Cade. In our home, you treat your elders with respect."

I shivered. That rule had been beaten into me, and it was now evident it would be beaten into this boy too. I'd been pretty sure that was why Daddy had told Carla he was going alone to pick up her son, so he could inform him of How Things Would Be in the Stark House on the way back.

Apparently, Cade hadn't quite gotten the message.

He would. Just not yet. "I apologize, sir," he said with dripping sarcasm. "It's been so long since I've had a real home, I guess I forgot my manners."

I saw my father's feet as he lurched for Cade, but this time Carla stepped in between them. "He's had a long trip, Langdon. He'll be better after he gets settled."

Keep your mouth shut.

I didn't know if I was thinking it for myself or for Cade. Despite being a flight away, I could feel him warring with himself not to say more, the same way I was fighting not to speak up in his defense.

It would only make things worse, I reminded myself. I was positive that even Carla's interference would have consequences, if not now then later.

A tense beat passed before my father backed down. "You can get settled then. Upstairs. First room you come to. The door should be open. I expect a new attitude when you arrive down here for dinner, which will be at six thirty sharp."

It was my cue to go back to my room, but I still hadn't caught Cade's face, and I thought maybe as he bent to reach for his duffel, I might catch a glimpse...

But he was too fast, grabbing the bag in a hurried swoop and then bounding up the stairs two at a time. He was at the top by the time I'd managed to scramble to my feet, and the second our eyes caught, I froze in place.

Because first of all, Cade Warren was not a boy.

Not like the boys I knew anyway. He was on the thin side, but he was broad, and he had scruff along his chin that actually looked capable of being a full beard. His jaw was chiseled and his cheekbones defined, and with his height, he could easily have passed for a senior in college rather than in high school. No, he wasn't a boy at all. He was a man.

And second of all, the real reason his intense stare had me pinned to my place was because Cade Warren was hot.

Generally, looks weren't something I noticed. I flirted and messed around with plenty of the guys at school, but that was always about me more than it was about them. I'd never really been interested. I'd never encountered one who made my heart speed up or my tummy flip or made me forget how words worked, and maybe it was simply because of the circumstances—me, caught spying; him, a stranger moving into the room down the hall—but looking at Cade made all three of those things happen, and now I was frozen and stammering and on the verge of a panic attack.

Plus, I was still wearing my school uniform—Daddy hated wasteful changes of clothes—and my lips were dry, and my hair was falling out of the ponytail I'd put it in that morning, and though he was in worn jeans and had been traveling all day, he looked a thousand times better than I did, even on my best days.

But despite me being nothing to look at, he was looking. Looking very intensely. Staring into me, and for the briefest of seconds, I was sure he could see all of me. All the lonely parts. All the dark parts. All the secret parts.

I wasn't sure if that made me feel comforted or scared.

"You're Julianna," he said. Not a question. I'd always hated the formal sound of my name, but I didn't mind it when he said it.

"You're Cade." Daddy and Carla were no longer standing in the foyer below, but I spoke only loud enough to be heard down the hall. I hadn't lost sight of the fact that I was supposed to be doing homework, and even if my father was distracted by Cade, I knew shirking my responsibilities wouldn't go unnoticed.

After the words were out, I wished I'd been even quieter. Wished he hadn't been able to hear me at all. *You're Cade. Great response, Julianna.*

Idiot.

He didn't react to my lame attempt at communication, seemingly more concerned with getting his bearings. "That your room?" He pointed his chin toward the door behind me. I nodded. "This mine?" He gestured now to the room in front of him.

I nodded again.

Now he looked toward the bathroom. "That just for me?"

Another nod. "I have my own."

He eyed the distance between us, thirty feet of hallway that passed by the bathroom and a guest room and a linen closet. "Plenty of space. You'll have no reason to get in my way."

With three steps, he was in his room, the slam of his door reverberating in the air.

I winced. Partly because Daddy didn't like slamming doors.

Mostly because Cade's remark had stung.

I didn't know there were pains that could hurt anymore. I'd grown numb to the slap of a hand. My mind went somewhere else during my father's darker tortures. But this—this I felt.

Maybe I'd thought there could be a camaraderie between us, me and this stranger. He could have helped carry the burden of living in the Stark household.

He could have made me finally feel less alone.

Stupid me. What was he possibly going to change? He wasn't here to save me. He wasn't a hero. He was only my stepbrother.

TWO
CADE

It took me less than twenty minutes to unpack, and that included going through the new uniforms that had been left on the bed and tossing the bag in the trash. Once upon a time, I'd owned more than could fit in an oversized duffle, but that was all I'd brought when my mother had dropped me off at Stu Goodie's house a little more than a year ago. I would have packed more if I hadn't been told I was only staying through the weekend.

Sometimes I wondered about the items that I'd lost in my mother's abandonment. Most were clothes I'd grown out of anyway, but there'd been a few things I'd cared about. The Nintendo Gameboy. A stack of Tom Clancy books. The keychain rabbit's foot that I'd had since I was five.

Well, they hadn't been waiting for me in this bedroom, which meant they were gone for good. I knew that without even asking.

A renewed sense of anger spiked through me as I slammed a dresser drawer shut. Why had I even bothered unpacking? Like hell was I staying.

I stormed out of the room and down the stairs and was grateful to find my stepfather nowhere in sight. Carla was easy enough to find. There was still twenty minutes before dinner, and having pegged

Langdon Stark as a traditionalist the minute I laid eyes on him, I was sure she couldn't be anywhere else but the kitchen.

I followed the scent of baked ham and found her bent with an electric hand mixer over a bowl of potato chunks. Her expression hardened when she saw me, but she only spared me a glance before turning her focus back on her meal.

"Tell me again why I couldn't stay in Kentucky?" I circled around the kitchen island so that I could face her but still have a barrier between us when we did.

A *physical* barrier. There were plenty of less tangible ones already.

"Because I'm here," she said without even a pretense of patience. "And because you're my son."

"So?"

Any response she gave would be a trap, and she knew it. "I don't have time for ridiculous conversations, Cade."

"The only thing that's ridiculous about it is you trying to suggest that parents should be with their children."

She set down the mixer with a thump. "I wanted to be with you. I've told you why I couldn't be."

"Actually, no. You haven't. But no need. I get that it was easier to catch your next man without a kid weighing you down."

"I was trying to build a better life for us. And I did. Look around you. We never had this type of security before. We never had the life that Langdon provides." She went back to her cooking, throwing the beaters in the sink then turning to stir the gravy on the stove.

I took a moment to sweep my eyes over the gourmet kitchen. It wasn't as fancy as the ones that were in the houses in the Parade of Homes shows she used to drag me to, but it was certainly way above anything we'd had in the past. Shit, we'd never even owned a dishwasher when we'd been on our own.

The reality, though, was that we were never on our own for very long. And the men that were with us in between never stayed.

Granted, none had ever put a ring on her finger like this one had.

I glanced at the diamond on her left hand and the plain gold band beneath it. "Do you get to keep that when he leaves you? I bet you could get some decent rent money with it."

"You're ungrateful and self-centered. Just like your father."

There he was—my mysterious father. Half of the time, she claimed that he'd been a one-night stand. The other half, she claimed she wasn't even sure who he was. And yet she knew enough about him to identify his hateful qualities whenever it was useful to her.

I'd grown immune to the mentions by the time I'd hit ten. "I'm the one who's self-centered? Okay. Sure. How about I offer a selfless act then and volunteer to get out of your hair altogether. Let you enjoy your new family unit without any extra baggage."

"Don't be so dramatic." She turned off the stove, setting the cooked carrots on a cool adjacent burner. "We want you here. *I* want you here. I always wanted you with me."

"You disappeared for a year! If you wanted me, why did you abandon me?" I hadn't minded her seeing my rage, but I could feel a more vulnerable emotion bubbling up in my chest, threatening to burst.

"I didn't abandon you. I left you with a good family—"

"They thought you were going for a job interview. We didn't hear from you for four months!" And then another nine passed after that before she'd informed the Goodies she'd gotten married and could finally take her son back. "How is that not abandonment?"

"I was doing what I thought was best," she snapped. She stared at me, her gaze heavy and loaded, and I met her back with equal venom.

"How could you do that, Mom? How?" I hated the way my voice cracked and how my vision suddenly felt blurred.

She opened her mouth, and for the briefest second, I thought she might actually give me something real.

But then a timer buzzed, and she jumped back to her duties, grabbing mitts before heading over to the oven. "It's complicated," she said as she took out the baking dish with the ham.

That's all it ever was with her—fucking complicated.

THE ONLY REASON I showed up to dinner ten minutes later was because I was hungry, and as much as Carla sucked at mothering, she was actually a good cook.

It wasn't at all to please Langdon Stark.

Sure, he'd huffed and puffed the whole ride, telling me about rules and manners and what to expect living in "his" house, but I'd seen this act before. Even the smack against the head wasn't anything new. Carla hadn't married any of her boyfriends before this one, but they all liked to assume authority over her son right off the bat, as if that quality would make them more attractive to her. Truth was, she just needed to have someone pay the rent, and she'd spread her legs. She couldn't care less if they were "good" with me.

Needless of my motivations, I walked into the dining room at six twenty-nine. The table had been set, all the delicious food my mother had been preparing now displayed in matching dishes. Julianna was already there, pouring water into glasses. She didn't even look up as I sat down across from her.

I chuckled to myself as the grandfather clock in the living room struck half past, and Daddy Stark still wasn't seated, but before the clock's song had ended, there he was, walking toward the chair at the head of the table with such precision, it was as if he were part of an automation.

My mother scurried in on his heels, her face red as she put down a tray of dinner rolls. "I'm sorry, Langdon. I didn't time the bread right."

Her husband gave her a disapproving look, but I had a feeling it was less to do with her two-second tardiness and more about me. The fact that all eyes had moved to me, the only one sitting, validated that feeling.

"Is this how you've taught the boy?" His admonition came out thick and ominous.

I had to shoo away the urge to protect my mother. She'd made her bed. If I got lectured along with her, so be it.

Besides, I honestly had no idea what I'd done wrong.

"He's been away for some time. He'll catch on quickly." She didn't look as sure as her words. She gestured toward me with her head, but I couldn't decipher her meaning.

Had I sat down in the wrong seat?

My mother started to explain. "We don't sit until—"

Langdon cut her off. "In a proper household, the master is the last to arrive, and the first to sit. As this is your first night here—and as you've likely been in a home led by less attentive adults—I'll give you an allowance for tonight's ill behavior."

"Wow, super kind of you." Was this guy for real?

His daughter's eyes went wide. My mother shifted nervously.

"Stop fidgeting, Carla."

Immediately, she became motionless. Everyone stood real still, waiting. It took a beat before I realized what they were waiting for. "You mean you want me to stand now?"

"I didn't explain how the dinnertime seating worked so that I could hear my own voice."

But hadn't he just said he'd give me an allowance?

I stood up, slowly, trying to decide if my mother's ham was worth this much trouble. When I'd been standing and nothing happened, I definitely was sure that it wasn't. "What did I fuck up now?"

My mother inhaled sharply.

Forget this. I was just about to ditch the bullshit when my gaze caught on the girl across from me. *Julianna.* My mother had told me about her in the same conversation that she'd told me about her marriage. A breath after she'd told me I was moving back, as though having a stepsibling might be enticing.

She hadn't mentioned that Julianna was also a teenager. Or that she had plump, raspberry-colored lips. And that her long, toned legs made a simple school uniform skirt look obscene.

Just my luck that my stepsister was a complete hottie.

It was her piercing blue eyes that kept me sitting there, and not because they were beautiful, but because they felt deep. Like what I saw was only wading in the shallows, and there was a whole ocean underneath. Those eyes were an anchor. They held me in place, and suddenly it occurred to me that leaving might be weaker than staying, and maybe this was a good time to show a bit of strength.

"Cursing in this house will be punished," Langdon said. "That will be your only warning."

"Like, you'll wash my mouth out or...?" I trailed off when I noticed Julianna frown. I'd yet to see her smile, and I was curious what that looked like.

Though with this hardass for a father, I doubted she did that very often.

Smarting off more didn't seem to be the way to go about seeing it, so I kept my trap shut. Tense silence strung out between the four of us as we stood at our places, waiting. Waiting.

"Could someone give me a little guidance here?" It was evident I was supposed to do something, and I still didn't know what was expected of me. The ham wasn't going to be any good if it was cold.

"Typically, when one insults their elders, it is customary for him to offer an apology." Stark had waited a handful of seconds before answering, almost baiting the others to answer first. I suspected that would have pissed him off, them talking out of turn and everything. I was starting to understand that this prick was after more than respect. He enjoyed this power game. Enjoyed the taunting and inciting.

He probably enjoyed the punishments that followed as well.

My mother had dated someone like that years ago, when I'd still been in elementary school. My middle finger on my left hand was crooked from an incident with that prick. I'd carried a ball of dread with me in my stomach the entire time Carla had been with him. I'd never slept better than the night we'd spent in a shelter after he'd kicked us out.

I was older now, though. In four months, I'd be old enough to go out on my own. In eight, I'd have a diploma. Whatever this asshole wanted to dole out, I could survive that long. I didn't need to bend to his whims.

Julianna's eyes stayed steady on me.

I found myself speaking before I made the decision to apologize.

"I'm sorry for my ill manners." Remembering a rule he'd given me in the car, I added, "Sir."

Stark's lips turned up slightly at the corners, but I sensed he was more pleased with my discomfort than my apology. "Not so hard, was that? Even the best dogs need training. You're a quick learner. I can tell."

He sat down.

I was smart enough to wait until the women started to sit before I followed suit, which they didn't do until Stark had given a nod.

Once seated, I reached for a roll, only to have a fork come swiftly down into the bread, centimeters from my finger. "Surely, you are not in the habit of eating before grace?"

The Goodies had been the pray-before-meal type as well. "We served ourselves beforehand at the last place," I said, which was a lie but not something he'd ever know, and did I really deserve to have my hand nearly jabbed for the "mistake"?

"How vulgar." He genuinely looked a little sick at the thought. "Who will volunteer?"

He was staring at me pointedly, a not-so-subtle hint.

Before I had time to decide if I was going to let him bully me into doing what he wanted, Julianna spoke. "I will."

Stark's eye twitched, but when he turned his gaze to his daughter, he beamed. "Of course you will, darling. Setting an excellent example. I wouldn't expect anything less."

She smiled, pleased to have him pleased.

A rule follower. My instinct to keep my distance from her had been right then. Likely, she was the type to tattle. Headmaster's pet and his daughter as well. Ten bucks said she had no friends. I certainly wasn't getting in line for the role.

She bowed her head and started reciting a memorized prayer. I turned to look at my mother, a woman who had never prayed once at the dinner table when I'd lived with her in the past, and found her eyes closed and her hands clasped, her mouth moving silently as Julianna spoke.

Great. Ma had found God. As if she didn't have enough dysfunctional relationships.

Rolling my eyes, I glanced at Stark. He hadn't bowed his head, and his stare was fixed on me, his expression cold and hard and menacing.

Quickly, I lowered my head, in time to hit the "Amen" and lift it again.

Serving began the instant the prayer was over, but only to Stark. Julianna placed a slice of ham on his plate followed by a spoonful of carrots. My mother stood and circled the table to dish him some mashed potatoes and gravy. It seemed I was expected to give him a roll since they were in front of me.

So I did.

Earning me a relieved smile from my mother.

When she sat down again, she waited expectantly for her husband to taste his food. All of it. Julianna sat still as well, though she was watching me, her face unreadable.

"Very good, Carla," my new stepfather said. "The ham is perfection."

I could feel her shoulders relax.

Then he went on. "Good thing it is too. It makes up for the lack of glaze on the carrots. And three starches in one meal? You know better than that."

She lowered her eyes. "The asparagus had gone bad."

"Then you'll learn to plan better. Won't you?"

"Of course."

He took three more bites before he motioned to us. "Go ahead. Eat up. It's already getting cold."

She and Julianna began dishing up their own plates. I waited until they were done, just in case there was a women-go-first rule I didn't know about, then served myself. Though, to be honest, I'd begun to lose my appetite.

Picking at my food, it began to return. The ham really was perfection. And the carrots were amazing the way she'd made them—with rosemary and oil. They'd been my favorite before.

I felt a softening toward her when it occurred to me she might have made them for me.

But then, out of the blue, she announced, "I'll do better, Langdon. I will."

"I know you will, dear." While I took those words as a threat, my mother glowed. As though fueled by her husband's support, ignoring the fact that she'd only needed it because he'd cut her down in the first place.

I knew then that I'd lost her. Knew that any hint of the woman who had once cared for me was gone. Knew that even if she'd chosen the carrots over the asparagus for me, she wouldn't do it again. That every choice after this would always put him first.

Once more I scanned the table—the do-gooder across from me, the stepfather with a need for control, the mother who'd abandoned her son.

I'd been without her for a while now. For the first time, I realized I was truly on my own.

THREE
CADE

"Look who's got the hots for New Boy."

I followed Troy's gaze to a group of girls in gym clothes walking the track, which was really just a quarter-mile gravel path that circled the school's main grounds. They were looking at us and giggling, suggesting they were talking about us as well, but I had no idea why he'd assumed it was me that had their attention.

"Which one?" Birch asked, more interested than I was. I'd already stopped looking.

"Amelia."

Birch nodded, as though his acceptance meant something to me. I hadn't decided yet if it did. He was definitely the popular man on campus, and befriending him would have its benefits.

Being a loner had benefits too.

Birch kicked at my shoe to get my attention. "Amelia would be a good starter girlfriend, Cade. I can hook you guys up, if you're into her."

Starter girlfriend. "Fuck you."

He laughed. "It's not a comment on your experience, asshole. There's a hierarchy. You can't get to the top-ranked girls without proving yourself with the lesser."

"He's not dicking with you," Troy said in a way that suggested it wasn't unlike Birch to bullshit.

I leaned back against the shed, turned off by both the idea of a ranking system with the girls and the notion that who you dated was just another way to show off status. It was true in my last school, too, but after only three weeks, I could tell it was worse here.

That was the whole environment at Stark Academy, though. All that mattered was power, power, power. Not only did the curriculum enforce the belief, but most of the students came from family backgrounds that exemplified it.

I was definitely the odd man out. In more ways than I could count.

Birch misinterpreted my silence as hesitation. "Come by my room tonight," he said. "I'll tell her you need a tutor, then I'll make myself scarce."

There was no doubt he could make it happen. Not only did Antoine Birch have the face and charm that girls went for, but he also had a pedigree that made him influential. His father was president of one of the nation's premier banks. His mother, a notable French actress who lived in London. His connections had the staff wrapped around his finger, and there wasn't a student on campus who didn't jump when he told them how high.

I actually could use some help with schoolwork, a fact I wouldn't admit to the guys. I'd gotten decent grades in the past; not from trying. Natural instincts weren't enough to survive at a prestigious school like the one my stepfather ran. I wasn't made for it. Not because I was afraid of hard work, an accusation I'd already heard from his lips a time or two, but because I wasn't made to be reined in.

But getting out of the Stark household, even under the guise of being tutored, wasn't a task I'd figured out how to manage yet. The few attempts I'd made had ended in menial punishments. No television privileges one night. No dessert, another. A backhanded slap across the face a couple evenings before.

I preferred to be seen as a tough guy, but I didn't know if I had the stomach for it. I was fully aware that I'd only scratched the surface of

Stark's wrath. I was already toeing the line by ducking out of study hall to sit out here and shoot the shit. I wasn't sure I was ready to push my luck with more disobedience.

"I'm not really interested in a girlfriend," I said finally, hoping the true statement would get me out of having to prove myself a rebel.

Birch pulled out a pack of cigarettes from his shoulder bag and stuck one in his mouth, a Zippo poised to light it. "What *are* you interested in? Fags?"

I cringed at the remark, even though I was sure he'd said it to be clever rather than homophobic.

"Fag. You get it? Because they call smokes fags in Britain." Troy was the perfect lackey. He'd probably suck him off, if that's what Birch wanted, and Troy had made it perfectly clear he was not into boys.

I ignored the invitation to pour praise on the top dog and answered the question. "Keeping my head down and graduating."

Birch passed the pack and the light to Troy. "Ah, I get it. You got a girl back home. Promised to be faithful?"

"No, no. I mean, there was a girl I fucked around with, but it wasn't like that." Well, it wasn't like that for me. I'd been clear from the start with Heather that relationships weren't my thing, which hadn't prevented her from latching on.

The sex had been too good for me to dump her altogether, but honestly, if there was anything good that had come from being suddenly transported to Wallingford, it was that I no longer had to deal with her constant attempts to make us a couple.

"So you want a fuck buddy." Cigarette lit, Troy passed the pack and the light to me.

I paused before taking one out. Though the shed and the grounds behind it were an area that seemed ignored by the adults, we weren't exactly out of sight.

On the other hand, I'd really missed smoking.

Fuck it.

I put the Camel between my lips and lit it. Then I set the pack and the light on the ground at my side. "I wouldn't mind a fuck buddy. If you could find me a chick that wouldn't get attached."

Birch looked back to the running path where the girls gym class was still walking the loop. "For that, I'd suggest *her*, but you know."

I took a drag as I again followed his line of sight and this time landed on Julianna. Her long hair was pulled back in a ponytail, her expression intent as she jogged past slower students. Her legs were more muscular than I'd realized. Her ass, more toned. She really was beautiful.

When she turned her head and saw me watching her, I smiled unintentionally. She didn't return it before moving her focus back to the path in front of her.

"Oh, yeah, Jules gives awesome head," Troy agreed. "You should definitely hook up with her."

Birch lightly smacked Troy's shoulder with the back of his hand. "He can't hook up with her, you moron. She's his stepsister."

"Right, right. It's not blood related, though. They could still get it on, couldn't they?"

Birch shrugged. "Kind of weird, if you ask me."

"Too bad. She's for sure the girl you want for no-strings-attached fucking around."

"You're bullshitting me." I'd spent as little time with Julianna as possible over the last month, which hadn't been hard since she pretty much stayed in her room and did schoolwork all the time that she wasn't in school or at mealtime. I had no doubt that my initial impression of her had been accurate—model student, model daughter, model everything. The image of her down on her knees did not fit into that notion.

It bothered me to even think about it. Which seemed strange. Maybe I had more brotherly feelings about her than I realized.

Except that didn't seem right either.

"No bullshit." Birch put a hand up as if to swear. "She gets around. Practically a rite of passage to have her lips on your dick."

"Have you fucked her?" I sounded more pissed than I'd meant to. I didn't feel quite angry, though. I felt something else, something I couldn't quite identify.

"He wants to," Troy said when Birch didn't answer. "He hates it when he's the only one who hasn't had access to something."

Birch scowled. "Like you've fucked her."

Troy shrugged. "But everyone else has."

I took another drag of my cigarette, hoping it would relax my suddenly tight muscles.

"Everyone else *claims* to," Birch corrected. "I don't actually know that anyone has. She might be a virgin with loose lips and that's all."

I didn't exactly feel relieved, but the tension in my shoulders eased slightly. "Does her father know?"

"That she's a BJ queen?" Birch stamped the cherry of his smoke out on the shed, then flicked the butt into a nearby trash can. "Fuck no. He'd kill her."

No shit, he'd kill her. "I'm surprised she takes the risk. I took her as a straight-liner."

"She usually is. Maybe she's hoping to get caught."

"Why would she want to be caught?" Troy seemed less aware of basic psychology than his friend.

Birch stood up and wiped the ground from his slacks. "I don't know. Some people get off on the taboo shit."

I barely knew her, but from my limited experience in the Stark household, I had a feeling it was less about taboo and more about control. It was the one thing she could decide for herself, and that had to feel satisfying. I could understand that. I could understand *her*.

If it was true, that was. I still wasn't entirely sure they weren't dicking with me.

Troy moved into a crouch. "You seen her titties yet, Warren?"

"Yeah, Troy. She parades around the house naked. Didn't you know?" I fought the urge to punch the guy in the nuts. I had a perfect opening. Such a shame.

He grinned, putting out his cigarette on the ground. "A guy can dream." He stood up. "You coming to Economics?"

I took a final drag, considering. It was tempting to ditch the rest of the day, but what would I do instead? No car, no funds, and a boarding school campus made for very few opportunities for fun.

Before I could answer, though, someone else answered for me. "He is not. He's coming with me."

I looked up to see the last person I wanted to see while I still had a lit cigarette between my lips—Headmaster Stark.

FOUR
CADE

"Hand them over," Stark said, his palm waiting.

For a second, I thought he meant the cigarette in my hand, but then I realized he meant the pack and the Zippo. I handed both over, then stood, swaying when I got to my feet. I'd smoked an occasional light back at my last school. The Camel was stronger than I was used to and made me especially jittery.

The anxiety of being caught doing something wrong didn't help my blood pressure.

"Who do they belong to?" Stark asked, eyeing the three of us. He lingered on me, a spark in his eyes despite his cruel expression before turning his focus to Birch. "You've been caught with cigarettes before. This brand, if I remember correctly. Are these yours?"

Logic said they weren't mine. If I'd brought them from Kentucky, it wouldn't still be a full pack, and when would I have had a chance to have bought them here?

But I was the only one still holding a smoke and too new to claim they belonged to anyone else without gaining a reputation I'd rather not have. Then, when Birch didn't respond, it seemed a clear message that I was expected to take the blame.

Fuck.

"They're mine, sir," I said, doing my best to keep my chin up and proud. If I was going to take the fall, I was going to be a man about it.

I swore I heard a note of glee in Stark's tone when he spoke. "Well then, Cade. It seems you will be accompanying me to my office. The rest of you—" He quickly scanned the small crowd that had gathered along. "Get to your next class."

Birch and Troy weren't even going to get detention for skipping study hall? Didn't seem fair. I supposed there was a chance he'd let me off as well when we were alone, that this was a demonstration to the school that he wouldn't play favorites, but from what I'd seen of him the last couple of weeks, the man didn't think he had to prove anything to anyone.

And even if he did, I certainly wasn't a favorite.

Resigned, I dropped the butt and stamped it out with my foot. Then made a show of putting it in the trash, determined not to add littering to my list of sins before following after my stepfather as he made his way to the administration wing of the main building.

We walked in silence, but there was plenty being said by others. Class had released, and students flooded the grounds as they hustled to their next hour. No one was too busy to notice the headmaster with a student in tow—his stepson, no less—and intense stares turned into rapid whispering behind our backs.

It had the potential of being embarrassing, though I couldn't decide who would be more scandalized by my crime. When I realized it was probably him, that the inability to keep his own stepson in line had to be quite a blow to his authority, the walk of shame became a lot less shameful. Soon I found a smug grin creeping onto my lips, emboldened by the fact that he couldn't see my expression when he walked ahead of me.

And what was the worst that would happen? I already spent all my evenings working on homework. I didn't have any possessions that I could have taken away. If my mother was upset, that might even be a step up in our relationship. It wasn't like I could get kicked out of school.

As for my peers, if they thought I was a bad boy, it was no skin off my back. If anything, a little trouble might make me popular. It would definitely improve my ability to get hookups to drugs and booze, and Birch and Troy had to have my back after I proved I had theirs. So I'd have to sit through a lame-ass lecture from my stepfather as punishment. All in all, it seemed worth the price.

My confidence only faltered when I saw Julianna.

She was back in her school uniform, a calculus textbook in her arms, her forehead still shiny with sweat from gym class. She stared, as everyone had when we walked by, but there was something else in her face—a flash of panic that had me craning over my neck to look again. Her eyes met mine then, and while I could understand how a goody-goody would see any act of discipline as terrifying, there was something about the fear in her gaze that rattled me.

My smile dropped, and by the time we got to Stark's office, my confidence was gone as well.

"Take a seat," he said, not bothering to look at me as he went directly to the cabinet behind his desk, pulled a ring of keys from his belt, and unlocked the top drawer before putting the keys, the lighter, and the pack of cigarettes on his desk and sitting down.

I hadn't yet been to my stepfather's office. My mother and I had spent an afternoon with the secretary down the hall, getting my transfer in order, but when she'd slipped down the hall to say goodbye, she'd gone alone.

I took it in quickly—it was dark and wood paneled. Cabinets and bookshelves lined three of the walls, making the room feel especially small and confined. Not that it was a very large office in the first place. The oversized desk took up a third of the space. Beyond that there were three chairs—one large and leather on his side, two plain armless chairs on the other. The only window had the blinds closed, and the overhead fluorescents were turned off, so the only source of light came from the desk lamp and a floor lamp in the corner.

I turned my neck to find the only wall space was behind me and covered with framed graduation certificates and certifications and awards, and I was still looking in that direction when he spoke again.

"I said to sit down."

His tone was sharper this time, warning me it wasn't a good idea to point out that he'd actually said *take a seat* and just go ahead and do it.

Once seated, with his stern face looking at me disapprovingly across his desk, I felt smaller. His chair was higher than mine so that he had to look down at me—purposely, I was sure—and the way the walls closed in made me feel both on edge and defensive.

"I didn't buy them," I said, excuses coming to my lips without willing them. "I found them. Someone must have left them. The lighter too. I only had that one cigarette. I'm not even a smoker. I just wanted to try it. No big deal. Send me to detention. I won't do it again."

"You *found* them?" He was obviously skeptical. "Is that the story you're sticking with?"

"Yes, sir."

He leaned forward, putting his elbows on the desk in front of him. "Let's cut the crap, Cade. We both know these cigarettes belong to Birch."

I hesitated, wondering if it was a trap to get me to narc, then settled on something I hoped wasn't too incriminating. "You think they were his?"

"I said to cut the crap."

My mouth clamped shut. I refused to rat anyone out.

"You want to know why you're in here instead of him, don't you? Go ahead and ask."

Him telling me to do a thing made me less want to do the thing, but I was starting to realize that he might actually have the power he was so intent on making me believe he had. "Um. If you think these belong to Birch, why am I here instead of him?"

He soured at my attempt to twist his instructions, but he let it slip by without remarking. "Antoine Birch is a serial troublemaker. He will spend this year in and out of detention, and each time I'll call his parents to inform them, and each time they will dismiss his actions with some version of the *boys will be boys* refrain. It's their prerogative to blow it off. All they care is that their son graduates and makes it into Harvard, where he will study medicine and eventually become a renowned doctor. His legacy will speak well for Stark Academy, so why should I feel motivated to correct the kid for being on the path that will most please everyone?"

"You shouldn't, I guess." Unless he cared about *being* an educator that deserved respect instead of just getting by as one, but apparently he didn't.

"That's right. I shouldn't. It's a waste of my time and energy." He brought his hands together in front of him with a clap. "You, on the other hand, stand to harm me much more with your offensive actions than Antoine Birch does. If you're allowed to get by with even a minor infraction, what sort of effect would that have on the student body? What if word got out to their parents? Can you imagine what people would say if it was reported that I couldn't manage the behavior of my own stepson? How many would whisper nepotism behind our backs? Have you thought of that?"

"No, sir." But I suddenly had a feeling that Julianna had thought about it. Or been told to think about it. Probably several times over her life.

Maybe labeling her a goody-goody had been unfair. She likely hadn't had a choice.

"Precisely. You hadn't thought of it. Which is why you are here in my office instead of Antoine Birch, because it is you that most requires to be taught a lesson, and acting as both your headmaster as well as your father, it is my duty to deliver that instruction."

"You are *not* my father," I said, probably more boldly than I should have.

"I'm the closest thing you'll ever get, and considering who you are and where you come from, you should consider it an honor to be my son. Place your hand on the desk in front of you, facing up."

A slap on the wrist, then—or palm, rather. With a ruler, most likely. It would sting, and it would be over, and I could go to class and forget the asshole shit he'd said and keep my head down for the rest of the year until I was free to get out of here.

Or I could continue to argue.

I wasn't sure if it was because I was smart or because I was scared, but backing down seemed to be the better option.

With a sigh, I placed my hand out on the desk in front of me.

Stark then picked up the pack of cigarettes and placed it in my hand.

"Sir?" I asked, unsure what he wanted from me.

"How many cigarettes are in there? Count them."

I remembered how many had been missing when I'd taken one out earlier, but I opened it and looked anyway. "Sixteen."

Next he handed me the lighter. "Smoke them."

Now I was definitely confused. "You want me to smoke one? Here? Now?"

"I want you to smoke them all."

It took me a minute, then I laughed. "You're messing with me. Funny. You had me there."

"I'm completely serious, Cade."

"You want me to smoke all of the cigarettes in here. All sixteen."

"Not at once, of course. One at a time." He leaned back in his chair. "Better get started. We're going to be here a while as it is."

I paused, still not sure. What if it was a trap? He wanted to see if I'd really do it, and then...

And then what? I was already in trouble. He didn't need to catch me in more. Was he trying to turn it into a joke? So that later he could tell my mother, *You should have seen him. He actually believed I wanted him to smoke sixteen cigarettes in a row.*

Or he really meant to teach a practical lesson—make me smoke a couple, and then when I was jittery and buzzed and feeling gross, he'd call it good, hoping it would turn me off from the damn things for good.

He was waiting. Only way to find out his intent was to light up.

It took seven minutes to smoke the first one. I watched the clock on the shelf behind him, the seconds ticking by at a snail's pace. When the ash started to fall from my cigarette, he dumped the change from a glass bowl on his desk and told me to use that.

He didn't speak again until I'd put the butt out. "Another."

I lit up again, already feeling lightheaded. I managed to smoke that one in just over six minutes. When he nodded, I lit the next one.

Halfway through the third, I'd reached my limit. "Okay. I get it. Smoking is bad." I rubbed the cigarette out in the glass bowl. "Thank you for the lesson. I won't smoke anymore."

"I told you to smoke all sixteen."

"Right. I get what you're trying to prove."

"I'm not trying to prove anything, Cade. Pick up the goddamn cigarette, and put it between your lips."

I stared at him. There wasn't a hint of amusement anywhere in his expression.

My stomach tightened. "I can't smoke anymore. I'm already feeling sick."

"Should have thought of that earlier. Light up."

"Look." I wiped my sweaty palms on my uniform khakis. "I can't. If you want to punish me another way..."

He stood up immediately. "Put both your hands on the desk in front of you. Palms up."

So now the ruler would come.

But when he stood and opened the drawer he'd unlocked earlier, he didn't pull out a ruler—he pulled out a long, black, skinny-tailed whip.

My breath caught in my ribs. Instinctively, my hands curled back toward me as he came around the desk to stand in striking position. The spark I'd seen in his eyes before was back. "Hands open, Cade. Now."

I looked at the door behind me, wondering what would happen if I just got up and left.

"Try it and find out," he said, reading my mind.

It would catch up with me eventually, this punishment. I couldn't escape the man. He slept under the same roof I did.

Tentatively, I laid my hands out and closed my eyes so I didn't see the whip as it lashed through the air.

But, fuck, did I feel it.

My eyes flew open, and I wasn't surprised to see bloody stripes along both palms. The sting was incredible. It was the kind of pain that lingered. The kind that I knew would take at least a week before it healed.

I reached for a Kleenex on his desk and dabbed delicately at the wounds. A whip. Was that legal for an educator? Was that even legal for a stepparent?

"Still prefer the whip to the cigarettes?"

"A little late to change my mind now it's done." But given the choice again, I wasn't sure I wouldn't pick the smoking.

"Oh, we're not done. You have thirteen and a half unfinished cigarettes. Either you smoke all of them, or you get thirteen more lashes. Your choice."

My head snapped toward him. "You're kidding, right?"

"I don't kid. Choose. Personally, I'm hoping you go with the whip. It will be the messier option, but it will be over quickly, and my office won't reek like an ashtray." He didn't hide his smile. The prick was enjoying this. "Choose."

I should have been angry, and I was. But more than that, I felt trapped. Trapped like I'd never felt before, and not just trapped between two options, but trapped in this life—*his* life. In his *school*. In his *house*. In his *family*.

He said he wanted me to make a choice, but he was actually pointing out that I didn't *have* a choice. Not really. He'd win, and I'd lose. There was nothing I could choose to make that end another way.

My hand shaking, I picked up the lighter. I wouldn't withstand fourteen lashes. And if I was going to lose, at least I'd make him waste a good portion of his afternoon on it.

It took almost two hours to smoke the rest of the pack.

I tried to take longer, dragging out each puff, delaying longer before I brought it to my lips again, but Stark watched me carefully and waved the whip threateningly every time I slowed down or didn't take a real inhalation.

I threw up after the eighth cigarette. He kicked his wastebasket toward me as soon as he realized I was going to heave. I threw up again after the twelfth, and still he made me finish the last one as well as the other half of the one I'd abandoned.

And through it all, he watched me with fascination. I'd never had someone's focus for so long. Never felt so intensely scrutinized. Never understood the real meaning of helplessness.

Finally, when all sixteen of the cigarettes were butts in the glass bowl, my punishment was finished. Without a word, Stark dumped the ashes in the wastebasket along with the empty pack and pocketed the lighter.

"Empty the trash on your way out," he said, pulling a file off a stack and opening it up, his attention now fully on work. He didn't spare me another glance. He was done with me. He'd moved on.

I stared at him, my head pounding, my body shaking, my stomach threatening to retch again, even though I'd emptied it completely.

Then, because he'd proven his point—that he was the one in control, and I had no say—I pulled the trash bag from the can and took it with me when I left.

FIVE
CADE

There was still one more class on my schedule, but I skipped it. I wouldn't have made it through the lesson, even if I'd wanted to. Just crossing the half mile to get to our house had felt like an achievement. I'd had to stop several times, my head pounding so hard I thought it would explode, my stomach churning like there was still something in it left to expel.

When the walking path made its final curve leading to our yard, I almost collapsed in relief. I'd never thought I'd be so thankful to see that damn front porch.

Even more reason to be thankful was the sight of my mother on her knees, weeding the flowerbeds in front of the house. We'd remained at odds since my arrival, but like the little boy I'd once been who sought her out to kiss away my boo-boos, she was exactly the person I needed now.

She stood when she saw me, bringing a glove-clad hand up to shield her eyes from the sun. "Cade? School's not over. Why are you home early?"

Then I was close enough for her to see me better, or the sun moved, because her hand fell, and her eyes grew wide. "What's wrong?" she asked, closing the distance between us. "You look terrible. Did something happen?"

I responded by bending over, my hands on my thighs, and retched in her petunias. They were pretty much dead, anyway.

"Oh, honey, are you sick?"

I felt too awful to give her a snide response—obviously, I was sick—and too grateful for the garden apron she handed me to wipe my mouth.

When I was upright again, she stepped closer, wrapping her arms around me while she pressed her lips to my forehead. "You're not warm. What's that smell?" Her nose wrinkled as she got a good inhale.

Immediately, she stepped away, her brief demonstration of compassion already over. "God, you smell like a smoking lounge on a Friday night. Was it just tobacco, or were you messing with marijuana? That stuff can be laced, you know. You have no idea if you're getting straight plant or if it's got some PCP, and if you're getting drugs from someone on campus, you need to let Langdon—"

I cut her off. "Langdon is the reason I smell like this." It was the first time I'd spoken since I'd left his office, and damn did I need a glass of water. My throat was on fire.

I crossed to the spout on the front of the house and turned it on, then cupped my hands to bring water to my mouth.

"Don't be cryptic, Cade. What are you talking about?" Annoyance was heavy in her tone.

I drank a little more, careful not to drink too much in fear of another bout of nausea, then turned the spout off and turned to her. "I'm talking about your husband. He's a monster. He made me sit in his office and smoke an entire pack of cigarettes. That's why I look like shit. That's why I'm puking in your flowers."

She visibly rolled her eyes. "I'm really not in the mood for whatever this—"

Angrily, I cut her off. "*You're* not in the mood? Do you think *I'm* in the mood to feel like this?"

"If you're messing around with cigarettes, then I'm sorry, but you get what you deserve."

"This wasn't me, Mom. Would you listen to me for half a second? Really listen?" I waited until she gave me her full attention. "Your husband—my headmaster—sat me down in his office for two hours with a pack of cigarettes and then made me smoke every single one of them." I spoke slowly, spelling it out to her like she was a child.

Finally, she seemed to process what I was saying.

Or at least tried to process. "What do you mean *made* you? You can't force someone to—"

"You can if you threaten them. Look." I'd almost forgotten about the stripe on my palms, too distracted by the effects of chain smoking. I showed her now. "This is from a whip he keeps in his office." I only now thought to question why he had it. What he used it for. Who he used it on. "He threatened to give me more lashes if I didn't smoke them all."

She took off her garden gloves and tossed them to the ground before reaching for my right hand. Then my left. Concern marked her features as she examined the marks, though I could sense she was still wary. "You didn't do this to yourself?"

"How could I do this to myself?"

"You didn't have a friend do this?"

"Why would I have a friend do this to me?"

"Because you want to make your stepfather into the bad guy. You wanted to frame him or something."

I was growing impatient. I'd come home intent on telling my mother right away what had happened. I didn't think I'd have to convince her it was true.

Still, I knew screaming at her wouldn't get me anywhere, so I took a deep breath and tried to remain calm. "I'm not trying to frame him, Mom, or make him a bad guy. I'm trying to tell you that he *is* a bad guy. I swear on my life, this was him."

She dropped my hands and hugged herself, as though she was the one who needed the comfort. As though finding out her new husband wasn't the knight in shining armor she wanted him to be would completely alter her world.

I supposed she wasn't wrong about that.

"Why? Why would he do something like this?" It no longer sounded like skepticism but an attempt to grapple with what I was telling her.

I'd spent the whole time in his office asking myself the same thing. "I don't know. He's cruel, I think. I think he liked punishing me."

I couldn't get the image of the gleeful way he'd looked at me while I suffered out of my head. He'd definitely enjoyed it. Thinking about it made me feel sick again. And small. And embarrassed for some reason that I couldn't explain.

"Why was he punishing you? Did you do something?"

"Well, I mean." I considered lying, then thought better of it. "Yes. I did something. He caught me smoking—"

"You said he *made* you smoke."

"He did! Not the first one, though. I was out with some of the guys, okay? It was just one cigarette. I bummed it from another kid. Stark caught us, and even though the cigarettes weren't mine, I'm the only one he took to his office. And then he spent the next two hours forcing me to smoke the rest of the pack. Sixteen cigarettes, Mom. One after another. No break."

"Oh, Cade." She let out another sigh, her head shaking as she dropped her arms to her side. "He was teaching you a lesson."

My heartbeat felt heavy. I was losing her. "That wasn't what that was."

"He was. He was teaching you a lesson about smoking."

"He was *torturing* a minor."

"You're so dramatic. It was a punishment with a moral. And, yes, punishments are uncomfortable. That's the whole point of them." She bent to pick up the apron I'd dropped and her discarded gloves, clearly having made her assessment of the situation and ready to move on.

I followed after her as she cleaned up. "This goes beyond uncomfortable, Mom. I'm pretty sure it's not even legal."

"It's extreme, yes. But sometimes extremism is called for. He's trying to teach you why smoking is bad. You haven't had a father in your life, so I can see why this sort of parental guidance could come as a shock, but honestly, you need this. This is exactly the kind of discipline you've been lacking."

I might not have ever had a father, but after a year observing Mr. Goodie with his children, I'd seen what responsible parenting looked like, and this was not it.

But that wasn't the part of her lecture that struck a nerve. "How do you even know what the fuck I need?" Her head snapped back toward me, her expression disapproving, but I wasn't going to apologize for my language or my outburst. "You abandoned me. For a year. How could you possibly have any idea that I need discipline?"

"I know by your own admission that you were caught smoking, so don't even try to play innocent with me."

"Fine! I was smoking, and I'm evil, and I deserve harsh and unusual punishments to put me in line. Is that what you want to hear?"

"What I want is a little gratitude."

"Gratitude." I repeated the word, as if I'd be less shocked hearing it from my own lips. "Unbelievable."

"Oh my God, Cade, please. Stop." She turned toward me, her body sagging with a weariness that was almost disturbing. "You've only been here three weeks, and I'm exhausted. And you can't even give this place a chance." Her voice dropped, low and convicted. "This is the best we've had it; do you realize that? You have one year to get through. One year, and this is the best chance you have for a future. This home is the best opportunity I've ever given you. Ever given *us*. So fine. Go ahead and ruin it for yourself, but you're on your own with that. You aren't going to ruin it for me."

I took a step backward, stunned by her words. Feeling them as what they were—another abandonment. Another betrayal.

Another step back, and this time I bumped into a body.

I turned in time to catch Julianna before she fell. "Sorry," she said, as if she'd been the one to bump into me. "I was trying to slip by without interrupting."

Her eyes stuck on mine, and I could feel my skin heat. Had she heard what we'd been talking about? I hoped she hadn't. Not because I cared if I'd destroyed her thoughts about her dear old dad, but because of that odd embarrassed element. There was something humiliating about being punished. About being weak enough to be punishable.

As little as I thought about my stepsister, I didn't like the idea of her finding me weak.

I definitely didn't like the weird, warm way it felt to touch her. As soon as I was sure she was upright on her own, I let her go, shoving my wounded hands in my pockets.

"You're fine, honey," my mother said, stepping around me, her voice full of cheer that hadn't been there a moment before. "We were just... Oh, look at this mess in your way." She bent to pick up the trowel she'd left on the ground and her gardening pillow. "I didn't realize how late it had gotten. I should be cleaning up and starting dinner."

She was terrible at a subject change, but Julianna followed her with it. "Um, about that... It's Dad's night in Hartford."

"Oh, that's right. The Council for Northeast Private Educators." Her expression eased with the reminder, and the cheer in her voice now sounded much more authentic. "Well, that changes things. Should we order pizza, or I could do grilled cheese?"

Julianna bit her lip, and I tried not to stare. "Actually, I was hoping I could go to my study group again. It was really helpful last time. I can grab dinner with them."

"Yes, yes. Of course," my mother said, and I could practically hear the wink-wink in her tone. "You'll be back before...?"

"He won't even know I was gone," Julianna said, then scampered into the house, closing the screen door softly behind her.

Under other circumstances, I would have tried to analyze it more—the conspiratorial interaction, the relief my mother had at a night off from her spouse, the knowledge that little-miss-perfect Juliana took advantage of her father's absence.

But I was too consumed with my own feelings. The words my mother had uttered before Julianna had shown up echoed in my mind. *You're on your own. You're on your own.*

"Do *you* have a dinner preference?" my mother asked when we were alone again, as though everything between us was fine and dandy.

Like hell was I playing that game. "I'm on my own, remember? Looks like you are too." I followed Julianna into the house, but when I went in, I let the screen door slam.

SIX
CADE

I slept the rest of the afternoon and into the evening. When I woke up around nine, there was a plate with two cold grilled cheese sandwiches on my nightstand and a can of Coke. Sugary drinks weren't allowed in Stark's household, so I had a feeling it was meant to be an offering, but I was still too pissed to accept it.

The sandwich, though, I appreciated.

I still had the headache from earlier, but my stomach had calmed enough to want food, even cold. After inhaling the first one, I slowed down on the second, taking a bite of it then crossing to look out at the front yard as I continued to nibble.

As much time as I'd spent in my room over the last month—mostly trying to catch up from my late start to the school year—I hadn't explored the window. There was no screen, I noticed now, and the roof over the porch extended seven or eight inches underneath.

Holding the sandwich between my teeth, I opened the window. It was only about a three-foot drop to the roof. Four at most. I could easily get out, and it wouldn't be that hard to get back in.

As badly as I wanted an escape from my life, this small discovery felt enormous.

After grabbing a hoodie from my dresser, I sat down on the sill, swung my legs out over the extension, and dropped. Easy.

Instantly, I had my own hideout. *Fuckin' A.*

I crawled more to the center of the roof then sat down, brought my knees to my chest, and finished my sandwich. It was chilly, and I was glad I'd donned the extra layer, but beyond that the night was clear and peaceful. The stars were out. The moon, bright behind the treetops. The only sounds were of the crickets and the occasional hoot of an owl and the rustle of a breeze through the trees.

Then something that sounded husky. A tortured moan.

What?

I listened. Waited to hear it again. Less than a minute later, I did.

No, that wasn't a *tortured* moan. It was an *aroused* moan.

I crept toward the edge of the porch roof and looked for the source, finding it quickly—two figures sitting on the metal garden bench my mother had placed two weekends ago at the side of the drive near the bird bath.

Well, one figure sitting, the other kneeling with its head over the other's lap, the shadows of the night making it impossible to make out either person's identity.

Who the fuck...?

The moon peeked up over the canopy then, shining light on the yard. Antoine Birch was the figure sitting, his head thrown back in pleasure.

And even though I couldn't see her face, the figure bobbing up and down over Birch's exposed cock seemed to have the shape of Julianna.

Then he wasn't talking horseshit earlier about her reputation.

It was startling. But I felt more than surprised. I felt...

I didn't know what I felt, exactly. My chest burned and my breath felt shallow, and I didn't want to be watching, but I couldn't force myself to look away.

If I had to put a name to the emotion, it was anger.

Except I wasn't quite sure whom I was angry with. Or why. Or what to do about it.

So I just kept watching, finishing my sandwich in angry bites despite having lost my appetite. And a few minutes later, when Birch's body got rigid and his moan elongated, I kept watching as she sat back on her knees and wiped the back of her hand over her mouth, apparently having swallowed.

Lucky Birch.

No, not lucky Birch. This was my stepsister. A girl I barely knew, but my stepsister nonetheless. There was no fucking way I was going to think about her like *that*.

But I was definitely thinking about her. More than I had before. Wondering how I'd been so wrong about who she was. Curious about what other surprises she might have in store, and if there was anything to learn that might be useful. Or illuminating.

I continued to watch as they chatted afterward, their voices too low to make out. There was no cuddling or kissing or anything to suggest the act had been romantic, and Birch didn't make any move to reciprocate. Prick. Eventually, he pulled out a pack of smokes and lit a cigarette which he ended up sharing with her.

Strangely, that seemed even more intimate than the blow job.

Also strange was how I was suddenly jonesing for a smoke myself despite how terrible I'd felt all day. *Great lesson, Langdon. All you got me was hooked, asshole.*

When the cigarette was burned down to a butt, the two stood up, and I crept back away from the edge, returning to my seclusion and my thoughts. Thoughts now centered less on my mother and the man she'd married and more on the other member of our household.

My solitude didn't last long after that.

"Oh, wow. This is really high," Julianna said, her voice behind me.

Startled, my head flew to my window where she was perched cautiously on the sill, peering down at the ground, obviously anxious about the distance.

I was equally anxious, but not about the height. *What the fuck was she doing in my room?*

"You're lucky," she continued, making herself comfortable. "My window doesn't have access to the roof like this. If it did, I'd probably be too scared to climb out." She shivered.

"It's not really that..." I was distracted by the length of her neck as she tilted it up to look at the sky. I hadn't realized how pretty her throat was. Or that women could have pretty throats. "What do you want?" I snapped, suddenly irritated.

She shrugged. "Just wanted to know if you enjoyed the show."

It took me a beat to get what she was referring to. "If you don't want to be watched, maybe don't do your thing in public."

"Not really many options around here."

"I guess not."

She didn't say anything after that, and I tried to ignore her. Tried to pretend she wasn't there, breathing the same night air, sharing in my escape.

But even silent, even not looking at her, she was still *there*. Present. With me.

"Brought you something," she said after an eternity had passed. "Though, after this afternoon, maybe you don't want them."

Intrigued, I glanced back to see her waving a pack of cigarettes and a lighter.

"How did you...?" Had she overheard me and my mother talking after all? I could feel embarrassment creeping up all over again.

"Antoine told me you took the fall for him and Troy. Figured you deserved them as a reward, but maybe you're done with them after getting caught."

So she didn't know the whole story. That was a relief.

Not willing to ignore a gift when I got so few, I crawled over until I was in reach of her. Then I stretched my hand out, my heart jumping when my finger accidentally brushed her skin as I accepted the offering.

Leaning back onto my heels, I took out a cigarette and lit it. When I tried to hand the rest back, she shook her head. "Keep them."

I shoved them in the pocket of my hoodie and kept one hand in there as I inhaled. "Are these from you or from him?"

"I asked him if I could have them. He didn't ask who they were for. I'm sure he assumed they were for me."

"Awfully nice of him to give up a whole pack. Especially when he lost one earlier." Though money wasn't an issue for him, it couldn't be easy to get smokes on a closed campus.

"Well, I'd been awfully nice to him, as you saw..."

For the briefest second, I wondered if that was the whole reason she'd sucked him off—so she could get cigarettes to give to me.

Then I realized how stupid that thought was. Not everything was about me. In fact, according to my mother, very few things were.

"Birch your boyfriend?" I knew from what he'd said earlier that they weren't together but was curious what she'd say.

She stared off in the distance. "Nah. Honestly, I don't even think he likes me very much. He just gets off on fooling around with the headmaster's daughter."

I wanted to ask her why she did it then, but that felt too personal.

Besides, the thought of her potentially gushing over Antoine Birch made me nauseated for some reason.

Actually, it was probably just the cigarette because I certainly didn't give a flying fuck about who Julianna Stark gushed over.

Did I?

"I have something else for you too." She shook a tin of mints. "I'll leave them on your dresser. Dad doesn't have the best sense of smell, but I'm paranoid."

"Thanks," I said, not sure what to make of her kindness. Not sure what to make of her at all.

"Anytime." She stood, but she kept her head out, and I could sense she had something more to say for several beats before she spoke. "It could have been worse."

"What could have?" *Did* she know what her father had done? Was she guessing?

She ignored my question. "It *will* be worse. You're going to have to figure out how you're going to survive here or..."

"Or what?"

"Or...you just won't."

Strange advice. *Ominous* advice. I took a long draw on my cigarette, stared into the night, and tried to process all of it. This house. This situation. This girl, with her pale eyes and serious expression and lush lips.

Lips that had, less than thirty minutes before, been wrapped around another boy's cock.

When I turned back to look at her again, I was surprised to find I was disappointed that she was gone.

SEVEN
JOLIE

Present

The house smelled exactly the same—a combination of Lysol and home cooking—and with a single inhalation, I was swept back to the past. With Cade right behind me, it was the good memories that came first. Some of the best moments of my life were associated with him in this place.

I glanced at the hallway upstairs, halfway expecting to see the ghost of my former self peeking through the railing. The first time I'd seen him, he'd stolen my breath. How long after had he stolen my heart?

But then came the other memories—the bad memories, the complicated memories—rolling in like a tornado, intent on destroying everything in its wake. My body had prepared for it before my mind, the constant fear. My shoulders were already tense. My ears were already straining for sounds of another person in the house. Hyperawareness switched on like it was a function of my autonomic system, as much a reflex as breathing and temperature regulation. *Where was he now? Was he close? Was he coming for me?*

The fact that I didn't hear him only heightened my tension.

"The living room's new," Cade said, reminding me that it had been seventeen years since he'd last been here.

Carla followed his gaze, her forehead creased. "I guess we had that redone after you'd gone. But it's definitely not new."

"A couple of years after graduation, I think," I said.

"So sorry I couldn't be here for that." Having been groomed to not display emotions in this household, Cade's voice seemed both out of place and to be expected. It occurred to me then that this might be harder for him than for me. I hadn't been thrown out of this house—I'd left voluntarily.

And damn, it was hard for me.

Without thinking, I reached out to take his hand and gave it a comforting squeeze. Who it was meant to comfort—him or me—I didn't know. I did know I couldn't imagine being here without him.

Carla cleared her throat. "I didn't expect to see you again so soon, Julianna. Considering how upset you were when you left, I'm surprised you're back."

Cade swung his attention toward me, eagerly picking up on details I'd continually refused to give him.

And now I had to give him something. Because if I didn't, he'd ask her. "I came last month. To ask my father for some money that he promised me years ago. He said no."

Put like that, it made it seem like the reasons I wanted my father gone were money related, which wasn't exactly the case. "It's more complicated than that," I amended. "But that's the gist of it."

He studied me. "He didn't need more reasons to be hated," he said, and I let out the breath I'd been holding, afraid that he'd press for more.

"No, he didn't." I was sure this wasn't the end of it, but at least it was the end of it for now.

"It's a good surprise," Carla said, her tone at odds with the statement, her eyes pinned on our interlaced hands. "Are you staying the night?"

"No, just dropping by." I started to drop Cade's hand, her attention making me feel ill at ease, but he wouldn't let mine go, a visible demonstration of defiance.

I didn't fight him, but the connection no longer felt soothing.

"You were in the area?"

"We, um." I looked to him, hoping he'd step in. When he didn't, I tried to remember what we'd practiced in the car. "We happened to both be in New York at the same time, and we met up, which led to a trip down memory lane, and on a whim, we thought we'd come up here. See how things have changed. See what's the same."

"My idea," he said, seeming to understand that that made more sense, considering the way my last visit had ended.

"He talked me into a day trip. I have to be back at my job on Monday." That last part was a spontaneous lie. An excuse not to stay.

Not a good enough excuse, apparently. "Monday is three days away. You can stay the weekend."

"I'm sure Langford would love that," Cade muttered too quietly for Carla to hear.

I jumped in with a smile before she asked him to repeat himself. "I think dinner is all we can promise."

"Then, I'll take what I can get." An awkward beat passed. "Well. I suppose we don't need to spend all evening standing in the foyer. Come on in."

She headed toward the dining room, leading us as though we were first-time guests and not family members. "It's nothing fancy tonight. You know I don't prepare extravagant meals when your father's away, so it's just homemade soup heated up, but I'll throw some rolls in the oven, and it should be enough."

I exchanged a glance with Cade. "Dad's not here?"

She grabbed a lace tablecloth from the dining hutch as soon as we entered the room—the table wouldn't be bare at this time of day if Dad was here.

"It was a testing day at school," she said, smoothing the cloth out and tugging one side so it fell evenly. "He doesn't need to be around for that, so he left early for the weekend."

"Left for where?" Cade asked.

"The cabin. Finally cold enough for ice fishing. It's the first time this season he's been able to get up there. Your father's gotten quite passionate about the sport."

"He's not my father." His hand tensed in mine.

In contrast, I felt mine relax.

He wasn't here. I didn't have to see him. What a relief. "He'll be gone all weekend?" I asked, just to be sure before I got too comfortable.

"Be back Sunday." She stood upright, the business with the tablecloth completed. This time when she smiled, it reached her eyes. "You could stay until then."

"We really hadn't planned—"

"We'll stay," Cade said, cutting me off.

I was too taken aback to hide my shock. "We will?"

He gave a one-shoulder shrug. "Seems silly to rush back. We have our luggage."

"Good," Carla said before I could argue. "You can have your old rooms. They both still have beds in them."

"They both have locks on the outside so you can keep us apart?"

This time she heard Cade's snide remark, and her smile fell. "I wouldn't know anything about that."

"No. Of course, you wouldn't."

"Cade..." I warned. I had no idea what his intentions were, but agreeing to stay then picking a fight seemed counterproductive.

"What?"

"Play nice."

The acid remained in his expression, but he did manage something that almost looked like a smile.

"Well," Carla said, breaking through the tension. "I'll put the bread in the oven if you want to set the table. We should use the china."

"The china?" I glanced at the cabinet against the far wall. We'd only ever brought the good dishes out on holidays.

"It's a special occasion," she explained, her tone flat. "Not every day my children return home for a visit. We should celebrate." With that, she disappeared through the swinging door into the kitchen.

As soon as she was gone, Cade dropped my hand—validating my suspicion that it had been a show—and opened the china cabinet.

"Why did you say we'd stay?" I hissed, taking the plate he handed to me.

"Why would we not?"

I set the dish on the table, then took the next one he offered. "Oh, I don't know. Because we hate it here?"

"Yeah. There is that. You could throw a plate. Maybe make you feel better."

"Very funny." The set was already missing a dish, and thinking about the circumstances surrounding that sent me down a rabbit hole of emotions, which was exactly why I didn't want to be here longer than necessary. Too many complicated memories.

Cade paused, holding the last plate instead of passing it over. "Did you hear her? 'My children.' Like we were once a happy family. And what's with this whole 'we should celebrate' act?"

There had been other parts of our conversation that had sparked my interest more than this, but I considered her words now. "Maybe it's easier for her to pretend that we were."

"That's an awfully generous outlook."

It was, I supposed. And maybe I was in a better position to have it than Cade since she hadn't been my mother, and she hadn't abandoned me.

More, though, I'd come to terms with something that I wasn't sure he'd yet realized. "To be fair, she was just as much his victim as we were."

His jaw tensed. "No." He waved the plate at me, emphasizing his point. "She doesn't get to be forgiven. She was complicit."

I didn't want to argue.

I also knew these feelings of his weren't going to go away. "Can you really spend two days here? Because I really don't know that I can."

He opened his mouth, then shut it.

When he opened it again, he sighed. "Look, I know it's not what we planned, and that this is awful. Probably even more awful than it seems on the surface. But this is really a blessing in disguise. It will give us more time to find the key, and who knows? Maybe we'll find something else useful. Or get something out of *her*." He gestured toward the kitchen, indicating his mother. "We have to remember why we're here."

Oh, I hadn't forgotten. The goal was to prove my father was involved in a sex trafficking ring or set him up for it.

"Besides, we can't go to the cabin while he's there. Might as well stay here until he's on his way back."

To succeed, we needed to get the key for the cabin safe from his home office and then use it to plant evidence, which meant my father couldn't be there. And he was right—staying here was our best chance, but that didn't uncoil the tight knot in my stomach. Even without my father present, fear remained. It was a stench soaked so deeply into the woodwork of our home that it lingered after the source was removed.

"And then we'll go to the cabin together, right?" I asked, needing confirmation that there would be something more between us before we had to be over.

Before he answered, his mother pressed through the swinging door with a crockpot full of soup in her hands. "It will be just another few minutes for the bread. Let me help you finish with the place settings."

We fell quickly into a rhythm from years ago—one of us putting out the goblets, another filling them with ice, the third following behind with a pitcher of water. The food came to the table in the same method, a practiced machine of serving, and when everything was in place—the head of the table left empty—several seconds passed before any of us dared to be the first to sit.

We'd been well trained.

It was Cade who pulled his chair out first. "Let's get at it. I'm starved."

We skipped the prayer, Cade immediately reaching for the ladle. I followed suit and put a warm roll on my plate before passing the basket to Carla. Once everyone was served, we preoccupied ourselves with eating, minutes passing with no one talking.

It didn't take long before the silence became heavy.

So much to say. So much better left unsaid. Opening conversation felt like walking into a minefield, and none of us wanted to be the one who took the first step. Even the most innocent comment could be a trigger.

I was the first to break. "I'd forgotten how good your cooking is, Carla."

"Hard to remember when you don't visit," she said.

And there went the first bomb.

I took a slow breath in but still didn't manage to hold back what came out. "Yes, I suppose missing out on your cooking is the price for my mental health and well-being. Perhaps it was a poor life choice."

Cade chuckled across from me.

"He looked for you, you know," she said casually, as though I'd simply been misplaced. "He wouldn't admit that to you, but he did."

I took a sip of water before I responded. "I figured he would. I didn't want to be found."

She shook her head in admonition. "Broke his heart when you took off. Broke mine too. It really wasn't fair to us the way you took off. It wasn't fair to—"

Wary of how she'd finish the sentence, I cut her off. "It wasn't fair to anyone. I get it. You want to know who it was fair to? Me. It was time I looked out for myself, and so I did." I stared at her pointedly, hoping she understood the boundaries that I'd set up for the conversation.

Hoping she wouldn't try to venture past them.

Thankfully, she stayed inside the bounds. "Seems to have done good for you. The blonde is a bit extreme, but you look well."

I gritted my teeth through the backhanded compliment. "Thank you. I am well."

"I have to say," she said, lifting her spoon to gesture toward her son. "I'm surprised you didn't immediately go looking for this one."

"I didn't want to be found either," Cade said, not missing a beat.

"I know. Your father looked for you too."

He was sitting across from me, but I could feel him go rigid as clearly as if I were pressed against him. "First of all, he's not my father. Second of all, if that man was looking for me, it could not have been for any good reason."

"I mean, do you blame him? After going to court like you did. After what you did to his daughter. And then just leaving when—"

"Carla," I interrupted quickly, not sure what to say but needing her not to finish her sentence.

Cade saved me from having to come up with more. "Have you somehow forgotten that he beat me to a pulp the last time I was here? I barely walked out of here. He broke two ribs. My face was swollen for a month. And you're talking to me about blame?"

"Rebellious behavior needs extreme parenting," she said, her volume reasonable, unlike his. "You kept pushing him and pushing him. What did you expect your father to do?"

Abruptly, he slammed his fist on the table, making his soup spill on the cloth. "He's not my goddamn father!" He stood up and threw his napkin on the table. "I've lost my appetite. I need a cigarette."

I watched Carla as she watched him storm away, looking for signs that she was upset. That had been the position I'd assumed as a teen— the peacekeeper. The comforter. The one who made sure no one else set off Daddy's temper.

Even in his absence, I found myself slipping back into the role. "It's hard to be back here."

Her eyes snapped back to mine. "You don't need to make excuses for him."

"I'm not. I'm explaining something about him. If you're looking to know your son, I thought it might help."

"So you know everything about the relationship between sons and their mothers, do you?"

"Carla... Please, don't make this bigger than what it is."

She ignored me. "And you know what's best for Cade?"

"I didn't say—"

"Is that why you haven't told him? Because you know what's best for him?"

I sat back, surprised she'd realized. Glad, too, since it would make this visit easier. Also, ashamed. Always ashamed.

"Or are you thinking about what's best for yourself?" she pressed.

I stared into my soup bowl. "You know why I haven't told him."

"Well, I wouldn't expect you to be completely honest about it. You never have been before. Why start now?"

The remark felt like a slap, but I tried not to react. It seemed like an especially bad idea since I didn't know if she actually knew the truth or if she was just referring to the truth she thought she knew.

For half a second, I considered just telling her. Considered clearing the air and putting everything on the table, and maybe I would have followed through if it were just the two of us.

But there was Cade.

And she was right—I was looking out for what was best for both of us, which meant keeping my mouth shut.

"I'm not trying to tell you what to do, Julianna," she said, her voice softer.

It's Jolie, I said in my head. "No, of course you're not."

"But this affects me too. What if I had said something I shouldn't?"

"You didn't. And I hope you won't. It would really mean a lot to me if you didn't."

She sat back in her chair, her expression thoughtful.

Like every other relationship in this household, my relationship with my stepmother was complex. For the most part, we'd understood each other, and when we didn't, we'd given each other grace, knowing that the things a woman did to survive weren't always easy to explain.

But that had been in the past.

We weren't the same women we'd been, and maybe her understanding had reached a limit. "He's going to find out eventually if you're going to keep up this..." She searched for the word. "This *couple* thing—"

"We're not a couple." We'd had one night together, but I wasn't stupid enough to think it meant anything. Not when he'd made it clear how angry he still was with me.

"You sure look together."

"It's temporary."

"Does he know that?"

I started to answer then got caught up in the possibility she alluded to. What if he didn't know we were fleeting? What if he wanted us to be more?

The bubble of hope quickly burst when I remembered why we could never be more. Because, as she'd just clearly pointed out, my secrets would eventually be revealed.

And this...this he could never know.

"I would have thought you would be happy to hear this was temporary," I said, swallowing past the lump in my throat.

She didn't hesitate. "I am. What the two of you are doing? It's sick. It was sick then; it's sick now. He's your brother."

And here was where *my* understanding reached its limit. "He's not my brother," I snapped. "He was never my brother. Just like you were never my mother."

She sat up straighter, taken aback by my outburst. "Ungrateful. Both of you have always been so ungrateful."

My first instinct was to backpedal. To apologize. To smooth her ruffled feathers and make her happy. Make her pleased.

But I was tired of those old habits. Hadn't I left them behind? Wasn't that why I'd run away and changed my name, so that I could be someone different? Someone who didn't kowtow and adulate and soothe? Someone who didn't stay and stay and stay, no matter what was said or done to me?

"You know what, Carla?" I threw my napkin into my soup bowl. "I'm not hungry anymore, either."

For the first time in my life, I got up from that damn dinner table and walked away.

EIGHT
JOLIE

I found Cade in his old bedroom, half sitting on the window frame with a lit cigarette, looking out over the front yard.

Leaning against the doorframe, I took advantage of being unnoticed and looked around. The room had been redone after he'd left years ago, and it had been redone again since I'd left. Now it seemed to function as a guest room, though I couldn't imagine who would ever visit. The walls had been painted real-estate beige, and the twin bed had been exchanged for a double with tan and gray bedding that was neither masculine nor feminine. The area rug that I'd helped pick last time was gone as well, leaving the wood floor exposed.

I tried not to make anything of the fact that my suitcase sat next to his against the dresser. Maybe he was fully intending to take mine down the hall and just hadn't gotten to it yet.

That was the scenario I should have been wanting, but a ridiculous flutter in the center of my chest said I hoped differently.

"Always the rebel," I said, ignoring my stupid, stupid heart.

He didn't startle at my presence, making me wonder how long he'd known I'd been standing there. After ashing out the cracked window, he held the pack out toward me. "Want one?"

His guilt-free smile made my stomach go topsy-turvy, and not just because his boldness made me nervous, despite my adult status and that I'd just been brave enough to leave the table downstairs. "No. I'm scared of getting caught." I shut the door, though, and crossed to him, reaching for his cigarette. "So I'll share yours instead."

He laughed, and this time my stomach did a complete flip. He'd so rarely been joyful in this house, and every time he had been, it lit me up like a firefly because his happiness was not only infectious, it belonged only to me.

It was scary how much I liked that it only belonged to me now too.

I tried to keep my head on why we were here. "Did you check out his office?"

"You didn't?" It surprised me when he shook his head. I'd thought for sure he would have done that as soon as he'd left me with his mother in the dining room.

"It was locked," he clarified. "Another good reason we're staying the night. I can slip down there after she's gone to sleep."

It needed to be him because he knew how to pick a lock, but I was the one who knew where he kept the spare key to the cabin safe and what it looked like. "We can slip down there together."

I waited for him to protest, but he didn't.

"This is new," he said, rapping a knuckle against the glass. It had been replaced after we'd been caught together with a window that only cranked open a few inches. "No late-night sneaking across the roof now. Yours got switched out too?"

"Naturally." I took a drag from the cigarette and blew it out the opening, watching the smoke mix with my breath in the cold air. "Except he didn't realize about the one in my bathroom."

His grin turned sly. "Too bad it's so cold. We could climb out for old time's sake."

It was a dizzying thought—going out on the roof always had my head spinning because of the height, but it was more than that. Recapturing even a sliver of that part of our lives was tempting. He'd been the most irresistible of drugs. A stimulant and an opioid all in one. One small hit, and I'd be paradoxically both soaring and numb.

But then I'd want more and more and more.

There was no more addictive escape than Cade Warren.

Was that really such a sin? Wanting to feel good? Finding pleasure and taking it? Finding love and holding it close?

Carla's accusations from earlier clung to me, and despite knowing better than to let her get to me, she'd gotten into my head. "Do you think we were *wrong*?" I asked when I handed back the cigarette.

He looked at me quizzically as he took a drag. "For us?"

"We were related."

"We weren't related."

"Related by marriage. We lived together."

"So?" He offered me the cigarette again, and when I shook my head, he tossed it out the window.

"So it's taboo."

That devious grin returned. "It's hot."

Unexpected arousal trickled between my thighs. He'd never acted like the wrongness of our situation had been a turn-on. "Yeah?"

"You're hot."

My breath caught as he wrapped an arm around me and drew me to him, standing up at the same time. My body flush against his, I could feel exactly how hot he thought it was. How hot he thought *I* was.

"It's funny," he said, his finger gliding along my collarbone, hidden beneath my sweater. "I thought you were hot *despite* being my stepsister back then. Now, being my stepsister might be part of what makes you so sexy."

His finger continued down, down, down. To my breast and tickled over my peaked nipple, drawing a gasp from me before he bent closer and danced his mouth over mine. "So. Fucking. Sexy."

The taunting made me insane, and I thought I'd die when he only brushed his mouth against my eager lips. Once, twice. I was on fire when he finally let me have his kiss, and though it had only been hours since he'd had his mouth on mine, it again felt new, like something I hadn't had in years. Decades.

It was intoxicating the way his lips pulled gently at mine, tugging and teasing before growing greedy, and the kiss turned sinful, his tongue giving an explicit demonstration of how deeply he wanted other parts of him to be buried inside of me. I gasped again when his hands slid inside my jeans and panties to grab my ass, and he hauled me against the rigid bar at my belly.

"I wasn't sure we were doing this again." It was true, but in the moment, I couldn't imagine the possibility of *not* doing it, and what I really meant was a warning for myself. *You really shouldn't be doing this again.*

It was a warning I had no plans to heed.

He nibbled along my jaw until his mouth was near my ear. "I hope that's not a problem because I really have to fuck you."

"I think I really need to be fucked." The words dissolved into a whimper as he pushed a long finger inside me and discovered how wet I was.

"Oh, baby, you do. You really, really do."

I spread my legs wider, inviting his finger to probe me deeper, even though the angle wasn't the best, and my jeans were restricting, and what I desperately wanted was much wider than his single finger. He humored me—or tormented me, depending on how I wanted to look at it—for a bit, kissing me and fingering me until I paid him back for the torture by rubbing my palm over the granite bulge in the front of his pants.

Abruptly, he broke away, and I was somewhat satisfied to find him breathing as heavily as I was.

Barely three seconds passed before he tore off his pullover and then reached for the bottom of my sweater to draw it over my head. He tossed it to the ground then palmed my breasts while I worked on unfastening his button-down.

"We never got to fuck in this room." He tweaked both my nipples at once, and I shivered from the jolt of pleasure-pain.

"There was that hand job that one Sunday." His shirt was finally open, and I paused to kiss the eagle tattoo across his chest. "When Daddy was at the cabin, and Carla was taking a nap."

"You kept stopping to listen because you swore you'd heard something."

"That must have been the worst hand job."

"The torture made me so fucking hot." He reached behind me to unclasp my bra. Once he'd freed my breasts, he gathered them in his hands, bringing me with him as he walked backward. When the back of his legs hit the bed, he sat down. Then he spent the next several minutes adoring my flesh with his tongue and teeth and hands.

"You were never this hot," he said after teasing one nipple to a swollen point. "And you were hot."

"You're misremembering."

"You were branded in my memory hot. I'm not misremembering anything."

My chest squeezed at his subtext—*I never forgot you. I never moved on.*

I knew it to be true without him saying it. Knew it as profoundly as I knew that I hadn't gotten over him, and the ramifications of that honesty ached so much that I pulled away with the noble intent of putting an end to this before we were further consumed by this desire.

But as soon as I was out of his arms, I knew the only place I was going was back in them.

"I got something when we stopped for gas," I said, giving a reason for my retreat by going to my bag and pulling out the box I'd purchased while he'd been in the bathroom.

He raised an inquisitive brow. "You didn't think we were still doing this, and yet you have condoms?"

"I'd hoped we would."

He reached into his back pocket and pulled out three single condoms, the kind that looked like they'd come from a restroom dispenser. "I'd decided we would." He stood just long enough to toe off his shoes and finish undressing. "Get naked, and get over here."

I stripped as quickly as I could, then grabbed a condom and straddled his lap. I'd never straddled him like this, never been the one to sheathe him, and yet there was a strange sense of déjà vu as I unrolled the latex over his length.

I might not have ever lived this, but I'd imagined it. Imagined it in detail. Imagined it happening in this room, in a smaller bed. Imagined it while...

Just before I climbed onto him, I was hit with a sudden memory. "You fucked Amelia in here."

It was a statement because in my gut I was sure, but it was also a question since I'd never gotten him to confirm.

Seventeen years later, his mouth split into a guilty grin. "I did. I did."

"I knew it!" That fucker. "I was so jealous."

"Get on my cock, and then you can tell me." He was already guiding me over his jutting erection, so all I had to do was sink down, and he was filling me.

"So, so jealous." I bit my lip, the sudden intrusion of him dominating all other thoughts and sensations. It felt like I was being stretched past my limit, not just physically but mentally. Emotionally too. Every part of me going taut as he pushed his way inside me.

"So jealous," he repeated. "I like you jealous."

I was still adjusting to him when he clamped his hands on my hips and tilted me forward, coaxing me to move.

At his urging, I lifted myself up an inch, then dropped back down. Then repeated the motion, forcing myself to ride him when a part of me wanted to simply sit still and feel him twitching inside of me.

"Yes, do that," he encouraged. "Bounce on my cock, just like that." He helped me, digging his fingers into my skin as he lifted me up and down, setting a rapid tempo.

"Did you listen at the door?" he asked, his eyes pinned to where we were joined. "Did you hear how hard she was trying to be quiet?"

Did he really remember that? It made my stomach burn to think that he did, but lower, my belly felt tight, and my pussy tingled.

And to be fair, I remembered distinctly what I'd been doing, and it hadn't been listening at the door. "I laid on my bed and pretended I was her."

His eyes flew up to mine. "Fuck, are you serious? Did you fuck yourself with your fingers and imagine it was me?"

"Yes."

He groaned, and I swore he got thicker inside of me. "What part of me did you think about? My fingers or my cock?"

Probably both, though I couldn't remember for sure.

But my uninformed fantasies were not as interesting as what had been happening in this room at the same time. Certainly not as interesting as the way my core pulsed when I thought about what he'd done with her. "You tell me, Cade."

Abruptly, he flipped me over so that I was on the bed, my legs wrapped around his waist, and he was bent over me. "You want to know what I did with Amelia?" His thrusts were slow and shallow. "Really?"

"I do." I lifted my ass, wanting him deeper, but he held my hips in place and refused to give me all of him.

"We kept our clothes on," he said, pausing to lick across my nipple. "We were wearing our school uniforms, so I got her panties off her." Another pause, another swipe of his tongue. "She had that little school skirt on, which made her cunt easy to access."

My pussy clenched with his coarse words.

"Then I pulled her onto my lap." He kissed me. "And turned her around. Because when she wasn't facing me, I could pretend the pussy riding my cock belonged to you."

He shoved all the way inside of me, drawing a whimper out of my mouth that he swallowed with a rough kiss. His mouth stayed locked to mine as he found a new torturous tempo. The bed squeaked, the headboard thumped against the wall, and while a part of me worried Carla would hear downstairs, another part of me was sorry the whole school wouldn't hear, and I urged him on.

"Faster," I pleaded against his lips. "Deeper. More."

He gave what I asked for, his pelvis rubbing against me in just the right way. Combined with the insanely erotic talk, I could feel an orgasm building, even without clitoral stimulation.

He was aware of me, could feel me tensing around him. "Don't come," he said sharply, his rhythm unfaltering.

I couldn't stop it. Especially now that he'd uttered the command, I was definitely going to come.

"Do not come, Jolie."

"I need to come," I begged.

"Don't. Don't do it. You should be as tortured as you made me that day with that hand job."

I couldn't stop it. I was on the edge.

"You should be as tortured as you made me every day that I spent in this house, thinking of you sleeping in a room down the hall. You should be as tortured as you made me every time I heard your shower go on, and I had to beat off in my hand while I pictured you naked under the water. Do you feel that tortured yet?"

If he only knew.

If he only knew how tortured I'd been then. How tortured I was now. How tortured I'd been all the years we'd spent apart, and I'd fantasized of only him.

I couldn't keep on being tortured. I wouldn't last. I couldn't...

I burst suddenly, like a rainstorm on a summer's day, heat and sensation flooding over me in a giant wave. My vision dissolved into several black spots. My limbs quivered, and pleasure invaded me as every nerve ending in my body pulsed like the heavy beat at a dance club.

"Oh, you're going to come all over my cock? You're going to make a big mess all over it?" Cade pushed through my tightened opening, and I could tell from his ragged voice he wasn't far from letting go himself. "Who said you could do that? Huh? Who said you could?" The last words came out gritted as his body tensed and sputtered before he collapsed on the bed.

He recovered before I did. My breathing still uneven and my heart still racing, he pulled me to my side to face him and anchored an arm at my waist.

Then he kissed me. Slow and deep and tender.

When he pulled back, he brought his hand to my cheek. "I can give you money, Jolie. No matter how much you need. More than your father ever promised you. I won't even miss it."

I'd hoped he would forget that exchange. I'd known he'd take it as a reason for why I'd come to him, and he wasn't wrong.

He just wasn't exactly right, either.

"It's not about the money." I brought my knuckles up to brush along the short hair along his jaw to let him know I appreciated the offer. "It's about…" I trailed off, not sure how to explain without telling him all of it.

Even then, I wasn't sure he'd understand.

Then again, maybe he was the only one who actually could.

"It's about everything he ever did to us," I said, giving it my best shot. "To all of us. Every pain and ache he caused. Every happiness he denied. And then fuck him for taking this too."

I didn't realize the tear that slipped until Cade was wiping it away with a gentle press of his lips. "We're going to destroy him, Jolie. I promise. We'll get him."

I believed him.

I only worried who else would be destroyed along the way.

NINE
CADE

Past

Amelia saw me as soon as I entered the library. "What happened?" she whisper-asked after throwing her arms around me in a blatant display of affection. "Did you get detention? Are you still going to be able to go on the New York City trip?"

She knew I'd just come from Stark's office—in trouble this time for walking on the lawn, which was dumb because *everyone* walked on the lawn without repercussions, not to mention that it was November, and we'd already had our first snowfall, and all the grass was dead.

But I'd become a target for the headmaster. I wasn't the only student he singled out, definitely wasn't the only one who got sent to his office, but when I'd compared my punishments to other kids, there was definitely a discrepancy. Birch usually got sent to detention for his stunts. Troy would be assigned extra papers. Alice Erickson had been scolded for not wearing an appropriate uniform and sent to her room to change.

No one I'd talked to had ever received physical discipline. No one else had been made to smoke entire packs of cigarettes or been struck with a yardstick along the back of their thighs or been locked in a cramped cupboard for several hours.

Today, I'd been forced to drink three 24-ounce bottles of water over three hours without being allowed to go to the bathroom. He hadn't stayed with me the whole time, thank God, but he'd strapped me to the chair so I couldn't leave. I'd considered urinating all over myself just to piss him off, but experience had told me that would only end up making the situation worse for myself.

I'd just gotten to the point where relieving myself was no longer a choice when he'd let me go.

I wasn't going to admit that to Amelia. It was too embarrassing. It made me feel weak. And what if she was like my mother and didn't believe me?

It was much easier to lie about my visits to his office.

"Just a talking to," I whispered after giving her a brief kiss. "You know how he is. He thinks he has to make examples of bad behavior or else no one will think he's doing his job."

"You have such a good attitude." She leaned in to kiss me again.

"Amelia Lu," Ms. Coates' voice cut sharply across the quiet library. "Study hall means study, not make-out sessions with your boyfriend."

"He's not my boyfriend," she muttered with an eye roll as she disentangled herself from me. Louder she said, "Sorry, Ms. Coates."

"And where are you supposed to be, Mr. Warren?"

"Mr. Garner sent me for a reference book," I lied. I was supposed to be in Physics with Ms. Ruiz, and I couldn't imagine a scenario where she'd send me to the library for a book during class.

"Better get to it then," Ms. Coates said before turning her attention to another student who had a question about the internet restrictions.

"I'll talk to you later," I promised Amelia, squeezing her ass quickly before letting her get back to her studying. She was a sweet girl—too sweet for me to be messing around with, probably, but she'd been the one to pursue me. When I'd told her I was only interested in a physical relationship, she'd shrugged her shoulders, got down on her knees, and sucked me off right then.

Who was I to question her ability to stay casual?

Okay, I knew there was potential to break her heart in the end; another Heather Price situation that would likely blow up in my face eventually. Her "he's not my boyfriend" statement had been made for my benefit, because she certainly acted like she thought I was her boyfriend most of the time, which was exactly why I should have been running in the other direction.

But doing the right thing with Amelia was hardly on my priority list. I didn't have the bandwidth for such nobility. School was harder than I was used to. Living in the Stark household was practically like living in a prison, and with him constantly on my ass, sex had been a welcome stress reliever.

After today, though, I needed more than an escape. I was worked up enough to seek an action plan. Since I had zero power in this situation, I needed an ally, and while I wasn't ready to share the truth with Amelia—she wasn't really in a position to help anyway—there was someone who I was pretty sure had some insight, and she had study hall right now too.

I found Julianna in a quiet corner of the library, alone at a circular table with several schoolbooks spread out in front of her, the picture-perfect student.

Except that instead of studying, she was wrapped up in a women's magazine.

It had to have been borrowed. Her father didn't approve of any reading that wasn't highbrow literature. She wasn't allowed much television viewing either, and the guy was so insane about her study habits that he sometimes bolted her in her room with a lock on the outside.

Because Stark was so controlling of her free time—and to an extent, mine as well—I'd barely talked to her since the night she'd given me the cigarettes. Every now and then I'd find another pack left in my bag that

I assumed was from her, but I suspected she passed them to me during school hours because we barely had access to each other at home.

She was sneaky about it, though. Most of the time she'd kept a distance. More than once, I'd tried to engage with her in between classes, but even if there was no one else around, she always managed to dodge me or brush me off. It wasn't even like all I wanted to talk about was her father and his abuse—though I definitely wanted to talk about that.

But I also wanted to just...talk. It was weird to live so close to someone who was practically a stranger. To look at her across the dinner table, unable to ask about her day. To work on my homework at my desk and know she was down the hall, her head buried in the same textbook. To stare at the ceiling when I couldn't fall asleep and wonder if she was awake as well.

My curiosity about her felt dangerous, though. For reasons I couldn't express, and so I hadn't made as much effort as I might have. I could have ditched Physics and cornered her in the library before now. Instead of hanging out at the school, I could have walked home with her once or twice. The night of Stark's November educator meeting, I could have tried to approach her instead of inviting Amelia over "to study," turning my radio on full blast, and fucking her with my eyes closed while trying really hard to keep my mind from wandering.

After this afternoon, I'd decided I needed to redefine dangerous.

"We need to talk," I said quietly, plopping in the chair next to her.

She jumped, instinctively trying to hide her magazine. As soon as she realized it was me, she pulled it out again. "No, we don't."

"We do." I pushed the magazine down to see her face. "Stop trying to avoid this. You're the one who warned me about needing to find a way to survive here."

"And it seems you did." Her tone was strangely bitter.

I followed her line of sight, my gaze landing on Amelia.

"Yes. She helps," I admitted. But that wasn't the point of me bringing it up. "How did you know, though?"

"Amelia has loose lips. She's told everyone she's with the new boy. Spoiler if you hadn't figured that out yet."

I fought off the impulse to be irritated about news that Amelia was indeed claiming me as hers. "I meant..." I paused when the librarian walked by until she was out of earshot. "I meant, how did you know I needed a method to survive?"

"I don't know what you're asking."

"You do, but you don't want to say it." I'd thought a lot about this over the last several weeks, especially today during those three hours strapped to Stark's chair, and I was convinced of my theory. "You *know* what your father does to me. At first, I thought you knew because he must have been abusive to everyone. That he punished lots of kids like that. But he doesn't, does he?"

She avoided eye contact. "I guess it depends on your definition of abusive."

"Cut the bullshit, Julianna."

She looked at me then, her jaw tight, her mouth a firm line. "What exactly are you getting at? If you want me to talk straight, maybe you should lead by example."

I thought I'd been pretty forward already, but I zeroed in even more. "Your father doles out severe punishments in that office of his. To me. Did you know that, yes or no?"

She let out a sigh before nodding.

"He doesn't severely punish other kids though, does he?"

Her shoulders sank as she shook her head back and forth.

It was a relief to be validated. Part of me had wondered if everyone was lying, all of us too scared to share our true stories.

But with validation came other emotions. Other questions. "Then how did you know? If he doesn't do this all the time, how did you know he did it to me?"

She shut her magazine, dropped it on the table, and stood up. Without a word, she headed down a row of biographies.

Like hell she was walking away from me. I jumped up after her. "How did you know, Julianna?"

She got to the middle of the row, then turned her head toward me and snapped. "How do you think I knew?"

We were deep in the stacks here, and I realized she'd led me here, not to avoid the conversation, but to make sure we had more privacy while we had it. "I think you overheard me telling my mother that day," I said, sure of it in hindsight.

"And?"

This was the part that I hated verifying, but it was the answer that made the most sense. "And because he does it to you."

"Ding, ding, ding, ding." She crossed her arms over her chest, like she was trying to guard herself from me, or from saying too much, or because admitting the truth made her feel exposed, which I totally understood.

What I didn't understand was why the hell she ever got punished. "But you never get in trouble."

"And maybe that's why he thinks his punishments work."

I had to think about that longer than I should have.

I was such an idiot.

Of course, that was why she was always so perfectly behaved. Because she knew the repercussions if she wasn't. Just because I'd never seen her get in trouble didn't mean she hadn't in the past.

"How long has he...?" I couldn't finish the question. He was her actual father. She'd lived with him all her life.

"It seems you're figuring that answer out for yourself."

That was hard to get my head around. I'd been dealing with the abuse for a little more than a month and was already at the end of my rope. How had she managed to cope?

Suddenly, I found her promiscuous behavior less curious.

After a silent beat passed, she lowered her defenses. "He's been better since you've been here. Sorry about that. I guess I should say thank you for giving him a distraction."

"You're not welcome."

She let out a defeated breath of air and her shoulders crumpled, and I worried she might cry.

"Don't, don't." I put my hand on her arm to comfort her and felt an unexpected jolt to my pulse that made me drop my hand instantly. "It's really not that bad."

"You don't need to lie."

"Okay, it's pretty shitty."

"I know." She tried to laugh, and it turned into a groan. "I know!"

She covered her face with her hands and shook her head, and for the first time since I'd arrived in Wallingford, I wasn't thinking about myself first.

And it wasn't for me that I said what I said next. "We could tell someone." I'd abandoned that idea after every attempt to talk to my mother had gone badly. With someone else to back me up, it was a different story. I was already trying to decide if it would be better to call the police or tell a teacher. "We could—"

She cut me off with a definitive, "We can't. We can't tell anyone."

"Of course we can. We *have* to tell."

"No one will believe us."

"With both of us—"

She interrupted that notion before I could finish forming it. "Did your mother believe you?"

The mention of my mother stung. I swallowed hard before delivering the excuse I'd formed for her. "She doesn't want to believe anything bad about her husband. She has a stake in the matter. It's not about me."

Julianna's expression softened. She started to reach a hand out to comfort me, but before she made contact, I casually stepped back and leaned a shoulder against the bookshelf, afraid that I'd feel that strange shock again if we touched.

Afraid she'd open up something inside me that I very much wanted to remain closed.

"This community doesn't want to believe anything bad about Langdon Stark," she said, rubbing her fingers against the binding of a random book, as though that had always been what she'd intended to do.

"Then we tell the police."

"It won't make a difference."

"You can't know that."

"I *can* know that. I'm telling you, Cade, all it will do is make things worse." Her subtext was clear—she was speaking from experience.

There was a rustling, and I peeked between the books to see a student taking a novel off the shelf on the other side. After he'd moved on, I asked, "When?"

She knew exactly what I was asking. "A while ago. I was thirteen."

I wanted to know all the details but was well aware of where we were, that we weren't exactly alone, so I focused on what was important. "You're older now. More reliable. Plus, with me—"

"No. No way." She turned and strode to the end of the row, and when she didn't seem surprised that I'd followed, I suspected that once again she hadn't been trying to run away from me.

Even if it wasn't about taking us farther from eavesdroppers, I understood. I felt that same restless burst of energy at times. That same need to run, even though there was nowhere to run to. No one to run to.

"No," she said again when she spun back to me. "I can't. I can't do that. Not again."

Imagining the worst, I tried to reassure her. "Whatever he did, I'm sure it was horrible. But if we get him arrested—"

She cut me off again. "It's not that easy, Cade. People don't want to believe these things about a respected member of the community, and if he finds out we said anything—"

She caught her voice rising and took a beat to calm herself before going on. "It wasn't like you think. It wasn't a big punishment for telling on him. He didn't even guilt trip me, exactly. He...he told me he understood why I was confused. Because I was young and didn't understand that love sometimes was uncomfortable, and that everything he ever did was out of making me a better person, and it was just as hard for him to know I was hurting as it was for him to do the things he had to do, and one day maybe I'd understand how much he truly loves me..."

A tear slipped down her cheek, and before I could think about it, I reached out and wiped it away with my thumb.

I'd been right. That same shock. That same stutter of my heart.

It didn't feel quite as terrifying as it had that first time.

Then because she was staring at me with so much vulnerability, and because she seemed so sad, and because I wanted so much in that moment to be the person who fixed everything for her, and because I'd never had anyone look at me like she did, and because her skin was so soft under my thumb, I trailed it down her cheek and traced her jawline.

"That's not love," I said, softer than anything I'd said so far in our whispered conversation, but with more conviction. Which was saying something, because I didn't have the slightest clue what love was, but I knew it wasn't that. "That's not—"

Another student came around the far end of the aisle, her eyes searching through the rows for a specific book.

My hand fell as Julianna instantly backed away from me, putting distance between us.

I hadn't realized we'd been standing that close until the foot separating us felt too far apart. I hadn't realized how good she smelled or how her bottom lip stuck out when she frowned, how it begged to be...

"It's my senior year, okay?" she whispered, her eyes glancing cautiously toward the student. "I'm so close to getting out of here for good. Six months, and I turn eighteen. Then I'm gone. Please, don't fuck it up by stirring shit now."

At another time, I might have thought it was an unfair request. She wasn't the one in his office every week, and if she'd really suffered at his hand in the past, then she had to know what a terrible thing it was she was asking.

Or I might have realized that I had other options. I could run away. I'd already turned eighteen in October, and even if Stark had the intention of paying for my college, I might have decided that it wasn't worth another six months of abuse.

But right then, all I could think about was the way my thumb was still burning from the touch of Julianna's skin and the trust she tried to hide in her eyes and the way that getting the chance to stand this close to her felt worth any price.

"I'll think about it," I said, storming off before she could stop me or ask any other impossible favor, terrified that next time, the only answer I'd be capable of giving her was yes.

TEN
JOLIE

"...And I'm thankful to have a husband who supports and provides for us like he does. And I'm especially grateful that he's made it possible to spend this holiday with my son, Cade..."

I was only half listening to Carla's gratitude spiel and was busy concentrating on what version of *I'm thankful for my father* I'd give this year. It was the only reason he made us play this game of Go Around the Table and Be Grateful, so he could hear praise heaped on him. For years, it had just been me and him on Thanksgiving, and I was having a hard time getting past what I really wanted to say, which was *I'm grateful to finally not have to bestow all the compliments myself.*

There were other things I was grateful for. Surely.

Careful not to be too obvious about it, I shifted my gaze from Carla to Cade, and my heart stumbled when I found him already looking at me. His expression was stone, but I caught his quick eye roll over his mother's profuse speech and found myself biting back a smile.

"Oh, is it my turn?" he said, quickly looking away from me to my father.

I hadn't even noticed the pause in conversation.

My father's irritation was apparent before he said a word. "It is."

"Sorry about that, sir. I wasn't sure of the order. Let's see..." He was getting better at kissing ass, which was admirable, and hands down it was better for him to stay in line and keep his true self hidden.

But it also made me sad.

I liked his true self. I wanted to know more of it.

"I'm thankful for this food, obviously," he said. "My mom's a great cook."

"And for the person who bought it for us," Carla coached.

He ignored her. "I'm particularly grateful for it this year since I didn't get to have it last year."

I had to pinch my thigh so I wouldn't laugh. He still got those digs in where he could, often to his detriment.

Thankfully, my father hadn't seemed to notice or didn't care since it hadn't been aimed at him.

"Oh, and I'm really grateful for the drama trip tomorrow. It's super cool of Ms. Stacey to arrange an opportunity to spend a night in New York and for our headmaster to approve it." Cade always found a way to avoid addressing my father. He refused to call him Dad, and that was pretty much the only thing my father accepted besides sir.

But that wasn't what had my attention. "Cade's going on the drama trip?"

Dad's eye sparked in that way it always did when he knew he'd upset me. I'd learned a long time ago that he liked me better unhappy, and I often performed that emotion just to stay on his good side.

These days, I rarely let him see any real pain he'd caused, but I'd been too surprised by this hurt to shield it in time.

With a slight smile, my father admonished me. "Wait your turn, Julianna. Cade isn't finished yet."

"Actually, I kind of—"

I stepped on top of his muttering. "Why does Cade get to go on the drama trip?"

The smile faded from my father's lips. "Julianna. You're being rude."

It was a tone I recognized, and usually I was better at heeding the warning. "He said he's done, which means it's my turn, and I'd be grateful to know why Cade gets to go, and I don't."

"This isn't the time to discuss this, Julianna." No, he wanted to discuss it later, when we were alone. When he could punish me immediately for every word that came out of my mouth.

I didn't know exactly what it was that made this battle worth fighting versus every other battle that I ignored, except that it had to do with Cade. Maybe it had been easier to accept that I was treated differently when I was the only child at the school from the Stark household. Or maybe it was because his going was more in my face than the usual extracurricular activities I'd been kept from.

Or maybe it was because I knew Amelia was going too, and thinking of him staying overnight in the city made my stomach turn to stone.

Whatever the reason, I pressed on. "You said it wouldn't be appropriate. Remember? That there was 'too much of an opportunity for corruption,' and that you 'couldn't risk allowing a representative of the Stark name to be put in that environment.' You treat him like he's your son in every other situation. Nothing against you, Cade, but what's different this time?"

"No offense taken," Cade said a bit too cheerfully. I had a feeling he liked someone else being the dissenter for once.

"Is it because he's a guy? Or because you don't care what happens to him in a corrupt environment? Or because you just like seeing me miserable?"

Carla fidgeted at my side. "Julianna..." she cautioned.

"If you must know," my father said over her—he hated when she tried to play peacemaker, preferring to be the one controlling emotions. "Carla signed the permission form without asking me."

"Right. That was me," she said, taking the blame.

Oh.

That's what had been behind her squirming. I saw it now—her downcast eyes. It had been an argument between the two of them, and

I felt a little guilty for bringing it up, except that it didn't explain why Cade was still going. Why hadn't my father overridden her permission?

He told me before I'd decided whether or not I was going to ask. "She understands her mistake, and to make up for it, she's agreed to go as one of the chaperones. If Cade gets out of line, the fault will be Carla's."

Wow. I didn't want to be in her position. Even if Cade behaved the entire time, my father would find a way to be angry with his wife. She was set up to fail.

Which, of course, was her punishment. I wondered if she realized that too.

It didn't do any good feeling sorry for her. Her bed had been made, and there was no reason I shouldn't be able to take advantage of it. "If Carla's going, then the problem is solved! She can chaperone me as well as Cade."

Mostly Cade, though. She could keep him from sneaking out of his room to be with Amelia.

"No," my father said. As expected. "I'm not going to put that much on Carla."

"I really don't mind—" she began.

"It's too much responsibility for you." Coming from someone else, it might have sounded like he was only looking out for his wife. From my father, it was clear to everyone that he didn't believe she could handle it. That he wouldn't even give her the opportunity to prove she could.

I wasn't especially fond of my stepmother, but we did share an unspoken camaraderie. The only two women in a traditional household—it was impossible not to be somewhat bonded. "She could handle it," I said, breaking one of the most important of my father's rules—no ganging up on him. "I wouldn't give her any trouble at all."

"I said no."

It was past the point of when I should have dropped it.

Still, I tried another of his favorite tactics: flattery. "You know what, Daddy? You should come too! Make it a family trip. You're so committed to your work and to us. When do you get a break? You deserve a—"

"I said no!" The table shook from the force of his fist against it. "Cade and Carla will leave as planned in the morning, and while they are gone, it seems you and I will need to have a lengthy discussion about your behavior today."

My stomach sank, taking my whole body with it. It had been a while since I'd had to suffer through "a lengthy discussion." I'd gotten so incredibly good at following the rules, and having Carla and Cade around had given my father other targets. With the two of us alone, it would be especially bad.

My fault. I'd known better. I shouldn't have pushed.

I couldn't swallow past the ball in my throat to offer an apology, though, and I knew he was waiting for one.

He only gave it a few seconds before lashing out again. "You've ruined Thanksgiving, Julianna. I don't even want to hear what you're grateful for now, and the food is getting cold. Pass the yams, Carla. Hopefully, the cooking will salvage the meal."

I tried to be thankful that I'd at least gotten out of the torture of that speech, but I knew it was another mark against me. Another thing I'd be "talked to" about this weekend. It was hard not to agree with him—I had ruined Thanksgiving. Not that the day was all that special to begin with. There wasn't any day in this house that was special. There were just days that were easier to survive than others.

Today was looking like an "other."

Heavy silence shrouded us for the rest of dinner. The cooking, it turned out, was not good enough to salvage anything. Not for me, anyway. Everything tasted the same, none of it very good, and soon I was moving things around on my plate more than I was putting them in my mouth. In the quiet, the rhythmic tick-tock of the grandfather clock sounded loud, boring into my head until I couldn't help but think it wasn't the clock at all, but the ticking of a bomb hidden deep inside me, getting closer and closer to going off.

The second my father put down his fork, I jumped up. "I'll start cleanup."

I gathered my dishes and Carla's—she was busy loading my father up with a second plate, which thankfully I wasn't required to sit through—and headed into the kitchen, but not before Cade jumped up as well. "I'm done too."

"You aren't going to eat more?" Carla sounded as hurt about this as if he'd turned down a hug. "It's Thanksgiving!"

"Saving room for pie," he said, then the door shut behind me, and I didn't hear anything else until he was pushing into the kitchen with his own dishes. "Thank God that meal is over. How about adding that to my gratitude list?"

I feigned a laugh, still too upset to give him anything sincere, and started in on the dishwasher. It was my nightly chore to load. Cade's chore was to help his mother clean up the table and then take out trash, and later he'd put the dishes away. Before he'd arrived, I'd been in charge of all of it and was generally happy with how the jobs had been divvied up, even if I found it a bit sexist.

Except it was a holiday.

Which meant we'd used a lot of cooking dishes plus the china. And that meant handwashing the china since it wasn't dishwasher safe, as well as the dishes that didn't fit in the first load since my father refused to let anything sit in the sink for more than the space of a meal.

So I was still elbows deep in suds by the time the dining room table was cleared and Cade had returned from his trip outside with the garbage.

I didn't turn to look behind me when he came back in, but the hair stood up at the back of my neck, and I could swear he was staring at me.

"Want some help?" he said after a minute.

Teeth gritted, I shook my head, quite used to being alone in my misery.

"Let me rephrase—because I'm pretty sure you don't know how to accept a favor—move over, and hand me a dish." He was reaching for the rose-patterned china plate in my hand before I'd even noticed he was next to me, sleeves rolled up, ready to rinse.

I scowled, unpracticed at receiving anything good—he was right about me there—but I handed him the plate all the same, and with him by my side, I wondered if I'd been too hasty the week before in the library when I'd told him we couldn't do anything about my father.

I hadn't changed my mind about the inability to get away with it. But I was mad, and anger made the revenge fantasy so much sweeter.

I didn't get even a full minute of daydreaming in before Cade interrupted it. "I'm sorry." When I didn't say anything, he added, "For the trip. I hadn't realized he was the reason you hadn't signed up."

I gave him an incredulous stare. "You can't be that naive."

He laughed. "I can be. Mostly because I didn't think too much about it. And I didn't think too much about it because I didn't want to feel guilty about it. I'm sorry for that too."

It helped, and it didn't. I wasn't ready to let go of my wrath, but it wasn't him I was mad at. "I'm the one who should be apologizing to you." I handed him another plate. "He could have said you couldn't go anymore just because I brought it up."

Of course, then he wouldn't have the opportunity to administer a lengthy punishment. Not that having Carla or Cade around made much difference. When my father shut himself in a room with someone, everyone else knew better than to interrupt.

"Wouldn't have been the end of the world," he said with a shrug.

Again, the look I gave him said I didn't believe him for one second.

He grinned. "All right. It would have sucked ass, but I get it. I didn't take it personally at all."

I hadn't really been feeling guilty about it, but I did appreciate the permission not to.

"And you didn't ruin Thanksgiving," he continued. "It was terrible to begin with."

"It was terrible to begin with," I said at the exact same time.

We laughed, and I handed him another plate. "I'm not usually so bothered by how terrible it is," I said when the amusement had faded.

"I don't look at it, really. But it all stacks up, and it's like there must be a sensor in my brain that doesn't register until the terribleness gets to a certain point, and then an alarm goes off, and I have to look, and when I do the only way I can react is to just...grrrr." My grip tightened on the dish in my hand as I pretended I was shaking my father.

"I honestly don't know how you do it. I think I would have gone crazy by now."

"Who says I haven't?"

"Even the way he talks to you is infuriating. 'Julianna, you're being rude.'" He mocked my father with an accuracy that made me have to attempt the same.

"'Julianna, don't interrupt.'" I scrubbed at the cranberry stain. "'Julianna, be perfect.' I don't know if it's the way he says it or the name in general, but I hate it. I hate what it stands for. I hate who she is. Julianna Who Does Everything Right. Julianna Who Never Upsets Him. She's so proper. So well behaved. What if that's not who I really am? What if I'm really someone else? Someone not Julianna."

"Julie," he suggested.

I cringed. "Too close."

"Jerico."

"Too far off." I sighed. "That's the problem. I've been so trained to be Julianna, I'd never look up if anyone called me something else."

I thought that had ended it, but then he said, "Jolie," and something happened in my chest. A pinching of some kind, like grabby hands clutching onto a much-wanted gift, refusing to let it go.

"Yeah, that's who I am. Jolie." Whether I liked it because it fit me or because he'd chosen it, I didn't know, but I instantly claimed it.

He tilted his head to study me. "Yeah? What are you like, Jolie?"

"Well, I'm not quiet, that's for sure." I passed the plate on, jolting at the zing through my body when I accidentally brushed his hand in the process. Hoping he didn't see my reaction, I turned away to grab another from the stack. "I'm very loud. And I openly smoke. And I kiss whatever boy I want when I want to. And I say 'fuck you' at the dinner table. And when I'm mad, I show I'm mad."

"Yeah, you do," he said, encouraging me. "How do you show you're mad?"

I let out an excited sort of giggle. Permission to express myself was not something anyone ever gave me, including myself, and it was empowering to imagine what I could do with that.

It was even more exciting that it was him who had given the permission. "I'd fucking tear out all the plants in that stupid garden of his, for one."

"Odd place to start, but I'll join you for it."

"And I'd take a sledgehammer to that lock he keeps on my door. And I'd take scissors to all his ties. And those short uniform skirts he makes us wear. And I'd break all his favorite albums in half. And his record player. I'd break everything I could get my hands on that he cared about. *Everything.* Every. Single. Thing."

The anger was too real, and giving voice to the things I fantasized made it too easy to get caught up in the destruction that I so very badly wanted to wield, and so when the impulse to throw the plate I was holding to the floor popped up, I didn't have time to calm myself down before I was hurling the dish across the room.

It hit the ground with a satisfying shatter.

Yes. That was exactly who I wanted to be.

We stared at the pieces of china for several seconds, my heart thudding like I'd just run the PE loop around the garden in record time.

"Oh, yeah," Cade said, and when his eyes hit mine, they locked onto some deep part of me, and suddenly, it felt like we were connected. Like the most basic parts of me were controlled by him. Like I didn't even breathe on my own anymore, and I didn't *want* to. I just wanted to keep being breathed by him.

Then reality hit. "Oh, shit."

I reached for a towel to dry off then went for the broom and dustpan. Cade was already stooped over the mess when I got back, several large pieces in his hands. "Probably too broken to just glue together."

He was joking. It was *definitely* too broken.

"He's going to kill me," I said, feeling that all-too-familiar panic. It was bad enough knowing I'd angered my father when I didn't deserve it. There was nothing I could do to prevent that wrath. When I brought it on myself, I only had one person to blame. "This was my grandma's china. I'm not going to be able to walk for days."

Cade's expression was hard to read, but his eyes looked…concerned? "Maybe he won't notice. We'll clean it up; I'll take the pieces to the trash. He won't notice until Christmas when there's a plate missing." He knew that meant we'd just be delaying an inevitable punishment, so he added, "We'll deal with it then."

I'd deal with it. Not *we*.

Because he hadn't been the one to throw the plate. It hadn't even been his chore to deal with the dishes in the first place.

But before I could correct him, the door opened, and there was my father. "What was that crashing sound?" His eyes landed on us, giving him his answer. "What the hell did you do, Cade?"

The *wrong* answer, it turned out. Since Cade was the one holding the pieces, it was easy to see where he'd gotten the impression.

"No, no. It was me," I said quickly. "My hands were wet, and it just slipped out of my grip." That didn't explain how the dish had gotten all the way over here by the wall, and my father wasn't stupid.

He'd add it to my previous transgressions. He'd be sure I suffered for it.

"Don't do that for me," Cade said, standing up in a rush. I gave him a puzzled look, but he'd turned his attention to my father. "She's trying to cover for me, sir. I was horsing around and dropped it."

My father adopted his Very Mad face, which looked a lot like a Very Happy face in some respects. "This was my mother's china," he said. "It's an heirloom. They don't make replacements."

"I understand, sir, and I'm sorry."

"To my office. Now." He didn't have to say he expected me to finish cleaning the mess up. "And you can forget about that drama trip of yours. Expect to spend this weekend with me."

I could have spoken up, and I should have. But Cade shook his head sharply when I tried, and I knew enough about my father to guess that, if I tried to take the blame now, he'd rather punish us both than exert the effort to get to the real truth.

But I thought about it. The words were still at the tip of my tongue when Cade headed off to where he'd been sent. Were on the brink of falling out when my father paused to kiss my forehead.

By the time he'd left, following after Cade, they'd dissolved into nothing.

I brought the back of my hand to my mouth, holding back a sob. Guilt shook my body, but that wasn't the most overwhelming emotion.

Finally, for the first time that day, I was grateful.

Grateful that he hadn't let me tell the truth. Grateful that he'd helped me with the dishes in the first place. Grateful that he wasn't going on that trip with Amelia. Grateful that he'd found a way into my otherwise terrible life. Grateful that he'd let my father abuse him this time instead of me.

So grateful that it didn't occur to me until later to wonder why.

ELEVEN
CADE

Grabbing both my sweater and my undershirt together as I pushed through the door, I had them half off when I noticed my room wasn't empty.

"Jesus, Julianna." It only took a second to recover from surprise and move on to panic. "What the hell are you doing? You can't be in here."

Nothing had ever been said about being in each other's bedrooms, but I didn't need to be given a rule to know her father wouldn't like it. He confined her to her own room most of the time and had a deadbolt on the outside of her door. It was pretty obvious he wouldn't want her down the hall in mine.

I might not have been so concerned about pushing my limits if I wasn't already coming directly from a punishment—a punishment that hadn't even been mine.

I still didn't know why I'd taken the fall for her.

Or if I did know, I wasn't interested in admitting it.

"I needed to talk to you," she said in a whispered tone, as if her father could hear what we said from the floor below us. I was pretty positive he couldn't really hear us, but I completely understood the desire to be cautious.

It was the same desire that had me desperate to get her off my bed and out the door. "This is really not a good time. You need to leave."

She stood up, which was a relief, but also a distraction, especially when she didn't make any other move to go. While I'd been in her father's office, taking the blame for the broken dish, she'd gotten ready for bed. Two months I'd been in her house, and this was the first time I'd seen her in anything besides her school uniform and father-approved casual clothing. Tonight, she was in a nightie.

And it was short.

And pretty damn see-through.

Fuck. I was going to hell for staring at her tits like I was. For wanting to touch them. For wanting to rub my thumbs over the taut peaks.

Of course, I was already *in* hell, so it probably didn't matter what shitty thing I did, except that it would be pretty goddamn embarrassing to get a boner in front of my stepsister.

I ran my free hand over my face. I'd skipped my shave since it was a holiday, and the feel of stubble on my palm gave me something to concentrate on so that the blood wouldn't run south. My other hand was at my neck, still clutching the clothing that I'd only managed to get half off, and after a few seconds, I realized that maybe that was a good thing because she was too busy looking at my bare chest to notice how I'd been staring at hers.

I knew it was stupid to make anything of that.

I had a normal, average teenage male body, nothing impressive. Whether she'd seen many men shirtless or not, I had no idea. Her reputation didn't shed any light on the matter. Shirts didn't have to come off to do the kinds of things she was known to do. So she was probably looking because bare skin was new to her. Or she was curious. Definitely not because she found me attractive.

Still, her eyes on me made me stand a little taller. And when she lifted her gaze and saw that I'd seen where she'd been looking, her cheeks flushed. "I'll be quick, I just need to know—oh, God. What did he do to you?"

I'd heard something—movement downstairs, and not a threat at all—but I'd made the mistake of turning back toward the door when I heard it, and that gave her a view of my back.

Somehow letting her see that was more embarrassing than an erection. "It's nothing; will you go?"

I started to put my shirt back on, but she was already at my side, already turning me so she could look at my lower back. "Just...let me see."

Her hand on my bare skin burned, almost the way the marks on my back had burned, and also not like it at all. Her burn hurt because it was dangerous. Because it was forbidden. Because I didn't want only her hand touching me but her whole body.

It pulled my focus long enough for her to get a look at the thing I didn't want her to see, especially when I'd yet to see it for myself, and when her breath hitched, I knew it was as bad as I'd feared.

"What?" I craned my head over my shoulder, impossibly trying to see the small of my back. "What is it?"

She brought her hand to her mouth, her eyes watering as she shook her head.

A flash of frustrated energy surged through me. I threw open the door and stormed down the hall to the bathroom. I didn't have a mirror in my room, and since I wasn't lucky enough to have an en suite like she did, I had to use the one down the hall.

Though, maybe I was the lucky one, because otherwise, I might have had a lock on my door too.

I shut the door behind me and took my sweater off the rest of the way, dropping it to the floor before turning my head to look in the mirror to examine what Stark had left on my skin. They were low on my back—he'd made me hold my shirt up while he'd done it. Not so deep that they'd scar, but deep enough that they were bleeding. Three words. Scratched into my skin with a piece of the broken china because he seemed to enjoy making the punishment fit the crime whenever possible.

I AM NOTHING

As sadistic as it was, it hadn't hurt as much as some of his other methods of discipline. It had been a constant pain, which was somehow easier to bear and prepare for than the surprise sting of a whip. I'd bit down on the back of my hand, which now had a pretty severe hickey, and had tried to guess the design of his strokes but had gotten lost with all the ups and downs of the M and the N and had no longer been sure he'd been writing words at all.

But of course he had.

Words that would hurt long after the physical pain subsided.

"It's not true, okay? It's not true."

I turned my head from the awful image to see Julianna had followed me into the bathroom. I should have locked the fucking door.

But it was already too late.

She'd already seen the words in my bedroom. She already knew.

My eye twitched, and I couldn't look at her. "Go away, Julianna."

"I liked it when you called me Jolie," she said, her back pressed to the closed door, as far as she could be from me and still be in the same room.

Yeah, right, it wasn't true.

"Go away, Jolie," I said, louder than I should have. I didn't care for the moment what happened to me if we were caught alone together, even though I really should care. Even though I would care about what would happen to her if I gave myself a second to think about it.

She took a timid step toward me, and despite feeling humiliated and raw, I caught myself stealing another glance at her breasts, and lower, the outline of her white cotton panties, and felt the blood rush to my cock.

"You can't let him get inside your head," she said.

Fuck.

He was already in there. And she was too. Two people who couldn't be more different. One pulling me into darkness. The other one...

The other one didn't belong.

"Go. The Fuck. Away." My jaw was clenched so tightly, the words came out focused and sharp and mean, and if there had been something satisfying to throw in that bathroom, I would have been hurling it at the door behind her, damn the consequences. I needed to be able to sit with this; alone. Needed to sneak out on the roof and smoke my cigarettes in the freezing cold.

She hesitated, the act of deciding written on her face. "I, uh—"

"Go!"

"But I need to know something first!" she said rapidly. Without giving me a chance to reply, she went on. "I need to know why."

My brows drew inward, and for a confused second I thought she was asking why her father had chosen to carve those particular words on me, then realized she was asking why I'd taken the blame.

Ironically, they were both sort of the same answer, but I really didn't want to get into that with her. "You've helped me too," I said, hoping a reply would get her out of there. "The cigarettes. The mints."

"It's not the same."

"How is it not the same?"

"That was camaraderie. This was... This was a sacrifice. I didn't risk myself for you. I didn't put myself on the line." She sounded angry.

Which struck me as ironic. Here I was with every reason to be angry at her—for breaking the plate, for making me want to act noble. For being soft and kind and out of place in a house that was only hard and cruel and punishing.

I let out a laugh as I reached for the towel to wipe off the blood on my back. I'd get in trouble for staining the tan fabric, but I was experienced enough now to know that toilet paper and tissue made the wound hurt worse when it stuck to the skin. "I didn't have an ulterior motive, if that's what you're asking. Don't worry about it, okay? Go."

"But why!"

Her tone was drenched in desperation, the kind of desperation that had a weight, and when it got its claws in you, and you pushed it away, it invariably took something from you at the same time.

From me, her desperation pulled the truth. "Because it *is* true. These words on my back? Your father carved them because he sees what I am. I *am* nothing, and I'll always be nothing, and it doesn't matter what happens to nothing the way it matters what happens to—"

I stopped myself. Partly because whatever came next would have been too much. Mostly because I hadn't quite formulated in my mind what it was that she was. But it wasn't nothing. It was very, very much not nothing.

She'd moved closer during my rant. Too close. And when she opened her mouth, I was sure she was about to deliver some consoling platitude or insist that I was wrong when it was so very obvious that I wasn't.

But instead, she stood on her tiptoes and leaned forward, and I was so stunned that her mouth was already brushing against mine when I had the sense to step back. "What the fuck are you doing?"

Her heels came back to the ground, but she didn't move. She kept staring at me, barely blinking, and I noticed for the first time that there were green flecks in her blue eyes, and that she had a sweet scent I couldn't place, and that I wished that I was dumb enough to lean in instead of away.

No.

This was trouble. *She* was trouble. Being anywhere near her would get us both in *too much* trouble.

"You can't fucking do this," I said, feeling like something more needed to be said. For me as much as her.

Then I dropped the towel and picked up my sweater. Trying my best not to let any part of my body touch her, I moved past her, out of the bathroom, to my room, and told myself I wasn't disappointed when she didn't follow.

TWELVE
CADE

I managed to avoid Julianna for a total of nine days.

Even when the trip was canceled, Stark made my mother still go—her punishment for signing me up in the first place—which meant the entire weekend was spent at his whim. Thankfully, he was on a kick about tidying up the school grounds, so I endured hours in the cold, cutting back dead hedges and picking up litter.

It was better than enduring time in his office.

I told myself it was better than being anywhere near Julianna, too.

Her punishment for speaking back at dinner was dealt with indoors, and as much as I wanted to know what it was, I knew it was best to pretend I didn't care.

When Monday came around, we were back to the school routine, and that was easier. Our class schedule dictated our separation. At night, we were in our rooms doing homework, like always. At dinner, I learned how to keep my eyes on my plate. I didn't offer to help her with dishes. I didn't even come in the kitchen to unload the dishwasher until well after I knew she'd be gone.

It was dumb. I knew that. Dumb to worry about being in the same room with her or what might happen if our eyes met. Both had happened plenty of times in the past, and her father had never cared. She'd never tried to kiss me. It wasn't like I expected she'd try again.

The problem was that I hoped she'd try again.

And if she didn't, there was a good chance I'd try to kiss her, and just thinking about kissing her got me all tangled up because then I wanted to think about what would happen next. And then next after that. But instead of staying focused on the next that would invariably lead to being murdered by my stepfather, I would get stuck on the next that had her in my arms. In my bed.

Under my body.

So I didn't only avoid her. I avoided thinking about her.

Easy enough until the following Saturday, Stark decided it was time to get the house decorated for the holidays. All for show, of course. Not for the enjoyment of the people who lived inside, but for what a Christmas tree in the window said to people outside.

"You can put up the lights on the house after you bring in the boxes of ornaments from storage," he said to me. "Julianna will take care of the tree."

He'd had that delivered, though he had threatened to drop me off in the woods and make me bring one back myself. He found my horror satisfying enough to not have to actually follow through, but I hadn't been entirely sure he wasn't sincere until the delivery man had shown up early that morning with a fresh-cut pine.

"And I'll fill the house with the scent of gingerbread," my mother said, cheerily keeping up her image as the dutiful homemaker.

Stark turned an accusing glare on her. "You've already forgotten I detest the spice? What do you use that brain for, Carla? Sometimes I think we need to enroll you in the academy, except that we have an IQ requirement, and I doubt you'd qualify."

Flustered, she somehow kept a smile on her face. "I meant poppyseed bread. I don't know why I said gingerbread. Vanilla is the spice you love. I didn't forget."

As much as I resented my mother these days, it enraged me to hear her referred to as stupid. Not that I was about to defend her—I wasn't stupid either.

Instead, I drew the attention back to me. "I haven't ever been in the storage shed. Will the boxes be easy to find?"

Asking questions was always a risk of its own. Stark hated explaining himself. On the other hand, he hated it when things were done wrong.

He narrowed his eyes at me, and I held my breath, waiting for the lashing.

What he said was worse. "Julianna? Go with and show him."

If she looked at me at all before saying, "Yes, sir," I didn't see it because I definitely did not look at her.

"Good. Dress warm. I wouldn't want you to already be frozen before you have to get on the roof."

Somehow I doubted his sincerity.

I took his advice, anyway, dressing in layers because it was a good way to stall, not because I was fearful of the cold, but eventually I couldn't put it off any longer, and the two of us set out to the rickety storage shed in the backyard.

"This is chaos," I said when I flicked on the light and saw the disaster ahead of us. Closest to the door was all the garden equipment—the mower and a wheelbarrow and hoses and shovels and rakes. There was also a generator along one wall. Beyond that were the totes. Dozens and dozens of them. None of them labeled or organized. Many, I suspected, hadn't been opened in years. "They have to be near the front, right? Since you used them last year?"

"Maybe." She didn't sound hopeful. "He had the generator set up last spring. Before that, a bunch of the totes were in its place. They've all been moved around now."

"Well, shit."

"Yeah."

She closed the door, and I tensed, wary about being in a confined space with her with the door shut, but as soon as I realized that it was warmer without the wind blowing in, I decided I was going to have to suck it up.

Though, the cold might have been easier to endure.

"Better get started." Faster we were out of here, the better.

It only took five minutes before I realized that this wasn't going to be a quick chore. Not with Julianna. A quick peek under the lid of each tote told me what was inside, and I was able to eliminate a whole tower of them right away. She, on the other hand, found a lot to distract her.

"My angel costume!" she said after opening one. She pulled out a headband with a halo and put it on her head, then rummaged around a bit before retrieving a crumpled set of wings. "This was my Halloween costume for third grade."

She stuck her arms through the elastics and turned around to shake the flimsy things in my direction.

Damn, she was adorable.

"Your father let you go trick-or-treating?" I couldn't imagine it. That was the only reason I wanted to know.

"Of course not. There was a parade at school, and he couldn't let me be the only one without a costume." She feigned a gasp. "What would people think?"

She took off the wings and tried to straighten out the bent wire. "He chose the angel. I wanted to be a witch."

Now that sounded like him. "I'm surprised he let you go to school at all before you got to middle school and he could police you all the time as the headmaster." Stark Academy started enrollment at sixth grade. I'd never wondered where she'd gone before that.

"It was almost worse that he did. I don't know if I would have realized that my family wasn't normal." She put the wings back in the tote and rooted around a bit more before returning the lid and moving it to the ground so she could look in the one underneath it.

It continued from there—every lid lifted revealing another memory.

I knew I should rush her along. But for some reason, I let her take the trip to the past while I worked, listening to her prattle on about this item or that, wishing I didn't like hearing her talk so much.

Most of it wasn't even happy talk. Every object held the same sorts of addendums—*This was how my father stained this memory. This is how he stained that one.* Every recollection another record of proof that Langdon Stark was a monster.

I'd gotten through almost half of the totes with no success when I realized she'd been quiet for a whole minute. I dared a glance at her and found her staring intently at a photograph.

I didn't want to be interested.

I really, really didn't want to be.

But there I was, setting down my tote so I could go and look over her shoulder. There was a woman in the image, with light eyes and long blonde/brown hair, the same shade as Julianna's.

It wasn't hard to guess who it was. "Your mother?"

"Yeah."

I bit my cheek and held my tongue. For all of ten seconds. "Do you remember her?"

"A little. I was only four when she died. But I remember that she hummed a lot, which irritated my father to no end. And she liked cats. She used to feed this black and white stray." She thought a minute, remembering that silly halo bobbing above her head. "I was so young...of course, I didn't really understand what death was, but when Dad said she wasn't coming back, that was what I was worried most about—that cat. Who was going to feed the damn cat?"

"What happened to it?" I whispered the question, sure I knew the answer, wishing I could ignore the need to have it confirmed.

"I fed him for a while. I'd run out every day as soon as I woke up and take a handful from the bag, just the way my mother did. But then the bag was empty. So I told Dad." She took a deep breath. "It didn't go well."

She smiled in that way that said what she was thinking about was terrible, but if she didn't show it, maybe it wouldn't hurt so much. "I think that was when I really knew, you know. Because he's always been like he is. That didn't just start after she was gone. He was always awful, and she was as helpless to it as we all are, but when she was here,

I always knew there was a lap waiting for me after. So that time with the cat—that was when I really got that I was alone."

I'd never been particularly empathetic, and maybe I wasn't then either, but it was the only word I had to explain the intensity of the need I had to want to console her. Console both the Julianna from the past and the one standing in front of me, though the one standing in front of me didn't necessarily look in need of consolation. She was strong. Stronger than me, in many ways. In most ways.

And the methods I would have used to console the Julianna from the past versus the one in front of me—well, those were very different. G-rated methods versus R. X, even, if I let myself think about it too long, which I knew better than to do.

"I'm sorry about the cat," I said, deciding it was the safest way around this conversation.

"Oh, the cat was fine. Janice ended up adopting him."

"Janice the gardener?" I'd worked with her a few times over the past months, usually as part of detention that I was sure I never deserved.

"Yeah. I don't know how she found out about the cat. Maybe I told her, or maybe he was never really a stray and was hers all along, I don't know. But she'd babysit me from time to time, usually at our house, but once I went to hers, and there he was."

I let out a sound that was almost like a laugh. "Who'd have thought there could be a happy ending in this place?"

"Right?" She cleared her throat, dropping the picture back in the tote before putting the lid back on it. "Anyway, the impression I have of my mother is that she was a lot like Carla."

I'd moved back to the tote I'd abandoned already but paused before I lifted the lid. "Subservient and neglectful?"

She gave a wry smile as she pushed the lid in my hand up farther to peek inside. "I meant traditional—a good cook and homemaker. A woman who made her husband feel important. But I could see how you'd label them both with less flattering adjectives. This isn't Christmas. Next."

I put the tote to the side and reached for the next one, puzzling over her choice of descriptors. She might be able to understand my labels, but I couldn't understand hers.

"You really only think those things about your mom?" As though she could see the inside of my head.

"Yes. Yes. Definitely yes." This tote had videotapes with handwritten descriptions like *La Bohème* and *La Traviata*. "Well, maybe that's not true. I should add manipulative and self-serving. She's real good at wooing men. Her problem is getting them to stick around."

"Move over so I can grab that one, will you?" I scooted her with my hip, regretting it as soon as our bodies met. Even through my coat and three layers of shirts, I felt the zing from the contact.

Either she didn't notice or she didn't mind because she moved, but not so much that we weren't still touching. "You really don't have any good memories with her?"

Fuck, were we still talking about my mom?

I considered not answering. This tote had ornaments in it. The rest of the ones we needed were probably underneath, which meant we were done and could get out of here.

But she was good at pulling things from me. Like a fishing line, except her hook didn't have any bait, and I didn't know why I kept swallowing it unless maybe I secretly liked the tortured feeling of saying too much to her, of being too exposed. Of splitting myself open and letting her see what was inside.

"She used to read to me," I said. "Picture books. Every one she could get her hands on. She was never really a library kind of gal, and we rarely had money for things, so she'd go to garage sales or take hand-me-downs. Dr. Seuss and The Wild Things one and Berenstein Bears."

"Beren*stain* Bears," she corrected with a grin.

"Whatever the fuck it was. I had *Inside, Outside, Upside Down* memorized. She'd use funny voices to keep me interested—or to keep herself interested—and run her hands through my hair. Kiss me on my head."

I barely recognized that woman in Carla.

I didn't recognize myself as that little boy at all. It didn't even feel like it had happened to me, but rather like a movie I once saw. "I think once I started to think for myself, she didn't know what to do with me. Maybe it got harder. Maybe *I* got harder. I don't know. Just... I learned to read for myself, and she stopped sitting with me, and she stopped getting me new books, and soon she stopped thinking about me much at all."

"We both lost our mothers young," she said. "Only you never knew, so you didn't get to grieve."

Yeah, that was it. That was...on the nose and so well said and no one had ever made me feel like they got it until right then.

Which made my chest constrict.

And my throat feel tight.

And the layers of clothing must have done the trick because I was suddenly hot and sweating. And she was standing so close, and I could feel her breath on my chin like the world's tiniest space heater. And all I wanted to do was capture that breath inside me, take it all in. Make it mine.

"You aren't alone anymore, Jolie." Goddamn hook. Tugging out words I shouldn't say. Calling her a name that was too intimate. Pulling my mouth down as hers moved up.

Something inside me was still thinking right because when her lips grazed mine, I said, "Don't." Which was the thing to say, and the thing to do.

But I didn't push her away, and she moved her mouth over mine again, softly. Teasing? Testing, before she closed her lips around mine.

I jumped back instantly. Fast, as though there'd been electricity in her kiss. "Don't," I said again.

Only one breath passed—a simple rise and fall of her chest—and then I was lunging forward, pushing her up against the tower of totes, my hands clenched around her upper arms while I kissed the fuck out of her.

Devoured her.

Like I'd never get a chance again, and there was a real good reason to think that was the case. Open-mouthed and punishing. Taking more than I was giving. Sliding my tongue in too far. Tasting her. Memorizing her. Kissing an angel.

She groaned, and I took that too, swallowing it as I pressed harder into her, grinding the ache in my jeans against her belly. I could feel her struggling, and I knew if I let her arms go, she'd touch me. Anywhere she touched me, any way she touched me, it would be heaven.

But I wanted her captive.

Needed her captive. Needed to feel like this was my decision instead of like I had no choice but to touch her. She made me too out of control, otherwise. Made me feel like I was a black hole, and whether I wanted to or not, I would draw all of her inside of me.

I would break her then.

Maybe not by my own hand, but she would be broken apart if she really got in. She'd be shattered, and her father would kill us both, and fuck. Fuck. I wouldn't care. For this one single moment, I wouldn't even care.

Abruptly, light spilled in the shed, and thank God for the yard equipment and that we were all the way in the back because even though we jumped apart instantly, we would have been caught otherwise.

"What's taking you two so long?" Stark said.

For the first time since I'd met her, I saw real fear in Jolie's eyes, a fear that somehow looked more severe with the halo on. I'd wondered before if her punishments were as severe as mine, if she really had a sense of how far her father could go. It wasn't the kind of thing I could ask, and she managed to piss him off so much less than I did, it was an obvious assumption.

Now, though, I was sure that she knew. She knew just how evil he was. She knew just how much she should be afraid.

Her fear sprung me into action. "It took us a while to find the Christmas stuff, sir, but these should be them." I lifted the last tote I'd looked in as evidence. "I should label them this year after the holiday before I put them back."

I did everything right. Called him sir. Assumed responsibility for making the task easier in the future. Let him know I was aware that I'd be the one storing them again.

I'd been learning from his daughter, after all.

"Smart thinking, Cade. Who knew you had it in you." He scanned his daughter then me, looking both of us up and down, his eyes lingering on her halo, and I silently prayed that he assumed her flushed cheeks and red lips were from the cold.

It felt like forever before he spoke again. "Make sure you clean off any mouse droppings before you bring those things inside. If any of us get Hantavirus, it will be your fault." He looked back at Jolie. "Probably shouldn't be handling anything in those totes, Julianna, but if you're determined, let him clean it off first. Better if he got sick than you."

I hated him. I legitimately hated him.

And even though he seemed to think better of her than he did of me, I hated him most because of whatever things he'd done to her. Because of that fear he'd programmed into her eyes.

She didn't seem to breathe again until he was gone. "I swear I almost had a heart attack."

My heart was racing too. For entirely different reasons than they'd been racing before. I set down the tote, and when I lifted my hands, they were shaking. "That was stupid. We were stupid."

"I know," she agreed, removing the halo and tossing it to the ground. "We have to be more careful."

My eyes flew to hers. *Be more careful?* No. That fucking couldn't happen again. No fucking way.

But it was hard to say when she was looking at me like that, like I was the only light in her world, and though it was possible I was just dark in disguise, I understood how much she needed to believe otherwise.

And I really did want her.

Wanted her to be my light, too.

She took a step forward, putting her hand on my cheek. "Cade..."

I shook my head, looking for strength I wasn't sure I had. If she couldn't protect herself, it had to be me.

"Stop. Don't do that. Don't say we can't have this. Don't say *I* can't have this."

Her pleading wore me down. It also hardened my resolve. "This is for *you*," I said, taking her hand from my face. I grabbed the other one with it, held them together. "It's not for me." I was pretty sure I'd suffer anything from her father's hand, if that was the only price to be paid.

But it wasn't.

"This can't happen again."

It was her turn to shake her head.

"It can't," I repeated. Bending in, I kissed her quickly, once more because I couldn't bear not to.

Then I picked up the tote and left, putting distance between us, determined that I would be the one to keep her safe.

THIRTEEN
JOLIE

I HATE HER.

The inside cover of my notebook was filled with that refrain, over and over. *I hate her, I hate her, I hate her, I hate her.*

I hated her pretty little laugh.

I hated her jet-black hair.

I hated her adoring smile.

I hated how nice she was.

Most of all, I hated that she had the one thing I wanted most: Cade.

The biggest problem with hating Amelia Lu was how much I actually didn't hate her. She'd been at Stark since sixth grade. We'd come into the academy together, and she was by all counts the sweetest girl in the whole school. We'd never been friends, per se—there was no being friends with the headmaster's daughter—but she'd been the closest thing to it. She'd never backed away when I entered a room or whispered behind my back as soon as I walked by. When her grandmother died the year before, she'd let me hug her when I gave her condolences, and she'd squeezed so hard, I'd been the one who had to pull away.

So it was a real shame to have such venomous feelings toward her now. Real, real shame.

I finished coloring in the block letters of the latest version of the phrase I'd drawn, this time on the borders of the Winter Talent Exhibition program, then stole a glance down the row to where she was seated.

Big mistake.

Because she wasn't just holding Cade's hand and giggling like she had been the last time I'd peeked. Now they were making out like they were at the local movie theater instead of in the school auditorium.

I REALLY FUCKING HATE HER.

I drew the words so aggressively that the program tore. It hadn't been high-quality paper, to be fair. My father boasted a quality school, but he was cheap when he had the opportunity.

The annual Winter Talent Exhibition, for example. Everyone knew it was a bullshit day. Half of the school had already gone home for the break. The rest of us had to endure ninety minutes of poetry recitations, piano performances, and choir renditions of holiday songs. With so many empty chairs in the three-hundred-fifty-seat auditorium, there was plenty of space for students to stretch out or break off in cliques.

Or, in Cade and Amelia's case, in couples.

And since my father had already left with an unruly bunch of tenth graders, the couples were now free to get coupling.

Another glance from me down the row—I couldn't help myself—this time my gaze smacked right into Cade's. He was still kissing Amelia, but his eyes were open, watching me, and as if to prove this whole relationship with her was only about pushing me away, he waited until he was sure I was looking before sliding his hand up her bare thigh.

I crumpled the flimsy paper without realizing what I was doing. God, I wanted to hate Cade. Wanted to wish him dead. Wanted to hate him so much that I would do something just as hurtful back to him.

No, I didn't.

I wanted to not feel anything for him at all. That's what I wanted. I wanted not to care. I wanted not to notice. I wanted to not be aware of every move he made in his room down the hall from mine. Wanted to not be counting the minutes of the two and a half weeks that had passed since he'd said *don't* and then kissed the air out of my lungs and made me light enough to fly.

He'd barely looked at me since then. Except times like now, when he would throw his relationship with Amelia in my face. Every time I saw him at school these days, he was with her. Holding her hand in the school cafe. Laughing with her in the hallways. Feeling her up in the library during study hall when he was supposed to be in Physics.

Well, I'd gotten the message. Loud and clear. He'd had a moment with me, but that's all it was. Anything more was too big of a risk, and I understood that better than anyone what that risk would cost. I wasn't worth that. I would never be worth that.

I wiped a tear and threw the crumpled program to the ground, then put my energy into applauding the solo modern dance routine from Isla Perez, hoping anyone who saw me would think I'd been moved by her performance. Who knew that I could still feel things? I'd thought I'd taught myself to bury any emotions. So close to getting out of this hellhole—five months before my eighteenth birthday and graduation—and *this* was when my heart started to beat again?

Not fair, God. Not fucking fair.

"Hey, Julsianna."

I didn't have to look up to see that it was Antoine Birch slipping into the empty seat at my side. Even if I didn't recognize his voice, he was the only person who called me that nickname. I'd liked it for a hot minute back in eighth grade when I thought it meant I was special to him, but as soon as I realized it was code for *I have something for you in my pants*, that liking had worn off.

I especially hated it after hearing Cade's name for me. Maybe the only difference was how I felt for the boy who'd said it, but I didn't think that was all there was to it. *Jolie* came all by itself, with no attachments. It felt more like a gift than a bribe. It was an invitation to be something more than I was. Someone different.

Julsianna was just an invitation to get on my knees.

As the applause died down, and Ms. Stacey's Advanced Drama

Class took the stage to perform a scene, I resisted the urge to tell Birch that I wasn't in the mood for him. That wasn't something Julianna would say. That was something Jolie would say, and as much as I wanted to be, that wasn't who I was yet. She was still just a seedling buried under my skin, waiting for the right season to bloom.

"What's up?" I whispered instead.

He leaned close enough that I could feel his breath tickle my ear. "This is bo-ring. Don't you think?"

I shrugged. To be honest, I'd barely been paying attention, and the show I was watching might have been devastating, but it definitely wasn't boring. Involuntarily, I slid my eyes back to Cade and Amelia. This time he wasn't watching me, and now she was on his lap, her legs spread slightly, his hand under her skirt.

The seedling inside me let out a string of curse words. Jolie, it seemed, had quite a mouth.

Biting down on the inside of my lip, I brought my ankle up to my opposite knee, facing away from Birch so he wouldn't be able to see my artwork, and took my pen to the bottom of my Mary Jane.

I Hate. Amelia. Lu.

I was too resentful to keep myself from using her name. Too consumed with rage to worry about what I'd say if my father discovered it. I'd have to pretend I was racist or something since he'd never believe anyone could hate Amelia. I couldn't ever let him guess the real reason.

"I swear the drama class does this *Steel Magnolias* scene every goddamn year," Birch said. "I think I have it memorized."

"Not many scenes with lots of characters, I guess." I doubted he'd paid enough attention to it any of the years prior to learn a single line, let alone memorize it, but that was Jolie who was contradicting him.

He let a good three minutes go by before saying anything else. "'...I've just been in a very bad mood for forty years!'" He laughed, quoting one of the more infamous lines from the scene.

I guess he did know the show after all.

I pretended to laugh. I was quite good at smiling while dying inside. I really should have been on that stage. If my father wasn't so controlling of all my extracurricular activities, maybe I would have.

"Whatcha drawing?" Birch stretched his arm on the seat behind me. Casually. Like he was just trying to make it easier to talk to me without disturbing the whole audience.

I wasn't stupid.

"Just doodling." I dropped my pen in my lap and crossed my legs, instinctively hiding what was between my thighs as well as what was on my shoe.

Like the single-minded sex addict that he was, he seemed to think I was flirting. He brought his hand up from the chair back to tickle along my neck.

My whole body tensed.

He ignored the cues and brought his opposite hand to my knee. "You should let me doodle." His whisper had grown husky. "My fingers are amazing at...doodling."

I knew how to get him to leave me alone. The same trick I used every other time he started to come on to me. By now, I had a feeling that he only offered to take care of me first because he knew I'd push his hand away and suck him off instead.

Not for the first time, I considered that it didn't have to be one or the other. It could be both. It could be neither. I could say no to all of it.

It was possible I didn't know how to say no. It had been so long since I'd actually tried it. It had been so long since I'd cared about saying no. There were benefits to being the girl who'd put out. There was satisfaction in getting away with something my father abhorred. I was careful about where and when I performed, and the boys definitely weren't going to confess to him.

And it made me feel wanted.

I knew that wasn't real—they wanted any hand around their cocks. They didn't care whose face the lips were attached to. They didn't want *me*.

But it felt close enough to real for me to accept it. To crave it, even.

And most days I was pretty sure it was all I was good for, so why not be the best that I could be?

It would be easy enough right now, in the dark. My father, preoccupied with dealing with the troublemakers in his office. I could slip my hand into his khakis and get him off. Birch was an early releaser. It wouldn't take more than five minutes. Maybe less since, knowing him, he'd probably find the whole public thing too hot to hold out.

It could even be satisfying for me, if I convinced myself that Cade would look down the aisle and see. If I could believe he'd care. I could fantasize his jealousy into something real instead of just a projection of what I felt inside.

"What do you say, Julsianna?" His fingertips had reached the elastic band of my panties.

I pushed his hand away. "Antoine..." I scolded in a tone that was more flirty than reprimand.

He took my hand with his. "Then maybe *you* could doodle instead." He placed my palm on the bulge at his crotch and helped me rub him. "You know what I like."

He liked what they all liked.

The same thing.

No commitments, no obligations in return.

Except Cade. I kept offering myself to him, and he hadn't taken. Was it possible he cared about me for more than just that? Or did he really not care enough to take the chance?

Back to that, always back to him. And I couldn't know what he thought or what he wanted because he wouldn't talk to me. All I could know was myself, and even if I meant nothing to Cade, there was Jolie now. He'd made her real inside me, and Jolie was faithful, if not to Cade, then to herself.

Jolie didn't want to be the school boy toy anymore.

Jolie knew how to say no.

Quietly, though, since she wasn't real enough yet to make a scene. "This isn't the best idea," I whispered, trying to extricate my hand from under his.

He clamped down on it harder, forbidding my escape. "That's what makes it such a fun idea. Come on. You can use my sweater to clean up if you don't want to use your mouth."

My stomach turned rock hard. I didn't want to fight him. *Please, don't make me have to fight him.* "I really don't want to right now, Birch."

"I'll be fast." He unzipped his pants with his free hand, not bothering with the button, and pulled out his dick from the hole in his boxers. "I'm already super hard. Feel it."

"No," I hissed, surprising myself. "No," I said again, stronger, when he tried to force my hand around his girth.

"Don't be like this, Juls. Don't play like you're suddenly a prude."

"I don't. Want. To." I glared hard at him, as though my stare could stand up to his strength.

"Why are you being such a bitch right now? I'm not even asking you to suck me. Just give me a little tug."

I was about to put my shoulder into pushing him away when suddenly he wasn't there anymore to push.

"She said no, you asshole!" Cade had lifted him out of his chair and was holding him by the scruff of his shirt, his expression brutal.

It was an unusual look on Cade. He was generally somber, but he wasn't a bully. And if anyone were to place bets, odds would probably go to Birch who was practiced at being a bully.

From my vantage point, though, where I could clearly see the look in his eyes—my money was on Cade all the way.

"Ah, I get it. Big brother's got dibs on you now, does he?" Birch didn't seem to have the same perspective I did.

Not until Cade's fist landed squarely in his face. With the sound of skin smacking against skin, I realized the stage had gotten awfully quiet.

The attention of everyone in the auditorium had turned to us.

Panic rushed through me—panic for Cade—as a familiar voice cut through the silence. "What the hell is going on here? Birch. Warren. In the hall."

My father had returned. *Fuck, fuck, fuck.*

Birch yanked himself away from Cade's grasp and wiped his bloody nose with the back of his sleeve. "I didn't do shit," he said, as he walked past me down the aisle, pleading his case while he used his sweater to help stop the bleeding. "He just hit me out of the blue. He's trouble, Headmaster Stark. You know he is."

It was absolute bullshit but an obvious line of defense. Everyone in the school knew how often Cade was in my father's office.

Cade didn't look at me as he followed after. He also didn't say a word.

"Ms. Stacey," Dad bellowed. "Tell your students to pick up where they left off." He opened the door to the auditorium and waited for the two boys to follow after.

I exchanged a glance with Amelia, who was sitting back in her own chair and appeared to want to stay out of the whole business. For the first time since I'd met her, though, her expression wasn't friendly. She looked very much like she was about to start writing **I hate Julianna Stark** on the bottom of her shoes.

I couldn't worry about her right now. What mattered was standing up for Cade.

Rushing out, I caught up with them still in the hall. "Cade was defending me, Daddy," I called out.

He stopped to throw me a look that I knew very well, one that told me to stay the fuck out of it or pay the consequences.

I was trained to step down with that look.

It took willpower that I didn't know I had to override that instinct. "Birch was getting handsy," I insisted.

And I swallowed. Because there was no way that my father wouldn't think that was my fault. There was no way that he would believe his daughter over the claims of one of the most important students in his student body.

"Now this dick is corrupting your daughter too," Birch said, with as much drama as the actors on the stage we'd just left, his words muffled through the sweater still pressed to his nose. "Un-fucking-believable.

You're not going to let him get away with that, Headmaster Stark, are you? My dad will be very disappointed."

"Watch your mouth, Birch." But my father was already talking softer to him. There was no way he was going to be punished for anything.

"She's telling the truth," a voice interrupted from behind me. "Antoine was trying to get Julianna to do something she didn't want to do."

Amelia had followed me out after all. Like I needed more reasons to feel guilty for hating her.

My father might be able to ignore what I said or what Cade said—he hadn't said anything, apparently aware that nothing he said would matter—but he couldn't just disregard another paying student's accusations. Could he?

"I didn't do—!"

"That's enough, Birch." My father's eyes scanned us one by one, the fury behind them growing as he evaluated his options.

I could imagine what he wanted from me. *It's no big deal*, he wanted me to say. Wanted me to save him from having to severely discipline a high-profile student.

It would be better for me to say it. I was already going to get in trouble for "provoking" Birch's advances. He might cut me a break if I took back the accusation now.

All I cared about was what helped Cade. And I honestly didn't know what that was, so I stayed silent.

Cade saw an opportunity to help himself. "Just looking out for my sister, sir," he said, looking directly at me with an expression that said there was no way in hell he thought of me as his sister.

My heart stuttered in my chest.

"Regardless," my father said after a beat. "You can't punch other students. That's behavior that should result in expulsion."

"Exactly," Birch said.

"Shut up, Antoine. If you don't want to face expulsion yourself, you'll take what you got as punishment and leave it at that."

So he'd get away with it. Of course, he would.

"Thank you, ladies," my father continued, dismissing us. "Please return to the assembly. I'll take care of it from here." He turned to Birch. "Get yourself cleaned up." Then to Cade. "My office."

I prayed Cade's punishment wasn't terrible. It couldn't be, could it? He couldn't risk Amelia Lu running home to her parents and complaining about injustice, and the best way to avoid that would be a slap on the wrist.

One look at Cade said he didn't share my optimism. But he stared at me for long seconds, then whispered, "Worth it," before following my father down the hall.

FOURTEEN
CADE

I turned off the water, grabbed a towel from the stack outside the boy's shower, and tied it around my waist. It had taken fifteen minutes before my fingers and nose didn't feel frostbitten from being outside, but all in all, it had been the easiest punishment Stark had ever given me. I would hands down choose an hour running six miles versus five minutes with the whip, any day, no matter the toll to my body.

While the physical pain had been more tolerable, I was still wrestling with what it had done to my psyche. I'd thought I'd already seen the worst of my stepfather, or imagined it, and yet I was still somehow surprised by his reaction to today's events.

I'd known he was a monster.

But even monsters protected their own children, didn't they?

Guess I'd been wrong because all Birch had gotten was what I'd given him, and in the end, that wasn't that much. I'd hit him hard enough to bleed, but the nurse had come into Stark's office while I'd been in there and told him his nose hadn't been broken. Disappointing. He should have been expelled for assault. He should have been in jail for what he'd tried to do to his daughter.

I would have killed the guy if Jolie was in any way mine.

I wasn't sure I wouldn't have killed him today if I hadn't been stopped. I sure fucking wanted to.

I shook my head of the thought, drops of water splattering from my hair to the tile, then walked out of the shower area toward the lockers.

Despite all the hard surfaces, the locker room was strangely peaceful when it wasn't filled with an entire gym class. I was actually glad Stark had suggested I clean up there after my run instead of going home. Of course, he'd passed it off as doing me a favor, and I was sure he'd lord it over me anytime he got a chance. How he'd gone soft on me. How there was no other student who could get away with violence and still be enrolled. How he'd have to think up some way to explain his leniency to Birch's parents.

He definitely wasn't done punishing me for this.

I forced myself not to dwell on it. It was no good wasting the present by worrying about what he'd do to me tomorrow, and honestly, he'd find something to do to me whether he thought I deserved it or not.

But when I wasn't thinking about what cruelty might come next, my head went in an even worse direction—Jolie.

Jolie, Jolie, Jolie. I didn't even think of her as Julianna anymore. Ever since that kiss, it was like she'd changed in my head, and there was no way to change her back. I knew too much about her and couldn't unknow it. I knew how good I could be to her. I knew how good she could be to me, and it drove me insane knowing how bad it would be for both of us if we tried to get together.

I couldn't have her. That was the hard reality. It could not happen between us.

And yet she was always on my mind. From morning to night. My thoughts ranged from the innocent to wildly dirty. I wondered what she was thinking when I sat across from her at dinner. I imagined what she'd say if we had a stolen moment together. It was Jolie's face I pictured when I fucked Amelia. Jolie's name that sat on the tip of my tongue when I whacked off in my bed at night.

The one girl I shouldn't want, and I didn't want anything in the world but her.

I saw her as soon as I turned down the first row of lockers, sitting on the bench between them. As if I'd conjured her up from a fantasy that had just been forming in the back of my consciousness—just the two of us here, me wearing only a towel, her panties on the ground.

Fuck, I was getting hard just from her presence.

This was the reason she and I could never be alone together. Why I'd worked so hard over the last couple of weeks to be sure we never were. Why I was in deep shit for being as happy to see her as I was cautious.

I forced myself to lean into caution. "You shouldn't be here." I didn't even want to know why she was there, because whatever reason she had, it was trouble.

"I had to be sure you were okay," she said, standing up, and I wondered how long she'd been waiting. The whole time? While I'd been naked in the shower nearby?

I tried to forget that I was practically naked now. "I'm fine. Now leave."

"He didn't—?" She cut herself off, and I could tell she was trying to decide what to say. It was funny how we did that—how we danced around the words of what her father did to us, as if they were worse than the things he actually did. "It wasn't too horrible? Just the running?"

She'd been looking out for me, then. I had a feeling she did that more than she let on, and I hated that I liked it. Liked it a real whole lot.

But she didn't know I liked it. And if I kept that to myself, there wasn't any harm in answering her. Maybe it would even send her on her way. "That, and he's making me take care of the grounds over break."

She didn't bother to hide her skepticism.

"I'm sure there will be more to it," I said. "He probably didn't have enough time to deal with me the way he wanted to with it being the last day of the semester."

"I'm betting I'll have to pay for it later too."

I felt a burst of heat run through my veins. "You? He had his dick out when you said no, and you're the one who has to pay?" My hand was balled up in a fist at my side, and the only thing keeping me from slamming it into the locker was the fact that it still hurt from punching Birch in the face.

"I was thinking more because I stood up for you, but I'm sure he'll blame me for Birch too."

"That's fucked up. That's. Fucked. Up."

"I know. But you know that's how it is. Don't worry about me."

It was like asking me not to worry about how I'd breathe if the room suddenly filled up with water. I couldn't help it.

I was worried about her now. "Whatever he's planning, it's going to be worse if he catches you in here. You really need to go."

She didn't move. "He's got parents arriving now until late. He's preoccupied. He's not coming back."

There came the water, filling in around me, because if I wasn't worrying about keeping her safe from her father, then I was thinking about...

Things I shouldn't be thinking.

"Go, Jolie."

Instead, she took a step forward. "Amelia asked me to give this to you."

The note was folded into a fancy square so that it tucked into itself. She'd done this a few times, passed notes to me, and it bothered me since it made it seem like we were more than we were.

But most of her messages were about when she'd be free to hookup, and it was the best way to communicate, honestly. Even if Stark had shelled out money for me to have a phone like the kids at his school, I wouldn't have wanted any records of correspondence. A note could be burned. A text could be read.

So even though this was standard between us, I had a feeling the tone of this note was different.

I took it from Jolie's hand, careful not to show her effect on me when my fingers touched her skin, but once I had it, I didn't know what to do with it. It wasn't like I had pockets, and reading it in front of Jolie felt awkward.

Then again, she might have already read it.

I opened it and scanned it quickly.

It's okay. I won't tell. If you need something from me, I'll help.

See you after the holiday.

xx

There wasn't any question what Amelia was referring to, and while I trusted her and felt relieved that she'd keep it hushed, having my secret called out—having it confirmed outside of me—made this thing I felt for Jolie real. Made it harder to put away and ignore.

"I think Amelia thinks..." Jolie was still standing there. Studying me.

"Thinks *what*?" I didn't know why I was daring her like this. Daring her to be bold and say the thing that shouldn't be said. I could feel my heart racing, like I'd just finished running the six miles instead of twenty minutes ago.

"Thinks there's something going on between us."

"Did you read it?" I asked angrily, though I wasn't quite sure why.

"I didn't have to."

Whatever she thought it said—whatever she thought it meant—she didn't *know*. And that meant I still had a chance to hide the elephant in the room. Could I really be surprised that Amelia had noticed? I'd been too obvious—always reaching for her as soon as Jolie showed up. Always letting her go as soon as Jolie left.

And today, I'd had my hands up Amelia's skirt, but my attention had been one hundred percent down the aisle. Thankfully. Or I might not have stopped Birch before he took advantage of her.

I really owed Amelia a fucking apology.

But shitty as it was, I was not thinking about Amelia right now.

I was thinking about Jolie's tongue sweeping across her bottom lip, and the way her throat moved when she swallowed, and how dark her eyes had gotten in the well-lit locker room, and how my skin was still damp and only a dropped towel away from being completely exposed.

I forced myself to look away. "Well, there isn't, so no big deal."

"Don't do that," she said, pulling my gaze back. The corners of her mouth had turned down, serious to a point I'd never seen. Scolding and imploring all at once. "We have to lie to everyone all the time, but I can't stand it if you lie to me."

The hair stood up on the back of my neck and down my arms, and I was suddenly aware how thin my defenses were, how she'd gotten behind walls I'd put up without realizing.

And fuck. I wanted her there, inside the fortress, with me.

But I wanted her safe, more. "I don't know what you're talking about."

"You do. You stood up for me."

"I would have stood up for anyone."

"You wouldn't have noticed it was happening if it was just anyone. Stop lying. Be honest with me."

She'd closed the distance between us, and I was so weak from the power of her that I couldn't even make myself step away. "Stop it. Stop this."

Her eyes sparkled with unshed tears. "I can't. Not any more than you can. It takes strength that I don't have to keep fighting it."

Strength I didn't have either.

"Jolie..." I was practically begging now, and I wasn't even sure anymore what I was begging for. For her to go? For her to stay?

"Please, Cade." She was begging too, and my eyes couldn't move from her lips.

I was being ripped apart, my head commanding me to step back, my heart wanting to lean forward. Stretching me beyond capacity to be stretched.

Barely able to keep my hands at my sides, frustration erupted from me. "What do you want from me?"

"I want you to love me!"

Instantly, Amelia's note fell to the ground, and my hands came up to grip her shoulders and push her into the row of lockers. "I do," I growled, unable to hold back the truth. "I already fucking do."

I hadn't even said it to myself, but with the words in the air, my chest released, and I felt the peace of surrender, the wild war that I'd been fighting finally at its end. I *did* love her, and it had been hard to admit or recognize, not only because of the odds against us, but because I hadn't ever really loved anyone before, and I had no idea what it was.

Now though, in this moment, there was no doubt. It was *this*. It *had* to be this. It was always and forever only going to be this.

In a blink, my lips were on hers, kissing her softly, trying to savor her. Trying to *show* her how I felt, that my love was patient and sweet and slow, nothing like what she'd been shown all her life from her devil of a dad.

But now that I was reconnected to her, I couldn't hold back, and quickly I was ravaging her, eating her up like the starving man that I was. My mouth wanted to know every part of hers, my tongue wanted to make its mark, wanted to claim her as mine. I didn't even notice my hands move from her shoulders until they were under her skirt, gripping her ass, pulling her pelvis against the hard ache between my legs.

Her hands were harder to lose track of. My skin burned everywhere she touched, leaving a trail of fire as her fingers skated down my torso to my waist, and even though alarm bells screamed in my head the whole time, it wasn't until I felt the towel loosening that I had the sense to pull myself together.

I brought my hand to her wrist to stop her. "That isn't the way I love you."

Hurt flashed across her mossy-blue eyes. "You don't want—"

"No, I do. I really fucking do." I wanted her more than I'd wanted anything, and I'd said it wrong. "I mean, I don't need this to love you."

"I know." She blinked at me like she might cry. "But I think I need this to know that you do."

She leaned forward and captured my mouth with hers, tugging me to her with a hand behind my neck. Her other hand had gotten beneath the barely-hanging-on towel, and with her fingers wrapped around my throbbing cock, it was extremely difficult to remember what was wrong with this. To hell that she was my stepsister—I couldn't fucking care less about that—but it was wrong to take what she was giving. She was an abused girl, and as little as I knew about life, I did know that I wanted to be different for her. I didn't want to be the person who required something from her. I didn't want her to think she had to earn me when the reality was there was nothing I could ever do that would make me worthy of her.

But her lips.

And her hand.

And the peek of her breasts as I unbuttoned her shirt and kissed my way down her chest.

And the dampness of her panties on my thigh that had somehow made its way between her legs.

There was no going back from what we'd started.

With a growl in the back of my throat, I pushed her panties down, letting them fall to her ankles before lifting her up, bracing her against the locker, which I doubted felt very good, but I couldn't seem to make myself care. Much as I wanted slow and sweet with her, this was what this love was going to be between us—rough and troubled and uncomfortable. It wasn't my choice to make. It was one that had been made for us—our lives, our circumstances—but it didn't make it any less beautiful, and all I could do was embrace it.

The towel no longer between us, she freed one foot from her panties and they dangled around the other as she wrapped her legs around me, pressing her heat against my cock. I tilted my hips up, sliding my length up and down along her slit, and grew immediately harder. She was so fucking wet. Dripping, like I'd already given her an orgasm.

On my next glide down, she tipped her pelvis forward and used her hand to guide me where she wanted me. "I need you here." Her voice was low yet heavy. "Inside."

My tip was already at her core, pushing in slightly, then pulling out. Teasing, which wasn't my intent. I was trying to convince myself to be smart. I was already an idiot for letting us get this far, but this right here was where I had to pause and think.

She sensed my hesitation. "I'm not a virgin," she said tentatively.

I'd tried not to let myself wonder, but when I did, I'd assumed she wasn't. Not with what I'd known she did with other guys. I was jealous, of course, but that wasn't why I'd hesitated. "I don't have a condom."

Surprisingly, she seemed relieved.

"Did you think I cared about that?" I couldn't keep myself from pushing my tip back inside her. She felt too good. Too hot. Too perfect.

"I didn't...I didn't know. I was afraid—"

I cut her off with a kiss. "It doesn't matter who you've been with before. I only care that you're with me now."

She tilted her hips again, drawing me deeper inside her, and I moaned. "Mmm, fuck. It doesn't change the fact that I don't want to knock you up."

"Pull out." She pushed forward, until I was practically spearing her completely. "I need you. I trust you."

I wasn't sure I trusted myself. I'd never been bare inside a girl. When I hadn't had condoms, I hadn't gone inside. It was my firm rule. There were other ways to get a release.

But all the rules were out the window with Jolie.

Against my better judgment, I told my head to shut the fuck up and thrust all the way in. "God, that's so good. You feel so good."

I hammered into her, setting a brisk though unsteady tempo, wishing I didn't need both hands around her to keep her up so that I could rub her clit and make it good for her too. I made sure to angle her against me instead, so that my pelvic bone knocked against her, hoping that would get her the friction she needed.

I couldn't think about it too much beyond that. I needed all my concentration to be sure I didn't accidentally come inside her. When she locked her ankles behind my back, making her feel even tighter, I was sure I wasn't going to last long. I could make myself think about her father (I didn't), and I probably would have been just as helpless.

It wasn't just the way it felt to be bare inside her that had me so turned on, though she did feel incredible. Like nothing else I'd ever known. It was also how much I'd wanted her. How I'd been denying her. That want had built up inside me. I was a powder keg giving off sparks. I was already so close to exploding before I'd entered her.

But mostly, the thing that had me so close to the edge was the pressure in my chest, a tightening that had nothing to do with sex and all to do with how I felt about her. She was the only star in a very dark night. She was a light that seemed to shine only on me, and the heat of that light—the fire of her attention—had me burning up from head to toe. My blood was blazing like a line of gasoline caught flame, and when her pussy clamped down around me, I knew I was a goner.

More abruptly than I intended, I set her down, pulling out as I did. Breathing heavily, I pressed my forehead to hers. She hadn't finished. It felt selfish to finish myself off like this.

But before even a handful of seconds had passed, her hand was wrapped around me again, tugging on my head while she kissed me. And forget about thinking about her pleasure. I was seeing fireworks, the base of my spine tingling as tiny rockets shot from my cock up and down my nervous system. Erupting wasn't a strong enough word for what was happening inside me. I was exploding. I was destroyed.

I let out a stuttering groan, coming all over her hand in ribbon-like spurts.

It seemed to take a lifetime before I'd caught my breath.

Her too, I realized when I could finally see straight again, her panting synced with mine. As my vision cleared, my head did too, and the enormity of what had transpired hit me like a wrecking ball.

I backed away from her quickly, then ran my hand through my hair that was as wet now from sweat as from the shower.

Jolie's back straightened against the locker, and she pierced me with a desperate stare. "Don't you dare pull away from me."

The thought had crossed my mind.

Briefly.

"No chance," I said honestly. Bravely. "You're wrapped around me like an anchor." I picked up my towel from the floor and cleaned off her hand before bending to wipe between her legs. I already regretted not spending more time down there. I wanted to fuck her with my fingers. I needed to fuck her with my mouth.

She pulled me back up to a standing position. "An anchor, huh? I go down, you go down?"

I'd meant it to be romantic, but I chuckled. She was probably more on point. "Sink or swim. We're doing it together."

Her breath shuddered. "Promise? You won't try to push me away again?"

I brushed my lips across hers. "Promise." I kissed her for real then, feeling the twin desires already wrestling inside me, the one that wanted to keep her safe. The other that wanted to keep her mine.

I'd have to find a way to do both because I couldn't give her up now. I was too selfish. I needed her to keep me from going insane.

Right now, though, while I was thinking rationally, I made myself do the smart thing. "But I need you to go. I know you said your father is preoccupied, but there are other people who could catch us. We have to be more careful than this."

"I know. You're right." She didn't let go of me when I let go of her.

"Jolie," I nudged.

"I love you," she said. "I didn't say it back."

I hadn't had time to wonder about it. I was still processing the fact that I loved her, and without having time to work it all out, I was already sure it was independent of how she felt about me.

But God, it felt good to know she felt the same.

I started to reach for her again and stopped myself before I got lost in another kiss. "Tonight. After your father's asleep."

"He locks me in with a key," she reminded me. "You can't get in any easier than I can get out."

Still high from the orgasm and from her loving me, I didn't feel the intensity of rage I usually felt when I thought about how much I hated that man.

Besides, I had another plan. "Don't worry about that. I'll get to you." *I'll always get to you.*

She didn't know it yet, but that was a promise too.

FIFTEEN
JOLIE

I was concentrating so hard on my bedroom door, listening for any sound on the other side, that the knock on my window made me jump.

Buzzing with excitement, I crawled across my mattress, threw back the curtain, and shoved the window up. It was the same kind we had throughout the second floor, the kind that pushed up with no screen, but unlike Cade's, the only way to the roof from mine was up.

My stomach was already in knots before I stuck my head out and looked above me to find Cade on his stomach. "Oh my God, you're going to fall!"

He grinned, half reassuring, half amused. "I won't. Just move out of the way so I can swing in."

"Oh no. No freaking way." I was so emphatic, I'd forgotten to be quiet. I clapped a hand over my mouth and listened for any sounds behind me before whisper-shouting. "Don't even think about it."

This time he actually laughed, and I realized I didn't ever remember hearing him laugh before. It mesmerized me so much that this time when he told me to move away, I did.

A tense thirty seconds later, he'd swung himself around, dropped his toes to the windowsill, then worked his way in, feet first.

After a surprised beat, I knelt on the bed and helped him—or pretended to help him. If he fell, it wasn't like I had the strength to pull him back up, but having something to do made me feel calmer, and besides, I really liked touching him.

I shut the window as soon as he was in, not wanting to let too much cold air in, then sat back, my legs curled under me, and stared at him.

Holy shit.

Cade was in my room.

The door was locked from the outside, and Cade was in my room, and my father didn't know, and I'd never been happier.

Until he reached his hand out and cupped the side of my face, which made me even happier.

I was also a nervous wreck. "You could have killed yourself."

"Doing that? Piece of cake."

"You should have come in the bathroom window." It faced the side of the house instead of the back, and the roof was easily accessible. I'd never climbed out that way because I was not too big of a fan of heights, but I was willing to try it when it was warmer.

"Too narrow for my shoulders," he said with certainty.

Which made me realize... "You've thought about this before. About sneaking in my room."

For half a second, I thought he was going to deny it. "All the fucking time."

My heart flipped, and I blushed. It could have been meant as a sweet comment or a dirty one, and instead of choosing which he'd meant, my body reacted to both.

Holy shit, Cade was in my room, and he was going to do sweet and dirty things to me real soon. Wildly dirty, maybe even.

Instinctively, I looked to my door. I'd never been granted happiness in my life without my father lurking in the shadows, ready to take it away.

Cade followed my line of vision. "He already came by, didn't he? I swear I heard him go downstairs before I came over."

"He did, but we should have a sign in the future. If you had knocked when he was in here..." My stomach tightened, thinking about the possibility of him coming over too soon.

"Next time, open the window a crack as soon as he leaves. I won't knock unless it's open."

I nodded, but I was still staring at the door. It was after midnight, and he'd already done his check-in, but I couldn't help worrying it would be one of those nights where Dad decided he wanted to say good night to me again. It was rare, but not out of the question. Especially if he'd punished me earlier in the day. He seemed to think an extra visit to my room could make up for whatever cruelty he'd dispensed.

"You think he might come back?" Well, now I was only thinking about my upper arm since his hand was stroking my skin there. "Will you feel better if we move the dresser in front of the door?"

It wasn't a very heavy dresser and wouldn't stop anyone for long, but any extra barrier seemed like a good idea.

Either he felt the same or sensed how I felt because he stood up to move it before I'd answered. I jumped up to join him, and together we pushed the dresser until it hit the doorknob and couldn't go any farther.

Once it was in place, Cade put his hand on the doorknob and turned it, testing it. "He really, really locks you in."

I nodded. I'd had years to get used to being treated like a possession more than a person. A lifetime trained to be the model daughter, only existing for my father's needs and nothing else. It had been a long time since I'd tried to remember that most children weren't treated this way, and though I had a feeling Cade's life hadn't been "normal" either, I also knew my father had to be a new kind of devil.

"How do we live like this?" he asked, and it was a rhetorical question, but I knew that the answer was that we didn't.

At least, I hadn't. I hadn't lived. I hadn't felt like I'd lived, anyway. Not until this year. Not until Cade.

And now it was just the two of us, alone in my room, and even after he'd been inside me only hours before, I suddenly felt shy. "Hi," I said.

"Hi," he said back.

He stood there and looked at me then, really looked at me, and with the moonlight coming into the room, I could see his eyes move down my body. Could tell when he noticed my nipples budding through my nightgown. Watched as he adjusted the crotch of his jeans.

"Are you cold?" But he was smirking, like he already knew the answer.

"I'm not cold." Immediately, I regretted my response. If I were better at being flirty or seductive, I'd have said something witty, told him I was freezing and needed him to warm me up.

It must not have mattered that I'd said something so lame because he prowled over to me anyway, like I was exactly as tempting as I wanted to be to him. He cupped my cheeks with his hands and moved his mouth lightly over my face, keeping his lips only a breath away. "There are so many things I want to do to you."

I closed my eyes, waiting for his kiss. "What kinds of things?" I could barely hear my whisper above my pounding heart.

"So many terrible naughty things that I fantasized about doing all those times I thought about sneaking in your window. It's going to take a lot of restraint not to do them all to you tonight."

"But you could do at least some of them."

"Maybe one."

My eyes flew open. "Only one?"

He chuckled, then kissed me quickly on the lips. "I'm serious about there being more than fucking between us." He took my hand and tugged me toward the bed. "Let's talk."

"We've had months of the 'more' between us. I think we deserve some time playing catch-up on the fucking." It wasn't that I was particularly into sex. I'd never done it for my own enjoyment. I'd never even had an orgasm.

But I knew what to do with sex. I knew how to use it to be worth noticing. I knew how to exchange it for a favor. I knew how it could make a boy say nice things.

I didn't know how to make a boy say nice things without it.

I didn't know how to be with a boy without it.

Yet here I was, climbing onto my bed with a boy who emphatically didn't want to just fuck.

I didn't know if I felt like flying or throwing up.

Cade propped himself up against the wall next to the window, then pulled me into him and wrapped an arm around me. "You're so tense," he said, his hand caressing my arm again. Goosebumps peppered across my skin in its wake. "Still worried we'll be caught?"

"I don't know."

His lips pressed against my temple. "You said no lying. Are you really that scared of letting me hold you?"

Yes.

But it was getting easier as the seconds passed, especially since I was facing away from him. "I guess it's not so bad. I just don't know what to talk about."

"Anything you want. Or you don't have to say anything, if you'd rather."

Both options sounded awkward.

But there was something I wanted to know. "What did Amelia's note say?"

"You said you already knew."

I hadn't read it. I'd wanted to, but I'd stopped myself, hoping that Cade would tell me himself. Even if he didn't, I'd seen the look in her eyes when she'd handed it to me. She knew whatever they had was over.

"I guess I don't care so much about what her note said. I care more about your reaction."

He pulled away so he could look at me. "Now I really need to hear what you thought it said."

"She broke up with you?" My voice squeaked, and now that I'd said it out loud, I was really afraid that it wasn't true.

"I guess she did? There wasn't anything to break up. She knew I wasn't into her. She just didn't know why until today."

"You really weren't into her?"

"Worse. I was using her. Do you think the worst of me now?"

"Using her to...?"

"To keep everyone from figuring out how I feel about you." A mountain fell off my shoulders. I'd told myself I didn't care what he felt for her, but it was a lie. I cared a lot. Especially since I was pretty sure they'd actually been fucking. It was a relief to know it had been the charade I'd thought it had been.

And I really loved hearing him talk about his feelings for me. It was probably going to take some time before I truly believed it, so I was glad he wasn't keeping it inside like a secret that only had to be admitted once.

"I guess it is more than my father who can't know," I said, realizing for the first time what it would look like to others. "People would probably think it's sick."

"Or kinky."

I let out a snort. Then second-guessed his meaning. "Is that what you think—?"

He cut me off with a kiss. "You know what we are. Better than I do, maybe. And I've already told you this isn't about sex for me. Isn't *just* about sex."

I wrapped my arms around him, and his hand grazed my breast as it skated down my ribs, making me very eager to climb on his lap.

Just as I was heating up, he slowed things down. "I think Amelia offered to help be our cover. I'll let that be your decision. Either way, even if I pretend to be with her, I promise I won't be with her again. Not like this."

I loved that he thought about my feelings. Loved that he was sure enough about me to make promises.

But he was still new to the compromises that had to be made on behalf of my father, and I didn't want to tell him that there were some promises that couldn't be made, but instead I said thank you and rested back into his arms, pressing my cheek against his chest.

We sat quietly for several minutes, his hand tracing up and down my arm, and soon I felt my body relaxing, the rock in my stomach lightening, and I could no longer hear my heartbeat racing in my ears.

I could hear his heartbeat, though, steady under my ear. It was so steady, I almost thought he'd fallen asleep.

Then he asked, "What happened after dinner?"

The bowling ball in my stomach returned. As I'd suspected I would be, I'd been called to my father's office. In all honesty, it had been a pretty typical punishment. Nothing I couldn't handle.

I really hated bringing that into this room though. I wanted Cade all to myself. "Do we have to talk about my father?"

I could feel him sigh underneath me. "No. Not if you don't want to. But I think you've never been able to talk to anyone about him, and I don't want you to have to carry that alone anymore."

But I'd carried it alone so long. I didn't know how to share it. I couldn't imagine letting someone else have to burden it with me, even though I was well aware that Cade already did share it with me, whether we talked about it or not.

I took a deep breath and tested what it felt to tell him...something. "He said he didn't believe Birch did anything that I didn't ask for, and if I got myself pregnant, I was out of here."

"In that case, maybe I should get you pregnant."

I ignored him because I didn't think he meant it and because I knew my father didn't mean it. He would never willingly take his hooks off me. "He also said if I hadn't asked for it, well, um. I shouldn't be surprised." I cleared my throat. "Shouldn't be surprised that boys like Birch treat me that way. Because that's what whores were for."

He went stiff. "He called you that?"

I was glad I didn't have to look at him when I nodded. It only felt hard to share because my abuse was different than his. It seemed my father's favorite weapon with Cade was pain. With me, it was humiliation.

He swore under his breath, then turned me so he could look at me.

"It's okay," I said, before he could give me his pity. "I'm used to it." Calling me a whore wasn't anything new. It was the first time I'd heard *cum bucket*, however.

"It's not okay, Jolie. And I'm never going to accept your 'it's okay' because you believe it."

Something cracked inside me. Some deep part of my foundation. No, I wanted to insist. *Of course, I don't believe anything my father says. He lies, and he's horrible and says things just because he knows they'll hurt.*

But of course I believed him. Why else did I do the things I did with boys? I didn't want to jerk them off. I didn't want their sweaty dicks in my mouth. I didn't want their cum down my throat.

I didn't know the tears were falling until Cade was kissing them off my cheeks, whispering reassurances. "It's not true. Even if you slept with every guy in the school, it doesn't make you a whore."

"Then why do you regret having sex with me?"

He looked at me like I was insane. "Why do you think I regret it?"

"Why do you just want to sit and talk?" I was being ridiculous, but I was upset and confused, and I didn't know what I wanted.

He kept calm despite my theatrics. "I want to sit and talk because I love you. And I want you to feel loved. It doesn't mean I don't want you, and it for damn sure doesn't mean I regret it."

"I don't know how to feel loved." I was kissing him now too, but my kisses were not soothing. They were hungry and needy and desperate.

Suddenly, I was on my back, my hands stretched over my head and held down, Cade's eyes dark. "Okay, I get it," he said, hovering over me. "Talking isn't enough, but I'm not about to stick my dick in you just so you can confirm that your father's right. How about we meet each other halfway?"

I'd been so surprised by being flipped that I'd stopped crying, but my eyes were still watery. "What do you mean?"

"You let me love you. The way you need to be loved." I was already tugging his sweatshirt off when he stopped me. "There's one rule: it's all about you."

I must have looked confused because he went on. "Trust me. Can you trust me?"

I'd never trusted anyone like I trusted him. He knew most of my secrets. I'd let him into my room. Why would he need to ask?

His smile appeared, startling when he'd been so somber only a minute before. "Well, then trust me all the way. Trust me to love you, okay?"

"Uh. Okay."

"Good. Second rule—"

"I thought there was only one."

"It's a subrule related to the first one." Now he had me smiling. "I get to touch you, but you don't get to touch me."

"Oh." I was beginning to understand. "Ohhh."

And now I was feeling terrified.

I started to sit up. "I don't think I can—"

He pushed me back down. "Can you let me help you try? I'm not going to do anything you don't want me to. I'll ask first. Can I take off your nightgown?"

It was light and practically see-through, and right now it felt as heavy as a winter coat on my skin.

But taking it off meant being naked, and naked felt very unbalanced if it was only going to be me. "Will you take off your clothes too?"

He shook his head. "You already got me naked. It's my turn to see you." He bent down to tug at my nipple through the flimsy material with his lips. "I'm dying to see all of you, Jolie. You have me going crazy imagining what you look like with nothing on."

He moved his mouth to my other breast, and I moaned, "Yes." Then, just in case I wasn't clear, "Yes, you can take off my nightgown."

"If at any time you want me to stop, you just say stop, and I will." He made sure I nodded consent. Slowly, gently, he pulled the gown up my body, over my head, then pinned my arms on the bed before really looking at me.

And the sound he made then as I lay there in only my panties, and he feasted on me with his eyes...

I didn't have the vocabulary to label it. It was raw and primal. A grunt and a growl and a sigh all mixed in one. Its baseness made me feel beautiful. In a way that I was used to feeling beautiful—with my body—but also in a whole new way because I didn't think anyone had ever looked at me so thoroughly. So completely, seeing all of me. The insides along with the out. The bad as well as the good and still wanting to see more.

"You're fucking gorgeous," he said, staring at my breasts like they were diamonds. My nipples were pointed so sharply, I swore they could have cut glass, but when he licked his tongue across one, it was me who cried out.

Seriously? Just having my tit licked felt that good?

I'd never had my breasts adored, never had someone kiss them and suck on them and squeeze them and nip at them until I was wet and writhing. It was more difficult than I imagined. More than once I tried to wrestle a hand free—so I could push him away or pull him closer, I didn't know—and every time he dominated me, keeping me restrained, reminding me he'd stop if I just said stop.

I didn't want him to stop.

As strange and vulnerable as he made me feel, I wanted more.

He took his time giving it. Slowly kissing down my stomach, fucking my belly button with his tongue before moving lower.

"Can I kiss you here?" he asked, hovering just above the very wet spot in my panties. And after I said yes, after he'd kissed me, "Can I kiss you without them on?"

"Please?" I was already about to beg him to take them off. Which had me topsy-turvy because I was a virgin at this part too—I'd never had a mouth between my legs. Never had anyone try to get me off. It was always the other way around, I was always the one giving or being taken from, and even before he had my panties down my legs, I could tell how different it was to be on the other side.

How vulnerable it made me.

How powerful. How wanted.

Even wanting them off, a rush of timidity came over me as he pulled the white flowered panties down my thighs, and I sat up suddenly.

"You're okay." He stopped, though, my underwear gathered around my knees, and of everything he'd said and done, that might have hit me hardest. "Is this okay?"

I had to look away. A deep breath later, I still couldn't look right at him.

"Did you hear something?" He was listening now, assuming that's what my problem was.

"No, I..." I had to decide quickly what to say. Another breath. "I want this. I just—"

He sat up now too. "We don't have to do this tonight."

"No! I mean, yes, we do. Because I want to. And yes, it's okay. Just, no one's done this to me before."

"Never?" He seemed surprised, and I almost wanted to ask what he thought my experience level was, but that wasn't a conversation I really wanted to have at the moment.

So I avoided the question. "I'm nervous."

He stroked the back of my calf, possibly subconsciously. "Nervous about what?"

"That I'll do it wrong."

"I'm the one who will be doing, remember?"

"Or that I won't be able to..."

"There is no end goal here." Now his caress became purposeful, up and down from my ankle to my knee. "If it feels good, it's working. If it's not, I'll stop."

Then there was the practical matter. "What if I...taste...bad?" I was glad it was too dark for him to see me blush.

"Your panties were soaked, Jolie. I could already taste you." He licked his lips. "And you tasted fucking good."

I lowered my face, trying to hide my embarrassed grin. "Okay, then. I'm ready."

I didn't lie all the way back this time. Keeping my elbows propped, I watched as he tugged my underwear off and tossed them to the floor. He kept his eyes on mine, checking in. Reading my every reaction as he gently pressed my knees apart.

I shivered when he finally tore his gaze from mine to look at what he'd uncovered. Again, his face lit up like he'd discovered buried treasure. Reverently, he ran a finger down my seam and up again.

"I'm going to lick you here," he said. "I'm going to put my tongue between your pussy lips, and then here..." He rubbed his finger around my entrance. "I'm going to lick you here. And here." He stuck it inside me, penetrating only as far as I imagined his tongue would go.

My insides clenched tight.

His finger was wet when he dragged it back along the path he'd drawn, landing at the hooded nub at the top. "I'm really going to lick this. Suck it too. Is it okay if I eat you, Jolie?"

My nod was eager.

If I thought describing what he was going to do was amazing—which I did—it was nothing compared to the actual doing. As soon as his tongue hit my skin, sparks shot through my body, awakening nerves I didn't know I had. "Ah!"

His head lifted, and I knew he was about to ask, so I beat him to it. "Still okay. *Very* okay."

He smiled briefly before—praise be—returning his tongue to my pussy. Just the swipe of it along my lips had my toes curling.

And still, my mind was a nosy bee. "Have you done this before?"

He paused to consider. The fact that he had to think was enough to make my body tighten because the answer wasn't hard. The only thing he could be considering was whether or not he should be honest.

Thankfully, he chose the truth. "Yes."

Or maybe not so thankfully because now my throat felt the hard knot of jealousy. "Amelia?"

"No." He laughed like that idea was ridiculous. "And it wouldn't matter if I had because you're the only girl I've done this to that I loved." He licked around my hole, which felt dirty and wrong and really fucking hot. "So I really haven't done *this* before."

"Okay," I said. There seriously wasn't room for any language in my brain anymore. And also, it really was okay. More than okay. It made me happy to be his first in some way.

It made me happy that he was *my* first in this too.

He took that okay as the end of discussion, which it was, and devoted himself to his task, starting over from where he first began and leisurely running his tongue all the places he said he would. He spent several minutes at my hole before completing his sweep back up my lips.

I was quivering before he even made it to my clit.

Then when he did... Fuck. I had to lie all the way down.

I thought for a moment, as he sucked the bundle of nerves into his mouth the first time, about how I'd describe the sensation. The words that came to mind were vague. *Incredible. Heaven. Ecstasy.* It felt like little fires everywhere in my body, furnaces turned to full blast. It felt like volcanoes. It felt like...

Indescribable, really.

So I stopped trying to name it and let myself relax and just feel, and pretty soon the fires began to build and blaze, and before I knew it, my hands were wrapping into the bedsheets and my entire body was trembling. I couldn't breathe. The ball of fire inside me was too big, pressing against my lungs, growing bigger, bigger still until I thought it might overtake me.

Then it did.

My chest lifted from the bed, and pure pleasure launched through me. I was buzzing everywhere, everywhere. There wasn't a fragment of my body that was untouched by bliss—pure and intense and encompassing.

And for the first time, I had a glimpse of understanding about sex, and why people were the way they were with it, and why it was such a powerful commodity, and why so many were obsessed with taking it even when it wasn't given.

But as wonderful as it was, it was over within a minute. And though I felt more relaxed than I'd ever felt, the orgasm didn't fix anything inside of me.

"Are you okay?" Cade had stretched himself out beside me while I recovered. I could feel the bulge in his jeans pressed against my hip, but

I knew he wanted me to ignore it.

For once, I did.

"I'm fantastic," I said honestly. Enlightened a bit, too.

Then I wrapped myself up in his arms and let him hold me while we talked late into the night.

SIXTEEN
CADE

Present

I jiggled the pick in the lock of Stark's office, grateful that Donovan had given me his jackknife pick set for the trip. It was taking me longer than I'd expected, partly because it had been a while since I'd had to engage in a task of this sort. Partly because I wasn't usually so distracted.

"It's like old times," I whispered. "Sneaking around your father's house late at night."

She laughed, making the light from the flashlight bounce. "I'm not scared enough for this to be like old times. And not naked enough."

Not right now, anyway.

I peeked over at her. Dressed in my T-shirt and drawstring gym shorts, she might as well be naked. She had the same effect on my cock. "We could fix that last part. Would you get any satisfaction from fucking on your father's desk?"

"Ew, no." She shivered in disgust.

Honestly, I wasn't sure I would either. Too many bad memories of that room. I probably couldn't even get it up.

"We'll get our vengeance." It sounded like a promise, and I wasn't so sure she should be that assured.

But she looked so adorable with that quirky smile, wearing my clothes, and I was pretty sure I'd just gotten the last pin lifted with the wrench, so I leaned over and kissed her.

Then I opened the door.

She smiled against my lips. "That's a pretty hot trick of yours."

So apparently I could get it up.

I could wait until we were back in our room to do something about that.

I pushed the door open, then reached in and turned the light on without crossing the threshold. Instead, I stood there, looking in at the space that had been the source of so many years of nightmares. It was almost an exact duplicate of his office at school with different books lining his shelves and a window that faced south instead of west. It was smaller than I'd remembered. Better lit. More mundane.

But those changes were all about me and my grown-up, distanced perspective, because on further examination, the room seemed basically unchanged.

Jolie hadn't yet moved either. "He reorganized the books," she said, indicating she was applying the same scrutiny to the room I was.

I followed her line of sight and saw it immediately—a minor alteration, unnoticeable to anyone who hadn't spent long minutes staring at the shelves, memorizing the titles to distract from the pain. My body shuddered, remembering.

Fuck. It was terrible.

Being back here was unspeakably terrible.

I grabbed Jolie's hand in mine, and she took it quickly as though she'd been the one reaching. There was no choice but to be together in this house. Now, like then, it was the only way to survive, and I didn't question the necessity of her. Didn't think about what would happen between us when we left. Future didn't exist when you were in Stark's world. There was only the present, anchored in a shitty past. There was only living through the moment.

I pressed my palm harder against hers. "Should we?"

"Yeah," she said, straightening. Steeling herself. "Let's get this over with."

Together, we crossed into the room.

Strangely, it was just as easy to breathe as it had been out in the hall. Back then, I'd been convinced the oxygen was thinner in Stark's office. It seemed I'd been wrong.

Maybe he had to be there for the air to constrict.

Realizing it was just a space like any other made it easier to focus, and I dropped Jolie's hand and headed straight for the desk.

"Which one did you say it was in?" I asked, already tearing apart the top drawer. This had always been planned as a quick in-and-out. We needed the extra key to the cabin safe, and that was all. Planting evidence in Stark's safe was the surest strategy, and there was no reason to torture ourselves staying longer than we had to.

She didn't appear to be as motivated to be done with our task. Instead of following me to the desk, she'd crossed to the bookshelves. "*Antony and Cleopatra. All's Well That Ends Well. As You Like It.*" She paused in between each title, as though searching for the next. "They're all still here. Just not in alphabetical anymore. It looks like they're grouped by genre now."

Not finding any keys in the first drawer, I shut it and moved on to the second. "Was the key all by itself, or is it on a ring?"

"The parenting books were the ones I found particularly ironic." I heard the sound of a book being pulled off the shelf. "*Positive Discipline*. It even looks like it was actually read. There're notes in the margins."

"Let me guess—he's arguing with his methods." The second drawer was also a bust, and the bottom drawers were locked, but the sight of an external hard drive had me reconsidering our strategy.

"*Her* methods. The writer is a she, and of course, that's what the notes are. I'm surprised he even bothered reading material written by a woman."

"We could just plant the flash drive here," I said, thinking out loud.

"Not after we've been here. It's too obvious. He could claim we planted it." She said it quickly, suggesting she'd already thought about it.

"Right, right." I would have gotten there too in a minute. And now it made me think of something else. "We should put the safe key back after so he can't say it was stolen."

Fuck. I didn't want either of us to have to come back.

"Could we get it copied tomorrow? Put it back before we ever go?"

She was sharp.

I should have been that sharp. "Good thinking." I pulled the jackknife pick from the pocket of my sweats. "You said the safe key was in a locked drawer, didn't you?"

"Bottom right, if it's in the same place it was before."

She put the book back and moved to the single bookshelf with pictures on display. A fleeting glance told me they were exactly the same photos that had been there years ago—a professional headshot of each of Stark's parents, a posed family portrait of Stark and his first wife with a toddler version of Jolie on her lap, a picture my mother had given him of me and her at my eleventh birthday party, and a formal photo from both his weddings, the first one framed and the second printed out and stuck in the corner of the glass covering the original.

"I always thought it was funny that he had these in here at all," she said. "They were always covered in dust. It wasn't like they meant anything to him, and it's not like he was putting them up to boast. No one ever came in here but us."

I'd stared at those pictures until I had every detail memorized, and I'd never thought too much about why they were there. They'd seemed incidental to me. A place he put these things that he didn't know what to do with.

I'd wondered if that's how he kept us in his mind too—relegated to a dusty shelf, never looked at, displayed exactly how he wanted us displayed. "They reminded him we were his," I said, sitting down in the chair to work on the lock.

"Was that it?" She didn't seem quite convinced.

The drawer was easier to pop than the door, and it was open almost instantly. "Got it," I said, looking up at Jolie.

She'd picked up one of the pictures from the shelf and was studying it. Now that she was holding it, I realized I didn't recognize the frame, and her earnest expression had me curious. "What is it?"

She let out a sigh. "Me. Graduation."

I knew better than to get distracted, but I needed to see it. "Show me."

She brought it over, and I stood to look at it with her. Seeing her like that, looking like she had the last time I'd seen her all those years ago, knocked the wind out of me. She looked exactly how she'd been etched in my memory—her hair a mousy brownish blonde, her face round. I could have conjured up the image of her in that cap and gown in a blink, and I hadn't even gotten to see her walk the stage. It was just another thing Stark had stolen from me. Another moment that I'd been denied.

I'd imagined it though. I'd sat in that stupid parking lot and fantasized the whole thing, waiting for her to hitch a ride with Amelia's parents and come meet up with me five miles away.

"You can tell I'd been crying," she said softly. "My eyes are puffy."

They were visibly red, and she hadn't even bothered to try to smile.

I realized what she was insinuating. "You'd already decided you weren't coming." I'd wondered for years. Wondered if she'd ever planned to come at all.

"I wasn't always not going to come," she said, reading my mind. "I'd meant it when I said I would."

And there it was—the part of the past we'd been dancing around. The thing I hadn't been able to bring myself to talk about. Because it hurt so much already, and I couldn't imagine that any reason she gave for not coming would make it better. Chances were, it would make it worse.

So I hadn't asked.

And she hadn't said.

But now it was there between us, picture proof that she'd suffered something.

I forced my eyes from the ghost in the picture to the woman at my side. "Why didn't you?"

Her lips turned down, and her eyes seemed to match the frown, but when she opened her mouth, it was another voice that spoke.

"Should have known that you weren't just stopping by for old time's sake. Should I call the cops and report a break in? There's nothing of value in there, I assure you."

Jolie jumped, and both of our gazes flew to the doorway where my mother stood in her bathrobe.

"It's not what it looks like. We were just…" As always, Jolie was quick to make amends. To smooth things over.

Fuck that. I wasn't explaining shit to my mother. "Do you even know what's in here? Have you ever taken the initiative to look for yourself? Hard drives. Locked drawers." I hadn't even gotten to the ones that held his instruments of pain.

"Your father—"

"Not my father," I corrected.

"Is the head of a prestigious school. He deals with private information all the time."

There was no use pointing out that data pertaining to Stark Academy should be kept at his school office, or that she couldn't actually know what was on all these drives unless she'd looked, which I was willing to bet she hadn't done. She'd find some way to stand by him no matter what was said, no matter what I found.

So instead, I cut to the chase. "Always so eager to defend him. To protect *him*. You're so good at it. I can't even imagine what kind of mother you would have been if you'd ever tried to use that instinct to protect *us*."

"There it is. The blame. I was waiting for it." She'd come into the office now, and if it felt like foreign territory or a line she shouldn't have crossed, she didn't show it. "You don't know shit about what I've done for you."

I let out a sardonic laugh. "I know what you *haven't* done. Frankly, that's all I need to know."

Her eyes flashed with anger, then looked at Jolie, who had slunk away to sit on the chair. Jolie had been raised to avoid conflict. I couldn't blame her for still having the urge to back away.

But that made me all the more eager to keep her out of it. "Don't look at her. She's not under his thumb anymore either. And despite not being your flesh and blood, she needed you to protect her too. We were kids, for Christ's sake."

She stared again at Jolie, pointedly this time. "You're really not going to say anything?"

I looked from one woman to the other, realizing there was an unspoken conversation happening between them that I wasn't privy to. "What? What am I missing?"

My mother folded her arms across her chest, and Jolie sighed. "Carla is the only reason I was able to get out of here, Cade. She helped me escape."

There were too many arrows in those two sentences. Too many hits to the heart. "My mother helped you? *Escape?*" The language alone shed light on what those years had been like after I'd left. He hadn't changed. Of course, he hadn't. It didn't matter that she was an adult.

So why had she fucking stayed?

There were other questions closer to the tip of my tongue. "And she knew where you were all this time?"

"No, no," Jolie insisted.

"I've had an email," my mother said.

"She had an email," Jolie confirmed.

Not only had she let my mother help her, but she'd let her stay connected as well.

This was the shit I hadn't wanted to know. This was the shit that only threatened to make painful memories hurt worse.

And the biggest sting? My mother had helped Jolie when she'd never helped me. "Fabulous. She can help you now then too."

For the second time that night, I stormed out on my mother.

This time Jolie followed sooner than she had before. She caught up with me before I'd made it to our room.

My room.

"Cade, please don't..." she said behind me on the stairs.

I swung around to face her at the top, sweeping my arm around her waist to catch her when my turn had taken her by surprise.

In my arms, she breathed a sigh of relief, and fuck if I didn't breathe it too. "Jolie...fuck," I said, pressing my forehead to hers, pulling strength from her touch.

"I'm sorry. I didn't know if I should tell you. I'm—"

"No, no. I'm just glad that you got out of here." It wasn't a lie. It just wasn't all the truth.

"I'm sorry," she said again. She wrapped an arm around my neck, and I could feel there was more she wanted to say, more she wanted to explain.

I just...

I couldn't hear it.

I forced myself to focus on something solid. Our plan. "I'll try to get back in there in a little while. There's still a long time before morning, and she hasn't kicked us out, so we still have a shot."

I sensed her smile before she leaned back, and I saw it. Then she held up her other hand to show me a ring of keys. "All the extra keys to the cabin. I grabbed them from the drawer while you two were arguing."

I almost laughed.

And then I did laugh. She hadn't been slinking after all. She really wasn't the girl she'd once been. She'd gotten a backbone, and I kept forgetting to see it.

I made a silent vow to recognize it more often. Then kissing her, I tugged her into our room—because as long as we were in this house together, it would be *our* room—and made another silent vow that, from now on, I was only concerned with the present.

The past needed to stay where it belonged—in the past.

SEVENTEEN
CADE

Past

"There are so many freaking bugs!"

I glanced up from my tire scrubbing, expecting to see Jolie swatting away mosquitos. Instead, she was frowning down at the windshield. "I never realized how dangerous cars were to insects. And what a terrible surprise that has to be, flying along, minding your own bug business and then wham! Their little guts are just caked on here, too."

I shook my head and stood up, then made sure to touch as much of her as possible as I moved her out of the way. "I'll take gut cleanup. You can take over scrubbing the tire rims."

"You mean you'll take over my dirty work for me?" She gave me the cutest little smile and blinked her eyes coyly, as if that hadn't been her plan with the comment all along.

"I wouldn't be too excited—the rims are covered in mud."

She scowled as she examined one. "How about I work on soaping up the rest of the car?"

I grinned. "Sure, sure." Honestly, she didn't have to ask. She knew I'd take all the shit parts of the task. I'd even let her sit the whole thing out if I didn't think her father would have something to say about it.

But she knelt down to work on the tire rim after all, and when I gave her a questioning eyebrow, she shrugged. "I felt guilty."

"For fuck's sake. Let me do the damn tires. Get scrubbing the hood."

She bit her lip and looked at me, wheels spinning, and I knew she wasn't thinking about whether or not to take me up on the offer but about how much she wanted to kiss me for it. Or just that she wanted to kiss me in general. It was a look I knew well. A look I often found myself giving her in return.

Four months into being a real couple, and the secrecy only got harder.

Only eight more weeks, I told myself. Eight weeks until graduation, and then we'd be gone. It was the mantra we'd adopted, the countdown. It was hard to imagine how we'd made it through before we had each other, because even with her, two months felt like an eternity.

Though, right at the moment, things weren't actually that bad.

Jolie echoed my thoughts. "I have to say, as far as chores go, I'd rather be scraping mud and bugs off Dad's car. It's almost not even a chore."

"I don't know. Could be better if you were wearing a bikini."

She blushed as she rolled her eyes. "You see enough of my body as it is."

"Never." Sneaking into her room every night was most definitely not enough.

But we were both in good moods, considering. The sun was out, a rare April Sunday when the temperature hit seventy, and we'd just come off of spring break. While Stark hadn't taken us anywhere, he'd gone up to his cabin for the week to hunt, which meant we'd not only had a vacation from his cruelty, but also we'd had more time to be with each other without him around, dictating our every second. We'd kept our hands to ourselves—mostly—since my mother was still around, and spent our hours reading to each other and listening to music and planning our future.

Best spring break I'd ever had, hands down.

I paused my bug scraping to watch her lift up on her tiptoes to clean the car roof. How a girl could look sexy in a white T-shirt and long swim shorts, I had no idea, but she did. Forget the bikini. I was half hard without it.

Walking past her to dip my sponge in the bucket, I glanced toward the house, wondering if anyone would see if I smacked her on the ass.

"Don't do it," she whispered.

She was so in tune with me, it was scary.

She turned her head to peer at me. "I heard Dad telling Carla he might take her away for a second honeymoon to the Bahamas. Which is a little weird since they never went on a first honeymoon."

Stark was such a tightwad with his money, I couldn't imagine him splurging on a vacation, but he'd been somewhat generous since he'd returned from his hunting trip on Friday, suggesting we get a new dishwasher and redo the driveway. "Maybe he lied about going hunting and went gambling instead. It's like he suddenly hit the jackpot."

"This car has definitely been to the cabin. And he gets like this sometimes. Splurges for a few months every couple of years. Not on us, of course. Stuff for himself. But point is, if they're going on a trip—house to ourselves." She tried to waggle her eyebrows and failed.

God, she was so adorable it hurt.

"Wait—your father's going to take a trip while school's in session?"

"No, the summer." She came flat to her feet, realization dawning on her face. We wouldn't be here this summer. "Oh." It took her a second, then she grinned.

It was strange to think of a future not tied to this hellhole, and I'd been here less than a year. I couldn't begin to understand how she felt. It was hard not to feel like her hero. We hadn't even left yet, but just knowing it was on the horizon made me feel like I'd already rescued her.

Cocky, maybe.

But I could admit she'd already rescued me too.

Her eyes suddenly focused on something behind me, and the grin disappeared. "That's for you."

Students had returned earlier that morning, but very few ever wandered all the way back here, so I already guessed who it was before I turned to see Amelia Lu standing at the edge of the property.

"Sure, Cade, I'll take over the work while you go get cozy with your girlfriend." As good as she was at hiding things, Jolie's resentment toward Amelia was obvious.

"You could come talk to her with me."

"Because it's natural for stepsisters to tag along like a third wheel," she said sarcastically. "Good thinking."

I wanted to tease her about her jealousy and then pull her into my arms and kiss her until she felt reassured, but both were off limits in the daylight. After dropping my sponge in the bucket, I took a smaller risk and playfully tugged on the back of her ponytail. "Be right back."

I jogged to the edge of the drive, Jolie's stare heavy on my back.

"Careful," Amelia said when I was close enough to hear her. "You guys look awfully cozy."

"We're washing a car together. I've barely touched her." It was easy to get defensive considering how much I knew I was holding back.

"You don't have to touch each other. You guys have googly eyes that can be seen for miles." She was teasing me, and she was warning me, all at once.

"Yeah, yeah. You're probably right." I sighed. "Is that why you're here? Checking up on us?"

"Figured I should probably come say hi to my *boyfriend* after being gone a week."

Amelia was the one person in the world who knew about me and Jolie, and no, I wasn't worried about her telling anyone. I'd been nervous about talking to her when she came back from winter break, sure that she'd guessed and intent on convincing her otherwise.

But she was too smart to buy it, and after everything, she deserved the truth. Thankfully, she'd promised to keep it hush. A few weeks later, she went a step further and offered to continue to pretend to be my girlfriend, to throw off any suspicions around campus. She had her own motivations, it turned out, since she'd moved on from booty calls with me to booty calls with the new Latin teacher and appreciated being able to use me to explain her frequent hickeys.

Jolie knew about the arrangement, of course, and appreciated Amelia for it, though she understandably didn't like it.

And I tried to pretend I didn't like how much it bothered her.

"I suppose that does make sense." Sure I saw movement at the front window, I stepped closer to Amelia, hoping we looked intimate. "I'll get in trouble if we talk long, though."

"With Headmaster Stark or Julianna?"

"Both." I laughed.

"Then I'll get out of your hair. But, hey—have you heard anything about Bernard?"

"Bernard Arnold?" I barely knew the guy. He was a junior, fairly quiet, the broody type. "What about him?"

"He's missing."

"Missing?"

"He missed check-in, so his RA called his family, and it seems there was a mix-up—dad thought mom had him, mom thought dad had him—one of those preoccupied and divorced parent situations. They're doing some investigating with other family and friends, but basically it looks like he never left."

"So he was here the whole time." There were always a couple of students who stuck around for the shorter breaks. Scholarship kids, usually. Kids who couldn't afford a quick trip home.

"No. No one's seen him since Friday before break."

"Fuck." I glanced back at Jolie, wondering if she'd heard anything about it. "Does Stark know?"

She nodded. "I heard the dorm parent called him a few hours ago to ask if he should contact the police. Stark said to give it until tomorrow."

He was so obsessed with his image, it totally made sense. The asshole probably wanted an internal investigation so he could clean up his rep before anyone found out one of his students ran away. "Let me know if you hear anything?"

"Yep."

This was the awkward part—the goodbye. If Stark was watching, and there was a fifty-fifty chance he was since he was hyper attentive where his daughter and I were concerned—then our goodbye would be best with a little oomph.

But I hated going that far with the ruse, especially when I knew Jolie was watching.

Amelia made the decision for me, pressing up on her tiptoes to give me a quick kiss on the lips. "It's just a kiss," she said innocently when I jumped away too quickly. "Julianna can take it. Heaven knows she's not a prude."

Sensing I was already in hot water, I didn't press the conversation further. "Bye, Amelia," I said and headed back to the car.

It was obvious Jolie wasn't speaking to me before I'd tried to engage her in conversation. Hell, I couldn't get her to even look at me.

"Come on, Jol. You know it's for show." I picked up the sponge from the bucket, but I was more concerned with her than the car. "And if you're going to be mad at someone, be mad at Amelia. It wasn't me."

I felt a little shitty for throwing Amelia under the bus, but it wasn't like it wasn't the truth.

"Mm-hmm."

Yeah, definitely not speaking to me.

Which was maddening on so many levels. Did she think I liked the situation any better than she did? Did she think I wanted to be making out with Amelia instead of her?

And what about Amelia's prude comment? It wasn't the only recent reference I'd heard to Jolie's past reputation. "At least I'm front and center about it. I have no idea what you're doing with the boys you're supposedly tutoring."

That got her attention. "Are you seriously suggesting I'm messing around?"

I already felt guilty for bringing it up, but now that I had, I wasn't sure how to back out of it.

So I shrugged. "How am I supposed to know?"

"That is some bullshit, Cade Warren. I'm upset about something I saw with my own two eyes, and instead of validating my feelings about it, you decide to make up some baseless drama about me so that you can feel better about yourself?"

"Not exactly baseless..."

I deserved it when she threw the bucket of soapy water on me.

She immediately clapped her hand over her mouth, but I could see the laughter in her eyes, and because I wanted to lighten the situation—and also a little because I wanted revenge—I picked up the hose, turned on the nozzle at the end, and sprayed her.

"Oh my God, you didn't." She looked down at her soaked shirt, her back arched trying to keep the cold, wet material from her skin.

"I did." I was still wetter than she was. "And guess what? I'm about to do it again."

With a shriek, she ran backward, holding her hands up as though they could protect her.

I followed after her, getting one more good spray in before abandoning the hose and chasing her. I caught up with her easily, and no longer in the sight of the front windows, I walked her back until she was pressed up against the garage.

"It makes me so fucking crazy to have to be secret about you," I growled. Her bra was thin under the wet, white T-shirt, and I could see the details of her hard nipples clearly. "It rips me apart to not be able to tell the whole world how I feel about you."

Unable to stop myself, I leaned in and devoured her mouth. And because I really was at the end of my rope—because I was so fucking worn out from having to be restrained—I slipped my hand down her swim shorts, inside her panties, and found the warm button between her legs that I'd become so familiar with in the last few months.

"We shouldn't do this." But the tone in her voice sounded more like *please, keep doing this*, and her own hand was stroking my cock through my jeans.

"I'm so fucking tired of *shouldn't*." I slid my hand lower, probing inside of her. She was so wet, and it wasn't from the hose.

"I don't know how to stay away from you."

"Someday, there won't be anymore sneaking around. Someday, it will be you and me going on trips to the Bahamas. Someday, it isn't going to matter how we met or what we were to each other. The only label that will matter is that you're mine."

Her hand lost its rhythm, and she gave up on fondling me, instead wrapping her fingers in my shirt, clutching on as though she needed the support to stand. I penetrated deeper, adding a second finger when her walls began to tighten around the first. Concentrating on her reactions, I moved my thumb against her sensitive nub, teasing her with a mixture of soft and hard strokes.

I was painfully hard, her breathy gasps sending more blood to my cock, and shit, it was stupid. So fucking stupid—to be kissing her so possessively, to be finger fucking her in the yard—and after the day in the locker room, I'd been so good about not being stupid with her. I only allowed myself to touch her in the middle of the night. I insisted on condoms, and if we couldn't get our hands on them, I didn't put my cock inside her, never again putting trust in pulling out. I didn't look at her at dinner. I didn't say her name. I didn't leave my room in the morning until I knew she'd already gone downstairs. I pretended I barely noticed her. I never let on that she was the only thing that ever crossed my mind.

I'd been painstakingly good for four months, and now any ounce of restraint I'd had vanished, and all I cared about was making her come all over my hand. She was there, so close, so almost there...

I don't know how I heard it. I was so completely wrapped up in our bubble—me and her, nothing else. Maybe we had an angel on our side, or maybe my ears had just become so attuned to always being on guard, whether I was aware of it or not. However it managed to register, I heard the footsteps in time, and I pulled away abruptly so that there was at least a yard between us when Stark came around the corner. "The car doesn't look done."

Jolie was used to thinking fast. She pushed away from the garage, her breathing still rapid. "Cade chased me with the hose," she accused.

She was pretty believable as a sibling complaining about her stepbrother's antics, as long as Stark didn't look at my crotch or think too much about the flush in her cheeks or notice how swollen her lips were.

My heart racing, I took my place in the scene. "She poured the bucket on me first."

"Accidentally. God." She marched toward the car and picked up her sponge, trying to pull her father's attention. I recognized the motives of her behavior better than I used to. *See, I'm doing what you want, Dad. There's nothing to be mad at.*

But he saw something to be mad at anyway.

I didn't think he actually saw my hand down her pants or my lips on hers, because if he had, he would have made a very big production about it. But he saw *something*. Maybe it was how we were so quick to move away from each other. Or the panicked look of my posture. Or maybe he saw the same googly eyes that Amelia claimed we always had for each other.

Or maybe I was being paranoid, and he was just pissed that we weren't finished with his car. "To my office, Cade."

Jolie went pale, and even though we'd promised not to draw attention to our relationship by sticking up for each other, she did anyway. "Why him? I said I started it with the bucket."

"I heard you. Your punishment is to finish washing the car by yourself. And Cade can explain to me why he thinks it's okay to waste my water, as well as why he finds it acceptable to distract my daughter from her chores. Are there any other transgressions you want to add to that?"

I could sense Jolie wanting to say something, wanting to save me the way she knew that I would want to save her if the situation was reversed. But I gave her a quick glance that warned her to keep her mouth shut.

Eight weeks. I thought the words loudly in my head, hoping she'd somehow hear them. Only eight weeks, and we were gone.

Meanwhile, I'd been fucking stupid today, and even if that wasn't what I was being punished for, I definitely deserved what I got.

EIGHTEEN
CADE

"Take off your shirt and put your palms on the desk."

It didn't matter how many times I'd been in his office now, I still found my entire body tensing up as soon as I crossed the threshold.

I was even more nervous today, the adrenaline from almost being caught still running through my veins, sending my anxiety to overdrive. My tension was validated with his initial instructions—the punishment was always worse when he started with bare skin.

Spring break was definitely over.

"It will be worse for you if you try to drag this out," Stark said when I hadn't moved past the doorway.

I'd already had the fortune of experiencing what happened when I wasn't quick to respond and wasn't about to test him again. His demeanor suggested he was in one of his more sadistic moods.

Lucky me.

Taking a deep breath, I forced my feet forward, stripping off my wet shirt as I went. Instead of dropping it to the floor, I set it on the desk before placing my palms on the wood. If this was going to hurt like I thought it was, I'd want something to bite on so I didn't chew up my tongue.

And so that I didn't scream.

Not that the happenings in this room were secret to anyone else in the house, but I preferred keeping a tough image. Even if Jolie knew it was all a facade, it kept her from acknowledging how completely awful it was, and for some reason, that made it fractionally more tolerable.

Eyes facing the desk, I shook my head from side to side, knowing that the more tense I was, the worse it would feel. After one particularly bad session a few months before, I'd found a meditation book in the library that happened to include a section on managing stress. The deep breathing techniques had been useful, both when I was facing Stark's latest punishment and when I was randomly seized by inexplicable panic.

I tried one of the methods now, engaging in a three-part breath—into the collarbone, into the lungs, exhale. I only managed to get two in before I heard the drawer open—the distinct squeak telling me it was the drawer that kept the whip—and my focus was thrown. I'd been listening for the rustle of his belt, hoping that would be his weapon of choice, or even the yardstick, which he was quite fond of and didn't leave lasting damage.

The skinny-tailed whip was the worst, and my wounds from the last time were less than three weeks old and just starting to really heal. I'd been hopeful they wouldn't scar, but if he reopened them today, there was less chance I wouldn't walk away with a souvenir. If Jolie still had Neosporin, she'd give it to me, and if not, she might know how to get her hands on more.

But I couldn't think about the later because I was still in the now, and the now required all of my attention.

Smack!

Stark liked to crack the whip through the air before using it on my skin. Warming up, maybe. He seemed to enjoy the shiver of fear it sent through my body as much as he enjoyed the actual torture. Anyone that suggested that anticipation was worse than the actual pain didn't know what the fuck they were talking about, but I would readily concede that it was far preferable to just get the shit over with.

This wasn't the crack of the whip, though. This was new. This was the smack of a thick cane against the desk. A cane that would surely feel a hell of a lot more substantial than the skinny-tailed whip.

It was almost impossible to suppress the instinct to run.

"You know why you're here today, Cade?" he said, slapping the cane lightly against the palm of his hand.

"Because I wasted water, sir."

In the early days, I'd argued my supposed transgressions. It was a natural defense mechanism, and even after I'd been given positive proof that it only made the punishment worse, I hadn't been able to shut my rebellious mouth.

Submitting to his power over me had never been an option until Jolie convinced me to try it. It had gone against every instinct in my body, but she'd been right. He wanted to see me on my knees—figuratively, if not literally—and the sooner I got there, the sooner he was satisfied.

He's even quicker if you cry, she'd said.

I still had a hard time letting him see tears. I'd discovered he also got off on bleeding, though, which I obviously had no control over.

But I could definitely lick his ass from word one. "I'm sorry, sir. It was impulsive, and I regret my actions." *Blah, blah, blah.* It wasn't even hard to sound sincere. Seconds from facing the pain, I was always genuinely regretful.

This should have been enough to get him going. Today, he surprised me.

"You think I give a shit about the water? With as much as we use to keep the grounds green, the amount you used today is negligible to our bill."

Of course, I knew that. It was a surprise that he did. Usually, *negligible* was not a word in his vocabulary. He was a tightwad, always harping on keeping the furnace no higher than sixty-eight, practically measuring out how much cereal I put in my bowl in the morning, as if he saw the world in pennies and nickels.

I hadn't realized I could get any more apprehensive, but apparently I could. My heart rate increased, and it felt like it was lodged firmly in my throat. Surprises were never good where Stark was concerned.

"Do you want to guess again?" he asked, slapping his palm again, taunting me with the way it smacked against his skin.

I really didn't want to guess again. Because if it wasn't the water, then it was Jolie. Had he seen us after all?

Well, I wasn't admitting shit. If he'd seen us, he'd have to put the accusation out there himself. I wasn't walking into a trap, and I wasn't bringing Jolie into it, no matter what he did to me.

"I'm waiting, Cade."

"It was taking too long to scrub the car," I said, knowing that wasn't it, but doing my best to paint myself as innocent of whatever it was he believed. "That was my fault too. Amelia stopped by and—"

"Since you aren't allowed to have guests when you have chores to complete, that's another infraction to add to your list, but you're still far from the reason you're here right now." He bent down next to me and clapped his hand around my shoulders, as though we were buddies. "You're a dumb one, but you aren't this dumb. You know what this is about."

"I really don't, sir." I could feel his breath on my cheek, smelled the lingering scent of the tuna fish sandwich he'd had for lunch. He wasn't usually this intrusive, and the new tactic upped my trepidation. I didn't dare turn my head, afraid my eyes would give something away. Because if he really had figured out our secret, there was no way I was leaving the room alive.

He pulled on a hair at the base of my neck, chuckling when I jerked. "You really think I'm the dumb one, don't you? Think you've been pulling the wool over my eyes for months, but let's be clear—the only reason you've gotten away with it is because I let you."

I moved from trepidation to out-and-out fear. "I don't think you're dumb at all, sir. I don't know—"

"It's okay, I know. I've seen you, Cade." His tone was suddenly gentle, coaxing. "You think I've missed the way you look at her across the dinner table? I'm a man, too. I remember what it's like to be a teen.

The hormones. The way anything with tits can get you hard. And my daughter is a looker. It's understandable."

My chest hurt, and it was getting increasingly harder not to piss myself. I'd thought I'd been so careful, trying to never look at her in case I let something on. The only glimmer of hope was that he was only talking about longing looks. And so far, he was only talking about me.

I'd never been big on praying, but I started right then, praying to whatever God there might be in the sky to please not be anything more.

"I figured no harm in lustful thoughts," he continued. "It seemed to be making you miserable, but no harm in a little suffering. Good for the spirit."

That was his life mantra spoken out loud right there.

"You know what was different about today?"

I couldn't help myself—I turned my head toward him, desperate to hear the depth of the shit pile I'd gotten myself in. The word what was on the tip of my tongue, but I forced myself to continue playing dumb. "I've never looked at your daughter the way you're suggesting. Not today. Not ever."

He went on as if I hadn't spoken. "Today, you weren't just looking at her with lust. Today, you were looking at her like you thought you could have her. See the difference there? See why there's no way that can't go unpunished? Because there is no way in hell you are ever getting your filthy bastard hands on my daughter. Do you hear me?"

It was surreal how relieved I could be while simultaneously feeling the weight of his threat. But fuck, I was slack with the relief, my eyes tearing. He didn't actually know anything. He hadn't seen. He had nothing but suspicions.

But if he ever, ever knew there was more...

"You do hear me," he said, clapping my back on my previous wound so that I would jerk again. "It's so gratifying to be understood. I'll make this memorable for you, so you don't forget. Go ahead, and let it out. Tears don't look good on a man, but we both know you're just a whiny little bitch. No use pretending otherwise."

I hadn't realized I was really crying, until he pointed it out. He hadn't even struck me yet, and a puddle was forming on the desk. By the time it smacked across my back, tearing and lacerating my skin, I was sobbing.

He only hit me once with the cane, but he followed with a smack of his hand against the wound, eliciting a higher-pitched cry from my throat. I could barely distinguish the next two slaps from each other because my whole body felt like a throbbing nerve. I didn't need to have the cane across my back to be in pain. It hurt just to exist, to have the mother that I had, to have to endure these punishments, to have to hide the only joy in my life from nearly everyone around me. It hurt to understand that this had been Jolie's whole life. It hurt to know we had eight fucking more weeks to survive, and it hurt to know that, even though our future had to be better than this, it was still uncertain.

And even though we were determined to escape, it hurt to know that we would never completely break free of him—he'd marked himself on our souls. He'd broken us in places that would never be healed.

I was so consumed by my crying, I didn't realize when the slaps stopped. It was almost like coming to—the way I suddenly became alert to my surroundings, the way that only a moment before I'd existed in some plane by myself—and in the shock, I didn't think before I twisted to look for Stark. It wasn't like him to have me linger after he'd finished his abuse, but I'd never broken down before, and now that I was aware of my skin, I had a feeling my wound was pretty bad.

It certainly hurt to turn, and I winced when I did, but the pain was momentarily forgotten when I saw my stepfather. His eyes were shut, so he didn't see me. The cane was hanging from his left hand, loosely at his side, and the right was fisted around his exposed cock, jerking himself rapidly, and judging from the expression on his face, he was very close to climax.

Bile rose in my mouth, and I quickly turned back to the desk, focusing my eyes on the wood so hard they physically hurt. *Unsee it, unsee it, unsee it.* I commanded myself to forget. It was such a brief look. So brief it didn't count. Like when I picked up a cigarette that I'd dropped on the ground and told myself *five-second rule* before picking it up and putting it in my mouth.

I didn't see it.

It didn't happen.

It *couldn't* be happening.

As terrible as everything else was, this couldn't be part of it. This would make it too terrible. This would make it that much closer to unsurvivable.

At the same time, another part of my brain tried to sort the new information. Tried to be reasonable. *You always knew your pain got him going. This is probably what he does every time after you leave. This isn't anything new. This doesn't change anything.*

But it changed everything.

I knew that despite not having time or capability to process it.

I knew this had inflicted a new pain that I couldn't begin to absorb.

This thing he'd done—was doing—*to me* without even touching me, it had an immeasurable weight. This was a trauma that couldn't be scaled against the other traumas. I was desperately trying to compartmentalize it, trying to stow it someplace I'd never remember, but it was too big to tuck away neatly, so instead it occupied every part of me, and still I was already trying to block it out, trying to paint over it. Trying to make it blend in with everything else so I could pretend it wasn't there. So I could make it go away. Make it not be real.

Just look at the desk.

Just see the desk.

Don't see anything but the desk.

I stared at that one spot, and didn't move for what seemed like ages. I managed to concentrate all of my attention on my throbbing back, so I didn't hear when he finished or when he zipped up his pants or when he finally walked to the drawer to put away the cane.

"When you're done sobbing like a little girl, you can clean up your tears and get out of here," he said.

He'd been so self-absorbed, he hadn't noticed I'd stopped crying.

That was good. I was glad he'd forgotten about me. It made it easier for me to forget about him.

I pretended to wipe the last of my tears away, grabbed my T-shirt to dry up the drops on the desk, then left without putting it on. Without looking at him. I always felt small coming out of his office, along with whatever pain he'd administered that session. Today, I also felt exposed. I felt naked, like I had more than just my shirt off, and it wasn't just my back burning from the slaps but all of me that burned with red-hot shame.

Eight weeks, I reminded myself as I climbed up the stairs to my room. Thank God Jolie wasn't waiting for me. I couldn't see her right now, and after this, we had to be cautious as fuck.

I wouldn't go to her room tonight.

I would avoid her.

We had to stop sneaking around. We couldn't risk being caught. I'd keep my eyes down through every meal. I'd lay low and keep her safe, and I swore to myself that I would never ever say a single word about what happened in that room to anyone as long as I lived.

NINETEEN
CADE

I was already most of the way through my physics assignment when the classroom door opened. My seat was near the front, so I didn't notice until Ms. Coates stopped her lecture. "Yes, Ms. Stark?"

As soon as I heard her say her name, I knew it was about me.

"Could you please excuse Cade Warren? His mother is here to see him about an important matter." She was all self-confidence. Not a note of anything unusual in her voice to betray the lie.

It helped that the lie was easy to believe. Most of the students boarded on campus, so parent drop-ins were not the norm, but everyone knew who my mother was. Just because she'd never called me out of class before didn't mean it wasn't possible.

"Did the office send a note?" Ms. Coates asked, following protocol despite the fact she was addressing the headmaster's daughter. Or perhaps *because*.

"No. His mother saw me in the hall and asked me to get him for her. Should I tell her to go to the office?"

My knee bounced under my desk, and I tried to keep my expression stone, even though I was freaking the fuck out. Whatever Jolie's scheme was here, there was every possibility it was going to blow up in her face. How could she stay so calm?

It was a needless worry because after a beat, Ms. Coates sighed. "Better take your things in case you won't be back."

It took me a second to move, a bit shocked that Jolie had managed to pull this off. Ms. Coates stared at me, waiting for me to leave before she went on, and that was all that I needed to get my ass in motion. Sticking my pencil in my pocket, I dumped my notebook and my textbook in my bag and scurried to the door where Jolie was patiently waiting, a twinkle of satisfaction gleaming in her eyes.

I followed her into the hall, neither of us speaking even after the door was closed behind us. There was no way in hell she was taking me to my mother. Carla would never dare to interfere in my school day, even if there was an emergency. I had zero doubt this was Jolie on her own, and there was something romantic about that.

But there was also an incredible risk associated, and with each step we took—each second that passed with the possibility of us getting caught—I found myself getting more and more mad.

What did I expect, though? After not talking to her for four days, did I really think she wouldn't do something like this?

Finally, she led me down the arts hall and into the empty choir room. As soon as the heavy door clicked shut, she turned to face me, and I dropped my bag to the floor, bracing myself for her inevitable rush into my arms.

A rush that never happened.

"What the fuck, Cade?"

I should have expected that I wasn't the only one who was mad. She had more right to be than me, honestly.

Even knowing that, natural instinct had me automatically jumping to offense. "Me, what the fuck? What about you? What kind of ballsy shit was that? What if Ms. Coates asks my mother why she needed me, or worse, your father? What if your father had seen us in the hall? Are you trying to get us caught?"

She rolled her eyes. "Ms. Coates never follows up on anything, and my father is preoccupied with the cops and Bernard's disappearance right now. You don't think I know how to be careful?"

Immediately, I felt guilty because of course she knew how to be careful, but also because she wouldn't have had to go to these lengths if not for me in the first place.

"And don't you dare turn this on me." She stepped close enough to poke me in the chest with her finger. "Why are you avoiding me? And don't you dare say that you aren't. You've barely looked at me since Sunday, and if you blame me for getting in trouble, fine, but at least talk to me about it instead of pushing me—"

"He knows," I said, cutting her off, knowing she'd understand immediately with only those two words.

They hung in the air, stealing the oxygen with their enormity. Admitting it made it bigger, for some reason, as if it hadn't been real enough already. The sting of the wound on my back certainly hadn't been imagined.

Her face went white. "He told you that?"

"Not in so many words."

Relief swept across her features. "He doesn't know. He *can't* know. If he knew, I would have been locked in my room permanently, and he would have definitely let me know that he knew. There is no way. There is just no way."

"He doesn't know about you," I clarified. "He only knows about me, and I've been avoiding you because I wanted to be sure and keep it that way."

It wasn't the whole truth, but it was close enough. Fear had been the main motivator. I wasn't going to admit the part where I'd also felt ashamed, and like hell was I going to tell her what had happened that had made me feel that way.

Her brows turned in, a mixture of puzzlement and concern. "What did he say to you? What did he *do* to you?" As if suddenly remembering I'd probably been physically punished, she started scanning me for injuries. "Was it your back again?"

"I'm fine. A single hit with the cane."

"Can I see?" She was already trying to turn me around, but I grabbed her hands and held them together with mine, happy to be touching her after several days of staying away.

"I'm fine," I said again, wanting to reassure her more than I wanted to be exactly truthful. The stripe hurt all the time, a constant reminder of why we had to be careful around each other.

Her body softened, seeming to be as comforted by my touch as I was by hers. "If you're fine, then why have you been distant? I miss you."

I bent my mouth to hers, kissing her softly.

"Are you over me?"

I laughed against her lips. "Fuck, no. Never." Wrapping my arms around her waist, I pulled her tighter against me. "But we can't do this for a while. Okay? He's onto me. He's seen how I look at you."

She leaned back to stare me in the eyes. "Is that what he told you? That you look at me...how?"

"Like I want you."

"And that's all? You didn't admit it?"

"I didn't admit shit, but he—"

"He doesn't know anything. Trust me." She let out a heavy breath. "You really had me scared there for a minute."

I didn't understand why she still wasn't scared. I was. "Are you not listening to me? He's watching us. He sees something between us, at least from my side, and that means he's going to keep looking for it."

"He hasn't seen anything. He's fucking with you."

"Jolie! How are you being so cavalier about this?"

"Because he does this!" She stepped away, flapping her hands in the air in frustration. "This is how he gets in your head. He makes you think he's seen you doing something bad so that you'll turn into a paranoid wreck. Remember when he said he'd caught you looking up porn sites and wiping them from the search history?"

"I swear to God I didn't do that." I'd never even heard of the sites he'd mentioned to me, but after getting punished for the thing I didn't do, I'd been extra careful not to use the home computer for anything but schoolwork.

"Exactly! He never thought you did. He sees a thing, gets an idea, and just fucks with you."

I wanted to buy her theory. I really, really did. "But this time his idea was right."

"It doesn't matter, Cade. It only matters if you admit it. Or if you start acting stupid. Believe me, he's loving how you won't even ask me to pass the peas at dinner anymore. He's watching you squirm, knowing there's nothing between us, loving every minute of it."

"Except there *is* something between us."

She brought her hands together in a prayer shape, placed them against her lips, and let out a small hum of frustration before speaking. "He doesn't know. I promise you, he doesn't know."

I considered the likelihood that she was right. We'd been so careful, never giving anything away unless we were completely alone. And when he'd come around the house, he really couldn't have seen anything but movement. Most likely, he'd interpreted the water fight as two teens having fun, which was enough to piss him off. He hated anyone being happy, least of all me. So was it possible he'd taken the opportunity to make it more? Just to have an excuse to give me pain?

Considering what happened afterward, it did seem more probable that the whole thing had been about scaring me, about making me miserable so he could get off.

And I'd played right into it, walking around the house like I was afraid any step I made would set off a bomb. He had to be loving every second of it.

But if there was any chance he really thought it was true...

I ran my hands through my hair. "Okay, okay. I'm probably overreacting."

"You are, but it's cute."

"But it's not a bad idea for us to be more careful, Jol." She was back in my arms, and I turned her around so that it was her against the door and not me. So I could put my weight against her and not have to worry about the pain in my back. "We should have a plan for how we'll talk to each other if something else happens." I brushed my nose along hers. "Pulling me out of class was not the most subtle of methods."

She laughed, and I could feel her breath on my chin, the tremble of her abdomen at my pelvis making my pants tighten. "Fine. Not the wisest of moves. But I was desperate. I really missed you."

Her sultry tone made my skin feel electric. I'd gotten so used to being in her bed every night that a few days had felt like a lifetime.

But fooling around in a classroom was not a good idea. Anyone could catch us, not just her father.

Besides, I was serious about having a plan. "We keep up the minimal interactions, but if you really need to talk to me, we should have a sign. Something our parents won't pick up on."

She thought for a moment, biting her lip as she did, making it hard for me to concentrate at the same time. "The shower curtain in your bathroom," she said. "No one goes in there but you, but I could easily have an excuse of needing to grab some toilet paper or whatever. If we need to talk to each other, we leave the shower curtain open."

Pretty clever since I always kept it closed. "That's good for you, but how will you know to go in there and look?"

"I have to walk by the bathroom on the way to my room. The door's already open. I'll make it a habit to look." Her cheeks pinked up. "I might already have a habit of looking," she admitted.

I didn't have to ask. I was equally attuned to her places. Whenever I walked in the lunchroom, I looked over to the spot she usually sat, even though we didn't have the same lunch break, just because I wanted my eyes to be somewhere that I knew she'd just been.

"So if it's open, then we meet after class at the greenhouse," I said. I worked there most days after school, especially now that it was spring. It was officially something I'd been assigned as a punishment, but Janice, the woman who oversaw the school gardening, had requested I stay on to help her with daily tasks, and Stark was none too happy to have me working and out of his hair. "Is it easy enough to find an excuse to come by?"

She nodded as she pressed an open-mouthed kiss on my chin. "I could come by for a fresh bouquet for the dinner table. Or even just to grab some of Janice's cookies. Really, I could stop by sometime even if the shower curtain isn't open. She'd never care."

Appealing as the idea of spending more time with Jolie was, that could not become part of her routine. "It needs to be only for emergencies."

She made a whiny sound that matched the pout on her lips.

"Jol, this is important. We have to take this seriously. There's only eight more weeks—"

"It's seven now," she corrected.

"Seven more weeks, and then we don't have to think about being careful ever again. But if your dad catches us before then?" He'd kill me. I was sure of it.

She knew it too, if her sudden seriousness was any indication. "I know. It's so close, and I want it to be here so badly. I guess I get a little stupid about it."

God, girl. Me too.

"The shower curtain and the greenhouse," I said, making sure our plan was solid. "And no more making eyes at me across the auditorium during assembly."

Again, she flushed, the color in her cheeks sending blood to my cock.

Her hand palming me might have also contributed. "Okay, but come to my room tonight. I've left my window open all night, every night this week, hoping you'd come, and it's not warm enough for that. Plus, I can't go this long without you."

I closed my eyes, doing my best to remember the fear that had kept me away from her for days. It wasn't hard to bring it back. The pain of it still throbbed on my skin, and thinking about it made my cock soften ever so slightly.

But there was no way I was going to make it seven weeks without her. And was there really any reason to try?

Well, we couldn't fuck in the music room. That was certain.

I placed my hand over hers, then brought it up to my lips. "I'll see what I can do about finding a condom. Now you should slip out before me. I'm going to need a minute before I can be in public."

Reluctantly, I stepped away from her. My chest ached every time I had to put space between us. Tonight, though, we'd be together. And soon we wouldn't have to be apart ever again.

TWENTY

JOLIE

I sat on my bed, leaning against the wall next to the open window, a blanket wrapped around me to keep away the spring night chill. Where the hell was he?

I stole a peek at my alarm clock only to find it hadn't moved since the last time I'd looked. To be fair, it had only just been an hour ago that I'd been locked in. Cade always waited at least that long, just to be sure. Thankfully, my father hadn't felt a need to come in and visit with me this time, but that also meant that he'd been gone quickly, and the wait for Cade felt longer.

Mostly it felt long because it had been four days since he'd snuck in at all. I was coming off of several nights of anticipation, and my whole body was jittery, and for no reason because there was no way that my father had figured anything out about us.

Or was I just telling myself that to make myself feel safe?

I'd become so used to manipulating my own emotions, I didn't know anymore which ones were real and which ones I created.

This isn't emotions; this is logic, my inner voice argued. My father didn't believe that boys had crushes without being provoked. I knew from experience that if my father knew someone liked me, I'd be punished for it.

My father hadn't laid a hand on me in over two weeks. He didn't know. He *couldn't* know.

I glanced at the clock again, glad to see the number had flipped, and just then, the rap came on the glass. Bolting into action, I flung the blanket and the curtain aside, lifted the window the rest of the way, then stuck my head out and peered up to be sure Cade knew it was open.

As soon as he saw me, he carefully turned around, and I held my breath while he lowered himself down to the ledge and worked his way through the window onto my bed.

"I swear I can't breathe every time you do that," I said, throwing my arms around him. Unable to resist, I glanced down. My bedroom was on the second floor, and the back of the house had a walkout basement so it was really a three-story drop. If he fell...

I'd read once that people couldn't survive any falls over four stories, so it wouldn't kill him for sure, but that didn't mean it couldn't.

"I could climb it in my sleep." He pulled away from me and shut the window then began to pull me back to him.

I resisted. "The dresser." We'd become lazy about moving it lately. It was overly cautious, not only because we'd been doing this routine for months and not been caught, but also my father had never in my life come back to my room after he'd locked the door.

If I trusted my logic, there was really no reason to be anxious about it now.

But logic also told me that I could be wrong.

Without arguing, Cade took his place on one side of the dresser and began to tug it into place while I pushed with my shoulder. "One day he's going to come up here because he hears us sliding the dresser against the door."

"It makes me feel better." That wasn't exactly true. The only thing that made me feel better was being in his arms.

I needed to be in his arms now.

Want felt warm in my belly and between my thighs. Four months into our physical relationship, and I was still blown away by the intoxication of lust. Before him, I'd only ever thought of sex as a means of negotiation. A price paid in exchange for attention, and usually scraps at that.

With Cade, it was almost always about me first. He'd given me permission to enjoy my body, and with that permission, I'd learned I could communicate with it as well. The form of expression was still so new and unexplored that I found myself choosing it over the methods of communication I'd used all my life.

I took Cade's hand in mine and pulled him with me back to the bed, letting this action tell him what I'd kept bottled for days: *I missed you. I need you. It's me and you in this together.*

He took my lead and pressed his mouth to mine, teasing me with soft kisses. I could practically feel him debating with himself about letting it become more. Four nights without each other meant four nights without talking, and that bond between us was equally important.

But words could wait, and when he slipped his tongue inside my mouth, I sighed with relief and wrapped my arms around his neck to pull him closer. As soon as I did, he retreated—not all the way, not breaking our kiss altogether, but slowing it down. Becoming less aggressive.

It drove me insane. The push, the pull. He was so good at teasing me like that. Giving just little tastes until I was near tears with want and then feeding me a feast. It didn't take long before I was breathless and clawing at his sweatshirt, needing it off. Needing his skin on mine.

Getting the hint, he broke away to pull the dang thing off. He threw it to the floor, and before he could once again take the reins of our speed, I pulled up my nightie and climbed onto his lap, a knee on either side of his hips so I could rub the ache between my thighs against the bulge in his jeans.

I bit my lip as my clit hit just the right spot, wishing I'd thought to take my panties off before straddling him. Wondering if I could shove them to the side and still get his cock inside me.

I was pretty sure he was thinking the same sort of thing, his hands moving up to cup my breasts through my nightgown, then letting out a grunt of satisfaction as he leaned back, taking me with him.

As soon as his back hit the window frame, he jerked.

Immediately, the bubble around us burst, and I remembered our reality and the latest beating he'd endured.

"Is it still really bad? Does it need more ointment?" I'd slipped him some Neosporin before dinner, but the tube had been practically empty. "I'm pretty sure I could get an antibiotic if I faked a sore throat."

He shook his head and moved himself over so his back met the flat wall instead of the window frame, taking me with him. "Carla had something from her last toothache that she never finished. I stole those. It's healing pretty well, I think." He'd told me it was only a single stripe, but he'd still been recovering from the whipping before that.

"Turn around. Let me see it."

He shook his head, and as I stared him down, I could feel myself turning protective. He was trying to be strong, and I admired that, but if he didn't want me to see it, it meant it was worse than he was letting on, which made me even more determined to see it so that I could be sure he was being taken care of.

But what was I going to do right now? He was already taking an antibiotic, and I wouldn't be able to try to get my hands on more ointment until tomorrow. Seeing it would only stir up more anger toward my father, and he already owned too much of our time. Too much of our lives. I hated giving him even a single minute more.

Would we ever belong completely to ourselves?

With a sigh, I climbed off his lap and stretched out half on top of him, half at his side. "How long do we have to hold on?"

I knew the answer, of course. I was counting down the hours. One thousand one hundred and seventy-six to go.

But the closer it got, the less it seemed real. It didn't seem possible that my life could be any different than what it was, and I needed Cade to reassure me, to say it out loud so that I knew it wasn't just a fairy tale in my head.

"It's only two months. Less, actually. Seven weeks." He brushed his lips against my forehead. "We just have to get through seven weeks, and then we're gone."

"Tell me again how we're going to do it."

As he had so many nights before, he spoke the details of our plan, falling into an easy rhythm born of repetition. "We'll walk the stage. We'll get our diplomas. Then after the ceremony, we'll leave. We won't even go to the after-party. We'll just be gone."

"And we won't take his car."

"No. We won't take my mother's either."

We went through the rest of the routine, and I played each step in my head, envisioning us behind the wheel of Janice's old truck, worrying if it would start, imagining what we'd say if we got caught.

I felt pretty sure she wouldn't turn us in. I would be eighteen by then, an adult. I'd known the gardener long enough to believe she'd support us there. She might even let us take the truck if we asked.

Of course, we couldn't take the risk of her saying no, but the fact that she would probably be on our side if we gave her the chance made me feel worse about stealing her truck. "We'll send her money when we can," I said, reassuring myself.

"We will. We'll be fine."

"And where will we go?"

He tipped my chin up toward him. My eyes locked on his, and I swept my tongue over my lip as I waited for his answer. He always said someplace new, and honestly, I didn't care. The truth was, we had no idea where we'd go. We had no money, no family. No jobs waiting for us. No place to stay. We were running off to be homeless and at the whim of fate, but we would be together, and I couldn't imagine anything better.

Instead of answering, he pressed his mouth to mine, his tongue tracing the path mine had taken across my bottom lip. Pulling my leg up around his hip, he turned so that his cock was once again pressing against the space between my thighs.

"I need to be inside of you," he whispered against my lips before kissing me long and deep. "That's the only place I want to go."

In sync, we began undressing, fast and furiously, a desperate eagerness growing between us. If it had been a race, I would have won, but I had less to take off, and he had the condom to retrieve from his pocket.

I sat on the bed to watch him as he rolled the latex down his cock, my pulse speeding up at the sight. For so long, I'd thought the male genitalia was ugly, and objectively it still was, but looking at Cade excited me. It was part of the gift he'd given me, that ability to find joy in sex, and the thrill went deeper than just feeling turned on. Was more profound. Seeing him naked and hard, his cock in his hand, *moved* me, and when he pushed me down to the bed, my legs wrapped around him like they belonged there.

He slipped a hand down between my legs, his fingers having learned their way around well enough that I was pretty sure he was now an expert. "Are you ready for me?"

God, yes. I'd been wet since he slid through the window.

He dragged the proof up my folds and teased the pad of his finger against my clit.

"Are *you* ready for *me*?" I arched into him, praying his answer was yes, yes, yes, because I wasn't just ready, I felt empty without him. I felt unwhole.

Hadn't that been exactly what I'd been before him? Half a person. Incomplete.

It was overly romantic to think in such platitudes. Love didn't fix all. It didn't win in the end. There was no such thing as soulmates.

But I believed it all the same.

He and I as one entity was the only sort of religion that made sense to me. I'd never seen proof of God. Prayer after prayer after prayer had gone unanswered. But Cade Warren gave me meaning. Without him, I was simply skin and bones. With him, my soul came alive.

At no time was I more alive than when he was inside me.

And since he was taking too long to get there, as soon as I felt his tip at my entrance, I lifted my hips and invited him all the way in.

I gasped at the feel of him, my pussy clenching and clinging to his cock as though afraid he'd leave too soon, though there was pleasure in his momentary absences when he dragged himself all the way out only because he immediately pushed back in. Electricity danced down my limbs and up my spine, and as deep as he was, I wanted him deeper, needed him planted. Needed him to touch me in every way he could, inside and out, so that the memory of him would linger in my body and get me through the long hours when we had to keep our distance and watch our gaze.

Some days that memory was the only thing that got me through.

When my thighs ached the next day, it would be proof that he hadn't been a dream. When I was scared and alone and trying to think of a reason to hang on, my body would remind me that Cade Warren loved me.

I brought my palms to his cheeks and kissed him. "I love you. I love you so much."

Sometimes, I thought he got off more on the words than the rest, and with my declaration, he released, grinding into me as his orgasm took over his body.

He so rarely came before me, and he was so beautiful doing so—his face scrunched up, his muscles tense—and I wanted to linger in that moment, wanted to savor the proof that I'd done that to him. I'd wrecked him so thoroughly with pleasure and unraveled him the same way he unraveled me, and wasn't that fantastic?

But that satisfaction was interrupted with an unexpected sound—a rattling at the door followed by a fist pounding against the wood. "What the hell is this, Julianna?"

My father.

Outside my room.

The dresser was already moving with the weight of his shoulder pushing the door.

Shit, shit, shit, shit, shit.

We jumped apart. I flung the window open while Cade threw on his jeans. He had his shoes in hand, but his shirt... "Where is it? *Where is it?*" His whisper felt like a yell.

"Open the door right this instant!" My father's voice boomed like he had a megaphone, and slowly the dresser was moving as he pushed harder to get in. "Goddammit, Julianna! When I get in there—"

I tuned out his threat. Whatever he dished out to me, I could handle. I'd handled him for almost eighteen years. I was a pro.

But what he'd do to Cade was a whole other story.

He had to get out of my room *now*.

He understood that as well as I did. Shirtless, he climbed up on the windowsill. "If you find it, stuff it under the bed."

I knelt on the bed, my hands laced together in front of me so that I wouldn't instinctively grab onto him and make him take me with. "Be careful." I glanced back at the door, the crack wide enough that I could see the side of my father's head as he gave another shove. "Be careful, but go!"

It was already too late.

Even if Cade hadn't hesitated to give me a reassuring nod, there wouldn't have been enough time for him to get in the position to climb out. He'd have to jump to the ground, and my heart was already in my throat, my chest splitting itself in two as I quickly reasoned which was worse: broken limbs or facing my father.

Light suddenly broke into the room as the door opened completely, and though my back was turned, I knew my father was towering behind me. The horror in Cade's expression reflected the terrifying sight. It wasn't one I had to see to understand.

"You're dead, Cade Warren." His tone turned my veins to ice, and now I had my answer—broken limbs were the better odds.

Even knowing it was the right choice, I couldn't help the scream that escaped my throat as he swung his legs out the window and fell to the ground.

I stuck my head out after him, too concerned with whether Cade was okay or not to worry about the fact that I was naked and about to be in trouble. Somehow he'd managed to land on his side. He rolled twice, then got to his feet, and while I could tell he was favoring one leg over the other, he disappeared into the dark before I could evaluate just how hurt he was.

But worry for Cade was suddenly superseded by pain as I was dragged back into the room by my hair.

"You dirty whore! You fucking whore. I knew you would spread your legs for anyone, but you had to go and prove it, didn't you?"

I didn't have time to respond before the back of his hand smacked across my face. He struck again before I'd finished staggering from the first blow.

"Trash is attracted to trash. I should have realized you'd invite him into your bed." With a roar, he used his fist this time, hitting me so hard I fell to my knees, nearly blacking out.

When I could see again, I saw him at the window, looking out at the yard. "He has no place to go. He'll show up tomorrow, and I'll take care of him then."

I wasn't sure if he was telling me or himself, but the message was clear—Cade would wait. In the meantime, he had me to deal with.

My face already felt swollen, tears were already streaming down my face. Usually, that's all he needed to be satisfied, but that was when my transgressions were small. He'd want a larger payment for this.

I was already bracing myself for it when he shut the window and prowled toward me. "Get the fuck up."

Cade's safe, I told myself. *Safe for tonight, anyway.*

Holding on to that thought, I found the strength to stand, trying my best to cover myself.

"You know the drill. Hands on the desk. Ass toward me."

I walked over to my desk and placed my palms down. My body tensed at the familiar sound of his belt unbuckling. It would have been worse for Cade if he were standing here. I knew that in my bones.

But it was still going to be bad for me.

TWENTY-ONE
CADE

I woke up suddenly, not sure what had woken me. I'd shivered for most of the night and only fell asleep when the sun came out. Even with the jacket I'd found hanging on the hook with the garden aprons, the temperature had been miserable. Only forty degrees, according to the thermometer hanging on the glass wall. It was definitely warmer now.

I stretched my neck from side to side. I had a kink from how I'd had to sleep, curled up inside the cabinet where the extra bags of soil were usually kept, and my ankle was throbbing so badly, I was beginning to wonder if it was broken. I tried to move it now, but it was too swollen. It needed to be wrapped. It probably needed an X-ray.

Uncomfortable as I was, I didn't think it was pain that woke me up.

I sat quietly, straining my ears.

"Cade?"

It was soft, but I heard it. Jolie's voice, quiet enough to still be called a whisper, but loud enough that I heard it in my hiding spot. It was too early for her to be done with school, and I hadn't expected her until then. Was it a trap? Cautiously, I opened the door and peeked out.

She'd passed by me, so I only saw her back, but it was definitely her. Fuck, I was so happy to see her, my eyes stung. "Jol!"

I climbed out of the cramped space and made it to a standing position just in time for her to rush into my arms.

"You're here!"

Thank God we'd chosen the spot the day before as an emergency meeting place. Even without the arrangement, I would have ended up there. I had nowhere else to go. "I hoped you'd find me. I didn't know if you'd think of it."

"I was so worried. I didn't know if..." Her voice was muffled in my jacket, but I could tell she was crying from the way her body quivered.

I wrapped my arms tighter around her. "I'm okay. Swollen ankle, but I'm okay."

At the mention of my injury, she pulled away and knelt down to examine my bare foot. I'd managed to take my shoes with me on my fall, but I didn't think I could fit into it if I wanted to.

"Shit, Cade. It's purple. Is it broken?"

"Just sprained." Maybe. Probably. "But what about you? What happened—?" Just then she stood up, and I got a good look at her face, and I didn't have to finish the question. The answer was black and blue across one side of her face.

I sucked in a breath. "Oh, fuck. Jolie."

I drew her closer, cupping her face on the side that wasn't bruised as I examined her marks. It looked like his fist had slammed across her cheekbone. She couldn't even keep her one eye open all the way.

I was going to kill him. I was going to fucking slip in the house tonight while he was asleep and slit his fucking throat with a knife.

"It looks worse than it is." She was as good at minimizing as I was. Better. "Doesn't hurt nearly as much as my ass."

Guilt sank through me like a stone in mud. I'd left her there to face Stark's wrath alone. He usually left her unmarked, but I knew what he was capable of. I knew how mad he would have been. I knew better. "I shouldn't have—"

"Stop." She put a finger up to shush me. "If you'd stayed, it would have been worse."

"Not for you."

"For both of us. I hurt when you hurt."

"Well, we're both in a fuck ton of pain right now then because I feel the same." I was suddenly very aware of the weight of it all, perched on my shoulders, and I slumped forward underneath it, resting my forehead against hers.

We stood like that, not talking, just breathing each other in and holding each other up for who knows how long. Hours, it felt like. Seconds. Time lost meaning with her. We forgot the world existed.

Right now, we didn't have the luxury of escaping like that.

I forced myself to take a step back, still holding her, just not so tight. "How did you get away? How long do you have?" I'd been hidden in the cabinet when Janice did her morning circuit through the greenhouse, and she usually didn't come out again until afternoon, so I wasn't worried so much about her.

Stark, on the other hand. I couldn't imagine that he'd have let her go to school with her face looking like it did. I also couldn't imagine that he would have let her stay home without keeping her locked up tight in her room.

"He's preoccupied," Jolie explained. "Bernard's parents got here today. He's meeting with them right now and the police. He doesn't know that I left class, and if we're lucky, he won't realize it until the school day is over."

I must have looked puzzled because she amended. "I told Ms. Stacey that my face was hurting too much. She sent me to the nurse's office, and the nurse sent me home. I ran there and got some of your stuff and then came here."

I only now noticed the duffel bag at her feet, but I was still hung up on something else. "He let you go to class with your face all bruised up? How did—?" My heartbeat felt heavy when I realized the answer halfway through the question. "He said it was me, didn't he? He made you say it was me."

The guy wasn't stupid. It was a brilliant tactic, actually. Tell the school that his wild and out-of-control stepson had attacked his daughter, then ran away, and suddenly he had everyone looking for me.

Now she was the one who felt guilty, if her tears had anything to say about it. "I didn't have a choice. He said I had to blame you or...or..."

If he'd been there right then, I would have punched *him* in the face, shown him how wild I could be.

But he wasn't there. Jolie was, and she wasn't who I was angry at.

I tugged her back into me. "You had to do what he said. You didn't have a choice."

Or maybe she did. With her face as evidence, if she and I both said something. "What would happen if you tell the truth? If you blamed him?"

Frustrated, she tried to pull away, and I didn't let her because that was the last thing I wanted. "I'm just asking the question. Wonder out loud with me, will you?"

She sighed, but she stayed. "I tried to report him once. I showed one of my teachers the belt marks I had on my back."

"What happened?"

"Teacher got fired, and I couldn't walk for a week."

I wanted to argue with her, wanted to tell her it would be different if we both went forward with the proof of our injuries, wanted to tell her that it didn't have to be like that this time, but I couldn't promise her that it wouldn't be.

It was too big a risk to take.

"You did the right thing," I said, absolving her from her guilty conscience. "You had no other choice."

I'd already decided that there was no way I could go back, but this sealed that. I would have to be a runaway like Bernard Arnold. I wondered if the police would even be called to look for me. I was already eighteen, and I had a damn good feeling that Stark didn't want me in his house again.

It was okay. It was going to be okay. We were already planning to leave. Just had to readjust our plans.

So then, what now?

Jolie leaned back abruptly, apparently following the same train of thought. "It doesn't matter, Cade. It doesn't matter what people think. We'll leave. Okay? Same plan as before, but we'll leave sooner. That's all. I should have packed some things for me, but that's fine. We have time. I can run back home now. Or...or I'll leave it all behind. I don't care about anything. Let's just go. Find the keys and go."

She was agitated and worked up, and even if she'd been calm, I would have wanted to give her what she wanted. It was definitely an option. We could go. I'd already checked to see if the keys to Janice's truck were where she'd shown me before. Like Jolie said—same plan as before. Just leave now.

But while I was unsure whether or not I'd be looked for, I was positive the cops would be sent after Jolie. She was still only seventeen. Knowing him, he'd come after her and charge me for kidnapping.

Jolie didn't need me to explain any of that. She already knew, and no matter how emphatic her plea was to run away, I could tell she knew she was lying to herself when she fell to her knees and brought her hands up to cover her face and cry.

I dropped on my knees in front of her, once again folding her into an embrace. "It's not that long, baby." I kissed her hair and rubbed her back. "It's seven weeks. Still just as long as it was yesterday. Only difference is you're going to have to be in that house alone, and I'm sorry about that."

She started crying harder.

"Shh, shh, Jolie." I wasn't used to seeing her so broken. So much of my own strength was stolen from her, and I didn't know if I could watch her crumble without crumbling myself. "Please don't, baby."

"I can't be there without you," she said, and I realized the reality of our circumstances must be just hitting her. She'd only packed things for me, so on some level she already knew, but knowing wasn't the same as accepting. "I can't. I can't without you. I'll die."

"You aren't without me. I'm here. I'm yours. Listen to me, Jolie. Look at me." I pulled her hands down from her face, made her look me in the eye. "You know this is the only way. You know it. Tell me you know it."

She blinked at me, her sobbing paused.

"Think it through. If you don't go back, he'll find us, and then he could keep us apart forever."

She hiccupped, her chin quivering. "But what about you? You can't stay here."

"No, I can't." I didn't know where I'd go, but that was less of a worry than what I'd survive on. I could sleep in the truck at the side of the road. I couldn't live without food for two months.

I didn't want that to be her worry. I had nothing to give her, but I could give her that.

Suddenly, her eyes widened. "The cabin! You could stay at the cabin!"

"Your father's cabin?" I'd only ever heard about it.

"Yes! You can go there!" She was excited now. "There's like a six-month supply of dry goods. You might have to break a window to get in. No, wait! He keeps a key hidden in the garage. On the boat, in a compartment by the front console. Oh, and the safe! There's probably a little bit of money in there. I think the combination is my birthday."

"Jol, I can't..." Could I? It sounded too easy.

"He won't go there again until school is out."

"How... I don't even know where it is." Or if the truck had enough gas to get to Sherman. Or how I'd figure out where Sherman was.

"The address is easy. It's Atchison Cove. Ten Atchison Cove. I was ten when he bought it, and I thought it was so cool that it was the same address as my age. Plus, it's on a big sign out in front. Ten Atchison Cove, Cade. It's only an hour away. You can stay there, and no one will know, and then come back for me."

"Come back for you," I repeated, readjusting the plan in my head. "After graduation. But I couldn't come back here." The truck would be recognizable.

"The C Town. We'll meet there. I'll find a ride."

"How?"

She shook her head like it was a trivial matter. "I don't know. Someone. There will be lots of people going that direction. Amelia! I can ask her."

"Okay. All right. I'll stay at the cabin until graduation. Then I'll come back."

"You'll come back."

"Yes."

It must not have been emphatic enough for her because she grabbed onto the jacket I was wearing, clutched on tight, as though I were the only thing keeping her from drowning. "Promise me, Cade. Promise me you'll come back for me. You have to promise me."

If I hadn't already been on my knees, her pleas would have pulled me there. "Oh, baby. I'm coming back for you. I'm coming back. I'll *always* come back for you."

I remembered the stupid pipe cleaner in my pocket, but pulling it out didn't feel ridiculous. It felt earnest and sincere. "This isn't what you deserve, Jolie." I laughed at how insufficient the comment was. "It's not even close to what you deserve, but what matters is what it means."

Taking her left hand, I wrapped the pink piping around her ring finger, once, twice, three, four times, until it was wound tightly. She was crying again, these tears falling silently and slowly down her cheeks.

"We can't have a real wedding," I said. Everyone we knew thought of us as siblings, but who did we even care about having there anyway?

"I don't care about that. All I care about is being with you."

"Be with me. Be with me always. Whether it's heaven or hell, whether we sink or swim, be with me, Jolie. Say you'll be with me."

"Yes, yes, yes." It was a litany. "Yes, yes. Yes, Cade, yes."

I stared at the pink decorating her finger. If I looked at her, I'd cry too. Shit, I might have been crying already. "One day, it will be a real ring."

"It doesn't matter. I love you." She placed her hand on my cheek, and I looked up then. "I love you," she said again. "You're everything, and I love you."

I kissed her like we had forever.

I kissed her like it was goodbye.

One of those was right for today. And then in seven weeks, it would never be that kind of kiss again.

TWENTY-TWO
JOLIE

Dad pulled the car into the garage and turned off the engine, the motorized whir of the garage door closing behind us the only sound.

I didn't move.

Everything hurt. Every part of my body. It wasn't like the usual physical pain I experienced, pain caused by abuse. That kind of pain radiated everywhere as well—it could make my head throb or my stomach hurt—but there was always a center. There was always a place where the pain originated.

But my father hadn't touched me in weeks, and this pain was different.

Every part of me ached. My feet, my legs, my chest, my ribs. My face. My teeth.

My heart.

I hadn't known it was possible to hurt like this. I couldn't have believed the magnitude until I'd experienced it, and for the first time in all my years, I understood what it truly meant to want to die.

My father sat next to me, seeming as unanxious to get out of the car as I was. We hadn't spoken on the ride back from the school, which took all of two minutes, and we didn't speak now, letting long breaths pass in silence.

"You must be tired," he said finally, his eyes focused somewhere vague in front of him.

Exhausted was a better word. I planned on sleeping for a week, if he'd let me, and he might. He'd been careful with me lately. He'd been nice—driving the short distance so that I wouldn't have to walk in my heels, for instance—which was almost more devastating than when he was cruel, because they always followed each other, and it was easier to be *in* the cruel than to be waiting for it.

Worse, this had been a particularly long stretch for him, going on three weeks. When the kindness dragged out, I started to get used to it. I found myself forgetting and making excuses and loving him. Actually loving him, despite everything he'd ever done to me. Everything he was still doing to me.

It was the part that made me feel the most ashamed—that I could care so much for the person who had been the most horrible to me.

"I am tired," I said, staring into the same nowhere that he was staring into. He'd let me stay out late, another example of his kindness, later than I'd ever stayed out before.

Of course, he'd stayed at the after-graduation party as a chaperone, so it was still a favor on his terms, but it was a favor all the same. One he would expect me to be appreciative of.

"Thank you again for letting me stay out." The words were mechanical. My thoughts were elsewhere. "What time is it anyway?"

I remembered the dashboard clock as soon as I asked and moved my eyes to check at the same time he said, "Almost one."

I swallowed hard past the ball in my throat. One in the morning. Three hours late for when I had agreed to meet Cade. Was he still sitting in that parking lot, waiting for me?

I'd thought I was all cried out, but my eyes pricked again, my vision swimming. It was too late to change my mind now. Even if he was still waiting, I'd lost any chance of sneaking away when the party had ended.

I glanced at the keys hanging from the ignition. I'd never been allowed to learn to drive. Was it something I could figure out on the fly?

I thought about Carla asleep inside the house. She'd come for the ceremony but left afterward. She'd shown little emotion over the weeks about Cade's disappearance and the accusations my father had hurled upon him, but tonight she'd been less cold. Her eyes had been sad, and when Dad had told her to perk up or take her mopey ass home after the ceremony, she'd chosen the latter.

Maybe she could drive me. I had the sudden urge to ask her. If I got her alone, if I begged, if I told her she could see Cade again, could tell him goodbye...

I closed my eyes, shutting down the inclination. I'd made my decision. I'd put careful thought into it. I'd considered every angle, every option. This was the only choice I could make. The only one I could live with.

But God, did it hurt like I would die.

With a sigh, my father opened his car door and got out. I followed his lead, letting his actions guide me since I couldn't trust my own will. Knowing he detested anything left in the car, I opened the back door and retrieved my cap and gown, wrinkled now after having been worn and discarded. Habit had me worrying that I'd be reprimanded for that, and when he was standing by me when I shut the door, I immediately got defensive.

"I should have brought the garment bag," I apologized. "I can steam it in the morning. Or tonight, if you prefer. It will be good as new."

He waved his hand dismissively, as though it was silly that I'd thought such a thing. "I just wanted to say how proud of you I am, princess. You're all grown up and graduated and making adult decisions. I couldn't have asked for a better daughter."

He put his hands on my upper arms as he bent down to kiss my forehead, and I tensed, as I always did when he touched me. My head could put moments into context, but my body didn't know when one of his nice touches would turn into a not-so-nice touch, and it often reacted before I could calm it down.

Unfortunately, he noticed. He often did, and it always pissed him off. "I can't even show you a little affection without you recoiling. I've gone out of my way for you, and this is how—"

I cut him off. "You just surprised me." I forced myself to relax. Forced myself to lean into him for a hug. "I appreciate all of it, Daddy. Thank you."

He took a beat before he returned the embrace, and I made myself go numb. Made myself focus on counting the seconds as they passed. *One one thousand. Two one thousand. Three one thousand. Four—*

Then it was over, and I could breathe again.

"Here. Let me take those for you." He took the cap and gown out of my hands, as if they were a burden to carry. Without them, I didn't feel any lighter. "Did I tell you how pretty you looked? The photographer said he got a real nice shot of you all dressed up."

He turned toward the kitchen door, then stopped when he saw the full garbage can. "Oh, shit, it's Thursday. You forgot tomorrow's trash day."

Even when he was being nice, he still was rigid. The chore had been my responsibility since Cade had left, and it didn't matter that I was tired or that I was in heels or that he was trying to win me over—if it was my job, I needed to do it.

I didn't have the energy to complain. "I better get it out then." With my elbow, I pushed the button to open the door again, then rolled the big can between the two cars, out of the garage, and down the driveway. When I got to the road, I dallied before turning back toward the house.

If I stayed here with the trash, would the garbage truck take me too?

I was still contemplating when a rock bounced on the road by my feet. I stared down at it, and another rock skidded by.

Abruptly, I turned around, my eyes scouring the dark landscape, looking for the source of the thrown rocks, a prayer whispering on my lips. *Please, don't be here, please, don't be here.*

But my heart was wishing for just the opposite, and I nearly collapsed with relief when his whispered shout reached me. "Jolie. Jol."

He was at the shed, crouched down in the shadows, but there was no question it was him.

Quickly glancing at the house to be sure my father was still inside, I rushed down the drive as fast as I could in the stupid dress shoes, kicking them off once I reached the grass. I was already almost to him when my brain stepped in to remind me this was over. It didn't matter. I couldn't help myself. He was here, and I had no choice but to run to him.

"Oh my God, I didn't know if you'd come out."

"You shouldn't be here," I said at the same time.

But I was in his arms, letting him hold me tight while I cried into his neck. It had been seven weeks since he'd asked me to be his bride. Seven weeks since I'd last held him in my arms. I'd imagined a million different lifetimes for him. Wrote and rewrote what happened to him next, and this was not in any of those endings.

I wasn't supposed to see him again. I'd thought I'd never hear his voice, never feel his touch.

I was practically breaking apart with relief.

I clutched him tighter, breathed him in. Had his scent changed in the last two months? It was still so...*him*...but different too. Older, somehow. More intoxicating.

Less mine.

No, no. This wasn't relief. This was torment. This was worse than never seeing him at all because his being here didn't change anything. It couldn't change anything at all.

And if my father saw him...

I tore myself away and repeated my words, as much for me as for him. "You can't be here, Cade. You can't. Why are you here?"

"I came for you. I came for you. I'm so—" He was emotional and had to swallow before going on. "When you didn't show up, I was so worried he'd found out. I thought he'd locked you up. I was ready to break into the house if I had to. Could you not get away? Could you not find a ride?"

I shook my head and tried to take a step back, but he grabbed my hands and held them between us. "What's wrong, Jolie? Whatever it is, it's okay. I'm here."

I shook my head again. "You have to go."

"We can go now. The truck's parked down the road."

"No, I can't. I can't." I pulled my hands away from him and brought them to my face as if that could stop the waterfalls of tears down my cheeks.

I felt his eyes land on my hand, the empty place where his pipe cleaner ring had sat the last time he'd left. "Jol?"

It was half a word, one syllable, and yet I could hear he was on the edge. This was my fault in every way imaginable, but I needed him to take some of the blame. I couldn't be the one who broke him. I couldn't, and yet I knew I was going to break him so hard, whether I witnessed it or not, but seeing him break…

I wasn't sure I would survive.

"Why did you come?" I asked again. "Why?" Imagining his pain had been bad enough. Seeing it was like looking in a mirror with a mirror behind me. The reflection repeated over and over. The pain went on and on and on and on.

"What are you asking? What…? I came for you, Jolie. We're leaving together. We have a plan."

Shaking my head was easier than speaking.

But it wasn't enough. He needed the words too. "That's not the plan anymore."

"Of course, it's the plan. Why are you doing this?" He stood up straighter, changing tactics. "We don't have time for this. We need to go."

"You need to go. I'm not. I'm not going."

"Don't do this, Jol. Why are you saying these things?"

I was shaking. This decision had been so much easier to get behind when I didn't have to face him. He was supposed to give up when I didn't show up. He wasn't supposed to come for me, but now that he had, I couldn't believe I'd been so stupid. So unprepared. Of course, he'd come for me, and when he was standing in front of me, I got confused. Possibilities blurred.

He saw my hesitation and took advantage. "Listen, baby. Listen."

He put his hands on my hips and leaned down so we were eye to eye. "The truck is in good shape. I stole a mattress from the cabin, and the shell on the back means we can sleep in it even if it's raining, and we can be someplace warm by winter."

He meant to be reassuring, but it only brought my focus back to reality. "We have nothing to live on. How are we supposed to survive?"

"We have money!" he announced suddenly. "There was more in the safe than you thought."

Hope fluttered through me despite myself. "How much?"

"Almost fifteen hundred."

My heart sunk. "It's not enough."

"It's enough if we have each other, Jol."

God, I still believed that on some level. He'd planted that idealism somewhere deep inside me, and I longed to let it bloom.

But I didn't have room anymore to make space for that hope. Reality was a voracious weed, and it choked every other chance for growth. Love did not save the day. Love did not put food on a table. Even sleeping in the truck, how long could fifteen hundred buy us? A month? Two at most. Then what? We'd have to use our IDs to get jobs and give references, both of which would make it possible for my father to track us down.

Which he would.

He would, and none of what I had to offer was fair to Cade.

My future had been set, and I loved him too much to chain him in it with me. "You have to go. You have to go."

He stepped toward me, and I stepped back. "We belong together. I love you, Jolie. You love me."

I did love him. So much that I would let him go.

My throat hurt too much to say it. I just shook my head, over and over and over until...

"Go back to the house, Julianna." My father's voice was steady and low and menacing.

The ground dropped beneath me, quicksand pulling me down, down, down, but somehow I was still standing upright.

Cade jumped back from me automatically. Then more boldly, as though he'd recovered some strength in his weeks away from this awful house, he stepped out in front of me, shielding me. "I'm not leaving without her."

Calmly, my father looked over his shoulder at me. "I'd say that's up to Julianna."

In another life, I would have taken Cade's hand, would have stood defiantly up to the man who'd raised me, who'd tormented me and loved me and fucked me up. In another life, I would have chosen with my heart.

But this was this life.

And this choice came from my heart too.

I walked around Cade, turning back one last time. My knees felt like they were going to buckle. My back hurt all the way down my spine. My throat ached. My chest felt split in two. "You should have let me go," I whispered. "You shouldn't have come."

"Go back to the house, Julianna," my father said again, and I did. I put one foot in front of the other, over and over and over until I reached the back door. I didn't look back. I couldn't. I could only move forward.

As soon as I was inside, I sank to the floor, brought my knees up to my chest, and buried my face in my dress. If I were a stronger person, I would have forced myself to watch from the window. I deserved to see what happened. I deserved to feel whatever pain my father put Cade through.

But I wasn't that strong.

I'd already used every bit of my strength to walk away. I was already in the worst pain. It wasn't possible for me to hurt more than I already did.

So I didn't watch. I hugged myself and rocked back and forth and didn't let myself think about the time that was passing or that it had been too long or that my father might not keep his word.

The material was soaked by the time he finally pushed the door open and found me on the floor. He looked down at me with as much disgust as I deserved. "Get up. Go to bed."

He was sweating, and his right hand had blood on it, blood that wasn't his.

Grief rolled through me. Regret. Anger. "You said you wouldn't hurt him. You promised, if I stayed."

He let out a laugh—a mean, gruff, calloused laugh. "I said I'd let him walk away. I didn't say he wouldn't be bleeding when he did."

My whole life with the man, and I still never quite learned that his terms were devil terms. The bargain made was never quite the bargain you got.

But as long as Cade walked away, I reminded myself, it was worth it.

And now he was in my past. I had to look forward.

TWENTY-THREE
CADE

Present

After our late night exploring and the activities that followed in the bedroom, we ended up sleeping away the morning. The bedside clock said almost noon when I opened my eyes. I stared at it, letting my vision focus, taking advantage of the particular stillness that occurs after waking to think about organizing my emotions.

I was half on my stomach, facing away from her, but very aware of Jolie. Sharing a full bed, we were close to each other whether we wanted to be or not, but she was pressed up tight against my backside, an obvious choice. And it was...

Right.

It felt right, which didn't mean it didn't also feel complicated and temporary, because it was all of the above and more. But right was an easy place to start, and so I breathed into that, and tried to let it be.

She was awake too. The stroke of her finger up and down my back gave her away. Her touch took a deliberate pathway, and though I didn't spend much time looking at that side of my body, I had a feeling she was tracing the faint scar left from Stark's cane.

Of course, that was the mark that remained. The one I was most ashamed of. The one that I couldn't ever quite reckon with.

"What do you tell women when they ask where this is from?" Her voice was morning-hoarse and sexy, and if she hadn't been bringing up such an unsexy topic, I would have rolled over and made my way between her legs.

Too bad for the mood killer since it would be awfully nice to have a subject-changer. This wasn't a conversation I was keen to get into, now or ever. There was shit from the past that still needed closure, but this was not one of them.

I closed my eyes, even though she wasn't facing me, hoping maybe she'd think I was still asleep.

"I know you're awake."

So much for that idea.

"I try very hard not to talk to women in my bed," I said, not moving.

A beat passed. The caress of her hand didn't stop. "Then I should feel special."

It was too ridiculous to let slide. I lifted my head and looked over my shoulder, giving her my best "duh" look. Seriously? She didn't feel special? She'd shattered my heart and still somehow roped me into helping her with the most outrageous of favors. It seemed pretty fucking obvious she was pretty fucking special.

Her hand stopped moving, but she kept it against my back, warm and firm. "I wish you wouldn't look at me like that."

"Like what?" I was curious how she'd interpreted it.

"Like you don't know what to do with me."

I rolled over the rest of the way onto my back and let my head sink into the pillow with a sort of huff. Because I *didn't* know what to do with her. I didn't know what to think of her or how to feel about her, and I sure as fuck didn't know how to be with her.

"I know, I know." She propped herself up on her elbow. "I ask too much, and then I ask too much again."

Her in a nutshell. At least she was self-aware.

Staring at the ceiling, I made an attempt to be equally mindful. "I wish I wanted you to stop."

It surprised her.

It surprised *me*, but it was the truth. Maybe it was all the shit Stark put us through. Maybe he'd turned me into a masochist, because as terrible and selfish as this particular ask was, it didn't scratch the surface of what I'd do for her. I'd hate it and be miserable the whole time, but I'd fucking do it. I guessed I had no sense left when it came to her.

And now I'd just outed myself. It was my weakness, and instead of keeping it hidden, here I was, showing it off. *Use me, Jolie. Trample me to the ground. Treat me like shit, I'm here for it. Every goddamn time.*

Honestly, she probably already knew. Still, I wanted the admission to mean something to her—wanted my loyalty to matter—but I couldn't bring myself to look at her to see her reaction. I just kept staring at the popcorn ceiling above me, breathing in. Breathing out.

The bed shifted, and in my periphery it seemed she'd taken the same pose. The silence between us was taut, a thick rope pulled so hard it was beginning to fray in the middle, and I wondered when it broke where I'd land. If I'd be standing or left in the mud.

"I'm going to ask too much right now," she said finally, and I was already feeling that cocktail of resentment and excitement that she stirred up in me. "When this stuff with my father is over, I don't want this to end with you."

The breath she let out was shaky, audible even over the sudden pounding of my heart in my ears. It was validating to know this was hard for her too, and maybe that should have been enough. Maybe it *was* enough, but fuck. Really?

Really?

Of everything she could ask...

"No, no, no. No." I shoved the covers off and got out of bed. I found my pants and shoved a leg inside, not bothering with underwear. "No."

"You feel pretty strongly about that."

I might feel strongly about it if it was real, but this wasn't real. "You're being nostalgic, Jol."

"I'm not."

"It's being here. In this house."

"It was before here."

I glanced at her and immediately regretted it. That downturn of her lip, that blinking of her eyelids like she might cry...

No. Wasn't doing that.

I turned my attention to finding my sweater, then putting it on, trying my best to ignore the part of my mind that wanted to play the fantasy out, see where it could lead. Consider it.

That was a stupid part of my mind. Incredibly stupid. And I intended on overruling it with the rational part of me, which was maybe only a very small part, but a very vocal part, and it knew where to draw the line. Apparently, I did still have some sense, and sense said this was too much. This was the one thing that went too far. If I trusted her that much—if I gave her whatever fragments of my heart that remained—and she fucked me over again, which she would undoubtedly do, then that was it. There'd be nothing left. I'd be destroyed.

I wasn't doing that again. I wasn't crawling away from her again.

"I know," she said solemnly. "I have no right to ask."

I spun back toward her. "You're goddamned right you don't."

"Not even a little bit."

She acted like she understood what she'd put me through, but she couldn't possibly. She couldn't, or she wouldn't have dared ask this. She wouldn't have dared come back into my life at all.

Did she not realize how much I'd fucking loved her? "Fuck, Jol. You don't even know, do you?"

"Know what?"

I shook my head. At myself as much as at her because the stupid asshole in this scenario was me. *Me*. Me who obviously still loved her or I wouldn't care so much about her bullshit, wouldn't wonder whether it really was bullshit, wouldn't hope that...

"This isn't fucking fair, Jolie." I shoved my foot inside a boot.

"It's not."

I found the other boot and put it on. I'd been dressing so I could run, and now that I was done, I wasn't ready to leave.

I paced the length of the room. Went to the window. Turned back to her. "This is because we fucked. I told you that you'd make it more than it is."

"Am I really making it more?" She asked so earnestly, and I wanted to shut her down with a definitive yes, but the word stuck in my throat, a lie too big to get out.

I ran a hand over my beard, trying to break the lie into something smaller. "You owe me too many explanations. You have too many things you won't share." As long as she withheld pieces of herself, this was only sex. It could only be sex. "You aren't relationship material."

The last one visibly wounded her, but I refused to regret it.

And she took it. Pulling the sheet up around herself, she sat up and nodded. "You're right. I could be, though, I think. If I told you everything."

"That would be a nice fucking place to start." I'd spoken before I really thought about it, and once I gave myself a second to do so, something warm stretched across my chest. A tiny ball of hope. Would she really give me answers? Would it really change anything?

My gut said that it would probably change everything.

There was something admittedly frightening about that. Just learning my mother had helped her escape had done a number on me. I wasn't sure I could take more truth.

She bit her lip, seeming to be worried as well.

I had a feeling her worries were centered elsewhere. "You're afraid to tell me because you think I'll walk out on this. That doesn't say much in your defense."

"I don't know how it will go, honestly. I think you'll understand me better, but I can't begin to know how you'll feel, so yes. You might decide you're done with me and leave me to do this alone, and that would be fair. I know I don't deserve—"

I couldn't take any more of this line, and I cut her off. "Stop, okay?

Stop with the 'I don't deserve and I'm to blame for everything' bullshit. Your father was to blame. Okay? For everything. All of it. It was his fault, and no one else's."

Now she was the one who looked hopeful. "Do you really mean that?"

Shit. Did I?

"I don't know." I'd been blaming her so long, it was hard to let that go. And yet... "I want to."

There I was again, showing her all my weak spots.

For some reason, I didn't feel that scared. Like when I'd woken up, it felt right.

I was going to need some time to process that. And to process whatever she had to tell me, but in order to do that, she had to actually tell me, and she wasn't going to do that without reassurances.

"Look." I took a step toward her, crouching down so I was on her level, close enough that I could touch her, but I didn't. "I'm in this. I'm not backing out. He needs to pay for his crimes, and if our plan backfires, I'm committed to finding another plan because it's way past time he goes down. Nothing you say to me is going to change that."

Before she could respond, my phone vibrated on the nightstand with an incoming call. I glanced over, intending to ignore whoever it was.

"Donovan," she said, apparently having looked too. "You should take it."

I didn't want to take it. I wanted to throw my cell out the window and finish this conversation. I wouldn't even bother to open it first.

"We'll talk later," she promised. "Take the call."

With a sigh that felt more like a groan, I picked up my cell. "What?"

"Hello to you too, sunshine." His voice was obnoxiously smug. "I'd expected a check-in last night and heard nothing. Forgive me for being concerned."

Fuck. I'd forgotten to let him know what was going on. I was going to need a smoke for this. "Yeah, we sort of had a change of plans." I put on my coat, made sure the cigarettes were in the pocket, then gestured to Jolie that I was headed outside. "Turns out Stark's at his cabin until tomorrow," I said to Donovan. "So Carla invited us to stay the night."

Jolie stopped me before I left with a tug on my sleeve. For a minute, I thought she was going to kiss me, but she was only handing me the keys we needed to copy. "You should probably take care of this soon too," she whispered.

"Right." Then I kissed her because it really needed to be done. "What were you saying?" I resumed the call as I left the room, shutting the door behind me.

"I said that has to be interesting," Donovan repeated, only mildly annoyed.

"That's one word for it. Turned out to be for the best since it took some time to find what we needed. Hey, hold on a second, D." When I reached the bottom of the stairs, my mother was heading toward me with an expression that said she wanted to say something. "Morning, Mom. What's up?"

"Afternoon now, actually." There was an obvious opinion about my waking time in her tone. "There's cereal in the pantry if you're interested in that. There's also eggs and deli meat in the fridge. Everything's pretty much where it's always been."

"Thanks. I think I'll hold off on food for a bit." I was about to go back to Donovan when she held up a cell phone.

"Julianna left this down here last night. She's missed a couple of calls. Should I take it up or...?"

"Maybe hold off. She's not dressed yet." It was liberating to flaunt our relationship, whatever it was, not just because it made my mother give a judgmental frown but because we'd never in our lives been able to be open.

I was smiling about it when I put the phone back to my ear. "I'm here."

"You still have space on your lower back, right? This tattoo would make a great tramp stamp."

Fucking Donovan. He'd bet that I'd be in bed with Jolie before the end of the week, and if I lost, he got to choose my next tattoo. "Yeah, yeah. Fuck you." And no way was it going somewhere people could see it. Whatever he picked was likely to be embarrassing as hell.

"Anyway." I opened the door to go outside and propped the phone between my chin and shoulder so I could pack the cigarettes.

"Oh, Cade," Carla interrupted again. "If you're going outside..." She waited until I gave her my attention. "I have groceries being delivered. Could you let the guy in when he gets here?"

"Sure." I stepped out onto the porch, letting out a sigh of relief when the door was closed behind me. It was harder to be in her presence than I wanted to admit. Thank God I had an errand to get me out of the house for a bit.

Thank God I wasn't here alone.

I lit a cigarette and spent the next few minutes bringing Donovan up to speed. By the time I'd gotten to the butt, I'd answered all his questions and promised to text him with updates, then promised to mean it this time.

I hung up just as a blue Nissan Versa pulled up in front of the house and parked. A tall kid got out of the driver's seat—well, not a kid since he was driving, but he couldn't have been older than twenty—then headed around to the trunk.

"Need some help?" I jogged down the steps, figuring I could help him bring in the groceries before I took off to get the keys made.

He seemed taken aback by the offer. "No, I got it."

Then instead of pulling grocery bags out of the trunk, he pulled out a duffel bag.

"Are you here with the groceries?" Stupid question since he most definitely was not. Visiting a student probably. Here for an overnight and came to the wrong place. It happened now and then in the past too.

He looked nervous. "No, uh. I was looking for—"

I heard the house door open behind me, then Jolie's voice, bewilderment in her tone. "Tate?"

The kid's features relaxed. "Ah. There. My mom."

WILD HEART

ONE
JOLIE

Past

THE SOFT LANDING of something on my upper back woke me up. I opened my eyes and rolled over to discover my father towering over me and a grocery bag on the bed behind me. I didn't have to look inside to know what I'd find.

"You know what to do." He handed me an empty plastic cup.

I stifled a groan, and simultaneously, I felt my stomach drop. Stuffing down my emotions often led to a sense of dread, but this was more than that. While the routine was familiar to me, I had real reason to fear today's results would be different.

I'd been trying not to think about that. I wouldn't be able to push it off now.

Out of habit, my gaze flickered to my window. He'd glued it shut the day after he'd discovered Cade in my room. He'd installed bars the following week, sealing me in a literal prison.

How long ago had that been now? Four weeks? Only four more until he came back for me. It already felt like a lifetime had passed, and graduation day seemed an eternity away.

"Hurry it up, Julianna. I need to be in early for a meeting with Sylvia."

No wonder my alarm hadn't gone off yet.

With a sigh, I threw the covers off me and picked up the bag. "We did this just two weeks ago," I said, but I swung my legs around and put my feet on the floor. Complaining about it wouldn't get me out of it.

"When you behave like a whore, you should expect to be treated like one."

My empty stomach churned, and I wondered if I could manage to throw up on his shoe if I angled myself right.

But the wave of nausea passed, so with the grocery bag in one hand and the cup in the other, I headed to the bathroom.

"Leave the door propped open," he reminded me when I tried to close it out of habit.

This wasn't new either. He always made me keep the door ajar, as though he thought I might have urine tucked away somewhere in my bathroom cabinets, and I'd try to substitute it out for mine. And even if I did, what good would that do?

It wasn't really about what I might do, though. It was about control. It was about me understanding that he was my lord and master. My prison guard. The person who controlled my fate.

What would he do when I ran away?

I almost wished I could be there to see his reaction.

A smile briefly bent my lips thinking about it, but it vanished as soon as I took the cardboard box out of the bag, and I was forced to face my situation. This was the whole reason I'd avoided truly fantasizing about the future with Cade this last week. This unknown could change everything, and I hadn't been able to process that possibility.

"Julianna?" My father was as impatient to get this over with as I was reluctant.

"Sorry. I was rereading the instructions." It was a lie that was hard to justify considering how often I'd had to take these—once a month since I'd started my period, more frequently since he'd caught me with

Cade—but I noisily tore into the box so he wouldn't feel the need to confront me on it.

Leaving the unpackaged stick on the counter, I took the cup with me to the toilet to do the deed. "This would really be easier if you just put me on the pill. Since you're so worried about me getting knocked up."

This was another familiar conversation, and he didn't even bother to give me his usual lecture about how preparation was an invitation and all that.

That wasn't the reason he didn't give me protection. It was another way he could control me. Plus, I was pretty sure he got off on how humiliating the whole thing was. *Sick fuck.*

I flushed the toilet and took the cup, now filled with my pee, back to the bathroom counter. After uncapping the stick, I dipped the end in and counted to ten. Then I put the cap back on and set it on the counter while I washed my hands, trying to ignore the current wave of nausea and the probability that I didn't need this test to know what was going on inside me.

As soon as he heard the sound of the faucet, my father nudged the door the rest of the way open and leaned against the frame.

His eyes were pinned to the test, watching as the pink control line brightened. "You know what happens if this is positive, right?"

This was another speech he gave every time. He would take me to the doctor to get me an abortion. I'd go through the procedure willingly, or he'd tie me to the bed and take care of it himself with a hanger if need be. There would be no bastard grandchild. End of story.

I couldn't bear to hear it this time. "Yes, I know."

"Are you sure? Maybe you should tell me so I can be sure you're clear."

"I know, Dad," I snapped. "I don't need to repeat it back to you."

His eyes darkened, and his hand twitched at his side while he tried to decide what to do about my disrespect. It was obvious he wanted to backhand me, and I wasn't sure why he even had to think about it since he rarely denied himself a reason to punish me, especially since the whole Cade incident. He'd been taking out his wrath about that on me for the past month.

Today, though, he let it go and glanced at his watch. "One more minute."

One more minute until the truth was confirmed. One more minute until I could no longer pretend my breasts didn't hurt more than when they did with PMS and that my exhaustion wasn't just about missing Cade and my missed period wasn't about stress and that the come-and-go nausea wasn't a weird stomach bug.

What if I was? What would I do then?

Tears pricked, and I shut my eyes, refusing to watch for the second line. I had forty-five seconds left before I had to figure anything out, and I planned on putting it off as long as possible.

My eyes were still closed when I heard my father move to pick up the stick from the counter. "How likely is it his?"

A sob threatened in my chest—or another urge to vomit—and I had to sit down on the edge of the bathtub for support. He knew the answer already, but he wanted me to know it too, and even though I already did, I did the math, figured out the calendar in my head, and thought about when I was most likely ovulating.

The thing was, I didn't know.

And there was no way I could know without a paternity test, and I didn't know if that was even possible before a baby was born, which meant I couldn't have an abortion, no matter what my father said. I wouldn't give up Cade's child. No way, no how.

But being pregnant put a wrench in running away with Cade. And if it ended up not being his, was it fair to saddle him with that burden?

"You need money to have a child," my father said, as if he could read my mind. "You need a home. Insurance. Healthcare. Baby clothes and furniture. Who's going to pay for diapers? And formula? Minimum wage isn't going to get you far. Even if you're both working."

I wasn't surprised that he had guessed I'd been planning to leave. I pushed him off every time he tried to talk about my plans after graduation, and he'd made it very clear he wanted me to stay with him while I got a degree in education so I could come help out at the family school.

What did surprise me was something else. "You'll let me keep it?"

He set the stick on the counter and came to crouch in front of me so we were eye to eye. He had his doting father mask on, which was probably the cruelest of all his masks because it confused me and tore at my emotions. "It will be very hard," he said softly, taking my hands in his. "And you'll need my support, but if that's what you really want, princess, of course you can keep it."

Silent tears streamed down my cheeks. I had no options. It was a facade of a choice.

So I took the devil's bargain, knowing full well that nothing he offered came without a cost.

TWO
JOLIE

Present

I PUSHED OPEN the front door and blinked, as if closing my eyes could make the boy and his duffel bag go away, but he was still very much there, standing in the yard when I opened them. "Tate?"

"Ah. There. My mom," he said to Cade, who was standing next to him with a look of horror on his face that had to match my own.

Immediately, the air went out of my lungs. The doorknob under my hand felt sweaty, and my heart was racing so fast and so hard, it felt like a trapped animal inside my chest.

This can't be happening.

After Cade left the room, I must have rolled over and fallen back to sleep, and now I was dreaming. There was no other explanation. Because the scene in front of me was plucked directly from my worst nightmare, and no way was it really happening.

The current dread was such a contrast from how I'd been floating on air only a few minutes before. Cade had promised he would see this through with my father, and maybe that was more about his own relationship with Dad, but I could tell things were changing. I could feel the tether between us—the one that had always been there, had never broken even when we'd been apart—and instead of yanking at it, trying to break free like he had earlier in the week, it had started to feel like he was shortening the leash, pulling me closer.

And I was ready to stop resisting being pulled.

I was ready to tell him everything, and that felt pretty damn good.

With the truth on my mind, I'd thought of Tate and reached for my phone. It had been a while since I'd checked in on him, and even though I knew he was mature enough to handle being alone with the neighbor keeping an eye on him, I still got anxious when I didn't hear from him for too long.

The fact that my phone wasn't anywhere in the room demonstrated just how distracted I'd been in my old home. Had I really not texted Tate since dinner? Panicking before it was necessary, I'd jumped out of bed and thrown on a change of clothes so I could go look for it.

Then, when I'd come downstairs, the sound of an engine drew my gaze to the window, and I saw a car I recognized—a Nissan Versa that I'd signed a lease on only three months before—and any chance that it could just be a coincidence disappeared when the engine stopped, and the driver who stepped out had a face I knew by heart.

A face that had earnestly sworn to never take the car out on the highway if I wasn't with him when I'd handed over the keys.

And the only way to get here from Boston was by highway, so either he'd broken that promise—and he was not prone to breaking promises—or I was dreaming.

Definitely dreaming.

Because why would Tate even be here? He thought I was at a conference in New York. He didn't have any reason to think I'd be elsewhere, and even if he did, he couldn't suspect I'd be at my childhood home, and he certainly had no way of figuring out how to get here. He'd been only seven when we'd last been here together. He didn't know the name of this town, let alone the address, and that was why he couldn't be here.

Could not. There was no way. This was not how Cade was finding out about him.

But the cold of the air blowing through the open door was undeniably real, proof that this wasn't a dream, that I was standing on my father's porch, that I was watching my son have his very first conversation with the one other man who meant the most to me, and I was seriously about to have a panic attack.

"Jolie's your...*mom*?" Cade's expression had gone hard. He was good at shutting down his emotions from view, a skill he'd perfected when we'd lived together seventeen years ago to help him survive the monster who was my father.

The skill *I'd* perfected back then was freezing up, and I was frozen now, my chest tight and my head screaming to *do something*, my body unable to move.

"Um, yeah. I wasn't sure I was in the right place." He gave his best grin. "But I guess I am. I'm Tate, by the way."

It was just like my kid to befriend a stranger. He was always sweet and polite, and for the most part, unafraid. I'd done my best to give him a life that allowed him to trust that people were good. It was the life I'd longed for and so it was the one I'd wanted for him, and in any other situation, I'd have taken this as a win.

But now I saw how I'd done him a disservice because I loved Cade—I'd both fallen for him again, and I loved him still—but I could admit he wasn't ready for this, and rightly so, he might lash out. As much as I wanted to fight to preserve whatever had been repaired between us over this last week, I had to think of my son first.

With that thought in mind, I could finally move.

I took a step out, then drew back quickly when I remembered I was still barefoot, and the ground was covered with snow. "Tate, get in here," I snapped, ignoring the strong desire to ask what the hell he was doing here. That could wait. This, however, was immediate. "Now. Right now."

Confusion marring his brow, Tate took a step toward me, but Cade grabbed his arm, sending warning signals shivering down my spine. "Wait. How old are you, Tate?"

"Leave him alone, Cade." Keeping the front door ajar so I could hear what was happening, I opened the coat closet, remembering I'd seen Carla's house slippers in there when we'd hung up our coats the night before. "Tate, come on. Get in here."

I had one slipper on and was looking for the other, when instead of listening to me and coming in the house, my son answered. "Almost seventeen. You're...*Cade*?"

"Tate!" I hadn't used that sharp of a tone with him since he almost stepped into the road chasing after the cat when he was eight, but this conversation couldn't happen like this. Absolutely could not.

Fuck the other slipper, I was going out like this.

Except then Carla popped up behind me. "Ah! He's here!"

Hold up. She was *expecting* Tate?

I spun back toward her. "This was *you*?" I couldn't imagine how she'd done it, but if she was somehow behind my child being somewhere he absolutely should not be... Rage surged through me, curling my hand into a fist when I'd never hit anyone in my life.

"What month?" Cade asked, ignoring Tate's question.

Fuck. I didn't have time for Carla.

Turning away from whatever bullshit response she started to give me, I ran down the steps so fast I didn't even feel the cold on my one bare foot, reaching Tate just as he said, "What month is my birthday? January. January sixth."

It was easy enough math, and I saw Cade doing the calculations, saw him figuring it out or thinking he'd figured it out, and there was nothing I could do but stop it. "Tate, please." I pushed him toward the door. "Go inside."

His expression gave just as much away as Cade's. "But Mom—"

I cut him off. "Seriously, Tate. Go. In. The. House. I'll be there in a minute."

"Jesus, okay. Fine."

I cringed. His choice of language was pretty trivial in light of everything else, but motherly instinct wasn't always great at prioritizing, and I had to resist the urge to correct him.

With his duffel bag in hand, he brushed past me, and while I wanted to follow him up the stairs and apologize and explain, I had to say something to Cade first.

Cade. My love. My only.

Cade, whose eyes pierced me like nails, accusing and angry, holding my gaze to his, demanding explanations that I couldn't give until my son was out of earshot.

"Come right on in, Tate. I'll get you some hot chocolate."

Goddammit. Carla.

I tore my eyes from Cade and swung my head around. "Don't fucking say a word to him until I'm in there."

She glared as Tate walked past her into the house. "I'm just warming the kid up, Julianna. No need to go all mother bear on me."

She hadn't seen mother bear. This was a kitten in comparison with what I felt inside, and her play-innocent gaslighting wasn't helping calm me. Acting as if I hadn't just sent my child into a house with a wolf when her teeth were practically bared. I almost left Cade to go deal with her instead.

"You didn't tell me? You weren't going to fucking tell me?"

Just like that, my focus was back on Cade. "You're wrong. It's not—"

He cut me off. "No, *you're* wrong. What you did is wrong. What you did—"

I raised my voice, trying to get a word in edgewise. "I didn't do what—"

"—is unforgivable. You *robbed* me—"

"He's not yours!" It came out as a shout, and immediately, I worried I'd been loud enough to carry inside. But the front door was still closed when I glanced behind me, and now I had Cade's attention, so I said it again at a more reasonable volume. "He's not yours."

It was a gut punch for me to say it, even now, after all these years.

It had to be just as bad to hear it.

"But his birthday...?" As hard as his mask was, I could see the hope flicker.

Or maybe it wasn't hope but the flame of resistance. The desire to see the past as he believed it to be, that belief so strong that it was easier to bend the facts to fit around that than consider he'd never known the truth.

The truth he now had to consider was probably earth-shattering.

And while the whole truth might make it better, it would take so much more explaining than what I could give to him standing outside, perched on one foot so the bare one didn't hit the cold ground while my son got interrogated by his step-grandmother in the house behind me.

The whole truth was hard enough under the best of circumstances. I still had a hard time saying it out loud.

"If he's going to be seventeen in January..." Cade wasn't going to give up so easily. "That means you got pregnant your senior year. Nine months. That means you were pregnant at graduation."

I wished I could lie, but all I could say was, "Right."

Then he understood. His shoulders slumped, his expression fell. I'd gotten pregnant while we were together, and the baby wasn't his, and that meant...

"Oh." He took a step backward. Then another. "I see."

But he didn't see, and while he now realized I hadn't robbed him of the chance to watch his child grow up, I wasn't sure that this new epiphany was any easier to forgive.

"Cade." It came out like a plea, even though I knew that wasn't fair.

He shook his head at me, confirming that I had no right to ask him anything now—maybe not ever again—and took another step backward, another step away from me. "I'm such an idiot."

"No." I stepped after him, reaching for him. "You're not."

"Such a fucking idiot."

"You aren't. I need to explain. I need to—"

But he wasn't hearing me. As though in a daze, his head still shaking, he turned toward our rental car. "I, uh, have to get to the locksmith."

He couldn't hide the hurt on his face, though he was trying. And as many times as I'd imagined telling him, his reaction was somehow way worse than any scenario I'd thought up on my own.

I'd broken him.

Again.

How many times could I do this to him and still hope that he could be put back together?

I felt the ache as though it were mine.

Whatever was happening inside the house, it was suddenly not as important as this. "Cade, wait. Please. Let's talk." I chased after him.

He was at the driver's side of the car. "I can't." He opened the door. "I have to…" Instead of finishing the sentence with words, he held up the keys to my father's cabin that we'd found while searching his office the night before, the keys he planned to take to town to get copied.

I didn't have my coat or my purse or a proper pair of shoes, but I ran to the passenger door. "I'll go with you." I pulled on the handle, but it was locked. I pulled again, as if that would magically make it open. "Please, let me come."

He paused, one foot in the car, refusing to look me in the eye. "I'd really rather be alone right now." He nodded at the house. "You should go be with your *son*."

He threw the word like a dagger, and while I knew this was the worst way for him to find out and that he might understand if he heard all of it, I also felt validated. This was why I hadn't told him. This was why I'd kept this secret, even when I'd come back into his life.

Because the only thing he could do with this information was hate me.

Or I could tell him more, and he'd hate himself.

I honestly didn't know which was worse.

So I let him get in the car, and when he started the engine, I backed up and let him drive away.

THREE
JOLIE

Cade took a piece of my heart with him as he tore out of the driveway. But the other piece of my heart was inside the house, alone with a woman who could destroy what Tate believed the same way I'd just destroyed Cade.

My focus had to be on my son.

Back in the house, I didn't bother to kick off the slipper and instead went looking for Tate. I was already headed down the hallway toward the dining room when he called out. "Mom?"

I turned around and found him with his phone in hand, sitting on the couch in the living room, a space that was a complete contradiction to its name. Growing up, we'd only ever used the room for guests, and since I was very rarely allowed to have people over, I spent very little time there. I'd gotten so used to thinking of it as a useless room, I hadn't even bothered to look there, and now that I was looking, it felt odd to see Tate sitting there, being treated like a stranger in a house I knew so well.

It wasn't a bad thing.

In fact, I preferred it, but I was surprised that Carla wasn't beside him, telling him all sorts of things I didn't want him to know.

"Mom, what's going on? You're being so weird, and that man

outside—"

I cut him off. "No, no, no. You don't get to ask questions until I get answers. What the—?" I paused to take a breath in and out before going on. However he got here, it wasn't on his own, and that meant I shouldn't be taking out my frustration on him. Slightly calmer, I asked, "What are you doing here?"

He looked at me like I'd grown two heads. "Are you messing with me?"

"No. I'm one hundred percent not messing with you. Why are you here?"

"You're scaring me right now, Mom."

Whether he deserved it or not, my rope was at its end. "Tate. Just answer the goddamn question."

"Why are you yelling at me? You told me to come!"

"I did not! When?"

With a huff of frustration, he clicked a few things on his phone and then stood up to show me. "Last night. Were you drunk or something?"

I read the last text he'd sent a little before ten.

> Maps says I'll be there in an hour.

The text before that from me had been sent a few minutes before.

> When do you think you'll be here?

Except I hadn't had my phone all morning, and I had definitely not sent that text.

A kettle whistle went off in the background. Carla fixing the cocoa. *Fucking Carla.*

I snatched the phone out of his hand. Anger stirred through me, my body vibrating as I scrolled up through several texts until I found the last text I'd sent the night before at dinner, reminding him that he couldn't have anyone over and that I didn't want him driving after ten p.m.

I'd stormed off from the table, leaving my phone behind before he'd responded.

> Tara and I are going to hang with Ben over at her place. I'll take the train back if we're out too late.

If I'd seen that, I would have told him to be sure he didn't stay out too late.

Instead, the screen showed I'd responded around eight.

> What are your plans for tomorrow?

> Homework and cleaning my room. Duh.

A winking emoji followed.

> Why don't you drive up and join me instead?

I stifled a growl.

> In NY?

> No, I'm in Connecticut now.

> Wth r u doing in CT?

> Change of plans. You should drive up. It's only a couple of hours away.

> Tonight?

> No.

There had been a pause before "I" added,

> Tomorrow morning. First thing.

He must have tried to call after that because his next message said,

> Mom, answer!

> Can't talk right now. Let me know when you're on your way in the morning.

The address followed that as well as a link to directions on Maps.

> Okey dokey.

The next text came from Tate as well, sent a little before nine this morning.

> Still want me 2 come?

> Yes. Bring an overnight bag.

> Should I tell the Burritts?

> I'll call them later today.

Then I was back to the text asking when he'd arrive, and it took everything in me not to throw his phone at Carla's curio cabinet.

"What's going on, Mom? Am I in trouble? You're really freaking me out."

Another breath. I'd worked really hard to be sure that I always handled anger constructively in front of him, and I wasn't going to let Carla's meddling be the reason I ruined that now. "It's, um, no. You're not in trouble. I just... I didn't send these messages."

The color drained from his face. "What do you mean? They say they're from you. How can they not be from you?" He took the phone back from me and clicked on one of my texts, bringing up the contact info, verifying it had indeed been sent from my phone.

"It did come from my phone. I just wasn't the one..." He looked terrified and confused, and I hadn't seen him in a week, and suddenly, I really needed to hug him. "It's fine," I assured him as I wrapped my arms around him. "I'm glad you're here. I was just surprised, is all."

"I don't understand." He pulled away, much earlier than I would have liked, but I couldn't be too disappointed since he'd let me hug him longer than usual. "If you didn't send..." He seemed to have a thought. "When I turned onto the road and saw the school, I thought you were going to tell me you got a job here or something, but then I got to the house—this is where you grew up, isn't it?"

"I..." I wasn't prepared to talk about this. He'd been seven when we'd left—old enough to have memories of the place—but I'd hoped those were few and faint.

Of course, when he was standing in the very house, it was harder to expect he'd forget.

"Do you remember living here?" Carla came in carrying a tray with three mugs and a plate of cookies, as if she'd been waiting in the wings to enter at the right moment.

I wondered if the chocolate was hot enough to scald if I threw mine in her face.

"Vaguely," Tate said, looking around the room.

I didn't like this. Didn't like him coming back here. Didn't like him wondering about that time or our life here or anything before that. "Hey, kiddo, I need to talk to—"

But Carla spoke at the same time, and she was the one who got his attention. "Do you remember me?" She set the tray on the coffee table and stood up straight so he could get a good look at her.

"You're..." He squinted his eyes in her direction.

"Married to my father," I finished for him.

Again, Carla spoke over me. "Cade's mother."

"Cade?" Tate perked up immediately.

Just like I feared, she had opened a can of worms that I was not ready to deal with. The situation was too complicated, always had been, which was why I had never wanted him to come back here. Now all my secrets and lies were threatening to unravel, and I needed to take control of the situation, right the fuck now.

"Okay, Tate. How about you go upstairs and rest for a while. I need to talk to Carla real quick." *And maybe murder her a little bit while I'm at it.*

I tried to nudge him toward the stairs, but Carla took that moment to put her hand in her pocket and retrieve my cell. "Oh, Julianna. You left this downstairs last night."

Tate didn't budge. "Julianna?"

I grabbed my phone out of her hand, wishing I could yank her arm out of the socket with it. Stupid me for leaving it out of my sight. Stupid me for using Cade's birthday as my lockscreen pin. She was probably the only person in the world who could guess it. Stupid me for not changing it before I'd stepped foot in this fucked-up house.

"Hold on," Tate said, pointing his finger in Carla's direction. "You had my mom's phone?" He was too bright of a kid to miss anything. "So who was texting me last night?"

This time, I didn't let her say a word. "I'm going to find all of that out, okay? I'll fill you in after. You can get a little rest before you have to go back home. Upstairs. The room at the end of the hall."

"Don't forget your cocoa." Carla looked smug as she tried to hand him the mug.

He ignored the mug and spun toward me. "You're making me go back home already?"

Whoops. Not the thing to say at the moment. "We can talk about it in a bit. Go lie down."

"I'm not tired, Mom. I haven't even had lunch. And why can't I be here for this conversation? I'm obviously involved."

"Do you want me to make you a bite to eat?" As annoyed as I was with Carla's innocent/sweet step-grandparent routine, I was grateful for this suggestion.

"Awesome idea." I took the mug out of her hand and put it in Tate's. "You can stay here and eat some cookies, and I'll help in the kitchen." I nodded for Carla to go ahead of me, but she only took one step before he stopped us.

"Wait a minute, Mom. Please."

I smiled at him impatiently. "What?"

"Just tell me one thing." He put the mug down on the tray, seeming disinterested in the drink. "That man—Cade? That's Cade Warren, right? And don't tell me it's not the same Cade like you did when I looked him up that one time because you can't say that's not him if he's here. That's too big of a coincidence."

I'd hoped he wouldn't recognize Cade in person. It had been a year since he'd gone looking online for the name he'd been hearing about for years, determined to find the man who I insisted had disappeared. Thank God the name wasn't that uncommon. He'd shown me face after face after face, and each time I'd said, "Not him."

Then he'd actually shown me Cade—my Cade—dressed in a suit, listed as a co-owner of a huge international marketing firm, and my stomach had turned over on itself while I'd repeated the same "Not him" response.

I'd been caught out, and my face must have shown it because Tate looked hurt. "Why didn't you want me to meet my father?"

I could feel Carla's glare at my back. Shame flooded through me, the kind of shame I hadn't felt in years. Shame for the lies. Shame for not being able to tell the truth now. "Oh, sweetie." I tried to hug him again, but this time, he pulled away.

"Don't treat me like I'm a kid. Does he not want to meet me? What is he even doing here? Is that why she brought me out here?"

I was a shit mother. This whole thing he'd walked into had to be even more confusing and fucked up to him than it was to me—and it was pretty fucked up to me—even though it wasn't my fault that he was here, it was my fault that he believed the things he believed.

And my fault for perpetuating the lies. "He doesn't know," I said softly before I'd completely committed to saying it.

"He doesn't know I'm his kid?"

Now that I'd started down this path, it was easier to keep running down it. "He doesn't know he has a kid at all. He left town before I knew I was pregnant, and then, like I told you, I didn't know what happened to him..."

"But then I found him on the internet—"

"You did. And I lied about who he was because, if I admitted it, you'd want me to reach out, and it's just..." I glanced back at Carla who now had the decency to look as pained by this conversation as I was. "It's just that it's complicated, honey. And that's not fair to you, and I'm sorry, but please, can I just have a few minutes to talk to Carla? Then I'll try to answer whatever questions I can." It wasn't just about laying into her any more about the mess she'd put me in, though it was that too. Now, I needed her to help me figure out how to get my fucking story straight.

And maybe a moment to cry without Tate seeing.

He cast his eyes down and flipped his phone around in one hand, over and over, something he often did absentmindedly while he thought things out. "Complicated because Carla is both married to Grandpa and also Cade's mother?"

Yep. Exactly because of that, kid.

Surprisingly, it was Carla who had the comforting words. "They were seniors in high school when they met, Tate. It wasn't like they were brother and sister, but yes. As you can imagine, it does make things complicated."

My eyes started watering, and I had to blink fast. "Look, you have every right to be mad at me, and I promise I'll straighten everything out soon, okay?"

"And you'll tell him the truth about me?"

That was easy to agree to since I already had outside in the driveway. It was Tate who I had to come clean with. "Let me talk to him first?"

Reluctantly, he nodded.

"Cool." This time, he let me give him a quick hug. "Now I'm going to go help Carla make us some grilled cheese, and then we can all sit and talk some more."

Of course, it was going to be hard for Carla to sit down with my fist shoved up her ass but no less than she deserved.

FOUR
JOLIE

Past

I TUCKED my feet underneath me, tossing the ice pack I'd had on my breasts to the ground. They were so engorged, every little movement hurt. The hospital nurse had been the one who recommended the icing, but they only stayed icy for about fifteen minutes—ten with the stove in the den going—and I really wasn't convinced it was helping anyway. Now my tits were just sore and cold.

The nurse had also said it would take a week or so to dry up. Considering it had only been a day since my milk had come in, the near future promised to be more of the same. I groaned thinking about it.

"It's not too late to change your mind about nursing," Carla said from the rocker in the corner.

I glanced over at her, my eyes resting on the baby in her arms. My chest tightened whenever I looked at him, a pain that had nothing to do with my breasts, and I had to swallow before I could respond. "I'm still thinking about it."

"I don't know what there is to think about. It's healthiest for the baby and for you, to be truthful. Not to mention how much money we'll save. Formula is expensive."

Everything was expensive—formula, diapers, doctor visits. The bill I'd been shown before I checked out of the hospital said I would have owed eighteen thousand dollars without my father's insurance.

That had been one of the primary reasons I hadn't left with Cade.

The other reason was why I had initially decided against nursing. The same reason the baby had yet to be given a name. I was trying my best not to bond with him until the DNA results came back.

What happened after that was beyond my ability to consider. It was one sleepless hour at a time right now. I'd deal with *what next* when it became *what now*.

"Who has a full tummy, huh? Do you have a full tummy?"

It was weird to watch Carla cooing over anything. I'd never imagined her having any maternal instincts at all, not just because I'd never witnessed that side of her but also because of the stories I'd heard from Cade. Maybe she was only good with babies.

Or maybe she was only good with babies who weren't her own.

She'd been a great help with the feedings, at least. The less I held him, the better. Because every time he was in my arms, I'd stare at his full lips and his wrinkly eyes and try to see Cade in his features. More times than not, I'd find him.

And until I knew whether those glimpses were real or not, I had to stop looking.

Carla unswaddled the baby, put him over her shoulder, and rubbed his back in circles. "Come on now. Let it out." She kissed his head and then looked at me. "Cade used to take forever to burp too."

Apparently, she was looking for him in my baby too.

It would have made me hopeful if I thought she suspected the truth. But she took it for granted that he was Cade's son, and so of course that's what she saw.

And I wanted him to be Cade's so badly that of course that's what I saw too.

A door shut in the front of the house. I hadn't realized it was so late. Day and night had blended together in the five days since I'd given birth. I'd been surprised when I'd come down for breakfast only to find it was time for lunch. Now I was surprised that my father was already home from his first day of the new term.

"Shit." It was under her breath, but I still caught the curse. "I haven't started dinner."

"Julianna?" He sounded like he was calling up the stairs.

I didn't answer. Instead, I held my hands out toward Carla. "Give him to me." Not because she had to go cook but because my father would find me soon, and bonded with the baby or not, I knew it was my responsibility to protect him from the evils in the world.

The biggest evil I knew lived under the same roof.

She swaddled him back up and brought him over to me. "He still needs to burp," she said just as my name was called again. "Your father is not going to be happy if he has to go upstairs looking for you only to find you're not there."

I hadn't been trying to keep on his good side for months now. Pregnancy had seemed to place me off-limits, and for the first time in my life, he'd left me alone for weeks at a time.

But I wasn't pregnant anymore, and I wasn't stupid enough to think a baby in his life would make him any less sinister.

"In the den," I shouted before taking the baby from Carla.

It was an awkward exchange—it always was, it seemed. It was like I made myself forget how to hold him, or I wouldn't allow myself to let the instincts of mothering take over.

But every time, as soon as I had him in my arms, he settled magically into the curve of my elbow—like he'd always been there, like he was an extension of me—and this time was no different.

"Hi." I couldn't help smiling. The corners of my mouth rose all on their own.

His eyes got big, and he made an O shape with his lips, as if I was the most fascinating thing he'd ever seen.

That tightness returned to my torso, and it suddenly felt hard to breathe.

Outside the den, my father must have bumped into Carla. "You're not in the kitchen." The words were innocent enough, but his tone was clearly displeased.

"I thought I'd do something simple tonight. Sandwiches and soup since it's so cold out." She tried to sound light and breezy.

There was a silence that I guessed was being filled with one of his seething stares.

"'Only peasants eat sandwiches for dinner,'" I whispered to the baby, quoting one of my father's convictions. "Learn that now, and you'll be ahead of the game."

Except it wasn't going to matter. Whatever we found out about his parentage, he wouldn't be subject to my father's cruel rules and specifications.

"I'll do a pasta with meat sauce then," Carla said.

"I'm presuming dinner will be late?"

"Not by too much. You'll see."

I'd wondered sometimes if Carla was subject to my father's wrath the way Cade and I had been, but if I believed she was, then I had to wonder if my mother had been too, and I didn't like thinking about that.

In instances like this, I was sure she was a victim as much as any of us. I could hear the nervousness in her tone. Could sense the subtext in my father's question about the lateness of the meal. There would be repercussions for this, it said.

God, what a nightmare this place was.

"You'll be okay, Tate. I promise."

"Tate?" My father had entered the room too quietly for me to hear. "Is that his name?"

I hugged the bundle closer to me, ignoring the pain of the pressure on my breasts. "Trying it out, is all."

"It's nice to see you holding him for once. It seems like he's been attached to Carla since he came home from the hospital."

These were the kinds of remarks he was famous for—seemingly

innocuous but loaded. *You're causing my wife to be distracted*, was what he really meant for me to hear. *I'm not going to tolerate that for long.*

I hated him.

I hated him, I hated him, I hated him.

"She's been great. Thank you for letting her help."

He stared at me. I could feel his eyes as I stared just as hard at the baby in my arms. His stares were almost worse than his subtle threats. They were harder to translate. What did he want? Would I be in trouble if I didn't anticipate whatever it was?

"You're leaking," he said after a long stretch of silence.

I glanced at the wet spot on my T-shirt and missed the cardboard envelope he threw at me, barely missing the baby's face as he said, "Oh, and this came."

I'd given him my share of glares over the years, but usually behind his back since looking at him "wrong" could earn me a week of not being able to sit down. This glare, however, I delivered right to his face, feeling a surprisingly intense and ferocious need to protect.

But before I snapped at him about his aim—which was likely purposeful—I saw the return address on the envelope label. **Science-Life Labs**.

"Are these the results?" My father had swabbed me, Carla, and the baby only a few hours after I delivered and took care of mailing them off for a paternity test. He'd said we'd get the results quickly, but this had been fast.

"I'd suspect so."

I hadn't even opened it, and my eyes were already tearing up. My heart was in my throat. I'd been waiting for this since I'd first seen the plus sign on that stupid pregnancy test. This moment would be the one that determined the rest of my life. The rest of this baby's life, too.

It was too much. Too fucking much.

"You're not going to open it?"

I was still staring at the label—the envelope in one hand, the baby in the other. He suddenly felt heavier than he'd been, and I wanted to put him down, wanted to put him in the portable bassinet and leave the room to read the results in private.

But I wouldn't leave him with my father.

"I could open it for you, if—"

I cut him off. "No. I'll do it." I ripped open the envelope—clumsily with the better part of one arm preoccupied—and pulled out the document from inside. It wasn't fancy but official looking. The ScienceLife logo sat in the top left corner. My name and address were typed below it. Then in the center of the next line, the words **Paternity Test** were in bold.

DNA MOUTH SWABS *were examined from the following individuals:*
 HNDS1987655Mother
 HNDS1987656Child
 HNDS1987657Alleged Paternal Grandmother

A BUNCH of technical speak followed, then a chart comparing the alleles found in our samples. I turned to the next page and scanned past everything to the heading at the bottom.

BASED ON OUR ANALYSIS, *it is practically proven HNDS1987657, the Alleged Paternal Grandmother, is not related to the child, HNDS1987656.*

MY VISION CLOUDED. If there was more to read, I couldn't see it. The paper fell from my hands, and I bit my lip to keep from losing my shit. *He's not Cade's. He's not Cade's. Oh, God, he's not Cade's.*

I felt sick to my stomach. Bile filled the back of my throat, and it burned when I swallowed it down. The worst part was that I didn't even have the luxury to grieve. A decision had to be made. *What now* was here. And I was not at all prepared to figure that out.

I could sense my father's glee as he sat down in the armchair next to the couch. He didn't have to ask what the report had said. It had to be written all over my face, and this kind of disappointment was exactly the kind of thing the man got off on.

Fucking psycho sadist.

"Are you going to hunt him down and join him?" My father didn't speak Cade's name anymore, but it was obvious who he was talking about. "Saddle him with a child that isn't his? Will you tell him, or will you lie?"

It was an option, one I hadn't wanted to consider. I didn't think I could tell him the truth, not all of it anyway, but I wouldn't lie.

And why would he still want you?

If he still loved me, I couldn't expect him to love me enough to accept this kind of baggage. It wasn't fair to force him to make that choice.

"Or are you considering adoption?" My father was exceptionally skilled at getting inside my head. He loved that as much as he loved any other form of torture, and right now, it was very much torture to hear him lay out my options, including the downsides, with pointed accuracy. "Is that why you haven't named him yet?"

I hated how well he knew me. No matter how hard I tried to hide myself from him, he still figured out so much.

Could I really give this baby away? A baby who wasn't Cade's but had been made from me and lived inside me and had been the only reason I'd had to push on for the better part of a year?

I brushed my finger against his tiny cheek. His skin was so soft, it felt unreal. And those eyes! The only other person who had ever looked at me that intensely was Cade. He looked at me like I belonged to him, and I did. I really did.

Because even if he wasn't Cade's baby, he was mine.

And that meant he was my responsibility. It was my job to do what was best for him, and what was best for him was giving him up.

A tear slid down my cheek. I'd told myself I could remain detached, but that was a big fat lie. I'd been attached to him from the second I'd found out about his existence inside of me.

Giving him up was going to hurt like hell.

But I would. For him. And then I'd go to Cade.

"You don't even know where that boy went off to," my father said, once again inside my thoughts. "How do you expect to find him? Are you expecting fate to bring you together? What a romantic notion. I've coddled you too much if that's what you're thinking."

Another tear fell. What if I never found Cade? What if I gave up my baby and never found him?

I pressed a kiss on his tiny forehead.

"You could always leave him here with us."

My head shot in his direction. "Never."

I knew I'd made a mistake the minute the word was out of my mouth. I'd walked right into his trap, and there was no way to get out of it because now he knew my price.

He smiled as though he'd already won, and honestly, he had. The rest was just going through the motions. "No judge in the county will deny me if I make the request to keep him."

I shook my head, trying to pretend he wasn't saying what he was saying.

"I'm a well-respected member of the community."

"I'm his mother."

"An unfit mother. If I say you are."

I'd fucked up. Fucked up so bad. I should have gone with Cade. We would have figured it out. Poor and uninsured people had babies every day. And I would never have gotten a paternity test. We could have gone forever not knowing.

But that wasn't what I'd done.

"Why would you do that?" I asked, already knowing the answer.

"For the baby, of course. I couldn't let a baby with Stark blood be raised by a stranger. Not when we could offer him the best life here."

It was all a bunch of lies. This was the worst life, and he didn't give a shit about a baby with his blood. He only cared about keeping me here. Keeping me under his thumb. Keeping me his.

I kissed my baby's head again. Pressed my cheek to his and rocked him back and forth. When I straightened up again, I lifted my chin defiantly. "You will *never* lay a hand on him. Do you understand?" I didn't have any power here, but I played it like I did. Because if he *did* hurt my child, I would find the power, whatever I had to do to get it, and he would regret it.

"Whatever you say."

"And I am his mother. He's mine, and I decide what's best for him."

He nodded, a smug smile on his lips. "Of course. Just like I decide what's best for you."

I squeezed my eyes tight against the onslaught of tears. They were still closed when I felt his lips on my temple. "Don't cry, princess. You're doing the right thing. I'll take care of you both."

It was fucked up how a part of me could still believe him when he said things like that. Fucked up that I *wanted* to believe him. Fucked up enough that I probably deserved whatever I got.

When I opened my eyes, he was collecting the dropped paternity results. I watched as he opened the door to the stove and threw it into the fire. A few minutes later, it was like the report had never existed.

No one knew what it had said but the two of us.

"What will we tell Carla?" She thought the baby was her grandson.

He shrugged. "Let her believe whatever she wants." That kept it easy, at least. He nodded to my shirt. "You should clean up before dinner. I'm going to go change myself."

Just like that, everything was settled.

Another wave of grief rolled through me. Another sob threatened, but I choked it back. This didn't have to be forever. It would just be for now. We'd get out of here eventually.

In the meantime, I had to be strong. For *him*. For Tate.

"I guess you have a name now." I swore he smiled, though the textbooks said he was too young, and it was probably just gas. "It's you and me, little guy. I will always try to do the best I can for you. I swear it on my life."

And ten minutes later, when dinner was announced, I did what was best for the both of us—I stayed in the den and taught my son how to nurse.

FIVE
CADE

Present

THE SOUND of a car honking let me know the light was green. I drove through the intersection, then pulled into the first parking lot I came to. I'd been driving around so aimlessly, I didn't know where I was or how much time had passed. I'd gone numb. Like I had when she'd first shown up back at Reach. Completely numb.

Now, with the car idling and the windows fogging up, emotion pushed at the edges of whatever box I kept it in, wanting to get out. Wanting me to feel. Wanting me to acknowledge.

I'd wanted to know, hadn't I? Whether she'd ever loved me. This proved that she didn't—at least not the way I'd loved her because I'd been faithful. There had been no one but her. There was *still* no one but her.

And for her there'd been...

I couldn't let myself go there. I'd already tortured myself over the years, wondering who had been in her bed. Who she'd given her lips and body to.

But the curiosity was always about the time after I'd left. I'd never believed there could be any reason to doubt her fidelity while we were together. We'd been devoted to each other, hadn't we? Even if it had happened right after I'd left, it would have been a betrayal. What had I missed?

My mind scanned through hundreds of memories, looking for a clue. Her in my arms. Her at my feet. Her on my lap.

I landed on a time in the shower, when she'd snuck in just as I was about to get out.

"Dad left early for school, and Carla has a doctor appointment," she'd said when I told her it was too risky. "I need you. I'll be quick."

He'd been mad at her the night before, and I hadn't dared sneak into her room. It was spring, close to the end, when even speaking to each other felt dangerous, and yet we couldn't bear to stay away. In the same breath I'd told her she should go, I lifted her up and braced her back against the tile wall. Her legs immediately curled around me, and I slid bare inside her.

"I love you," I'd said as I pounded into her. "Only you. Only you. I belong only to you."

"I love you, too."

Had she said she'd belonged to me too?

Had she ever?

I'd made promises to her over and over, always telling her there was no one else, but had she? What had she said exactly?

As hard as I tried, I couldn't remember.

My jaw tightened. It was seventeen fucking years ago. It shouldn't matter. I should have moved on. It shouldn't hurt like it was fucking yesterday.

But God, it did. Like the knife had been lodged there this whole time, and now she was twisting it with all her strength.

I took a breath in and let it out. Curled my fingers around the steering wheel and tried the old trick of tracing the tattoos on my hands with my eyes, hoping it would calm me down. Get my head focused. Bring me back to my prison of numbness.

But I didn't even get through one time across both knuckles before my mind had wandered; not to her this time. The boy. The kid with her eyes and my height.

And when I'd seen him, when I'd realized he was hers and in the minute that followed when I thought that meant...what it *had* to mean...

That was maybe the best and worst minute of my life.

Everything I'd missed was front and center—most people don't meet their kid when he's already full-grown, and the birthdays and milestones that had gone on without me were unforgivable even before I'd had the chance to recognize them.

But I'd wanted him all the same.

Wanted him to be my kid. *Our* kid. Made out of our love.

I'd wanted that to be her secret, and then I would hate her for keeping him from me, but I would love her too, and I would love him enough to make up for everything else.

"*He's not yours.*"

Fuck.

I punched my fist into the dashboard so hard I wondered for a moment if I'd sprained it. Even that pain wasn't enough to dull the ache of the other pain.

I shook my hand out and stared out the window. I'd pulled into the parking lot of a CVS. There'd been a Blockbuster next to it when I'd been in high school. Now it was a Dollar Store.

Nothing stayed the same.

Nothing changed.

Her son was what she was going to tell me about when all this was through, I realized. The reason why she thought I wouldn't want to help her with her father. A natural supposition. It made the imbalance between us obvious. She had her own life, her own world—her own *family*—and I was just the fucking tool she knew she could use.

Or I was the jackass who couldn't separate one thing from another.

Fact: Her father was a monster.

Fact: He was selling kids, and he had to be stopped.

Whatever had happened between me and her, that much was true.

He was the true bad guy here. I hated him without her in the picture. His crimes against me had nothing to do with her. He needed to be destroyed.

And I had the literal keys to his demise resting in my pocket.

I pulled up the car's GPS and located the nearest locksmith, then put the car in gear. This was what I had to focus on. Bringing down that motherfucker. Making him pay.

Figuring out how to feel about Jolie was going to have to wait.

SIX
CADE

The locksmith held up the key ring I'd handed him, singling out a small gold one. "I can copy all of them except this one."

That was the key I needed most, of course. The words *do not duplicate* engraved on it made it pretty obvious that was the cabin's safe key.

I'd been expecting this. I'd lucked out when the person who'd come to the counter to help me was a man. Women, I'd learned over the years, were more likely to follow the rules. Some heavy flirting could maybe win one over if she already hated her job, but it didn't work as often as it did.

Men, on the other hand, were much easier to entice.

"I was hoping you might reconsider," I said, handing over a Benjamin that I'd previously pulled out of my wallet for this specific situation. "It's sort of an emergency situation."

He blinked at the hundred, and considering he looked fresh out of high school, I wouldn't have been surprised if it was the first time he'd seen that big of a bill or at least the first time he'd been given one for himself.

"Uh..." He glanced at the front of the hardware store, likely looking out for a boss before he took the money and pocketed it. "I think I could help you after all."

"Thanks. Appreciate it."

He took the keys and began working, duplicating the engraved key first, his eyes darting back and forth from the machine to the front counter. "Stark Academy," he said, a nervous twitch in his voice.

It took me a second to remember the key chain I'd given him had the school's logo on it.

Dumb move. I should have taken it off before handing them over and would have if I hadn't been so distracted.

"Yeah, my, um, kid goes there." It was a better answer than the truth, but I was cursing at myself for having brought attention to me at all.

Though the hundred-dollar bribe had probably already made me memorable.

But now I was thinking about having a kid old enough to go to Stark Academy, and wouldn't you know it, the kid in my head had green-blue eyes and dishwater-blond hair.

"Son or daughter?"

He's not yours.

I cleared my throat, and the image in my head dispelled. "Daughter."

"Nice."

I was about to excuse myself to smoke a cigarette rather than continue to engage in painful small talk, but before I could, he started up again. "Crazy what happened there, isn't it? With the missing girl. Did your daughter know her?"

"Missing girl?" I was all ears.

"You didn't hear about it? I thought they would have sent some sort of notice home to parents."

"My ex gets all the school notices. I get weekends." I faked a laugh, as if the kid could understand custody arrangements. He laughed too, pretending he could. "So what happened with the girl?"

"I don't know a lot about it. Only reason I heard anything about it was because my dad's a detective with the police, and he said another student had accused someone who worked at the school of being involved with her disappearance. But then he said that that student was caught with a bunch of drugs and wasn't really reliable, and the girl was most likely a runaway. So I guess it wasn't really that crazy of a situation after all."

No, it was a crazy situation all right. And right on brand for Stark.

"When did this happen?" I already had my cell out of my pocket. "Do you know her name?"

He shrugged. "A couple of weeks ago? Thanksgiving weekend, I think. I don't remember her name, but I bet your daughter would know."

"Yeah. Probably." I dialed the last number that had called me and put the phone up to my ear. "Mind if I step away to make a phone call?"

"Sure. It's going to take me a bit to get—"

Donovan answered before the kid finished his sentence. "What's up?"

I stepped away from the counter, heading down an empty store aisle. "Another kid went missing over Thanksgiving. A girl. Don't know her name."

I could hear the sound of typing. Donovan Googling the information, I suspected. "Are you sure? I don't see anything about it when I search."

"Being labeled a runaway."

"Of course. How did you hear about it?"

I wasn't going to admit my slipup with the key chain. "Overheard someone talking about it at the hardware store. Here's the thing, though —apparently, there's another kid who came forth and accused someone who works at the school of foul play."

"Daddy Stark?"

"Possibly. The cops dismissed it because the kid who came forth was in possession of drugs."

"Sounds a little convenient."

"That's what I thought." A partner in the police might explain how Stark had gotten away with his dirty side hustle for so long. "But also, you don't understand how that man is revered around here. He doesn't need anyone doing him favors. People believe the best of him already, no matter what proof is brought against him."

Donovan considered. "This is good actually."

He was often several steps ahead of me, but I didn't see anything good about another missing kid, and I said as much.

"No, but it's recent, and that's good." Another creak of his chair, and he was typing again. "Getting that drive in his safe is only step one, you know. It isn't going to bring him down until it's discovered, and it's not going to be discovered until there's reason to look. A recently missing kid could be exactly the flag we need, especially if there's a witness, and we can establish a pattern. Didn't you say that Arnold kid who went missing when you were there happened over a long break?"

"Spring break." And this had happened over Thanksgiving.

"I'll go back and see if I can detect that sort of pattern with the other missing kids. Meanwhile, think you can talk to the witness?"

I rubbed my forehead with two fingers, trying to ease the ache. "I don't know the name of the missing girl or the student who said it was foul play or how I'd get access to speaking to him, but sure. Why the fuck not?"

He didn't seem to catch my sarcasm. "I know someone who should be able to hack into the police file. If I can get that info back fast, you can make a stop at the school and play private detective."

"He might not even still be enrolled after being caught with drugs."

"Kicking him out would give the student more reason to voice his accusation. Stark is smart. He'll be there."

"I don't know, D..." I trusted Donovan with my life, but I was wary. As far as I was concerned, Stark was guilty, but getting a charge to stick —real or not—wasn't easy, from my experience. And it definitely wasn't going to work if we could be accused of setting him up.

Donovan knew what I was thinking. "It's harder to prove child abuse, Cade. This shit he's involved with now isn't going to go away just because you're caught asking some questions."

Except I wasn't just asking some questions. I'd also searched Stark's home office, was copying his keys, and was planning on planting incriminating evidence in his safe.

But Donovan was right when he said this missing girl thing was good because following this lead would be a distraction.

And I definitely had shit I wanted to be distracted from. "Get me the info, and I'll do it. But it has to be today."

Stark was due home from the cabin tomorrow, and I planned to be gone when he arrived. Then I'd head up to the cabin myself to put the flash drive in his safe, and while I didn't know yet what I'd do after that, I did know one thing for sure: no way in hell was I ever coming back here again.

SEVEN
CADE

I paused on the steps to the house to smoke a cigarette even though I wasn't really in the mood for it, needing a beat before I faced the situation I'd left. The drive back from the locksmith, I'd been focused on the conversation with Donovan and the next task on our Bring Down Stark agenda, but now that I was here, I was reminded of the rest.

It twisted me like someone had tightened a cord around my middle, making it hard to breathe. Which was another reason I shouldn't have lit the smoke, along with all the other reasons cigarettes were terrible, especially when just a few weeks ago I'd considered myself in excellent shape.

Didn't stop me from taking another puff. At this rate, I was going to have a habit that needed to be kicked when I got back to Tokyo.

Tokyo.

The place I'd considered home for the last handful of years felt so far away. So *not* home. Where was home then? It sure wasn't the place I was standing now. It was stupid to think that it might be the woman inside, but my head kept going back to her.

Just like my heart.

Stupid fucking heart.

It was beating faster by the time my cigarette burned out, both from the nicotine and from the anticipation of what awaited me inside.

Focus on what I'd found out in town.

Everything else was just noise.

Not quite convinced, I dropped the butt to the ground, hardened my features, and forced myself through the front door, not worrying this time about knocking.

My heart rate didn't slow any when I got inside and saw the kid—Tate, she'd said—sprawled out on the rarely used living room couch, typing furiously into his phone. He didn't see me, too wrapped up in whatever conversation he was having, a big goofy grin on his face.

I took advantage of the moment and surveyed him. He had Jol's nose and her thin fingers. His forehead wasn't hers—it was broad and protruded slightly, more like mine. It was a common feature, but I couldn't help myself from wondering—could she have been wrong? How did she know he wasn't mine? Was she really sure?

I knew better than to question a woman about her body and her cycle, but now that I thought after learning that she'd never felt the same as I did about her, could I trust her? Maybe she'd lied. Maybe she didn't want him to be mine, and so she'd decided he wasn't.

Or was that just wishful thinking?

I was studying him harder now, looking for something else that I could lay claim to, but before I found anything, he noticed me and sat up abruptly. "Oh, shit. I mean...hi. I didn't hear you come in."

He tossed his phone to the coffee table as though he'd been caught doing something he shouldn't have been doing by someone who would know or care, which of course I was neither. Maybe he was just a nervous kid.

"Yeah, I..." I pointed at the door behind me. Stupidly. Like he wouldn't know that was where I'd come from.

Fuck, maybe I was nervous too.

It was just because he was a teenager, and I was rarely around them. No other reason. I couldn't think of the last time I'd dated a woman who had a kid. Actually, I'd never dated a woman who had a kid. For one thing, fucking probably wasn't the same as dating, and that's pretty much all I did.

For another thing, Jolie and I were definitely not dating.

I don't want this to end with you.

Had it really only been this morning that she'd said that? It felt like another life. A life I wasn't sure we could go back to.

A life that didn't have a scrawny blue-eyed teenager staring up at me like I was an idiot.

I shook my head free of my meandering thoughts. "Know where Jol—?" I made myself stop. Made myself say it. "Your mother is?"

"She's in the kitchen with your mom. We had lunch, and I would have helped clean up, but then she said they needed to talk. They were going to talk before lunch, except someone came with groceries, and by the time my mother and I had gotten them unloaded, Carla had food ready, so we ate, and now here we are."

He was babbling. Definitely a nervous kid.

He must have read my face because he blushed and lowered his head. "You didn't ask for all that. Sorry. She's in the kitchen." He wiped his palms on his jeans, and I wondered if they were as sweaty as mine.

"Okay. Cool." It was my cue to exit this awkward scene.

But I couldn't get my feet to move.

"You should probably take your boots off if you're going to sprawl out on the couch like you were," I said, as though he needed parenting. And what the fuck did I care about his feet on the furniture? After all the months I'd lived here making sure to follow Stark's rules to the letter, I kind of wanted to put my feet on the furniture too. "On second thought, forget I said that."

It was too late—he was already pulling the second one off. "Right, right. Sorry about that."

"No, really, kid. It's not my house. I honestly don't give a shit what you do to it."

"My mother would."

"Eh, I suspect she doesn't care much about this house either." I didn't know anything about Jolie's parenting style, but considering that she'd lived with the same strict rules for even longer than I did, and from the attitude she'd had so far in the day we'd been here, it seemed fair to presume she felt the same.

He frowned, thinking that over. "She really doesn't like it here, does she?"

Now I frowned. What had she told him about growing up? How did anyone explain to their kid that their grandfather was an abusive asshole? "Uh...no. She really doesn't."

"She told me some."

"Did she?"

"I mean, not a lot. Just that she and my grandpa don't get along."

Well, that was one way to put it, I supposed.

And since I knew I couldn't be as courteous when I discussed our childhood, I took that as another cue to leave.

He stood up abruptly. "She told me about you," he said hopefully, almost like he'd sensed I was about to leave, and he really wanted me to stay. "Cade, right?"

Curiosity, probably. How often did he meet someone from his mother's past who could spill some inside dirt? Not that there was anything I felt safe spilling.

Problem was, I was just as curious. "Really? What'd she say?"

"Oh, uh." He flustered again. "Well, that um... She said you used to be in love?" He said it like it was a question, not like he wasn't sure, but like he wasn't sure he should say it.

My mouth fell open. I'd hoped that I hadn't been relegated to "Uncle Cade," but no way had I expected that. Especially after finding out she'd been pregnant with someone else's kid. If she'd really loved me, how did that happen?

But why would she tell her son that she had? Why would she have mentioned me at all?

"She didn't tell me that your mother married her father?" Again, another question; this time he seemed uncertain. "I'm just working that out as of today."

Yeah. I would have left that part out too.

It was strange, though, hearing it put that simply. We'd been convinced we would never be able to tell people how we'd gotten together, but all these years later, it felt more like an anecdote to tell at parties.

How did you two meet again?

Funny story about that...

Still, it was probably a little bit of a shock for Tate. "Yeah, it's not quite a traditional romance, that's for sure." Wary I shouldn't say too much, I couldn't help but add a clarification. "You know, we weren't ever like brother and sister. I didn't even live here a year, and more than half of that time, Jol and I were..." I reminded myself that he'd said it first. "In love."

He grinned, like my repeating of the term validated his sharing. "She told me you broke up because your family kicked you out, which now I'm realizing that your family was her family. Is that why she hates her dad so much?"

"Yeah..." I scrunched up my face. "I think it's safe to say she didn't like him before that."

This conversation was a land mine waiting to happen. I needed to extricate myself from it ASA-fucking-P.

But when I took a step, he took one too. "I'm Tate, by the way." He rocked back and forth, as though deciding if he should shake my hand or something.

He kept his arm down in the end, so I walked over and held out mine. He shook it quickly. A kid inexperienced with many formal introductions. "Just Tate?"

His phone buzzed on the table. He ignored it. "Tate Jacob Warren."

I froze, his hand still in mine. I'd half expected he'd have my last name—she'd taken it as her own, after all. But she'd given him my middle name too.

What the fuck was this woman playing at?

"Wait." He dropped my hand, his eyes wide in horror. "Is that weird? It's probably weird that I have your name. I shouldn't have said that. I'm sorry. Fuck. I mean, not...sorry for cursing."

I really wanted to hear what he'd been told about why he had my name, but I also had the inexplicable urge to make him feel better.

The latter won out. "Nah, she told me. It's a good name."

"Phew." His relief was like a firework in my chest. "I didn't know... Hey." His phone buzzed again, and this time, he glanced at it quickly. "Can you tell me what's going on? Like...why I'm here? Because my mom didn't know I was coming, and this whole week I thought my mom was in New York, but then I find out she's here, and she's with you, and she'd said she didn't know where you were..."

He trailed off. Really, what was there to say at the end of that?

And what was there to say in reply? "Honestly, I'm not sure I know myself."

"But could you tell me what you do know? How did you two hook up? Has she been in contact with you all along?"

"First time I heard from her since high school was about a month ago." This conversation felt increasingly unsafe, so when his phone buzzed again, I nodded to it. "You need to get that?"

"No, I mean..." He sighed as he bent to pick it up. His eyes scanned over the screen, and that same goofy grin appeared.

"A girl?" Except it wasn't polite to presume that these days. "A boy?"

His neck got red, the same way Jolie's did when she blushed, except his didn't reach his cheeks. "A girl."

"A girl...friend? Or a girlfriend?" I didn't know why I was asking or why I was talking to him at all. It was possible I was stalling. The longer I stood here talking to him, the longer I could avoid talking to *her*.

And I liked this nervous kid. He was friendlier than I'd been at his age. Less hard, and just like he seemed to like what he could learn about his mother from conversing with me, I liked what I was learning about her from him. It was evident she'd made sure his childhood had been easier than hers had been. He didn't *yes, sir* and keep his mouth shut and his eyes down the way she and I had been trained.

In some way, that felt like a victory.

"Friend," he said uncertainly. "Or both. I don't know." Now the blush moved up his neck. "I asked her to the winter dance next week, as friends. We're going with a group, so not really a date thing, or I didn't think it was really a date thing, but since I asked her, we started a private chat, and I don't know." He shrugged. "I just like talking to her."

"That's how it starts." I could remember that feeling with Jolie like it was yesterday. Remembered trying to keep her at a distance, trying to keep her off-limits, trying to ignore how good it felt just to have her look in my direction.

"Well, now I don't know if—when I take her home at the end—do I try to...?"

"Kiss her?" He might have been insinuating something else, but I was fairly sure it wasn't appropriate to be giving Jolie's kid advice on anything besides kissing.

It probably wasn't appropriate to be giving him any advice for a myriad of reasons, starting with how much I liked the way it felt for him to ask in the first place.

"Yeah, kiss her," he agreed, and when he looked up at me with his wide trusting eyes, I knew that was another reason I should be walking away.

Still, I stayed. "I think you have to feel her out that night."

"Was that what it was like with you and Mom?"

My breath moved uneasily through my lungs. Thinking about the first kiss with Jolie was a tornado all on its own. Telling her son about it, his ears perked like it meant something, was a whole other storm system.

And if I stayed standing here—if I kept opening up and sharing and *bonding*—I was going to start to want him.

I was going to want him as much as I wanted his mother and the family the two of them made together.

But he wasn't mine.

And unless Jol had lied, he would never be mine.

There was an ache in my side every time I thought of that—low and sharp, buried in between my ribs—and I had a feeling that even when I had time to get used to it, that ache would still live there. A hard, malignant mass that never went away.

"Where did you say your mother was again?" It was an abrupt change of subject. Rude, too, and I knew the answer, but I thought it was better than just walking away.

Though, if I'd walked away, I would have missed the disappointment in his eyes, and that was both unexpected and brutal.

"The kitchen." The kid had tenacity, it turned out, and optimistically added, "Maybe we could talk more later?"

All he was asking was for a conversation. Probably wanted to hear more about his mom when she was younger. I'd already been haunted by the past since she'd shown up in New York. Why not share some of that out loud? Take him along for the trip down memory lane. Bring Jolie along as well, if she wanted to. What could it hurt?

The answer was me.

It could hurt me.

"I'm not sure about that," I said. "I've got a lot on my plate right now." I started toward the kitchen before he could respond, refusing to look back.

This time, if he was disappointed, I made sure I didn't see.

EIGHT
JOLIE

As soon as the kitchen door swung shut behind me, I tore into Carla. "How dare you?"

The words had gathered in my chest and had been worming their way up my throat for the last hour. I'd been ready to talk to her somewhat calmly when I'd first offered to help her with lunch, only to be interrupted by the grocery delivery. Tate had jumped to help—because he was a good kid, not because he was frightened of what would happen if he didn't—and I'd been proud of that, but it had left confronting Carla until later.

By the time groceries had been put away, she'd had lunch ready. Sitting at the table, listening to Tate politely answer her questions about his life, should have given me an opportunity to compose myself and find the best way to approach my stepmother and her outrageous behavior.

It's not so bad, him being here, I'd told myself while he blushed when asked about the women in his life. He was the best part of my life. I always wanted to show him off, and Carla had helped so much in his early years. It could have been a tender reunion.

Except I couldn't forget Cade.

Couldn't forget that pain washing over his face, and sure, it was going to hurt him no matter when he found out about Tate—and I had definitely planned on telling him—but finding out the way he did, with no buffer, with no chance for me to explain...

No. It shouldn't have happened like that.

He shouldn't have had to hurt like *that*, and it was Carla's fault that he did.

And when I thought about how many times Carla had hurt him over his lifetime—how deeply and how unforgivably—my anger built.

Not to mention that her method of interfering was an egregious breach of privacy, which should have been the main reason I was angry at her, I realized when I thought about it. As recovered as I was from my childhood, I still found it hard to put *my* feelings first. I'd spent so many formative years only caring about my father's feelings that sometimes it was hard to even figure out what my feelings were.

But given the time during lunch to evaluate the situation, I'd definitely figured out that I was downright pissed.

"How fucking dare you," I repeated, low enough to not be heard by Tate in the other room but with enough fury woven through the words that there would be no mistaking how enraged I was.

With a roll of her eyes, she turned away from me and started on the dishes at the sink. "Oh, settle yourself down, Julianna. He got here in one piece. No harm, no foul."

I bristled at the name that I considered dead, even though I preferred that to having my real name poisoned on her tongue, but when she got to the *no harm, no foul*, my spikes were fully out.

I wondered if she'd learned how to gaslight from my father because this was a load of lies if I'd ever heard any, and I'd heard plenty. *Lots* of harm. *Lots* of foul.

"You had no right. *No right.*" I was so mad, I was shaking. The stack of plates I'd brought in from the table rattled quietly in my hands. "To log into *my* phone? And talk to *my* son? Pretending to be *me*? No fucking right."

Her back still to me, she shrugged. For the first time in my life, I wished I had the power to instill fear the way my father did. Or at least the power to draw attention.

Desperate for her to take me seriously, I took the top plate from my stack—the same china she'd insisted we use the night before, the set missing a piece from my tantrum all those years ago—and threw it across the room.

The dish shattering made a satisfying sound.

It also got me what I'd wanted—Carla's attention. She turned first toward the mess I made, then toward me, her expression mean. "Real grown up."

"No, no, you don't have any right to tell me how an adult should behave, just like you had no right to interfere with my child."

"*He* had a right to know," she said definitively before turning back to the dishes, and I didn't think for a moment that she was talking about anyone other than Cade.

"You did not get to decide that for me. That was *my* decision to make, on *my* timeline." I resisted the urge to tell her that I'd already planned to tell him. I didn't need to defend myself to her. "It was none of your business."

"You made it my business the minute you showed up here again bringing Cade with you. You expect me to stand by while you string my son along? Keeping secrets from him that he deserves to know. He should have known back then."

"Oh, please." I slammed the rest of the plates down on the kitchen table and was admittedly disappointed when they all remained intact. "It's a little late to play the good mother routine."

"I don't have to explain myself—" She cut herself off and swung toward me, a bread knife in her hand that she pointed in my direction. "You know what? How dare *you!* How dare you keep Tate from me all these years! I helped you get away. You think I would have given away where you were? You should have kept in touch."

She looked down at the knife in her hand, surprised, as though she hadn't realized she'd been holding it. Calmer, she set it down on the counter, but her back was still straight and her voice still firm when she insisted, "I deserved to be part of my grandson's life."

A whole new onslaught of angry words gurgled inside of me, but they caught in the back of my throat.

So that was what this was about.

I could argue that the way she'd treated Cade was cause enough for termination of any rights to his offspring, but that was neither here nor there considering the truth. And while I really wanted to lay into her for decades' worth of hurts, I knew the most productive use of my energy was to simply set her straight. "He's not your grandson."

"Don't do that, Julianna. You can't cut me off from him just because—"

"He's not Cade's son," I clarified.

She frowned. "But you had a DNA test. And Tate...you just told him that—"

"I know what I said, and..." I sighed. "I lied."

"You lied to your son about who his father is." It was less a question and more of an accusation.

At least, that's how I heard it.

Which was about right because I felt pretty damn guilty about it.

Funny how I'd never regretted the lie before now. I'd never expected I'd be caught in it, and the story was much more tolerable than the truth.

I half sat/half leaned against the table. "The DNA test showed Tate had no relation to you. I didn't tell you because...well, honestly, it was easier. And you never asked. Maybe that's not fair because I knew what you believed, and I let you believe it because, like I said, it was easier."

She let the water keep running, but she turned around so her back was to the sink and leaned heavily against the counter. So heavily, I wasn't sure she'd still be standing if she didn't have it to keep her up.

As if I needed more guilt.

I hadn't realized it would matter so much to her. It wasn't like she'd ever acted like she cared about any one of us.

"Look, I'm really sorry." The words came out so naturally, especially being here in this house, and a beat had to pass before I took them back. "No, actually, I'm not sorry. I didn't realize it affected you, and maybe if I had I would have told you the truth, but I'm not sorry for letting you believe what you did because it made it easier for *me* to believe it, and I really needed to believe he was Cade's."

She was quiet.

I wasn't sure what I was waiting for her to say, but I let several seconds go by in case she felt the urge to fill them. "I think I actually convinced myself he was Cade's. So by the time Tate started asking about his father, I didn't even think before I told him. If I had thought, I would have probably chosen the same answer. I just..." I rolled my neck, trying to loosen the tension that was most definitely related to the headache that was suddenly pounding behind my eyes.

And I thought about my reasons.

And reminded myself I didn't owe Carla anything, but saying it out loud was helpful because I was trying to understand my reasons myself. "I just wanted my child to have all the love possible. I wanted him to feel wanted, even if he was unplanned. I wanted him to feel like he came from something beautiful because I know firsthand how ugly beginnings breed hatred and self-loathing. I didn't want him to ever feel ugly. He's the most beautiful part of me, even without the lie. You know?"

"I know." Her voice was soft, and I had a feeling she was thinking about how Cade was the most beautiful part of her too, and as much as I didn't like her, she got credit for recognizing that fact at least.

"And that's why I hadn't told Cade yet. Not because I was trying to keep his son from him but because I knew he'd hurt when he found out that I had a son who wasn't his."

Carla lifted her head, and I thought I saw a flicker of regret in her eyes. Then defiance. "But he has Cade's lips," she said.

I'd thought that before myself. "He has Channing Tatum's lips too. If you look hard enough."

"Who's Channing Tatum? His real father?"

I chuckled. "No. It doesn't matter."

The door swung open, and I stood abruptly and threw Carla a *shh*, expecting to see Tate on the other side.

But it was Cade who walked in, his large frame filling the room. He hadn't taken up so much space when we'd worked side by side in the kitchen all those years ago. He'd outgrown the space over the years, and now he looked incredibly displaced.

I wondered if I looked the same to him or if I looked like I was right where I belonged.

The thought made me sick.

Seeing him made me sick.

It made my chest warm, too, and I wanted to reach out and touch him so badly it hurt.

"Hey," he said, his eyes darting from me to his slumped mother to the broken plate on the floor. He didn't seem to find any of it unusual, and his eyes swept back to me. "Can we talk in private?"

"Yes!" It came out too eager. "Yes. Of course. I didn't hear you come in." I'd spent the whole time he was gone thinking about what I had wanted to say to Carla and didn't have anything prepared for him, but I was beyond relieved that he wanted to give me a chance to explain.

I hadn't let myself acknowledge the thought, but now that he was here, I realized how scared I'd been that he might not come back. He could have gotten in that car and kept on driving, and I wouldn't have blamed him at all.

He half shrugged, as though he didn't know what to say to that. "Got here about ten minutes ago."

I cringed inwardly, afraid of whatever conversation he might have had with Tate. It was Cade who had come looking for me and not my son, though, so if anything had been discussed, at least Tate wasn't upset by it.

It was only a partially soothing thought. Eventually, I had to talk to Tate about Cade, and I didn't imagine that conversation was going to go well at all.

One aggrieved man at a time.

"Should we go upstairs?" I offered. "Or I can get some shoes, and we can go on the porch?"

He looked down at my bare feet and back at the broken plate, and even though he didn't express any concern out loud, my chest felt warm.

"You can have the kitchen," Carla said, turning off the sink. "I'm not in the mood to deal with the dishes." Her gaze also drifted to the shattered dish before coming back to me. "The broom's where it's always been, Julianna."

"Yes, I'll clean it up."

She'd left the room before I'd finished speaking.

Cade looked questioningly after her, but he refrained from asking.

"I've managed to piss off both the Warrens today it seems," I said, trying to lighten the mood.

He didn't even hint at a smile.

"Listen, Cade—"

He cut me off. "Here are the original keys. You should get them back to where you found them as soon as possible, in case Carla goes looking and finds them missing."

I took the keys from his outstretched hand. "You got them copied?"

"I left the spare set in the glove box. I didn't want to chance leaving them here or having them discovered."

"Good thinking." I slipped the keys in my pocket and took a step toward him.

He stepped away, so casually I wasn't sure he'd meant to avoid me or not, especially when he reached for a glass from a cupboard and filled it with water. "Is the office still unlocked, or do you need me to pick it again?"

Carla and I had left my father's office at the same time the night before. "I think it's still unlocked."

"Let me know."

"Okay." I took another step toward him while he gulped back the water, and this time, I was certain he was keeping his distance when he once again stepped away. "Can we please talk about this?"

"Nothing to talk about."

"Don't say that. You know there's a lot to talk about, and I'm here and willing—"

He interrupted again. "You had the right idea when you said we should hold off having any serious conversations until this is over with. We need to keep focused."

I'd thought it was the best plan at the time, but that had been before Tate had shown up, and the way Cade kept moving away from me had me worried that if we didn't talk about it now, he'd be too far out of reach to talk about anything at all when this was over. "I think it might be better if I can just explain—"

"Another kid's gone missing, Jol."

"What?" If he'd meant to distract me, it worked.

He pulled his phone out and unlocked the screen, then handed it over to me. "This girl. A few weeks back. I heard about it in town, and Donovan emailed over what he could find. Apparently, there's someone at the school who made a report, but the cops aren't following up on it. D arranged for me to go over and conduct an interview. I only stopped by here first to make sure you got the keys put away."

He was obviously avoiding all talk of Tate—I didn't blame him—but as much as I wanted to demand that we have a conversation, another missing kid was certainly more pressing. "Let me finish getting dressed. I'll come with you."

"I can handle this on my own."

"I know you can, but you're not going to."

"There's no need for two of us—"

"Cade, we're doing this together. This isn't up for debate. Don't forget what happened the last time you tried to keep me out of a part of this plan."

His mouth tightened as he remembered when I'd followed him to meet up with Donovan's contact, and I tried not to see Tate in the shape of his lips. He was about to argue with me, but when I handed him back his phone, I let my fingers brush his, and even though he yanked his hand away, the touch softened him.

Not much, but enough. "Fine. I'm not going to waste time or energy arguing. Hurry and get dressed, and put back the keys, and I'll..." He looked once again at the broken plate. "Clean up your mess in the meantime, I guess."

Apparently, he didn't need any explanation to know it had been me who'd thrown it. I suspected he was only volunteering to take care of it so that he wouldn't have to deal with Carla or Tate while he waited.

Fair enough.

But before I could let it go... "I know you don't want to talk about this right now, but there's something I have to—"

"You don't have to say anything."

"No, it's not what you think. It's just..." God, this would have been easier if I could have told him everything else too. But we were on a time crunch, and this needed to be said now. "Tate thinks you're his father."

He stood up taller, drawing more away from me without physically taking a step. "And why would he think that?"

"Because that's what I told him. Not today. Before today."

His jaw went tight. I could see the muscles straining all the way down in his neck, and the space between us felt heavy and hard, like an invisible boulder had been lodged there. "You sure know how to keep the hits coming, don't you, Jolie?"

I deserved that.

I deserved worse than that.

"I'll tell him," I promised. "But not here. I can't—"

"I don't really care what you tell him, Jolie," he said sharply. "Not my kid, not my problem. Just don't expect me to play daddy anytime soon or ever." He shoved away from the sink and walked around me toward the door. "I'll be on the porch. If you're down in ten minutes, you can come with me. Carla can clean up the goddamned china herself."

I winced as the door banged shut behind him. Winced again as his words echoed in my head and tried to tell myself it was a good thing that for once he wasn't the one cleaning up my mess.

NINE
CADE

"You're sure he's not mine?" I hadn't meant to ask. I hadn't meant to talk to her at all, but there it was, out of my mouth the minute we stepped onto the sidewalk that led to the dorms.

With her eyes pinned to the horizon, she sighed, her breath coming out in the cold air in a cloud. "Yes. I'm sure."

"Why? Because of timing? Because he doesn't *not* look like me."

"I had a DNA test done."

It was strange how I could feel disappointed yet again. When had I even gotten my hopes up? And why?

And why was I letting myself think about it right now? "The dad can't be in the picture, though, if you told him he was mine."

She shook her head, her mouth opened as though she were about to say something, but I cut her off before she could start. "And you thought he *could* have been mine. Or you wouldn't have gotten tested."

And if he could have been mine, then why hadn't she told me back then? "Did you know you were pregnant when I came here that night?"

She stopped, her hands shoved in her pockets, and stared at me. "Do you want to talk about this? Because if you want to talk about it, then you have to really let me talk about it."

Of course, I wanted to talk about it.

And also, I didn't.

It was definitely not the best time to discuss it. I glanced at my watch. The afternoon was getting away from us, and we needed our heads elsewhere. It was a legitimate reason to put this conversation off.

Still, I couldn't help but be an ass about it. "I don't think I can hear anything you say right now."

"Then maybe we shouldn't talk at all."

There was a note of pain in her timbre that matched the hurt in her eyes, and I tried to feel satisfied about it. She *should* feel hurt. She should share this pain with me the same way I was sharing the pain from her father with her.

It wasn't the same, and deep inside, I knew it too well to feel anything but guilty.

We walked the remaining ten minutes to the dorms in silence, but my head was still wrapped up in the past.

Being on the school grounds didn't help. Even if I wasn't focused on everything that happened between me and her, there were a hundred other ghosts there to haunt me. There were a few new updates to our surroundings—the greenhouse had been expanded, and there was a new building with a sign that said computer and library services—but mostly it all looked the same.

The same dull winter-white landscape.

The same asphalt pathway.

The same girl at my side.

The same monstrous headmaster dictating my day.

It felt like putting on an old pair of polyester pajamas. The fit was familiar, which might have been nice, but they still made me itch. This particular itch could never be scratched away.

It was better when we reached the dorms. There were fewer memories in the long stretch of student apartments since, for the most part, Jolie and I hadn't been allowed to visit anyone in them. If we'd had class projects or study groups, Stark had insisted they be held in the student center or the library. I'd managed to sneak into Amelia's room a few times to fuck quickly before the RA came by, but I couldn't have said now what floor she'd lived on.

I didn't remember the dorm lobby either. It had changed beyond recognition, or perhaps I'd only ever gone in the building through a side door using Amelia's key because nothing about the space was familiar. It was small with only a single couch and a handful of chairs next to a water dispenser. It was empty except for a student behind a glass-enclosed desk at the far side of the room. She had textbooks spread out in front of her and headphones on, and when I knocked on the window, she jumped in surprise.

"Hey." She slid the headphones down to wrap around her neck and slid the glass open. "Need something?"

When it came down to it, Donovan's version of arranging a visit with the purported witness actually meant just providing me with a name as well as verification that he was indeed still at the school. "Yeah, we're here for Terrence Moore."

My eyes flicked to the sign taped up to the glass with visitation rules, and though we were well within visiting hours, I'd forgotten that only family members were allowed to meet with students. Stark sure did know how to run a prison. "I'm his cousin," I added before she asked.

The girl's forehead wrinkled as she studied me. "*You're* his cousin?"

Jolie jumped in to rescue me from my apparent mistake. "Cousin by marriage."

"Oh. I'll call his room." She shut the glass again before looking something up on the computer, and I was half afraid she was hitting some secret buzzer that notified the cops about an intruder.

I felt slightly better when she picked up the phone. She spoke loud enough for us to hear her side of the conversation. "Terrence? You have a visitor." She paused. "I don't know. He says he's your cousin. He's a white guy."

Fuck me.

Yeah, it hadn't been the best tactic, I admitted. I had planned to say I was a private detective, which may have gotten us past the student "guard" despite the "family only" rule, but I'd changed my mind spur of the moment when I'd seen the sign.

Frankly, I blamed this on Donovan. He could have gotten us more information or arranged a face-to-face that sounded more legit.

The student was nodding now while eyeing me suspiciously. Fearing this visit was over before it began, I managed to slide the glass window back open and pointed to the phone. "Can I talk to him a quick second?"

The student seemed unsure, which was nothing compared to the look Jolie was giving me, but she put him on speaker. "Hey, Terrence, it's me, Cade. I'm a cousin on your mother's side. We've never met, but I thought we could talk a few minutes since I'm passing through town."

The speech was for the girl so that she'd feel all right about buzzing us in. Now I had to pray Terrence was curious enough to give her the okay.

There was only a fraction of a pause. "Give me a few minutes, and I'll be down."

I gave a smug smile to the student who still didn't look convinced. "ID and sign in, please," she said, pointing to a clipboard hanging on the edge of the desk.

I handed over my license, and when I realized she was only giving a quick glance at the picture before handing it back, I scribbled down a fake name on the sheet. Hopefully, she wouldn't remember my real name if anyone asked later.

As soon as I was finished signing, a buzzer sounded, and a door to the side of the enclosed desk opened. "Parents' lounge is the first room on your right. Make sure you sign out again when you leave." She put her headphones back on and returned to her work, already done with us.

"Ladies first." I felt unreasonably self-righteous as I stepped aside for Jolie. Truth was I should have been more prepared. It wasn't like me. I was too distracted. Too invested. Too off my game.

She seemed to share my frustration. "Way to assume everyone's white," she scolded as she walked past.

"I'm working with what I have, okay?" I hissed back, trying to ignore the cherry-blossom scent trailing after her. Why had I let her tag along again? She was the cause of my distraction. If this wasn't Donovan's fault, then it was definitely hers.

The parents' lounge looked much like the lobby except with more furniture. It was also empty, which was natural at this time of year and this time of day. If any parent was actually in town, they would have picked up their student earlier and taken them somewhere or gone up to their room. No one actually used the lounge for visiting.

That would be good for privacy, considering the conversation we needed to have with Terrence.

It wasn't good, though, for the meantime while we waited for Terrence to show up because once again, I was trapped with Jolie and the past, and this time, after pacing the room several times didn't calm my brain, I couldn't keep my mouth shut. "Who was it? Birch?"

God, I was an asshat.

I couldn't help thinking about whoever had been with her. Wanted to put my thumbs in his eye sockets and press hard.

Confusion skidded across her face, then dissolved into sadness as soon as she understood the question. "It's insulting you'd ask that."

"It's insulting that I *have* to ask." I wasn't proud of myself for it. I'd seen her fool around with Birch willingly, so it seemed a reasonable enough guess, but I'd also seen him try to take advantage of her.

The possibility that she might not have participated willingly in the act that knocked her up sat at the periphery of my mind, but I couldn't let myself consider it. That was a pain I wasn't sure I could live with. I preferred the pain of being betrayed, and so I focused on *that* pain until the possibility of anything else disappeared entirely. "If not Birch, then who?"

She nibbled at her lip for several long seconds before responding. "Does it matter who?"

Honestly? No.

The only thing that mattered was that it wasn't me. There wasn't a single name that she could give that would make that hurt any less.

It felt too vulnerable saying that, so I shrugged the question off and paced to the lounge door. I looked out into the hall and found it empty. "Where is this kid?"

"He'll come."

If he was there right now, maybe I could stop obsessing about her.

But he wasn't.

And wrong time, wrong place, but I was a jackass, and I really needed her to feel as bad as I did. I shut the door again. "Do you even know who it is? Were you fucking everyone?"

She leaned against the wall and rolled her eyes in a way that made me feel like I was the immature one. "That's not fair."

"I'm not really sure you have a right to talk about fair right now." Looking at her made me all twisted inside, so I looked away.

But not looking at her made me feel twisted up the other way, so I paced back over to her and looked her dead in the face. "It might not have been a real ring on your finger, but we were engaged."

As far as I was concerned, we were anyway. She'd said yes. We'd made love in celebration. Anyone else she was with, she'd been cheating.

She shifted, giving me her profile, but I still caught the glimmer of tears in her eyes. "It was a long time ago, Cade."

"It doesn't matter if it was a long time ago or yesterday. I'm finding out now, and I deserve a chance to process it."

"Which was why I was waiting to tell you until after all of this other bullshit was done. So you could have the time and space that you needed."

"Because you were always planning on telling me eventually."

"Not always, no. But that changed. I would have told you."

I believed her.

Which made me a sucker.

And I didn't want to be a sucker, so I tried to play like I didn't believe her. "Sure, sure. You would have told me everything, just as soon as I gave you everything. Again."

I paced back toward the door but only made it halfway there before a torrent of emotion swept over me like a flash flood.

I spun back toward her, my finger pointed at her like a weapon. "You know, it was real for me. I was in fucking love."

Her breath shuddered through her, and as many times as I'd seen her cower in front of her father, I'd never seen her look so small.

I felt even smaller for condensing her to that, and before I could think what I was doing, I reached for her.

Then her eyes flew to a point behind me, and when I turned around, I saw that the boy I presumed was Terrence Moore had arrived. "Don't mean to interrupt whatever this is, but I'm guessing you're Cade?"

A minute ago, I'd been desperate for him to disrupt this conversation. Now that he was here, I wished Jolie and I were still alone.

But Terrence was why we were here.

I answered the obvious with the equally obvious. "I'm guessing you're Terrence."

He came closer, looking me over. "Before you try to sell it to me again, you and I both know you aren't my cousin."

His dark skin made any blood relation improbable, and I had a feeling he knew his family tree too well to try to convince him I was connected by marriage. "You're right, and I'm not going to try to sell it. I just needed to get past the desk. Thank you for being intrigued enough to meet me." I held out my hand, figuring a formal introduction might be a good idea at this point. "Like I said, I'm Cade."

He took it, his eyes darting to Jolie, then back at mine in an unspoken question.

As much as I preferred leaving her out of this, she was here. I debated introducing her with a fake name. "This is Jo," I said, compromising. "My, um...partner."

Sure. Partner worked.

Terrence's face lit up with excitement. "I knew it! You're here from the police, aren't you?"

Uh... "Yeah." Jolie shot me an unsure glance. "I mean, why do you think we're from the police?"

He dropped my hand and shoved it into the pocket of his hoodie with the other one. "Besides the fact that no one else ever visits me? Look, it's cool. I know the official word is that Cassie ran away, but I heard the detective at the precinct talking with the FBI agent about the down-low investigation going. Don't worry. I won't say anything. Mum's the word. So are you here undercover or what?"

Jolie and I exchanged a look.

I was definitely rolling with this. "Obviously, we can't confirm that." I gave him my best nudge, nudge, wink, wink. "But I'm also not going to deny."

"Got it, got it." He beamed, thrilled to be in on whatever it was he thought he was in on.

"You said there was an FBI agent at the precinct?" It wasn't where I should have started, but an investigation directed by the police was one thing. An investigation involving the FBI was a whole other ball game.

Unfortunately, it wasn't subtle enough, and suddenly Terrence looked less sure. "Don't you already know? Isn't that why you're here? Is this a test?"

Jolie rushed forward with an encouraging smile. "We need to be sure we didn't miss anything from your initial interview and to make sure there aren't any contradictions. I know this is a total pain, but we need you to pretend this is the first time you're meeting with us, and we're going to ask you questions as if we know nothing about what you've told us before."

"Oh, okay."

"And I'm sure I don't have to tell you this," Jolie continued, "but it's my job to say it—it's best if you don't tell anyone at all about this visit. Is that cool?"

Whether it was her experience working with students or just her natural charm, she had him reeled in. "Totally cool. I wouldn't want to do anything to jeopardize finding Cassie."

"Of course not. Thank you, Terrence. We appreciate it." She gestured to one of the seating areas. "Should we sit?"

A handful of seconds later, and we were seated around a small table, my phone in hand, ready to take notes. I hit record on my voice recorder too, discreetly, though I had a feeling the kid would have agreed to being taped if I'd asked. "I'm going to ask you to start at the very beginning, but before we dig in, let's just clear up what you overheard. You're sure it was an FBI agent that the detective was talking to?"

"Yeah. He introduced himself as Agent Jones. He wasn't there the first time—"

"You were interviewed twice?" Jolie interrupted.

"Yes, which is why I didn't believe them about Cassie running away in the first place because why would they need to talk to me twice? And why would they bring in the FBI?"

Exactly what I was thinking, Terrence.

Jolie was stuck thinking something else, it seemed. "They interviewed you two times without your parents there? That's not legal."

"I'm eighteen. Technically don't need them, and it's a good thing because my mother wouldn't have let me say anything if she *had* been there. She doesn't like to get 'involved.'"

He made quote marks with his fingers as he said the word *involved*.

I didn't give a fuck whether he'd been interviewed legally or illegally. I wanted to know more about what he'd seen and who was being investigated. If the FBI already had their eyes on Stark, that changed everything. "So Agent Jones told the police that there was an ongoing investigation?"

He got nervous, his eyes bouncing from mine to Jol's. "I don't want to get anyone in trouble. Detective Aquilla didn't know I was there, or I'm sure they wouldn't have said anything. They'd dismissed me, but I thought I'd left my phone, so I'd come back to the room, and then I realized my phone was in my coat pocket, and I should have turned around then, except I heard Agent Jones ask if he thought I was going to tip anyone off about the investigation, and Detective Aquilla said he was pretty sure he'd convinced me that Cassie had run away, and he wasn't worried." He ran a palm over his thigh. "I wasn't going to drop it before that, to be honest, because I know what I saw, and if I didn't think they were going to get them, I would have made my parents pull me out immediately. Or I would have run away myself, I guess, since I'm old enough, and my parents seem to think I made the whole thing up, and no way could I stay here if I didn't think Stark was going down. Plus, who would want to miss out on that? I'm hoping they arrest him on a school day. That would be epic."

The kid talked so quickly, it was hard to follow.

It probably didn't help that we were only pretending to be on the same page as he was.

Fortunately, Jol seemed to have kept up with him. "Just to clarify, you think Langdon Stark is the person responsible for Cassie's disappearance?"

"I know he is. I saw her get in that car." He was convicted now, his expression solemn. "But it's not just a *person* who took Cassie. Headmaster Stark wasn't alone. He wasn't the only one."

The hair on the back of my neck stood up, and my skin felt prickly. "Who was he with? Do you know?"

"Oh, yeah. I don't know her name, but I know who she is—the headmaster's wife."

TEN
JOLIE

Cade immediately called Donovan from the dorm lobby after we'd finished talking to Terrence, and by the time we started home, the sun was beginning to set.

"Donovan knows that Agent Jones guy because of course he does," Cade said, a cigarette in between his teeth as he searched his pockets for a lighter. "He's going to reach out and see if he can get some inside information about the investigation."

He lit up before thinking to offer one to me.

I shook my head.

"You're so good." He inhaled, and I pretended it was the cold giving me the chill and not the compliment. "How you can manage to be here and not pick up old habits beats the hell out of me."

"I guess there are other old habits I prefer." I said it before thinking how it might sound. He was definitely the habit I preferred, but I hadn't *picked him up* because I needed the crutch. Or that wasn't the only reason.

But amending the statement was impossible without returning to the conversation he'd started before Terrence had interrupted us. It was a conversation that needed to continue, but it wasn't the most pressing topic.

Besides, I wasn't sure either of us were in an emotional state to handle it. Particularly him, after learning what he had about Carla.

That was a conversation that needed to be had too. If he'd let me have it with him.

He looked at me after the habits comment for a beat. I could feel his eyes on my profile, and I wanted nothing more than to turn toward him and show him everything I held inside. I wished it was the right time. Wished he would let me mean the things I felt.

I was strong, though, counting the steps in my head before I felt his gaze fall off me to the sidewalk in front of us.

The silence that had accompanied us earlier on our walk was too heavy to carry this time. Too many words needed said, and since he didn't seem to be interested in saying them, it fell to me. "If there's already an investigation on my father at the federal level..."

I wasn't quite sure what the question was pressing to be asked.

Fortunately, Cade did. "Then do we still plant the files we were planning to plant?"

"Yeah."

"That's the question, isn't it?" He inhaled and exhaled. "The FBI might already have copies of what's on that drive."

"That doesn't really put us in a different position than before." It was possible my father already had copies of the "receipts" we'd obtained for the sale of children—God, it made me sick to even think about it—hidden away somewhere amongst his things. They'd most likely been written for him in the first place. The problem was that we didn't know for sure, and making sure the damning evidence was in his possession had felt critical.

Still felt critical.

"But if there's a chance that planting evidence interferes with their investigation..." He didn't have to say more.

"That seems more of a risk now than before, doesn't it?"

This time, when he turned to look at me, I was already looking at him, and he quickly flicked his eyes away. "We should wait to find out what Donovan learns before making a decision about what to do next."

"Will he really be able to discover anything more? FBI agents don't just go spilling information, even to their friends."

Cade chuckled. "They might if their friend is Donovan."

Good point. With only a few brief interactions with the man, I had a feeling Donovan was good at ferreting out everyone's secrets. He'd wiggled some of mine loose, and given more time, I was pretty sure he would have learned more.

Briefly, I wondered what secrets Cade had shared with him.

The prick of jealousy was unreasonable. I didn't deserve to know more of him, not without letting him know more of me, and still a part of me felt that I had a right to every part of him.

He certainly owned every part of me.

I resisted the urge to tug on his jacket and make him face me while I gave him all the parts I'd kept hidden.

Not now. Not yet.

"We'll wait then." I bit my lip to keep from saying more.

He took another drag from his smoke before tossing it into the next garbage can we passed along the path. "He's smart. Real smart."

"Donovan?"

"Well, I'd never say it out loud," he admitted. "But I was talking about Stark."

I liked it when he referred to him as *Stark* instead of *your father*. It was one of the reasons I'd changed my name in the first place. It let me disconnect from the monster. Let me be his victim instead of his daughter.

As for his intelligence, I wasn't about to be so kind. "He's not smart. He just bullies anyone who challenges him, and so people assume he's smart."

"There's truth to that for sure. But he's been clever about the way he's gone about this. I'd wondered how it had been so easy for everyone to write these kids off as runaways. Didn't they have belongings they'd left behind? Didn't they have friends?"

That had been one of the most useful things we'd learned from Terrence—Stark's method. At least the method in which he'd reeled in

Cassie. He'd chosen a girl who'd kept to herself, which had to be purposeful. A girl who had been known for ditching class and wishing herself elsewhere. A girl who very might well have run away eventually.

Then, according to Terrence, he'd offered her something she couldn't resist: a chance to escape.

He'd sworn her to secrecy, of course. I was familiar with the ways he managed to be sure a girl wouldn't talk. Whether he was smart or not, he was particularly good at manipulation. The only reason she'd told Terrence was because she'd bumped into him outside after curfew, smoking a joint, when she was sneaking out with her packed suitcase.

She must have been too excited at that point to keep it in. She'd told him that Stark had gotten her an audition with a modeling agent in New York City, saying they'd let him bring one girl only, and that he'd selected her.

Terrence had promised not to tell anyone and bid her farewell, then watched her from the shadows when Stark's car pulled up. The cab light had gone on when she'd opened the door, and he'd seen Carla behind the wheel.

"If it had just been Stark, she might not have agreed to go," I said. The girls in my classes were smart enough not to trust an older man by himself, no matter what position he held in their lives.

But a married couple? That was harmless.

"Maybe not." Cade's voice was tight, and I suddenly felt like an idiot. It wasn't that I'd forgotten that Carla's involvement might be a shock to him—it had been to me—or that he might have feelings about it. There were just so many elephants in between us, it was hard to navigate without hitting at least one.

I fretted for a few steps, wondering if I should say something more about it. If he needed to talk, I wanted to be the one he talked to.

Honestly, I was the perfect person for him to talk to. Not just because I felt so much for him, but because I knew what it was like to realize you shared DNA with someone capable of evil. It was kind of a refreshing change to not feel alone in that regard.

Though, to be fair, maybe I was jumping to conclusions. "She might not know, Cade. He could have lied to her too."

He didn't ask who I was talking about. "We both know it's more complicated than that." He pulled out another cigarette from his pack and lit it.

It was complicated, and it wasn't. Maybe Carla hadn't known what she was part of, but she'd still driven the car. And maybe she hadn't known what he'd done to us, but she'd still let it happen. Maybe she hadn't known the truth about her husband's evils, but she'd been willfully ignorant.

No matter what grace anyone tried to give her, she was still guilty.

Yeah, I understood how that could be hard to talk about.

I turned the focus, instead, to myself. "I thought I'd made peace with everything my father had done years ago." As much as I hated acknowledging our relation, sometimes it had to be faced. That was something I'd learned about healing over the years. It's important to realize the past doesn't have to define you, but burying and forgetting wasn't really moving on. "I mean, it was over and done with. What was the point of holding on to it? I had Tate, and I needed to be in the present for him, and I couldn't do that with this huge weight dragging me down."

Cade looked at me intensely, not backing away this time when I met his eyes. "You just forgave him?"

"No," I scoffed. "No, no, no. Never." I reached out and swiped the cigarette from his hand, bringing it to my lips.

I broke into a coughing fit mid-inhale. "Fuck, how do you smoke these?" I asked when I could breathe again.

"If you don't like it, don't smoke it." He tried to take it back, but I moved it to my other hand, out of his reach.

Then I took another drag. Smaller. More manageable. "I like punishing myself."

"I'd tell you not to do that except pot, meet kettle."

"Oh, I know." I passed the cigarette back. "Anyway, not forgive, but forget. Or I didn't feel like I needed to confront him about it. I still don't. Not really."

"You don't?"

I shrugged. I'd imagined it for a long time—telling him off. Unloading and unleashing every stored pain. Preferably while inflicting pain on him. "I suppose I don't think he deserves the recognition. He'd enjoy it too much."

Maybe he wouldn't enjoy the hurting part, but despite everything, I was pretty much a pacifist. Any inkling toward violence made me feel too much like him.

"Yeah. He probably would." He passed the cigarette, and I took it, my skin sparking when my knuckle brushed his. "You said you *thought* you'd made peace. Does that mean you really didn't?"

"Obviously, not now. Not when I discover he's doing this. To other people? It was one thing when it was just me."

"And me," he reminded me. As if I needed reminding.

"And you." I inhaled. "But you were gone. So it was just me again."

"It was still bad when it was just you, Jolie."

I exhaled, pretending it was the smoke making my eyes prick. "Yeah. It was. I didn't always realize that."

It was sad how I'd minimized my father's behavior for so long. As if I didn't count. As if I didn't deserve to be treated humanely and without cruelty.

If I thought about that too hard, I'd break down, and we were too close to the house for that. I didn't need Tate—or Carla, for that matter—seeing me lose my shit.

"Anyway, again." I regrouped. Brought us back on topic because I knew what it was I was trying to tell him now. "I'd thought I was past it. Thought I could live with him, and it would be okay. He was awful, but not always. Sometimes he was not awful at all. And he was my father. He'd been all I had for most of my life, and I'm—this is embarrassing to admit—I, um, I think I really believed it was love. How he treated me. I hadn't really had a whole lot of experience otherwise."

He opened his mouth to interject, but I didn't let him. "Until you. You were so different and so incredible. So unreal. It often felt like there was no way it could last, and I sort of kept waiting for the other shoe to drop. Which is partly how I was able to let you leave. It was going to end anyway."

Again, he opened his mouth, and I wanted to hear him say what I knew he was going to say—that he wouldn't have let it end. That he'd loved me. That it would have been forever.

It didn't matter if I believed it. I would have liked hearing it. Even now.

Especially now.

But that would have been said for me, and I was determined that this be for him. After he kept giving and giving, I needed to be able to give him something too, small as it was.

So I beat him to it. "It's not the point, Cade. The point is that I thought I'd made my peace, and it was fine as long as it was only me—"

"It wasn't fine," he muttered.

"—and then it wasn't only me." I let that hang in the air, letting him figure it out on his own. It was too hard to say it out loud. The guilt from this was the one guilt worse than hurting Cade.

"Tate," he guessed. We were at the bottom of the porch steps now, and he stopped and turned to me. "He hurt Tate."

I swallowed, afraid to talk.

Then I grabbed the cigarette from him, needing the buzz to distract me from the overwhelm of emotion. "He was, um, six." My hand trembled as I brought the stick up to my lips. "He'd sworn to me—" I shook my head, realizing I hadn't been clear with my pronoun. "My father had sworn to me that he wouldn't touch him. And I believed him. Because I was gullible and stupid, and I don't know, because I wanted so badly to believe that this human—this tiny miracle of a person—had changed his life as much as he'd changed mine."

Another drag. I was feeling nauseated, unaccustomed to the nicotine, but it was a much-needed crutch, and I understood one thousand percent why Cade was constantly sucking on one since we'd arrived. "I don't know how many times it happened. Or how bad it was. He'd made Tate promise not to tell. Scared him into secrecy saying I'd go away if I knew."

I shuddered, as I always did, when I thought about the psychological damage that had potentially been done to my son. He was as well-adjusted a teenager as I'd ever seen, and I still worried about it.

Cade's expression softened. "You don't have to—"

"Let me finish," I insisted. This was the hard part because it came with admitting my failure as a parent, but while it was something that I had fully intended on eventually telling Cade, it was the part after this —the easier part—that I was trying to get to. "It was purely an accident that I figured it out at all. Tate was practically never out of my sight. Or when he was, he was also out of my father's sight because I worked shorter days at the school than he did. So I didn't think it was even possible, and if I hadn't been paying attention, I would have missed it altogether."

"Jolie, it's not your fault." He took a step toward me, and as much as I was aching to be in his arms, I knew I couldn't touch him and not fall apart, so I stepped backward, putting my hands up to stop him.

"He was playing with his dolls—he loved playing house—and I happened to overhear him. Something the father doll said to the baby doll." I couldn't remember it now, but when I'd heard it, the hairs on the back of my neck had stood up straight, and I'd known. I'd just *known* because there was no way that he could know about discipline like that. "So I'd asked him about it, and he tried to deny it." I pointed the cigarette toward the house as a substitute for my father. "Because that fucking asshole knows how to keep a kid's mouth shut, but then he admitted it, and I realized what I should have always known—my father would never change. He was incapable of it. He *is* incapable of it. He was always going to get worse and worse and worse. It was never going to be fine."

I swallowed past the lump in my throat and hugged my arms

around myself, careful not to burn my clothes with the cigarette, not ready to put it out.

Cade seemed to understand my need to say this now, and he waited patiently instead of trying to fill the silence.

It took several seconds. "I didn't have anything. No money. No education. Nothing but Tate, and I knew we had to disappear, or he'd find us. Which," I let out a gruff laugh, "might have been an unfounded fear. He told me time and again that he'd come after me, but that could have been fearmongering and manipulation. Who knows?"

"You had to believe it could be true."

"Yeah. I did. I knew I couldn't get anywhere without help. I really wished for you then. I can't even tell you—" Deep breath in. Then out. "I broke down and asked Carla. Told her the truth. Expected her to brush it off, but she didn't, Cade. She got me the money and helped us leave, and you know that couldn't have been easy. Not the way Dad is. You know she paid for it somehow, and *that's* the point of me telling you this. It's too little, too late for you, I'm sure, but for me and Tate? She changed the course of our lives for the better."

I was the one who stepped toward him now. "And whatever things she knew about or did—whatever she's guilty of—she also saved us. So when you're hating yourself for coming from a woman who could stay in an evil relationship—because I know you, Cade Warren, you will try to hate yourself for it—just remember you also come from a woman who would risk herself for us."

Maybe it was even partly why he was so good at rescuing me.

This time, when he reached for me, I didn't stop him. He put his hands on my waist and bent his forehead to mine, not quite an embrace. My arms were still folded across my chest between us, but his touch anchored, and his skin was warm. "I'm so sorry, Jolie."

"Goddammit, Cade. I'm trying to give you something here." But there wasn't any energy behind my words. I *wanted* to give, but maybe I really needed to take too.

"And I'm taking it. Thank you for telling me."

"That wasn't what—"

"I know, but it was what I appreciated most." He lifted his chin so that he could skim his lips across my skin, then returned to leaning his forehead against mine.

"Okay," I said. "Okay." Because if I said anything else I'd cry and because I'd give whatever he let me. "It should have been you she saved."

"It should have been both of us."

I didn't know how much time passed with us like that. I was so intensely present, so completely absorbed in the moment, that it felt like hours. But the cigarette still had its cherry when the door banged open, and we jumped apart like two teens caught making out.

"Tate!" I sounded guilty.

Seeing him, it was a whole new guilt that rippled through me. The guilt of lying to him about his father and the guilt of whatever he might assume having found me in Cade's arms.

"Mom, you're smoking?" he asked, eying the cigarette in my hand.

Fuck. Another guilt added to the mix. "No! I was just..." I blinked, no excuse coming.

"Holding it for me," Cade finished.

But I didn't want to feed Tate more lies. "I *used* to smoke. I was reminding myself how awful they are."

"They're fucking terrible," Cade said, taking the cigarette from my hand. He dropped it on the ground and crushed it with his boot. "Nasty habit to break. Don't ever start."

"Yeah. Don't ever start," I agreed.

"You used to smoke?" Tate asked.

I put my hands to my face and groaned. "Isn't it dinnertime yet?"

Tate shrugged. "Carla said something about having a headache, and we could fend for ourselves."

Good. I had not been looking forward to another meal with her.

Honestly, I didn't want to go back in her house at all.

Cade's expression said he felt the same way. "Hey, what do you guys say to bowling and pizza?"

It was a dangerous offer. One I shouldn't accept. Tate was instantly excited—too excited—and every minute he spent with Cade without knowing the truth would make it harder to come clean later on.

But I was fragile and only human. So I said yes and let Cade rescue me once again.

ELEVEN
CADE

Watching Jolie shoot little green men on an arcade screen was the first thing that had made me laugh in days.

"Why aren't I getting any points?" She shook the plastic gun, as if there might be a "bullet" stuck inside, even though it worked with a digital sensor. "Is it broken? I think mine might be broken."

Beside her, Tate was racking up the points, eliminating aliens with the skill of a pro. He gave her a side glance, so quick it didn't mess up his current hit streak, and shook his head in a way that clearly meant *God, Mom, you're so not cool right now.*

She glared at his profile, then tried pointing the gun at the screen again, her aim nowhere near any of the targets. "It's seriously not working." This time she turned to me. "Are you laughing at me?"

I stifled the laugh but couldn't rid myself of the smile. "Maybe this isn't your game. We should have stuck to bowling."

She'd been a shark in our earlier match, pretending she was only a fair player in the first round until Tate accused her of holding back on purpose. The next two games, she slaughtered us both.

Since we'd finished our pizza by the time she was officially crowned the victor, we'd abandoned our lane and wandered over to the arcade section of the entertainment center, and while Jolie had held her own on most of the games we'd played so far, her skill apparently didn't extend to shooting.

"There was no way we could have bowled more. I couldn't handle how embarrassing it was for the two of you."

I gave her my best *fuck you* face, which I suspected looked more like adoration than wrath and only prompted her to give me a sassy smile in return.

Tate paused as the scene changed to nudge her. "Mom! The game?"

Even if she suddenly became an expert shot, there was no way she was catching up with his lead. Still, it was probably less fun to win if she didn't even try.

"Yeah, let's talk about embarrassing," I said, stepping toward her. "Let me help you."

I considered coaching from the side for all of two seconds before I threw that out the window, stepped behind her, and wrapped my arms around her. She stiffened in surprise, her breath hitching, then relaxed into me as I clasped my hands around hers and the gun.

Fuck, she smelled good.

Felt good too. Warm and soft, and I hated myself for grabbing the excuse to touch her like this. I'd tried to be careful all night, steering away from any sort of intimate connection, not just because I was concerned about giving her son the wrong idea about us, but also because I didn't want her to think she and I were suddenly fine.

We weren't fine.

And it wasn't like we'd been exactly fine before the whole *I have a secret kid* thing, but we'd been close enough that I'd thought being fine with her might eventually be possible.

After Tate showed up, I wasn't so sure we could ever be fine.

But for the past two hours, it had been hard to remember that. The activities we'd engaged in had required being in the moment, and as the present became more pronounced than the past, I felt...better.

Better than I had in a long time.

My body didn't hold its usual tension. My head didn't feel on the verge of a migraine. My stomach didn't feel like it was trying to digest a twenty-pound medicine ball, and air moved in and out of my lungs easier than it had in years.

So when I put my arms around her, it was only a little bit because I thought it was the best way to help her shoot. Mostly, it was because I wanted them there. Wanted to feel her heat and smell her hair and be fine with her.

"You don't get any points by just shooting everywhere and hoping you hit something," I said, my mouth near her ear. "Better to take your time, line up the shot..." I directed her arms so that she was aiming at one of the aliens. "And...shoot."

She turned her head to look at me, her lips so close I could kiss her if I wasn't focused on the shot and very aware of her son at my side.

I gestured toward the screen, needing her attention somewhere other than my mouth.

Slowly, she turned her head. "Ah!" she squealed. "I hit one! I hit one!"

"Amazing work, Mom," Tate said flatly. The Game Over words flashed onto the screen. "Maybe you can hit two next time."

"Oh, no. I'm not playing again." She escaped from my arms, and instead of putting the gun back in the holster, she handed it to me before walking out of range.

Tate looked more interested than he had a minute before. "What do you say?"

I paused, gun in hand. He wasn't my kid.

He wasn't my kid, and he thought he was, and that made this entire outing the worst fucking idea ever. Not just because he might develop some sort of attachment but because...

Nah. I couldn't go there. Couldn't think about it even a little. "Is it time to get some dessert? I think I saw an ice cream counter up by the bar."

"You scared I'm going to whip your ass?" He wasn't just taunting me for taunting's sake. He really believed he would.

Which made it much harder to walk away.

"Swipe the card," I said, taking the gun. "It's on."

Tate easily won the first round, but I held my own enough for him to prod me into another, and the second time, I'd gotten used to the game and edged out ahead at the last minute. So of course we had to play a tiebreaker.

Jolie cheered for both of us, praising Tate one minute and me the next. After her son performed a particularly good shooting streak, she frowned. "Should I be worried about how good you are with that gun?"

He rolled his eyes. "Because I might turn into one of those angry white boys who shoot up a school? Not the same, Mom."

"But if you—"

I cut her off. "Not the same, Jol."

And it wasn't. Not at all. I'd held a gun in my hand a hundred times. Aimed it plenty. Shot one off a few times, too, though never to kill. The weight of the real thing made it impossible to forget it wasn't a game, and the trigger required intentional pressure.

It didn't mean I didn't think Tate was capable of terrible things—anyone could be when put in the right situation—but I definitely didn't believe a source of entertainment was a predictor of such actions.

I mean, I was killing it in the game, and I wasn't running to gun down Stark. And I even had plenty of fucking good reason.

Tate grinned, obviously appreciative that I backed him up, and before I could stop myself, I grinned back.

"Good game," I said afterward, extending my hand toward him. "You pulled it out there at the end. I have to be impressed."

He scowled at my hand. "What? Are you an old man or something?" He curled his fingers into a fist and then pushed it toward me in invitation.

"It's traditional to shake the hand of the winner." But I bumped my fist to his.

"That's weak sauce. Let's go find the ice cream." He headed off in the direction of the concessions.

I turned to Jolie. "Weak sauce?"

"I think he's saying you're a loser, and not just in the literal sense."

The way she was looking at me, she thought I was exactly the opposite of a loser and might even be about to tell me so.

I didn't want to hear it. Couldn't stand there while she thanked me for being cool to her son, as if I was doing it for her. Or him.

And saying it was about me didn't make sense even to myself.

So I made sure she didn't get a chance to speak. "We better catch up with him before he needs a credit card."

I took off after Tate, not waiting for her to go first.

Twenty minutes later, we were sitting in a booth with two sundaes (me and Tate) and two beers (me and Jolie).

"Are you going to finally tell me why I'm here?" Tate scooped up a spoonful of his sundae, making sure to include lots of chocolate sauce before putting it in his mouth.

I could feel Jolie tense from across the table. When I looked at her, I could see it too.

Tate, who was sitting next to her, didn't seem to notice. "Because you were clearly surprised to see me, and then I found out you didn't even have your phone all night."

I'd been curious about his arrival myself, and now I realized exactly what must have happened. "Carla," I guessed, wondering if Tate had assumed it was me.

He put his spoon down. "That's what I thought. But why would she want—?"

"We can talk about it later, Tate." Jolie plunked the cherry off his sundae and brought it to her mouth, and while it was distracting to watch her bite into the juicy fruit, I wanted to have the conversation now, suddenly curious what she'd tell him.

"Don't put it off on my account." I finished off my beer, then raised my hand to signal the drinks girl to bring another.

She shot me a glare. "You know how Carla is..."

I almost felt bad for Jolie, having to juggle whatever stories she'd told her son with the fact that I was sitting right there in front of him.

But not bad enough not to stir the shit. "She broke into your phone and pretended to be you texting Tate? That's a new brand of bitch for

Carla. Usually, she's a stand-by-and-watch-the-fire-burn kind of gal. Not a start-the-fire herself kind."

Jol chewed her lip, probably deciding how to navigate the mess before speaking. "I think she just wanted to see how you've grown up. She was around for the first seven years of your life, you know. She had to be curious."

"Then why didn't she just tell you to invite me? And why didn't we just keep in touch with her?"

"I've told you—my father and I are estranged. Keeping in touch with Carla would mean keeping in touch with him, and I didn't want him to know where we were." Her tone was tight, and there was no questioning she thought this should be the end of it.

I had a feeling Tate got the message but just didn't care. "Were you scared of him or something?"

She fidgeted nervously with the salt and pepper shakers on the booth table. "I really don't want to talk about this right now."

"Did you fight with him because he kicked Cade out?"

Jolie's neck went red, and I saw her debating whether or not to grab that as an excuse.

Obviously, she hadn't told her son much about her father at all.

It wasn't my place to interfere.

No matter how many times I told myself that, I couldn't quite latch on to it. Every time I looked at Tate, all I could think was *If he were my kid...* I'd never felt that way about a teen before. Or a child of any age, for that matter. I'd never wanted to be woven into a person's DNA the way I wanted to be woven into Tate's, and it was truly fucking with my head.

So much so that, even though I knew it wasn't my place, I went ahead and acted like it was. "Your grandfather is a monster, Tate. No other way to say it. An abusive, fucked-up asshole."

"That's it. Conversation over. We should get going." Jolie started gathering the napkins strewn across the table as if she were cleaning up to go, neglecting that neither Tate nor I were finished with our sundaes and that I had another beer on order.

She was on the inside of the booth, though, so Tate would have to stand up to let her out, and he wasn't budging. "Abusive?"

Admittedly, it wasn't just that I wanted to have an impact on this kid. It was also the resentment I felt toward Jolie that had me poking holes in whatever story she'd told about her past. Or as it seemed, *hadn't* told. It gave me a sense of power in a relationship dynamic where I was otherwise insignificant. "You know what a sadist is?"

"Cade!" Her tone was sharp and warning. "He's a kid."

"He's nearly seventeen. That's practically a full-grown adult." I gave her a glare as sharp as her words. "And don't tell me you didn't know the meaning at his age, in action if not the word."

She clamped her mouth shut, probably because she couldn't refute it without outright lies, and anything she said to clarify or smooth over would be an admission of truths she didn't appear to want to share.

Tate pressed on despite his mother. "It's a sex thing, right? Sadists are people who get off on pain."

My spine stiffened. Sex had generally not been a component of Stark's punishments. I didn't talk about the one time he had brought his pleasure into it. It was too humiliating. Too shameful. I'd never told a soul.

But we were talking in a general sense about Stark, not specific. "Pretty much, yes. In some relationships, the pain inflicted is consensual. No judgment if that's your thing—"

"Oh, my God." Jolie crossed her arms over her chest and sat back against the vinyl seat, her irritation displayed in a cute little pout.

"I'm not..." He shook his head, deciding to ignore his mother's reaction rather than address it. "And that was what my grandpa was into?"

"I don't know what went on in his bedroom, but I can tell you without a doubt that he derived pleasure from inflicting pain. Getting kicked out of that house was a blessing, not a curse. The terrible part was not that I left but that your mother wasn't able to leave with me."

I didn't want to know her reaction to that. Fortunately, the drinks girl picked that moment to deliver my beer, so I had a good excuse not to look in Jolie's direction while I dealt with payment.

After she left with my drink in hand, I studied Tate instead, watched his furrowed brow as he scooped ice cream into his mouth and worked the bits and pieces he'd collected into a picture of some sort. "He hit me, didn't he?"

Jolie's anger dropped instantly, concern taking over her face. "You remember that?"

He shook his head. "Not really. It just feels like I know he did." He angled toward her. "Why didn't you tell me?"

"You had counseling at first. The therapist said he thought you were dealing with it well, and there was no need to bring it up unless you brought it up. We can talk about it later, if you want."

I tried not to feel left out. Not my kid, not my duty to be part of his emotional health. He was lucky, really. To have forgotten. Amazing what a mind could do in order to protect a growing child.

Too bad Jolie and I hadn't had the same method of coping.

"Is that why we left?"

"Yeah, tiger." She brushed a hand through his hair, and he pushed it off with an irritated shrug. She did a good job of not being offended. "I vowed he would never lay a hand on you again."

"Makes sense, I guess." He took it like it was no big deal, and it probably wasn't to this teenager who didn't have fear branded into his everyday life. Or maybe he was blowing her off because he was unhappy that she'd kept these things from him, which was understandable.

Either way, it was a real gift she'd given him—one not every mother gives her children, despite it being their job—and I suddenly wanted him to know that. "You would have had a very different life if she hadn't gotten you out of there. Whatever you might feel about her not telling you, and whatever struggles you may have experienced being raised by a single mom, she rescued you from hell. No other way to say it."

He looked at me with somber eyes. "Okay," he said, and though it was only two little syllables, I could tell he understood the seriousness of the facts if not the complete story they told.

He scooted to the edge of the bench, leaving an undeniable space between him and his mother. A beat passed in silence. Then another.

He didn't speak again until he was scraping at the last of the chocolate in his bowl. "I guess what I don't get is why you two went back there then. If he's so horrible."

Jolie sighed, and I could feel the weight of it like it was my own. I couldn't imagine the burden it must have been over the years to carry the remnants from her past while caring for a child.

It pissed me off all over again that she'd thought she'd had to do it on her own.

Pissed me off mostly because it was easier than feeling hurt.

My own feelings aside, her son had a question that likely was not an easy one to answer. It was one thing to make sure he knew what kind of man his grandfather was. Quite another to tell him what his mother had wanted to do about it.

I considered letting her address this one herself, but she didn't jump to explaining, and I could see from her posture that she was weary from the stories.

Without ever having a kid of my own, I knew that I was a transparency-and-no-bullshit kind of parent, and even so, this wasn't the place to be completely honest. "We bumped into each other unexpectedly in New York," I said, selling the lie we'd sold Carla. "After a bit of reminiscing, we decided to go back to the house."

"That doesn't make any sense."

No. I was sure it didn't. "When you've suffered the kind of abuse that your mom and I did, it haunts you. Sometimes the only way past it is to face it head-on. Does that make sense?"

"Sort of."

My skin pricked at the judgment in his tone. "Hey, Tate." I waited until I had his eyes on me. "You can't judge the choices she's made. You weren't there. You don't know."

He shrugged in response, obviously not wanting to let go of his irritation.

Yeah, I knew the feeling.

He might not have understood her, but I sure as hell understood him. Understood how anger was easier than forgiveness, anyway.

To be fair, his feelings likely extended beyond the secrets about her father to the secrets about *his* father. There might be a real chasm between them when she finally told him the truth.

What if he never had to know?

Was it selfless for me to consider that or selfish? Or just plain stupid?

Not your place to consider it at all.

"We shouldn't stay there tonight," Jolie said decisively after a short but heavy silence.

"We could get a hotel." I pushed my beer away, ready to leave it only half gone.

"Yeah. That's..." Her shoulders sagged. "Dammit. I didn't get a chance to put the keys in the office."

"We have to go back for our things anyway." Maybe she could return them quickly then, though after being caught in there the night before, it might not be quite that easy to slip in without Carla's notice.

Tate looked up from his phone. His ice cream gone, and at least some of his questions answered, he'd been texting for the last few minutes. "Will your dad be there?"

Jolie shook her head. "No, he's at his cabin. We were planning to leave tomorrow before he got back."

"We might as well stay then." There was defiance in his tone, as if he was daring her to insist otherwise.

Instead of answering, she looked to me to back her up. Tate looked to me as well.

Part of me wanted to earn points with her because I always wanted to earn points with her. Another part of me wanted to let her down.

Another part of me wanted to sneak her to the bathroom and fuck her against the wall. Fuck her mean. Fuck her a little sweet too.

It was confusing to be so conflicted.

So I chose my response without factoring in my feelings about her at all. "We should leave first thing in the morning. You two can take the beds. I'll sleep in the den." I made sure she understood my reasoning. "We may need the night to get the keys back in place."

Plus, we still hadn't made a decision about what we were doing next. I didn't want to cut off our access to the house just yet in case we needed it.

Her nod was reluctant. "All right. You're right. We should go then."

"I'll meet you outside," Tate said, holding up his phone. "I need to make a quick call."

Jolie's brow lifted in curiosity.

"The girlfriend?" I asked before taking another swig from the beer I'd meant to abandon.

"Yeah." He gave an embarrassed smile and slid out of the booth, bringing the phone up to his ear as he did.

"Girlfriend?" Jolie called after him in surprise. "What girlfriend?"

Before she could chase after him, I put an arm out and stopped her. "Leave him be."

I braced myself for admonition. I'd been crossing the line for the last hour, and she'd yet to call me on it.

Instead of letting me have what I deserved, she let out a breath. "I just didn't know he had a girl."

"Not usually something a kid wants to talk about with his mom, even when their relationship is a good one."

She scrutinized me, as though she was unsure why I continued to try to reassure her. Or why I tried to do anything nice at all, for that matter.

Fuck if I knew myself.

"You're good with him," she said, and now I wondered if I'd been off base about her thoughts. Maybe she'd gone in an entirely different direction.

I hesitated.

Because what I wanted to say was that I could have been better for him. I could have been *there* for him, if she'd let me. Despite not sharing DNA.

I could be good with him in the future.

I could be good with her, too.

But that would mean I'd have to take my own advice—stop judging the choices she'd made. Stop holding on to my resentment. Stop picking apart the past.

And while I'd accepted I'd do pretty much anything for her, I wasn't sure I was capable of doing that.

TWELVE
CADE

It was almost ten when we got back to the house. It was dark, but the porch light was on, which I would have attributed to habit before the conversation with Terrence.

Now, all of my mother's actions felt suspicious. Was the welcome gesture a ruse?

I left the car idling. "She wouldn't have called him, would she? Let him know we were here?"

I expected Jolie to brush off the idea right away. Instead, she chewed her lip and considered. "She helped me and Tate leave. It wouldn't make sense for her to turn on us all of a sudden." But she didn't make any move to get out of the car.

In the back seat, Tate leaned forward, poking his head between us. "There aren't any new tire marks on the snow. If he's here, where's his car?"

Good point. Tate's Versa was blocking the empty side of the garage, so there wasn't a vehicle hidden in there.

I looked again at Jolie to be sure.

She let out a tense laugh. "He's not here. We're paranoid. Come on." She pushed open the door and got out.

"Paranoid? Scarred is more accurate." I was talking to myself since Tate had gotten out too.

I turned off the car and followed after them. Whither she went, so did I, it seemed.

Still, after everything, she had me on a fucking leash.

Whatever had motivated my mother to leave the light on, she'd had to consciously leave the door unlocked, and it was. No one greeted us when we stepped inside, but I knew for sure he wasn't there. The air felt thick, but I could breathe. Stark had a presence that smothered, even from rooms away.

Tate picked up the duffel bag that he'd left inside the door. "Upstairs?"

"The room at the end of the hall," Jolie said, then turned to me. "I think I'll take a shower."

It could have been an invitation. Yesterday, I'd have taken it as such. Part of me still wanted it to be—a big part of me—and I had a feeling that I could easily change her mind if it hadn't been.

But I was afraid she'd take fucking as a sign that things were settled between us, and I wasn't sure I was ready for that.

Her son only a handful of feet away didn't make it a good idea either.

"I'll come up with you to get my things."

I could see her lip twitch, the urge to say something more, but whatever it was, she let it pass with a nod.

A few minutes later, with my bag in hand, I found my mother watching some crime procedural in the den, dressed in a zip-up robe, her feet curled up underneath her. She reached for the remote as soon as she saw me and turned it off with a click.

"You don't have to do that on my account." Not that I planned to stay in the room if she did, but there were other places I could be.

"It's over anyway." She stood up, her eyes landing on my suitcase. "You'll keep up appearances for the boy but not for me?"

Her wounded act would never have worked on me. Tonight it had a particularly sour taste. She'd driven the car while her husband had abducted a teenager. She'd possibly done more. Any chance of excusing her as another of Stark's victims had been erased with that knowledge, and now I could barely look at her. "I can sleep in the living room, if you'd rather."

She let out a huff, irritated that I hadn't picked up on her cue. "Here is fine. I can get you bedding."

"You still keep linens in the hall closet?" I waited for her to say yes. "I can get it myself then." Anything to get rid of her. If I didn't, I'd tear into her with accusations, which might feel good in the moment but wasn't in our best interest. If I wanted the investigation against Stark to come through, I couldn't let her see our cards.

Thankfully, she took the hint. "Good, then I'll be off to bed myself. You're still leaving in the morning?"

"Unless you think your husband will be back sooner."

"He won't be back until afternoon."

"Then we'll be sure we're gone by then."

She gave a nod, then started to leave.

I let her get past me before the niggle inside me grew into something I couldn't ignore. "I'm not asking why. I'm not demanding anything you should feel the need to defend. Just answer me one thing—you know he's a bad man, don't you?"

She had the nerve to look angered by the question. Then she almost blew me off but at the last second turned back. "I never wanted you here, Cade. Not back then, when the only reason I sent for you was because he demanded it, and not now. Take that however you will."

I stood in the same place for several minutes after she left, not dissecting her words but convincing myself I didn't care. Whatever message she meant to give me, I did not care. I did not care. I did not care.

Said enough times, maybe I'd start to believe it.

It took all of two minutes to grab a blanket and sheets, having decided not to bother with the pull-out bed. The couch would be fine, not that I expected to get much sleep. The ghosts were too present tonight. It had been different last night, with Jolie distracting me from them. Without her, they were everywhere, filling every corner of my mind.

I managed to avoid them by concentrating on every sound in the house, waiting to be sure that Carla was asleep before returning the keys we'd stolen to the office. Pretending that was all I was listening for and not straining for signs that Jolie might still be awake.

What would it matter if she was? Nothing good would come from going up those stairs. Not a goddamned bit of good.

As convinced as I was, the temptation and the memories kept me restless. For the next hour, I paced the den like a lion in a cage, wishing I had a punching bag to direct some of my energy. I took my boots off. Texted Donovan, who didn't respond. Did fifty push-ups. Stood perfectly still when I heard a door close upstairs.

Silence followed, and any wish that she might be sneaking down to see me vanished when five minutes passed, and I was still alone.

I wished I hated her.

After her betrayal, it was almost possible.

But if I really hated her, I had to be done with her, and if I was done with her...

I wasn't sure I could ever be done with Jolie. Seventeen years had gone by, and I hadn't been able to let her go. Would it really be any easier now?

Maybe the things she had left to tell me would help push me away.

In which case, I wasn't so eager to hear them.

It was close to midnight when I felt confident that my mother was truly asleep. I managed not to glance up the stairs at all on my way to Stark's office. The door was still unlocked, so it only took a couple of minutes to return them to the place Jolie had told me she'd gotten them from. I made sure to latch the lock on my way out.

Then, because that was off my plate and all my bandwidth was available to fixate on her, I climbed the stupid fucking stairs.

It can be like old times, I told myself. Sneaking in to be with her, but through the door instead of the window. We could leave the lights off. We wouldn't have to say a word. Just burn off some of the tension like animals in the night.

At her door, I grabbed the handle, then changed my mind and lifted my fist to knock.

Then thought about how little I had left to lose to her, and that got my head in the right place.

I let my hand drop, turned around, and went back down the stairs.

This time, when I got to the den, it wasn't my mother waiting for me. My deliberation at her door had been in vain. She hadn't even been in her room when I'd stood there. I hadn't heard her when I'd been in the office.

Jolie sat on the couch, wearing nothing but the T-shirt she'd stolen from me, her hair tousled from being left to dry naturally, her lips wet from the run of her tongue. In the soft glow of the one lit lamp, she could have been an angel if I didn't know she was a temptress.

Maybe I did hate her after all.

Hated how she owned every single part of me, from my heart to my pride. Hated how I wanted to hurt her and heal her all at the same time.

"Are you here to talk, or are you here to fuck?" I asked, my cock already hardening behind the zipper of my jeans.

She stood to face me, and there was something in her eyes—a window of sorts—and for a moment, I thought she might actually be ready to tell me all her secrets. Thought she might push to put everything on the table and see what was left between us, when all I wanted at the moment was to be with her.

But she surprised me when she spoke. "I'm here for whatever you'll let me have."

I closed the distance between us, on the verge of letting out a laugh until I realized none of this was the least bit funny. "I'm feeling mean, Jolie. Do you want that too?"

My hand settled on her throat before she'd answered, so I could feel her swallow and the rush of her pulse.

I squeezed ever so slightly, so her voice was strained when she spoke. "I want it all, Cade."

No sooner than her consent was past her lips, my mouth crashed against hers, hard and aggressive. I kissed her like a thief—taking, taking, taking. Barely giving her a chance to breathe. Pushing my tongue into her throat when her kiss came too easily. Biting her lips. Sucking them raw.

I'd been so gentle with her in the past. I hadn't known how to fuck rough, and even if I had, I hadn't wanted to ever show her anything but kindness.

Now I touched her like it was punishment. For staying with him instead of going with me. For letting him have more of her life than she'd given me. Maybe if I'd hurt her then, she'd have chosen differently. Maybe she needed to be bullied into her love.

They weren't fair thoughts—they definitely weren't thoughts I'd have outside the moment—and as out of control as they felt, I still couldn't make myself truly hurt her. I couldn't even bear to put enough pressure on her neck to leave bruises despite the fact that she was practically asking for it, pushing her throat up against my hand, whispering, "More," whenever I gave her a chance to speak.

I was as mad at my inability to damage her as I was at her ability to damage me. I fought against that reality, trying to take some of that power for myself, and the next time I had her lip between my teeth, I bit hard enough to taste blood, only to soothe it with a gentle swipe of my tongue.

With a frustrated growl, I wrapped my hand in her hair and pulled her away from my mouth, pulled her downward, to the couch. Her legs opened slightly, and I could see she'd come to see me without any panties on. Had she never really planned to talk, or did she just know what I'd choose? Either answer fucked me up inside.

Yeah, I did hate her.

Roughly, I wrenched one of her legs up over the arm of the couch, spreading her into an uncomfortably wide position, then dropped to my knees. Without any preamble, I began lapping at her cunt. Lapping like a dog that had gone days without water. Like her sole reason for existence was to provide for me.

"This doesn't feel very mean." She was breathless, her back arching, giving away that her words were a lie with the way she quivered from the cruel assault.

But if she was going to taunt me...

I sucked her clit hard. Hard enough that she gasped.

Then she started to beg, her body jolting as I added teeth. Alternating between nips and sucks, I took her quickly to the brink.

Just when she was about to go over, I broke off entirely.

See? I could be mean.

I ran my fingers along her inner thighs, pinching her skin until it was bright red as she bucked her hips toward me, urging me back to her cunt, which I only returned to when I was good and ready.

Then I repeated the attack, winding her up, backing off abruptly, until she was crying and pleading and drenched with sweat and pussy juice.

But I wasn't even mean enough to deny her an orgasm forever.

As soon as I shoved three fingers inside her, she erupted. I didn't even need to push in with a second stroke. It would be easy and cruel to demand another one from her right after, which made the idea tempting, but my cock was a fat steel bar, and I chose it for my next weapon.

She was still shuddering while I worked the shirt over her head and hadn't recovered by the time I got my jeans down and my cock covered with the condom I'd retrieved from my wallet. Limp as a rag doll, she was easy to manhandle, and I moved her how I wanted her—pulling her ass up to the arm of the couch, yanking her to the edge so I could shove inside her balls deep.

"Oh, God," she moaned as I drove in.

She was slippery but tight, and I didn't give her a chance to adjust before pummeling into her. Her breasts jiggled from the impact, and I liked that—liked seeing her out of control too—so when she moved her hands to hold them, I smacked them away and increased my brutal tempo.

Hard, hard, hard, over and over, and it still wasn't enough. Wasn't mean enough.

I straightened one of her legs against my torso and pushed forward, bending her as far as she could go, and gripped one nipple, pinching at it until she whimpered and arched her back, trying to ease the pain.

"You want it all, Jolie?" I was in her face. "I would have given it all to you. I would have given you everything."

"Give it to me now."

It pissed me off, how she could plead so sincerely for something she'd once thrown aside.

Pissed me off more that I couldn't stop myself from giving.

Still pinching her breast with one hand, I shoved my other fingers in her mouth—three of them. The same fingers that had been inside her. I fucked her mouth with those fingers as savagely as I was fucking her cunt, until she was drooling and choking, and still, when I gave her a second of reprieve, she again begged for more.

"You're so fucking greedy. How much is enough for you? Should I take your ass too?" She couldn't respond—I shoved my fingers farther down her throat when she tried—but she gave no sign of resistance, and that made me mad too.

Because I wanted an excuse.

I wanted something I could point to that would prove this couldn't work between us.

I wanted to be able to accuse her of giving up, like she did back then, because if she was going to break my fucking heart again—if she was going to destroy me like she so very much had the power to do—I wanted it done sooner rather than later, when there was still possibly something left of myself to salvage from the wreckage.

But she didn't give me that excuse.

And when I finally pulled my fingers out of her mouth so I could pull her other leg up against my chest as well, she looked me dead in the eye. "I want you, Cade. All of you. I won't give you up this time."

She was crying, I noticed. Truth be told, I might have been crying too. "You have me. You already fucking have all of me." She clenched tight on my cock, but I didn't slow my assault. "No, you don't get to push me out now. You asked for it, and now you have to take it."

And she did.

Took all of it.

Even though I fucked her like I was trying to tear her apart—and maybe I was, and maybe it was too rough—but when she whimpered my name, she was still asking for more, and when she came again, it was a whole-body orgasm that shook through her like an earthquake, wrecking her completely.

Wrecking her as thoroughly as she always wrecked me.

I came right after, groaning and grinding into her with an orgasm that reached every end of me—to the tip of every finger, down to my toes, up my spine to the top of my head—and held on for long seconds, as if I was indeed giving her everything I had, everything I was. Everything until there was nothing left of me alone, and all that existed was the me that was part of her.

It was freeing to feel linked to her like this, and with my eyes closed, I imagined that when I opened them again, I would somehow see the joining. That we would be soldered together with alloy. That our bond would be obvious to anyone.

Of course, that wasn't the case. We were united only by my half hard cock, still buried inside her pussy, and the tear-stained woman that laid depleted beneath me was not only separate from myself, but someone I had just selfishly used.

"Are you okay?" I let her legs fall to the floor and drew her to me. "I shouldn't have... Did I hurt you? I'm sorry. I'm so sorry, baby." I spattered kisses across her cheeks and nose, so intent on delivering my apology that I barely recognized she was giving one of her own.

"Stop. Don't say that. I loved it. I'm the one who's sorry. I'm so deeply sorry."

I pulled back to look at her when I realized her apologies had nothing to do with what had just occurred, and for once, I was able to hear it. Suddenly, I could believe that the years she'd spent without me had been a torment for her, that the ache inside me was shared.

That we were on the same side. That we'd always been on the same side.

I kissed her. Desperately. "How could you think that I wouldn't want both of you?" I cradled her face between my hands and stooped so she had no choice but to see me at eye level. "I would have been his father. Even if you didn't love me, I would have loved you enough for the both of us."

Fresh tears sprang in her eyes. "I loved you too much to saddle you with my baggage."

"The weight of being without you is heavier than any baggage you could have put on me."

"I didn't know. I didn't know." She started to break down, but I wouldn't let her, kissing her until I was her focus, and not her guilt. Forcing her to be here with me instead of locked inside whatever prison waited for her in her head.

We'd both been locked up too long.

We both deserved to fly away. Together, this time.

With my hands still on her face, I pushed my forehead to hers. "I won't lose you again, Jol. I hurt right now from every secret you've kept, but this hurt feels better than the hell of being without you."

"I don't deserve you."

"You better fucking try. Because I'm not letting you go again, whether you want me or not."

She smiled, but it brought another round of tears. "I want you, Cade. I've always wanted you. There's nothing I've ever wanted but you."

"I mean it." I brushed the wet from her cheeks. Crying and sex-rumpled and wrecked, she'd never looked so beautiful. "You're stuck with me from here on out."

"Stuck is my new favorite." She brought her hands to my neck and gripped on as tight as if she was drowning, and I was the only thing keeping her afloat.

If she was going under, fuck, so was I.

As if she could read my thoughts, she trembled. "Are you scared?" I asked.

She shook her head. "'Sink or swim, baby.'"

Except this time, I wasn't wrapped around her like an anchor. This time, our heads were both above water, and I was pretty damn sure I could see the shore.

THIRTEEN

JOLIE

After several more lingering kisses, Cade took care of the condom then cleaned me up with the T-shirt I'd worn.

"Now I have nothing to wear when I go back upstairs." Obviously, I'd steal another of his shirts.

"Guess you'll have to stay down here."

"Well, it was either that or take you up with me, but with Tate down the hall..."

He chuckled. "As if you don't know how to be quiet."

Even after what we'd just done, it made me blush to think about how I'd had to learn to keep my pleasure inside all those years ago, afraid we'd be heard. "And we got caught anyway."

Too late, I worried that I'd said the wrong thing, that I'd sent him down the path of darker memories, and he'd go cold again.

He did just the opposite. "You're so beautiful," he said, staring at me with hot eyes that reminded me that I was the only one of us who wasn't wearing any clothes.

I shivered from the intensity of that stare, but he must have assumed I was cold since the next thing I knew, he pulled me off the arm of the couch where I was perched and wrapped a blanket around the both of us. "There's less room down here than in the twin upstairs, but I promise I'll keep you warm."

"Skin to skin would do that job best." I slipped my hands under his sweater, but he caught me at the elbows before I could try to take it off.

"We both know where that would lead, and you're still catching your breath from the last round."

I didn't have a chance to respond before he was kissing me again. No wonder I couldn't catch my breath. I wasn't complaining.

And when he pulled me with him to lie on the couch, I didn't complain about that either.

For long moments, we lay like that—stretched out, face-to-face—sometimes sharing deep kisses. Sometimes just looking at each other. It had been so long since we'd been wrapped up together, and now that we were, I couldn't imagine how we'd survived so long apart.

I'd only made it through because I'd had Tate.

How had Cade managed?

Thinking about it made me too regretful and sad, so I pushed those thoughts away and did something I hadn't done in years—daydreamed about our brighter future.

"What are schools like in Tokyo?" I asked, tracing the curve of his lip with my finger.

He thought about it a second before realizing why I was asking. "You're not moving to Tokyo."

Panic rose quickly in my chest. We'd just said we weren't letting each other go. "Your company is—"

He cut me off. "I can work at whichever office I want. I'm an owner. I don't have to work at all, if I don't want to. I get a portion of the profits no matter what, and it's more than enough to take care of us quite comfortably. I don't need the salaried position on top of that."

"But I'll move to Tokyo if that's what you want."

"I want us to decide what we do together. What do you want?"

It had been so long since anyone had asked me that. The last person who had might have even been him. "Honestly? I just want you."

He gave the smallest smile, but it lit up his entire face, and then of course I had to kiss him. Or he had to kiss me. Whichever, we were kissing again.

God, I'd forgotten how nice it was to just kiss and be held. There'd been men from time to time over the years, but only one came close to being serious, and no relationship had felt this intensely affectionate. Like we were teenagers all over again.

"We're going to have the academy to think about," he said when he eventually broke away. I must have looked confused because he clarified. "When your father gets arrested, the school is going to be yours."

"I hadn't thought of that." How had I not thought of that? I'd based my career choices on that one-day possibility, even after I'd left him, assuming that one day I'd be left everything.

Of course, that had been before my last encounter with him, when I realized he would cut me off entirely. "He'll give it to Carla," I said.

"She doesn't have any interest in running it. Trust me. She wouldn't know where to begin. And after today, it sounds like there's a good chance she'll go to jail too."

That was weird to think about. It had to be weirder for him than for me, and I started to say something that would allow him to talk about that if he wanted, but he'd read my mind and shook his head before I got any words out.

So I stayed on topic instead. "Whatever happens, he'll leave it to someone else."

"You're his only living relative. Who else is there?"

"He'll give it to charity. He's already told me he's not giving me anything of his. He'll sell it, and donate the money." I let out a sharp laugh. "No, he'll use the money for his legal defense."

Cade didn't blink. "Then I'll buy it."

"You will not—"

"You're right. *We'll* buy it. I'm not used to thinking in the plural."

I was too happy to refute him. "We're really a we now, aren't we?"

"Yes. We really fucking are." He placed a kiss on the side of my mouth. "We could have our wedding here. On the grounds. That would piss your father off to no end, wouldn't it? Replace his legacy with ours."

"You're planning our wedding now?"

"We'll go all out. Make it huge. We didn't think we'd ever be able to be public, but fuck that. Unless you'd rather not have anything to do with this place."

"No, I love this place." I rethought that. "I mean, I love parts of this place. I love the you parts. I hate the him parts."

"We'll get rid of all the him parts."

Years had passed since I'd truly known Cade, but I knew him well enough to know that he didn't make idle plans. He meant the things he said.

Suddenly, my chest didn't feel big enough to hold what was inside of me. "Is this your way of asking me to marry you?"

He shook his head. "No, no, no. I'm not doing that again. Not without a real ring. The fake one didn't take so well."

I giggled because he made me feel dizzy and light. I still had that pipe cleaner tucked away in a jewelry box.

And then I sobered up because there was also so much between us that was still unbearably heavy. "It took the first time, Cade. I just—"

This time, he cut me off with a kiss. "Later, okay?"

I got it. He didn't want to talk about Carla. He didn't want to talk about the past. He wanted to be here, enjoying the present. Planning the future. Blotting out the bad stuff.

That had been the way with us back then too, and in the end, that might have been to our detriment. If we'd been honest about what had been going on—if *I'd* been honest—maybe everything would have been different.

I worried that we'd get stuck in that same bubble this time too.

"We *will* talk about it," he assured me, reading my thoughts. "But not here. We need to be on neutral ground when we do. There are enough ghosts around us here."

"Okay."

He ignored the reluctance in my tone. "Tate still has another year and a half before he graduates, doesn't he? We probably don't want to uproot him before that."

It was a good distraction. Hearing him talk about my son was fucking sexy. "He's really happy where he is."

"And there's the girlfriend. We wouldn't want to break them up."

I playfully slapped his shoulder. "Who is this girlfriend? I haven't heard a word."

"I think it's a new thing. He's still feeling her out. He'll tell you. When he's ready."

A knot pulled in my belly. I had things I had to tell my son, and I didn't think I'd ever be ready for this truth. "I have to tell Tate."

I could tell he knew what I was talking about when the corners of his mouth fell downward.

"I know—we're only thinking about good things right now, but I can't let myself dream so much that I end up putting this off. I have to tell him soon."

"Do you?"

"Yeah. It's not fair to have kept him in the dark this long. Each minute he spends with you, he thinks he's getting closer to his father."

Cade brushed my hair away from my face then caressed my cheek with the pad of his thumb. "So maybe you don't tell him at all. Maybe you just let him keep this one lie."

"You don't know what you're offering." I wasn't considering it yet—that would be a whole other thought process that required some deep evaluation about whether or not I still wanted to be the kind of mother who could lie to her child.

Right now, though, I was only thinking about Cade and the weight of what he was suggesting.

He propped his head up on his hand. "I think I do."

I mirrored him. "This is the kind of thing you can't decide on a whim. You'd be tied to him. Forever."

"What is it you think we've been talking about here?"

I blinked. "We've been talking about you and me."

"And he's part of you. You're a package deal. I'm well aware of that."

I shook my head. "No, this isn't the same. You can leave me. You can't—"

He wrapped his hand around my jaw. "I can't leave you, Jol. It's not happening."

"I know, but—"

"I should have been his father. In practice if not in blood. You should give me the chance now that I should have been given then."

That got me in the gut.

Before I could process enough to say something, though, he spoke again. "Think about it. You don't have to decide right now."

I couldn't decide right now even if I wanted to. Making those kinds of plans required everything on the table. This was why the past had to be discussed. It kept popping back up whether we wanted it to or not. Our future didn't exist without the past. They were also a package deal.

I tucked the blanket around my bare chest, as if that would make me feel less vulnerable, and sat up a little more. "We should talk about that, Cade. What happened. Why I didn't go with you back then. About Tate's father. It could change how you feel about us."

He sat up as well, moving so he was sitting next to me.

Side by side made the conversation safer somehow. Because we could look straight ahead instead of at each other. Looking in his eyes was what felt most dangerous.

"First of all, we have enough on our plate right now planning what's next. With your father, with us." He took my hand in his and laced our fingers together. "Second—and most important—it's not going to change things between us. What part of I'm not letting you go do you not understand?"

When I'd let him go all those years ago, I'd given up on any chance of ever having him. The possibility of us still felt so unreal, and admittedly, it was going to take a whole hell of a lot of talking about it and seeing it happen before I could really believe it in my bones.

I knew that. I understood that about myself.

What I didn't understand was how he could believe in us. "I just don't know how you can trust me." I swallowed, surprised by how much this meant to me.

"And you think I'll trust you more once you've told me everything you need to tell me?"

"I think I'll be more trustworthy when I don't have any more secrets."

"Yeah, I suppose you will be." He turned his head toward me but tilted it down toward my shoulder instead of my face. "I know trust matters. And maybe I'm not quite there yet, but you aren't either, or you wouldn't be worrying about me."

"But..." I didn't know where I was going with that, only that it hurt not to have his faith, which I knew I had no right to ask for, and I wanted to believe that everything we were saying tonight had a chance of being real.

What was the point of any of these words?

I repeated what he'd said only moments before. "What is it you think we're talking about here?"

He opened and closed his fingers around mine. "I think we've been talking about our future. Do I trust that you mean it?" I felt him shrug. "I know that *I* mean it. And I know that even after what happened in the past, I still want you. I still love you. Try as I might not to. So the way I see it, I have two choices: I can either not trust you and be alone and miserable forever like I've been for the last seventeen years, or I can try to trust you and maybe get everything I've ever wanted. Either way, I still love you. Seems my odds are better if I stick around."

My vision blurred. It was more than I deserved. So much more.

I twisted to face him. "You really still love me?"

"I think it's pretty fucking obvious."

"I really still love you too."

His breath seemed to catch. And then he was cupping my cheeks, bringing my mouth to his for a salty kiss. "It wouldn't matter if you didn't. I'm still not going anywhere."

"But I do. So much."

"I'm going to give you everything, Jolie." We spoke between kisses that were getting progressively deeper. "Everything you ever wanted."

"You're what I've wanted."

"A real family."

"A baby?"

He pulled away to see if I was serious. "Tate's almost grown up. You want to do it all over again?"

"With you, yes."

"I want that." He grinned. "I want a baby with you, Jolie, very much."

"I'm thirty-five, though, so we should get on it soon."

The next kiss took us back to a prone position. This time, when I tried to take off his sweater, he helped me get it off. He stood to get out of his pants, and then there he was, standing like a naked god, pumping his hard cock in his fist.

Be still my heart.

"We could start right now," he said, looking at me so fiercely I could have gotten pregnant from his gaze. "I don't have to put on a condom."

"Condoms aren't only to prevent pregnancy." It was the kind of decision that shouldn't be made in the heat of the moment.

On the other hand, if he was clean, I didn't really have to think about it. "I haven't been with anyone except you in more than a year."

Damn, I sounded pathetic. I knew he'd been with someone else as recently as last week.

"I haven't been bare with anyone but you, Jol. Ever." Another stroke of his cock, and I didn't know if it was his words or his actions that had my stomach flipping. "Tell me now because I need inside you."

I nodded.

Was still nodding when he stretched out beside me. He put a hand on the side of my neck, firm and sure, but nothing like the last time when he'd put pressure on my airway. I'd been really turned on by that version of him.

This version of him took me to another plane of existence.

He pulled me snug up against him. I lifted my knee to his hip, and immediately, I could feel the thick crown of his cock nudging at my entrance. I tilted up in invitation just as he pushed forward, sliding in easily like a key in a well-oiled lock.

"Cade!" I threw my head back in pleasure, fighting against the instinct to close my eyes. I wanted to see him. Wanted to see everything he said without words. Wanted to see how I affected him. Wanted him to see how he affected me.

He kept hold of my gaze, kissing me reassuringly. "I'm right here with you, baby. Me too." He threaded himself in and out of me, slowly, making sure every stroke was felt by every part of my insides. "Fuck. It's incredible. You feel..." He finished the sentiment on a low growl.

"I know." He felt hotter without a condom separating us. Skin to skin with our most intimate parts. I was already clenching around him. "It's good. It's really good."

Another kiss. I loved that he was a kisser, that he was reaching to me with his mouth as often as I reached for him.

He was restraining himself, but I couldn't tell if it was for me or for him. And then he asked, "Was it too much? Before?"

"No, I loved it. I wanted it." I shivered as he hit a particularly sensitive spot. "But this..."

"This is special," he finished for me.

I had to blink back tears. Shit, I was an emotional mess. "This is love."

He surprised me with a shake of his head. "This is trust. I'm completely vulnerable right now. Completely bared."

I clung harder to him, digging my fingers into his back when he adjusted his angle and hit me even deeper. "It's love, too," I insisted.

"Yeah. It is."

We stayed like that, him rocking in and out of me, whispering I love yous, both of us clutching to each other. Trusting each other. Loving each other. If we didn't conceive a child tonight, we were still planting something new. Something that would grow. Something that would bind us forever.

Whatever came tomorrow, whatever our future brought, neither of us were going to face it alone.

FOURTEEN
CADE

The first thing I was aware of when I woke up was my phone buzzing.

The second thing was that Jolie wasn't in my arms.

Trying to ignore the panic of her absence, I checked who was calling then answered. "About time you checked in."

"It's not even nine yet," Donovan said, sounding like he'd been awake for hours. Likely the man never slept. "I figured you'd still be sleeping."

"I figured I'd hear from you last night." I pulled the phone away to check the exact time. Eight thirty-seven. The alarm I'd set was due to go off in eight minutes. "It's not like we're under a time crunch here."

"Forgive me for having my own long-lost love to woo."

"God, no. I can't picture you wooing." In my mind, Donovan's version of the term looked more like a kidnapping and hostage situation.

"I get it. The kids never like to think about their parents having sex. Daddy won't talk about it anymore."

"Fuck, don't. Do not ever refer to yourself as Daddy again." I shuddered.

"I think I just proved my point."

"Can we please get to what you've found out?" The longer we

stayed in this house, the more my skin itched. It didn't help that I'd woken up alone.

"Not a lot, but enough. Leroy said the investigation is real top secret, but he let me know that he feels pretty good about it. They apparently have an informer and tabs on the girl who went missing before Thanksgiving, Cassie Benito, and they haven't made their move yet on Stark because they want to be sure they can get her out before anyone gets tipped off. But it's looking like an any-day-now bust."

I waited for relief to sweep through me, something that I wouldn't truly be able to feel until we were gone. "In other words, it's time to get out of here."

"That would be my advice."

I scrubbed my face, trying to wake up enough to get me thinking what was next.

Donovan was ahead of me. "Are you wondering if you should still plant the drive?"

That was exactly what I was getting to. "An informer doesn't necessarily mean the deal is sealed."

"It was a different situation when you tried to press charges," he said, knowing exactly what I was thinking. "The FBI wouldn't be involved if they didn't have something more solid. With that said, you know what I'd do."

Donovan didn't let anything happen without being sure it would happen how he wanted it to happen. He'd still plant the drive.

I'd promised Jolie I'd destroy the motherfucker, and for that reason, I was leaning toward D's thinking.

On the other hand, I was feeling...good. For the first time in a real long time. Vengeance wasn't as high on my priority list as it had been a few days ago.

"I'll leave it up to Jol." This had been her show from the beginning. I wasn't going to take over calling the shots.

"Pussy. Oh, while we're on the subject. Hold on a sec." The sound muffled, but I could hear him saying something to Sabrina about naked breakfast in bed, an indicator that this call needed to be over ASAFP.

"Whatever you decide," he said when he returned to me, "let me know when you're ready for me to set up an appointment for that new tattoo of yours. Nate has a guy if you'll be back in the city soon."

That goddamned tattoo bet he'd made with me only a week ago. He'd said I'd be in bed with Jolie before the week was out, and if I was wrong, he got to pick my next tat.

"Fuck off," I said. Wasn't Sabrina enough to occupy him? He still had to keep his fingers in my business as well?

But I supposed it was his need to meddle that had gotten us this far, so I thanked him for the information and told him I'd keep him updated before I hung up.

Awake now, I stretched and sat up. Except for my state of nakedness and my T-shirt wadded up on the floor, there was no trace that Jolie had spent the night in my arms. I might have thought I'd dreamed it all without that bit of proof. Had that really happened? Had she really told me she loved me? Did I really fucking believe her?

Fool that I was, I really fucking did.

I was eager to go find her, not completely because I doubted anything that had happened, but also because I wanted to spend as little time apart from her as possible.

First, though, we had to work on getting out of the house before Stark showed up.

I dressed quickly, stowing yesterday's clothes in my suitcase, and was folding the blankets I'd grabbed from the linen closet when I became aware of someone in the room behind me.

I was smiling when I turned, expecting to see Jolie. Instead, I found Tate, rumpled but awake, already wearing a snow cap as though he was headed out. "We're ready to go when you are."

"Your mom send you?" Why hadn't she come herself? I told myself I wasn't worrying, but it was a lie. She'd burned me before. It was only natural that our new status felt fragile.

"No, she's doing her hair. I'm supposed to be loading up the car—which I did—and then I thought... I don't know. I guess I was just wondering when you wanted to take off."

He was nervous, too, I noticed now. Of course he was. He thought I was his father, and I hadn't yet acknowledged him as my son, and here we were getting ready to head out, and the poor kid probably didn't have any idea where that left us.

No wonder Jolie had been fretting about him last night. This was a big thread to be left dangling.

I ran my hand over my beard, trying to decide what I could say to make this better for now without stepping on his mother's toes. Things said in the dark didn't always hold as much weight in the light, and I thought about the offer I'd made. Tested whether I still meant it when I said I'd be his father if she'd let me, and I wasn't surprised to realize I still did.

I hoped she let me.

But that was her decision to make and not one I could pressure her into, so I'd have to give different assurances to Tate for the time being. Which wasn't hard because, regardless of what I was to him, I had once been a teenager whose mother had brought a new man into my life. I knew what it felt like to have no power in that situation.

Whatever else I was allowed to give him, I could at least give him the opportunity I never had. "I'm ready any time," I said, "but listen, Tate. I'm glad you came back here. I had something I wanted to talk to you about."

He perked up like I'd just offered him the keys to Donovan's Jag. "Yeah? Sure. What is it?"

"Well." I leaned against the arm of the couch, careful not to remember how I'd had Jolie propped up there while I'd fucked her the night before, hoping the reduction in my height made me a little less formidable. "I wanted to let you know that I am..." I hesitated, not because I was unsure of what I wanted to say, but because it was the first time I'd declared it out loud to someone other than Jolie. "I am very much in love with your mother. Always have been, to be honest. We'd lost each other for a while there, and now that we've reconnected, I'd very much like to be in her life. In your life, too. If that's all right with you?"

He blinked a few times—his excitement wasn't so palpable—and I had a feeling he was getting choked up. "Yeah, yeah." He cleared his throat. "That would be all right with me. Does Mom know?"

My smile came easily. "Yes. I've discussed it with her."

"Oh. Okay." He shifted his weight from one foot to the other. "And did she say anything to you? About me?"

I knew what he was asking and quickly choreographed my own dance around it. "Some. I'm eager to learn more. Like I said, I want to be in your life as well as hers. I don't want to take her from you, and I don't want you to feel like I'm only interested in her. Though, I know it can be hard letting a stranger in, especially at your age. I certainly didn't have a good experience with my stepfather."

"Stepfather?"

Fuck. I saw the natural leap he'd made after I'd said it. It was what I intended to be to him—if not more—but that was jumping too far ahead. "I just meant... Well. Maybe eventually. Or not... Look. I was trying to relate as best as I can."

I sounded like an idiot.

I wiped my sweaty palms on my jeans and straightened to my full height. "The point is, I really want you to be okay with...um, me. Being around."

He returned my grin. "I'm okay with that. For real." His eyes drifted somewhere behind me while he considered something. "My grandfather was really that terrible, wasn't he? Like I know he was. It would just help to have some details?"

I nodded.

He had a right to know, didn't he? He'd been a victim himself, even if he didn't remember it very well, and Stark was part of him, awful as that was to think about.

But opening up about the details was a fucking hard ask. Jolie and I hadn't even ever talked about it. Not really. We knew we were both suffering, and that was enough. It wasn't any wonder that she hadn't wanted to tell her son about it.

I would tell him, I decided. I would take the burden from her, if she needed me to, but that had to be her choice. "We'll talk about it," I promised. "But not today. In the meantime, I think you should ask your mother about it."

"Yeah. Okay."

"And don't feel like it has anything to do with you if she has a hard time talking about it, okay? It's going to be a hard conversation for her. She carries a lot of hurt from that man."

He nodded, and I knew he understood when he spoke next. "I hope that means you'll be extra careful not to hurt her too."

I'd spent so much time concerned with how she'd hurt me that imagining the flip side was possible almost made me laugh. "She's lucky to have you, kid. And I would do absolutely anything for your mother. Anyone who hurts her, I will take them down, including myself if necessary. I promise."

"Good. I'll hold you to it." He looked down at my suitcase, possibly searching for a change of subject since this one had gotten so heavy. "Is this ready? Want me to put it in your car?"

That was a good question. Mine was the rental, and whether or not I held on to it for much longer depended on what happened next. "I'd appreciate that. Thanks."

"Anytime."

I let him get a head start, eliminating any more awkwardness he might feel by my presence, then followed after him to the front of the house and then went upstairs where I assumed Jolie was still getting ready. I slipped into her room—my old room—without knocking and found her bent over, ass in the air, tugging on a boot.

"What a lovely sight," I growled.

She twisted her head to give me a mock scowl. "Predator."

"If you're the prey, then definitely yes." I pulled her into my arms before I thought about it too hard. She hadn't showered, and this close, I could smell the faint whiff of sex on her, and it was all I could do not to press her against the wall and fuck her again right now. "I woke up without you."

She placed her palms on my chest. "I wanted to be there, trust me. I didn't think Carla would appreciate walking in on us naked on her couch."

"Might have been fun to scandalize her, though."

"I was more worried about Tate," she admitted.

"As long as you still..." I didn't know how to finish it, so I trailed off, letting her assume an ending.

"Oh, I still. All of it." She tipped her chin up, begging to be kissed, but when my mouth was an inch above hers she asked, "You, still?"

"Every single word." I pressed my lips to hers, and the commitment she'd made in words was verified with her kiss, a kiss that went on a little too long, and by the time I pulled my mouth away, my pants were uncomfortable.

"How did we ever manage to keep our hands off each other?" I stretched the distance between us so our bodies were no longer flush, but I held on to her waist.

"Then or this past week?"

"I don't think we actually managed this past week. Then, well, I suppose your father was deterrent enough."

"Yeah." Her body sagged at the mention of Stark, and I hated that he still had that effect on her. Hated that I couldn't make everything disappear just by holding her in my arms.

At least I could give her some good news. "Hey, I heard from Donovan." Quickly, I filled her in on the status of the FBI investigation and what I'd learned from my earlier phone call.

"So we don't have to plant evidence," she said when I'd caught her up.

"It couldn't hurt, I don't think. But it sounds like they have a solid case without it." I tried not to let my preference show in my tone so that this decision would be all hers.

She looked down at her hands as they played with the collar of my flannel button-down. "Is it terrible if I just want to walk away right now and never look back?"

"Why would that be terrible?" It was a fucking relief.

"Because I dragged you into this, and everything you've done so far, like coming here, would be a waste of—"

I cut her off. "None of this past week has been a waste." I lifted her chin so she would look at my eyes. "I'm walking out of this house with you. And with Tate. There is nothing more I could want or hope for, so don't even go down that road of regret. You hear me?"

She took a breath in, her chest stuttering as she did. Then she smiled. "I love you."

"Just keep telling me that." I kissed her quickly. Then again. Then not so quickly.

When her arms snaked around my neck, I knew I had to come to my senses before our clothes ended up on the ground. I pulled farther away from her this time but held her hands in mine. "I'm guessing Tate needs to be in school tomorrow. And you as well?"

She blinked, as though she'd forgotten the world that existed outside of our bubble. "Yes. I suppose we do."

"Okay then. I'm coming with you to Boston." I wasn't asking. "We can figure out what's next from there."

She was beaming now. "All right. There's got to be a place to return the car in Hartford. We could meet there and then drive the rest of the way together."

It wasn't a bad plan, but I'd already thought this through. "Actually, I was thinking I'd return the car in Boston."

Her forehead creased in question.

"It's only a two-hour drive, and I thought you might want the time alone with Tate."

"Oh." She let go of my hands, taking a step back, and I hoped it wasn't because she thought I'd overstepped with the suggestion. "I haven't..." She started again. "Did you really—?"

Again, I interrupted. "I said I meant everything I said last night, and I really do. Even that. I will be his father, in whatever way you'll let me, and you don't have to decide that right now. But even if you leave that for later, he needs to hear something about me from you. About what you want me to be in your life. It's not fair to just bring me in without that conversation."

"Ah, fuck. You're right." She ran her hands through her hair. "I can't believe I didn't think about that. You must think I'm a terrible mother."

"God, no." I closed the distance between us. "Never. I'm elated that you're as wrapped up in me as I am in you, and the only reason I'm letting you out of my sight for two seconds is because I don't want anything to fuck up what's going to be between us—between *all* of us—including starting off on the wrong foot with him."

"He's going to be happy about this, you know."

"I know." She gave me a suspicious look. "I might have already laid the groundwork with him."

"What did—?"

"It doesn't matter. You can talk to him, and when we meet up in Boston, we'll go from there."

I would never get tired of her adoring gaze. "Did I mention that I love you?"

"I love you, too, baby." What I meant was I love you more, but that wasn't relevant. "We should get going. Your father might have gotten an early start, and we don't want to be here when he shows up."

Fifteen minutes later, after Carla had given them a stiff goodbye, I put Jolie in the passenger seat of Tate's Versa with a promise to follow soon behind. I wanted to do a final sweep of the house first to be sure there wasn't any evidence of our visit, and I supposed I wanted to be alone for my own goodbye with Carla.

Not *wanted*—needed.

She'd been as much of a hanging thread over the years as Jolie had been, and while I was now certain I wanted to follow Jolie's string, I was also certain I wanted to cut my mother's completely.

As if she suspected as much, she was waiting in the foyer when I walked back into the house. "Langdon called while you were out there. He's on his way home. Should be here in less than an hour."

"Good thing I'm about out of here then."

"Yes, quite good. You don't want him to find you here."

My curiosity got the better of me. "What would he do if he did?"

"Probably kill you."

"And you'd let him?"

She stared at me indignantly, as though she couldn't believe I'd need to ask.

I couldn't believe she thought I already knew the answer.

"Never mind," I said, realizing I probably didn't want to know.

I also realized there was nothing more I needed from her. There wasn't a loose end here. I'd already put her in the past, and when I walked out that door, if I never saw or heard from her again, I wouldn't be disappointed at all.

Without another word, I brushed past her upstairs to do my final walk-through and then back downstairs to check out the den.

I found nothing. We'd left the place as we'd found it. As though we'd never been there. As though we hadn't found ourselves again inside these walls.

The house was perhaps a harder goodbye than my mother. I hadn't gotten a real chance for one the first time I'd left, and this time...

It should have been easier to part with this place, with all its haunted memories. The problem was that, as horrible as those memories were, I couldn't separate them from the moments that I'd had with Jolie. They came together—the good and the bad. Without one, there wasn't the other, and I wouldn't trade anything for what I had with her. Not even the hell that we'd been through.

But that hell was over now. Only heaven on the horizon.

The sooner I got to that horizon, the better.

When I came back to the foyer, my mother was still in the spot I'd left her. "Are you going home with her?"

I considered what answer I wanted to give her. She wasn't important enough to be considered an enemy any longer, but she didn't deserve anything satisfying. "It doesn't matter," I told her eventually. "None of us are your concern any longer."

She stuck her chin out defiantly. "Tate's phone number had a Massachusetts area code. And it only took him a couple of hours to get here. That doesn't make it hard to guess where they're living."

My back went straight. "Is that some kind of threat?"

She held her stance for several seconds before she sighed. "I don't know what it is, Cade. I was trying to point out that I already know more than you want me to know, so does it really matter if I know anything else?"

"I'm going home with her." I only told her because I wanted her to realize I'd be with Jolie going forward, in case she did mean her statement as a threat. "I'll be staying with her from now on." I'd have a really good security system installed if Jolie didn't have one already.

"All right then." She looked like she wanted to say more, but I didn't care enough to pry it from her.

I turned to the door, and maybe it was easier when I wasn't facing her because she spoke to my backside. "There's one thing, Cade, that you should know."

Jesus, not this.

I couldn't take anything she had to offer—an explanation, an apology, a final defense. Whatever it was, it wouldn't be enough, and if it wasn't enough, it wasn't worth hearing.

Telling her as much was a waste of energy.

Without acknowledging the remark, I put my hand on the doorknob.

"It's about Tate's father. Did she tell you who it is?"

How she was able to find the one weakness she could exploit, I had no idea. Maybe she'd learned from her husband.

I debated. Told myself to leave. Told myself the answers were waiting for me, already on the road to Boston, as soon as I was willing to hear them.

But if they were already waiting for me, what was the harm in hearing what it was that Carla thought she had to add to the conversation?

I turned my head toward her. Then my whole body. Didn't say a word. I refused to give her more than that. I shouldn't be giving her even this.

"I let myself believe he was yours," she said. "Because I wanted him to be, I admit that. It was naive. But if he's not yours, then it has to be..."

Shit, I was exhausted. "Spit it out, Mom. It has to be...who?"

"My husband."

FIFTEEN
JOLIE

A month ago

MY HEART TOOK off at a gallop with the sound of a door banging shut in the kitchen. I hadn't heard the garage open—a sound I'd been listening for—but Carla had mentioned that it had been replaced recently. Apparently, the new one was whisper quiet.

I shouldn't have had feelings about that, but I did. The whine of the old one had frequently acted as an alarm, telling us my father was home and to be en garde. Even though it had been years since I'd lived in the house, the missing siren felt like a victory in his favor. Just one more way that he could control the lives of those around him. Keep them on edge and unaware of when he'd next return.

It was only Carla living here now, of course, but I was definitely on edge at the moment.

This was a bad idea. I shouldn't have come.

The only movement I made was to strain my ears, listening for conversation that would verify his presence.

"Whose car's outside?" he asked.

Carla's voice was too hushed to hear her response, or maybe I wasn't trying hard enough since my head was suddenly distracted with paranoia. I'd taken the train and rented a car so that he couldn't trace my license plate, but with my father came unreasonable fears. What if I'd forgotten something? Had I left my rental receipt with my information on it in the front seat? Had I locked it? I could picture him opening the door and sniffing around, never mind that whoever owned the car might think it a violation. It was parked in front of his house, and that was all the permission he needed.

Anxiously, I found the key fob in my pocket and clicked the lock button. The beep that sounded meant it had already been locked.

That was good. Still, I didn't feel relieved.

And I wasn't at all ready when a moment later, the kitchen door swung open, and there he was, tall and looming, as formidable as ever.

I scrambled to my feet, an automatic act of respect that I immediately regretted. I'd told myself I'd carry myself with confidence. He didn't have any power that I didn't give him and all the other sorts of mantras therapists had given me over the years.

They seemed easier to believe when he wasn't standing in front of me. Now my knees were shaking, and though I hadn't tried to use it yet, I knew my voice wasn't all there.

He stared at me for what seemed like an eternity, and I couldn't help wondering about what he saw. How mad was he about the dyed blonde hair? Did he notice the fifteen pounds I'd gained since I last saw him? Did he prefer me with the curves?

I was disgusted with myself for caring, and yet I couldn't deny that I did. Despite everything he'd done to me, not as intensely as I'd once cared, but blatant enough to have to acknowledge. I shouldn't have expected less. The desire to please him was so ancient within me that I often wondered if it had been the first part of me to form when I was still a cluster of cells in my mother's womb.

No, that was the lie he'd convinced me of.

I didn't really want to please him. *He* wanted me to please him, and he'd groomed me to believe it was my choice instead of the other way around.

But I could tell myself that all day, and it still wouldn't feel any different standing in front of him. Wherever the desire came from, it was there, and it was persuasive, so when his lips curled in revulsion, I felt the shame he meant me to feel.

"You have some nerve showing up here." He hadn't even bothered to take his coat off. His careful, meticulous self had been shocked enough by the announcement of my presence to forgo his coming-home routine. That should have felt like a win. "What's it been? Eight years now?"

There was a trick here somewhere. Had he really not cared enough about my absence to know how long it had been, or was he trying to throw me with his air of disinterest? Was he trying to figure out if I knew the correct answer?

Like always, I found myself questioning my response, as if it might be tied to a punishment.

He doesn't have any power that I don't give him.

I gave the truth. "Ten years."

"A decade. Well." He wore a satisfied smile when he looked me over this time, and I couldn't decide if that meant I'd said the right thing or the wrong thing. "I suppose you aren't here for a social visit."

I shook my head.

"Of course not. To my office then."

I felt the color drain from my face. "I'd prefer we stay here to talk."

As soon as I'd said it, I knew I'd fucked up. Letting him know what I wanted gave him the upper hand, and he didn't hesitate to play it. "The dinner table is for eating. You're more than welcome to stay for a meal, but if you want to have any real discussion, it will take place in a room suited for such."

I looked helplessly to Carla who stood behind him, as if she had any ability to save me. Her blank expression was a reminder for how to school my own as I pondered my choices. If I said no, this conversation was over before it started. If I said yes, he'd win the round. But maybe that would make him more amenable to losing the next?

I knew right then it was a lost battle, no matter what I did. That I should march out the door without another word, and never look back.

If I'd come for myself, I would have.

But I'd come for Tate.

"Lead the way," I said, surprising myself with the steadiness of my voice. It didn't have to be a lost battle. I'd known how to appeal to him at times in the past. I could find a way to appeal to him now.

Whatever bravery I'd found to follow after him, it left me at his office door. I stood on the threshold, watching him as he took a seat behind his desk, unable to move my feet any farther. This room had been a place of torture for as long as I could remember, and while I tried not to bring the past to mind, countless atrocities played out before me. They rolled together. A snatch from one incident layered with a scrap from another, turning a lifetime's worth of memories into a short reel of terror.

It's just a room, I told myself.

Standing in the hall wouldn't erase the things that had happened inside the room. Walking in willingly might even help me take back some of what I'd lost every time I'd walked in by force.

It was complete bullshit.

"I'm moved to see you hesitate, Julianna. It appears you consider this place as I do—special."

He was trying to goad me, and it worked. I stepped into his lair. "If by special you mean should be burned down, then yes. I do feel that way."

He let out a patronizing chuckle. As though he thought me adorable, and I hated myself for giving off that appearance. Adorable meant vulnerable. Vulnerable meant able to be hurt.

"We haven't even begun the discussion, and you've already moved to hostility." He clicked his tongue. "This might be a fun evening after all."

He'd changed. Once upon a time, he would have pretended he didn't find any delight in the things he did to me. Now, he was brazen enough to flaunt it.

. . .

I TOLD myself it was courage on my part—not fear—that dared to not close the door behind me when I crossed to the chair in front of him. Dropping my purse on the ground next to me, I sat down, keeping my spine straight.

He eyed the open door with an eyebrow raised but didn't fight me about it. I told myself that was another win for me and that it meant I was safe.

Stupid me, I felt the need to test it. "Careful. You'll give Carla the wrong idea."

"My wife respectfully stays out of my business, whether the door is open or not."

My stomach dropped until it felt like it was hanging between my knees, and I had to coach myself calm. Just because he thought that was the case didn't make it true. She wasn't completely devoid of humanity. She'd helped me leave. She'd help me again if I needed her.

I hoped to God she wouldn't get the chance to prove me wrong.

Before I could get my wits enough to drive the conversation, my father spoke again. "I'm sure you have an agenda, Julianna, but considering how you left without a note or warning or forwarding address, I believe I should be allowed to ask some questions. Where are you living these days?"

I shook my head, half in response to him and half to myself. I'd already lost any advantage I had by surprising him, and I had no idea how to take back the reins. I'd vowed to myself that I wouldn't tell him anything about my life, and I intended to keep that vow, but I hadn't expected to be grilled. Which made me an idiot because of course he'd grill me.

"You don't think I have a right to that. After all this time. What are you afraid I'll do with that information?"

Come after me. Hurt me. Hurt Tate.

Honestly, my fears weren't even that tangible. I didn't really expect him to get in his car and drive to Boston and torment us. I didn't want him to know where I was because I didn't want him to exist at all, and that meant he couldn't have access to me in any way, shape, or form.

When I remained silent, he poked again. "I at least deserve to hear about Tate."

Red flashed before my eyes. He didn't deserve shit, and I had to fight the urge to tell him exactly that. It was only because that was what he expected that I was able to bite my tongue.

"Actually, Tate is the reason I'm here," I said, seeing the opportunity to take the wheel. I swallowed the bad taste, ashamed of myself for using my son as bait even while knowing it was the most sure way forward. "He's a very smart kid with a promising future. I'm pretty confident he could make it into one of the best schools for college, though probably not with full rides. You know how little financial aid covers, and I don't have the means to pay the difference."

I tried to give as little details as possible, leaving out that Tate was hoping to study engineering and looking specifically at MIT. He could live at home then, which would eliminate the expense of room and board.

"Of course he's a smart kid. It's in his DNA."

He was complimenting himself, but I knew he wanted me to say thank you, and the words slipped out before I had a chance to think about them.

It didn't earn me any points. "That's pretty ballsy of you, don't you think? Showing up here after a decade to ask for money?"

I'd expected this, and I managed to remember the comeback I'd prepared. "No. I think it's pretty reasonable. Legally, you have a responsibility toward him."

"Is that a threat? Because the statute of limitations is in my favor."

"Yes, you made sure to keep me under your thumb until that expired."

"I'm sorry that's how you choose to view my love and care."

I bit back a laugh and reminded myself that riling him up wasn't the way to get what I was after. "I'm not threatening you, Dad. I'm here because you promised to take care of him, and I have faith you'll live up to your word."

"Is that right?" His smile was smug. He knew the tactic I was playing, which meant it was a failed move. Flattery had always been the way to win his favor, but not if he didn't believe it was genuine. "I seem to remember that promise came with the agreement that you'd stay here."

"The agreement was that I wouldn't leave *then*." I couldn't bring myself to mention Cade, afraid I'd be too emotional if I did. "I didn't realize it relied on me staying forever."

"That's why you should have had a conversation with me about it before you took Tate and ran away. I have rights where he's concerned, and as he's not yet eighteen, those rights have definitely not expired."

Now *that* was a threat.

He wouldn't follow through, would he? Admit to everyone his relationship to my son?

I ran through the logic behind it in my head. Too much time had passed for him to be arrested for what he'd done to me, but his reputation would be destroyed. The school would have to close. He wouldn't allow that to happen.

Which meant I could use it against him. "Go ahead and claim those rights then. I dare you."

He almost looked proud when he smiled this time. "I wouldn't want to drag Tate through the scandal, and I doubt that you would want that either."

"No." It was why I hadn't gone that route already. "So let's stop with the threats and just focus on him. A good education is what he needs, and I'm asking you to provide that for him. That's all. Nothing more."

"You want me to write you a check and just let you leave with it? No questions asked?"

Ideally. "That would be great."

"How about this." He stood up and casually circled around in front of his desk while every muscle in my body went on high alert. "I'll pay for Tate's education in full. If he graduates from Stark Academy."

"Oh, no. No. No." The suggestion alone made me want to scream.

He leaned against the desk, unbothered by my refute. "We're a prestigious school, Julianna. Only the top kids in the nation make it in. He'll get into any college he wants with us on his transcript. This is the offer of a lifetime."

"No, not happening. Not a chance."

"You don't want good things for him after all? What if I promised he could stay in the dorms?"

I didn't even take a beat to consider. "There's no way in hell I'm letting you anywhere near him. Ever. You got that?"

"Ah, so you don't really want what's best for him. You want what's best for *you*."

Despite my better instinct, I let him get to me with that. "Fuck you." How many times had he pretended what was best for him was really best for me? "You're a hypocrite to say that to me, and you fucking know it."

"The mouth on you. You used to always be so prim and proper—yes, sir, no, sir. Where did that come from? I like it."

My stomach curled, and this time I nearly choked on bile. "This was a mistake." I picked up my purse off the floor and stood.

But before I could take a step toward the door, he'd grabbed my arm.

"Don't touch me," I snarled. I tried to pull away too, but he held me too tightly. A panic that I hadn't felt in years spread through me like a wildfire in the brush, and since there was no longer a chance of me controlling what showed on my face, he knew exactly what was going on inside me.

There was no doubt that he liked that, too. "You don't like that option, princess, then I'll give you another." He wrapped his other arm around my waist and wrenched me closer. So close my face would be mere inches from his if I wasn't leaning back as far as I could, and I didn't have to ask what his other option was because it was very much implied.

It was also crystal clear that he wasn't really giving me the option. "You can keep struggling, if you want," he said, his eyes dark. "You know it will go fast if you cry."

"You disgust me." I disgusted myself as well. Tears were already falling, and I could feel myself turning back into the girl I'd always been with him—a girl who didn't fight back. A girl who knew there was no escape. A girl who had learned that fighting only drew it out longer.

No. I wasn't that girl anymore. I was a full-grown woman. I was a mother. I was not his to use and defile and humiliate.

I lifted my knee, intending to aim for his crotch, but he closed his thighs tight around mine, restricting my movement. "The more you fight me, the more I want to hurt you."

He would, too. He'd hurt me in so many vile ways that I'd come to prefer the rape. Sometimes, I'd even believed that I should be grateful for it. I was ashamed of how many times I'd thanked him afterward. How I'd even thought that it was somehow a show of his love.

I was ashamed now that I'd thought the same man who'd raped and abused me for years might have had enough heart to help take care of Tate.

I was such an utter fool.

But I still had a free hand. And whether it was foolish or not, I brought it up to his throat and squeezed. As hard as I could. Digging my nails into his skin and pressing against his airway.

"Let me go!" I screamed, knowing it was futile. He was bigger and stronger than me, and when he wrestled out of my grip, he'd make me pay, but I put all my energy into it, and when he let go of my other arm so that he could pull at the hand choking him, I added it to the effort, squeezing and squeezing and squeezing until he punched me so hard that I saw stars, and my grip loosened involuntarily.

Before I got my balance again, he'd grabbed both my wrists.

"Langford?"

He froze at the sound of Carla's voice. I turned my head to find she was standing in the doorway, and though she managed to not look surprised at what she saw, she did look intent.

"Not now, Carla," he said, a dismissal.

Help me, I said with my eyes.

She barely looked at me, but she didn't leave. "Dinner's ready. You won't like it if it's cold."

He took another several beats to make his decision. When he finally let me go, he did it with a push, sending me to my knees. "Perfect timing. Julianna was just leaving."

I scrambled to my feet, then backed away from him, afraid to take my eyes off of him before I made it to the door. Once I did, Carla made room for me to pass by without actually looking at me. "Sorry to hear that. I'll be sure to clear up the extra place setting."

Maybe it was the best she could do without getting herself punished. She'd most likely suffer later for her intervention, and maybe I should have felt grateful to her for that.

But the only thought in my mind as I drove away was too loud and persistent to drown out everything else, and I committed to it fully before I considered the consequences or whether or not it was even feasible—one way or another, my father had to die.

SIXTEEN
JOLIE

Present

WE ONLY MADE it fifteen minutes before I made Tate pull over so I could take over driving.

Once I was behind the wheel, I turned off my phone, wanting to model appropriate driving behavior, then reassured him as I pulled out into traffic. "It's not that I don't trust your skills behind the wheel."

I cringed at the lie. It was exactly the reason I'd made him switch places. "I mean, you're a good driver. I just have more experience, and the roads are slick."

"I drove down here without a problem." It was impossible to tell how upset he really was since his general teenage demeanor was sullen, even when he was in a good mood. "Seems that should have been enough to prove myself."

"That was different."

"Because you hadn't wanted me to come?"

"Because I hadn't been in the car with you." I reached over and slapped his feet down from where he had them propped on the dashboard.

Now he scowled at me. "It's my car!"

"That I pay for."

He harrumphed. Then he turned up the radio and curled up as much as his long body allowed, his head facing the passenger door. "I'd rather you drive anyway. I'm gonna sleep."

I considered letting him. His weekends were usually spent sleeping in, and even though it hadn't been me who had requested his presence in Connecticut, it had been because of me.

Plus, I needed to talk to him about more than just Cade's role in my life, and I was dreading it. Putting it off another few hours was tempting.

But procrastinating made it harder and harder to want to tell him the truth at all. And maybe it was for the best that I didn't. Why not take Cade up on his offer to keep up the ruse? I'd already been lying to my son for years. If I hadn't brought Cade back into his life, Tate would have never known he wasn't really his father.

Except that wasn't true either.

Eventually, Tate would have gone looking for Cade. He'd already done an internet search, and telling him he'd found the wrong guy would have blown up in my face when he got serious about his hunt. He would have realized the Cade he'd found had been the one in my life. A paternity test would be ordered...

I shuddered thinking how Tate might have discovered the truth.

With Cade's offer to step into the role of father, that potential disaster was averted. I should grasp onto the suggestion and let Tate continue to live a sheltered life.

It was what I wanted to do.

Nothing would have made me happier.

But the weekend back at my house had taught me there was no escaping my past. It didn't matter how much I ignored it or ran from it or kept it from my son—it was still there, buried under the foundation of my being, a fundamental element of who I was.

Having Tate there had made the lesson learned even more poignant.

Less avoidable anyway. Tate shared that history, and if he ever decided he wanted to know more—especially when my father was arrested and his life was scrutinized—what Tate could discover would be terrible and shocking.

It would be better coming from me.

And it would be best if I didn't try to pick and choose the secrets to keep and admitted everything.

I turned down the radio. "Before you drift off—"

"Too late. I'm already asleep."

"You're talking pretty clearly for someone who's asleep."

He groaned but turned his body so he was upright. Or as upright as a sixteen-year-old ever was when riding in a car. "What?"

"We should talk about your father." There. I'd said it. There was no going back now.

"Oh, I already know."

I glanced quickly at him in alarm. Cade wouldn't have told him the truth, and Tate's face was too passive to suggest that he'd somehow figured it out. "You know...what, exactly?"

"About you guys. Like, it was obvious anyway, the way you keep giving each other those starry-eyed lovebird looks. And Cade's suitcase was in your room, so I'm guessing he slept in there the night before I arrived."

"You saw that." It wasn't a question. More of a statement of acknowledgment on my part. An embarrassing acknowledgement. I could feel my cheeks go bright red. "I didn't realize you noticed."

He made an annoyed sound and followed it up with one of his favorite phrases. "I'm not dumb."

I somehow managed to refrain from rolling my eyes and tried to figure out what parental thing I should be saying. Not having dated much during his life, Tate wasn't used to seeing his mother as a woman, and I hadn't prepared how to talk to him about it. "That was probably awkward for you to see. I'm sorry about that."

He did roll his eyes. I could feel them rolling without looking. "Mom. I'm not twelve. I get how the birds and the bees work.

Remember that uncomfortable conversation that one day after fifth grade? Trust me, I know about sex."

Immediately, I wanted to know exactly what he knew about sex and how well he knew it, as well as who he might know it with, but I remembered Cade assuring me that Tate would tell me when he was ready and forced myself not to ask.

"Okay. Well. Okay." If he wasn't going to be embarrassed about my sex life, I could try not to be as well. "Glad you understand."

"Anyway, he told me he's going to be a part of our lives now and all that, and that's cool with me."

"Oh. He said that?" More and more, I was feeling I did not have the upper hand in this discussion.

Tate shifted in his seat. "Yeah. This morning. He said he was coming home with us and asked if I'd be okay with that."

That must have been what he'd meant about laying the groundwork. "And you are? Okay with that?"

He was quiet, and when I glanced at him, I found him studying his thumb, wearing a contemplative expression. "I'm okay with it for me, definitely. I guess I'm a little worried that you might not be okay with it for you, though."

I considered his thought process. He wanted to get to know the man he thought was his father, and that made sense. But why he thought I wouldn't want Cade around was a mystery to me. "I want him with me, Tate. I really do. I've never gotten over him, and I'm...well, I'm a little scared to have him back in my life, but just because relationships are always scary, and I'm out of practice with them. But I'm willing to take that risk because of how I feel about him and because I think he feels pretty strongly about me too."

"No, he does." He turned his head in my direction. "He told me he's in love with you anyway." Now he blushed.

God, what a character. Sex didn't faze him, but emotions got him flustered. It was sweetly innocent somehow, and if I hadn't been driving, I would have wanted to give him a hug or ruffle his hair.

Which would have annoyed him, so it was probably for the best.

"So you knew how he felt. Were you worried I might not feel the same?"

Out of my peripheral vision, I saw him give a one-shoulder shrug. "You just so rarely do anything for yourself, it seems. So if you're inviting him into your life because you want him to be there, then I think that's a really good thing for you, but if you're inviting him because you think that's what I want, then I'm going to feel really guilty about it."

My chest tightened. He was a thoughtful, caring kid, and I was bursting with pride about it, but now I also worried that I'd been too selfless in my child-rearing. Had I really made it seem like everything I did was for him? On the one hand, that was what a parent was supposed to do, wasn't it? My father certainly hadn't, and I'd promised myself I wouldn't be like that, but maybe I'd gone too far in my efforts and put a different sort of weight on my child's shoulders.

God, parenting was hard.

And I was good at overthinking. "It's not for you. I promise."

"Good." He grinned. "Then I'm really okay with it."

"It will be weird having someone else in our house. It's going to take some getting used to on both our parts, and if it's not working out for you, then you need to tell me, and—"

"We'll figure it out," he said, cutting me off before I once again offered to sacrifice my happiness. "I'm only around for another year and a half anyway."

I did not want to think about him leaving. So I didn't.

And I tried not to think too hard about how much damage could be done in a year and a half. Cade had only been in our household for a year, and that had completely changed the trajectory of his life.

Besides, Cade was not my father, and I was not Carla. "Yeah. We'll figure it out."

With that sorted, I tried to find another pathway back to my agenda.

Before I did, he spoke again. "Can I ask something, though?"

"Sure."

"If you both were so hung up on each other all this time, why did you ever get separated in the first place? Your dad kicked him out, right? But that didn't mean you couldn't keep in touch behind his back."

When I tried to look at the situation from his point of view, it seemed ridiculous. The easy answer could have been to blame it on poverty. Tate was a privileged kid in many ways—we'd struggled, but we'd never gone without the internet or a cell phone. Cade truly had nothing when he'd left, and explaining that to Tate was probably all he needed.

But that wasn't the truth, and I'd started this talk wanting to be honest. "It's complicated," I said. "And I'm not saying that as an excuse because I'm going to try to explain, but I'm also going to ask you to forget about logic when you're trying to understand because sometimes humans aren't logical, for a lot of different reasons, and that can make people seem really stupid, when in fact, some things are just *really complicated*."

"Uh...okay..."

Great preface, Jolie. Way to make things clearer.

I turned the radio from a low hum to off. "First, you should know, I had meant to run off with Cade after graduation. But then I found out I was pregnant with you." This didn't seem like quite the right moment to say that I'd been unsure of paternity, so I skipped that particular detail. "And I knew that if I left with Cade, we'd have nothing. No money, no healthcare, no family—and I didn't think that was the best situation to bring a baby into.

"And I didn't tell Cade that was why because I was afraid that if he knew, he'd try to change my mind, or he'd stay nearby, and I was pretty sure that if my father ever saw him again, he'd kill him."

"Literally kill him?"

I took a deep breath before I answered. "Yeah. He beat him up pretty badly as it was, and my father promised he wouldn't go after him if I stayed."

"He would have really gone after him?"

That was one of those questions that made me look stupid in retrospect. Feel stupid, too. "He said he would. And I believed him. That's one of the complicated things that's hard for me to explain because on the outside, it seems like I had so many other options. And I probably did. We could have gone to the police. We could have found a shelter. We could have tried to get the help of friends."

I paused for a moment, struck by all the ways I could have done things differently.

Then I shook off the regret. "But here's the thing about abusive relationships—the abuser wields all the power. I believed my father would do the terrible things he promised because he'd taught me time and time again that he would. It was impossible for me to see myself as capable of fighting back. I'd tried to report him in the past, and no one believed me, but my father knew what I'd tried to do, and I got punished for it. I got punished for anything and everything that I did that wasn't perfect, and after so many years of that, I had been trained to just try to make him happy. So it didn't matter if he would actually have gone after Cade—I believed he would, and that was enough to scare me into staying.

"And he was my father, Tate." I glanced at him and found him staring straight ahead, a slight frown on his face. "I thought he loved me. I thought that's what love was. I loved him too—almost as much as I hated him. He was the person who'd raised me. I trusted him. Trusted that he'd be awful. Trusted that he'd come after me. Trusted that he would always have power over me. He broke me before I'd finished forming, and that kind of broken is really hard to fix. Does that make any sense?"

Another shrug. "A little, I guess. It's hard to understand."

"It is. I get it." A car passed me, and when I looked at the speedometer, I realized I'd slowed down while I was talking.

I resumed my speed before going on. "The other thing that comes with abuse is shame. It doesn't make any sense to blame yourself for what happens to you." Realizing I sounded like the text on a support website, I shook my head and rephrased. "I was embarrassed about the things he'd done to me. It felt like it had to be my fault. That there was something wrong with me, and so when Cade showed up, and my father hurt him too, I did feel less humiliated. Less alone, at least. But I still wasn't able to talk about it, and not talking about it meant that I never told Cade everything that my father was doing."

"Like...what?"

I could hear a rhythmic flicking sound, and when I peeked at him, I saw his foot was resting on his other knee, and he was picking at the sole of his shoe.

"You mean, what did my father do to me?"

"Yeah." *Pick, pick, pick.* His focus was glued to his sneaker.

"Well." It was a fair question. Abuse ran the gamut, and I'd been pretty vague in most references to it so far. "Physically. He hit. And whipped. He liked to slap me a lot, but he rarely broke my skin. Cade, on the other hand—he especially liked seeing Cade bleed."

That was Cade's story to tell, though.

I needed to stick to my own. God, this was hard.

"Mental and emotional abuse was his specialty. He would degrade me. Call me worthless and stupid. He liked to confuse me and manipulate me. And he, uh." They were just words. I could say them. "He would do sexual things to me. That was what I never told Cade. And I think that was another reason why I didn't run away with him. Maybe even the main reason. I was afraid he'd find out, and I was just so, so ashamed."

I'd talked about it a lot in therapy those first years after I'd left home. Discussed and analyzed until I'd felt like I'd gotten a pretty good handle on how to move on.

Then I'd put all those memories in a box, buried it deep inside of myself, and tried never to think about it again. I'd been pretty successful until I had gone back home a month ago. One little encounter with my father, and the box flew open, and the memories and self-loathing were as vivid as ever.

My eyes stung as the fog of shame shrouded me now, and I made sure not to look at Tate until I was sure that no tears would fall.

When I was certain I wouldn't break down, I looked at him again, only to find he was fighting his own tears. Less successfully than I had.

"Oh, honey!" I put my hand on his thigh and quickly found a place to pull off the highway.

As soon as I had the car in park, I took off my seat belt and stretched my arm awkwardly over to rest on his shoulder. I desperately wanted to pull him in for a hug, but he was almost seventeen and self-conscious of any vulnerability, and he was already leaning as far from me as possible as he pinched at the corners of his eyes.

I had to settle for patting his shoulder. "I didn't mean to make you cry. Talk to me, can you? Tell me what you're feeling?"

He shook his head, refusing to look at me. "It's just... It just sounds really awful."

"Yeah. Yeah." I opened the glove box looking for a napkin or tissue and found only junk, so I shut it again. "Yeah, it was pretty awful. Which is why I haven't talked about it."

"But I wish I'd known."

"I know. I know." I *hadn't* known. It hadn't ever occurred to me that he would want to know. I was just talking, trying to say reassuring words. "I should have told you. It's hard to talk about. I didn't know how."

I remembered my purse on the floor in the back seat, and I reached in and dug around for a Kleenex while I patted his thigh. "I can tell you more, too, if you need me to. Not right now because this has already been a pretty heavy conversation, and I need a break from it, but if you need to know more in the future."

"Okay." He sounded choked up but less on the verge of breaking down.

Finally, I found a tissue, and he took it from me gratefully. He blew his nose, and once he was done sniffling, he said, "I'm sorry that happened to you."

"I am too," I said.

He looked at me—finally. "I suppose you want me to give you a hug now."

"I'd love one."

He took his belt off and reached his arms around me.

"I love you, kid."

"Love you, Mom," he mumbled.

He let me hold him for longer than he had in years, and even though he was the first to pull away, I was sure the hug had been for him as much as for me.

In typical fashion, he handed me his used tissue. "Do I look like your trash can?" I teased.

He gave a slight smile then swiped it from my hand, only to toss it in the back seat. "I think I know enough now, if that's okay. I don't need any more details."

"It's okay." It *was* okay. For now, anyway. Telling him who his real father was would probably count as more details, and considering how hard this had been on him, I imagined that conversation was going to be a doozy.

That could wait, though. This had been more than enough for one day.

"You okay enough for us to get back on the road?"

This time, his grin reached his eyes. "Can I drive?"

"Nice try."

"Fine." He gave a fake pout and refastened his seat belt as I steered the car back onto the highway. "I guess while you're driving, I'll tell you something."

"Tell me what?"

I could feel his blush even before he spoke. "Well, you see, there's this girl…"

SEVENTEEN
CADE

I had every intention of driving straight to Boston.

Or maybe I had no intentions at all. My mind was a storm. My vision was bright red. I had a surreal sense of both not being connected to my emotions and also being nothing but emotion, and that emotion was rage, rage, rage.

Blinding rage.

I didn't remember saying goodbye to my mother, or if I even did, I didn't remember getting in the rental car or pulling out onto the drive. Like the day before when I'd grappled with the knowledge that Jolie had a son, I was aimless. Then, though, I'd been numb.

Today, I was the exact opposite of numb.

I'd break my fist if I tried slamming the dashboard today.

And that was precisely what I needed to do—I needed to hit. I needed to pound. I needed to destroy.

Disconnected as I felt, somewhere a code of logic processed. I found my phone shoved into a pocket and tried to call Jolie. When it went straight to voicemail, I dialed again. This wasn't a conversation to have by phone. It was definitely not a conversation to have by voice message, but when she didn't answer the second time, I heard myself leaving a response. "You didn't tell me. How could you not. Tell. Me?"

Then I hung up and beat the phone against the dashboard until I lost my grip, and it flew out of my hand and into the back seat.

"Fuck!" I screamed into the empty car. "Fuck, fuck, fuck, fuck, fuck!"

Cursing and smashing my phone weren't helping. The storm inside me only escalated, the energy gripping me so tightly, I couldn't sit still. Rocking back and forth, I blinked the red from my eyes. Where the fuck was I?

The school was on the outskirts of Wallingford, and luckily, I'd driven away from the city rather than into it where there was no traffic on a Sunday because when I finally brought my focus to the road, I was well above the speed limit and wasn't even driving between the lines.

I moved the vehicle to the right lane, slowing down enough to realize I was near the reservoir, which was by a gun range. Maybe that was what had given me a course of action—the sign inviting me to practice my shooting. The reminder that I had Donovan's semiautomatic with me.

I pulled into the range's parking lot, hit the button to open the trunk, and left the car running when I climbed out. The gun was where I'd stashed it on Friday night, tucked into the inside pocket of my suitcase. I'd loaded the magazine when we'd arrived at Stark's house and hadn't taken it back out, which was not the way to store a gun, but it had made me sleep better in that suffocating hellhole knowing I had a loaded weapon within easy access.

Now, I tucked it into my coat pocket and closed the trunk, not bothering to zip the suitcase again. I glanced in the back window of the car as I passed on my way to the driver's seat and saw my phone lying on the floor. The screen was cracked. I wondered if it still worked.

I didn't wonder enough to find out.

If I had, maybe that would have thrown me off my current trajectory. I might have tried Jolie again and gotten her. I might have tried Donovan, who would have instantly given me a better plan. I might not have called anyone at all, but just the distraction of checking out the phone, that simple moment of pause, might have given me a chance to think. A chance to reason. A chance to acknowledge that if I got behind that wheel, there was no going back.

I didn't take that moment, and when I climbed in the front seat, I didn't hesitate at all before throwing the car into gear and peeling out of the icy lot.

Ten minutes later, I was back at the academy. As my emotions felt disconnected from my thoughts, so did my actions, and yet whatever part of me that was controlling my decisions had some sense of sanity because instead of going to the house, I found myself in the school lot.

So he won't know I'm waiting.

It was my own voice in my head and someone else's entirely.

I parked and locked the car, then set out on the mile trek to the house, careful to stay near the trees. When I got close enough, I veered off the path so I could approach from the back. As if I were a burglar daring enough to strike during daylight, my gun was pulled out and poised while I jogged hunched over until I got to the door that led into the garage. I peeked in the window.

Still only one car.

I checked my watch. It would be soon.

And as if the universe was for once working in my favor, a vehicle pulled into the driveway just then. I wouldn't have heard the garage door open after if I hadn't been listening for it, the lift was so quiet. A moment later, a car door slammed.

That quickly, he was here.

Or maybe the universe wasn't working in my favor because if I'd had to wait, I would have had time to think. Right now, I wasn't thinking at all. Not my conscious mind anyway. It was something more primitive driving me. An instinct. An impulse.

Favor or not, he was here, and reason was not.

I hugged the wall, my breaths coming fast but even, and even if I couldn't hear him inside the garage, I would have known when he passed by me. His essence inked dark and evil, and I could feel him through the layers of wood between us, shuddering through me like a ghost.

I waited until I'd heard the door to the kitchen close.

Counted to a slow ten.

Then tried the door to the garage.

It had rarely been locked during the day when I'd lived there, and it wasn't now. The kitchen door was never locked period, but it was solid with no window to peer in, and I wanted to keep the element of surprise on my side. I pressed my ear against it, listening. The sink was on. Then it turned off.

"You forgot ice," Stark said, his voice muffled but understandable.

"Ice maker's broken again," she said. "I already have a repairman coming tomorrow. I can get you some from the tray, but I know you prefer crushed."

I recognized the trepidation in her tone. She knew she would be blamed for the situation, but she was hoping she could soothe him anyway.

I hadn't forgotten that feeling. Remembering it made the hurricane of rage spin faster inside of me.

"This will be fine." His subtext said it clearly wasn't. "Fish is in the cooler. Don't leave it."

"I'll put it in the freezer now." Frantically, I looked for a place to hide, afraid he'd left the cooler in the car, but then she said, "You caught some big ones this time."

He grunted, unsatisfied with the praise.

"The weather's so good, I'm surprised you came back so early in the day. I figured you'd want to get in more time at the hole."

"There's a game at noon." College hockey, no doubt. He'd always enjoyed watching "young men duke it out." All the anger and aggression in the game, it was a sport made for him. "I wanted to be sure I was back in time."

"I'll make fried chicken then."

His voice was closer, and if she was across the room putting fish in the freezer, his back would be to me.

Again, it was instinctual. The thoughts didn't come fully formed. I just knew their likely arrangement, knew how they'd be standing when I quietly pushed the door open. Wasn't surprised to find I was right.

"Potato salad too," he demanded as I crept up behind him.

"Red potatoes okay?" When she turned back from the freezer, she saw me. There was no doubt. Our eyes met.

But though her brow wrinkled slightly, she didn't say anything until I had the gun out and pushed to the side of Stark's head. "Give me one good reason not to blow your brains out right this minute."

"Cade." My mother didn't sound at all surprised. It wasn't even an admonishment. The only emotion that I might have detected in her single word was relief.

I ignored her, lasering my attention on the man in front of me and repeated myself, slower this time. "One. Good. Reason."

His body had gone stiff, as any reasonable man's body would when the barrel of cold metal was pressed at his temple, but he played it cool. "So the prodigal son returns."

I wondered if he would have recognized my voice if my mother hadn't said my name. Wondered who else he might have thought was coming to get their reckoning. I'd always thought it had just been me and Jolie who deserved the gun-pointing kind of wrath. Then I'd learned that he'd been selling teenagers, and I'd realized there were plenty of others who would want to be in my position now.

Still, despite all the sins that he'd surely committed against countless others, all I cared about were the things he'd done to Jolie. The horrific, unspeakable, heartless things.

I was glad it was me here. Me with the weapon. Me who would make him pay.

I suddenly felt like this was what I'd been born for. This was the reason fate had brought me into the Stark household, into Jolie's life, and I was electric with the responsibility placed in my hands.

"Mind if I turn around?" he asked.

It pissed me off because I should have had him turn around already so I could keep an eye on his hands. Now if I let him, I'd be giving him power, and I refused to give him even a drop of it. "No. Hands up, and then don't move."

To his credit, he did as I said, and I actually thought he was taking me seriously for a moment.

Until he spoke again. "Call the police, Carla."

"Leave her out of it," I said.

"He won't shoot his own mother, and he's too smart to shoot me. Call them."

He was talking directly to her, so I did too this time. "You pick up the phone, and I'll kill him, Mom, so help me God."

She looked from me to him, to the gun, and back to me. Without saying a word, she turned and left the kitchen.

Shit.

For the first time since I'd left the house more than half an hour ago, I became aware of myself. Became conscious of thought. Became more than just blinding emotion.

I had a gun pointed to my stepfather's head, and my mother was likely calling the police.

What the fuck was I doing?

Fuck, fuck, fuck!

"Keep your hands up and walk." I was improvising. With the gun still at his temple, I put my other hand on his shoulder to guide him through the kitchen door into the dining room.

My mother wasn't there. Wherever she'd gone, it wasn't within sight. The smartest idea was to follow after her and be sure she didn't make any phone calls.

But none of this was smart, and when focused on that feeling I'd had of being fated for this, I knew exactly what I was doing. And that meant I didn't care if Carla called the cops. I just needed to be sure I did what I meant to do before they got to me.

I thought quickly.

The living room and Stark's office had windows open to the front. If the police came, I'd see them in time to act. The former had too many access points. His office was more contained. Since it had always been a place of torture, there was irony doing this there. I steered him in that direction.

I'd forgotten that the door would be locked when we got there.

"The key's in my pocket," he offered. He started to lower his hand.

"Keep your fucking hands up." I didn't trust him. I pushed the gun so hard against his skull that his head leaned to the side, reminding him who was in control.

His hands went back up.

"Which pocket?" I asked.

"Left coat."

I dropped my hand from his shoulder, stuck my hand in his pocket, and found his key ring. After making sure there wasn't a Swiss Army knife or anything on them, I handed them over. "Unlock the door, then drop the keys on the ground."

Collected as he seemed, I realized it was at least somewhat of a ruse because his hand shook as he fit the key in the lock.

Not that brave after all.

That was satisfying. And not altogether shocking. In my experience, the biggest bullies were usually the most terrified when they were bullied in return. A sick glee surged through me. How far could I take this? Could I make him beg? Could I make him cry? If he shit his pants, I'd be overjoyed.

I'd never felt so delighted about the prospect of hurting someone else. Was this what it felt like to be him?

A dissonance rang in my body. I wouldn't become him. And he had to suffer. Both were true, and I didn't know if they could coexist because I would take pleasure in making him suffer, and that was the very definition of becoming him.

What the fuck am I doing?

Back to that, it seemed.

One thought at a time.

"Open the door slowly, then hands back up, and walk in. I'm right behind you." I moved the gun so it was at the back of his head, still pressed to his skull so he wouldn't forget for a second that it was there. It was damn gratifying to realize my hand was steady as could be.

I didn't pull the door closed behind me. I liked having it open so I could hear my mother if she returned. The curtains were already open, so no one was sneaking in on me there. I'd been in here a couple of times, but the situation had been different. This time, I did a quick scan, noting the everyday objects just waiting to be turned into a weapon if given a chance. When I felt I had a proper inventory, I pushed Stark away from me then told him he could turn around.

"Keep your hands where I can see them," I warned.

He turned, flashing his hands like he was a magician trying to show there was nothing up his sleeve. That's where my attention was first—his hands—and then finally, I looked at his face for the first time in seventeen years.

He studied me as I studied him. He still had his coat on. He'd aged, of course. He didn't seem quite as tall. His hair was entirely gray now. The wrinkles in his face more prominent. Even still, he looked younger than he should. Was that some sort of magic trick of his? When he'd stripped his victims of their innocence, had it gained him his youth?

He didn't deserve to be so untouched by time, and he most certainly didn't deserve to look so smug. I felt an overwhelming desire to bring my hand with the gun down hard across his face. See how smug he looked then.

It was so fucking tempting.

I took several steps until I was right up in his face and placed the tip of the Glock under his chin. "One reason, Stark. Give me one reason why you deserve to wake up another day on this planet."

The gun moved with his throat as he swallowed. "I have a feeling you'd find it more satisfying to tell me why you think I don't."

"Don't fucking be smart with me."

"Wasn't trying to be. I know we parted badly, but it's a surprising reunion to say the least."

"You should have been scared to wake up with me putting a gun to your face every day of the last seventeen years. I should have done this sooner."

"Then do it."

I felt my finger tightening on the trigger while simultaneously, my bicep shook in restraint. *Do it. Fucking do it. Just fucking do it. For what he did to her.*

It was thinking of Jolie—not what he'd done to her, but of her face, telling me she loved me—that gave me pause.

With more strength than I knew I had, I pulled the gun down and turned it to point at him again. Then I took several steps back, keeping it pinned on him as I did. "Tell me—do you know you're evil incarnate, or do you really think you're a stand-up guy?"

He started to say something, but I could tell it was going to be another wisecrack. "The truth, asshole. Do you know what you've done to people? Do you know how you've ruined lives? Do you care at all?"

He sensibly considered before speaking. "Yes, I know that my actions have an effect on others. It's not in my nature to care."

"So you don't even feel bad? Of course, you don't." I hadn't ever believed that he felt bad for what he'd done to me, but to Jolie? I thought he'd at least pretend remorse. "Just one more reason why you shouldn't live."

He tried to shrug, like he didn't care whether he did or not, but it ended up looking more like a twitch. "It might help if you tell me what I'm on trial for."

"You know what you've done." Listing his crimes would only bring him pleasure.

"And you're planning to shoot me for it? There will be repercussions, I'm sure you realize that. Your mother is a witness. Will you kill her as well?"

I hadn't thought any of it through, obviously.

Because yes, I came back with one intention only, and it was to shoot him between the eyes. I'd wanted to watch the life fade from his body, I'd wanted to know he suffered, and I'd wanted him to know who was responsible and why.

But I'd hardly thought that far, let alone about what happened after.

I'd go to jail for Jolie. I would. I'd serve the time without blinking an eye.

But I couldn't stop remembering her in my arms the night before. The promises we'd made. Promises to be together and to never let her go, and if I killed her father...

Fuck.

There was no way Carla wouldn't turn me in. Would I ask Jolie to live a life on the run?

Stark had to see the battle in my eyes. "It's not too late to change your mind. Walk away now. I'll give you my word not to say anything."

"Like your word means anything."

"So it would be your word against mine. If you left before the police showed up, there would be little to press charges on."

He was trying to manipulate the situation, and I wanted to shoot him in the teeth for that alone. "Shut up for a minute. Just...shut up."

He was going to go down anyway. The FBI had him under investigation. He was already going to be destroyed. I really could walk away.

Would that be enough? Would he suffer enough?

"YOU DON'T HAVE A PLAN." The conceit had returned to his expression. "Which means you came here on impulse. What triggered you, I wonder."

"I said shut the fuck up!" I was in his face again, my hand on his throat, the gun at his temple. I'd lost control, if I'd ever had it in the first place. I wanted to shoot so badly I could already feel the kickback from the gun. Jolie had wanted him dead when she'd sought me out. If I'd known what he'd done to her, I would have agreed. I should shoot him right now and get it over with.

"How could you do that to her?" My hand squeezed at his throat. "Rape your own child. Get her pregnant. I should shoot your dick off, that's what I should do. Let you bleed out from it. That's what you deserve."

"Ah. You found out about Tate." He sounded more relaxed than he had, which was the only indicator that he hadn't been relaxed before, and that made me all the more eager to inflict the pain I'd offered.

"Yeah. I found out, you bastard. Did you get off on hurting him too?" I tasted bile in the back of my throat. Jol said she'd left because he'd hit him, and while I could barely stand to think about the possibility, it occurred to me now that it could have been more. "Did you rape your son like you raped your daughter?"

"Of course not. What I had with Julianna was special." I squeezed harder at that, and his next words came out more like a rasp. "Besides, Tate isn't my son."

I let go of his throat, only to strike him across the face with the gun. "You're trying to mess with me. That's not helping you any."

His nose cracked loud and began to bleed. "No, it's the truth."

"I already told you I don't believe a word you say." This time, I pressed the tip of the gun up to his eyeball.

"Fine, don't believe me," he spat. "But I had a vasectomy. The boy is yours."

I wouldn't fall for his lies. This was his specialty—the mindfuck. He knew exactly where a hit would land, and I would not give him that satisfaction. "She told me he wasn't, and I'm sure as hell not going to trust you over her."

"She told you that because that's what she thinks. I'm the one who told her that, and she believed it."

My hand was back at his throat. I didn't believe him for a second, and yet I couldn't stop myself from asking.

"It was the only way I could guarantee she wouldn't go running after you," he continued despite struggling to breathe. "I asked for two reports. One had Carla's swab. The other had a swab from some woman I paid on the street. I have the proof."

His face was starting to look blue. I squeezed harder. Harder.

Then I dropped my hand and stepped back.

"Where is this supposed proof?" I hated myself for falling for his trick. It was a terrible trick at that because he hadn't denied raping his daughter, just fathering Tate. Langdon Stark still needed to die.

But like I said, he knew where to throw the punch.

And this punch hurt.

Stark rubbed at his neck and did a good job at not appearing to be gasping for air while doing just that. He gestured behind him. "In the desk. Key's on the same ring as the door."

So this was the trick. Get me digging in the files, distracted, so he could overcome me or escape.

Without taking my eyes off him, I backed up to grab the keys off the floor. Then I brought them to him. "Get it."

He hesitated, calculating, maybe. Or still just trying to breathe.

After a moment, he took the keys.

He circled behind the desk and dropped in his chair. Just as he bent over, it occurred to me that I'd only looked in the locked drawer on the bottom left. I hadn't opened the bottom right, which meant I didn't know what he kept in there. I knew he had a gun in his bedroom nightstand. For all I knew, he had one there too.

"Wait. Which drawer is it in?"

He looked at me strangely. "Bottom drawer."

"Which side?"

"Left."

The keys had been in the front. Behind it had been hanging files that I hadn't looked through. There definitely hadn't been a weapon. "Okay. Go ahead."

I watched him as he bent down and jiggled with the lock. It clicked, and he slid the drawer open then flipped for several seconds through files.

"Hurry up, Stark. You're stalling."

He glared at me then pulled a folder out and dropped it on the desk. "It should be in here."

He sifted through the pages, and while it still wasn't quick enough for my taste, at least I could watch him do it now. "Here," he said eventually. He turned the report around to face me and handed it over.

I snapped it out of his hand but scanned it cautiously, keeping my gun trained on him. There was a lab logo at the top corner—Science-Life—followed by Julianna's name and address. Then in the center of the next line, the words **Paternity Test**.

I threw my gaze back to Stark. He hadn't moved.

Back to the report. It listed two swabs had been collected—one from Tate, one from his suspected grandmother. I skimmed to the end.

Based on our analysis, it is practically proven HNDS1987656, the Alleged Paternal Grandmother, is related to the child, HNDS1987519.

My chest felt like it was yawning. Like something inside me was opening up and reaching out toward the possibility of something that should have been impossible. Something I was too scared to imagine was true.

I shook my head. "How do I know this one isn't the fake?"

"It's much easier to get a report that says negative than one that says positive. You think I've been sitting here with it in my drawer all these years just in case you came in with a gun and demanded to have proof?"

I shook my head again. He couldn't be that cruel. "If you really had a vasectomy, why get a test at all?"

He sighed impatiently. "Because vasectomies aren't one hundred percent, and I wanted to know if she'd been fucking anyone else."

"She hadn't been." I knew that as sure as I knew anything.

"If she was, they didn't get her knocked up."

I stared at the report again, wanting to read every single word in search of the flaw, but my eyes were too blurry to see anything. If he wanted to hurt me, this was the way. Convince me it was true and then tell me it was all a trick.

Actually, he wouldn't even have to do that. It hurt just as much if it was the truth. Tate was practically grown. If he was my son—we'd get a test to be sure, but something had lodged itself in that opening in my chest, something that said he was and refused to budge—then Stark had stolen his entire childhood from me. I'd missed everything. And he'd taken from my son the exact thing I'd yearned for in my own life: a father.

The rage burned hotter than ever within me, but now it was shrouded with a thick cloud of grief.

A sound I didn't recognize fell from my mouth. Something between a gasp and a sob. "Is it really true?"

But I'd taken my eye off Stark for too long, and while I'd been distracted, he must have opened the other drawer, or he'd gotten into some other secret hiding place because now when I looked at him, he was the one pointing a pistol at me.

I felt the blood rush from my face.

Then the sound of a gunshot cracked through the air.

EIGHTEEN
JOLIE

I moved the curtain back so I could see out the living room window. The street looked just as quiet as it had when I'd looked out five minutes ago. As if the view might be different twenty feet away, I crossed to the dining room window and peeked out there. This time, I saw car lights coming down the street, and I stretched my neck to get a better view of the vehicle.

It was a suburban.

Not the rental car that Cade and I had picked up.

Biting my lip, I let the curtain fall and crossed back to the front door to make sure the porch lights were on.

"You're making me anxious," Tate said.

I turned toward him and blinked until my own anxious thoughts parted long enough to register him. His textbooks were spread across the dining room table, his headphones wrapped around his neck, a bag of Lay's Cheddar & Sour Cream Flavored Potato Chips open in front of him. He reached in and brought out a handful of chips.

"Why are you snacking before dinner?" I marched over and grabbed the bag and moved it to the kitchen so he couldn't eat more.

"Because it's seven o'clock, and you haven't started cooking anything."

Was it really already seven? We'd arrived home just before noon, and I'd expected Cade to show up soon after. When he was still MIA at two, I had my first doubts—was he not coming? Was this his revenge? Him bailing on me this time?

It was Tate who reminded me I'd turned my phone off during the drive, and I brightened considerably when I saw a voice message waiting from Cade.

Until I listened to the message.

Ever since then, I'd had a lump in my throat and a bowling ball in my stomach and a sense of foreboding that increased a degree every time I replayed the message—which had been plenty—even though I'd immediately memorized both the words and Cade's gut-torn cadence. *You didn't tell me. How could you not. Tell. Me?*

There was only one secret I was still keeping from him. A secret I'd tried to tell him last night. He couldn't have found out on his own, could he? But what else could he mean?

And as each quarter hour passed without word from him, years of shame felt validated. Who would want a woman who'd been raped by her father? Who would want a woman who loved and raised a child born from that abuse?

My greatest fear, and the one that had kept me from telling him, was that Cade would think differently about me once he knew. I'd known rationally that it was a silly worry, especially back then when we were both under my father's thumb. Part of me even thought he already knew. At times, it had seemed like it couldn't be more obvious—the way my father treated me. How he locked me up. How he did a bedroom check on me at least once a night. I'd thought Cade had figured it all out and that he hadn't cared.

Wishful thinking on my part.

I'd hoped he'd known, but deep down, I knew he didn't. And I hadn't told him myself because I was ashamed. Because I was afraid it would matter to him. Plus, keeping it secret made it easier to pretend it wasn't happening. I'd dealt with it for so long that I'd learned how to tuck it away from my reality. Once I said it aloud, it would have to come out of the dark, and that would make it real.

And it was the worst real thing.

"Mom?"

I shook my head out of the shame spiral and tried to remember what we'd been talking about. "You could make dinner yourself, you know."

I immediately regretted snapping. "I'm sorry." I crossed over to him and gave him a hug. "I'll order Panda to make up for it."

He tried to shrug me off, but I wouldn't let go. "It's fine. Panda's good. I don't need the hug."

"The hug is for me." I hugged him tighter.

With a sigh, he put his hand over my arm. "Maybe he had car trouble. And his phone died. Or he decided to stay with his mom longer."

"Maybe. Maybe."

"He wouldn't have talked to me about being in our lives if he was going to ditch us."

"Yeah. Right. I'm not worried."

He was kind enough not to address my blatant lie. I was out-of-my-skull worried. Barring a horrible accident—and God, that would really be horrible—there was no plausible excuse for his absence, and we both knew it. If he'd had car trouble, he would have called. If his phone had died, enough time had passed for him to have charged it. If he'd decided to stay longer at the house, he would have seen my father.

This was the excuse I couldn't stop thinking about because it was the worst of the bunch and also somehow the most likely. Even more likely, I imagined, than Cade having second thoughts about us. Especially after the message he'd left because if he meant what I thought he meant, who could have told him except Dad?

If they'd had an encounter, I almost hoped that Cade had been too grossed out by the truth and that was the reason he wasn't here now. It was better than the alternative—that my father had prevented him from coming.

I couldn't let myself think about that.

Realizing I was squeezing my child probably a little too hard, or at least harder than he would have liked, I let him go and returned once again to the window. Then I pulled out my phone and made sure it was still on. That the ringer was up. That I had no messages. I called his number. It went instantly to voicemail. I hung up and tucked the phone back into my pocket.

"Mom?" he said impatiently. As if I'd forgotten something.

But when I replayed our last words, the conversation seemed to have stopped in a natural place. I drew my brows together in question.

"Do you want *me* to order Panda?"

Ah, right. Dinner. "Yes. Sorry. I'm...Please. Do."

He pulled his laptop closer and started typing. "What do you want me to order for you?"

"Nothing. Anything." I wasn't hungry.

I crossed back to the living room window.

"Should I get extra in case Cade—?"

"Yes." I wasn't going to lose hope. I refused. "He'll be here."

Then, as if declaring it out loud had summoned him, my phone rang.

I answered before there was a chance for a second ring. "Oh, my God, where are you? Are you okay? Is everything okay?"

"Jol?" He sounded exhausted, and that mattered, but it was better than not hearing a sound from him at all.

"I'm here." I tried not to speak so quickly this time but didn't do well at succeeding. "Where are you? Did you get lost? Are you...okay?"

"No." He cleared his throat. "I'm not lost, I mean. I'm sorry, babe. You must have been worried."

"Yes, I've been worried!" I could feel Tate's eyes on me, and I turned to him. "I expected you hours ago. What happened?"

Tate made a gesture that said, *Well?*

I gave him one back that said, *I don't know.*

"I'd really rather talk to you in person." Cade didn't just sound exhausted—he sounded run over. "I just wanted to call now that I had a chance. I, um. My phone broke."

He had more to say, but all the nervous energy inside of me pushed me to interrupt. "Your phone *broke*? How did it break?"

He tried to chuckle. "I might have beaten it against the dash a few times."

"You...what?"

"Listen, I'll tell you everything when I get there. I would have called sooner, but the broken phone thing, and I didn't have your number or your address anywhere but on my cell—trust me, I've memorized them now—so I had to stop in Hartford and get a new one."

"Hartford? You're in Hartford now?" He was giving me information, but it wasn't enough or it wasn't connecting. I still felt as confused as I'd been before I answered. "But you're still coming?"

"I'm headed to you now."

"Okay, good. That's good." I did the math. "You'll be here about nine then."

"Yeah. I will." I heard the car turn on then, and I pictured him sitting in the parking lot of the phone store, calling me before he got back on the road.

But Hartford was only twenty minutes from Wallingford. Where had he been for the eight hours before that?

He'd said he'd beaten his phone against the dash. It had to be connected to his earlier call. *You didn't tell me. How could you not. Tell. Me?*

"Cade...the message you left..."

"I'll explain everything when I get there, Jol."

I didn't know if I could take another ninety minutes plus of anguish. But he'd called. And he was coming. And I trusted him. "Okay. See you soon."

CADE MUST HAVE SPED because he pulled into my driveway less than ninety minutes later. The kitchen window looked out on that side of the house, so I pretended to do dishes and sneakily watched him get out of the car, stretch, then look from the side door to the front of the house, as if not sure which to use.

When I felt his eyes move toward me, I made sure to lower mine. As anxious as I'd been for him to arrive, I was also nervous about him being here. I was pretty sure I would have been nervous if he'd shown up when he was supposed to. It was one thing to cling to each other when we were surrounded by memories of the past. It was quite another to bring him into my present.

Now he was showing up late. Add to that his mysterious voice message and evasive phone call, and I felt unmoored.

He ended up choosing the front door, and as I opened it and invited him in, I regretted not running out the side door to greet him as soon as he'd driven in. Greeting him here was too formal. Like he was a guest coming to our house rather than a man who was coming home, and of course, that's what he was—a guest—but it wasn't how I wanted him to feel.

It wasn't how I wanted to feel about him.

The awkwardness could have been fixed with an embrace, but I couldn't bring myself to take the step toward him. There was a wall around him, thick and impenetrable, and instead of feeling natural with him like I had in the early morning hours in his arms, I felt like I had when I'd arrived at his office in New York more than a week ago.

It didn't help that he hadn't brought his suitcase from the car.

All of a sudden, I wanted to cry.

I feigned cheerfulness instead. "You found us all right?"

"Yep." He shut the door behind him and scanned his surroundings.

I tried to see it from his eyes. The hotel we'd stayed in this past week had been bigger than my main floor. The furniture nicer, too. My fifteen-hundred-square-foot HUD home looked shabby in comparison.

"It's small." It was an apology.

"It's nice."

"Not what you're used to, I'm sure."

"I love it." He was too polite. He was too distant. "What I can see of it."

"Oh. You want a tour?" It would take two minutes to show him the whole house.

"How about later?"

"Yeah, later's good."

It wasn't really my home I was ashamed of. He knew what it was like to be dirt poor, and we were much better off than that. He had money now, but I knew he wasn't materialistic.

The shame came from somewhere else, from the thing I thought he knew. That was the thing with shame though—it grew like ragweed, rapidly spreading from only a small seedling. It wouldn't have mattered if I was inviting Cade into my twenty-million-dollar mansion. I would have still felt unattractive, out of place, and a pest.

But maybe I was jumping to conclusions, and he really didn't know, and I was freaking out for nothing. "Are you hungry? We ordered Chinese. Not good Chinese. The franchised kind. We didn't know what you'd like, so we have a bit of everything."

"Thank you. I picked up something on the road. I'm sorry."

"No, no worries. Now we have an easy dinner for tomorrow." I tried to laugh, but it didn't sound natural. He was definitely acting weird, and I was definitely acting weird, and in my heart of hearts, I knew that something was very, very wrong.

I could feel rather than hear Tate coming up behind me. His presence was confirmed when Cade lifted his chin in his direction. "Hey."

"Hey," Tate said back.

"Homework?"

"Taking a break."

He studied Tate for a long moment. Too long, and I knew then, knew without a doubt, that Cade had found out. He was looking at him with new eyes. Trying to see any defects that children born of incest sometimes display. I, too, had looked for those traits over the years. It was natural when I did it.

I didn't like someone else looking at him like that. Not even Cade.

Irritated about that and about the tension between us and about feeling less than and about the hours he'd kept me waiting and about the answers I'd yet to receive, I decided I was done with the bullshit small talk. "What the fuck happened today?"

If Cade was surprised by my directness, he didn't show it. He glanced again at Tate. "Do you want to talk alone?"

"No." Talking alone was never good. "Tate's been anxiously waiting for an explanation as well. He deserves to hear it."

Cade didn't argue. "Why don't we sit down?"

"I don't want to fucking sit down. I want you to stop fucking stalling and tell me what the fuck's going on." Not being prone to cursing or outbursts, the two used in combo tended to do an excellent job of getting people's attention.

In turn, he got to the point. "Your father is dead."

"Wha?"

It was more of a sound than a word, but he understood enough to repeat himself. "Your father. Langdon. He's dead."

"He's...? For sure?"

"For sure."

The air was suddenly thin.

Or absent.

I was stunned.

Or relieved.

Or sad?

My heart thundered for a few erratic beats. "I think I should sit down."

I felt disconnected from my feet as they took me into the living room. When I sank down on the sofa, Tate was suddenly at my side, his arm around my back. "Mom? Are you okay?"

Cade was there too, kneeling in front of me like he was about to propose, and though I didn't feel him taking my hand, he was holding it in his when I looked down. I watched him rub his thumb across my knuckles, and I thought, *that feels good.*

And I thought, *this is why he's acting weird.*

And I thought, *I should have dusted the floor.*

And I thought, *my father's dead.*

"I don't know how to feel." I was skipping ahead. "How?"

Cade didn't take his eyes off of mine. "Gunshot wound."

Someone had a vise grip around my torso, and it tightened around me. "You?"

He hesitated, and again, I couldn't breathe.

"No," he said finally.

The grip on my chest loosened. Slightly.

"I wanted to," he continued. "I would have. I went there planning..." He glanced at Tate and seemed to regret what he'd been about to admit.

"From what I hear, he deserved it," Tate said.

That encouraged Cade. "He did. I'm not ashamed to say I don't feel bad about it at all."

"Don't you dare feel bad about it." My vision was swimming. I brought my hand up to my cheek and found it was wet. Which was confusing because I'd wanted my father dead. Truly.

So why was my eye leaking?

I ignored it. "You saw him? You saw it happen? What happened?"

"I left soon after you did. But I went back." Cade gestured something to Tate.

Tate's arm left my shoulder so he could reach over to grab a Kleenex from the box on the side table. Then he thought better of it and grabbed the whole box.

I took one, but my attention was pinned on Cade. "You went back?"

"I did. I..." He hesitated long enough for me to know he was leaving something out. "I wanted to make him pay. For everything. Everything he's done to...us. And I meant to do it, Jol. I was going to make him suffer. But then he pulled out his own gun and pointed it at me."

The vise grip tightened again.

"And then Carla shot him," he said.

"Carla?" The shock momentarily stopped the tears.

"She came in behind me. I didn't have any idea she was there. She must have grabbed the gun that you'd said was in the bedroom, and when your father pointed his gun at me, I thought I was dead. I swear I saw my life flash before my eyes. When the gun went off, I actually looked down, looking for the wound. I thought it had been me because it wasn't my gun that had gone off.

"But then I saw your father. A shot right between the eyes. He fell over his desk, and when I looked behind me, there was Carla, holding a pistol with both hands wrapped around it."

"Carla," I said again. Because it was easier to think about that part than the part where Cade had almost been dead. "Carla shot him."

"I was surprised too. Who would have predicted?" He was trying to hide his emotion, but I heard it now. All the years that Carla had stood by while her husband had abused her son... Cade had never believed his mother cared about him at all. It had to have an impact on him.

My hands flew to cup his face. "Oh, Cade."

He brought one of his hands to cover one of mine. "I'm fine."

He couldn't be. He'd been upset enough to confront my father—upset enough to want to kill him in cold blood—and then my father had pulled a gun on him...

The tears turned into full-blown sobs.

Obviously, I was *not* fine.

"I'm so sorry, Mom." Tate patted me in that way he did whenever I got emotional, and I'd already broken down once on him today. Poor guy didn't always know how to react when I showed vulnerability.

Cade, however, did.

He sat up so he could wrap his arms around me. I clutched onto his shirt and cried on his shoulder while he rubbed his hand soothingly on my back.

"He. Had. A. Gun. Pointed. At you," I said, stuttering through sobs. It wasn't the only reason I was crying, but it was the easiest to explain, even to myself. "You could be dead. It could have been you."

"I'm not, though." He kissed my hair, then hugged me tighter. "And he is."

"And he was so awful."

"Yes, he was."

"Then why am I sad?"

"Oh, baby." He rocked me back and forth. "He was your father, and now he's dead, and every possibility of him being something better or different to you is gone."

"Yeah." That was probably it.

"And you loved him."

"I think I sort of did."

"Of course you did. And that's okay."

I'd thought my tears were slowing, but another wave crashed over me. It was complicated, all the things I was feeling. They rolled together into a muddy mess. I wasn't entirely sure that I wasn't crying partly in celebration.

A large part of it was definitely relief.

Relief that my father was dead, and Cade was alive. Relief that he was here, holding me.

Relief knowing that whatever came between us from here on out, it would no longer be Langdon Stark.

The cage door was open, and this bird was finally free.

NINETEEN
JOLIE

Fortunately, the crying didn't last too long, though it left me weary and with a headache. Tate still had homework, but he made me a cup of tea before retreating to finish it in the basement. He'd adopted the extra room down there at the start of the school year, abandoning the bedroom upstairs next to mine for his own space.

Once he'd gone, Cade had insisted I take a bath. He drew it up for me using generous amounts of the cherry-blossom bath salts I kept on the shelf, then helped undress me and get settled. I'd been disappointed when he hadn't joined me, but once I was alone in the steamy room with a washcloth on my forehead, I appreciated the privacy.

I would need a lot of these moments, I realized, before I fully processed everything that had happened with my father.

Not just today, but over the course of the rest of my life. I'd done work in therapy to deal with a lot of it, but he wasn't like a tree that I could hack off and be done with. He was seeded into me, a stubborn weed that mingled with other growth, sprouting when better parts of my life were in full bloom. I would dig him out at the root then, but that didn't mean he wouldn't return again and again and again.

This time, when I hacked at the plant, I'd manage even better because Cade would be next to me. Right?

He said he would. I had to believe that he still meant it.

By the time the water was cold and my fingers were pruned, I figured I'd done enough weeding for the night. I climbed out, toweled off, and put on the white fluffy bathrobe that Cade must have found in my closet and laid out on the counter for me.

I wasn't sure what I'd been expecting when I came out, but when I opened the bathroom door, I had to lean against the frame because the sight in front of me made me dizzy.

"You look good on my bed," I said. He was stretched out on top of the covers, his phone in his hand, and he didn't just look good—he looked divine. It helped that he wasn't wearing anything but his black jeans. Something about seeing him barefoot as well as shirtless did extraordinary things to the space between my legs.

It was strange to acknowledge sexual thoughts after an evening spent dealing with Dad, but that had frequently been my way of coping. He'd ingrained a desire to please. Taught me that was the way to receive love. It took work to separate the real from what he'd programmed. Was sex what I really wanted right now? Or was it enough that Cade was here?

It would have been enough if I knew he was *really* here, and I was too scared/tired/unsure to find out, so yes, sex would substitute nicely.

He'd been focused on whatever he was reading and must not have heard the door open because he looked up in surprise at the sound of my voice. Avoiding my comment, he set his cell down on the nightstand and swung his legs over the side of the bed. "How are you feeling?"

"I could be feeling better. You could make me feel better."

His eyes darkened as they swept over my body, but he followed with the words I'd been wanting to put off. "We should talk."

I wondered if I could convince him to put it off.

But I'd promised him I'd tell him. Since he'd found out before I'd had the chance, I couldn't let him wait longer for that discussion. He deserved this.

And his shirt was off, and his suitcase was leaning against the wall, so he planned to stay for at least tonight.

"Okay."

He didn't start, though, and knowing where to start myself was daunting.

Well, if I got to choose, I'd start where I wanted to. "Your message. You asked why I hadn't told you..." I swallowed. "How did you find out?"

"Carla guessed."

I let out a sound that was half *ha* and half *huh*. Decades too late, but good for her.

I wanted to care how she'd felt about it.

No, actually, I didn't even want to care. I wanted to want to, but I didn't. I only cared about Cade. "That was why you broke your phone. And why you went back to the house. With a gun."

"I..." He took a breath in. Let it out. "Reacted."

He didn't add *poorly*. Most people would expect that word to follow.

Most people didn't understand what we'd dealt with.

He'd reacted *naturally*, as far as I was concerned. I'd wanted to kill my father as well.

Still, it was moving. That Cade had reacted like that. That he'd been upset enough to want to kill the man who'd hurt me. It affected me deeply, but it didn't tell me everything I needed to know. Just because he'd been angry enough to kill didn't mean everything was okay between us. Was I the same person in his eyes knowing what he knew now? Was Tate?

There was definitely something that had changed. Something he had yet to say that he hadn't. "Go ahead," I coaxed. "Say what you need to say. I'm ready." I wasn't ready.

He let out a slow breath. "I understand why you didn't tell me. I shouldn't have inferred that I didn't."

I hadn't seen that coming. "Because it's a terrible thing, and you'd rather not know?"

"Because it's a very terrible thing, and I'd rather it hadn't happened. And I wish I had known. I wish to God that I had known."

"Because it changes how you think of me?"

"No." He jerked like I'd slapped him. "No."

"Why then? Do you think there was something you could have done to stop it?" It came out harsh. A judgment.

I expected him to be defensive.

Instead, he responded honestly. "I'd like to think I would have tried. But I hadn't tried to stop any of it."

"Exactly." I didn't add that it would have gotten him killed because I was being an asshole. Everything was coming out mean, and I felt shitty about it, but I couldn't stop myself. It was like I was so afraid he was going to hurt me that I kept trying to hurt him first.

He understood that. Somehow. And he didn't let my bullets land.

He didn't let me shoot again, either, because he stood up and crossed to me. When he put his hands on my waist, I was disarmed. "I wish I'd known, Jol, so that you could have leaned on me. I wish I'd known so you wouldn't have had to carry it alone. I could have done that for you."

My lip quivered. "I didn't want you to have to carry any of it."

"I get it." One hand swept the damp ends of my hair off my shoulder and rested on my neck, and I liked feeling held, but I also felt vulnerable because I didn't believe he did get it. He *couldn't* get it. How could he? I barely got it, and it had happened to me.

It was like he could read my thoughts because he used his thumb to tilt my chin up, and he said, "I promise I get it, Jolie. Because I didn't tell you either."

Now I didn't get him.

And then I did, and my stomach dropped. "You... What did he do?"

"Nothing compared to what he did to you. It only happened once. Near the end. I'd cried—I usually didn't—and I guess that...aroused him. The beating stopped, and when I got brave enough to look behind me, he was...taking care of himself."

"Cade!" My arms dropped, and I brought my palms to his chest. The horror made me forget about protecting myself, and I only cared about protecting him.

He covered one of my hands with his. "Like I said, it was nothing comparatively. He didn't do anything but that. He never touched me in a sexual manner. And I was still so fucking humiliated by it. I couldn't bear for you to find out."

"Yes." Oh, my God, yes.

"I wouldn't have even known how to say it."

"That's exactly it. And I thought you'd blame me."

His eyes met mine for the first time since his admission. "I would never have blamed you for that. *Never*."

"I know. I really do. It's stupid when I say it, but I felt it. I worried you'd think I was *too* broken. That you wouldn't want to touch me, knowing I wasn't just yours."

He cupped my face. "Baby, you were always just mine, no matter what he did to you. He stole that. It wasn't his to take. And if I'd known, I would have touched you more. I would have tried to erase every memory of his touch from your body."

"You did. You did that without even knowing."

"I wish I'd done more. I wish I'd stolen you away from there."

"I was pregnant. The odds of Tate having a severe defect were fifty percent. We couldn't have handled that on our own. Without money? Without support? It wasn't a risk I could take."

"I need to—"

But I wasn't done, and this was important, so I cut him off. "By the time I knew he was okay, you were long gone. And even if I'd found you, I didn't know that you could love me after... I didn't know that you could love *him*."

He knew that what I was really saying was, *Can you still love him?*

"About that..." He dropped his hands from my face.

No.

I took a step back. Away. Tate and I were a package deal. He couldn't accept what my father had done to me without accepting him. Without loving him.

But Cade hadn't been pulling away. He'd only let go of me so he could take something out of his pocket—a paper, folded up into a square. No, two papers, I realized as he unfolded it. A familiar logo at the top caught my eye.

I'd seen that report already. It was burned in my memory and then burned in the fire. How did he have a copy? Did he think I didn't know?

He held it out toward me. "Your father showed me this."

"I've seen it."

"The one you saw was fake."

My heart did an involuntary flip before I got control of myself. "It wasn't fake. Did he try to tell you it was?"

"Maybe it wasn't. But he said he'd gotten a swab from a woman on the street for the one you saw. This report is the one that had Carla's DNA."

I was immediately angry. At my father, not at Cade. Though a little bit at Cade for being swept into whatever last game my father had tried to play. And a little less mad than I'd ever been at Carla for making sure he couldn't play any games again. "He was lying to you."

But I took the report from his hands because I was also gullible where my father was concerned and because I was as desperate to believe another truth as Cade was.

"You're right. He could have been lying," he said as I read. "I acknowledge that. But he said he'd had a vasectomy. Did you know that?"

I didn't. Could that really be true?

"He made me take all those damn pregnancy tests." I was skimming the text as I had back then. Seeing a different outcome this time—an outcome I really wanted to believe.

Had my father known every time that those tests would come back negative? Why *had* they? He'd been raping me since I was thirteen. Cade was the only other man I'd let inside me.

"And that last night we were together?" There was a thread of excitement in Cade's voice now, just barely there, as if he was trying to contain it. "I'd thrown my jeans on, but the condom was broken when I finally got a chance to dispose of it."

"It was broken?"

"I'd figured it had torn in my escape, but it could have been torn before."

It would have been the right timing. Even if it hadn't been that night, there had been other times we'd been less than careful.

"And Tate has my earlobes. I noticed tonight. Your lobes attach to your head at the bottom. So did your father's. Not Tate's."

I looked at the sides of Cade's head and saw ears that I'd seen every day for almost seventeen years. I couldn't remember what my mother's ears had been like. Had they been attached?

"I love him no matter what, Jol." Now he was definitely excited. And sincere. "We can get another DNA test, if you want, but he's mine. I don't need a test to know it."

Honestly?

I didn't need a test either.

I already knew. I'd always known. I'd always seen Cade in my son and had excused it as seeing what I'd wanted to see, but I'd also somehow known. It was partly why I'd told Tate that Cade was his father in the first place. Not just because I'd wanted that but because I'd *known*. The only reason I hadn't ever gotten a second test was because I'd been afraid that finding out that what I knew to be true was wrong would have destroyed me.

Now my father was dead, and Cade was standing in front of me, claiming my son as his. I could question the report in my hand, say we needed to verify it, and give my father another chance to take this moment from us too.

Or I could accept what I'd always known as truth.

"He's yours," I said. Relieved. Joyful. Exhilarated. "We don't need a test. He's yours."

His grin reached his eyes. "He's ours."

"He really is—"

And then it hit me in full.

What this meant.

What I'd done.

"Oh, Cade." My legs couldn't support me anymore. He tried to catch me on my way down but only managed to hold on to my arms as he came with me to the ground. This time, my sobs came without tears, shuddering through my body like mini earthquakes. "Cade. I kept him from you. You missed so much. You missed everything."

This shame felt entirely different from the humiliation that came from my father's assault. That shame focused on myself. This shame came from outside of me, came from recognizing what I'd done to someone I loved very much. Two someones. This shame was majority guilt, and the pain of it was like none I'd ever known.

"Baby." We were both on our knees, and he tried to pull me into his arms, tried to comfort me.

I couldn't let him.

I braced my hands on his shoulders to keep him from me. "Don't you dare tell me this is okay. This is unforgivable."

"This isn't..." He closed his mouth, wisely realizing he should consider before he said anything he didn't actually mean.

I knew what I meant already and didn't have to think about it. "You can't tell me it's not. You missed your son's whole life."

"His life isn't over. It's just beginning."

"You missed him growing up. You missed years you can never get back. You will never be able to repair that completely. It's not okay."

"I know, okay? I know. Believe me, I know. I've had hours to think about it, and I know." His eyes were glossy.

That got mine flooding as well, and I clutched onto his shoulders, my nails digging involuntarily into his back. "I'm so sorry. I'm so, so sorry." I could barely get the words out.

This time, when he pulled me into him, I let him hold me, let him rock me back and forth. Let him cry with me.

When my sobs began to be less violent, I let him pull me with him to the ground so that we were lying face-to-face.

He calmed faster than I had, and he whispered soothing words that I was unable to hear and stroked my hair with more love than I'd felt in years.

When my hiccups slowed, he wiped my face with his palm and tried again. "Jolie, this is not your fault."

"It is! I could have—"

He caught my eyes with his. "This is. Not. Your. Fault. It's not. This is him. No one else. Blaming anyone but him gives him yet another win. After everything he's taken, we can't let him have this too."

"But I left him a decade ago. I should have—"

"No!" He said it so sharply, it startled me to attention. "No more regrets. We can't go back, and I don't want to. I want to go forward with you and my son." His voice cracked on the last word, and I'd never heard anything so beautiful.

Still, I couldn't let go of what he'd lost. What Tate had lost. "You don't know him. He doesn't know you."

"But I will. He will. I'm going to spend so much time with that kid, he's going to be sick of me. I'm not missing a single moment from now on."

"Not a single moment." Admittedly, I liked hearing that for selfish reasons. If he was here for Tate, he'd be here for me.

"And we'll have another baby." He tucked a piece of hair behind my ear. "I know that won't make up for what I missed, but you'll tell me. Every milestone that our baby goes through, you'll tell me what I missed with Tate."

"Okay."

I must not have sounded sure because he asked again. "Okay?"

And since it seemed he really wanted to know, I thought about it before I spoke. "It's never not going to be sad."

"No, it's not. But we can grieve together." He swept his knuckles across my jaw. "I have to tell you, Jolie—I'm sad, but also I'm so tired of life without you. Exhausted from it. There isn't any pain I can't get over as long as I can suffer it next to you."

My next breath quivered, but it was an afterquake. I was feeling calmer now. The ground solid beneath me, both literally and figuratively. "I don't think you can understand how in love with you I am."

"Don't bet on that." He stroked my skin, his touch soothing and intimate, and I let myself feel how much he loved me as his fingers explored my neck and collarbone, his eyes never leaving mine.

God, he loved me. He did, and I knew it as surely as I knew that Tate was his. He'd proven himself and beyond. "You would have killed for me."

"I would have." The depth of his love was in his sincerity. "I wanted to hurt him for hurting you."

"I think he hurt anyway because he knew I loved you more than him."

"It wasn't enough. He deserved much more pain."

"He doesn't deserve to take any more of our energy, though. Or our time. I don't want to give him any more of me. I want to give all of that to you."

"I'll take it." His face was nearer to mine than it had been. Had he moved closer, or had I?

I was just thinking I wanted more of him—all of him—when his lips found mine. His kisses were slow. Not hesitant but lingering. Between, his mouth worshiped my jaw and my neck and my throat, always returning to my lips before they had a chance to feel neglected.

It was a natural progression for his hand to slip inside my bathrobe. For his thumb to rub over my nipple and then slide between my legs where I was already swollen and waiting. It was nothing at all for him to make me come, and he swallowed my whimpers, not because we were afraid of being heard by an abusive father, but because he liked the taste of them.

He chased my cries with my pussy juice, licking his finger clean before divesting me of my robe entirely. Then, taking my hand in his, he rose from the floor, pulling me with him and over to the bed where he laid me out and feasted on me with his eyes while he took off his jeans.

Then he climbed over my body and slipped inside me, and I felt joined to him like I had that day that he'd dressed my ring finger with a pipe cleaner and asked me to be his wife, and also not at all like that day. Because that union had been fragile, and even when I'd earnestly said yes, I'd known the obstacles in our way. Then, yes had felt like a wish.

Now, yes was a promise, and I said it over and over as he thrust inside me. Yes, yes, yes. From this day forward, let us never be apart.

After, when the lights were off and the covers pulled over us, I nuzzled my face in his neck, relishing the smell of man and sex that had been absent from my room for way too long.

"I feel good about that round," he said, kissing my hair. "Those were my best swimmers."

I laughed, my nipples sharpening as my breasts brushed his chest. "I'm not as young as I once was. We might have to do that a lot."

"Oh, we're definitely doing that a lot." This kiss he planted on my lips. "Do we need to tell Tate?"

"That we're doing it a lot?"

"That we want another. Will he feel…replaced?"

There was a delicious pinch in my heart. He was instantly a good father, and I'd never been happier. "I don't think so, but we'll make sure he knows that's not the goal."

"Maybe we should save it. Let him get used to the idea that I'm in his life for good first."

"Yeah. We should tell him that part. Soon."

"That I'm his father?" He corrected himself. "That I know I'm his father? What time is it? Should we do it now?"

I laughed again, animated by his eagerness. "It's late, and if he's not asleep, he's finishing homework."

"Tomorrow."

"After school," I specified.

"After school," he agreed. "Tell me about him, will you?"

I smiled and wiped the tears that had gathered in the corners of my eyes.

Then, my fingers laced through his, I told my true love all about our son.

TWENTY
CADE

I woke up alone. The scent of bacon filled the air, though the placement of the sun said it was closer to lunch than breakfast. Since we'd stayed up talking until almost four, I wasn't surprised that I'd slept in, but I was surprised how good I felt. It was the first day since I'd seen Jolie that I hadn't woken up reaching for a cigarette.

Good thing, too, since the pack I'd bought was empty, and I'd vowed to not buy another.

I wouldn't have minded reaching for Jolie, though.

I threw my legs over the side of the bed, and while I was considering whether I wanted to take a shower before or after I found her, a buzzing came from the nightstand.

My new phone.

I hadn't bothered with the charger, and I'd expected it to be dead, but apparently, Jolie had plugged it in.

Good woman.

I wasn't used to being cared for. Most women I bedded were usually kicked out before I went to sleep. This was different. This was fucking fantastic.

But the buzzing...

I managed to answer before it went to voicemail.

"About time you fucking answered. You leave me a message like you did yesterday and then don't take any of my calls? You're lucky I didn't drive out there myself looking for you."

Donovan didn't just sound concerned—he sounded pissed off.

"I expected you to call back last night." He'd been the second call I'd made after I'd bought the phone. I'd called him again when Jolie had been in the bath. It wasn't like him not to return a call that involved topics like guns and death and DNA tests.

"Yeah, well, I have shit of my own, you know. I don't just sit around waiting to fix your life."

Beyond pissed off. That's what he was. I could tell from its intensity that the emotion had nothing to do with me and rather was applied to everything in its way.

Which wasn't like Donovan either. He tended to be in control of everything, most notably his own emotions.

"What bug got up your ass?" I asked, but the tone was playful.

"My ass is bug-free, asshole."

"That true?"

He took a beat. "No. But that's all I'm giving you."

Had to be about Sabrina. I debated pushing him—I imagined the guy needed someone to look after him sometimes, the way he looked after everyone else.

Problem was that he wasn't prone to letting anyone in, and no one knew how to bully their way past personal boundaries as well as he did.

I ran a hand up and down my thigh, not sure what to offer him. "Anything I can do?"

"You can shut the fuck up, and let me update you on what I know."

I stifled a laugh. I'd barely given him any details when I'd left the message for him, and of course, he knew more now than I did. That sounded about right.

"Shutting the fuck up now."

"Spoke to Leroy, my FBI guy. A big bust went down this morning, seventy men arrested in total for charges of human trafficking. It's on all the news, if you haven't looked already. Stark would have been part of that, as well as your mother. You saved the government the cost of a trial, which I'm sure someone appreciates because he most definitely would have been in cuffs today."

My breath came in sharp. "My mother?" She'd gone willingly into custody after the shooting the day before, though the detective in charge had said she'd likely be let go as soon as they investigated since it was essentially a case of defending others.

"Figured that was what you'd pick up on rather than the seventy people involved in human trafficking. This was way bigger than your douche of a stepfather. Real finessed operation. Several others involved had access to kids the way Stark did—some other private school teachers, coaches, one was a librarian. They were spread across the nation, and they rotated abductions so no one looked suspicious."

"Blamed them all on runaways," I interjected, understanding how it worked.

"Correct. The abductor would take the kid to a meetup and be paid in cash for delivery. It's been going on for over two decades."

And Stark had been involved for probably all of it. "What happened to the kids?"

"Most were sold overseas. Imagine what you will what kind of slaves they became."

I shuddered. My skin felt like it was crawling. "They're going home now, though, right?"

Donovan's pause told me the answer before he spoke. "They've been able to locate a few that were in domestic situations. International is harder to track down, but there are a lot of people working on it. I know Edward Fasbender from Accelecom has been working with my FBI friend, Leroy, and financing rescues. You want in on that?"

"Yes. Yes, I do."

"I'll set it up for both of us. Meanwhile, this is a big takedown. The spotlight's everywhere on it. You may want to lay low. That school is going to be crawling with press."

"We're in Boston now, so I think we're good."

"You are? Good." He wasn't often surprised, and I couldn't help feeling smug that I'd managed to keep something off his radar for once. "As for your mother—are you ready for this?"

So much for feeling smug. With that lead up, I had a feeling whatever he said next was going to throw me for a loop. "I'm sitting down, if that counts."

"She's been Stark's wingman since the beginning. Before they even got married, but according to her, she was basically blackmailed into it. She says she accidentally found herself doing a favor for him while they were dating—a favor that basically threw her into the business of sex trafficking—and then he used that to keep her under his thumb for the next twenty years."

"Sounds like a likely excuse."

"Maybe that's all it is, but this isn't what she told them last night—this is what she told them a month ago. That insider giving info to the feds was no other than Carla Stark, neé Warren."

I blinked. Then ran a hand over my face. "Okay?"

"Okay? That's all you have to say about that? Dude, it's your mom."

I rolled a kink out of my shoulder, turning my head in time to see Jolie walking through the door with a tray of breakfast wearing nothing but my T-shirt.

At least, I assumed it was only the T-shirt. I'd have to do some investigating to be sure.

Whoa, I mouthed with a smile, then responded to Donovan. "I don't know what to say, Kincaid. Is that supposed to make up for all the shit she overlooked over the years? Am I supposed to think of her as just another one of Stark's victims?"

"No. You aren't supposed to think anything. Just thought you'd be more interested."

Maybe I would have been. Before Jolie and I had decided to put the past behind us and stop giving energy to the people who had hurt us. "Does this mean she's going to jail?"

"If she does, it will be a light sentence. That was her exchange for providing information willingly. Want me to keep you updated?"

I almost missed the question. Jolie had bent to lower the tray to the dresser, and I was too busy tilting my head to see if I would catch a peek of something naughty. "Uh, nah. I'm good."

"You're good," he repeated. More bewildered than questioning. "Didn't she save your life yesterday?"

"Look, D. The first time she gave me life, she fucked me over repeatedly afterward. I'm grateful she was there, and I told her as such before she left with the police, but now I'm going to cut my losses and be done with her. I told her that as well. She seemed to understand."

"Huh. That's a surprisingly grown-up attitude."

With a piece of bacon in hand, Jolie came over then and sat on my lap. She offered the piece toward me as she whispered, "Donovan?"

I nodded as I took a nibble. "Maybe I don't need Daddy anymore."

"No, you need Daddy."

"Hi, Donovan," Jolie said loud enough that he could hear.

"He says hi back." He hadn't said it, and he wouldn't, but she didn't need to know that. "Actually, I do need something from you, D. I need to take a leave of absence."

"Of course. How long?"

I shrugged even though he couldn't see me. "Indefinitely, I think. All this is going to stir shit up, as you said, I imagine for quite a while. We'll want to lay low, and I need to give all my focus to my family."

I could tell that Jolie liked it when I said that. She grinned so hard, she glowed.

"Take the time. I'll take care of getting you replaced. You want me to tell the guys?"

I trusted the men at Reach, I did. But I also liked the idea of being off the grid. "Let's keep it just us."

"Sounds like a plan."

I caught him before he hung up. "Thank you, Donovan. I mean it. We both really appreciate this."

"Told you you still need Daddy."

The dial tone followed, and maybe I should have called him back and offered to help again with whatever troubles he was going through.

But on the other hand, there was the underneath of a shirt I needed to explore.

I TOOK one step down the stairs then immediately turned around.

"What's wrong?" Jolie stood blocking my way. Not intentionally, but the fact remained that she was there, and if I wanted to get off the stairs, I either had to go down or she needed to move.

I scratched the newly buzzed hair at the back of my neck. We'd arrived late to the day, but we'd been productive with what we had left. After returning my rental car, she'd given me a trim, then after a nap that consisted of no sleep, we'd gone to the store to buy ingredients for dinner, discussing parenting methods while strolling down the aisles.

It was reassuring that we agreed on most everything. For the rest, I'd agreed to defer to her until we were all more settled as a family, at least. Providing stability for Tate was important to both of us, second only to making sure he knew he was loved.

Jolie and I had been cooking together—something I hadn't done with someone since I'd cooked on occasion with my mother before she married Stark—when Tate had come home from his after-school activities. He'd asked what we were cooking, sniffed suspiciously at the pot of beans on the stove, then disappeared down to his room.

It had been Jolie's suggestion that this was the time to talk to him.

Having been excited about it all day, I'd eagerly taken that first step after him. Now, I was having doubts.

I considered playing tough guy for all of three seconds before I remembered I didn't want to hide my emotions from Jolie anymore. "I'm really nervous all of a sudden. What do I even say?"

She wrapped her hands around my neck. Being a stair down from her put her at my height, and that felt ridiculously comforting at the moment. "You'll figure it out."

"Will I? This conversation doesn't seem all that intuitive."

"It will be awkward. For both of you. But beginnings often are, and you can't get to a place where you're both comfortable until you get past the beginning."

"But maybe you should be there to smooth the awkwardness."

"I think you need to do this alone. Your relationship shouldn't be about me."

I groaned and dropped my head dramatically to her shoulder.

She gave a pitying laugh. "You've been through harder things."

"I don't think I have." My voice sounded muffled from her shirt sleeve.

"Seriously?" She wasn't really questioning the statement since she knew the things I'd been through and was instead questioning my attitude.

I lifted my head so she could see my pout.

She kissed it off my lips. "I'll come down in twenty minutes to check on you. How's that?"

"I'd be happier if it was fifteen."

She glanced over at the kitchen timer counting down the minutes until the ham casserole would be done in the oven. Sixteen and thirty-two seconds. "I'll pull out the food and then I'll be down."

I considered stalling for a couple of minutes, but she knew me too well. "You got this, babe. Now go get it."

Sighing, I turned back around and pushed myself to walk down. I totally had this. I'd dealt with all walks of life. I'd managed lowlifes and arrogant, rich assholes. Surely, I could get through a conversation with my son.

Though, just thinking of the term made my throat tight. I had no fucking clue how I was going to succeed in saying it.

I paused at the bottom of the stairs. Jolie had given me a quick tour earlier, which hadn't actually included Tate's room—respect for his privacy and all—but I knew where it was. Even if I hadn't been down here earlier, the steady beat of a rap song coming from behind a closed door led like aural breadcrumbs.

I stood outside long enough to recognize the artist (Eminem) and that it was a song I wasn't familiar with, suggesting it was likely one of his newer hits since I regularly boxed to his older albums and knew them inside out.

Kid had good taste in music.

The common interest gave me courage to knock.

"Yeah?" he yelled over the music.

Did that mean come in? Jolie let Tate treat his room as his own safe space. She'd never felt she had that growing up, and I respected passing that on to our son, so I called back to be sure. "Mind if I come in?"

Immediately, the music turned down, and a moment later, the door opened. "Oh, sure. Come on in."

He stepped back, and I tentatively walked in, taking in everything around me like his room was a personal guidebook to Tate Warren. "So this is your place."

Shit, I sounded like an idiot.

"Uh, it's kinda a mess. Sorry."

I hadn't been allowed a messy room when I'd lived in the Stark household, and as itchy as I got seeing the stack of discarded clothes on the gaming chair and the desk that had so many books and papers piled up that there wasn't any space to work on it, I appreciated that Jolie let the state of cleanliness be up to Tate. "Hey, it's your room."

Yeah, this was definitely awkward.

He stood watching me, probably waiting for me to hurry up and announce why I was intruding and then leave. I didn't want to rush this, though, and I wasn't going to miss this opportunity to examine all the ways his personality was expressed in his space.

I let my eyes drift to the decor now. White walls were peppered with promo posters of various PC games. I recognized several of the names, including a popular driving game that had hired Reach for their marketing campaign. Red LED lights ran along the baseboards. The bedding was black. Textbooks and his backpack were spread across the mattress, and I guessed that he did his schoolwork in his bed since the desk wasn't usable, though maybe he also used the draft table that was in the corner. There were drawings strewn across the surface, and I crossed to study them.

"You do these?" I'd expected anime figures or drawings of girls with overly large breasts, and instead I found sketches of architecturally complex buildings.

He came up next to me, and I could feel his urge to reach out and hide the drawings.

"Sorry. I should have asked." I pulled my attention away from them.

"No. I'm just not used to people looking at them. Yeah. They're mine."

Pride burst through my chest. "Really? May I?" I reached out toward one, waiting until he gave permission before picking one up to examine the modern house design. "This is really good."

He gave an embarrassed shrug. "I'm fascinated by, um, the geometry of architecture."

I'd been good at math too. The art skills, he definitely didn't get from me. "Thinking about being an architect?"

"Maybe. Lots of school." He let out a nervous laugh. "I'd rather see the world's famous structures in person than study them in a classroom."

"Me too, kid. I spent several years working jobs that took me everywhere." Fuck. I'd tell him if he asked, but I preferred to let him get to know me a little better before confessing to dealing in illegal art.

I steered the conversation back. "I know you need a degree to be an architect, but maybe you can take some time off to travel first."

"I've been thinking about that."

I handed the drawings to him, and when he set them down, he straightened all the papers on the drafting table at the same time.

I used the opportunity to put a little bit of distance between us physically and crossed to the desk on the other side of the room. I leaned against the edge and folded my arms then dropped them then stuck my hands in my pockets (what the hell were my arms supposed to do?) then cleared my throat. "So...I hear we're related."

His back was to me, and he got real still before turning around. "Yeah, Mom told me she told you."

"She did?" This was news to me. "When did she tell you?"

"She'd promised to tell me as soon as she told you, so she texted me this afternoon."

"Ah. Good mom." Yep. Fucking awkward.

Now what?

"You've known about me longer than I've known about you." I didn't know if that made this easier for him or harder, and I wasn't exactly sure what I meant by saying it out loud because he already knew that. I shifted my weight onto my hip and decided to just ask what was foremost on my mind. "Is it...weird?"

"Meeting you?" Another shrug. "I dunno. I guess. It's cool, too." He swallowed. "Is it weird for you?"

I rubbed again at my buzzed hair. "Like I said, I didn't have any inkling you existed. But there was a time that I imagined a family with Jolie so vividly that...I don't know. It's weird, but it also feels like it's just...right."

A smile fluttered quickly across his lips. "Yeah."

I let my smile stay longer, but I aimed it at my shoes. "Even feeling right, it's going to be new—for both of us. I already told you I plan to be in your lives from here on out, and I am, but I also want you to know that I don't want my relationship with your mother to have anything to do with us. I'd like to get to know you, and I don't expect that to happen all at once. But maybe we can spend time, just the two of us, sometime if that's cool?"

"That's cool."

I bit back a laugh. I supposed I'd been quiet as a teen too.

"And when you need some normality and you want to just spend time with your mom, you let me know. Or her know. Okay?"

"Okay."

"And just so you know, I'm not going to come in here and make everything different. I'm not going to try to be all 'I know best' or any of that. I don't know shit, to be honest. I'm figuring all of this out as we go."

"Okay."

"But you can come to me. We can talk things out. I'd love your help when I fuck things up—and I'm definitely going to fuck things up. Like, am I not supposed to curse? Is there a swear jar or something?"

Now he laughed. "No. Mom believes in free speech, but she does encourage more complex language choices when possible."

"Of course she does." I smiled, and this time, I met his eyes.

He smiled back.

Then again it disappeared. "Uh, so what should I call you?"

Dad. I wanted to say, *Call me Dad.*

But I didn't want to push. "Whatever you're comfortable with. You choose."

He dodged my gaze, looking everywhere but at me while he considered. "Could I...?" He wasn't bold enough to say what he wanted.

"Yes," I said, pretty sure I could guess what he was wanting. "Call me that."

"Okay. Thanks...Dad."

I would not cry. I would not cry. I would not cry.

I managed to keep my eyes from watering, but I couldn't talk. I crossed back over to him and clapped my hand on his back, an invitation for more if he chose to take it.

He did. He turned toward me, and for the first time, I hugged my son.

IT SEEMED like a blink before Jolie knocked on the door. She didn't wait for an invitation before opening the door—so she was still a mom about the privacy she granted. I couldn't help adoring her for it.

She found Tate sitting on the gaming chair—he'd tossed the laundry to the floor—and me on the bed with one of his notebooks in my lap and a pen in my hand.

"You boys doing okay?" She couldn't see Tate's half eye roll—I wasn't sure he even realized he'd done it—and another burst of warmth spread through me at the knowledge that he was enjoying his time with me enough to not want to be interrupted.

But this conversation involved her, and as devoted as I was to growing this relationship with Tate, I was still very much obsessed with his mother. "We're planning our world travels," I said. I motioned her over to me.

She came and sat next to me. "World travels?"

"Instead of college," Tate said.

"A gap year," I corrected, well aware this probably should have been a discussion I'd had with her first. "College after that."

"Uh, do I get a say in this?" She settled her chin on my shoulder, looking at the list I'd made in the notebook.

"Of course you do. We're just talking right now." I twisted my head to kiss her cheek. "We thought it might be fun to spend some time together—all of us as a family—seeing the world before the kid leaves home."

"It was Dad's idea."

Fuck, I'd never get used to hearing that. It was overwhelming and wonderful.

"Dad," Jolie whispered so only I could hear, obviously as moved as I was.

"I know, right?"

"And these are all the places you're thinking of? Can I add to the list?" She was already taking the notebook from me before I said yes, which I was totally going to do. Truthfully, I didn't care where we went. I just wanted to be with her.

With both of them.

They were my family, and wherever they were, there was my home.

I handed her the pen.

Tate leaned forward, trying to see what she'd write. "Don't add too many!"

"Why not?" I asked.

At the same time, Jolie said, "We can vote for where we want to go most."

"But I want to go so many places. I need to see the Parthenon in Greece. And the Taj Mahal in India. And La Sagrada Familia in Spain. And Hagia Sophia in Turkey."

I was impressed. I couldn't name half of the buildings my son had mentioned let alone where they were.

"We'll use ranked choice voting," Jolie said, adding the Galapagos Islands and Myanmar to the already long list.

"Or we just go to all of them," I suggested. "We'll have a year."

"Really?" This from Jolie.

"We're just dreaming," Tate said. "I know a trip like that would be expensive as hell."

I'd been a dad for a little more than a day, and I already knew the feeling of wanting my teenage son to think I was cool. I leaned forward, as if I was about to admit a secret. "This might be a good time to tell you, Tate—I'm loaded."

His eyes went wide, and he looked to his mother for confirmation.

Her nod felt reluctant. "It doesn't mean anything changes. We're not spoiling you. Are we, Cade?"

I wasn't sure I could commit to that. If I looked at her, she'd know.

"Cade!" She slapped my shoulder when I wouldn't meet her eyes.

"Okay, okay. We're not spoiling you. But college is paid for, and we are going on a world trip where I'm going to spoil you." I directed this *you* to her. "And Tate's invited to come along." I winked at him.

He winked back.

She pretended to deliberate, but she wasn't fooling anyone. She knew we deserved happiness after everything we'd been through. We deserved to be spoiled for the rest of time. "All right. I'll let you spoil me."

I kissed her quickly, which elicited a groan of annoyance from Tate, but his smile said he wasn't *that* annoyed.

"So let's see where we're going." I pulled the notebook back from my wife-to-be—there'd have to be an engagement and a wedding thrown in all of our plans at some point, but I wasn't worried about it too much. It would happen. "We have Scotland, Paris, Greece, Turkey, Spain, Rome, India, Japan—I already have an apartment in Tokyo, so we can stay a while; there's so much I want to show you there—the Galapagos Islands, and Myanmar."

"And Iceland," Jolie added enthusiastically.

"And Iceland." I wrote it down, about to burst. Was it possible to hold this much joy inside? Even when we'd dreamed about a future together as kids, I'd never been this happy. It was an entirely different thing to anticipate something that I knew would happen than something that I hoped would happen.

And I knew our trip would happen.

Or if it didn't, it would be because we chose something else that was better. I had no doubts. Nothing stood in our way of taking everything we reached for. A glance at Jolie said she was bursting with the same joy.

"Fucking good itinerary there." I ignored Jolie's frown at the swearing and looked to Tate. "How does it sound to you?"

He took the words right out of my mouth. "Sounds wild."

EPILOGUE
CADE

Eighteen months later

Jolie jumped and grabbed on to me as the cork came out with a loud pop.

"I wasn't expecting that," she said as laughter rippled through our group.

"I wasn't either." Weston held the bottle away from him, though the champagne was already dripping down his sleeve, so I didn't really see the point. "Guess it got shaken up in the process of opening it."

"My carpet appreciates it," Donovan said with smug sarcasm. "How about I open the next one?"

"I got you, I got you." Weston's wife, Elizabeth, came to the rescue carrying two flutes. She positioned one under the nozzle as he poured then replaced it with another when she handed off the first to Jolie.

Sabrina came up behind her with more flutes, and between the three of them, we soon all had glasses in hand except Tate.

Elizabeth held the last flute in front of him and looked toward us. "Is this okay?"

Tate raised a hopeful brow, and Jolie frowned.

"Come on. We're celebrating," I said to my fiancée.

"Which is a fine excuse for your drinking, not for our eighteen-year-old." Jolie had been my rock when I'd decided to cut back on alcohol except for wine at dinner, for a myriad of reasons—health and being a present parent topped the list.

"He's going to be able to legally drink tomorrow when we're in France."

"But today, we're still in New York." God, she was adorable when she was ridiculous. As if Tate hadn't snuck a sip or two from our wine glasses in the past.

I might have even let him have one of her margarita coolers when she was out of town last spring to deal with the final sale of the school property to a rehabilitation organization for women and children who had been rescued victims of human trafficking. Did she really think I'd been the one to dig into her stash?

"Ah, for Pete's sake, let the kid drink." Donovan swiped the drink from Elizabeth's hand and gave it to Tate then raised his own glass in the air before anyone could object. "To safe and adventurous travels."

"Thank you," Weston said, as if the toast was meant for him, which he probably assumed it was.

Jolie sighed, but she raised her glass with everyone else. "Here, here!"

Clinking glasses and cheers followed, and when everyone drank, Tate made a big show of being disgusted with the taste for his mother's sake but not so disgusted that he relinquished the glass. In my arms, Devyn stiffened at the commotion.

"Hey, baby bird. Did that startle you?" I bent my face down to reassure my seven-month-old daughter. As soon as she saw my grin, she gave me one of her own.

"Her smile kills me," Sabrina cooed. "Those two little teeth are so cute."

Jolie reached over to straighten her jumper. "Not so cute when she's biting on my breast, but yeah. We like her."

Fuck yeah, we liked her.

For so long in my life, I'd believed the best I could be had passed.

Once upon a time, I'd been the boy Julianna Stark had loved, and nothing could top that.

Then I met my son, and the whole universe shifted. Being his father had become my gravity. It held me in place and was such an essential part of my reality, I couldn't comprehend anymore that I'd once existed without him.

I loved him and his mother with every cell in my body, and when Jolie got pregnant a few short months after our reunion, I'd been surprised to find there was room inside me to love more.

The first time I'd held her, I thought I was going to explode.

If sobbing like a baby counted as such, then I did explode. One of the happiest days of my life, and there'd been plenty of those in the eighteen months since I'd taken a leave from Reach.

Including tonight, celebrating Tate's recent graduation with friends before we took off on our year-long trip around the world.

"I can't believe you're traveling with an infant," Elizabeth said.

I looked up to find her so baffled she was shaking her head. I supposed it was to be expected from a woman who was celebrating her babymoon sans baby in her womb. To be fair, she was the heiress to a giant media company and loved her career. So instead of taking time off to have a baby on their own, Weston and Elizabeth had asked the mother of Weston's son from a previous relationship—if a one-night stand could be called a relationship—to surrogate for them.

If it worked for them, who was I to have an opinion?

"We have a nanny traveling with us," Jolie said.

"An old lady nanny," Tate added. "I still say we should have hired the twenty-five-year-old."

"You have a girlfriend," his mother reminded him.

"We're on a break," he reminded her.

Having lost so much time together, it was difficult for Jol and me to understand Tate and his girlfriend wanting to spend any time apart. Ironically, he'd credited our relationship as the inspiration. *True love will still be there when we get back to it*, he'd said. *If it's not, then it's not true love.*

He was a wise one. I wasn't jerking his chain whenever I told him I looked up to him.

"Anyway." Jolie turned her attention back to Elizabeth. "Even with the nanny, we intend to take Devyn with us as much as possible."

"We're a real together sort of family." If I sounded proud of the fact, I was.

Weston moved over to join the conversation with a four-year-old wrapped around his leg like that was everyday for him. "So we've discovered. So tight-knit you didn't tell anyone where you were for more than a year and a half." He paused for dramatic effect. "Oh, wait. I mean since you didn't tell me where you were."

Donovan and I exchanged a glance. He'd taken me seriously when I'd asked him to keep our lives hush-hush. The rest of the firm had been told nothing except that I'd been on sabbatical. Weston had only been caught up on the events of my life in the last hour over dinner hosted at Donovan's. He'd been playing hurt ever since.

I stuck my tongue out at Sebastian—the three-year-old wrapped around Weston's leg—before responding. "Look, I'm sorry I didn't tell you. There was a lot of media—"

"So much media," Sabrina agreed.

"We even covered it in the European markets," Elizabeth added.

"And we were trying to maintain some normalcy." Too much of our lives had been not normal. Choosing to drop off the grid had been one of the best choices I'd ever made.

"I get it," Weston said in a tone that said he really didn't. "I just thought we were closer than that, you know? You came all the way from Tokyo for my wedding—and it hadn't even been a legit wedding."

"He didn't really come for your wedding," Donovan said, flat-toned.

Weston went on as if he hadn't heard the interruption. "At least you're here tonight. We only get to the States once a year, at most. It was really great of you to come to New York to see us."

"He didn't really come to New York to see you." Donovan again.

I only somewhat successfully bit back a smile. "Wouldn't have missed tonight for the world." Because it was the first leg of our trip, not because of Weston. I hadn't even known he'd be in town when I'd told Donovan we'd be there.

Weston appeared somewhat mollified. "Is it safe to assume we'll get an invitation to your wedding?"

Jolie and I looked at each other. We still hadn't decided if we were going to do something big or something quiet. Truth was that we hadn't spent any time at all planning the event. When she'd found out she was pregnant, she'd wanted to wait until after the baby was born. And then we were so busy planning the trip, we decided to push it until after that.

At least, she was wearing a ring now. I'd officially popped the question on Valentine's Day with a gorgeous diamond ring surrounded by Tate and Devyn's birthstones (garnet and topaz). As far as we were concerned, that was more ceremony than we needed, but the idea of celebrating with friends did have its appeal.

"When we get around to figuring out what that will look like, sure," I said.

Sabrina linked her arm through Donovan's. "Watch what you're saying in present company. Donovan will surprise you with a wedding if you're not careful."

Everyone laughed because it was true.

"He throws good weddings," Elizabeth said.

I groaned. "Please, don't encourage him."

"I don't know. Seems sort of fitting since he's practically responsible for you being together. According to him, anyway." Sometimes Weston was clueless, but sometimes I thought he stirred shit on purpose.

I sent a pointed glare in Donovan's direction. "Oh, is that right?"

"I didn't say it in quite so many words. But while we're on the topic, how about you show them?"

I didn't have to ask what Donovan meant.

Rolling my eyes, I finished off my champagne in a single gulp and handed the flute to the asshole before offering Devyn to whoever volunteered.

"I got her." Tate had been as excited as we were to add her to our family. Sometimes I wondered if he was more of a third parent than a brother. I worried about him eventually going away to college. It was going to break her heart.

Okay, it was going to break my heart.

Which was why I wasn't thinking about it until I had to.

With my hands free, I loosened my belt and lifted up my button-down so I could display **I love D** tattooed on my right hip.

Elizabeth's eyes went gleefully wide, and she covered her mouth.

Weston didn't bother hiding his laugh at all. "Seriously, Cade? You let him put that on you permanently?"

"Well, I didn't ink it on him myself," Donovan said, obviously pleased with himself despite the fact.

"A bet's a bet," I said. "But the joke's on him." I pulled my pants down a bit so everyone could see what I'd had added to the tattoo since Donovan had last seen it—**EVYN**.

"I love Devyn," Weston read out loud.

"You motherfucker," Donovan muttered. "I call that cheating."

"I call it genius." Sabrina didn't even look sorry when her husband threw her a look. Honestly, the whole exchange seemed like foreplay.

I definitely didn't want to think about that.

"I got two other new tattoos when I had that one done." I showed everyone the open birdcage on the left lower side of my back that matched Jolie's tattoo and then rolled up my sleeve to show off the house that had been an original design. "Tate did that one."

"He's really good."

I puffed up from Elizabeth's praise as if she'd been praising me and glanced over at Tate for his reaction. He was plopped on the ground now, trying to draw on his iPad while Devyn crawled back and forth over his stretched-out legs, and though he didn't look up, the color in his cheeks said he'd heard the compliment.

The kid was too humble for his own good. I would have boasted more if he hadn't been present. There was still a chance I'd boast more before the night was over.

"Yeah, yeah, we know," Donovan pretended to grumble. "You're a family man now. And I'd had such high hopes for you."

I shot him a glare.

Then decided on another tactic. If he was going to poke, it was only fair that I poke back. "And how about you, D? You're married now. You planning any mini Kincaids?"

She made it seem casual, but Sabrina chose that moment to step away from her husband and crouch down by Tate to see what he was drawing.

Weston bent down to pick up Devyn who had taken Tate's distraction as an opportunity to reach for the first editions on Donovan's bookshelf. "You're going to have to babyproof, if you are."

"You know what? Mind your own business," Donovan said.

Yes, we definitely laughed.

"That's rich coming from you," I said.

"I have no idea what you're talking about. How about I break open another bottle?"

It was a change of subject if I'd ever seen one, and I might have pushed him on it if it was the old days, when it was just the two of us. When all we had of the women we loved were wild memories and deep regrets.

That wasn't us anymore.

Thank God.

I wrapped an arm around Jolie's waist and pulled her to me while Donovan worked on opening the next bottle. "You happy?" I asked.

"Impossibly."

And when Donovan handed me my replenished glass, I didn't need an excuse to celebrate. My impossibly happy life was reason enough.

Keep reading for a bonus story in the Dirty Universe!

Don't miss the next Dirty Universe installment

Kincaid

Past and present weave together in Donovan's point of view for the next chapter in Donovan and Sabrina's life.

She was supposed to save me.

In a twist of fate, I rescued her. Since then, I've lived for her, breathed for her, overreached with my love.

She's still here, so I must be doing something right. But now I want more.

Except, a dangerous secret from my past threatens to come between us, forcing me to confront what kind of man I am.

And whether I'm the one who can save our future.

Get Kincaid now.

If you're not caught up on the Dirty Universe, start with The Dirty Duet or check out the reading order at the back of this book.

Turn the page to read Ten Dirty Demands, a bonus story in the Dirty Universe.

THE DIRTY UNIVERSE CONTINUES...

Meet all my Dirty Men.
Dirty Universe reading order

The Dirty Duet - Donovan Kincaid

Dirty Games Duet - Weston King

Dirty Filthy Fix - Nate Sinclair

Dirty Sweet Duet - Dylan Locke

Dirty Wild Trilogy - Cade Warren

Dirty Sweet Valentine & Other Filthy Tales of Love

Ten Dirty Demands - Donovan Kincaid

Kincaid - Donovan Kincaid

ALSO BY LAURELIN PAIGE
WONDERING WHAT TO READ NEXT? I CAN HELP!

Visit www.laurelinpaige.com for content warnings and a more detailed reading order.

Brutal Billionaires

Brutal Billionaire - a standalone (Holt Sebastian)

Dirty Filthy Billionaire - a novella (Steele Sebastian)

Brutal Secret - a standalone (Reid Sebastian)

Brutal Arrangement - a standalone (Alex Sebastian)

Brutal Bargain - a standalone (Axle Morgan)

Brutal Bastard - a standalone (Hunter Sebastian)

The Dirty Universe
Dirty Duet (Donovan Kincaid)

Dirty Filthy Rich Men | Dirty Filthy Rich Love

Kincaid

Dirty Games Duet (Weston King)

Dirty Sexy Player | Dirty Sexy Games

Dirty Sweet Duet (Dylan Locke)

Sweet Liar | Sweet Fate

(Nate Sinclair) Dirty Filthy Fix (a spinoff novella)

Dirty Wild Trilogy (Cade Warren)

Wild Rebel | Wild War | Wild Heart

Men in Charge

Man in Charge

Man for Me (a spinoff novella)

The Fixed Universe

Fixed Series (Hudson & Alayna)

Fixed on You | Found in You | Forever with You | Hudson | Fixed Forever

Found Duet (Gwen & JC) Free Me | Find Me

(Chandler & Genevieve) Chandler (a spinoff novel)

(Norma & Boyd) Falling Under You (a spinoff novella)

(Nate & Trish) Dirty Filthy Fix (a spinoff novella)

Slay Series (Celia & Edward)

Rivalry | Ruin | Revenge | Rising

(Gwen & JC) The Open Door (a spinoff novella)

(Camilla & Hendrix) Slash (a spinoff novella)

First and Last

First Touch | Last Kiss

Hollywood Standalones

One More Time

Close

Sex Symbol
Star Struck

Dating Season
Spring Fling | Summer Rebound | Fall Hard
Winter Bloom | Spring Fever | Summer Lovin

Also written with Kayti McGee under the name Laurelin McGee
Miss Match | Love Struck | MisTaken | Holiday for Hire

Written with Sierra Simone
Porn Star | Hot Cop

A NOTE FROM THE AUTHOR AND ACKNOWLEDGMENTS

Welp.

I said this was the last trilogy in the Dirty Universe. Then, when I was mid through this final book, I started thinking more about what I wanted to write next. I get an email or message at least once a week asking for another Donovan book, and when I tried to imagine him in the epilogue for Wild Heart—because if this was really the finale, we had to see where everyone was—I realized I couldn't just slap Donovan and Sabrina with a baby on the way and call it quits. Their relationship is too complex for me to imagine what that would look like without a thorough exploration.

So there will be more of the Dirty.

But that's getting ahead of myself. Now is about Cade and Jolie. I always knew their story was going to be more heart wrenching than sexy (though I hope it's sexy too), and I knew they were going to wreck me to write, and I am so grateful that I had such amazing people to support me while I did.

Instead of going through and saying who did what and what position they have in my team/bubble/life, I'm just going to dump a bunch of names here, in no particular order. Names of people who have been extremely important to me this last year and always:

Candi Kane, Melissa Gaston, Roxie Madar, Kayti McGee, Sarah Piechuta, Amy Vox Libris, Erica Russikoff, Michele Ficht, Kimberly Ruiz, Liz Berry, Brandie Coonis, Ann R. Jones, Rebecca Friedman, Kim Gilmour, Andi Arndt, Sebastian York, Lauren Blakely, CD Reiss, Melanie Harlow, Orion Allison, Open Cathedral, my littles (who aren't so little) and the adulters (who only sort of adult) in my household, and the Higher Power who leads me through all the chaos.

Last but not least, thank you dear readers who pick up the book time after time after time. If I were to fill a book with enough words to express my gratitude, it would never be finished.

XO,

Laurelin

ABOUT LAURELIN PAIGE

With millions of books sold, Laurelin Paige is the NY Times, Wall Street Journal, and USA Today Bestselling Author of the Fixed Trilogy. She's a sucker for a good romance and gets giddy anytime there's kissing, much to the embarrassment of her three daughters. Her husband doesn't seem to complain, however. When she isn't reading or writing sexy stories, she's probably singing, watching shows like Billions and Peaky Blinders or dreaming of Michael Fassbender. She's also a proud member of Mensa International though she doesn't do anything with the organization except use it as material for her bio.

www.laurelinpaige.com
laurelinpaigeauthor@gmail.com